# A Man of Property

# A Man of Property

### Davidyne Saxon Mayleas

McGRAW-HILL BOOK COMPANY

New York  St. Louis  San Francisco
Toronto  Hamburg  Mexico

2 3 4 5 6 7 8 9 D O C D O C 8 7 6 5 4 3

ISBN 0-07-041208-1

LIBRARY OF CONGRESS CATALOGING IN PUBLICATION DATA

Mayleas, Davidyne Saxon.
A man of property.
I. Title.
PS3563.A9635 1983     813'.54     83-5390
ISBN 0-07-041208-1

Book design by Roberta Rezk

# Part One
# *1940*

# *Chapter 1*

THIS Sunday morning was like other Sunday mornings in Carson House. The family, William Carson and his two sons, Francis and Henry, rose early to go to morning services at the Episcopal church about a mile away. By the time they finished breakfast, the chauffeur had the black Cadillac limousine in front of the house. The three men climbed into the back of the car for the short ride down the driveway, flanked by white stones and the bare bones of elm trees stripped of their plumage by the undeniable demands of nature. If William could, he would have held nature at bay when it came to the elm trees. But he had learned long ago that nothing could hold nature at bay.

For once, the boys—boys no longer at twenty-three and twenty-four—were quiet. William could hardly remember a time when they had been quiet in each other's presence. After his wife, Nathalia, had died years ago, William had taken to riding between his two sons to see to it that at least on Sundays, on the way to church, they would be unable to get at each other. In the beginning they had tried, but each attempt was met by a solid smack on the side of each boy's head. William didn't care who started the trouble. Each was smacked. That way he did not have to worry about mishandling justice. Eventually, the boys learned that on the way to church they had to behave.

The big car turned out of the driveway onto a poorly shoveled, icy, dirt road. The ruts were still frozen, so the car bounced and skidded along.

When the car stopped in its unofficially reserved space in front of the church, the Carsons got out. The three men stood for a moment on the freshly shoveled sidewalk, then proceeded up the broad path leading to the small, white, wooden Episcopal church.

William, well over six feet tall, had white-blond hair that had in his youth been lemon-yellow. His head was large even for a tall man, but his features were strangely delicate. Only a square jaw and startlingly bright blue eyes hinted of the power of the man. Until he stood next to

3

a man of average size, he gave an impression of slim elegance. Then the width of his shoulders, length of his arms and size of his hands would make any observer question a description that included, even vaguely, the idea of "delicate."

Francis was in William's image but larger. It was as though nature had tried out the model using William as the prototype and then made Francis into the final form. He was six feet five inches in his bare feet, 225 pounds of bone and muscle. He had hair that looked sun-bleached even in the dead of winter and a perfect profile. Francis was the *beau idéal* of every woman, married or single, in the county. He looked so alive he seemed to walk in bright sunshine even on the bleakest wintry day.

Henry was the smallest of the three. Though as tall as his father, he seemed shorter because of the size of his body. Henry did not have a chest, waist, arms and legs in the usual sense. His body was like the trunk of a tree: huge, massive. He had no elbows or wrists. His arms were one solid column that, unexpectedly, could bend for there seemed to be no elbow. His thighs and calves were sized to carry this massive torso, narrowing slightly at the ankle. Unlike his father and brother, nothing about Henry seemed graceful or delicate. Henry was pure power. Surprisingly, the body was topped off by a face with features only a shade less perfect than Francis', a head that seemed too small for his torso, a mop of unruly, carrot-red hair and sea-green eyes.

When the three stood in the church door, the door was filled. The aisle was too narrow, so they walked single file to their pew in the front of the church. As though on cue, the service began.

That Sunday the sermon was about the war going on in Europe. The minister offered a prayer for the brave Englishmen fighting and dying to save their country and the western world from the German dictator. He also offered a prayer that the United States not be forced into the war, that its young men not have to fight and die for democracy. The inconsistency was noted by all three Carsons.

The service ended, the church gradually emptied. Greetings were exchanged among the minister, William, his sons and the small group of parishioners who were among their acquaintances. Several men asked William if the afternoon's entertainment were still on. William said it was, and they went away satisfied.

The weather had warmed up by the time the Carsons headed home. The ice and dirt on the road had softened, and the heavy car didn't bounce quite so much. On other Sundays they would have gathered for lunch in the glass-enclosed porch overlooking the south lawn. But because of what was going to happen at three o'clock today, there was no lunch. Each Carson was given that time to prepare, in his own way, for the afternoon's "entertainment."

During most of Saturday and Sunday morning, a large number of servants and extra laborers, hired for the occasion, had been working steadily. Two brightly colored pavilions were in place next to the stables. A grandstand, large enough to hold several hundred people, had been erected in the riding ring. Paths had been shoveled from the house to the pavilions and grandstand and covered with fresh, dry straw. Finally, a twenty-foot square had been dug out of the snow with two five-foot squares at diagonal corners. The twenty-foot square was covered with a padded canvas that was held in place by wooden stakes driven into the slightly thawed ground. The two smaller squares were covered with straw, and each had a low stool in the center.

Large poles, six inches in diameter, had been hammered into the ground, and heavy ropes hung from the poles outlining the twenty-foot square and the smaller squares. It looked exactly like what it was: a boxing ring. Under the shelter of the pavilions, the house servants had set up several bars and tables with all kinds of food ranging from huge steaks to a brace of geese. Alongside these hot dishes were mounds of freshly delivered caviar and shrimp. Everything was ready. At about two o'clock the first guests arrived. Slowly, but in ever increasing numbers, the county was gathering. Drinks were drunk, food was eaten, and the voices grew louder and louder as the crowd waited.

Henry's room on the second floor overlooked the lawn that led to the stables. Still wearing his underwear, Henry watched the crowd below with increasing fascination. He had eaten a huge steak with the usual side dishes. His one concession was the omission of a good bottle of Burgundy to go with the steak.

The most distinctive features of Henry's room were its size, the beautiful oak beams that ran the length of the ceiling, the heavy oak furniture, and the huge bay window through which Henry was now looking.

He watched a bookmaker, hired for the occasion by William, taking bets on the event. Henry rang for his valet. When the man arrived, he told him to place $10,000 on Henry William Carson to win and a second $10,000 that the fight would last longer than twenty rounds. The odds did not matter. When the bets were placed, he was to return and help Henry dress. This done, Henry turned away from the window to reflect on how this "charade" had come about. Why he hated Francis so much and could never tell anyone. Why, in his darker moods, he even hated his father.

Francis was also resting in his own room. He had not bothered to change from the clothes he had worn to church. Like his brother, he was also thinking about the past. He had reached puberty unusually early, and being an extraordinarily handsome boy, he'd had what he considered a stroke of luck. The house was being redecorated for the first time since their mother's death. A husband and wife team had been hired to supervise the work. Francis was their natural prey. First he was seduced by the wife. Then "accidentally" discovered by the husband. Under not too much duress, Francis agreed to become part of a three-way arrangement.

To his surprise, Francis found that he had a preference for the man. He found he preferred that hardness of the male body to the softness of the female.

Francis fully understood that, while William might have complained about an affair with an older woman, if he discovered the homosexual affair, complaining would hardly suffice for what would happen. In any case, the redecorating was completed all too soon, and the couple left for the city. Except for two trips to New York, it had been a long, dry period for Francis.

So he had made a plan involving Henry, but Henry's reaction made the plan impossible. Actually, Francis did not remember disliking Henry before, but the whole incident and the fear of what Henry might say to their father combined to turn all his brotherly feelings into pure hatred. And now, years later, they were preparing to settle their feud in a thoroughly barbarous way. Just the kind of thing his father would invent and Henry would love.

He had no serious doubts that he would win. He was taller, faster, almost as strong; and, what neither William nor Henry knew, Francis had learned a lot about boxing. One of his male lovers had been a well-known prize fighter. The cruelty of the sport appealed to Francis. It remained the only sport where the intention was to hurt your opponent. Admittedly, the boxer was smaller than Francis, but when the time came to end the affair, Francis had little trouble beating his about-to-be-ex-lover into a pulp. Yes, both his father and Henry were in for a surprise.

Now it was time to change. Francis rang for his servant to remove the food. He went to his dresser, opened the bottom drawer and took out his boxer's jock strap. No punch in the balls was going to end this fight unless he did the punching.

\* \* \*

At two-forty-five, William ended the eating and drinking and proceeded to the main event. He signaled the two men he had selected as seconds for Henry and Francis, sending them to the house for his sons. Turning to the assembled group, he requested everyone to go to the places in the stands assigned to them. The plates of food and glasses of drink were set down, and in minutes everyone was in place.

There was total silence. Francis, followed by Henry, could be seen walking with their seconds down the straw-covered path between the snowdrifts toward the ring. They were dressed alike. Each wore ankle-length sweat pants and a long-sleeved sweat shirt made of light cotton. Each wore high, rubber-soled black shoes. Only the colors of their sweat pants and shirts were different. Francis was in blue, Henry in gray.

Francis and Henry climbed through the ropes of the ring and settled themselves on the low stools. Each second carried an oddly shaped piece of rubber in his left hand and a bucket of water in his right hand. Under one arm each carried a bottle with a rubber nipple. They also carried a number of towels.

William was now ready. He was dressed in a similar sweat suit, but his was black and contrasted with his silver-gold hair. As he spoke, his breath was visible. "I would like to explain what we are doing here, why we have chosen to do this, and why, in my opinion, it is necessary to do this in exactly this way." The "in my opinion" was a concession very few people had ever heard William make.

Those who felt they knew William Carson took it as a sign that, for all the preparation that had taken place, William was not that certain it was a good idea. They were correct. It was not the event that concerned him, but the outcome; if he was wrong about that, he would have to accept it. And William accepted very little he did not like.

He went on. "We are witnessing a boxing match between my two sons. The match will take place under 'Old Time' rules. They are as follows: no boxing gloves will be worn; this is to be a bare knuckles fight. With gloves there is a greater risk of brain damage. A fighter can hit the other fighter's head harder without much risk of breaking a knuckle, and the blow is spread over a larger area, thus doing more damage. Without gloves, there are more facial cuts and more blood, but a little blood does not compensate for brain damage. So any lady, or gentleman for that matter, who is upset by the sight of blood, may leave without any loss of my personal esteem."

He paused. There was some stirring and shuffling of feet, but no one left. "In addition, there will be no rounds with pauses between. At the sound of the bell, the fighters will move to the center of the ring and 'toe the line.' They will touch fists and begin to fight. *A round will end when one of the fighters is knocked down.* The fighter still standing will go to his corner and wait. The fighter who has been knocked down will be assisted to his corner by his second. The fighter will be allowed one minute to recover. A bell will then sound, and both fighters will 'toe the line' and start again. Any delay on the part of a second in getting his man to his corner will start me counting prior to his getting there. If a fighter is knocked through the ropes, his second will be allowed to help him back into the ring. If he is unable to 'toe the line,' it will count as a knockdown, and the rules I have just outlined will go into effect. *The fight will end when and only when one fighter is unable or unwilling to* 'toe the line.'

"There will be no butting, gouging, hitting below the belt, rabbit or kidney punches. If such an event does take place, the round will end, and the fighter who has been the recipient of the foul will be given five minutes to recover. Three such blows on the part of a fighter loses him the fight. Each fighter will wear a mouthpiece. I think that covers the rules, but if either fighter or anyone in the stands has a question about them, I will try to answer it now." Henry and Francis were silent. They had heard the rules three months ago when William first proposed the match. There was one voice from the audience. "William, I question your decision about the gloves and rounds. After all, this is 1940. We have progressed from the nineteenth century. This is a throwback."

"Robert, your question is noted. But by 'question,' I did not mean to include your opinion of how I am handling the fight. I merely wanted to be certain you understood it. And I take it you do understand the rules. Does anyone else have a question?"

Once again William paused to give his audience time to reflect. Francis sat erect on his stool with his arms hanging loosely at his sides. They actually touched the ground. He was looking across at Henry. As he listened to his father, Henry seemed to become a ball. His arms were wrapped around his stomach and his knees tucked up under his chin. All one saw was the top of his red hair and a huge hulk below.

"Now I come to the reason why we must do what we are doing. As you know, the Carson Company was founded by my grandfather. He had the good sense to create one son and a number of daughters. In time my father took over the company, and he continued his father's practice. He also had one son. Me. And he had no daughters. Upon reflection, one might say he had improved upon his father. There were no confusing questions about sons-in-law and the like." By this time a few people in the stands had begun to understand where William was heading, and a slight murmur broke out. William waited for it to subside. "I had the foolishness not to follow my grandfather and father's admirable practices. Not only did I sire two children, I sired two sons. And as you know, they are not exactly the best of friends."

This gross understatement brought a burst of laughter from the very tense guests. Francis smiled a little, and Henry looked up. Those who could see his face were startled at the strange contorted look. It was almost as though Henry were trying not to cry. The difference between grief and great rage is small.

"What we are settling is the eventual succession to my position as Chairman of the Carson Company. The winner of this fight will work with me at the company. The loser will be given a large amount of money in cash or an annual income and be free to do whatever he wishes. He will be welcome at Carson House at all times, but the company will be barred to him. This division is necessary. If I left my two sons to run the company after I died, they would destroy themselves, the company and everything for which three generations of Carsons have worked.

"I have tried to decide which of my sons should inherit, but I have been unable to do so. So I went back to an even older time when succession was determined by weight of sword or lance. My sons are reasonably well matched physically, each having advantages and disadvantages. Sword and lance seemed a little out of date, so I decided on fists. Finally, I want to emphasize the point that both my sons have agreed to abide by the results of this fight, and you people have been chosen to witness the event in case witnesses are ever required." There was not a sound.

Moving quickly, William went to the side of the ring. He turned to face his sons. Both Henry and Francis stood up and removed their sweat shirts. The size and strength of the two naked torsos brought gasps of disbelief.

"Are you ready, Francis?"

"Yes!"

"Are you ready, Henry?"

Henry nodded.

William motioned to the side of the ring, and a loud bell, more like a gong, resonated over the entire area. Francis and Henry walked slowly toward the center of the ring to "toe the line" and touch fists. As their fists touched, Henry's kept going, hoping to catch Francis unready.

Francis moved his head slightly to the right, and Henry's blow went by. Francis pivoted quickly and caught Henry with a solid left hook to the ribs, following it up with a straight right cross to the head. Henry went down on his back. He was up before his second could move, but William called a round, and they returned to their corners for the minute's rest.

This set the pattern for the first part of the fight. Francis knew far more about boxing than Henry. So much more that a few onlookers wondered where he had gotten the experience. But as big and strong as Francis was, Henry was actually much stronger. The next four rounds ended as had the first one. Henry was flat on his back, and Francis walked slowly back to his corner. Each time Henry got up faster than was necessary.

In the sixth round Henry landed his first real punch. As usual, Francis had slipped Henry's right hand lead, but instead of punching back, he stood there, leaning slightly away, and laughed. The laugh ended almost at once as Henry moved much faster than before and hit Francis right in the middle of his exposed stomach. The blow doubled Francis up, and Henry followed up with an uppercut to the jaw that sent Francis staggering back across the ring and right over the ropes. His second ran around to help him back into the ring, but Francis pushed him away and climbed back in without any help. Henry was waiting. They "toed the line," and Henry swung a roundhouse right. Had this punch landed, the fight would have been over. But Francis was ready and blocked it. Seemingly unhurt, he moved sideways, blocking everything Henry could throw. Suddenly he counter-punched, and once again Henry was on the ground. Now there was a cut over Henry's left eye that began to bleed. This time Henry waited for a moment and allowed his second to help him to his corner.

For the first time there were mutterings among the crowd. They had begun to question William's earlier statement that the two brothers were fairly well matched. Francis knew what he was doing, while Henry had nothing but extraordinary strength, and that strength would soon be exhausted. One voice came out of the group asking William to call a halt and declare Francis the winner before any real damage was done. In between rounds the bookmaker was making new odds and taking new bets. With each knockdown the odds on Francis grew shorter. By the time Henry was cut and the first objection heard, one dollar bet on Henry would receive five if Henry won.

Sitting on his stool, Henry heard the cry to "stop the fight." He stood up and bellowed in rage, "Get that bastard out of here. Ten thousand dollars more on me to win." The bookmaker nodded and made note of the bet. Francis decided to take no more chances. He would tire Henry before knocking him out and, in doing so, cut him to pieces. If Henry wanted to play bull to his torero, let him.

During the next forty-five minutes there were eleven knockdowns. The fight had gone eighteen rounds. Henry was bleeding from the nose and from cuts over one eye; more seriously, he was swallowing blood from a badly cut mouth. Still he came on. Francis decided that now was the time to end it. He had heard about the fight going twenty rounds and decided that Henry should lose all bets.

Throughout the fight William had watched and moved in only to break up clinches and count between rounds. Even so, his face had grown a little paler.

They came out for the nineteenth round. The pattern seemed to repeat. Henry moved forward, and Francis sideways and backwards. Once Henry committed himself to a punch, Francis would either block or slip the punch and counterpunch. This time there was a change. Before Henry could move, Francis hit him with a straight left jab. It caught Henry coming in, and his head snapped back. The jab was followed by a combination left hook to the head, right to the ribs, left to the head, and a perfect right cross, with every ounce of Francis' weight and strength behind the blow, to Henry's jaw. Henry went down on his face as though he had been poleaxed.

He lay there for a few seconds before rolling over. His second rushed to his side and dragged him over to his corner. Henry weighed too much to be lifted to his stool without help, so he sat on the ground. He was on his knees when the gong sounded for the start of the next round. He pushed himself up and staggered rather than walked to the line. Francis met him at the line and hit him with a blow that was supposed to end the fight—another perfect right cross that hit Henry flush on the chin. Henry staggered backwards but did not fall. He leaned against the ropes, holding himself up with one hand. Francis moved forward to finish it. By the time he reached Henry, Henry had covered his face and body with his two massive arms. Francis threw punch after punch trying to bring down Henry's arms, but they stayed in place.

Frustrated, Francis stepped back. For the first time he felt a little weary. Henry had taken his best punches and was still there. Then Francis remembered something his former fighter-lover had told him. There are fighters who simply cannot be knocked out. They could be beaten, but it had to be on points. He could not knock Henry out.

Now he knew. William had meant exactly this to happen. He had chosen Henry to succeed him and had arranged the only kind of fight that Henry could win. He had avoided wrestling where Henry had a great advantage. That would have been too obvious. It had to be boxing, and boxing under these rules.

The slight pause in the action had an effect on the crowd. Cries of "Get with it" and "Fight or quit" were heard. Francis knew how blood-mad a boxing crowd could become. It was happening here. Henry heard the crowd and, carefully, he peeked out from between his arms. There was Francis about six feet away. He could see him clearly out of one eye. The other was almost closed. Moving to Henry's blind side, Francis hit Henry again, and again Henry did not fall. He backed away, blocking Francis' following right. Francis didn't follow Henry. He stood and motioned Henry to come to him.

Through a bloody mouthpiece, Henry muttered, "Not yet, brother, but soon enough."

The pace of the fight slowed. Then very slowly, like a wounded tank, Henry moved toward Francis. He reached for Francis with a lazy left hand from which Francis leaned away. He had gotten a little tired, and the lesson of an earlier round was forgotten. For an instant his solar plexus was exposed. It was all Henry needed. Putting every ounce of his enormous weight and strength behind the punch, he hit Francis right in the center of his solar plexus.

Francis doubled over and fell to the ground. Henry wavered to his corner where he vomited blood and bile onto the edge of the square. Francis lay still. His second tried to lift him, but the punch had temporarily paralyzed Francis' legs. Francis' second dragged him to his corner, and the count began. It was over before Francis could move his legs. Still spitting blood, Henry moved to the center of the ring to "toe the line." William rang the bell and walked over to meet Henry.

"I declare Henry William Carson to be the winner of this fight."

A doctor entered the ring. He went over to Francis, flexed his legs and helped him up. By this time Francis could stand. It was an odd sight. He did not have a mark on him except for a red blotch on his stomach that would turn black and blue during the next week and then disappear. Henry was cut, bleeding, swaying on his feet. His face would need stitches. But he had won the fight.

Without a word, Francis slipped through the ropes and walked up to the house. This was Henry's day, but by the terms of the agreement, Francis was free. Although he had never really wanted to run the company, he had desperately wanted to keep it from Henry. Now he'd lost to Henry. But some day he would win. He'd stake his life on it. He had no idea how or where or when, but the day would come.

Everyone's eyes were on Henry. Slowly and very carefully the doctor and his second helped him to his stool. After cleaning the cuts, the doctor poured liberal amounts of iodine into them. Henry was so numb he barely felt the sting. The doctor was anxious to check for internal bleeding, but Henry waved away that part of the examination.

They left the ring and started up the same path Francis had taken a few minutes earlier. As they moved up the path, their way was blocked by William. He and Henry looked at each other for a moment. Then Henry said, "It took a son of a bitch like you to figure out this was the only way I could beat him. You wanted me to run the company."

"That's correct."

"Francis would have been wrong?"

"Very wrong. But if you didn't want the company badly enough to take the beating, then you also would have been wrong."

"I'll run it." Henry looked at his father with his one open eye and added, "You know, at the end Francis realized what you did."

"I expected him to realize it. That way you'll have no further trouble with him."

Henry nodded, too exhausted to talk further, but he knew that, for the first time in his adult life, his father was wrong. Flat out wrong. Henry would never be rid of Francis.

# Chapter 2

THE DOCTOR insisted that Henry rest for a week. It would take at least that long for the stitches to set. Henry would have a slightly crooked nose for the rest of his life, but nothing would get him to a hospital. He just wanted to get into bed and sleep as long as necessary.

When Henry finally woke up, he was very stiff and sore. He soaked in a hot tub for a long time. Then he dressed in a pair of warm pants, a shirt and sweater and went downstairs to eat. Francis had left the day before. He had called and requested that his personal things, including the furniture in his room, be made ready for a mover. "Did Mr. Henry have any objections?"

"What did my father say?"

"He thought you should decide what Mr. Francis could or could not take." It took a moment for Henry to digest his new status. A household decision was left to him. He wondered if a study of history would show any relationship between cuts and bruises and the right to make decisions. Probably, and it was William's way of telling everybody where matters stood.

"Let him take anything he wants in his bedroom and study."

The servant left, and Henry settled down to a large breakfast.

He felt much better after eating and debated ignoring the doctor's instructions. He just might pay a visit to the plant. The idea was dropped when he was met in the hall by a company messenger carrying a huge pile of carefully wrapped documents and a white envelope. Henry signed for the package and envelope and went into the library.

Of all the important rooms in the house, the library was the one with which Henry was least familiar. It was in the southeast corner of the house, with two sets of French doors opening out onto the terrace. This was the room used most often by William. It was completely masculine. He went directly to his father's desk and sat down. Sitting in his father's chair turned Henry's thoughts to his father's life.

Henry was well aware that William had had numerous affairs in the twenty-two years since his wife's death. But at no point was there even

14

a rumor of an impending marriage. Why? Wasn't it possible that a new mother, a stepmother, would have provided a better example for Francis and Henry than the succession of private tutors and prep schools in which they grew up? Not only did they not have a mother to raise them, but due to business trips, late evening conferences and the like, William was absent from home much of the time. So they had little of a father's care as well.

The demands of the Carson Company dominated William's life, and therefore, indirectly, it dominated both Henry's and Francis'.

Henry walked around looking carefully at the walls full of books. He marveled at William's thorough organization. He wondered what William would do if someone placed a book from the west wall on the east wall? Even more interesting, with every shelf full, how did William plan to keep the library current? There were several couches and easy chairs, all brown or dark red leather. The carpet was a huge oriental that had seen better days. Henry made a mental note to talk to William about replacing the rug with something new, knowing his father would answer, "No!" The rug was a tradeoff. What Henry wanted was his own desk in the room. He would insist on that.

After completing his inspection, Henry returned to the desk and opened the white envelope. He read the handwritten note inside. It was from William. He was taking the Twentieth Century Limited to Chicago to meet with their Midwest representatives. Then on to St. Louis to meet with their southern representatives. He would return in seven days. If he were late, he would call. Meantime, Henry was to "read and learn what we do in the Carson Company." There was a postscript. When Henry had reviewed the material, he should call Mary O'Toole, William's private secretary. Then a special packet would be sent over. Henry should give particular attention to the contents of that packet. They would discuss it when William returned.

Henry opened the large package to find a note from the same Mary O'Toole:

*Would Mr. Henry be kind enough to read the reports in the order in which they are arranged and not skip anything?*

He wasn't disturbed by the assumptive tone of the instructions. If this was the way his father wanted him to learn the business, there was a good reason for it, and he would follow instructions. There would be time in the years to come to have his own opinion. And when it was time, he would have good reasons and not object for the sake of objecting.

He started to read the report on top. It was a current report on the

Carson Company dealing with the divisions, products and breakdown between sales, management and production. Henry started to make notes. The first one was, "Where is the research on new products being done?"

The Carson Company seemed to have two main divisions. The larger of the two sold products to the public: bandages, tape, disinfectants, cough medicine you could swallow or suck on, and something called a mouthwash or rinse for which extraordinary claims were made. The second division was smaller; it sold products to hospitals. Henry quickly realized that the products sold by both divisions were about the same. The difference was in the packaging.

The second report was a combination of historical and current financial information on the company. The company was almost 100-years-old and had been started in New England by his great-grandfather, Francis Carson. The first product was a "medicine" sold from the backs of horse-drawn carts. His great-grandfather had started with one cart in and around Boston. There was no information as to what was in the "medicine," but Henry suspected it was mostly alcohol and a pain killer such as codeine or morphine. Probably highly addictive, which might account in part for the ten-year growth in the number of carts. Francis Carson had finally settled in the Back Bay section of Boston and hired men to travel around New England in wider and wider sweeps.

By the time his grandfather and namesake, Henry Carson, was born, the business had taken a major step. The Civil War had begun, and the Carson Company supplied bandages to the Union Army. The war added to the product line by increasing the sales of bandages along with pain killers. Henry's grandfather was the one to make the next big break. It was geographic. Railroads were being built across the United States. The terminal for the railroads was New York City, and the Carson Company along with the Carson family moved to New York City.

It was during the first Henry's time that the company started manufacturing some of its own products. A building on Greene Street in New York was purchased. Germs had been discovered. Those microscopic monsters could turn a scratch into the loss of a leg. This resulted in disinfectants such as iodine making their appearance in the Carson Company catalogue. Chloroform was added. When William Carson was born, in 1890, the company was grossing more than $5 million per year. It had come a long way from selling patent medicine off the backs of horse-drawn carts. The only thing that disturbed the upward spiral of the family was the sudden, violent death of the first Henry Carson.

Although the report did not explicitly state it, it seemed to Henry that Grandfather was a ladies' man. He was shot to death by a male employee. The trial was a thirty-day sensation in the Yellow Press. The murdered man was portrayed as a seducer of women who deserved to die. Whether the murder was deserved or not, the murderer was found guilty and sentenced to death. In accordance with the customs of the day, the sentence was promptly carried out.

At the age of twenty, William Carson inherited control of the Carson Company. Within five years he moved the factory and family out of New York City and up to Westchester. Carson House was built in Pleasantville. A short rail spur was constructed connecting the factory at Hastings-on-Hudson with the main New York Central rail line. Later, a pier was built into the Hudson River. Boats and barges could dock at the Carsons' private pier. By the time the World War had ended, the company had doubled in size. It was one of the major suppliers of bandages, disinfectants and chloroform to the Allies and then, later, to the United States Army.

After the United States entered the war, William made several attempts to enlist. Because of the importance of his work, he was rejected each time. Henry wondered exactly how hard William had tried. It was difficult to see his father being stopped by any petty official from doing something he really wanted to do. This was not something about which he would inquire.

Through the 100-year history of the Carson Company what stood out was its steady growth and the concentration of power in the hands of one man: a Carson.

The history now reached the Great Depression, a depression that William had foreseen. Unlike most people, William had sold all his stock holdings in 1927 and was in a cash position when the crash came. There was another note in William's handwriting telling Henry the country and the stock market would recover and stocks were now selling at bargain prices.

In spite of the depression, the company did very little retrenching. Its products were good products, and if sales dropped and profit margins were pinched, it meant little to William. He had no stockholders to answer to. Not a man was fired from the Carson Company. When President Roosevelt declared a "bank holiday" and closed the banks, William again had planned ahead. Substantial sums of cash were in the company safe. The 800 employees were paid in cash until the banks reopened.

The report ended with the current Audited Statement of Income and a 1939 Balance Sheet. The company was grossing in excess of $50 million per year. It was netting over $8 million per year after taxes, and there was not one cent of either long- or short-term debt.

Somewhat awed, Henry put the report of the history of the family and the company face down on top of the first report. He glanced at the next document. It was a long, detailed statement of William's personal holdings. On the most conservative evaluation, his father was worth over $60 million. He had just begun to reinvest in the stock market. Most of his wealth was in cash and real estate. He owned several large buildings in New York, one in Chicago and, for some reason that Henry would have to discover, William had purchased a large tract of land about fifty miles south of Los Angeles. Henry wondered when William had been to Los Angeles. It was unlike his father not to have made the trip if only to see what he had bought. But he couldn't remember a time when William had been away from the factory long enough to have made the train trip to the West Coast and back.

As for the Carson women, there was no mention of any. It was as though three generations of male Carsons had been born and raised by invisible attendants. Henry knew his mother had died shortly after his birth during the great influenza epidemic of 1918.

Henry spent the rest of the week going over the mountain of reports. The notes grew. On Friday morning, William telephoned.

"How is it going, Henry?"

"Fine. I finished reading that avalanche of paper you dropped on me, and I'm going to call Miss O'Toole for that special package."

"Very good. Read it carefully. And think. Don't just skim it."

"I don't skip-read business matters."

"This isn't all business." William coughed. "Well, I'll see you in the office Monday morning. I'm spending the weekend in New York."

"That's nice. Happy hunting." Henry hung up while William was sputtering that he never hunted. They were already caught.

Miss O'Toole had been waiting for Henry's call. Within an hour a messenger arrived from the plant with a sealed package that he refused to hand over to a servant. His orders were to give it to Mr. Henry Carson himself. When Henry appeared, the messenger handed him the package, and Henry signed for it. The package was wrapped in such a way that any tampering with the seal would be easily apparent. Henry went into the library and carefully opened it. A photograph of a girl fell out. Henry looked at the picture as it lay on the desk. She was young. Not pretty but not hopeless. Her hair was dark and cut short. Her lips thin. Probably the worst that could be said was that the face did not look as if she smiled very often. He placed the photograph to one side and removed the rest of the documents. He was surprised to find that it was a report of another company, a competitor of the Carson Company.

He read the report carefully. Although smaller than the Carson Company, it was a respectable operation grossing over $20 million per year. When he turned to the Profit and Loss Statement, he noted that for the last two years it had been losing money. He put the financial report away and turned to the next document. It was a yellowing four-year-old newspaper clipping announcing the untimely death of a Mr. John Wilkenson from a heart attack. He was survived by a wife and daughter. Henry picked up the picture of the young woman. He now knew what William had in mind, and for the first time he felt a prickle of irritation at his father's highhandedness. There were limits to what William had a right to expect from him. Henry would have to know much more, and the reasons would have to be damn good ones.

The next document was a report from a senior research chemist at Wilkenson, Inc. The report was stamped CONFIDENTIAL on every page. Henry wondered how William had gotten his hands on this. But this too was something he was not going to question. If William chose to tell him, splendid! If he didn't, he didn't. The report dealt with a new product. Not only a new product but a new concept and even a new industry. Henry read the report twice, and still he wasn't certain he understood it. The broad claim was that people who were nervous, upset, jittery could swallow the product, and it would calm their nerves. The chemist referred to the product as a "tranquilizer." Even if Henry didn't understand the technical matters discussed, the importance of the invention and its potential wide use was obvious. It had been in development for years, and patents on the basic chemistry were currently pending.

The next document was a copy of a letter from William to Mrs. Evelyn Wilkenson offering condolences on the death of her husband. It went on to suggest a meeting as soon as she felt it fitting and proper. There were copies of a series of proposals from other companies suggesting a similar meeting and couched in similar terms. Obviously, the sharks were gathering to fight over a choice piece of meat. One could smell the blood. Again, Henry wondered how William had obtained carbons of the offers of competitors.

There was a proposal from William dated about six months earlier suggesting the Carson Company would be willing to purchase Wilkenson, Inc., lock, stock and barrel for $10 million. Henry whistled. Ten million dollars was money. He whistled a lot louder when he read the next group of papers. A bidding war was going on, and the price had reached $25 million.

The final paper was another note from William. It stated that $10 million was a good price, and one might even stretch it to $15 million, but as in most auctions the bidding had gotten out of hand. Much as he might like to, the Carson Company couldn't or wouldn't compete. Henry was to look at the enclosed picture and see if anything came to mind.

What came into Henry's mind was very clear—a dynastic marriage. Not as in the old days for land or military power, but for a new product. A new product that would spawn a new industry and that was, in William's opinion, worth a great deal of money. Henry looked again at the picture. He wished she would burst out laughing at him as he looked at her. Maybe there was a home movie in existence? Probably not. Obviously they would have to meet. William would see to that. Then Henry would have to think about it.

Henry's bedside alarm went off at five-thirty. He'd been up for ten minutes waiting for the alarm. He'd spent yesterday going over the reports for a final time, studying the questions he would ask and the questions he would not ask. And looking at the picture of Miss Wilkenson. The more he looked, the more his opinion shifted. This was a bad picture of a very pretty girl. This was a good picture of a plain girl. This was a wonderful picture of an unattractive girl. Reluctantly, he placed his bet on the last option. A pretty girl would not let a bad picture be printed. Or she would have other pictures from which to choose. No. This was not a pretty woman.

After showering and shaving, he considered what to wear. Henry had no idea of his position or responsibilities. Or even where he would be working. It could range from the shipping room to an office adjoining his father's. An office was more probable, so he chose a tweed suit with a vest. To maintain a routine, he had his usual huge breakfast though he was too excited to be hungry.

Then he went into the library, picked up the briefcases and checked each package of papers again. He called for his car to be brought around to the front of the house. Although he would have preferred a sports car, his bulk made the small, bucket seats impossible, so he had settled for a two-door La Salle convertible. He left the house at seven-thirty. The office opened at eight, but he hoped to be there waiting for William rather than have William waiting for him. Any advantage, no matter how small, could only help.

Henry arrived at the plant and stopped at the gate to let the guard identify him. While he was waiting, he studied the three-story red-brick converted factory building which served as headquarters for the Carson Company. The building was long and squat. To Henry it looked old and unattractive. A more astute onlooker would have noticed the neatness of the window trim, the sharpness of the pointed brick, the general air of prosperity exuded by the converted factory building. However, even the most astute appraiser would have been startled upon entering the building. A second guard/receptionist sat at a good copy of a nineteenth-century English desk with a guest book before him. A visitor signed the book giving his name, the company he represented or where he was from, whom he wished to see and the time he entered the building. He was given a card which he clipped to his suit coat pocket. Only then was he allowed to pass the guard and enter the waiting room. Meanwhile, one of a dozen boys sitting on two benches across from the receptionist was dispatched to the member of the company being visited to tell him that Mr. X had arrived and ask for instructions.

While this protocol was followed, the visitor sat in the huge, three-story waiting room. The room had good oil paintings on the walls, oriental rugs on the floor, heavy easy chairs, couches and many lamps to make the wait as comfortable as possible. There were daily newspapers as well as weekly and monthly magazines to read.

If, for some reason, the visitor did not have an appointment, the receptionist would inform him that it was impossible for Mr. So & So to see him that day, and in the future would he please call for an appointment. In the matter of appointments, there were only two ironclad rules: anyone with an appointment was seen; anyone without an appointment was not seen.

After completing his identification, the guard told Henry he was expected. Would he please park his car in the space where his name had been painted? Henry drove down the paved driveway and found his name in the second space from the end, next to the area marked out for William. He wondered if the procedure would have been the same had Francis won the fight. Including Miss Wilkenson? He grew impatient with himself for thinking about Francis.

When he entered the building, the guard/receptionist rose to greet him.

"Welcome to the Carson Company, Mr. Carson. My name is Carl." He turned to the boys sitting on the benches. "Lads, this is Mr. Henry Carson." Twelve bodies shot to their feet and stood at military attention.

Henry didn't know what was expected of him so he contented himself with, "Good morning, lads."

"You've been expected, sir. Just take the elevator there." He pointed to a small door on the right. "Ring. When you reach your floor, you'll be met."

"Thank you, Carl." Henry walked to the elevator. He didn't have to ring. As he got there, the door opened, and the elevator operator pulled back the brass gate. Henry realized there had to be some kind of buzzer system that told the operator the elevator was wanted. As soon as Henry entered and the door and gate shut, the elevator rose to the third floor and the operator opened the door.

Henry glimpsed one of the messenger boys scurrying through a door marked EXIT. He pictured the boy leaping up the stairs to let someone know that Mr. Henry Carson had arrived. The boy had beaten the slow-moving elevator by minutes.

Henry's thoughts were interrupted by a bright voice. "Mr. Carson?"

"Yes." He turned, and standing there was a middle-aged lady in a soft, gray woolen dress, gray shoes and neatly-bobbed gray hair. She was slim and youthful in spite of all the gray. Her voice had a slight chirp that Henry felt came from excitement. He was certain that, normally, her voice was as well modulated as her looks.

"I'm Mary O'Toole, Mr. Carson's private secretary," she said with a note of pride in her voice. "Mr. Carson planned to be here to meet you, but he's been detained. So let me show you your office."

Henry smiled, partly out of politeness and partly out of pleasure. He had beaten William to work. Score one for the visiting team. They walked down the thickly carpeted hallway, the carpet a medium shade of brown that blended well with the oak-paneled walls. And it didn't show dirt. Henry wondered if the same decorators who redid the house were also responsible for the offices. He thought not.

They passed a number of openings with room numbers next to them. Peering in as he went by, Henry saw that each opening had a secretary. In one of the inner offices where the door had been left open, he saw a man at a desk that reminded him of his father's desk in the library. At the end of the hall was a set of double doors. There was no number beside them. Henry waited for the secretary to open the door.

They entered a large outer office. On the left was an empty desk. Miss O'Toole's? At the desk on the right sat a much younger, very pretty girl with blue eyes and a mass of dark, curly hair. She stood up. Henry kept his face blank, but it took an effort. The girl was special. Her full breasts and hips were emphasized by the slightly too-tight dress. In keeping with the fashion, the dress was far too long to give him any idea what her legs were like. Just like William to set this dazzler before him to throw him off balance.

The name plate on her desk said Margaret Rhodes. "Good morning Miss, or is it Mrs., Rhodes?"

"Good morning, sir, and it's Miss." Her voice was almost as low pitched as a man's.

"Will you come this way?" Miss O'Toole resumed command. They went through another set of doors. "I must apologize for the smell, but the painters finished only last night. I stayed until the work was done."

"On Sunday?"

"Mr. Carson left instructions that the painting had to be completed before his return, and things went more slowly than we expected."

"I'm certain my father will appreciate your efforts. I know I do." Henry looked around. What William had done was to break down the walls between two offices, making one huge room. There was a desk on the left with an old brass name plate and the name William Carson etched into the brass. Other than the name plate, the inevitable inkwell, penholder and leather desk pad, the desk was bare. The desk on the right was an exact copy of the one on the left. Everything was the same except for the name Henry Carson etched into a new brass name plate. Obviously, he wasn't going to work in the shipping department, or even have an office next to his father's. They would share an office. Score one for William.

His father felt strong enough, smart enough, confident enough to be able to ignore the daily pressure from his highly competitive son and eventual successor. In spite of himself, Henry wondered what had been done with the name plate that must have been prepared for Francis. He frowned at the thought. He had to stop it.

Ever sensitive to moods, Mary O'Toole asked, "I hope you like what we did. The smell will be gone in a day or two."

"It's perfect." Henry was delighted. His father had meant what he said. Henry was going to be trained to run the company, and William was going to do the training.

Suddenly there was the sound of a door opening and banging shut. Then the inner doors burst open, and there stood William.

"Please get us a pot of coffee, Mary. Mine as usual, and my son likes sugar and cream." He opened a door near his desk. Henry caught a glimpse of a well-equipped bathroom. While waiting, he stepped around his desk and sat in the chair. William had supplied him with a large, heavily reinforced chair that could support his weight. He placed the briefcases that he had been carrying on top of the desk.

William returned in a few minutes. "Sorry I'm late. It seems you found your way without too much trouble."

"Everybody was helpful." They were both formal and a little uncomfortable. An awkward silence was broken by the return of Miss O'Toole with the coffee.

"Thank you. Now I would appreciate it if you would hold all calls except anything on the Wilkenson matter or a genuine emergency."

"Certainly, sir." She closed the door softly behind her. The coffee had been left on a low, mahogany table that stood between a leather couch and several large leather chairs against the wall opposite the desks.

William poured himself a cup of black coffee. "Help yourself." He sat on the couch and waited. Henry poured his coffee, adding sugar and cream. He sat down in one of the large chairs on the other side of the table. Henry studied his father carefully, thinking William was looking a little tired. Either the trip had been rough or he had had a tough night. Or, and this made him smile, it was both.

"What's so funny?" William's voice was slightly defensive. A change was coming, and although it had to happen, he didn't have to like it. Both Henry's arriving first and his grin weren't helping.

Henry tried to hide his grin. "I was thinking Marion gave you a hard time last night. Or maybe the reverse?" William smiled too. The two men finished their coffee at the same time, placed their cups on the tray, each waiting for the other to speak first. Finally William said, "Have another cup of coffee, Henry." He was buying time, trying to work out the best way to lead up to the subject uppermost in his mind: the Wilkenson deal and the picture.

Henry knew it as well, so he decided not to give William any more time. "No, thank you. Now that you've called us together . . ." His voice trailed off, leaving William to finish the sentence.

William took the cue. "I presume you've read the reports?"

"I have."

They got down to work, spending the rest of the morning going back and forth on the material. Henry asked questions, and William answered them. William asked questions, and Henry answered them. But while Henry was asking for information, William was making certain that Henry actually understood the material in the reports. Finally Henry came to a key question. "What about the research and development of new products?" William looked at his watch and suggested a break for lunch.

"We'll eat in the cafeteria. I want everyone to meet you." And although he didn't say it, he also wanted them to know that he had returned. The cafeteria was divided into three rooms: a large room for most of the office staff, a smaller room for middle-level executives and executive secretaries, and a rather smallish room that held four round tables with six chairs per table. Status at the Carson Company was lunch in the executive dining room. The food was the same in all three rooms, and nobody paid for their lunches. That was a company perk. But the executive dining room had table linen, china and four waitresses to serve and clean up.

The two men entered the dining room where fifteen men were already seated and eating. William asked for a moment of quiet. "This is my son, Henry Carson. He's joined the firm. As soon as you've finished eating, I'll introduce you to him."

Both William and Henry knew everyone present had heard about the method of selection and were curious to meet Henry. When everyone had finished eating, they rose and lined up for the introduction. The names and titles were a blur, but Henry knew time would solve that problem. The men filed by to shake hands. Some of the welcomes even sounded sincere.

Near the end of the line, a large man was introduced. "Morgan, this is my son, Henry Carson. Henry, I'd like you to meet our Executive Vice President for Manufacturing, Morgan Easton." They shook hands. The man's grip was firm, and Henry waited for his hand to be released. It took several seconds for him to realize that too much pressure was being applied to the grip. The pressure increased. Henry thought, "Oh, shit!" It tightened even more. Finally Henry had enough. He stopped holding his hand still and returned the pressure. He could feel the man's knuckles grind. He was strong, but not the way Henry was strong. Five seconds were enough, and Henry let go. Easton's face had turned white. He walked away quietly, unwilling to reveal what had happened. Henry turned to look at William. His father had missed nothing and muttered something that sounded like "Damn fool." The introductions over, they left to go back to work.

Back in their office, William returned to the incident. "Morgan responds to a whip, and I haven't been around to whip him often enough. You just inherited the job."

"Why keep him?"

"First lesson in administration. No one is perfect. He's a bully, but in manufacturing you have to be a bully or the foremen will walk all over you. Also, he's a damn good executive when it comes to getting a product out the door."

Henry nodded. The lesson was learned. Without breaking pace, William changed the subject. "I've called us together because I want to talk about the Wilkenson situation." The suddenness of the shift threw Henry off stride so he said nothing. "You asked me earlier about research for new products. The Wilkensons have patents pending on one hell of a new product." He grew expansive. "It's more than a new product. It's actually the birth of a new industry. We have a man working in the same general area. They're about ten years ahead of us. I want that product, but I'm not going to get into the auction. The price is already too high. We couldn't meet it if I wanted to." He looked sharply at Henry. "I asked you if you could think of another approach. Have you?"

"Is she as unattractive as her snapshot? And what's her first name?"

William had the grace to sigh. "Yes, she is as unattractive as she looks. And her first name is Selma."

"Selma Wilkenson. Not that Selma Carson sounds any better."

William exploded. "I don't give a damn about her name. Do you have any objections?"

"You mean about my forthcoming romance with Miss Wilkenson?"

"Will you agree to the idea if we can convince the lady?"

"Let's say I'll agree to meet the lady. After that, we'll see. How do you plan to make the introductions?"

"We might start by asking the ladies and their lawyer to spend the weekend with us."

"Why their lawyer?"

William paused. He cleared his throat. "Henry, I'm certain you recognized there were a number of documents in that file that I had no business having." Henry nodded. "Let's say their lawyer is not above listening to a reasonable proposal. Providing, of course, the proposal contains a little something in it for him. He's far too fond of cards, dice and ladies. Also brandy. A man should have certain pleasures, but not when they bring him to the point of personal bankruptcy." William's face dissolved into a big grin. "Since I've given you the stick, I have a carrot for you."

Henry understood.

"You're going to need someone to show you around the facilities, building by building. Miss Rhodes has been with the firm for a number of years. She started on the production line in the factory. I had her trained as an executive secretary in preparation for today."

Henry was astonished. "You've been planning this for years?"

"Precisely. From the day I read of the death of John Wilkenson. Survived by his wife and young daughter."

"What makes you think I can't find my own consolation prizes? I've never needed help before."

"True. But I suppose I felt a mild, a very mild, twinge of guilt at the sacrifice I planned to ask of you. For the Carson Company. Selma Wilkenson is likely to be quite a dose to swallow. And given the volume of work here and the duties of married life, I felt there might not be much time for your usual scouting."

"Thank you for the consideration."

"Your sarcasm is not appreciated. Anyway, I consider it my duty to keep my son and heir both fit and happy."

"Her name is Margaret Rhodes?"

"Yes. And Miss Rhodes has a clear idea of her duties. In fact, I believe she looks forward to her new responsibilities. Certainly, she's dressed for the part."

"Am I to assume you've already broken her into the Carson way of doing things?"

William was indignant. "You may assume no such thing! I'm not offering you used merchandise. At least not merchandise used by me."

Henry looked at his father. The idea that his father had thought four years ago that they might be sitting in his office having this conversation and had planned far enough ahead to have picked out an alternative to an unfortunate marriage, should one be necessary, was quite a feat. Even for William. He started to laugh. "Why not? Let's give Miss Rhodes her chance to be a hero. Or is it heroine?"

They stood up together. William went to the door. "Miss Rhodes, would you mind joining us for a moment?"

# Chapter 3

**W**ILLIAM CARSON had picked Maggie Rhodes out of the production line. He had her educated and trained to be Mary O'Toole's assistant. And for a long time Maggie wondered why she had been selected. When she finally got up the nerve to ask Mary, the answer was not an answer.

"I have no idea. Mr. Carson doesn't confide in me. But he has his reasons." Maggie thought about what those reasons might be. It seemed to her that there was nothing exceptional about her. Nothing that would have caused him to select her. Yet, select her he did. It must have to do with something she didn't understand.

She was the youngest of five children: two boys and three girls. Her father, Arthur Rhodes, was a reasonably successful real estate broker who dabbled in land speculation. During the twenties things had gone well for the Rhodes family. Westchester, especially that part located near Long Island Sound, was rapidly developing into a series of "bedroom communities" for New York City. By the time Herbert Hoover was elected president, the Rhodes family had moved to a large fieldstone house on East Lincoln Avenue in Mount Vernon, and two new maids were hired to help Mrs. Rhodes run the establishment. Maggie attended the Woodrow Wilson Junior High School. A bright, attractive child, she was clearly the daughter who inherited her mother's beauty.

Then came 1929, 1930, and finally 1931. With the stock market crash, real estate values crumbled and Arthur Rhodes stopped earning a living. First the servants were let go. Then, late in 1931, unpaid taxes and overdue mortgage interest payments forced the Mount Vernon Savings Bank to foreclose on the fieldstone house. The Rhodes family had to move into a four-room apartment on the third floor of a ramshackle wooden building on the wrong side of the railroad tracks.

Four of the five children were old enough to work. The two boys, having no place to sleep in the new apartment, chose to leave home and try their luck in other parts of the country. The two older girls were glad to have found permanent employment as sales girls in Genungs

Department Store, the largest store of its kind in Mount Vernon. They arranged for Maggie to work there after school and on Saturdays. The three small incomes were barely enough to hold the family together.

Every day Arthur Rhodes went to a rent-free office and waited for the phone to ring. It didn't. Finally the telephone company, finding that Arthur was six months in arrears on his phone bill, cut off the service. Without a phone, there was no use in Arthur's going to the office, even if it was rent free. He was reduced to walking the streets canvassing for possible leads to people who needed help or advice in real estate matters. At this point he had a stroke of luck. A real estate firm that had survived the depression needed an office manager. They were located only a few blocks from where the Rhodes family was living. The job paid $50 per week. It seemed for a while that, bad as things were, the family would manage to ride out the depression.

Maggie was then sixteen years old. She was a tall, dark-haired young woman whose potentially excellent figure and beautiful face were often hidden under clothes that were too large and hair that was a tangled mass. In spite of everything that had happened to the family, she retained her optimistic disposition.

Then the short spell of good fortune was abruptly cut short. One morning Mrs. Rhodes felt a lump in her breast. An examination at the Mount Vernon Hospital showed she had cancer, and the cancer had spread so far it wasn't operable. She would die quickly. After her mother died, Maggie had to take over the shopping, cooking and cleaning on top of her schoolwork at A. B. Davis High School and her afternoon and weekend job at Genungs.

In the limited privacy of his room, Arthur Rhodes grieved in silence. Losing his wife and his business was too much. One morning he didn't feel well, but there was work to be done in the office. Crossing Fifth Street and Second Avenue, he felt a painful vise close around his chest. He collapsed before reaching the other side of the street. An intern from Mount Vernon Hospital pronounced him dead on arrival. Massive heart attack.

The double tragedy left the family without any guidance. Maggie's sisters offered to stay together if Maggie would continue to shop, cook and clean for them. That way she could finish her senior year at high school. They meant well, but Maggie had had enough of being an unpaid housekeeper. She answered an advertisement in the *Daily Argus* for factory workers at the Carson Company, spending ten cents to make the two-hour trolley and bus ride to Hastings-on-Hudson. The ad promised clean, inexpensive apartments for those young ladies who were hired. The apartments were located next to the plant and were to be shared by up to four girls per apartment with no more than two girls per bedroom.

Because of her clean, pretty face, her excellent though incomplete academic record, and her respectable family background, Maggie was hired to fill one of the openings. There was a tearful farewell when she said goodby to her sisters and left home for the first and, she knew, the last time.

It didn't take Maggie long to discover she had merely exchanged one form of drudgery for another. While she was no longer expected to shop, cook and clean for her sisters, she still had to shop and cook for herself. That in itself was all right, but her three roommates had no interest in house cleaning. Once they discovered Maggie would not live in a dirty apartment, they took advantage of the situation. If Maggie didn't clean the apartment, the apartment remained dirty. There were unmade beds, clothes thrown all over, scraps of food on the floor, dirty dishes piled up in the sink and spilled makeup in the bathroom sink. They didn't care. The mess was something all three were used to. Their mothers had done only what was necessary, so why should they be different? They thought of Maggie as a dumb, stuck-up snob.

What really mattered to them was having a date on Friday and Saturday nights. Men didn't care about a clean apartment; they wanted a sexy looking girl to fool around with. The question always was, should they or shouldn't they "go all the way"? Since the three didn't trust one another, Maggie became their unwilling confidante. She learned each did "go all the way" all the time. If they didn't, the boys would take out other girls who did.

Occasionally, one would return from a date with a few bruises. "Mickey got drunk and slapped me for dancing with Pat." None of the bruises were serious, and the girls considered them part of the price to be paid for Friday and Saturday dates. Serious beatings were reserved for after marriage. They knew. They'd watched their parents go at it often enough.

Maggie did not understand any of it. The girls didn't seem to enjoy the sex, and she found it difficult to distinguish between Mickey and Pat. She had never seen and couldn't even imagine her father getting drunk and hitting her mother.

On the few occasions when one of her roommates had a date who happened to have an available friend, Maggie was considered "safe" to be included as a blind date. She would never make a pass at her roommate's guy. But she had no idea what to say or do on a date. As soon as the friend found out she wasn't going to "go all the way" or even any part of the way, she wasn't asked out again. For the most part, her time after work and on weekends was spent listening to the radio when she was home alone or going alone to the local movie. She saw films in which men and women lived lives that filled her with awe—and a deep resentment that she would never have a chance to experience firsthand what she had seen on the screen.

And then there was the job. She worked in the division that rolled and packed gauze bandages. All day long she and nineteen other girls sat at a bench. The girls all wore white smocks and white caps to keep their hair out of the packages. What they wore under the smocks was a matter of personal choice. Some wore dresses, some slips and a few almost nothing. It wasn't unusual for a girl to slip off to a special area in a loft for a "quickie" with one of the men. Usually a few dollars were exchanged.

The gauze came in pre-cut rolls. The girls wrapped the rolled gauze and then placed it on a cart behind them. When their cart was full, they would ring a bell. There were times when as many as fifteen or twenty minutes would go by between the ringing of the bell and the cart being wheeled away. The other girls on the bench enjoyed the "free time." They would whisper and giggle among themselves about who was going out with whom and who had finally got Jack or Charlie to pop the question. Maggie was shut off from all this. She would sit staring blindly into space and try to close off her mind. Her thoughts would keep returning to the films and radio dramas and the dreams of a life she was missing.

Lunch break consisted of more of the same. The girls brought their own lunches and sat in their white smocks and caps at the long tables with backless wooden benches on each side, chattering. Always about the same thing: Jack, Joe, Charlie and Bobby. Though Maggie was surrounded by them, she was alone. Rarely was she included in the conversation. The isolation had nothing to do with any attempt on her part to be different. She was different without knowing it, but the girls knew it and resented her for it.

Once she had an idea that there would be less time lost waiting for the carts to be moved after sounding the bell if the boxes were also stacked on the carts. The girls could do their own packing. Once the gauze was in a sealed box, the cart could be pushed aside and another one put in its place. They could all be collected two or three times a day. Loss of production time would be cut to a minimum. So would the "free time." Maggie suggested the change to the foreman, Mack Parker, who told her to go back to work. Two weeks later the change she suggested was put into effect. Parker took the credit.

The long days became weeks, the weeks months, and the months years. The work remained the same. Boring, endless. Maggie ached for some relief. Anything. She understood why the girls wanted to get married so badly. It was an escape. Her memories of another life when she was young and lived in the fieldstone house faded beneath the reality of the factory and the apartment. Maybe she could find a boyfriend who was nice, who wouldn't insist on sex in the rear seat of a car, who wouldn't get drunk and beat her up if they were to marry. Maybe she had no other choice.

Maggie's loneliness was verging on desperation when, after three long, soul-stifling years, William Carson picked her off the production line and selected her for her present job.

Since Mary had given her no information, Maggie decided to accept her good luck and adopt a wait-and-see attitude. About a week later, she got a partial answer. Mary told her, "I don't know why you were selected, but I've found out what you're going to do."

Maggie didn't know whether to be glad or scared. "What is it? Please tell me."

"It's a marvelous opportunity, but it's confidential. Understand? Completely confidential."

Maggie understood. Confidential!

"You're going to be Mr. Henry Carson's private secretary." Before Maggie could ask the question, Mary added, "Yes, Henry Carson is Mr. Carson's son. He's coming into the firm."

"I didn't know Mr. Carson had a son. He's never mentioned a son. And I don't think the son has ever been here."

"He has two sons." Maggie was wide-eyed. "That's right, but you'll be working for Mr. Henry. I understand he'll be starting in a year or so."

Mary went back to her work, leaving Maggie to ponder the news. It was pointless to ask Mary how she knew, because Mary wouldn't tell her. It was privileged information. Maggie's thoughts were in a whirl. What was Henry Carson like? What did he look like? How did he behave? Would she like working for him? Lots of questions and no answers. She thought she might try to see the mysterious Henry Carson. Should she? Yes? No? Why not? Of course she should see him! But how? Where?

Then her dilemma was solved. Mary O'Toole happened to mention that Mr. Carson and his sons attended church every Sunday, the Episcopal church in Pleasantville near their home. So one fine winter morning, with the new-fallen snow covering the unplowed road, she borrowed a car and drove, skidding and sliding, to the small, white wooden church in Pleasantville. She arrived early and waited in a pew in the rear of the church. Sure enough, just before services began, Mr. Carson and two young men entered the church, marched up the aisle and sat in the places reserved for them. But which son was Henry? The tall, handsome blond man or the shorter, red-haired one?

Maggie prayed it was the blond. He was so handsome. Of course, the one with the red hair wasn't bad. Far from it. But the more she stared, the more she prayed, "The blond. Please. The blond!" She fantasized Arabian Nights of romance with a blond Henry.

When the service ended, a discreet questioning of the minister told her her mistake. Her daydreaming began again, but this time the new man was slightly shorter and had bright red hair. A little later she wondered what would become of the blond-haired son whose name she had just learned: Francis. Maybe another secretary had been chosen for him?

While this answered the questions of what her job would be and for whom she would work, one nagging question remained. Why her? Why had Mr. Carson taken the trouble to have her trained to be his son's secretary? A perfectly competent professional secretary could have been hired. He had even given her time off to complete her high school education and receive an academic diploma. Why? It didn't make sense.

The winter of 1939 was particularly harsh and long. Colds, grippe and pneumonia were rampant. Even the indestructible Mary O'Toole was forced to take to her bed with flu. This left Maggie handling William Carson's secretarial needs. Her two-year apprenticeship had given her both the technical skills and the knowledge of office routine she needed to carry on with little loss in efficiency.

It was during this time that she made a discovery. One morning when she was opening the office mail she came across a curious envelope. First, the envelope was hand addressed, and the word Mr. was omitted before William Carson's name. Second, the return address was a handwritten name and a post office box number. There was nothing on the envelope to indicate either that it was personal or confidential. So she opened it along with the other mail. She was startled to discover that the contents were a combination of a carefully typed technical report, a handwritten note, and finally a picture of a rather unattractive young lady. She blinked as she realized that both the note and the report were written on the stationery of a rival concern, Wilkenson, Inc. She also realized she had made a mistake in opening the envelope. But how was she to know? After gathering the part of the mail she would give to Mr. Carson for his personal attention, she knocked on the door to his office.

"Come in."

She entered and handed him his mail. Her voice was shaky as she apologized for opening the envelope.

William frowned a little and shook his head. "Don't worry. It's hardly your fault if someone is careless enough not to mark a confidential document 'confidential.' " He looked directly at Maggie. "You do understand that this matter is confidential? I mean totally."

"I understand, sir."

William leaned back in his chair. "Sit down for a moment, Maggie. I think this might be the moment for us to talk."

"Yes, sir."

"Unless my eyes have done me a disservice, I've seen you at church in Pleasantville lately. Could it be for the excellence of the service?"

"No, sir. Er, I mean, yes, sir. The services are excellent."

"And our minister's sermon? Also excellent?"

Having been caught out, Maggie realized she had best go along with the charade. "Inspiring. Far superior to our pastor's."

"Inspiring? Isn't that a bit of an overstatement?"

Maggie shook her head. "They are inspiring."

"I see." He grinned a slightly lopsided grin and moistened his lips. "I don't suppose you noticed my sons in the midst of such inspiration?"

Maggie couldn't control her enthusiasm. "I think you have two very handsome sons."

William paused, and wanting to leave before the conversation went any further, Maggie started to rise. William signaled her to stay. "I know you have extra work with Mary out sick, but this won't take much longer." She settled back and waited. "Did you happen to notice the picture of the young lady that was in the envelope you opened?"

"Yes, sir. It fell out."

"As a woman, what did you think of her?"

"Oh! Well, one can't tell much from a picture, but she seemed nice."

"Would you say Selma Wilkenson is pretty?"

So that's who the girl is. Selma Wilkenson. Maggie thought before she answered and chose her words very carefully. "Pretty? No, not really. But I'm sure she has many excellent qualities," she added cautiously.

"Are you? Why?" William asked, a bit sourly. "Because she's an heiress? That's not a good reason for anything. Actually, she's a foolish, unattractive young woman. The picture is flattering."

Maggie wondered why Mr. Carson was telling her this. Why was he interested in her opinion about a woman she did not know and would never know?

Abruptly he changed the subject. "Have you ever heard of the English king Henry II and his wife, Eleanor of Aquitaine?"

Maggie was glad to end the discussion of Selma Wilkenson. She did know something about Henry II. Years ago, she and her mother had talked about England and Scotland. "My mother was Scottish. I think we talked about Henry II, but I don't remember what we said."

"It's not important. Eleanor was the mother of four kings."

Maggie was suitably impressed.

"Would you like to learn about Henry and Eleanor?" William was hard put not to laugh at what he was about to say. "I happen to have a book about them. It's called *England Under the Normans*, but it's mostly about Henry and Eleanor. Why don't you borrow it?"

For some reason, William Carson wanted her to read this book. Of course she would. It might even be interesting. "I'd love to."

William handed her a book which had been lying on a table behind his desk. "Now I've taken enough of your time for today. When you've finished the book, we'll discuss what you've learned."

Maggie left the office feeling as confused as she had ever been in her life. Why was Mr. Carson interested in her opinion of a woman she didn't know and would never know? And then the book. She had a strong suspicion he had bought the book for her and was only waiting for the proper moment to give it to her. But why? Why a book about an English king. Maybe reading the book would tell her why.

It took Maggie almost a month, reading at night and on weekends, to finish the book, but it was fascinating reading and made her regret all the more her lack of a good education. She put the book into a manila envelope and brought it back to the office. It looked as clean as when she first took it home.

By this time, Mary had recovered and was back in the office, so it took a week for Maggie to find an opportunity to let William know she had read the book and would like to return it to him.

"Good! Would you mind staying a little later tomorrow evening? I'd be interested in hearing your thoughts on the book."

Maggie was sharing an apartment—the cooking and cleaning—with one girl, Anna Jaskowicz. But tomorrow would be Friday, and the girls took Fridays off. Maggie had planned to see a movie alone, and she knew her roommate would be out until dawn with her latest "steady." Sometimes when her body ached with loneliness, she wondered why no one came along for her.

"Yes, sir. Tomorrow would be fine."

"Tomorrow it is. I'll be at the factory during the day, and I'll meet you here between five and five-fifteen."

Maggie returned to her desk. Mr. Carson was being very strange. She felt like a detective searching for clues.

William Carson watched Maggie leave the office. Although he had masked his feelings, he was more than a little apprehensive about tomorrow's meeting. It occurred to him that when he had started this venture, he had created a far more complicated situation than he had bargained for. So, in a totally uncharacteristic gesture, he had put the meeting off until tomorrow.

It had seemed so much simpler when he had first selected the girl for the job. There was, of course, her beauty. The color of her lips, eyes, hair, all glowing with the brightness of her so-alive nature. Her body was rich and supple, and although she was quite tall, she seemed to spring up and carry her head high. And yet, there was an odd mixture of elements in the girl. Her beauty was nothing for which she took credit or to which she gave much thought.

Then there was her intelligence, which, unlike education, was something that William was able to attribute to possibly one person in a thousand. Several of her suggestions on assembly line changes had been very astute and were adopted. He had let the foreman take credit for the ideas, but his spy system informed him of the actual source.

Last and most important was a very special instinct he had about women, a result of his long years as a widower. This instinct told him that Maggie Rhodes had a rare, if untapped, quality. He knew that there were some women who did not enjoy the sexual act, and others who delighted in it but only with a particular man. And then there were a few women, Marion being of the cast, for whom passion was a necessity of their nature. To make love, to give and receive physical pleasure, was an irresistible demand of their blood. It was a gift, but a dangerous one.

Maggie Rhodes had that gift. He suspected she would cause considerable confusion among the young men she met.

While her stunning good looks and exceptional figure should have drawn them to her, her too-prim dress and her reticent, even remote, manner created a barrier that kept them at a distance. Had she dressed and behaved more obviously, the men would have been standing in line. As it was, William would not have been surprised if she were a virgin. And profoundly unconscious that she, by her true nature, was made for love.

It was this final intuition that made him decide to have her trained as Henry's secretary. But this evening in the privacy of his own office, alone with his thoughts, William questioned the wisdom of his original plan. He felt it was shabby and he was more than a little dismayed at its crudeness. And no longer was he confident about what Maggie's reaction would be.

That evening, after her roommate had gone to bed, Maggie settled herself in the most comfortable chair in the living room and began to think. What did she know?

She knew Mr. Carson had two sons, and she was going to work for one of them, Henry Carson. She knew there was something confidential going on between the Carson Company and Wilkenson, Inc. She also knew there was a Selma Wilkenson whom Mr. Carson thought unattractive. What else did she know? Not much, except that Mr. Carson had wanted her to read a book about Henry II and Eleanor of Aquitaine. Why?

What was in the book that related to her? A twelfth-century English king and his queen? She picked up the book and thumbed through the pages. What was it? Where was it? She thought about the lives of Eleanor and Henry. About Henry's struggle with Thomas à Becket. Was William referring to this? Was there a struggle between William Carson and someone? Between William and Henry maybe? Was she possibly being warned who was still king at the Carson Company? Was there a struggle between Henry and Francis? Quite likely. But how did that relate to her? Apparently Henry had won or would win. But these were struggles for power between men. Concentrate on Eleanor and Henry. It had to be reasonably simple or Mr. Carson wouldn't have hoped the story would tell her something. But she wasn't getting anywhere. Go over the story. Eleanor, Countess of Aquitaine, had been married to the king of France. Her marriage was annulled, and she married Henry, thus uniting her own vast holdings with those of Henry.

Wait a minute! The picture! Selma Wilkenson!

Maggie knew she had found something. It sounded outlandish, but it made good sense if you knew the rich and powerful. Times hadn't changed that much for them. In the middle of the twentieth century, William Carson was planning a dynastic marriage between Henry or Francis and Selma Wilkenson. A marriage that would unite not land but companies. That was it! She was positive that was it! What a shame for one of those sons. Both Henry and Francis were so good looking, and Selma was, well, so plain. She stopped dead.

Suddenly she understood, and in a rage at the understanding, she slammed the book to the floor and screamed, "The bastard! The goddamn fucking bastard! I'm to play Rosamund. Damn it! Henry's mistress! Bastard!" The questions were answered. The picture was complete. But she hated it.

The bedroom door opened, and a very sleepy Anna looked out. "Are you all right, Maggie? Did you scream?"

"No, I'm not all right. Oh, Christ! Yes, I'm fine. I'm just angry."

"What are you so mad about?" There was concern in Anna's voice.

Maggie looked at Anna. Her face was swollen with sleep, her makeup still on. "I'm fine. Just fine. Go back to sleep."

The face disappeared, the door closed, leaving Maggie with her fury. She would confront William Carson in the morning. No. In the evening. She would quit on the spot. There were plenty of jobs for a trained secretary, and that's what she was. A very well trained secretary with a high school diploma to boot. He'd see!

She looked down at the book she had slammed to the floor in her burst of rage. It was a fine book. She picked it up, and seeing that several of the pages were creased, she tried to smooth them out. It looked almost as good as new, but it wasn't. And she wasn't. She felt dirty, betrayed. A used piece of merchandise.

Gradually, Maggie's rage began to recede. She was still angry, but other factors were beginning to emerge: who she was, who she had been, who she wanted to be. Yes, she would listen to the offer. Unless she totally misjudged William Carson, he wasn't going to have such an easy time making it. That was why he had given her the book. Maybe that was why that special envelope was not marked "confidential." She was supposed to open it, to know what was coming, and by knowing, make it easier for him.

She wasn't going to make it easier for him. If William Carson had something to say to her, he was going to have to say it. Word by word.

Then she would walk out. Yes, she would! Walk out! She wasn't a whore, and she wasn't going to be treated like one. Maybe she would stay home tomorrow and show up just in time for the meeting. No! That would make him suspect, and she didn't want him alerted. She'd be composed. Puzzled. Let him sweat.

It took hours before Maggie was ready to climb quietly into her narrow twin bed that stood next to Anna's. The clock with its shining radium dial said two-thirty. Lying there in the dark room, Maggie reviewed her situation again in the crude light the nearness of her roommate shed on it. Anna, with her half-washed face, her too-frequent affairs, her limited opportunity to meet different types of men. Maggie knew that as a factory worker, she, like Anna, had had little to look forward to except a life of struggle, a marriage to another laborer, a bunch of kids and growing older. Her chance for happiness would have rested entirely on her choice of a husband, and there wasn't much choice. She had seen and heard too much of the desperate lives the women lived once the first sexual excitement had faded and the children, the boredom and the grinding money pinch set in. Girls who had been round and firm grew fat and sloppy. Young men who had been lean and muscular grew paunchy and dull. And there were the stories of the drinking and wife beating. She knew all about the ugliness of their lives. And what really frightened her was the knowledge that without William Carson's help, she would have had to accommodate herself to that life.

This fact brought into sharp focus the misery from which she had been rescued. In objecting to his offer wasn't she sacrificing herself to one of those abstract notions of what was and what was not moral? What debt did she owe a social order that had condemned her father, her entire family, to destitution? Why should she hesitate to make private use of an advantage she was offered? The disgrace in the act lay in the name attached to it. Call it "whore," and it became unthinkable. But describe it as a business arrangement, and it was something else again.

Throughout the night the two forces fought their battle in her mind. When she rose at six the next morning, exhausted from lack of sleep, she hoped her moral scruples had won. But she wasn't sure.

William spent the day at the factory. He had two motives in mind. First, there was the matter of maintaining his usual high visibility. Second, he didn't want to see Maggie before their meeting. That way he hoped to make it easier to present his proposal in all its tarnished glory.

Maggie was glad not to see him. The day slipped by in a routine fashion. Mary O'Toole sensed that something was wrong, but since Maggie said nothing, Mary just watched and wondered.

Finally it was five o'clock. After Mary left, Maggie brought a small bag out from under her desk. She packed it very carefully, taking only those things she considered hers. When she walked out, she would not have to return on Monday for her belongings. No false exits for her. The bag was barely packed when William arrived.

"Good afternoon, Maggie."

"Good afternoon, Mr. Carson."

"If you'll give me five minutes, I'll buzz you, and we can have that chat we agreed upon."

"Certainly, sir. I have plenty of time."

Something in Maggie's voice caused an alarm to sound in William's brain. He looked sideways at her for an instant. Her face was composed, but her body was tense, leaning forward. He noticed the book on top of her desk. She meant to return it that evening. She knew! She had put the pieces together and knew what they were going to talk about. But what would she do? He couldn't tell. He glanced at the mail. There was nothing to give him an excuse for further delay, so he buzzed for Maggie.

The buzzer sounded much louder in the quiet, empty office, startling Maggie and forcing her to her feet. Controlling herself, she picked up the book and walked slowly toward the office. Even though he had just buzzed for her, she knocked on the door.

"Come in."

She entered the room. William wasn't at his desk. He was sitting in one of the huge leather chairs on the other side of the room. This was not to be strictly a business meeting. Seeing him gesture toward either the couch or another chair, Maggie chose the couch. It wasn't quite so deep. It would be easier to get up and leave.

"How was the day? Fridays aren't usually that busy." William hoped to smooth the way with small talk.

"Routine." She would be as patient as he. More so, if necessary.

"Did the new mimeograph machine arrive?"

"I think so. Mary got a call from Receiving. Something arrived."

"Good." William knew he would have to come to the point. "Tell me what you thought about the book on Henry II and Eleanor."

"Very interesting. I'm sorry I know so little about history. One can learn from the past."

"And did you learn from this book?"

Maggie smiled. He was pushing her. "I don't think Henry really meant to have Thomas à Becket killed."

"Most historians would agree."

So they talked about Eleanor's imprisonment, about her four sons who became kings. Clearly, Maggie had spent time and care in her reading. But the one subject William wished to discuss seemed to have eluded her. Once, when he brought up Rosamund and Henry's love affair, he thought they would get to the point. Instead, she made an observation about how Henry changed the English system of Common Law.

Actually, Maggie was having as much trouble with the conversation as William. The hard cutting edge of her anger had been dulled by her long night of thinking. Added to this was her liking and respect for William, and her gratitude for having been taken off the production line and given an opportunity to live another sort of life. Her great fear lay in her old incurable dream of poverty and the life which poverty forces one to lead, in her fear of the mounting tide of squalor against which her mother had so valiantly fought—a fight which she had been spared. It was with a feeling of resignation that Maggie finally decided to come to the point. She said, "Mr. Carson, I enjoyed the book very much, but I have two questions I'd like to ask you."

"I'll try to answer them."

Maggie took a deep breath. The temptation of the idea which her first, instinctive reaction had forced her to reject with rage now tugged at her will. How much strength had she left to maintain her position? "Why did you select me to be trained as an executive secretary? There are many women here who were far more qualified than I. Or you could have gone outside for a top professional."

"I could have. But I checked. I know who suggested the production changes for which Mack Parker took credit. You are unusually intelligent. And there are other reasons."

"Leaving aside my small qualifications, why did you give me a book on Henry II to read? Please, Mr. Carson. As you said, I'm not stupid, and I'd appreciate a straight answer."

"You are far from stupid, so I assume you've guessed."

"I'd like to hear it from you." Maggie was making a strong effort to remain calm.

William found he was more affected by her attitude than he had expected. Much as he disliked doing it, he would try to explain. "Maggie, having seen both my sons, do you have any opinion about them? Aside from their good looks, that is."

"No. How could I? I don't know them." Maggie knew she was lying. She recalled her romantic fantasies first about Francis and then Henry, but she would never admit this to William Carson.

"I assume that Mary did her usual excellent job, and you are aware of what is to happen next year."

"I understand that Henry Carson is coming to work for the company, and I'm to be his secretary."

William smiled. It was a forced smile that went no further than his lips. The closer they got to stating openly what he had planned, the more impossible it seemed. "That's correct, but I—er—I have something to add to that." He looked carefully at Maggie. She was wearing a dark dress. Her black curly hair was neat, and her beauty wasn't marred by excess makeup. What had made him think that she would agree to a backstairs affair with his son? He had had some vague idea that her ambition and personal sexual needs could be used, but now he knew better. She would hear him out, and she would leave. She wouldn't like leaving, but she would.

Maggie noticed his hands resting on his thighs. The long fingers clenched, then relaxed, only to clench again. Maggie realized the possibilities of embarrassment the whole subject held for him.

"Maggie." He paused, thought and made a decision. He couldn't do it. For one of the few times in his life William Carson was thoroughly dismayed with himself and his judgment, the values he had placed on another human being. "Maggie, I had an idea. I now realize it wasn't a very good idea, and I think it might be just as well to drop the subject right now."

After making his little speech, William slumped back in his chair, but the view of having failed to live up to his image of himself drove him to continue. If she had not been aware of what he had planned, he could have ended the discussion, gone home and licked his wounds. As matters stood, he felt something further was called for.

"Under the circumstances, I feel you are entitled to certain options." Maggie made a gesture that was meant to indicate that there was no need for him to go on, but he ignored it. "You've become an excellent secretary and have many other admirable qualities. For reasons of which we are both aware," he continued, admitting for the first time that he knew she understood the purpose of their meeting, "you may wish to leave the Carson Company." As he said the words, he knew that her leaving would cause him a genuine personal loss. The depth of the loss surprised him, but he had to continue. "If you do wish to leave the company, I will see that you receive the finest of references, and I will call a number of men who I'm confident can make good use of your loyalty and skills. However, if you choose to stay with us"—he was indulging himself in some wishful thinking—"I will find you a job in another division."

A blush of surprise rose to Maggie's face, and it deepened into a glow in which humiliation and gratitude were mingled. "Thank you, Mr. Carson. Give me a minute to decide what to do."

In the silence that followed, Maggie had a clear picture of her choices. She could have a job with another company or a different job within the Carson Company. Or could she stay where she was? He hadn't said so, but she could, couldn't she? She thought about Henry Carson and how attracted she had been to him. She thought again about other men and how unattractive she found them. She felt an urgent desire to find someone special, but every time she tried to focus her attention on a single man, she found herself put off by what she saw him to be. Henry Carson was the first exception. She understood William's plan, and the yearning to go along with it was insidious. Not only was her mind pulling her, but the needs of her body were also nagging. Would she have rejected Henry if there were no strings attached? She doubted it. More and more the pursuing Furies took the shape of childhood memories. Of her losses. Of her broken and destitute family. And now of her desires and needs. Why shouldn't she explore the opportunity for personal satisfaction when she was not under any obligation to do more than either her feelings or pride inclined her to do?

Why should she resign? Hadn't Mr. Carson made that decision unnecessary? For some reason he had changed his mind. She would not be forced into an unwanted relationship. So Maggie made her decision. She looked up at him. "I think, sir, I'd rather stay here. Right here."

William stared at her. Having so thoroughly shamed him, she now seemed interested in some form of accommodation, and he tried to understand this turn in her logic. "I'm not certain I'm following you."

"Your son does have to have a highly skilled secretary, and I certainly know the company routine and procedures thoroughly. I'm probably as good a secretary as anyone you could find for him."

William felt slightly ridiculous. The years of despair and hopelessness spent in the factory were all still so very real to the girl. He had been thoroughly dense. Beneath Maggie's veneer of pride and independence was a very frightened young woman who had had a terrible time with life. Then there were the things in her nature that he had sensed in the first place. There had been no need for him to meddle. Events would have taken their course.

He believed that to some extent Maggie was deceiving herself into thinking her role might begin and end with secretarial work. The key word was "might." It also "might not." Now William understood that her dignity had to be preserved. Matters had to be arranged to enable romance to have its best chance to flower. He would play the game her way.

"I'm delighted that you're willing to stay. Henry will need all the professional help he can get." He thought for a moment. "And in consideration of your increased value not only as a secretary but, shall we say, as aide-without-title, I think it's only reasonable to start by increasing your salary."

Maggie understood.

"As of Friday, we will increase your salary one hundred dollars per week. You'll be paid the same amount as Mary. She earns enough to afford her own house."

"Oh?"

"I don't think you're quite ready for a house, but you certainly will be able to afford your own apartment. And a nice one at that." He knew that any relationship between Maggie and Henry required that the girl have her own apartment. And that was only the first step. "Further, the company will give you the opportunity to enter its executive education program so you can continue your education both in business and the arts. The company will pay for your courses, and if you continue, it could lead to a college degree." If Maggie was going to attract Henry for something more than a quick weekend, she would require additional education.

Maggie listened to William. She knew everything he said had a rational basis, but she also knew that he, like she, was not entirely sincere. The awareness of her past only served to enhance the concrete gains now being offered. The terms of the deal, so to speak. The arguments pleading for her to accept them were the old, unanswerable ones. Why should she hesitate in accepting them? Because they would make her more attractive to Henry? Because they would make her more susceptible? If they would, they would.

Looking directly into his eyes, she said, "I'm very grateful to you, sir, for all you're doing for me."

"Don't be grateful, Maggie. I'm only doing what's right and proper. You'll find, in life, that most people get about what they deserve."

Maggie was silent for a moment while William's eyes continued to search her, consider her, question her. Then she nodded, belatedly noticing that his hand was extended toward her. It had an instant effect.

Without hesitation, she took his hand in hers and clasped it. Hard. She realized without a word passing between them that they were shaking hands on a deal. Afterward she dropped her hands back into her lap, exhausted. Then, gathering her strength, she rose quickly to her feet. "It's getting late, Mr. Carson. I should be getting home now."

"Yes, you should. Good night, Maggie."

William watched her leave the office. As she closed the door after her, he felt a sense of failure. Too late he realized that he wished she would walk out on Henry and the Carson Company.

When Maggie reached home, she found the apartment empty. She walked into the bedroom and slowly began to undress. As she did this, she thought about her conversation with William Carson and what had come of it. For one thing, an apartment. Her own apartment! Imagine it! Living alone would certainly make it easier to invite a man over, if only for dinner. And, of course, having a roommate had made many other things impossible. In her own apartment she'd be free, free to do anything. Even to have a man over and make love. She thought, almost with awe, of the depth of William's understanding. How well he knew her. Yes, in her own apartment she could make love to a man. She closed her eyes. If she chose, she could even make love to Henry Carson. If she chose?

But could she choose? Her body was completely uneducated, untouched. She was a virgin who knew nothing about making love. She understood—only from the giggling, half-sentences she had overheard on occasion—the basics of sex, but she was far too private a person to ask anyone for more information. Gently, she slid two fingers into her vagina and moved them around slowly, hoping to feel something. Anything. But she felt nothing. Not the faintest sensation. Only the soft, wet slipperiness of the inside of her body. Some mistress! What a prize William had selected for his son!

Now she stood naked before the bathroom mirror. Suppose this was her own apartment? Hers alone? She thought of Henry, and the idea that they might make love filled her with a kind of recklessness. She thought of his face, his hands, his touch. All the years of repressed desire, all her long-controlled sensuality started to awaken, to flare up free for the first time. She abandoned herself to a passionate fantasy of Henry. Clasping her arms around herself, she hugged herself tightly, and the arms around her became Henry's; as she sank to her knees, her body bent forward. The very air of the room seemed to touch her skin like a caress.

Minutes passed before she fully recovered her senses. She still knelt naked on the floor. If she could arouse such sensations in herself, the thought of the delights a man might provide made her tremble with anticipation.

At length, she stood up and put on a bathrobe. She went to sit in the living room and consider her situation in the light of her new knowledge. It would be unthinkable to deny her body the wonders that making love promised. On the other hand, the puzzle of finding the appropriate man remained. The kind of man she could respond to and who would respond to her. Someone to teach her.

What was it that Mr. Carson had also suggested? She should register for classes in a nearby college. Wasn't it possible that she might meet such a man at one of those classes? A man who would attract her and be attracted by her. Certainly the men who attended night school at college were a different type than the factory laborers and junior office clerks who had been her only dates. Perhaps, and she colored at the thought, Mr. Carson would somehow have a hand in solving the problem of providing a man. He had solved so many other problems. Why not this one?

After her meeting with William, Maggie did register in night school at Iona College in New Rochelle. She was in search of an education of both mind and body. As she had hoped, in regard to her body, here and there in a class she did meet a man to whom she was quite attracted. Usually these men were older, better educated, more worldly. To Maggie's relief, the men to whom she responded were usually attracted to her. The result was that, on occasion, she was able to choose one from among those who invited her to dinner to "help her with her studies" and also to initiate her into the pleasures of lovemaking.

While she did not know for certain, she suspected that William had somehow arranged for appropriate men to be in her classes. She was right. However, he did no more than provide the opportunity, counting on Maggie's beauty to do the rest. The Carson Company Education Program plus the Carson Company Scholarships for Working Executives were long-established traditions. They brought ambitious men, intelligent men, responsible men into night courses at various colleges. These men usually had expenses that made the free education very desirable. Often they were married men who might be interested in an adventure, not a disruption of their marriage.

Maggie Rhodes was ready for the call from William Carson. She had been waiting for over a year for this day, and a year is a long time for a twenty-two-year-old girl to wait for anything. Knowing that she would meet her new boss the following day, she had bathed and washed her hair the night before. A carefully selected dress was ironed and placed on the back of a chair along with her most seductive underwear: black silk panties trimmed with fine lace, a three-quarter-length matching slip and bra, and a very light girdle. At the last minute, she decided not to wear either the girdle or brassiere. Her body was firm enough.

William waited for Maggie to appear. Henry watched her cross the floor. She stopped at a point where she could see both men.

"Henry, this is Maggie Rhodes. I've chosen her to be your private secretary and guide until you learn for yourself where things are. Maggie, this is my son, Henry Carson."

Henry held out his hand. "Miss Rhodes."

Maggie shook hands. "Good afternoon, Mr. Carson."

They stood holding hands, not knowing exactly what to do next. It amused William to wait and see who would let go first. Finally, Maggie dropped Henry's hand and turned to William. "A slight problem, Mr. Carson."

"Oh? So soon?"

"Yes." She smiled. "Not earthshaking. How will Mary and I address you? There are now two Mr. Carsons."

William stroked his chin. "Yes. I see the possible confusion." He went to the door. "Mary, would you mind coming in for a moment?" Mary appeared looking puzzled. She hoped things were going well.

"Maggie has made me aware of a minor problem. Exactly how will you distinguish which Mr. Carson you want?" William was hard pressed not to smile at the foolishness of the situation. But there certainly were two of them now.

Mary rose to the occasion. "I have a suggestion, sir."

"Good. Our two young people seem to have no ideas." Neither Maggie nor Henry missed William's deliberate joining of them.

"Could we refer to you as Mr. W and Mr. H?"

William wasn't ready for equality yet. "A nice idea. But I think, for the moment, I'll remain Mr. Carson. Henry, would you prefer Mr. Henry or Mr. H?"

Henry smiled inwardly at the obvious positioning of the titles. William was still in charge. His turn would come. The years were on his side. "Why not Mr. H? It has a nice rakish sound."

"Mr. H it is. Does that solve your problem, Maggie?"

"Yes, sir." Actually, Mr. H had a nice sound, and there would be time in private to call him Henry. Should that time ever come.

"Good. I enjoy solving problems." The pompousness of the remark almost made Henry laugh out loud. He could never tell when William was being serious. Complicated, important problems might be solved with a word, while trivia could, if William was in the mood, require endless delicate discussion. "Maggie, I'd like you to plan a tour of the factory for Mr. H tomorrow. Spend some time at the R and D facility as well."

"Certainly, sir." She turned to Henry. "Would eight-fifteen be convenient to start?"

"I'll meet you here at eight. We'll have a cup of coffee and be on our way." After the two women left the office, Henry asked, "Incidentally, Mr. Carson, when you retire, will I become Mr. Carson and you Mr. W?"

Always the direct attack. The bludgeon not the rapier. William refused to let Henry see how well he had scored. "When, and if, I retire, you can be anything you like. I'll probably be in my grave."

"Somehow I think not. In any case, let's get back to the Wilkenson patents."

"Agreed. Again I suggest we start with a weekend at the house."

Mimicking William, Henry said, "Agreed. Again I ask how you plan to arrange this fateful event?"

"Again, you are forgetting the lawyer."

"Again, I am not forgetting the lawyer. By the way, what's his name?"

"Craig Spears."

"By the way, what makes you think he's your man exclusively? Couldn't he be passing the same papers around to all the suitors?"

"I like that." William sat down. Suddenly aware that they had been having this conversation on their feet, Henry also sat down. The seat creaked in protest. "Say, Henry, watch your weight. If you get fat, not only will you fail to survive me, but we'll have to be constantly refurbishing the office."

"Unfortunately, you had a Neanderthal somewhere in your ancestry." He studied his father thoughtfully. "Exactly what did I say that you liked?"

"You recognized that Spears might be no straighter with me than he is with his employers. Of course he isn't. That's something we'll have to deal with later. In any case, do you have the papers on Wilkenson, Inc.?"

"No. I flushed them down the toilet. They were much too incriminating."

"You what?"

"Nothing. I was kidding. Of course I have the papers."

"That's not funny." He stopped. Henry had done it to him again. "I agree many of the so-called business problems can be amusing. But you must learn when, on rare occasion, they are not. This is one of those rare occasions."

"Sorry." Henry knew he had gone too far, but it was necessary to keep William as much off balance as possible. Otherwise Henry would be walked over. He went to his desk, opened one of the briefcases, separated the special envelope from the rest of the documents and handed it to his father.

William noted approvingly that Henry had carefully resealed the envelope. "We can expect Mr. Spears at any moment. He's due at four."

"Why didn't you say so?"

"I did say so when I was ready."

Henry bristled at the answer. William liked to play games with him. He had to admit that he liked to do exactly the same with his father. They were a well-matched pair. He would have to learn not to react to every one of William's needles. "All right. What are you planning when our pigeon walks into our web?"

"Don't mix your metaphors. Just sit still and listen. If you have to answer a direct question, grunt."

"Will a cough do?"

"Yes." A knock on the door interrupted them. The door opened, and Mary O'Toole entered.

"There's a Mr. Spears downstairs who insists he has an appointment with you. It's not in your book, but he insists." The last words were said in a slightly accusing tone. How could Mr. Carson have an appointment about which she knew nothing, that wasn't even in his book? It reflected on her competence.

"I'm sorry, Mary. I made the appointment last Friday in New York and forgot to tell you."

The apology mollified Mary. "Shall I have him shown up?"

"Would you mind going down and getting him? I don't want him wandering around the offices unescorted."

Mary smiled. She liked being entrusted with special duties and possibly Mr. Spears was special? "I'll take care of it at once."

"Leave the door open for now. When you show him in, close the door. If we run after five, there's no need for you to stay."

With the door open and Maggie at her desk going over her plans for tomorrow, they weren't going to be able to talk about anything important. And that was the point. William had had enough of sparring with Henry. He wanted to get ready for Craig Spears.

A few minutes later, Mary came in followed by a short, portly man with thin brown hair carefully combed to cover a growing bald spot. His cheeks had a red tint, and one could see the fine veins in his nose.

"Hello, Craig. Come in. Come right in."

Henry was reminded more than ever of the spider and the fly. Craig Spears entered the room, and Mary shut the door. He sat in the seat William offered him.

"Before we get down to business, Craig, I want to introduce my son, Henry. He's totally familiar with the situation."

Spears looked at Henry, nodded curtly, then turned back to William. "I don't like it. We agreed everything was to be confidential."

"Henry is absolutely discreet. And Craig, he is my son. Should anything happen to me, you'll do business with him."

"I still don't like it."

"I'm sorry, but from now on, there are two of us. However, if you'll think of us as one, you'll recognize nothing has been lost."

Henry listened to William being high-handed with Spears. This was a side of his father he knew well.

Spears gave up. There were now two Carsons. "You asked to see me, and here I am. What may I do for you?"

"For all of us, Craig. All of us. First, where are we in the bidding war?"

"The price seems to have stabilized at about twenty-five million dollars."

"Too high!"

"Who knows? It's a seller's market. The current business isn't worth that much, but there are the patent applications. They're worth whatever someone will pay."

"Of course payment needn't be made strictly in cash."

"I'm not sure I understand." Spears was watching Henry out of the corner of one eye. He hadn't noticed a single muscle move. Henry might as well be a piece of furniture. But there was something about that inert lump of a man that communicated noise even when he was silent, projected action even when he was still. Whatever deficiencies of character Craig Spears might have as a man, he had not become general counsel for Wilkenson, Inc. by being stupid.

William went on. "For one thing, there's the possibility of an up-front payment and then a downstream royalty."

"I could propose that to the family. One can never tell."

"I have an additional thought. The royalty agreement I have in mind calls for mutual trust and a form of partnership." He leaned back in his chair, folding his hands over his waist. "Craig, I think it would be helpful if we met Mrs. and Miss Wilkenson. Could that be arranged?"

"Not easily. The day-to-day running of the business is in the hands of division heads. My job is to see that the Wilkensons don't get screwed too badly."

Henry tried not to grin at the thought of this little man being a watchdog. Who then watched the "watchdog"?

"I wasn't thinking of a business meeting. What I had in mind was a social occasion. A weekend in the country for the ladies, properly chaperoned by you of course, might place the negotiations on another level."

Spears shot a second glance in Henry's direction. His red head had not moved. So this was what William had in mind. "Your son will be present for the weekend?"

"My son and between twenty and thirty other people, and a larger party later. The Wilkensons could come up Friday for an evening of bridge. I seem to remember reading that Mrs. Wilkenson is very fond of contract bridge. On Saturday, we'll have a gala dinner."

Thinking about the plan, Spears rather liked it. Not that he thought it would do William any good, but it would give him a chance to play some bridge, which he liked as much as Mrs. Wilkenson. Also, if the stakes were high enough, he might win enough money to make the weekend worth his time. He would stash his latest girlfriend at a nearby inn and spend a long Saturday afternoon with her. He could envision a series of such weekends during which the various companies bidding for the Wilkenson patents would duplicate William's idea. Several of them even had sons to interest Selma Wilkenson, although he wasn't sure why anyone would want to pay such a price. There would have to be much more in it than a corporate win for him to put up with the likes of Selma Wilkenson. Maybe that was why he was a corporate lawyer and not chief executive officer. He wouldn't pay the price.

"I think a weekend at Carson House is a fine idea. Of course, I can't promise anything, but they might be persuaded. Mrs. Wilkenson does like to play bridge."

"Talk to them tomorrow and let us know."

Spears nodded. "Do you have anything else in mind at the moment?"

"No. Just set up the weekend. There'll be other things later."

Listening to Spears and William talk, Henry couldn't understand what his father hoped to accomplish. It was obvious that Spears would inform the competition of the planned weekend. A number of them would propose the same personal approach. Whatever initial advantage might be gained would be lost in the duplication of events. Surely William recognized that. It was time he entered the conversation. As agreed, he coughed. "Father?"

"Yes, Henry."

"Before this meeting ends, could I have a word with Mr. Spears?"

"Certainly." He ignored the plan that Henry would observe and do nothing more, being curious as to what Henry had in mind. Henry stood up and walked toward Craig Spears. Looking at the size of the young man approaching him, Spears instinctively cringed a little. As Henry neared Spears, his movements quickened. Before Spears could gather himself, he found himself on his feet and then dangling in midair. As though he were holding a child under the arms, Henry carried Spears to the center of the room. Once there, he dropped him, unceremoniously, onto the floor. Spears looked up and saw Henry smiling down at him as though nothing unusual had happened. William was still sitting in his chair with his arms folded over his waist, observing the scene.

"Exactly what is this all about?" Spears' voice sputtered with rage and fear at being so manhandled.

"Nothing. Let's call it an example. You see, I don't like you. And I certainly don't trust you. I think you intend to go to our competitors and suggest to them that they get to know the Wilkensons personally." He reached down and lifted the plump lawyer to his feet. "Now I suggest you do no such thing. I don't need to hire bully boys to do my work for me. I promise you that if you do not do exactly as my father has suggested, without relaying any information to the competition, I personally will take you and rip each leg from its hip socket." His voice became almost a croon. "Don't be too alarmed. With modern surgical methods, they will have you out of a wheelchair and onto crutches within a year. Though the doctors don't promise much beyond crutches for this kind of injury." Henry smiled and reached out a hand to touch Spears. The lawyer shrank away from the hand, silently cursing the genetics which had made him short and plump, and his mother who had made him into a coward.

He stammered a denial. "I really didn't expect this kind of treatment from friends and gentlemen. You have no reason to be suspicious of me."

He could hear William chuckle. "Quite true. And we want no reason. My son was merely illustrating a point. Of course we're friends and hope to remain so. As for being gentlemen, neither of us claim that title. You may choose to fool yourself. We don't."

Henry returned to his chair and waited for the act to be played out.

"I suggest we point for a weekend toward the end of the month. That will give you time to make the arrangements." He turned to Henry. "Don't you agree?"

"Absolutely. Accept my apologies, Mr. Spears. But as a student of human nature, I find sometimes that direct action is the best way to make one's position clear."

Still somewhat in a state of shock, Spears muttered, "Yes, I see."

"Good. Then we can count on your cooperation?"

"Absolutely!" He made an effort to pull himself together and looked at his watch. "If you gentlemen"—the word was said without any inflection—"will excuse me, I'll be on my way. I'll try to get back to you tomorrow or Wednesday."

William smiled thinly. "Thank you for coming on such short notice. Henry, would you mind seeing Craig to the elevator?"

The lawyer was on his way out the door. "Please don't bother. I can find my way."

"Allow me. One can have manners without being a gentleman." He draped a heavy arm over the shoulders of the smaller man and conducted him to the elevator. Henry surrendered his charge to the operator with the words that he was to see Mr. Spears out, personally. Returning to the office, he was ready to face William in whatever mood he found him.

"That was a novel approach to a business meeting."

"Something was necessary to force him to play it straight."

"Yes. I think we can count on his full cooperation. By the way, what was that business about new medical techniques and crutches?"

"Pure nonsense. But I think it was effective." Henry felt a little smug. Somehow William had not considered the possibility that Craig Spears might double-cross them.

William picked up the phone by his desk and dialed a number. "Hello. This is William Carson. That's right, Jack. Mr. Spears will be at the gate in a moment or two. Please put Plan Two into effect. That's right. Plan Two. Good. I'll count on that."

Henry listened. He didn't feel quite so smug. "Father, exactly what is Plan Two?"

"Spears be allowed to leave and drive home."

"I see." He considered Plan Two for a moment. "If there's a Plan Two, I assume that there was a Plan One?"

"There was."

"And what was it?"

"Spears would be allowed to leave and then followed home."

"Might I also assume that the trip home would not have been uneventful?"

"Decidedly not!"

"Then my act was wasted." He sounded a little like a small boy whose pride had been hurt.

"Not at all. You were far more effective than any hired 'tough' could ever be. I've rarely seen a man more ready to cooperate. Now I think it's time we went home. I could use a drink before dinner."

"Splendid suggestion." Henry admitted to himself that William was still William. He could learn from his father. "I have my car. I'll drive you home."

# Chapter 4

AFTER her meeting with Henry Carson, Maggie Rhodes spent a restless night full of troubled dreams. Most of them dealt with Henry. A year of examining him, studying him from a distance, hadn't prepared her for the face-to-face impact. Along with his size, she had recognized another quality. He represented what neither life nor any other man she had ever met had given her; not simply wealth and the services wealth rendered, but the many more things she lumped together as "breeding." And there was something else. It was to Maggie's lasting honor that she knew on the spot she was in the presence of a "man." The fact that he was young was irrelevant. She had known too many forty-five-year-old "boys" who would remain "boys" all their lives. She couldn't define exactly what she meant, but Henry Carson, like his father, was a "man."

The next morning she dressed for work in one of her most tailored dresses. She would appear cool and businesslike, though she knew she was only deceiving herself and, hopefully, him. She tried to tell herself she was merely curious to find out how good a case he might make for himself as a would-be lover.

Maggie was at the office promptly at seven-forty-five. This gave her time to prepare the coffee and go over the plans she had developed for the day.

Before going to bed, Henry had set his alarm for six-thirty. He was up with the first sound of the buzzer, telephoned the kitchen to announce he was up and would be down to breakfast at seven. As usual, he had slept soundly through the night. At four minutes past seven he sat down to his usual sizeable breakfast. Remembering his father's sarcastic warning, Henry decided he would eat a little less. With his bone structure and weight of muscle, as he got older weight might become a problem.

Henry allowed twenty minutes for his drive to the office. He waved at the guards, wondering which one had been selected to give Spears a lesson. Since he was early, he sat in his car and thought about Maggie.

What kind of woman would lend herself to this scheme? Where did she come from? What was her family like? She had to be able to do more than satisfy him sexually, or William would never have chosen her. But she was a beauty! It might be amusing to let her wait a bit. Anyway, it was always better to let the woman make the first move. And he doubted that a woman, given a choice, would select a desk top or a conference table as the ideal place to begin an affair.

He smiled inwardly. William would most certainly be kept informed by the lady. It amused him to keep William waiting as much or even more than it did to keep Maggie waiting.

He was greeted at the front door by the same guard at the same desk. "Good morning, Mr. H." The boys on the benches shot to attention.

Henry appreciated Mary O'Toole's efficiency. The guard had been instructed to call him Mr. H. Probably a carefully typed and mimeographed notice was sent to all those who might be expected to come in direct contact with the Carsons and should know the limits set on the use of the Carson name.

Once again the elevator door opened before he could ring. The operator took him to what he now recognized as the executive floor. The double doors at the end of the corridor were closed. He debated knocking and then smiled. What nonsense was this? This was his office. He walked in.

Maggie was waiting. She had placed a pot of coffee on a large silver tray. There were two cups and saucers as well as silver serving pieces containing sugar and cream. Several spoons and neatly-folded linen napkins were also on the tray.

"Good morning, Mr. H."

"Good morning, Miss Rhodes." Henry decided that formality was in order for now. It was well enough for William to call the ladies by their first names. "Will you please give me a few minutes, and then bring in the coffee?"

"Certainly, sir."

Henry entered the office and looked at his father's desk. It was clear of all papers. Either the mail had not arrived or had not yet been distributed. His own desk still had the briefcases with the documents he had studied the previous week. He noticed that several wooden file cabinets had been added overnight and set against the wall next to his desk. Miss Rhodes could organize a filing system so that his desk would be as clear as his father's. He looked around the room and was childishly pleased to find that nothing had changed.

Carefully balancing the tray, Maggie set it on the table and waited. After a short, awkward pause, Henry realized she was waiting for his instructions. He wondered what would happen if he were to tell her to pull up her dress and lie down? She just might, and then they would be interrupted by William's entrance.

He could see his father's impassive face studying their movements and making wise comments on his lovemaking technique. The absurd fantasy made him laugh out loud, but he couldn't help it. Restraining himself, he asked, "How would you like your coffee?"

"Black, please."

"Just black? No sugar or cream?"

"No. There's quite enough of me already."

"You look splendid. A few pounds more or less would make no difference." After that bit of gallantry, he poured her black coffee and added sugar and cream to his. Then he asked for the day's itinerary.

"As you know, all our manufacturing facilities are at the river plant. We'll start here with the offices and then drive to the factory. If things go on schedule, we should arrive at the factory in time for lunch."

"That sounds all right, but I have a question."

"Yes, sir?"

"First, let's drop the 'sir' routine. My father may have been knighted, but I haven't. Mr. H will do. Second, let's have lunch on the way to the plant. I know a small restaurant that serves far better food than our cafeteria."

"What a lovely idea." The charm of the idea glowed in her eyes. To forget about the office, the routine, the schedule with such an attractive young man.

In the middle of sipping their coffee, William arrived. Remembering his earlier thoughts, Henry burst out laughing.

"Exactly what is so amusing?"

"Nothing. The joke's on me. Miss Rhodes, I suggest we be on our way."

The trip through the converted loft building was uneventful. Henry paused in the reception room to study the three large oil paintings on one wall. Small, elegantly-etched brass plates announced the first to be a portrait of Francis Carson, 1835–1886. Henry's great-grandfather. Henry looked at the portrait searching for a likeness.

"I understand that the painting was done from a Mathew Brady daguerreotype after his death." Maggie was a mine of information.

"I don't look much like him."

"A little, I think. Mr. Carson does though."

Henry nodded. Allowing for a painter's desire to please his client, there was a resemblance in features. Especially in coloring. The first Francis Carson had a lean face and thick, blond hair. But the face was unmarked by either emotion or intelligence. It was a pity the painter didn't know his subject. No face as vacuous as the one in the portrait could have founded the Carson Company.

He moved to the next painting. Henry Francis Carson, 1865–1910. Better. The first Henry had actually sat for the painter, John Singer Sargent. One felt the vitality of the man flowing out of the picture. Henry had been well aware of the scandal connected with his grandfather's death long before he read of it in the papers his father sent over. The face fascinated him. He imagined he saw something of himself in it. The first Henry's hair was also blond, but the face was fleshier and the body thicker than the man in the first portrait. The eyes were electric blue and seemed to leap across the space to drag you into the painting and the life the man led.

Once again Maggie was ready with a comment. "He looks like you."

"You think so?"

"Yes." She may have sounded spontaneous, but in reality, she had studied the paintings for the last year. She decided Henry did look like his grandfather and meant to say so.

The third and last painting was William Francis Henry Carson, 1890–, with a blank space on the brass plate. William was still alive. Henry looked at the picture and mentally added NEVER in the place where the date of William's death would someday be etched. His father would live forever. He was sure of it.

"Your brother, Francis, looks like him." Even as she said the words, she regretted them.

Henry stared at her. "Where did you see my brother?" His voice was hostile and accusing.

Trapped by her loose tongue, Maggie fell back on something resembling the truth. "When Mr. Carson told me I was going to work for you, I wanted to see what you looked like, so I went to your church one Sunday and saw both of you."

"You saw us in church? Only in church?"

"Where else would I see you? We don't travel in the same circles."

"You'd be surprised at some of the circles Francis travels in and some of the people he's met."

"Maybe so, but not mine and not me!"

Her vehemence struck Henry, and he dismissed his unexpected

jealousy. "I'm convinced. You never met my glorious brother." He turned from the paintings. "Now where?"

"Lunch. At the factory or a restaurant." She offered a silent prayer for the restaurant but was prepared for the cafeteria if her mention of Francis had cooled Henry's cordiality. What she didn't realize was that once Henry was satisfied, the subject was closed.

"I thought we'd agreed upon a restaurant."

"Oh, yes. Of course." She stammered with pleasure. "We did, didn't we?"

He drove Maggie to a small restaurant in Tarrytown, overlooking the Hudson. After the maître d' seated them next to a window overlooking the river, Henry asked Maggie what she would like to drink.

"A very dry martini with an olive. With lots of ice."

Henry signaled the waiter and ordered two martinis, one on the rocks and one straight up. Maggie, fascinated by the river, kept staring at the view.

Absorbed in her memories, she didn't notice that the drinks had arrived. "A penny for your thoughts," Henry prodded.

"Oh—" Maggie turned from the river. "I was thinking of your namesake."

"My grandfather?"

"What a one-track mind you have. No. Henry Hudson."

Henry grinned sheepishly. "You mean the explorer? Too bad he came to such a sticky end."

"He did?"

"I'm afraid so. He died on an ice floe somewhere in northern Canada. His crew mutinied, though no one knows for certain what actually happened."

"How awful."

"I agree."

"And how awful that I didn't know. My education is full of holes." She reached for the martini and drained it in one gulp. "I think I'll have another. As an educational experiment. I've never had two."

"Never?"

"Not consecutively, I mean. I'm afraid of being drunk. I've seen too much of it, and it's stupid not to be able to hold your liquor." She sighed. "I have so much to learn. About everything. Next semester I'm taking a course in Early American History. I'll learn about Henry Hudson then."

"You're leaving the Carson Company to go to school?"

"Oh, no! It's night school. I've been going for a year."

"A job and night school. That's a full load."

"It's a question of what you want out of life."

The waiter approached with a menu, and Henry ordered a second martini for each of them. "What do you feel like eating?"

"I'll like anything you choose. I've heard what a good restaurant this is." She smiled. "Thank you for bringing me here."

Her pleasure was childlike, direct, open. It made Henry like her even more.

All too soon for Henry, Maggie looked at her watch. "It's after two. We're behind schedule. Dr. Flam has been waiting for us since one-thirty."

"Who's Dr. Flam?"

"I'll tell you on the way." They started out of the restaurant. "The check?" Maggie reminded him.

"They'll put it on my tab. We're late, so let us go, then, you and I . . ."

"While the evening is set out against the sky . . ."

"Nice. You like poetry?"

"What little I know, yes. I don't need a school for that. Just a library. Or a bookstore."

A young romantic. He liked her even more. He took her arm and guided her through the maze of tables. She pressed her arm against her side, bringing the back of his hand against the edge of her breast. It was soft yet firm. He held the contact only until they reached the street. When he let her arm go, the back of his hand seemed to burn.

Watching her settle herself in the seat, he wished again that he had found her without William's help. It never occurred to him that, given her life and his, without William's intervention they would never have met. And if he had met her, he would not have noticed a factory day laborer. He was too young, and he wasn't William.

As with the offices, there was an iron fence around the factory grounds and a guard at the gate. They were expected, and the gate swung open.

The factory was a complex of three parallel, one-story, red-brick buildings with a large, paved parking lot between two of them. The property sloped down to a long pier that extended out into the Hudson River. Maggie told Henry that goods were shipped and received both by rail and by ship. There was a second loading dock adjoining building number three which was used to receive trucks. William believed that trucks were the way of the future for shipping lightweight cargo, so he'd planned ahead. Trucks had the advantage of being able to handle small shipments and take them directly to their destination without the necessity of loading and unloading ship cargo or train carloads. Henry saw at once his father was correct.

Having quickly gone over the external operations, Maggie turned to the buildings. She pointed to a small, one-story white structure with blue glass windows. "That's the R and D lab. The factory buildings are fine for anything we currently make, but there was no way to set up a first-class laboratory in them. Mr. Carson had that building built for the lab." She added, "There are plans to double the size of the building over the next few years."

"Why the blue glass?"

"It has something to do with the kind of light scientists like to work in. In fact, whenever we build any new building, it will have blue glass. It's cheerful. Even when it rains." She led Henry into the lobby of the laboratory. A guard with a holstered revolver was seated at the entrance.

"Good afternoon, Miss Rhodes. You're expected."

"Thank you, Slim." She signed the register. Slim handed her a badge which she pinned to her dress.

Then Henry signed the register.

The guard looked at the signature, straightened up and glanced at Maggie, who merely nodded.

Henry pinned on his badge and followed Maggie through the door that led to a long, tiled corridor. When they came to a door on the right, Maggie knocked. The door was opened almost at once by a short, plump man with heavy features, thin dark hair combed straight back, thick glasses and a spotless white coat.

"Come in. Quickly! Or we let too much air in." The voice was pleasant and heavily accented. Henry identified Middle European with an overlay of something else.

They entered, and Maggie made the introductions. "Dr. Flam, Mr. H. Mr. H, Dr. Flam."

"What's this Mr. H shtick?"

"My father and I feel two Mr. Carsons are one too many."

"Mr. H?" Dr. Flam showed his scorn.

"I agree. It's ridiculous. Please call me Henry."

"Fine. You call me Felix."

"Dr. Flam, would you tell Mr. H what you're working on and why it's so secret?"

"Henry, what do you know about chemistry in general and organic chemistry in particular? Also drugs?"

"I know there are such things as test tubes, Bunsen burners, distillation processes and the like. So much for chemistry. The only thing I remember about organic chemistry is that there's a carbon molecule somewhere. I know more about some drugs. The nasty kind, that is. They tend to be habit-forming and rotten habits to form."

Maggie left the two men and walked over to a barred, blue glass window. She wanted to compose herself. Henry had aroused her more than she had expected. After calming herself, she glanced at the two men floundering in their conversation.

Felix was trying to explain his work to Henry. It was heavy going. Finally Henry said, "I just don't follow you. Take it from the top and go slower."

"From the top? Oh! You mean begin again." Dr. Flam looked at the huge man struggling to understand simple chemistry. What kind of a country was this where a man who understood nothing about science was placed in charge of a business such as the Carson Company? It would never have happened in Europe. Felix Flam had taken his degree at the University of Vienna and, being Jewish, left just before the Nazis occupied Austria. It had been hard to find work in America. He, his wife and family considered themselves very fortunate when William Carson hired him.

Now he had the problem of explaining what he was doing so Henry would understand. Indicating that Henry and Maggie should follow him, Felix led the way to his office, which contained a desk, a wall of files, a blackboard and several chairs. Henry and Maggie sat down, and Felix went to the blackboard.

"I'm going to give you a rough explanation of what we are trying to accomplish, but it will not be very satisfactory. You will have many questions. But we must start somewhere."

When Dr. Flam finished, Henry had no questions. He also had few answers. He thought it might be a good idea if he joined Maggie in night school to take a few courses in chemistry.

After they said goodby to Dr. Flam, Henry asked Maggie, "How much of this does my father understand?"

"He knows what Dr. Flam is trying to accomplish, but I don't think he pays much attention to the actual science. I know Mary brings him weekly reports. And every month he spends a morning with Dr. Flam to be brought up to date."

Knowing his father, Henry said, "Then he understands the science. It's either the craziest idea I've ever heard of, or it's the birth of a new industry." He made up his mind that, come what may, they must control the Wilkenson patents. He and William would have a lot to talk about.

During the rest of the afternoon, Maggie took him on a whirlwind tour of the production facilities: supplies, receiving, storage, production, packaging, shipping. Everything. They met Morgan Easton in the factory and heard him give a foreman a very rough going over for allowing the incorrect labeling of a shipment of hair tonic. The man was good. This time there was no foolishness when they shook hands. Easton returned to his work as quickly as politeness permitted.

Maggie hesitated and then said, "You don't like each other?"

"No, we don't. But I respect his competence."

"And I respect your ability not to let your feelings color your judgment."

"Don't respect them too much. Sometimes they do."

They drove back to the office in semi-silence. It was after five and dark when they arrived. Henry parked his car next to Maggie's. She got into her car and looked up at him, his bulk filling the entire window opening. She felt his eyes on her face. If he kept them there much longer, she was afraid she would start to tremble. "Do you have anything planned for tomorrow? Mr. Carson's instructions only went as far as today."

"We'll meet tomorrow morning for another cup of coffee."

"Eight o'clock?" She didn't want to look at him now or even have much more conversation. It was partly his manner, so self-contained, as if he knew how hard her heart was pounding. And it was partly her own emotions that frightened her.

"Right." He turned away and then returned. "I want to compliment you on the tour. It was very well done. Also, the company was delightful." There was a quick smile. "See you tomorrow."

She put the car in gear and drove off slowly. She realized again how attracted she was to the man. The sensation filled her with a kind of awe at all it implied. But she would not let the accident of her feelings make any difference. He would have to make the first move. Illogically, she grew angry. Did he think he only had to nod and she would fall at his feet? Think again, Mr. H. But she had to admit he had neither nodded nor asked anything of her. She would have liked him less if he had.

# Chapter 5

**I**T TOOK Spears longer than he expected to arrange a weekend with the Wilkensons. It was too cold, too snowy, they had other plans: the opera, the ballet, a dinner party. Finally the date was set for the spring equinox, March 21, the only provision being that the ladies be escorted to church Sunday morning. Fortunately, they were also Episcopalian, and once Spears explained to Mrs. Wilkenson that the Carsons went to church every Sunday, that difficulty was resolved.

During the six weeks since Henry had started work at the company, he and William spent a great deal of time together. There were ever-present signs of "men at war," but the war was kept to verbal sparring. William did not want direct conflict. He wasn't sure what Henry would do when he lost, and Henry, knowing he would lose, didn't want a showdown.

Henry had made the difficult decision to keep Maggie at arm's length. Not that she pressured him. It was her presence, the closeness of her, the sensuality she exuded, that pressured him. He wisely maintained a relationship with several agreeable ladies to keep his physical needs in check. His reservations came out of hope, a sentiment in which there was only a little romantic feeling. He had definite ideas about marriage; he hoped Selma Wilkenson might satisfy them, hoped she might not prove as dismal as her picture. There are many ways to judge a woman above and beyond good looks. He expected his wife to be loyal, devoted and unresentful of his commitment to the Carson Company. He would like her to be reasonably sexual, and he hoped she would have a mind that would not be small and stifling, that would make her an easy, animated companion in their domestic life. When they had children, the vacant corners in her life would be filled. Selma Wilkenson might be just the wife he was looking for. Poets made too much of love. In any case, he would wait. And it was none of William's business.

As for Maggie, the lack of any overtures on Henry's part was causing her more and more difficulty. It seemed a cruel joke for William to have implied another kind of relationship and for Henry's attitude to turn out to be such a complete contradiction of all her expectations. Despite her nagging conscience, she had privately prepared herself to accept him. She had stopped seeing other men in an effort to be completely free for Henry. But to what purpose? Henry did nothing. Nothing at all. They saw each other every day, had lunch frequently, and when she worked late, an occasional dinner. The result was always the same. He would wait in the parking lot and watch her drive away. Almost as though she posed some kind of challenge. Though only a few weeks had passed, her ordeal of waiting had become so personal and painful, she made herself sick wondering if and when he would ever come around. If there was any comfort in Maggie's situation, it was that she knew nothing of the reasons that compelled Henry to keep his distance.

All plans were completed as the weekend for the Wilkenson visit approached. William had arranged for the Glenn Miller band, which was playing an engagement at the Glen Island Casino, to provide the dance music. The weekend program included bridge on Friday night, a dinner party for thirty on Saturday evening and open house for the neighborhood and assorted acquaintances from New York after dinner. Sunday morning was for church. The afternoon was free for the Carsons and Wilkensons to follow their inclinations.

The groundskeepers had been planting, trimming and cutting for several weeks. The gravel driveway was freshened and the bordering stones painted white. A small army of servants had gone over the house, inside and out, leaving it spotless. Even the weather had cooperated. An early spring had come, and the snow had melted. The weekend weather prediction was for fair and unseasonably warm temperatures.

William and Henry left the office early Friday. The Wilkensons were due around five o'clock. Craig Spears was in high spirits. His wife, Myra, had predictably chosen to stay home and nurse a migraine. As the Lincoln turned into the Carson driveway, Craig thought of his current girl at a nearby inn. He would spend most of Saturday afternoon with her. And possibly Sunday morning. Unless Evelyn objected, he had better things to do Sunday than listen to a sermon.

Both Henry and William were waiting on the flagstone terrace. They wore dark-blue blazers and dark-gray slacks. The one difference was their ties. William had a Black Watch stripe and Henry's matched the Cameron clan. The low afternoon sun cast a long shadow, and the bare trees traced a spidery network on the newly defrosted lawn. The south and west windows were bathed in the last golden rays.

After the chauffeur opened the door, Miss and Mrs. Wilkenson got out of the car. Craig Spears joined them. William descended the steps to greet them. "Welcome to Carson House. We're delighted you could find the time in your full social calendar to spend a weekend with country folk." The flowery speech was accompanied by a broad welcoming smile, and for once Mrs. Wilkenson felt the importance of her presence had been given its full value. William continued, "I would like to introduce my son." Henry walked slowly down the steps.

As he approached the group, he glanced quickly at Selma and thought, Christ, the picture was flattering. "Ladies, allow me to add my welcome to that of my father." He reached for Mrs. Wilkenson's hand and brushed his lips lightly over her dark glove. Then, turning to Miss Wilkenson, he reached for her hand.

Hesitating only slightly, Selma shook hands. He was so different—both the Carsons were so different—from her late father. It had been comforting to learn that they attended church every Sunday. Men who prayed to God for safety and salvation should be men one could trust. But glancing up at Henry, he seemed to fill the landscape. She wasn't able to see anything else. Selma had a gentle, delicate, timid nature, and she couldn't help wishing he weren't so big. She wondered if it was natural.

Craig Spears was amused. For the first time he felt there was a chance the Carsons might pull it off. That church bit was a winner. And they really did attend church. It was too good to be true.

The chauffeur and servants whom William assigned to help were busily removing the luggage from the car. William led the way into the house. Henry offered his arm to Selma as they climbed the wide steps. She placed her hand on his forearm, uncomfortable with the necessary familiarity, and tried not to show she was nervous. Henry thought about the way his hand had pressed against Maggie's body after that first lunch. There certainly was a difference.

On entering the house, they found the estate manager, Oscar, waiting. Following William's instructions, he had arranged for the guests to occupy adjoining rooms on the second floor. The suites consisted of two bedrooms, two private baths and a common sitting room. They had been redecorated years ago with the thought that at some time there would be female guests in the house. There were fresh flowers on the dressing tables and on the tables beside the beds. Flowers on the carved fireplace mantelpieces as well. Both rooms were papered with a very delicately tinted wallpaper. The women were surprised and delighted with their quarters. They had seen their equal on occasion, but this was a house run by men. Men, in Evelyn's opinion, sadly lacked the more subtle senses.

Alone with her mother, Selma asked, "What do you think of them?"

"Charming! Absolutely charming! Mr. Carson is one of the most distinguished men I have ever met." After placing her imprimatur on William, she asked Selma about Henry.

Selma was more cautious. "He seems nice." Then she added, "But isn't he terribly large?"

"Yes, he is. But remember what they say about large animals. The large ones are the gentle ones. It's the little, yapping dogs that nip your ankles."

Selma always accepted her mother's appraisals, and now she saw Henry in a new light. He was a large, docile animal. Like a big dog. Maybe a Saint Bernard? She smiled as she pictured Henry with large, liquid eyes, floppy ears and a wagging tail sitting quietly by the fireplace while she and their minister talked. She glanced at her mother, and as she did, she had an instant, intimate contact with her mother's mind. "Mother?"

"Yes, Selma?"

"Mother, do you think the Carsons have a special reason for inviting us to visit them?"

Evelyn Wilkenson's mouth turned slightly upward while her lips remained closed, until it almost reached a sad smile. "Of course. People always have a reason for inviting us."

Selma was not stupid. She was painfully shy and only secure in her sense of duty to God and Church. As far as she could conceive Christianity, she tried to be a perfect Christian. Her devotion to her religion made it difficult for her to think about anything else—people, politics, ordinary emotions and desires—in any but the most superficial way. Normal human relationships did not exist for her. Her world was occupied by a deity and his representatives on earth. The day began with prayer and ended in prayer, often with a prayer or two in between.

Had fate made her a Catholic, she would have entered a nunnery and resolved the question once and for all of where her pleasure and duty lay. But she was an Episcopalian. And rich. She knew what had to happen. She knew her mother was stronger than she, and she would submit to her mother's will. She knew her fate was to marry and bear children. The idea made her body rigid with aversion, but if she were not to be permitted the life of a higher being, there must be a reason. She would do her best to accept what she must.

That a number of ambitious men had already approached her mother seeking Selma as a wife was a fact with which Mrs. Wilkenson thought it best not to burden her daughter. There would be time enough to tell Selma when she had selected the right man. A man who would run Wilkenson, Inc. A man who would listen to her, follow her instructions, respect her values. Most important, a man who recognized exactly how important the research and development of the new tranquilizers was. It would make Wilkenson a household word for generations. The current auction was a means of putting herself in contact with prospective husbands for Selma.

Henry Carson might well be her man. She would see.

William had scheduled an early dinner to allow time for a long session of bridge afterward. So, promptly at seven o'clock, Mrs. and Miss Wilkenson descended the broad, oak staircase leading to the main hall. Oscar was waiting and ushered them into an enclosed porch which, due to its rattan chairs and sofas and bare stone floors, had an outdoor feeling. Cigarettes were available although neither William nor Henry smoked, occasionally enjoying a good cigar after dinner.

William rose from where he had been chatting with an Englishman. He hurried to greet his guests and introduce them to Godfrey Moore. "Welcome, ladies. Might I offer you a drink before dinner?"

"Not I, sir. I never drink," murmured Selma.

Mrs. Wilkenson permitted herself to be talked into a sherry. "Not too sweet, please."

They chatted about the latest bidding techniques which had just begun to complicate the game. Half an hour later, still discussing the fine points of bridge, they went into dinner. Since a gala had been planned for Saturday, Friday's meal consisted of a seafood buffet. A fine white wine was served with the fish.

"This poached salmon is superb, Mr. Carson. The sauce is so delicate." Mrs. Wilkenson was enjoying the good food.

"I'm pleased you like it." He turned to the man standing behind the serving tables. "James, give my respects to Reginald. He's equaled himself. One cannot expect more."

Dinner over, William suggested they gather on the porch in thirty minutes for bridge. Craig had been waiting for the game. His only question was, would Evelyn play for money? It surprised him to find included a player of the reputation of Godfrey Moore, who had written one of the early books on contract bridge, but since they would revolve partners he would have the same chance as the rest to make use of Moore's talents.

Henry was the only person at dinner who was suffering. The more he listened to Selma's childish preaching, the more he thought of Maggie. Though Henry had thought he would always prefer a woman's company to bridge, listening to Selma made bridge attractive indeed. But he was stuck with Selma. "Miss Wilkenson, would you like a tour of the estate? We have enough exterior lighting so there's a lot to see, even at night. Why don't we go and explore?"

Evelyn answered for Selma. "She'd be delighted. Wouldn't you, dear?"

Given her mother's approval, Selma agreed. He was a church-going man. She had nothing to fear from such a person.

Henry suggested she wear her warmest coat. He had a surprise waiting for her. Worrying about the surprise, Selma sent for her coat, mink-lined boots and mink hat. Henry put on his usual Burberry.

William had been watching them, excused himself before the game started and hurried over. "You've got Selma bundled up for a sleigh ride to the North Pole, not a drive around the estate. What's going on?"

"Miss Wilkenson is properly dressed." Henry laughed. "Come see for yourself what's outside."

William stepped onto the terrace of the great house. There in the driveway was a horse-drawn carriage with a driver perched on the high front seat. The carriage stirred old memories in William. The last time he could remember using it was when he and his wife used to take rides around the estate. Nathalia loved the rides as much as he did. He remembered once driving the carriage to a remote spot and making love to her under a hot summer sun. It might have been that afternoon that Henry had been conceived. He hadn't thought of the carriage in twenty years, and his eyes misted a little. It had been such a long time. As Henry led Selma into the carriage, William returned to the porch.

The other guests were preparing for the game. Two unopened decks of cards along with a printed score pad were on the table next to the seat that had been established as "north." The three people seated at the table were absorbed in their own thoughts.

Craig Spears hoped that Evelyn wasn't one to play for pennies. What a pity if she objected to decent stakes, and he lost an opportunity for a big win.

Godfrey Moore thought how different his life might have been if bridge had not been invented. But he had become a world class professional, and now, twenty-two years later, here he was at the invitation of William Carson, not the worst of hosts by any means, applying a small part of his education and a large part of his public school accent playing a ridiculous game that amused people with nothing better to do. It might have been worse, and who knows if it could have been better?

Evelyn Wilkenson was thinking about the game. Bridge was a drug to her. She loved the combination of skill and luck. She delighted in estimating each player and adjusting her game to her partner while trying to confuse her opponents.

William took charge. "I suggest that Mr. Moore be a constant north, and we revolve every two rubbers. He can keep score, and we all get the same chance to play with him as a partner." Everyone agreed. "I also suggest the game be limited to three rounds of two rubbers per partner. Eighteen rubbers. No time limit. When the game ends, the winners can cheer, and the losers can have a drink. Otherwise we might play all night." Again there was agreement. Then came the most delicate question, the stakes. He had no idea what Evelyn considered reasonable, and had settled privately with Moore to make good Moore's losses and have Moore keep his winnings. If the stakes were so small as to make the winnings meaningless, he would pay Moore $1,000 for the evening's work. William accepted that, as a professional, the evening was work for Moore. Spears could be counted on to agree to anything. So he turned to Evelyn.

"I think we should play for something. Do you agree?"

"Yes. I've found that without meaningful stakes, the game tends to disintegrate."

"What would you consider meaningful stakes?"

Evelyn liked his tact. "May I assume you've made your arrangements with Mr. Moore?"

The astuteness of the question surprised William, but his expression did not change. This was not the ingenuous lady Spears had described. "You may assume so."

"No offense intended, Mr. Moore."

Godfrey looked at her with level eyes. "No offense taken, madam." He was a professional.

William could see Evelyn mentally rubbing her hands together.

"Gentlemen, I suggest ten cents a point!" Her voice held a rising note of triumph.

William pursed his lips. "Mrs. Wilkenson, not to be impolite, but you do realize that at ten cents a point, down two doubled, vulnerable, means a loss of fifty dollars?"

Evelyn stiffened. "Thank you. I can both add and multiply."

William looked around the table. Something was happening. At ten cents a point, a great deal of money could be lost. She could afford it. So could he. So could Moore, with his backing. But could Spears? Was the lady out to get her own lawyer?

Spears did not see the danger and actually beamed at the possibilities. This was better than he had hoped. Now all he needed was luck.

Moore opened the two decks of cards and placed the cellophane in the bottom of a free-standing ashtray that had been provided at each of the four corners of the table. He caressed the cards almost as sensitively as he would have caressed a woman. Or a man, for that matter—a very private taste he had developed as a youth at an English public school. They cut for partners. The game was to start with Craig Spears and Evelyn Wilkenson as partners versus William and Moore.

Moore dealt the first hand.

The weather bureau had been correct. The night was windless, balmy, with a glowing full moon. Almost anyone but Selma would have been overdressed. As they drove around the estate, Henry took care to point out the barns where the corn and grain were stored. They got out and walked through the stable to see the horses. Dim yellow bulbs cast a golden glow on the fresh straw. Henry took pride in the workmen. Even the stalls were spotless.

After they returned to the carriage, Selma gathered her courage. Hesitatingly, she mumbled, "I wonder, Mr. Carson, would you call me Selma?"

"Of course. But only if you'll do me a favor."

Still shaken by her own forwardness, his words alarmed her even more. She hoped he wouldn't be improper. "What is it?"

"Why, you must call me Henry."

Her relief was visible. "Henry is a very nice name."

"Good. Let's continue." Henry rapped on the back of the driver's seat. "Robert, drive us around the lake. I think the path is still firm enough."

"It is, sir. I tested it this morning."

He noticed Selma starting to huddle in her coat. Henry wasn't sure if it was fear of him or the night air that made her shiver. "Would you like a blanket, Selma? We have several on the rack."

She smiled wanly. "Thank you, Henry. I do feel cold."

He took the blanket out from under the driver's seat, and managed to tuck it around her without actually touching her. It was a feat requiring very delicate hand motions.

"Is your minister a good speaker?" Selma asked, settling into the blanket. "It's so important for a minister to have a good voice."

Henry had never considered Dr. Carlson's speaking voice. Actually, it was nasal, but it certainly was loud enough to fill the church. "It does carry well. You'll have no trouble hearing him."

"That is important. Once when Dr. Jeffrey was sick, his substitute spoke so softly, I had no idea what the sermon was about."

Henry found it astonishing that in an age when many people denied the existence of God and others were agnostic, God and Church played such an important role in Selma's life. As their ride continued, their conversation became more relaxed if not more intimate. Selma had no knowledge of religion in all its complexities and contradictions. Her notion of God was akin to a big, kind Daddy in the sky who brought good to his flock. She was pleased to find that her feeling for Henry began to resemble her feeling about God. He was kind, too, his manners gentle. She noticed how his eyebrows almost met, red and very thick. She supposed he was attractive. And if not quite a "Daddy," he was a huge, friendly, red-haired dog with a wagging tail just as her mother had suggested.

From the start, the game did not go well for Craig Spears. The cards were not coming his way, and when they did, something tended to go wrong. First Evelyn misplayed a three notrump defense so that instead of setting the hand by two, William made an overtrick. Then she bid a natural four heart contract to six hearts and went down two, doubled. So it went.

It took a little while for William to accept an astonishing fact: of the four of them, Evelyn Wilkenson was the best natural player. Technically, of course, Moore was faultless. He and Spears were not far behind Moore. But for brilliance and an intuitive grasp of the game, Evelyn was in a class by herself. Except when her partner was Spears. In bridge, when the four players are more than competent, it doesn't take much to alter the flow of the game: a missed lead, a blown end play, a tossed aside squeeze. Evelyn Wilkenson was trying to make sure that Craig Spears lost a great deal of money. And she was successful.

By the middle of the second round of partner shifts, there were three winners and one loser. Spears had lost over $2,000. At this point, his play began to disintegrate. With the cards and Evelyn working together, the lawyer lost his head. He began to overbid and misplay his cards. Once the pattern was set, Evelyn shifted her tactics. She played as well when she was Spears' partner as when she was anyone else's.

They were about to start the last round of rubbers when Henry and Selma returned. Seeing them standing in the doorway, William proposed a short break.

"Did you have a pleasant ride?" Evelyn asked Selma.

"Beautiful, Mother. The estate is wonderful, and Henry showed me the lake. The moonlight made it look like a huge silver disk."

First names. This was even better than William had dared to hope. "I'm delighted you enjoyed yourself," he said.

"Yes, we did. Now I think Selma is a little tired. And I could use some sleep. So unless you have another idea, Selma, why don't we leave these bridge addicts to their vice and turn in?"

Evelyn had also picked up their use of first names. Apparently their time together had not been wasted. "Go along, Selma. I'll be up shortly. If you're awake, we'll chat."

"I'll wait up for you. I want to tell you about the ride."

They said good night to Spears and Moore. William decided that Evelyn was as pleased as he was. It occurred to him that a woman who could deliberately cause her lawyer to lose more money than he could afford could also conduct an auction without ever intending to bring down the gavel. Meanwhile, there was the final demolition of Craig Spears to be taken care of.

And a demolition it was. When the allotted rubbers were finished, Spears had lost over $10,000. More than half had been won by Godfrey Moore. William had won some $3,000, and Evelyn slightly over $1,500. It took some vehement insistence that they stick to the agreed-upon rules before Spears accepted that play was over.

As they were going up the stairs together, William resisted the impulse to ask Evelyn why she had done what she had done. Spears had stayed downstairs to have a final brandy. He had given the winners checks that William was certain would bounce when presented to his bank. Sometime over the weekend, Spears would ask him for a loan to make them good. With luck he would have had an opportunity to talk to Evelyn. That would help him decide about the loan. He'd wait until tomorrow to talk to Henry. Silently and for the last time he congratulated himself on the wisdom of choosing Henry over Francis. There was no way he could ever have convinced Francis to go along with his plans for Selma.

After breakfast the next morning, Henry agreed to squire the ladies on a tour of the countryside. As expected, Spears bowed out, saying he had an old friend in the neighborhood he wished to visit. William did not doubt that the "old friend" was female and reasonably priced. But as long as the lawyer was back for dinner, he was satisfied; he even lent Spears a car for the day. He and Godfrey Moore stood on the terrace and watched the cars leave.

Once they were out of sight, William remarked, "Godfrey isn't the devious nature of the human female awesome to behold?"

"You do have Mrs. Wilkenson in mind?"

"Yes. You realize the dear lady sabotaged Spears last night?"

"And a beautiful job it was."

"Why do you think she did it?"

"I haven't the foggiest."

"Nor do I, but I'll wager I'll know before the weekend is over."

"I believe you will." He studied William. "By the by, what do you suppose I should do with the bad check he gave me?"

"How do you know it's bad?"

"One of my more useful talents is an ability to read upside down. Learned it during the war. Kept me out of all sorts of sticky situations."

"And?"

"And reading Mr. Spears' checkbook, he had exactly $1,264.85 in his account as of last night."

"He may have other sources. Other checking accounts. A savings account."

"Would you like to make a small wager? Say my check against yours for one thousand dollars?"

"Of course not. Anyway, we agreed I would guarantee the game. That covers bad checks as well. In fact, if you'll come with me, we'll make the exchange right now."

"A pleasure."

William led the way into the library, which he now shared with Henry, wrote a check for $5,862.50 and handed it to Moore. He glanced at the check he received in return, tossing it in the center drawer of his desk. "I still wonder why she did it."

"The predatory instinct of the mating mother."

"What do you mean?"

"I think she's looking for a husband for Selma."

"What makes you think that?"

"I've been the target often enough. Of predatory mothers. I can smell one at fifty feet."

"But why sabotage Spears?"

Moore smiled again. "I'll let you find out for yourself. You'll enjoy it more that way."

"That's unfair."

"I never promised to be fair. I only promised to play a good game of bridge, not to drink too much and not to make passes at any of the guests. Male or female. Nothing more."

William considered his options. On one hand, he could offer Moore enough money to get him to talk. On the other hand, as Godfrey had said, it would be more amusing to do his own detective work. "I'll make you a sporting wager."

"Oh! I do so like sporting wagers. Actually, I've seen so few of them."

"Go over to the other desk and write your opinion of why she wrecked him. We'll put it in the safe along with Spears' check. When I find out from Mrs. Wilkenson, if you're correct, I'll add another five thousand dollars to the check you already have. If you're wrong, you'll return me my check, and I'll give you back Spears'. Collecting will be your problem."

Moore considered the proposition. Ten thousand dollars was a deal of money, and he was certain he knew what the lady was up to. If he had to, he just might be able to get Spears to cover part of the debt. All in all, why not? "Agreed."

"Done." William watched as Moore sat down, took a piece of note paper and, picking up the desk pen, wrote two lines. Moore then folded the paper and put it into an envelope that was also on the top of the desk. He handed the envelope to William, who added Spears' check to it. Turning to a painting behind his chair, William carefully moved the painting and spun the dial of the now visible safe. He placed the envelope, still unsealed, in the safe.

"Er, I say, would you mind terribly sealing the envelope? You know . . ." The sentence was left hanging there.

"Of course. Who knows what scoundrel might open the safe, change the paper, being careful to copy your handwriting?"

Moore turned a brilliant red. "I must apologize." He decided to recover a bit of his own. "I like keeping an eye on my investment, and you miss the point. Three spins to the left. Stop at thirty-two. One complete turn to the right and stop at sixty. Two more turns to the left. Stop at three. Move to five. Open safe. I could also change the papers."

"Very astute. I'll have to be more careful." He wasn't the least disturbed. How was Moore to know that he hoped the Englishman was as shrewd as he appeared? If he was, William had work for him worth far more than $10,000. He thought of the Swiss, unaffected by the war, doing work that might parallel the Carson Company. As his man in

Switzerland, Godfrey Moore would indeed earn far more than $10,000. But that was for a later day. "Incidentally, what, if anything, do you have on schedule today?"

"I'll stroll around the estate. The air and exercise will do me good. I spend too many hours in smoke-filled card rooms. And what will you do?"

"Some last-minute arrangements for tonight. And then I'm going to sit and think about the Wilkensons."

After Moore left the library, William leaned back in his chair. He had an idea and debated its wisdom. Then he picked up the phone and dialed a number, more conscious of his purpose than of possible consequences.

Maggie was sitting at the small table in her kitchen, sipping coffee. Last night had been worse than usual. She couldn't eat, she couldn't sleep, at intervals she burst into angry tears. She was baffled by Henry and enraged at herself. Obsessively, she reviewed the options William Carson had offered her more than a year ago, and she was bitterly sorry at not having chosen another career. Then she asked herself if she was brave enough to ask for a change now. The answer was No! For the reality was that, wounded and outraged though she was, the fact of Henry had sunk into her heart, into the very core of her being. So she spent the night caught between her physical desire for Henry and her frustration with her own inability either to satisfy or to control that desire.

Then the phone rang. She put down her coffee and went into the bedroom to answer it.

It was William Carson.

"Good morning, Mr. Carson." For a moment Maggie's self-possession deserted her. Why was William Carson calling on a Saturday morning? Her eyes widened. "Of course, Mr. Carson, I have an evening gown." She listened. "I beg your pardon, but would you repeat that?" A limousine would pick her up at seven. She was to be dressed and ready. They were giving a large party at Carson House, and it occurred to Mr. Carson that she should attend. Not as a secretary working for the company, but as Maggie Rhodes, a member of the community whose mother had been a schoolmate of William's dead wife. No, she didn't have to understand anything else. Just be dressed and ready. That is, of course, if she was free. Yes, she was free, and yes, she would be delighted to attend the party. The idea of seeing Henry outside the office was overwhelming in its possibilities.

Only after she had prepared her gown for a final pressing did she stop to think why she had been invited. She had no idea and didn't care. Things planned by William Carson had a habit of working to her advantage. The only thing that hadn't happened yet was she and Henry. Maybe tonight would improve matters?

A long line of elegant cars drove up the torch-lit driveway of Carson House, everything from Rolls Royces to an MG-TC. They were handled by a team of waiting drivers who, after the owner got out, drove each car to its allotted space. There were lined spaces for 150 vehicles, and an additional fifty spots for the Glenn Miller Band and other entertainers and extra servants.

The formal dinner was held in the great, oak-paneled dining room, in use for the first time in years. The room had a high ceiling with huge wooden beams stretching from wall to wall. In between the beams the plaster had been painted a light blue with soft clouds that seemed to float across the space. There was a fireplace at each end of the room. Oscar had seen to it that both fireplaces were lit. A single, crystal chandelier lit the long, narrow table, and there were matching crystal sconces along both sides of the length of the room. The combination of electric and firelight reflected off the crystal, producing ever shifting prisms of color. The pegged oak flooring, waxed to a high sheen, added to the play of light.

Seated at the head of the table, William scanned the group. There were fifteen men and fifteen women. The ladies ranged in age from twenty-three to sixty-five. The distinction of being sixty-five belonged to a near neighbor, Mrs. Rochelle Guilder, who, though she made little of it, was a Roosevelt of the Oyster Bay Roosevelts on one side and a Grosvenor on the other, having a pedigree of landed Dutch gentry that went back to original land grants from Peter Minuit. At the other end of the age range was Maggie Rhodes, erstwhile secretary and co-conspirator with William, whose land grants ran back to an apartment acquired a year ago and whose pedigree was a figment of William's imagination.

William had to smother a laugh as he remembered the look on Henry's face when Maggie was announced.

"What the devil is she doing here?"

"I invited her."

"Obviously. But why?"

The conversation was conducted in the lowest of whispers. "I'm smoking out Mrs. W."

"And Maggie is the fire. Does she work for us?"

"Certainly not."

"Do I know her?"

"Yes."

"How well?"

"Not that well, but you'd like to."

"I see. I'm to pay equal attention to Cinderella and her sister."

"That's an unflattering comparison."

"You're right. Selma is a nice young woman whose brain has been allowed to atrophy."

"Enough. Duty calls. Go talk to the ladies."

Henry was at the other end of the table, seated between Selma and Maggie. He was doing his job well. Both ladies were given equal attention. William spoke to Evelyn. "Don't they make a beautiful couple, Mrs. Wilkenson?"

Evelyn looked down the length of the table. There they were: her vacuous, undeveloped daughter, Henry and a dark-haired young woman who was far too striking and far too much Henry's equal in so many ways. Lucid, hard-headed woman that she was, she had to admit that Henry and Miss X seemed a perfectly matched pair; Selma was the "off horse." "I'm not sure which couple you're referring to," she remarked grimly.

"Why, Selma and Henry of course."

"Of course." She smiled her narrow smile. "Who is the young lady in the black gown on the other side of Henry?"

"That's Maggie Rhodes, an old family friend. Her mother and my late wife attended school together." He added, "She was left a reasonable income which I manage for her. It's enough to allow her to live and travel." He paused to take another look at Maggie as though he hadn't really noticed her before. "Yes, she has grown into an attractive young thing. Her mother would be pleased."

"Does she know Henry well?"

"No. Though I suspect she'd enjoy knowing him better."

"And how do you feel about the idea?"

"Does how I feel make any difference?"

"It might."

"Frankly, I do not find the subject of Henry's interest in woman and vice versa very stimulating. There must be more interesting topics."

"I like kitchen gossip, but let me think. We could tell jokes. Or discuss the weather. Or astrology."

"I prefer kitchen gossip." William watched Craig Spears pick at his food. "Take Craig. He took a bad beating last night. And I think another today. I believe our friend spent the afternoon with a companion who asked more of him than he was able to provide."

"I will never understand the way some men choose to take their pleasures."

"Nor will I. Still, to each his own."

Their conversation was interrupted as Oscar entered pushing a large serving cart. The cart contained a huge rib roast, a deep pan with roasted potatoes and several smaller pans in which a choice of vegetables from lima beans to squash was being kept warm.

Rank has its privileges, and at this table on this night, Mrs. Wilkenson outranked the other guests. She was offered the first choice of meat. To William's surprise, she chose a very rare cut and added a bone. A generous helping of potatoes and squash completed her selection. When the serving cart reached Spears, the lawyer selected a rather small slice of an outside cut and added only a few potatoes and a very small sampling of vegetables. However, he was making a good job on the wine which was constantly having to be added to his glass. William hoped he could hold his liquor. A drunken guest is almost as bad as a fist fight in terms of spoiling a party. With his employer on hand, William expected Spears to stay reasonably sober. Nonetheless, one could take precautions. He motioned for Oscar and suggested that Spears' glass be allowed to remain empty as long as possible.

After Oscar left, Mrs. Wilkenson whispered, "I approve. A drunk at a party is a bore. I used to have my husband's wine watered. The poor man never understood how much he could hold before he became incoherent and noisy."

Another fact for William to digest. He hadn't known John Wilkenson had a drinking problem.

"Very few people knew John was a drinker." She looked at William thoughtfully. "This is, of course, confidential."

"Of course."

"And now that we speak in confidence, I would like a private meeting with you after lunch tomorrow."

"Certainly. We can closet ourselves in my study for as long as necessary." He risked teasing her. "I'll even lock the door unless you think your reputation will be compromised."

"My dear William, I am too old and too rich to be concerned with such trivia. Lock the door."

There it was. The real game had begun. Possibly this whole boring party would prove worthwhile.

Craig Spears knew why his glass was still empty. It was empty because William Carson thought he had had enough to drink. Damn Carson. He needed a drink.

He had no idea how he would make good on last night's losses. His bank would not lend him another nickel. His wife had stashed her remaining jewelry in some safe-deposit box. And William could turn out to be a dangerous source of funds. What if he let the checks bounce? Impossible! But what could he do?"

He turned to the maid who was serving and asked for another glass of wine. There was a pause while he waited, afraid that his request would not be honored. That would call for a reaction on his part. But what kind of a reaction? Fortunately the question never had to be answered. Oscar appeared with a bottle of Nuit St. Georges and poured him a reasonable amount. He hadn't been cut off, merely put on shorter rations. Probably a wise thing at that. Spears was an optimist by nature, and he decided to try eating something. Very slowly but with increasing appetite, he began to eat. After all, as Scarlett said, "Tomorrow is another day." Tomorrow he would see what could be done.

Maggie was having a wonderful time. She had never been to a party like this before, and she was impressed by everything she saw: the room, the furniture, the servants, the lights, the food, the people, the men in white tie or tuxedos, the women in formal gowns and jewelry that wasn't from Woolworth's. Henry had been trying to divide his attention between Selma and her. He was chattering to Selma and having difficulty concentrating. She knew his mind was on her, and she had a strong sense of her physical attraction for him. Watching him, listening, hugging her silence, she suddenly bubbled to the surface with a splash of talk.

"Selma is such a pretty name."

"Do you think so? I think Maggie is also a pretty name. Don't you, Henry?"

"Yes."

Selma glowed with the attention of her two dinner partners. Tossing aside her well learned sense of position, she whispered to Maggie, "Call me Selma. We're about the same age."

"I'd love to, and you call me Maggie."

Henry was not pleased. The idea that his possible wife should become friends with his probable girlfriend was something for which he hadn't bargained. And it was his father's doing. They would have to have a talk at the earliest opportunity. It was going to be hard enough without Maggie and Selma becoming friends.

Maggie was aware of everything. She had no need to worry. Henry belonged to her no matter what else happened.

The meal was concluded with sachertorte and coffee. William stood up at the end and announced that the rest of the evening would be spent dancing, playing cards or listening to a jazz group he had brought up from Fifty-second Street in New York. He told where each of the entertainments was going to take place. The house was large enough and the walls thick enough to separate the jazz from the Glenn Miller Band.

The after-dinner guests had been assembling in the main ballroom. Henry continued to try to divide his time between Maggie and Selma, but most of it was spent with Selma. Maggie had no trouble attracting other men. They gathered around her in a general explosion of talk and laughter.

While dancing a fox trot with her, Henry held her close and felt her breasts pressed against his chest. During a deep dip, he let his knee slide against the ridge of her pelvis and was rewarded with a low, involuntary moan.

She murmured, "Please! You're taking unfair advantage."

He tightened his arm around her back, and moving slowly so that her back was against the wall, he dropped his hand to cup her buttocks. "No girdle?"

She leaned on his shoulder and shuddered violently. Henry could feel his erection coming to full hardness. They were interrupted by a tap on Henry's shoulder. There stood William, half grinning.

"If you two want to go upstairs and play 'doctor,' do so. But not on the dance floor. And not where Evelyn Wilkenson can see you. I'm cutting in. Henry, why don't you leave by that convenient door until the evidence of what you had in mind disappears?"

Henry shook his head to clear it. "You are a bastard." But the advice was sound. Marriages of state are just that. They are not affairs of passion. After he calmed down, he would find Selma.

When Henry discovered Selma, she was talking to her mother. Before he could ask her to dance, Mrs. Wilkenson claimed the right. Once again the music was a slow fox trot. Henry danced in silence thinking about a life of slow fox trots with Selma and Evelyn. His thoughts were interrupted when Evelyn asked him a question. "Sorry. I was listening to the music. Would you repeat that?"

"I asked you what you thought of my daughter."

"I think she's charming."

"Not to be compared with your Miss Rhodes, though."

"My Miss Rhodes? She's not my Miss Rhodes."

"Come, Henry. I watched you two dance before your father had the good sense to cut in." There was very little he could say to the unspoken accusation. "We'll drop the charming Miss Rhodes for the moment. Henry, it would please me if you called on Selma from time to time."

"I was planning to."

Evelyn marveled at how well he and William worked together. "Good. And I have another favor to ask of you."

"If I can oblige you, I will."

"It should cause you no trouble. Tomorrow, after lunch, I want a word with your father, alone. Both my daughter and lawyer will be in the way. Do you think you could keep them amused for several hours?"

"We could visit Playland. In Rye. There's indoor ice skating. We'll be busy for hours."

"Fine. Now push me back to where Selma's standing. She looks so lost. It isn't fair to deprive her of you any longer."

Unlike his father, Henry recognized how much more there was to Evelyn Wilkenson than he had imagined.

Slowly, inevitably, the evening wound down. At three a.m. the band played its last set, ending with "Good Night Ladies." By four the guests had gone. The only people remaining were William, Henry and their weekend guests. During the time he had spent with Selma, Henry had managed to keep a watchful eye on Maggie. Though not certain, he was fairly confident she had been driven home, alone.

Whatever came of William's meeting with Evelyn Wilkenson, Henry had a purpose now beyond the demands of the Carson Company. It was Maggie Rhodes. She was meant for passion. She was meant for him, and fulfilling his purpose was now only a question of time.

# Chapter 6

CHURCH services went well. According to Selma, Dr. Carlson had a fine voice, both in volume and resonance. For her part, Evelyn noticed that services did not commence until they arrived. This agreed with her opinion of her own worth and confirmed again that the Carsons, too, were a little more than equal among their equals.

When they arrived home, they found Spears still there, but Godfrey Moore had decamped for the city, leaving William a note. Excusing himself, William went into the library to read the "thank you" note. A postscript said Moore would call in a day or two to find out if he had won his wager.

After lunch, Henry organized the skating expedition with Selma's gushing approval and Spears' grudging acceptance. Before leaving, Spears had a quick word with William about a private meeting. William suggested Monday, and Spears asked that it be as early as possible. Then they left for Playland.

William smiled at Evelyn. "Alone at last. Now we can settle the affairs of the world."

"Not the world. Only our portion of it." As agreed, they retreated to the library, where Evelyn settled herself in a deep chair. William sat behind his desk.

"We should have quiet here. For the afternoon at least."

Evelyn nodded. She looked around the room appraisingly. She asked in a voice of approval tinged with envy, "Has anyone climbed the ladder recently?"

"Weekly. The servants have to dust, you know."

"I deserved that. Books are a bit of a hobby of mine. Collecting as well as reading. My envy was showing."

"My father started the collection, and I've continued to add to it. In fact, Henry remarked the other day that we'll either have to break down a wall or build an annex."

Evelyn gave her opinion without being asked. "Build an annex.

This room is too perfect to change. Speaking of Henry, will he listen to your advice should our talk make it necessary he listen?"

"He might. Depending upon the advice."

"I'll be blunt. I've watched the growth of the Carson Company for a number of years. You've done an excellent job. We need the same kind of management at Wilkenson. So I would like to propose a merger between our two companies. And," she added, her mouth twisted slyly, "our children."

"A merger?" William elongated the word, almost savoring it. "What kind of a merger, if I may ask?"

Evelyn snorted in mild disgust. "Stop it, William Carson. You know exactly what kind. That's why we were invited to spend the weekend." She stopped, suddenly having another thought. "And speaking of the weekend, exactly who is Miss Rhodes? No more stories about your dear departed wife. The truth, please."

"Very well. A truth for a truth."

"What do you mean?"

"Why did you sabotage Craig Spears on Friday night?"

Evelyn Wilkenson leaned back in her chair. This time when she smiled her eyes gleamed. "So you noticed."

"Of course I noticed. So did Moore. Again, a truth for a truth."

"If I tell you my little secret, you'll tell who the girl is?"

William nodded.

"Very well. I dislike traitors. I dislike them even more when I'm the one who is being betrayed. It's bad enough when I have to hire industrial spies. It's far worse when I'm the one being spied upon."

"You believe your lawyer is a spy?"

"How else could you have obtained all your confidential information about my company?"

William politely shook his head. "I'm not aware of having any confidential information about your company."

"Please. I know you do. And I can make a good guess at exactly which information you have and when you received it." She opened her large purse and produced a notebook. She read the times and dates of Spears' visits to the Carson Company and noted certain telephone calls that had passed between them.

"I take it you've had him followed?"

"For months."

"Madam, my admiration overflows." And William really did admire her. She had recognized there was a leak in her company, discovered the source of the leak and plugged it. He could have done no better. "So you taught Craig a nasty lesson." He mused over that information. It was pretty much as he had thought. "How do you propose to let him know he's been taught a lesson?"

"I've fired him. His dismissal is on his desk. He'll pick it up Monday morning."

Even though he would have done the same thing, William felt sorry for Spears. And he had a twinge of guilt at being the cause of the man's loss of his job. The least he could do was make good his gambling losses. And, of course, pay him a fee when the deal closed.

As though reading his mind, Evelyn added, "Don't feel too sorry for him. Or blame yourself. He sold the same information to the Johnsons, the Bristols, the Lamberts and other companies I know of, plus a few I don't yet know. And now for your truth. Exactly who is Miss Maggie Rhodes?"

"I'm sorry to disappoint you, but she is exactly who I said she was. The daughter of a schoolmate of my wife."

"I'm disappointed in you. In fact, so disappointed that I think this meeting is about to end."

William stood up. "Before you leave so hastily, permit me to show you something." Evelyn sat back and waited. "You asked me if we ever use our ladder. I will now." He moved the ladder across the room and climbed the steps until he was able to reach the top shelf. There was a small group of scrapbooks lying flat on the shelf. He picked up the top one and leafed through it. The wrong one. The second produced no better results. But part way through the third book he made a pleased sound and jumped to the floor holding the book. He opened the book and showed Evelyn a page. "Please read that clipping and several that follow."

Evelyn looked at the yellowed clipping and turned the page and read the next two. Without a word she handed the book back to William and sat silently while he replaced the scrapbook. When he was seated across from her, she simply shook her head. "My apologies. It seems that she is the daughter of a schoolmate of your late wife. What can I say?"

"Nothing. Nothing at all." He congratulated himself on having the foresight months ago to have had several articles printed about Maggie Rhodes and her mother, providing her with the background he claimed. He had won the gamble that Evelyn Wilkenson would not be aware of the small printers around Times Square who would slug in any article on yellowed newspaper, so that only an expert could recognize that the article had been added at a much later date. "But I can certainly understand your doubts. She is a beautiful young woman. Let us continue with the reasons for this meeting."

Seemingly convinced, Evelyn agreed. "I would like to see both our companies and families merged."

"Why?"

"I've told you why."

"Let's start with the companies. Why the Carson Company? No more games, Evelyn. Since you believe you know how much I know about your business, let us assume that I also know how high the bidding has gone. Too high for my taste."

"Not for mine. But there are other things besides money."

"What things?"

"Your son for one. For another, I want the Wilkenson name to remain before the public. Especially as concerns the new products. Not disappear into the maw of a huge public company."

"I see. That might be a problem."

"Your son? Or the name?"

William thought for a moment. "Let's settle the easier problem first."

"All right. Which is the easier one?"

"The merging of the families. I believe I can speak for my son. So I, William, father of Henry, do ask you, Evelyn, mother of Selma, for the hand of your daughter in marriage to my son."

Evelyn laughed harshly. "Why not? I, Evelyn, mother of Selma, accept the hand of your son, Henry, for my daughter in marriage."

Thus the engagement was sealed.

"Now that that's settled, let's get to the real problem. I really don't want your company. I only want those patent applications."

"One goes with the other."

"Not necessarily."

"Necessarily! And furthermore, so does the name. I suggest Carson and Wilkenson as a proper name for the merged entity."

"Madam! Excuse me, Evelyn. Your company is losing millions every year, and the bloodletting will increase."

"My name must remain before the public."

"Why?"

"Because I choose it to."

"Not the best of reasons, but one with which I can sympathize."

Evelyn waited for him to continue.

"I wonder if, by using our best efforts, we can reach a compromise."

"Compromises are what make the world go round. Suggest one."

"First, let's summarize. I don't want the company, but I do want the patent applications."

"Anyone with reasonable ability can make money with Wilkenson, Inc. Anyone except the idiots now running it."

William reminded her gently that those "idiots" were men she chose.

"I didn't choose them. My late husband did. And assuming we can't reach an accommodation, I will clean house. Spears is only the first to go."

"As I understand you, you not only want your products continued, you want them continued under your family name. That's why the merger." Evelyn kept nodding her agreement. "And we don't want a merger. A family merger, yes. A corporate merger, no. Hmmm. I may see a way."

"I never doubted that a brain as fertile as yours would."

"What would you think of a Wilkenson Division? No—better, a full subsidiary? Wilkenson, Inc. in very large letters. In small print, a wholly-owned subsidiary of the Carson Company. One would have to read the package with a magnifying glass to know we had anything to do with the product. Especially the tranquilizers."

"We would specify the size of type to be used in the contract?"

"Of course. We could even stamp Wilkenson, Inc. on the pills themselves."

"Yes. I can agree to that. Now as to the money?"

"A detail. After all, won't our children inherit everything? Whatever is paid will eventually belong to our grandchildren."

"Yes, William. But the grandmother in me wants to know what my grandchildren will get. Let's agree on a payment of twenty-five million dollars to me, the grandmother-to-be."

"No. I told you I have no intention of matching bids."

Evelyn frowned. She had forgotten for the moment that William knew what she had been offered. And it was true that he had added his son to the bid. Now what was Henry worth? "When do you suggest the wedding take place?"

"When do you suggest?"

Evelyn thought about her daughter and the strain she would be living under. Was she doing the right thing for her daughter? Probably not. But that hardly mattered. It was the right thing for the family name, and that was what counted. She considered her lack of traditional motherly tenderness and dismissed it. That, too, didn't matter. Henry wouldn't injure Selma, and Selma would learn to accept his physical needs. All women learned about men. Children would come and she would adapt. In full justice, she accepted that Maggie Rhodes would make a far better mate for Henry than Selma. And remembering Maggie prompted her decision. "Let's give them as little time as possible to get to know each other."

William raised his eyebrows. "As little time?"

"Yes. We don't want the daughter of your late wife's schoolmate to become an obstacle, do we?"

William remembered Maggie and Henry at the dance. He may have borrowed trouble by trying to sweeten Henry's future. "Evelyn, you're a wise woman. Exactly how little time should we allow them to get to know each other?"

"They've now known each other for two days. Pity they had to meet at all. It might have been simpler as it was in the old days when the betrothed couple met in the church." She tugged on her lower lip considering alternatives. "A three-month engagement. I believe that's time enough. They'll be married on June twenty-first. The first day of summer."

"I agree. Now, if I may return to the financial side, I suggest a payment of five million dollars to you against a royalty of five percent on all new products. The royalty to go to Selma and Henry and eventually their children."

"Against, did you say?"

"I did."

"Ten million dollars to me plus, not against, a five percent royalty. I agree the royalty should go to Selma and Henry and then to their children."

William knew he could negotiate a little harder and settle for something less, but he liked the idea of the royalty remaining in the family. Why push any further? "You drive a hard bargain, but I think I can live with those terms."

"Suppose you make a few notes on what we've agreed to, and we can have the lawyers start on the contracts tomorrow."

It took three pages of carefully handwritten sentences to set down the terms of the acquisition. Evelyn read it over word by word and agreed without a single change. He copied the pages, handed her one and put the other in the safe. "I believe a glass of champagne is in order."

"A glass? Don't you think we might open a bottle?"

William dialed a number on his desk phone. "Oscar, please bring that special bottle I placed on ice Friday to the library with two glasses."

"You knew?"

"Let's say I hoped."

The champagne arrived, and the two parents toasted themselves, toasted their company and finally toasted their children. Evelyn excused herself. She wanted to rest and think about what she would say to Selma. She paused at the door and looked back at William. "I suggest you not show those clippings of your late wife's friend's daughter to others. The name of the typeface escapes me at the moment, but it wasn't used until about 1930. That would make Maggie Rhodes about ten years old today. However, I'm certain Henry will be discreet. In fact, I'll count on it." She left the room, leaving William stunned. He would have to check out that typeface. He wouldn't put it past that woman to throw it at him with nothing more to go on except a hunch. In any case, he had work to do. Several hours went by while he reread the reports on Wilkenson, Inc. She was right. The management were a pack of fools. It looked as though the company was being milked. Absentee ownership made it easy. He could have it in the black within six months. A year at the most. The sound of a returning car barely gave him time to return the papers to the file.

An excited Selma rushed in followed by a tired Spears and a very curious Henry. Evelyn appeared at the door. She too had heard the car returning. Seeing Spears, she said, "Craig, leave us alone. I'm certain you could use a drink and some freshening up. We have private matters to discuss."

William stopped him. "Craig, you wanted to speak to me? I'll have time to chat before you leave. Oscar will let you know when."

"Thank you. I'll be waiting."

"Why do you bother with him?" Evelyn was peevish.

"Because he asked to speak to me earlier."

As Selma looked at her mother, she became unsure of herself. Something had happened but she didn't know what, and she felt a flash of fear. Henry was waiting for a sign from William. He was rewarded by a brief nod. It was enough.

"I assume you've reached a meeting of the minds?"

"We have, Henry. In all areas." Evelyn answered before William could.

"Then suppose Selma and I take a stroll, and I'll explain what has happened."

In spite of all the preparation that had gone into this moment, Henry could not help feeling annoyed. He had known Selma for forty-eight hours, and now he was going to propose. He didn't doubt she would accept him. What the marriage would be like was another matter. In a burst of optimism, he actually thought that once released from her mother's hold, Selma might grow. If this marriage was possible, anything was possible.

They walked through a privet hedge maze that occupied one section of the formal part of the garden. He remembered how he and Francis had played hide-and-seek in the early days before their hatred made play together impossible, and for a brief moment he regretted the loss of his brother.

"You look so sad, Henry. What is it?" Her mother had encouraged their going together into the garden, so it must be all right.

"It's nothing. I was just thinking about my brother, and I guess a part of me wishes it would have been different."

"Then make it different. You can, if you and God wish it."

"I rather think God likes it the way it is." They had reached the center of the maze, and Henry pointed to an iron bench. "Let's sit here. I want to talk to you."

Selma felt an impulse to turn and run, but instead she sat down. Her mother wanted her here, and here she must stay.

Seated by her side, Henry began. "Selma, do you like me?"

"Oh, yes. I think you're about the nicest man I've ever met." She said it brightly, but her spirit quivered and waited.

"I mean really like me?"

Though she was nervous and afraid, there was something about him that fascinated her. "I swear under God that I like you." What more could she say?

Henry realized the importance of what Selma had said. He pressed on. "Do you think you could love me someday?"

"Oh, Henry." Her heart hurt in her body. This too she had to accept. It was God's will.

"You see, Selma, your mother and my father have arranged for our families to be joined. Your mother has agreed that I may ask you to be my wife."

"You want to marry me?"

"I want to marry you." This was far more difficult than he had imagined it would be. "Will you marry me, Selma?" He felt furious and helpless. What was there in him that made him consider the possibility of marrying Selma Wilkenson? He had a clear view of the future and the dreary nature of their life together. She was naive. She was not sexual. She would be happier in a convent. Even knowing this, he could not stop himself from proposing to her. Why?

He stared into his mind, seeing William. Never having guessed the depth of William's loss when his wife died nor sensed the cry for help from a man who would never cry, Henry accepted that his father's deepest commitment had always been to the Carson Company. He took it for granted in the manner of information learned in childhood and never questioned. William took more pleasure from his work at the company than he did making love to any woman—and Henry was William's son. He nodded his head in unconscious agreement with his logic. That was the heart of the matter, why he was as he was. That was why he, like his father, lived with a kind of chastity of spirit that made him shrink, not from the physical pleasure of making love, but from any intimacy with a woman that required she come before the company. He was a monk dedicated to the service of a faith that was his one true passion, the Carson Company. For such a religion, Selma would do as well as any wife. Better, in fact, when he thought of her dowry. Of course he would propose. He could do no less.

"What I'm trying to explain to you is that arrangements our parents have made include our getting married."

"My mother agreed?"

"Would you be here if she didn't?" He got down on one knee before her. "Selma Wilkenson, with your mother's permission, and God's, I ask you to marry me."

Selma hunched forward almost in pain. Then she straightened up and said what she knew she must say. "Yes, I will marry you."

Henry could feel the effort she was making and was touched with pity. "I will treat you with kindness and goodness always." Then he helped her rise, making certain that he didn't touch any part of her body; then he pressed his lips against hers. It was Selma's first kiss from anyone other than a parent, and that was always on the cheek.

She pulled her head back sharply. "Your lips are wet, Henry."

"I'm sorry. I'll try to keep them dry."

"Thank you." Her fear had changed, becoming puzzlement. Without realizing it, she leaned forward, magnetized by Henry. Shuddering, yet drawn, she pursed her lips and touched them to his. They stood very still, inches apart, Henry holding her hands and their lips touching lightly.

Then she drew back. She felt dragged to earth, a rabbit some dog had got down in the dust. She knew her life would be unhappy. She knew what she was doing was wrong. But right or wrong, she would obey her mother. Henry tried to comfort her, but he wondered how Evelyn Wilkenson had permitted her daughter to grow up so isolated, unwarmed, with no hold on real life. He had told the truth. He would do his very best.

"We had better go back and tell them we're engaged. Though they've probably selected the ring and the wedding date and decided where it will be held."

"The ring? The wedding?"

"That's what people who become engaged have. A wedding, dear."

"I understand." And she did. She knew her days of grace were numbered.

After the couple entered and Henry made the dry announcement that they were engaged, William relaxed. He had never been certain Henry would do it. The open bottle of champagne was still in the ice bucket. Two more glasses were called for, and there was just enough flat champagne left for William to toast the couple. Then Evelyn and Selma left to pack for their trip home.

When they were gone, William looked at a solemn Henry and observed, "You'll live happily ever after." He told Henry the terms of the deal he had made with Evelyn.

"It's a coup, Father. But you weren't in the maze with Selma. In every deal someone gets less, and she's the one who's getting short-changed. I feel sorry for her."

"Sorry enough to back out?"

"No. But it is a pity. At least I get something from the marriage. I don't know what she gets."

"You. You're worth something. And you can never tell what marriage will do for Selma."

"I can tell." Henry let out a deep breath.

"We'll talk later." William watched Henry leave, the glow of triumph fading from his face. He had refused to let any doubts surface in front of his son, but they were there. He knew he had set in motion events that would not bring happiness to the people involved. But happiness is an accident of circumstances that can never be guaranteed. It was no longer relevant to life as he saw it. Life was what it was. That reminded him of Craig Spears.

Spears entered and came right to the point. "I believe I've earned my fee, and I'd like to collect now."

"All right. What would you consider a reasonable fee?"

Spears hesitated. William might be in a generous mood. Why not ask for more. All he could do was say no. "Fifty thousand dollars."

William considered. That was one-half of one percent of what he would pay Evelyn, and without Spears, there might not have been any deal. However, if he agreed too readily, Spears would think he had asked too little. "I'll make a counter offer. Fifty thousand dollars is high, and we haven't signed the contract. How much did you lose Friday night?"

"Over ten thousand dollars."

"Final offer. No negotiation. My personal check for ten thousand dollars now, and because I'm in a good mood, forty thousand dollars when the deal closes." He could feel Craig weighing the offer. Should he try for more? "Don't do it, Craig. I said no negotiations."

Spears surrendered.

William wrote a check and handed it to the lawyer. Now came the difficult part. "Craig, Evelyn knows what you've been doing."

"You bastard! You told her."

"Don't be a fool. She's had you shadowed for months. She knows the other companies you've been dealing with. Even where you spent Saturday afternoon."

"Then I don't have a job?"

"No, you don't. It ends tomorrow."

"Tomorrow! That bitch!"

"Stop it. You're a big boy. You were playing with fire and got caught. Besides, I've just given you enough money to tide you over. And when the deal closes, you'll have enough money to live until you relocate. Your story is you were phased out in the merger. I'll write you a reference."

"Thanks. That ten thousand dollars will just cover my losses."

"Not quite that bad. Wait outside for a moment?" After Craig left, he opened his safe. He glanced at the memorandum of agreement and removed Godfrey Moore's sealed envelope. He opened it and read: *You've been using Spears in some way. She found out and gave it to him right up the old ass.* It was signed with a large G. Moore had won his wager. He lit Moore's note and dropped the ashes into the ashtray on his desk. Then he called for Spears to return. William handed him his two checks, one Spears had made out to Moore and the other to himself. "Take them. The only check you have to cover is Evelyn's. But count on it, she will deposit hers."

Cash his check after firing him? Hardly! He'd put a stop payment on the check before going to the office. Then he'd have the full $10,000. He muttered a thanks and left to dress for the drive back to the city.

# Chapter 7

**W**HEN HENRY and Maggie met at eight o'clock on Monday morning, it was hard to tell who was more nervous. They sipped their coffee in silence. Then, without introduction or warning, in an oddly unstressed voice, Henry told her his news. "Congratulate me. I'm going to be married."

"Congratulations, Mr. H. It's a pleasure to know a man who sees where his duty lies." She knew she had no right to be angry, but she was.

"Does your congratulations reach far enough to celebrate by joining me at dinner tonight?"

"It does."

"Where do you live?" She gave him the address. "I know the building. It's right on the river."

"I have a beautiful river view."

He hesitated. "I thought I might provide a steak and the fixings. We could spend some time together without worrying about the waiters. That is, if you think you'd like that."

"I'd like that very much."

"What's the apartment number?"

She told him. In spite of the knowledge that he could have arranged to have dinner with her at any time during the last few months, Henry felt a little like a schoolboy on his first date. "You're sure you're free tonight? It's short notice."

"I'm free. I'd have told you if I weren't." She no longer cared if Henry guessed, or anyone else. Her desire for him had passed all reasonable limits. The fact that he was engaged didn't matter. It would be a marriage of state. It didn't count. The idea that he might love Selma would have hurt beyond bearing; it would have made anything between them impossible. But he didn't love Selma. And what she did not realize was that Henry's thoughts exactly echoed her own. If he had cared for his wife-to-be beyond the merest flicker of human feeling, he would never have suggested dinner with Maggie.

"Would seven be all right?"

"Seven is fine."

He glanced at his watch and switched gears. His tone became more formal, business as usual. "Since the Wilkenson acquisition is going through, I'm going to spend the morning going over the reports on the company."

"I'll get them for you."

While he waited for Maggie to return, Henry thought about his father and himself again. He thought about William's lack of jealousy with regard to Marion. William paid for what he received. He was not ready to pay more, either in money or emotional commitment, and he got his money's worth. No more and no less.

Henry thought he was the same kind of man. If he was going to have a wife and a—a what? a girlfriend, mistress, sweetheart?—like his father, he wouldn't expect more than was reasonable from the arrangement. Essentially he was a monogamous man. It suited his nature and his sense of an orderly world. If Selma had been Maggie, he would have no need or desire for another Maggie. But Selma was Selma. There were problems inherent in the business of royal marriages. They would force him to live a divided life. He would live it.

The morning was spent going over the Wilkenson reports, and he was amazed at the company's mismanagement. The difference between the Carson Company and Wilkenson, Inc. was a matter of management rather than product. With very few exceptions, there was a complementary mix between the products of the two companies. They could support each other. Of course, if the combining of the drug research resulted in their being able to market the tranquilizer in the near future, the corporation would have to reallocate its resources. The less successful products from each company would have to be dropped.

Lunch time arrived too quickly, and Henry and Maggie went their separate ways. He wouldn't see her again until late that afternoon. The lawyers had telephoned from New York requesting that current audited financial statements of the Carson Company be prepared. Auditors from Price Waterhouse & Co. would be arriving shortly, and Maggie was to show them where they were to work and help them get started.

At lunch, Henry thought about Evelyn Wilkenson and admired her foresight. She was not going to buy a pig in a poke. As far as Evelyn was concerned, the Carson Company's reputation for financial soundness was pure hearsay. She wanted the real numbers. So Price Waterhouse was going to review the company books and issue an audited report. This made Henry think again about his "limbo" position in the company. His authority had never been clearly spelled out, and the uncertainty bred executive resentment. If it continued too long, he would have to insist on having something spelled out. But he preferred to have it come from William voluntarily. After all, any authority that he might be given could only be given at some sacrifice of William's own authority.

He arrived at the lab at three, signed in and took a badge. He liked the idea of not having Maggie with him. If they were going to have a private relationship, he would find another spot for her in the company. A spot other than that of his secretary. It was too much of a good thing and would get in the way of work. Henry entered the lab without knocking. It looked empty. Then the face of Dr. Flam appeared from behind the corner of a bench. He had been lying on the floor, completely oblivious to his ridiculous position, studying a number of caged mice.

"What are you doing on the floor?"

"Watching the mice frisk and frolic. They refuse to be tranquilized." He sounded irritable and his accent was heavier.

"Could we go into your office? I'd like to be brought up to date on the project."

Before he answered, Felix gave one last, unloving look at the hyperactive mice. Then he led Henry into his office which was, if possible, more cluttered than when Henry first saw it.

Henry made a sour face. "How can you, a man who must keep his mind orderly, work in this mess?"

Felix looked around. "This, maybe, is worse than usual." He suggested Henry place a pile of papers that were on a small chair on the floor. Henry could sit on the chair. Felix would stand.

Henry followed instructions, and as he sat on the chair, it creaked under his weight. "Have you any idea of the time frames within which we're working? Assume for the moment we can combine the Wilkenson work with what you're doing here. When do you think we might be marketing the tranquilizer?"

"No one has even begun to test the product on human beings."

Henry revised his remaining questions. Tranquilizers were not going to drain any resources from current product marketing. "I don't want you to think I'm putting you under any pressure, but off the record, how much more time will you need before testing on humans can begin?"

"It's pure guesswork, but if the work at Wilkenson is where I think it is, we'll need two more years of lab work before we can think about testing on people. We'll file additional applications with the patent office long before that, but it takes time. We can't afford mistakes."

Henry crossed his legs, and the chair began to give. He stood up before it caved in. "May I move those reports off the couch? This chair won't have me."

Felix went through the pile of documents. "These are a year old and belong in the files." He took an armful of reports, notebooks and loose papers and went over to one of several file cabinets. When he opened a drawer, Henry wasn't surprised to see that the file was empty. He repeated the process until the couch was empty and the file was full.

Henry was in a state of shock. "That was well done. Now, tell me, how are you going to locate the papers in that file when you need one?"

"I'll look until I find what I need."

"Don't you have a secretary?"

"What would she do?"

"Keep your files in order, for one thing."

"I don't think there's room."

"We'll make room. At least a part-time secretary with a desk somewhere else. And I think I know just the right person."

Felix was about to object. He didn't want a strange secretary arranging his precious papers. Maggie had entered, overheard and understood Henry's thought.

"The right person, Dr. Flam, is someone so gifted she can handle two jobs at the same time. On cue, I appear."

This was exactly what Henry had in mind. "There's a fine idea. Maggie's being underused. She can easily work for you as well as for me."

Felix remembered how skillfully Maggie had adjusted during his first meeting with Henry, watchful of their moods, quick to speech or silence as the conversation required. And now the ease with which she picked up the thread of their talk. Such facility puzzled him. Was she really only a lighthearted, very pretty American girl? That was the effect she wished to convey. Yet it seemed to him then that the situation for her must indeed be desperate, desperate enough to require such alertness, such adroit handling. It was as though she walked with slow, careful steps across a very narrow plank spanning a deep crevass, never looking down, knowing if she did she might lose courage and fall. She reminded him of himself before William Carson had hired him, making his bridge across the crevass safer. Though Maggie was American-born and he was a Jewish refugee from Vienna, he saw in her the same "outsider" he saw in himself. This recognition of another hard-pressed spirit, as much as any need for a secretary, decided him to accept her. He would widen the plank to make her crossing safer. He said, "Henry thinks this office is a mess. Can you help me with it, please?"

"Of course." Knowing Dr. Flam's eccentricities, she was glad he had accepted her. There really wasn't enough to do working for Henry. And seeing him all day, as well as, hopefully, many evenings, could make things very difficult. "But will Mr. Carson agree?"

"Mr. Carson will agree," Henry answered firmly. The time was closer at hand than he had realized for there to be two Mr. Carsons. No matter what the confusion. "Felix, you said two years, more or less, before we consider testing the tranquilizer on people?"

"Two years if nothing goes too wrong. It's four-thirty. I have several hours of notes to enter before I can go home. Can Maggie start tomorrow?"

"Yes. The sooner we get this place in order, the better."

Henry and Maggie left together. "See you at seven. With the best of everything," he said as they stood close together in the parking lot.

"At seven."

He watched her get into her car. Then he drove back to his office. He wanted to talk to William, who was in New York. After that, he would select the perfect steak, several bottles of a fine wine and a few special items he had in mind for the evening.

William had had a difficult day in New York. First there was a meeting with his lawyers, Cravath, Swain and Moore. The copy of the Memorandum of Understanding that he had drawn up the day before was brought to their attention. When John Hillyer, the tall, red-haired partner who handled his work, had come to the clauses dealing with the royalties, he looked at William in surprise. He knew both Evelyn and Selma socially. He also knew William and Henry and Francis. The idea that Henry was going to marry Selma struck him as sheer lunacy, and he didn't hesitate to say so.

William held his patience for a brief period and then said very quietly, "John, it is not advisable for you to venture unsolicited opinions. I neither want nor need your advice as to the wisdom of our decision." He added, "Please remember I have never offered you advice on any of your personal affairs. I mind my own business. Pay me the same courtesy, please."

Hillyer stiffened. He was thirty-eight years old, a physically imposing man, actually taller than William, and no one had spoken to him that bluntly in years. "On precisely which aspects of my life would you choose to give me advice?"

"You want to know?"

"You're damn right I do!"

"Your choice, not mine. You had no business allowing that property on Thirty-eighth and Fourth Avenue to be auctioned. That land has been in your family for four generations. New York real estate will come back stronger than ever. I bought the property from the bank. If John Junior turns out the way we hope, I plan to make a present of it to him on his twenty-fifth birthday. You have no right to fool around with your family trust. Shall I go on?"

Hillyer almost choked on the words. "Please do."

"We're sharing Marion Wade. You take her far too seriously."

"We're what?"

"Sharing Marion. Damn it, John, I introduced you to her in the first place. How do you think I came to know her?"

"I have no idea."

"Think about it. Anyway, Marion had a few free nights. You seemed ideal. She tells me you're talking about love and commitments and being together always. Stop it. She doesn't want it. And if you persist, she'll cross you off her list."

Hillyer had the grace to flush. "I thought women like to be told you love them."

"Stupid women, on occasion. Wives almost always. Smart whores, never. If you mean it, it's a complication. If you don't, it's an insult. Gifts of jewelry are fine. Expensive pieces are even better. You can afford it. But for God's sake, keep the romance for your wife. She probably needs it. Shall I go on?"

"That will do. Are you the reason I'm not seeing Marion tonight?"

"I am. I have first call on Mondays, Thursdays and some Sundays. I understand you have Tuesdays and some Saturday afternoons."

"You know too damn much!"

"Stop it. She's a fine woman. If she's a bit too fond of money and doesn't choose to earn it by conventional means, that's her business. Now if you really want her deep appreciation, put her on the Class A list. She'd like that."

"The Class A list?"

"As distinguished from the Class B list."

"I don't understand."

William was growing irritated with his lawyer, whom he respected and wanted to continue to respect. But in terms of the sexual mores of their group, John was turning out to be a simpleton. "Okay, but this ends all discussions about women. Class A women are rewarded for performance by charge accounts in their own name billed to you, stock tips and, occasionally, some shares in a good company. The Class B list gets money, jewelry, trips. Anything lower doesn't matter. Do you understand me?"

Hillyer nodded. He would have to think about that. Money was one thing, but charge accounts and stock? That implied responsibility. Suppose Ellen found out. Despite his compulsive infidelity, he loved his wife, their marriage and their son, John Jr. Maybe William was right? He was out of his depth. They had better get back to work.

The next few hours were spent going over the agreement. Finally it was settled. Henry and Selma would marry at the same time the acquisition was finalized. A double ceremony. A prince and princess would be joined in holy wedlock, and their property would be united in one larger, stronger entity.

After leaving his lawyer's Wall Street offices, William was driven uptown to the University Club where he had lunch in the main dining room. He toyed with a piece of fish. Putting aside all his confident words to Hillyer, he had many qualms about the impending wedding. Where was the morality in creating a marriage between two people who were totally unsuited for each other? There was no morality at all. Of course, Henry could have refused after meeting Selma. But he didn't. To Henry, the Carson Company came ahead of everything. And from the corporate position, the acquisition of Wilkenson, Inc., with its patent applications on the tranquilizers, was the biggest step the company had made since it first began to manufacture its own products. Still, William doubted that given the choice he would have made the sacrifice Henry was making.

Of course, there was Maggie. Henry could find his pleasure outside of marriage. Most men did, no matter what vows they took in church. Or the intentions they had when they made the vows. If the results were more or less the same, what difference did "intentions" make? He doubted that they made any difference. This bit of sophistry made him feel somewhat better. William accepted that he was far from a perfect father, and perhaps less than a moral man, if judged by the moral code of our civilization. But civilizations change and morality along with them. What is right for one may be wrong for the next. Henry would marry Selma.

Wilkenson would be acquired. That was that, and the right and wrong of it would be left to a Higher Being to judge, always assuming that such a Being existed.

After lunch, William went down to the main reading room and buried himself in the *New York Times*. The war was going badly. He read a story about the bombing of London. There were pictures of the fires and the destruction that the bombings had caused. This reminded him of Francis. Using the utmost caution, he had kept track of Francis. A curious mixture of a man. Francis had joined the RCAF since the RAF wouldn't accept an American. He had become a Wing Commander with a truly outstanding record of achievement, highly regarded by both his men and his superiors. His height limited him to flying bombers, and although he was flying the most dangerous of missions, he brought back a higher percentage of his command than did most of his peers. And not because his missions were not being completed. Francis seemed to have a rare quality. He was both recklessly brave and shrewdly cautious.

On the other hand, heroics aside, the reports hinted at but did not detail an impressive list of vices. When off duty, Francis mingled in the highest social circles, and it is in just those circles that one finds the most corrupt elements of a society. They accepted Francis as one of their own with the result that he went from nights of total dissipation to days of astonishing courage. He was becoming a twentieth-century Dorian Grey.

Neither side of Francis either surprised or dismayed him. He had known more about the true nature of Francis than either Francis or Henry had given him credit for knowing. That was why he had never wanted Francis to inherit the Carson Company. He suspected that was the reason Francis and Henry had battled constantly. Francis was a born libertine. Henry was, in his own odd way, a highly moral man. In any case, Francis was earning the right to behave exactly as he wished by daily risking his life in a cause that, soon enough, would be America's as well.

It was four o'clock by the time he finished the *Times*, and he had to check in with the office. Mary answered his call. Things were quiet. The audit was under way. Henry and Maggie were over at the lab with Dr. Flam. William thought about Maggie. It pleased him that she was as attracted to Henry as he was to her. It was now time to play a game or two of squash with the professional, get a massage and dress for the evening ahead with Marion.

In the middle of the massage there was a call from Henry, who requested a private meeting in the office the next day. William knew the storm signals were rising. A little sooner than he had expected. He would have to decide what areas of authority he was prepared to cede. That was what they were going to talk about. Authority.

Maggie arrived at her apartment in a state of growing excitement. At last Henry Carson was coming to see her. It was five-thirty. One and a half hours to wait, and he would be there. The apartment was clean. All she had to do was strip the bed and put on fresh sheets. After that she undressed and ran a hot bath. The water would relax her. She felt desire spreading through her body, a tight pressure in her throat, in her stomach and, most of all, in her vagina. Then she felt a violent apprehension. What a terrible joke on her if he came for dinner, had dinner and went home. She would kill him, see him collapse and then she would kill herself.

She knew exactly what she would wear. Something feminine and simple and easy to take off. A wrap-around, pink silk dress that was held together by a sash and two snaps. Stockings held up by a garter belt. No panties. No brassiere. Black pumps and a pink band on her curly, black hair. A little eye makeup. No lipstick. No rouge. Just her own face.

The buzzer rang, and the doorman told her that a Mr. Carson was here.

"Send him up, Harry."

She went to the door, opened it and leaned against the door jamb. She felt a tense, joyous impatience as she waited for the sound of the elevator door. Then she heard it, heard Jimmy, the elevator man, giving directions to her apartment. It seemed forever until Henry appeared around the corner. He was carrying a large, brown paper bag and a brightly wrapped package. In the first moment of seeing him again, she felt such immense relief that she thought she might rise weightless into the air, such relief that she could find no words to welcome him and just stood aside allowing him to pass.

Once he was in the apartment, they looked at each other, and she knew that he understood. But what he said was, "Point me toward the kitchen, please."

She managed to answer, "Follow me." She led him down the short hall to the kitchen. He placed the paper bag on the counter and opened the package. There were two bottles of Burgundy and a bottle of brandy. She read the labels: Romanée Conti 1929 and Napoleon VSOP.

Henry wandered around the room looking at the stove, the sink, the table. He found what he wanted in the cupboard over the stove where the platters were stacked. He took out the largest platter and placed it next to the paper bag. Then he opened the bag and produced a porterhouse steak about two inches thick. There were Idaho potatoes and assorted greens for a mixed salad. The bag also held a cake box which he put into the refrigerator.

When he was finished, she said, "I have the drinks ready in the living room. It has a great view of the Hudson."

"I know. You told me." There was a bottle of gin and a small bottle of dry vermouth on the table. Maggie waited while Henry made two martinis. She wondered why she had bothered with the drinks when all she wanted to do was make love to him.

After pouring the drinks, Henry stood at the wide picture window, looking at the river. He had counted on Maggie's desire being equal to his own, and his ideas for the evening rested on this belief. He recognized that most men and women, no matter how sensual, had fantasies that were off limits as far as actual sex was concerned. He had no such limits himself, and he planned for Maggie to have none either. She would satisfy herself completely.

Maggie sipped her martini and looked at his back. He had changed into a gray tweed sport coat and gray slacks. Then she could no longer control her craving for him. She moved toward him, pressing herself against his back, running her arms around his body.

Henry put down his glass and turned in her arms. He bent his head down and brought his mouth against hers. She felt an exultant pleasure knowing that from here on the decision was his, that nothing was left to her except the thing she wanted most—to accept. Her mouth opened, and his tongue entered between her lips. It tickled, licked, probed, and then their tongues touched. Maggie felt her legs go weak. He reached inside her dress and felt her breast, gently rubbing his palm against her nipple. First one breast, then the other. She could feel his erection pressing against her. His hand moved lower onto her hip, and his hand touched her pubic hair, feeling how wet she was.

Suddenly he stepped back. She was left as though suspended in midair. He smiled and said, "We can make love, or we can do more."

More? Was there more? He seemed to think so. "I want what you want."

He took her in his arms again. She could feel his hands on all of her, touching, feeling, caressing, probing, entering her. She was about to have an orgasm, and he knew it. "Do you want to come now?"

She almost screamed, "Yes! God, yes!"

"Come to the sofa." He was going to explore the limits of her sexual appetites. He untied the sash holding her dress together and undid the two snaps. As she had planned, the dress slipped to the floor, leaving her standing naked before him, except for her garter belt, stockings and shoes.

He still hadn't even taken off his tie, but she was beginning to understand. "What about you?"

"I'm next." She could not look at him as he had looked at her. Her eyes were blurred by the depth of her feeling, and she closed them in suspense. By the time she was able to look, Henry had removed all his clothes and was standing as naked as she. His penis was erect and large, in proportion to the rest of his body. Oddly, his pubic hair was blond. Maggie had seen a picture of a statue of Bacchus in an art magazine. That was Henry. "Now I suggest we eat."

"Please!"

"Do you have a better idea?"

"Please make love to me."

He held her close and ran his hands over her body. She could feel his shudder and recognized his effort to maintain control. He wanted her as much as she wanted him. Why were they waiting? He carried her to the couch and placed her on it so that her legs were on the floor. Slowly, so slowly, he began to lick the insides of her thighs, coming closer and closer to her crotch. Then he was there. He put his hands under her ass and lifted it up until her vagina was arched against his mouth. His tongue went from clitoris to vagina and back again. Deeper and deeper. The orgasm started, and as the waves swept over her, she heard herself scream as though from a great distance. It seemed to last forever as wave after wave of pleasure rose, receded, only to rise again. Finally it began to subside. She lay back panting.

Henry waited until all the afterglow had faded before removing his tongue. He was a little surprised at the intensity of her orgasm, but wasn't this exactly what he had wanted? Yes! And yet?

After the multiple orgasm, Maggie thought that, though she still ached for Henry to be inside her body, she could wait if he wanted to wait. "I feel selfish. I've had so much and you've had nothing from me."

"I will. In good time." It was time to prepare the meal. When dinner was ready, they sat opposite each other at a small table in the living room. The Hudson was dark except for a very few ships that passed on their way to Albany. They could see the flickering lights of the small towns in Rockland County that fronted the river. They ate by

candlelight. The food was delicious. Even after the intimacy of masturbation and oral sex, Maggie was astonished to find herself wanting to
cover her breasts and crotch. Her nakedness. But now she understood
even more. It was a game. A beautiful, sensual, sexual game, and her
mind rose to meet the eroticism. She loved it. Eventually he would
make love to her the way she wanted it, but oh, the joy of waiting. She
wondered where he had learned so much about women in general, sex
and her in particular. Some day she would ask, but not tonight.

After dinner they sat in adjoining chairs drinking coffee and sipping
brandy. This time she didn't ask permission and settled herself on his
lap. He continued to sip his brandy and seemingly idly caressed her.
She could feel his penis pressing between the cheeks of her ass. She
settled herself so that it would reach deeper into her, and felt it slip into
her open, wet vagina. They stayed motionless for a while, each in their
own position. Maggie had never felt anything like it. A man was not
only inside her, he was part of her. As though they were one person.

Responding to her inner need and Henry's wish that she do anything
that pleased her, she began to move up and down on his penis. Henry
remained motionless, allowing her to enjoy her own desires fully. The
feeling inside her began to build again. She was so wet she was afraid
she might drown both of them. Her nipples extended and ached, but
she couldn't seem to reach her orgasm. Something that had been dormant
rose to haunt her. It was too much. Too much! Her private self was
being lost. She even felt ashamed at what had happened. Foolish thoughts
were getting in the way.

Henry sensed at once they were at a crucial moment. He had been
expecting it. If she was to be what she could be, what she wanted to be,
what he wanted her to be, he would have to bring her past the crisis.
"You're thinking too much. Trying too hard. Sit back and feel me inside
of you." She did as she was told, sitting quietly, trying to recapture the
intense desire of the earlier part of the evening. "Try to feel me with
every part of you."

It was beginning to happen again. She could feel him. All of him.
Her body welcomed him. He moved one hand over her belly and touched
her clitoris. Her feelings of shame and doubt disappeared. Whatever
they did was right. It was proper and belonged only to them. Her orgasm
began to well up, and when it finally came, it was stronger than ever
before. She gasped violently for air. As the pulsing of her body diminished, she collapsed against him. Only then did she realize that he had
not come to climax though his penis seemed to have grown and grown.

"My darling, what about you? When is it your turn?"

"Now. Now it's your turn to pleasure me."

She lifted herself off him.

"Wait one moment. I'll be right back." She went into the bathroom, sat on the toilet and let everything gush out of her. She thought how extraordinary their sex had been and how she had almost lost everything because of unnecessary shame. How could she please him? Far more important than anything else, she was in love with him. She thought again that she only wished to be an instrument of the satisfaction of his desires. And whatever pride of person she had, of her mind, of her freedom, she would offer gladly for the pleasure of his body. The fact that he wanted her was the greatest reward she could possibly have.

It occurred to her then that they should make love like two young lovers with no past. Simply, even innocently, as though they had never known anyone but each other.

When she returned to the living room, Henry was standing looking out the window again. She said, "Lie on top of me, darling. We'll make love as though it was the first time for both of us."

She spread her legs apart and drew her knees back, opening herself to him as much as possible. He lowered himself over her, and her hands grasped his penis, guiding it into her. He filled her fully, reaching the deepest part of her, even it seemed to her womb, inflamed with a passion that drew him on.

"Don't think of me," she panted. "Don't hold back. Just fuck me. Hard!"

First he moved slowly in and out, then faster, then still faster. His hands slipped under her, lifting her off the ground to meet the force of his thrusts. She felt his penis swelling inside her. Now he was moving in long, slow strokes, pressing up against her clitoris. Each stroke was an agony of tension and pleasure, making her dizzy with a desire that was like annihilation. He went on and on, cruelly denying his own release, only to drive them both to greater heights of passion. Finally he lost control and went wild, moving in and out like a piston, pounding, pounding.

They climaxed together, their cries of ecstasy mingling. Her legs went slack as his semen flowed into her body, and he buried his face between her breasts.

"Put your full weight on me. I want to feel you. All of you. Crush me!" He lay flat on top of her, his weight flattening her breasts and stomach. Only her pelvis was strong enough to hold him. She loved his strength and weight. She could smell his body as he pressed her down.

There was a stunned look on his face. Very softly and with an almost reverent tone, he said, "Oh, Maggie, Maggie. My God!"

In a sudden change of mood, he pulled out, and the same bubbling and gurgling sound came from inside her. "I think you ought to wash up. Douche. I didn't wear a rubber, and I don't think we want a baby."

"It's not necessary. My period's due tomorrow or the next day. I won't get pregnant just before my period."

"Are you sure?"

"I'm not that kind of a gambler."

"Then get a couple of towels so we can sit here and talk without dripping all over the furniture."

He watched her back as she walked toward the bedroom. In spite of his outward calm, Henry Carson was a very confused man. He had discovered a stronger sensation, a stronger flavor than he had ever known before. The smell of Maggie's hair, of her body, the strength of her as she enclosed him. In two short hours she had obliterated his memories of all other women. But what kind of a future could they have? His marriage to Selma wasn't fair to Maggie. And if he loved Maggie, that wasn't fair to Selma. He had counted on their sex being good, even orchestrated every nuance to make it better, but he had never considered the possibility of falling in love. He needed time to sort things out. Fortunately, he had time. Months. And meanwhile they had the rest of the night for each other.

# Chapter 8

THE SUN was rising when Henry dressed. Maggie refused his suggestion that she take the morning off. If he could work, so could she. But she understood that they must now return to behaving like their office selves, observing the arm's length formality of office protocol. It was going to be a difficult readjustment for both of them. Not only must they avoid physical contact, they must be careful of how and what they said to each other.

Henry decided that Maggie was to call in with an excuse and arrive later than Henry—about eleven. It would give her time to readapt. Henry would return home, shave, shower, change his clothes and ready himself for his meeting with William.

Walking toward his office, Henry had difficulty managing his thoughts. It had been an extraordinary night. He thought of Maggie and shook his head as if by doing this he could stop his mind from throwing up pictures, as if he could get rid of her, of the sensations she aroused. But he couldn't stop. Even in the cool, impersonal offices of the Carson Company, there was nothing that did not suggest Maggie. Much more had happened last night than he had anticipated. Beyond these passionate intimacies was a communication of spirit such as he had never before had with a woman. She was strong. She was brave. She was generous as only the strong and brave can be.

When he entered the office, Mary O'Toole told him Maggie would be late. Henry tried to review again the reports on the Wilkenson operation, but his mind kept returning to Maggie and then ricocheting off to Selma. Did he want to marry Selma? No! But without Selma Wilkenson as his wife, there would be no Wilkenson subsidiary. That was unthinkable. It was a matter of his commitment to the company, to the company's opportunity to expand into an entirely new area, an area more important than anything they were presently doing. To create a new Carson Company.

Precisely at that moment, eleven o'clock, Maggie arrived. She popped her head through the door and apologized in a loud voice for being late. Then she disappeared "to point the auditors in the right direction."

That brief glimpse of Maggie's face made an instant impression on Henry. It pointed up her existence in his world—how intimately, how inescapably she was joined to him. He knew her narrow hands, her long supple fingers. Above all, the fineness of her strong flexible body. He saw her as cluster of possessions of his own. Items in a full list, items catalogued, waiting through time, waiting for him.

But had they been waiting for him?

Could he jeopardize his heritage, the achievements of three generations of his family, for the likes of Maggie? He could thank his father for the grimmer vision Maggie had given him of what he would surrender by marrying Selma.

Maggie! She, not Selma, should be the one. She should be everything to him. Even his—abruptly, he checked the thought. Their night came flooding back to him. The ease and readiness of her acceptance, even her aggression, rose in his mind with an unexpected result. Her facility filled him with dismay. The very ease with which she met him more than halfway suggested an unusual variety of experience. Worse, long before he met her, she had entered into an understanding with William. She had not been coerced. She had accepted the arrangement.

The combination of what he thought she was and, most damning, his idea of her arrangement with his father, now forced his decision. She wasn't a whore, but she had too many of the whore's motives and skills. Thinking this, he confronted a startling revelation; his rejection of Maggie as a possible wife was as nothing compared to his contempt for himself. Even if he did love her, loved her beyond anything he had ever imagined possible, that he would consider sacrificing the Carson Company to such a love, to any love for that matter, was a direct attack on the foundations of his life.

William had meant no harm by meddling, but in the end it only heightened Henry's bitterness. He would marry Selma. He had to. Even though now he knew he was completely in love with Maggie.

Maggie was providing the auditors with the access to the files where more information might be found. As she went about her work, she remembered Henry sitting behind his desk. Originally she had been willing to be used, partly for her own sake, partly for the sake of William Carson who had helped her escape from the prison that factory life led to. But finally, it had been her intense desire for Henry that had smothered all moral objections. Now she was moving in a great new light of understanding. There seemed to be two people at war inside her—one drawing deep breaths of joy and exhilaration, the other gasping for air in a little black cave of fears. She had fallen in love, and in doing that, she had separated herself from continuing happiness by all the length and breadth of her vision of the future. The future that led to Henry's marriage to Selma Wilkenson.

It was characteristic of Maggie to feel the only problems she could not solve were those which she had not faced. So she faced her fear, recognizing it in Henry's aloofness in the morning and recognizing it was all make-believe. She had only to remember their night together, see his eyes as he looked at her to know he too remembered; he wanted what she wanted. Gradually the grasp of the captive within her eased. The horizon expanded. The air grew lighter. Since their relationship would continue, anything might happen. Hadn't a miracle already occurred?

Serene again, her mind turned to practical matters. It was fortunate she would be working for Dr. Flam. She would have only minimal contact with Henry.

William relaxed in the rear seat of his limousine. These days he preferred to rest after a strenuous night with Marion. As it so often did after leaving Marion, his mind wandered to thinking about his long-dead wife. He had been so completely in love with her, and her death, while still in her twenties, left a deep wound that had scarred over in time. But the psychological scar, like all scar tissue, remained rough and unresponsive. After Nathalia's death, William recognized he had lost the ability to maintain deep and continuing feelings for a woman. A part of him was buried and remained buried in Nathalia's grave.

This inability to make an emotional commitment extended, in part at least, to his sons, although as they grew older he had begun to see them as extensions of himself. The choice of Henry to succeed him was akin to the choice of a husband for a favored daughter, the Carson Company being his favorite child.

And that brought him to Henry and their meeting. He had run the Carson Company alone for thirty years, and he had no intention of retiring. But unless he'd badly misread yesterday's phone call, soon they would be sharing control. And he wondered if Henry would listen to him, or anyone for that matter, for more than a very few years.

He arrived at eleven-thirty. One glance at Henry told him that last night was a case of like father, like son. The slightly too relaxed body, the hint of hesitancy in the arm movements, the look of satisfaction.

Now he would find out exactly what Henry's price was. There would have been a price in any case. But having discovered Maggie after proposing to Selma, the price might have risen.

"Where's Maggie?"

"With the boys from PW. And she'll spend the afternoon with Dr. Flam straightening out his office. It's a mare's nest."

"Is that a temporary assignment?"

"No. Unless you object, I'd like her assigned to Flam from now on."

William understood the problem and saw no objection to Henry's solution. "Then you'll need another girl?"

"That depends, in part, on the results of our talk."

Ah, yes. The talk. He certainly didn't waste any time getting down to it. "And when do you want to have this talk?"

"Ten minutes ago."

"Oh?" William went to the door and spoke to Mary. "Hold all calls. I don't think I have any appointments today, do I?"

"No, sir."

"Mr. H and I are going to want privacy. We may take a break and ask you to order something from the cafeteria."

Once the doors were shut, William turned to Henry. "This is your show. How do you want to run it?"

Henry was ready for that. It was like his father to let his opponent make the opening move. "Let's sit where we'll be comfortable." He nodded toward the couch and easy chairs. Henry didn't want William to have a desk between them.

They both rose and walked around the opposite sides of their desks toward the couch. The timing and general symmetry of their movements had the look of a staged ballet. William sat down, crossed his legs and waited.

Henry looked at his father, crossed his legs and waited.

"Henry, you asked for this meeting, so you must have something in mind. Let's have it."

"When we spoke yesterday, I had a simple request. I wanted my areas of authority defined. As a free-floating apex, I'm not earning my keep."

"What areas do you have in mind?"

"That was yesterday."

"I see. Today you have other ideas?"

"That's right."

"May I ask what happened to change your plans?"

"One of your schemes came to fruition last night."

"Delighted. May I offer my congratulations?"

"Yes and no."

"I'm confused. If not congratulations, I hope the evening was pleasant?"

"Extremely!"

The tone of Henry's voice made William pay closer attention. "Extremely? I envy you."

"Don't. It poses a problem."

"You will tell me your problem?"

"Yes, since you arranged it. I'm engaged to be married to a woman I don't love. I'm not even sure I like her."

"Agreed. What else?"

Henry had considered a number of ways of saying this, and had decided that the flat-footed approach was best. "In addition, I believe I'm in love with Maggie."

"In love with—" William broke off his sentence. Was his grand plan about to founder on the rocks of a love affair? A sexual union was one thing, but a love affair? That was something else. For an instant William considered trying to destroy his construct, but he doubted Henry would listen. And when it came down to it, he admired Maggie too much.

There was a short period of silence. Then Henry probed, "Any suggestions would be appreciated."

"No suggestions."

"Come now, Father. You're never without a suggestion."

"Sorry. No suggestions."

"No sympathy?"

William laughed ruefully. "Lots of sympathy, but no suggestions."

"Suppose I said no deal? I want to marry Maggie. Not Selma."

"You won't." William relaxed. Henry had a deal in mind. It would work out.

"Are you certain?"

"I'm not certain. But you didn't say the deal is off. You said 'suppose.' Fine. Let's suppose the deal is not off. What then?"

Henry sighed. "My dear father, you can be a chore."

"My dear son, do you think you're an unmixed blessing?"

"I suppose not, but you've had more practice."

"And you're younger. You have less to lose."

"Less to lose? I don't understand. I'm the one who'll do the marrying."

"I'm a middle-aged man. The chance to control the birth of a new and very important industry, such as tranquilizers, doesn't come often. I doubt if I'll ever have another opportunity." He decided to take the further risk of complete honesty. "Did I ever tell you what my one real ambition has always been?"

Henry was very interested. They had never talked so openly before. "No, you haven't. Do you want to tell me now?"

William made his first physical movement since sitting down. He uncrossed his legs, placing his feet flat on the floor. The very essence of sincerity. "Yes, I think I do," William answered.

"If you only think you do, suppose I tell you."

"You want to tell me what my lifelong ambition has been?" He shrugged his shoulders. "Go ahead."

"You want to do more for the Carson Company than either your father or grandfather did."

"You're right. I inherited something, and I want to leave you a bigger, stronger, more important company than I inherited."

"And I am to marry Selma Wilkenson to achieve your ambition."

"I can't say I appreciate the way you put it."

"So don't appreciate it, but it's the truth."

William surrendered. "Yes, and I need your help."

"You've got it. For a price."

"What's the price?"

Henry sank back in his chair. Despite the polite words and offhand approach, the tension had been severe. Now his moment had arrived. He had been maneuvering the entire conversation toward this question. What was the price?

William was growing impatient. It was a new experience for him. Usually he was the one who sat while his opponent grew impatient. He spit out the words. "I asked you what your price was."

Henry had decided that his price was non-negotiable. William would either agree or he would not go forward. "I don't think we should work in the same office any longer."

"You want a separate office?" William looked startled.

"For openers. Then I want Maggie transferred to Dr. Flam permanently, and the R and D center enlarged with Flam at the head."

"I can agree to everything regarding the R and D facilities. I was planning that anyway. But will Maggie accept a transfer?"

"She'll accept it."

"Is that it?"

"For openers."

"Ah, yes. Openers. Let's have the rest."

"First, I want to be in personal charge of the labs, with everyone reporting directly to me. Including those working on the tranquilizers."

William thought about that for a moment. The R and D facilities were his pet, representing the long-range future of the company as well as the core of his plan. "Before I answer, what's the second request?"

"Got your feet on the ground?"

"That bad?"

"I don't think so. However, you may."

"Ummm."

"If I'm going to marry Selma Wilkenson, I want to be President and Chief Operating Officer of the Wilkenson subsidiary. Completely in charge of everything from product mix to production to sales and advertising. The works. Answerable to you only in terms of my achieving prearranged annual figures on gross sales and profit."

There was total silence in the room.

Suddenly William burst out in a wild whoop. He was holding his sides laughing so hard his eyes began to tear. When he managed to bring himself under control, he said, "Amazing. You've been here about three months, and you want to run a multi-million-dollar division. Nothing less will do?"

Henry felt grim. "That's right. Nothing less will do!"

Still fighting for self-control, William held out his hand. "You've got it. With one exception."

Henry looked at the hand. "What's the exception?"

"I won't give up control of the labs. The tranquilizer work means too much to me. But I agree to share decisions."

"Everything else? My presidency?"

"Everything!"

Henry and William shook hands, and William said, "Henry, I want to congratulate you. And myself, I think. I didn't realize you'd ask for the entire Wilkenson operation, but now I'm glad you did. In fact, I'd have been disappointed in you if you had asked for less."

"Delighted not to disappoint you."

William looked at his vest pocket watch. "Twelve-thirty. That didn't take too long. Time for lunch. Let's skip the cafeteria. I'm buying. The White Swan all right with you?"

"Yes." As they left, Henry told Mary O'Toole that Maggie would now be working for Dr. Flam. She should find another secretary for him.

# Chapter 9

**M**AGGIE lay on her bed, cold and passive, unable to sleep. She was thinking about the months that had passed. It was astonishing how fast they had gone. Henry lay beside her. Except for an occasional movement, he always slept soundly. Usually, satiated by their lovemaking, she slept too. But this night, for Maggie sleep never came. As the dawn broke, she had to face the fact that this was the day she had come to hate. This was Henry's wedding day.

Since their first night together, she had managed, for the most part, to avoid any thoughts about his wedding. When she thought about it at all, she was sure something would happen to save them.

That first night had been followed by a series of nights, and days and weekends that only served to deepen her feelings for him. She had poured herself into the relationship without any reserve, glorying in the joining of their bodies. Their sensuality and sexuality had continued to grow until gradually something happened between them that was more than making love. It was a knowledge of a feeling greater than an orgasm, than ecstasy, of being as one with each other and the world that provided their minds and bodies with such joy. Ownership is not made up of marriage vows and licenses. It is a thing of the spirit, and she believed she owned him, even as he owned her. They knew each other as thoroughly as two people can, knowing things that went beyond the senses.

Then as the time for Henry's marriage drew closer, this joy, just beginning to try its wings, drooped and finally fell to the ground. Maggie had recurrent glimpses of the future without Henry—a future that stretched out interminably, with her lonely figure moving down a narrow path, a mere speck in the solitude. So she had grappled all night with the fact of his marriage as though with some formless evil. Reason, judgment, renunciation, all the sane daylight values that guided her life were abandoned in the sharp struggle for survival. She wanted her happiness, wanted it as fiercely, as unscrupulously as ever a woman could. But she had no power to obtain it. In her conscious impotence, she lay shivering. Even hating Henry.

Last night was the last of the best of their relationship. With Henry a married man, it would change. Certainly their meetings would be fewer. He would have to spend some nights and most weekends at home with his wife.

The thought of his leaving so dismayed her that she slipped out of bed and walked, naked, into the living room, a room now flooded with the first soft-pink light of morning. Maggie buried her face in her hands, tears streaming down her cheeks. She felt a deep sense of injury. Was it her fault her father hadn't been rich and had lost what little he had? Was it her fault she had to work in a factory and escape from its bleakness as best she could? Even Henry had only the vaguest notion of what it meant to be poor. Henry could sympathize intellectually, but he had no sense of the desperation. No, it was not her fault, or his, that, unlike the drab, dull Selma, she had not been born into a world of money and power. But that fact was going to separate them.

She also saw herself as she must appear to him: a poor girl, perhaps very pretty, but with nothing really to offer. And, what was worse, a poor girl climbing her way out of the pit as best she could, by the use of her brains and body. It was true, as far as it went. But she had fallen in love with him. His money and position meant nothing to her. She loved him and had no use for him except for the uses love makes of all creatures.

It seemed incredible to her that Selma would want to be Henry's wife. She was incapable of loving a man, any man. But, obedient daughter that she was, she was capable of marrying a man to meet her mother's dynastic goals. And, reluctantly, Maggie admitted that it took no deliberate effort on Selma's part to rob her of her dreams. That she was heiress to Wilkenson, Inc. was an accident of birth, but given Henry's nature, it sufficed. He could neither make himself change nor spare himself any demand the Carson Company might make. And the company granted no mercy. Selma's inheritance was a siren song. Maggie, the human girl on the shore, was helpless against the siren who desired her prey.

Then she felt a breathing warmth behind her and a pair of hands slipping over her breasts.

"Hold me, love! Hold me," she moaned. "I've been thinking terrible thoughts." She rested her head against his shoulder, and, unconsciously, pushed herself against his naked body, pressing to make the contact closer. She could feel his penis beginning to rise between her legs. This was his wedding day, and perhaps it was wrong to make love on such a day? But she needed something. Some show of his continued love. She had spent all night in a well of despair, and it had become an urgent necessity to be as they had been just once more—even though she accepted the fact that Henry's love could never be her final refuge. Still, it would be so sweet to take shelter in his arms while she gathered courage to go on.

She bent forward, resting her arms on the window sill, and pushed her buttocks against his body. He stood quietly as she reached between her legs, taking his penis in one hand and guiding it into herself. The touch of his flesh brought a flush of relief. They were one again, and the awful night seemed to change to day. They melted together in one great wave. Maggie came first, followed almost immediately by Henry. She felt his orgasm exploding inside her, his semen flooding her womb. They had neglected to use any contraception, and swallowing half a sob, she pulled away.

"I'd better douche. This is my fertile period, and it's not the best time for you to become a father. At least not the father of my baby."

Henry tensed at the warning. "You're right," he said, disgusted as much with himself as with the situation. "Go ahead. Then let's talk before I leave." He knew he had no one to blame but himself for the suffering they both felt. If he had not agreed, there would be no marriage to Selma. Then he would be free to offer Maggie the possibility of having his child. Or would he? The sight and nearness of Maggie dazzled but did not blind him to the facts. He was aware now, as he had always been, of exactly how he came to know her. His mind turned to William's words.

"She's not a used piece of merchandise. At least not used by me." But used by how many others in her climb out of poverty? The strength of his love for her, the intimacy they shared, the range of her rapidly-developing intelligence, the total of her was still not worth the sacrifice of the Carson Company. His surrender to his love for her was complete. But it was always followed by a reaction of resistance and withdrawal. Aside from its value to the company, his marriage to Selma had a deeper value. It would confirm the distance he had to establish between Maggie and himself. He had good reason to be afraid of what he might do if he were free to choose.

When Maggie reappeared, she was wearing a long housecoat. Her fully covered body made him aware of his nakedness. "Wait a minute. I want to put something on."

Maggie was sitting in her favorite chair, waiting. He looked at her and thought that a subtle change had taken place overnight in the quality of her beauty. It seemed now to have a transparency through which the fluctuations of her spirit were tragically visible.

They sat for a while holding hands and saying nothing, each thinking his own thoughts. Maggie had never seen Henry so little the master of a situation. It occurred to her that his awkwardness might be due to his fear of what she would do. The thought produced a touch of bitterness in her first remark.

"I suppose congratulations are in order?"

Henry met this directly. "No, I'm not to be congratulated. It's simply the way things are."

"You arranged things as they are. You could change them."

"I accept that."

"So do I."

"It doesn't change my love for you."

"Or mine for you. But it will change our lives."

"What do you mean?"

"I mean you'll be married. Things will have to change."

"Only if you want them to."

The harshness in his voice might have shown her how much effort went into the words, but she was in no state to consider his feelings while hers were in such revolt.

"I don't believe what I want or don't want will weigh that heavily in the future. Probably far less than in the past."

Henry released her hand and faced her. "Does that mean you don't want to see me again? If you don't, I'll hate it, but I will respect your wishes."

"You misunderstand me. I want to see you as often as we can manage it. Do you think it could be otherwise?" She paused, then added, "You see, I love you. But you'll have other duties. Other responsibilities. For instance, if you're not on your way shortly, your bride will be waiting and worrying at the church." The words served to harden her for what had to happen. "And I must bathe and dress as well, so I can watch the happy pair stroll down the aisle."

"Watch us what?"

"Watch you get married. You didn't know I was invited to the wedding? And the reception?"

"No, I didn't. Why the hell didn't you tell me?"

"I assumed you knew, that you'd arranged it. Haven't you seen the guest list?"

"I left that to my father and Evelyn."

"Splendid! I'm on the list. And your mother-in-law-to-be added a handwritten note asking me to please attend. She invited me as the daughter of a close friend of your mother."

"And you're coming?"

"I thought you wanted me there. Anyway, I enjoy attending the weddings of lovers."

"Now I wonder what that lady has in her devious little mind."

"When I find out, I'll tell you."

By unspoken but mutual consent, Henry dressed quickly. Maggie walked with him to the door. "See you in church. I'll be the one without the veil."

Henry took her in his arms and held her close. The smile she gave him summed up their case. But he could not let her go. He was still very young, and it was possible for him to feel many conflicts without knowing they were conflicts. His head and his body did not seem to belong to the same person. He was in love the way one loves the first person who truly touches the heart. He would never love anyone else in quite the same way. In the years to come, he would continue to hear her voice in his head, feel her presence in his heart. Her memory would be with him forever. But it was no use. He accepted for the first time that everything was not possible. Even a Carson could be left without a choice. His hands dropped to his sides.

"See you in church." What else could he say?

# Chapter 10

AFTER the wedding service, the bridal couple walked back down the aisle and out the great front doors of St. Thomas's into the brilliant sunshine and the waiting limousine on Fifth Avenue. The rest of the guests waited for William and Evelyn to follow before joining the general exodus. Selma looked charming, if frightened. She was dressed in a fitted white satin gown, trimmed with seed pearls embedded in Irish lace. Henry wore a morning coat, striped pants, a double-breasted gray vest and striped ascot, with not a crease or wrinkle to mar the fit.

Maggie had been assigned a seat in a special section, and on her arrival found a note telling her she was to ride in limousine number four. The bride and groom rode in the first car. The second was full of bridesmaids. The third carried the ushers. Maggie and a few friends of both families were in the fourth car. She was astonished at the attention she was receiving.

The ride from the church to the black stone townhouse on Beekman Place took only a few minutes. A police cordon had been thrown up, and the press covering the event was everywhere. Photographers were snapping pictures of the bridal couple while the guests and Maggie got their share of attention. The marriage of two companies and two families as renowned as the Carsons and Wilkensons, plus a guest list of social and business luminaries and a generous sprinkling of theatrical and political celebrities made it a full day for business journalists and society reporters.

Once inside the house, Maggie asked for and was directed to the second floor where a luxurious powder room was available. She locked the door and studied herself in the mirror. What she saw pleased her. Despite the tears she had wept at the wedding, her face was now calm, even contented. William had sent her a dress ideal for the occasion, a light-blue silk print with a wide skirt falling away from a laced empire bodice. A wide-brimmed floppy hat in a matching material completed the ensemble. After repairing her mascara, Maggie left the powder room and glanced at the small group of women waiting in line. Who was she? they wondered. She was too pretty, too well dressed and too important—she had arrived in the fourth car—not to be noticed. A society reporter stepped out of line to interview her.

"How are you? Remember me? I'm Bea Fairfax. I believe we met at the Belmont party."

"No, we didn't. Sorry." Maggie moved off.

In the library, another ceremony was in progress. Evelyn Wilkenson had insisted there be no closing until Selma and Henry were formally married. An engagement was not good enough. Her position was simple: no marriage, no acquisition. And William had agreed, so there they were—William and John Hillyer on one side, Evelyn and her new lawyer, Kenneth Keith, on the other. The presence of Keith made William curious about Craig Spears.

"William, I have no idea and no interest in what has happened to him."

Keith spoke softly. "He's tried most of the good law firms. They won't hire him. It's a pity. And my wife tells me his wife has tossed him out."

"If you bump into him," William said, "ask him to give me a ring."

Evelyn stared at him. "Are you thinking of hiring him? Again?" There was no mistaking her meaning.

"I might."

"Don't!"

"Let's not quarrel. We have papers to sign. Why don't we get on with it so we can join the celebration?"

The documents were produced, signed, witnessed and notarized. William handed Evelyn a certified check for $10 million which, without more than a glance, she stuffed into her bag. The Carson Company had acquired a subsidiary, added fifty percent to its sales, gotten a jump on the world in a new area of business, and it had only cost some money and three lives.

Henry Carson had a new job as well as a new wife. Keith left with a signed set of all the papers. Hillyer, as a personal friend of William's, exercised his option to stay for a glass of champagne. Now that the legalities were in order, Evelyn asked William if he could find Margaret Rhodes. She wanted to have a private chat with the young lady.

"I warn you, Evelyn. Maggie's no fool."

"I'm aware of that. Neither am I." She looked at him. Who

was he protecting? She decided it was Maggie. "Don't worry. I won't eat her. In fact, if she's so intelligent, we'll have a very profitable chat."

William left to find Maggie. She wasn't hard to find. She was far and away the most attractive woman in the room and was surrounded by a large group of men. He managed to catch her eye, and she went to him directly. "I hate to spoil your fun, but Evelyn asked to see you. She's in the library."

"She mentioned wanting to talk to me in the wedding invitation."

"Very interesting!"

"I assumed you knew. In fact, I seem to have assumed a number of things about my invitation that were not accurate."

"Such as?"

"Henry had no idea I'd be here."

"Interesting and still more interesting."

Lowering her voice, Maggie asked, "How much does she know, or think she knows, about me?"

"Enough. She knows that you are not the daughter of a friend of my late wife."

"That will do!"

"Yes, it will. However, Evelyn Wilkenson can be an educational experience. Also, I'm curious. A report would be appreciated."

"You'll get one. Lead on, MacWilliam!" Suddenly she realized to whom she was speaking. "I'm sorry, sir, but I don't know how to address you at the moment."

"William will do very nicely. My dear, you're about as close to being a member of the family as a woman has been in years."

"Except for Selma Carson."

Recognizing the pain implied, William did his best to sound casual. "Of course. Except for Selma and Evelyn." Once he had ushered Maggie into the library, he bowed himself out.

The room was a typical library in a New York townhouse with the exception that more loving care had been lavished on it than on most such rooms: mahogany bookshelves from floor to ceiling on three sides, a large desk with its back to a series of French doors that opened out onto a small garden overlooking the East River. There was a set of chairs and a table, and another larger group of a leather couch and two leather club chairs and an Edward VII leather-topped table between them. The pieces were all good and all authentic.

Evelyn was seated on a small chair facing the door. The table held a pot of tea, assorted glasses, cups and saucers and an ice bucket with two bottles of champagne.

She made a slight gesture indicating that Maggie should sit in a chair next to her.

"You look lovely. I'm delighted you were able to attend our little reception, Miss Rhodes."

"It was kind of you to invite me."

"Will you join me in a toast?"

"Yes, thank you." She watched as Evelyn carefully filled two tulip-shaped glasses from the already opened bottle.

"To the bride and groom. Health, wealth and happiness." Evelyn raised her glass.

"Health, wealth and happiness." Maggie's irony cut deeply.

"You realize I had a reason for wanting this little talk with you."

"I suppose so."

"Good! Then I shall begin at the beginning."

"I tend to like beginnings. It's the endings that turn out troublesome."

"The story starts with me, Evelyn Wilkenson. First, Wilkenson is my maiden name."

Maggie gave the woman a startled look. It was a moment for tact, for the quick bridging over of gaps, but she couldn't come up with any trivial phrase of politeness.

Evelyn's small eyes lit with amusement. She was pleased at the effect she had created. It told her so much. "No, Selma is not an illegitimate child. And I understand your surprise. But Wilkenson was my father's name, not my husband's. When I married John, he changed his name to Wilkenson. Our family is a very old one. Not as old as some of the Dutch, but old enough, and I have always been concerned with the family name. Unfortunately, I had a daughter, not a son. Problems with Selma's birth made it impossible for me to have another child." Evelyn brooded about this for a moment. "There is another problem. Selma has inherited the worst characteristics of both John and myself. My most serious mistake was in not recognizing her shortcomings earlier." She shook her head slightly as she contemplated her loss. "I could have done a great deal with a daughter such as you."

She laughed with a touch of asperity, and there was an odd look of envy on her face. "If I were a chronic invalid, perhaps Selma would have been the ideal daughter. But I'm not. If I could not have had a boy, I would have been glad to settle for a brilliant daughter. I've never understood why I was punished with Selma."

Maggie thought of how both of them had failed. Life is so full of blunders. What a mother Evelyn Wilkenson would have made for her. Together they . . . "I think you overrate me."

"No, I don't. I appreciate you and resent my cross. Nonetheless, it's my cross, and I bear it. Which brings me to my final problem with Selma and our need for this talk." Evelyn paused as though to consider what to say next. "As I said, Selma has inherited the worst traits of both John and myself. John's was a lack of intelligence. Mine, though I never really thought of it as a handicap, is both a lack of good looks and a lack of interest in sexual matters. I married to have children to carry on the family name and the family company." She poured herself another glass of champagne and sipped it slowly, sinking into meditation for a moment.

Like two long-time friends, the older and the younger woman were silent together, each engrossed in her own thoughts. Abruptly, Evelyn broke the silence. "As I said, Selma, like myself, is not a sexual woman. Worse, she is totally ignorant of sexual matters. And she has just married a highly sexual man. I'm afraid I'm forced to be somewhat indelicate." Evelyn considered Maggie with the eye of a physician estimating exactly how much information she could impart to her patient. "I must question you about your relationship with my new son-in-law."

Maggie took a long swallow of champagne. "What relationship with your new son-in-law?"

"Would you like the dates over the last several months when Henry has spent the night with you?" Maggie blushed under her makeup. "Don't be upset, Miss Rhodes. Of course he's been followed. Would I let him marry my daughter without knowing everything I could about him?"

Evelyn didn't seem the least bit angry. Maggie wondered why. "You may have reports you believe are accurate, but according to mystery stories, private detectives can show great imagination in order to earn their pay."

"True. So, for the sake of discussion, suppose that, hypothetically, the reports are accurate."

"But only hypothetically."

"Now that Henry is married, what do you propose to do about your hypothetical relationship?"

Maggie had learned from working with William that to attain her ends, she had to use a circuitous route of working with other people's goals. She hesitated only for an instant. "Conclude it, of course."

"Of course." Evelyn refilled Maggie's empty glass. "I would like to make another suggestion."

Maggie was beginning to feel a little lightheaded. "Mrs. Wilkenson, I'm open to all suggestions."

"Very well. I would like you to continue your hypothetical romance with Henry Carson."

"Your daughter's husband?"

"My daughter's husband."

"For how long?"

"For as long as it pleases you."

Maggie ran out of questions, so she finished her champagne. Then she said with some impatience, "I'm not a fool. Do you really expect me to believe you?" She placed her glass on the table and prepared to leave.

A struggle was going on behind the carefully controlled mask of the older woman's face. "Believe me, Miss Rhodes"—she said it almost pleadingly— "unless you continue your relationship, I doubt the marriage will have any chance of lasting."

The two women stared at each other. Maggie murmured, "Oh," and rubbed her forehead with her fingers.

Evelyn waited nervously for another word of response. None came, and at length she had to ask, "You think I'm an unnatural mother?"

Maggie's eyes filled with tears. "I think you're an excellent businesswoman, and I wish you hadn't spoken to me."

"I had to. Married to my daughter, Henry is going to need another woman. I believe he would rather be a faithful man. He has been faithful to you, and you've been faithful to him. You're both honorable. I wouldn't like Henry to have to replace you. He might not make as suitable a choice next time."

In spite of a moment of sympathy for the older woman's plight, Maggie felt the request was anything but a compliment. "So, to save the situation that you created, you want me to be Henry's whore?"

Very quietly, even resigned to failure, Evelyn answered, "Not his whore. I think of you as the woman Henry loves."

There was silence in the room again. At length Maggie said, "And this is what you wanted to speak to me about?"

"Yes."

"I'm sorry for you. For me. For all of us."

Maggie needed fresh air and space. She left Evelyn to her champagne and her qualms, and slipped out through the French doors into the garden. Under her angry recognition of the perverseness of things was an absolute necessity to rid herself of her overwhelming feeling of loss. She needed something or somebody to replace her thoughts of Henry and what might have been.

A tall man with red hair much like Henry's saw her in the garden and left a group of celebrators to join her. "This is luck," he said. "For a moment the prettiest girl at the party is alone. My name is John Hillyer."

"John Hillyer? I know. William Carson's outside counsel."

"That's right, but how did you know?"

"I'm Margaret Rhodes. I work for the Carson Company. I've seen your name on documents."

"Margaret Rhodes! You're Maggie Rhodes! William thinks highly of you."

"And I think very highly of William Carson. My mother was a close friend of his wife. He's been kind enough to give me my start in business."

"So that's how you know him?"

There was a slightly unpleasant note in his voice that implied some doubt of her history. Maggie wondered if he knew about Henry. Or was it something else? Whatever it was, she decided to put him in his place. "Yes, he's been very kind to me. When I was younger, I used to call him Uncle William. How else did you think I knew him?"

Hillyer reddened slowly, shifting from one foot to another. He didn't believe her for a moment. She was not an "old family tie" type. And if she was, "Uncle William" wasn't helping her out of the goodness of his heart. She was too pretty, too female, too tempting a morsel. It would take a saint not to want a taste, and William Carson was not a saint. "I really didn't think much of anything. Would you like some champagne and food? The lobster mousse is delicious."

There was a sudden commotion and applause from within the house, and Maggie, forgetting Hillyer completely, hurried to the doors that led to the living room. She saw Selma running up the stairs to the second floor while a blonde young woman cradled the bridal bouquet she had just caught. Henry had already vanished. Maggie didn't notice that Hillyer had followed her. Her sense of great loss gave way to a feeling of desperation. She felt a light touch on her arm. It was William. She tried to give him a cheerful welcome, but the best she could manage was, "Hello, William."

"Maggie, my dear." His voice was full of fatherly concern. "Will you excuse us for a few minutes, John. I'd like to have a short talk with Maggie." Without waiting for an answer and ignoring John's supercilious smirk, he linked his arm with hers and guided her back into the garden. He found a stone bench and sat down beside her. "You're not enjoying the celebration?"

"Did you expect me to?"

"You didn't have to come."

"I regarded it as an obligation to the Carson Company." She lifted her head, making an effort at lightness. "And I did have a handwritten invitation."

"A true heroine." William was prepared, in his own manner, to supply the ease he knew would be lacking in her. Also, he felt a strong need to justify to himself what he had done. "We all knew the plan. You did. Henry did. And I suppose Evelyn has figured it out as well. Isn't that why she wanted to see you? To discuss Henry and you?"

"Yes." Her lips began to tremble, and she was afraid the tremor would appear in her voice. "She's had us followed. Dates. Times. The whole thing. Except pictures." She gave William a teasing smile. "Do you suppose she's had you followed as well?"

"Of course." Actually he hadn't considered detectives, but given Evelyn's history, he should have. "A very astute woman indeed."

"More than you know."

"She quite lives up to my expectations. I suppose she asked you to continue your relationship with Henry?"

"She did."

"What did you say?"

"I said I felt sorry for her. For all of us."

William knew Maggie had been traveling a difficult path, and for the moment he permitted himself to feel the tragedy of her life. He couldn't see the course her grief might take, and this lack of vision added to his concern. "Would you like to be driven home? My car is outside. I can walk to my evening appointment."

"I don't want to go home. I don't want to be alone. Not tonight."

"All right. But don't waste your time on John Hillyer. He's a fine lawyer and not a bad man, but not for you. Let's say his code of romantic conduct is as dishonest as his legal principles are honorable."

"Maybe it's time I took a course in shameless dishonesty? I've had a strong dose of, shall we say, virtuous sinning?"

William had no answer. What she said was true.

On the second floor in a suite set aside for the purpose, Selma was changing for the long trip to the bridal suite at the Plaza, physically a ten-block trip, but psychologically light years away. Henry stood with his back to the room trying to make himself as invisible as possible. He had already changed and was waiting for Selma. He saw Maggie and William sitting in the garden, and it seemed to him they were very close. Too close. Possibly it was this marriage that he hated so much or possibly the inevitable loss of Maggie which he saw so clearly, but he felt a strong burst of jealous anger at the two of them. Why were they so close? What was going on? William had said at the start that there was nothing between them, but was it true? He knew his father was capable of lying whenever he found a lie necessary. Would he lie about a matter such as this? Would he lie to his own son? At another time Henry would have answered, "No!" But the recognition that he would lose Maggie was so vivid that it reinforced the strong but usually sublimated streak of jealousy he felt toward his father. He couldn't quiet his doubts. And the two figures seated so close together seemed to confirm all his fantasies.

William shrugged. "All right. Just watch out for Hillyer. His kind of dishonesty takes practice. I know from experience." He rose. "In any case, let's get back to the party or people will have second thoughts about us." He laughed. "Innuendo and insinuation are everyone's second favorite pastime."

John Hillyer had been keeping a weather eye on the garden door, and he joined William and Maggie as soon as they entered. "I thought you'd given me the slip." His voice had a too-familiar note that irritated her.

"Why don't you go home to Ellen?" William asked.

"Because Ellen is visiting her mother, and I'm looking for a dinner companion." He'd been drinking, and it showed. "Would the two of you like to join me?"

William stared at Hillyer. "I'll see you Monday morning." He turned to Maggie and made one last try. "May I take you to the car?"

She looked at him helplessly, a frightened child. "No, thank you. I'll find my own way."

William surrendered and left. Hillyer assumed that this was one of William's nights with Marion. It angered him beyond reason, and his anger made a decision for him. If he had anything to say about it, they would share Maggie as well. What right did William have to every beautiful woman in New York?

By six-thirty the party had thinned out, and it was time to go. John and Maggie, who had separated and come together all afternoon, now stood on the sidewalk. They were deciding where to go for dinner. Maggie realized again that, now and forever, Henry was out of her reach. He had married into his heritage. What was left to her were the crumbs of his life. Foolishly, all morning long a childish part of her nursed the secret hope that he would stop the wedding and, by some magic hocus-pocus, substitute her as the bride. The old Cinderella story. However, life is no Cinderella story. It grinds up those who don't discover this fact early enough. So here she stood with a pale, red-headed copy of Henry about to go to dinner at some expensive restaurant and pretend to be charmed by his attention. Well, she thought, isn't this rich, gracious living?

They ended up at the Beekman Tower Room on the corner where Forty-seventh Street, Beekman Place and First Avenue almost meet. John Hillyer was well known there, for the maître d' greeted him effusively and led him to "his table."

From where she sat, Maggie could look south to the tip of Manhattan and east across the East River. It was June 21, the longest day of what she would think of in the future as her longest year. The day had not yet turned into night, and lights were just beginning to appear to the south. It was a splendid, magnificent, romantic sight, and she didn't feel a thing.

The waiter arrived, and without asking, two martinis appeared. Maggie realized with some amusement that John was going to try to get her drunk. Let him try. What difference did it make?

John suggested they walk around the terrace. She agreed, and they took their drinks with them. He led her to a door that opened onto a narrow terrace with a shoulder-high parapet. John had chosen both poorly and well—poorly because this was a place for lovers and she wanted Henry, but very well because it made her longing to be with someone even greater. She sipped her martini, and they walked around the terrace looking at the city from all four directions. Then they stopped in front of the door that let them out. She looked at New York City where the majesty and grandeur of the city almost competed with the sky, and she came to the decision she'd been reaching for all afternoon. Tonight, Henry would be with a woman about whom he didn't care. He would be unfaithful to her. Tonight she would be with a man about whom she didn't care. She would be unfaithful to him. No matter what, she wouldn't spend the night alone. She leaned back against the parapet. Her breasts thrust forward against the thin fabric of her dress. Hillyer's eyes grew round, and he caught his breath.

*    *    *

After Selma finished changing, the couple stole down the service stairs. Their limousine was waiting, and they were driven across town to the Plaza. They had been registered that morning, and their luggage was already deposited in the bridal suite. Henry realized it would be wiser to go first to the restaurant. He and Selma would have dinner at the Oak Room and retire to their suite at the hotel for their first night together as man and wife. The Oak Room was one of Henry's favorites. The food wasn't really that special, but the quiet stability of the room satisfied his need for order in a world he believed had gone temporarily insane.

Evelyn had never taken Selma to the Oak Room. Everything was new and surprising to her. Henry ordered a martini for himself and a glass of sherry for her to get her a little drunk, not too drunk but a little drunk, before going upstairs. Even with the greatest patience, it was not going to be easy to make love to her. He had to be certain that he could maintain control, so he restricted himself to one drink while insisting on several sherries for Selma.

Maggie and John ordered two small steaks and two more martinis. The drinks came rapidly and the food slowly. Maggie was getting drunk, and in the slight haze that covered her mind, John Hillyer's profile began to resemble Henry's. The food still had not arrived when they finished their second martini, so she suggested they have another while waiting.

At the Plaza the food came and went, veal for Henry and filet of sole for Selma. Henry struggled to keep a conversation going, but it was reduced to a monologue. The only areas of interest Selma had were those with which she was familiar—charity work and a desire to do God's will on earth. Her knowledge of religious philosophy was limited to that expressed by the minister at her church. She knew only a few Catholics and had never knowingly met a Jew. Time passed, and Henry grew more desperate. Soon he would have to take her into the gilded, wrought-iron elevator for the trip to the bridal suite. What would he do then?

Hillyer was becoming more confident, and as they sipped their third martini, using his hand to make a point, he placed it high on Maggie's thigh. She didn't move her leg away. Instead, she placed her hand on top of his and pressed it harder against her. At this point, much to his irritation, the steaks finally arrived. He had to remove his hand. After all, he couldn't cut the steak and eat one-handed. Stupid ass! Why hadn't he ordered fish or soup?

Henry needed to postpone the inevitable, so he ordered a brandy for himself and a Grand Marnier for Selma. Selma was drunk. She had probably consumed more alcohol during this meal than she had in her entire life. The dining room was empty, and the bus boys were setting up the tables for tomorrow's brunch. Henry realized his wedding night was upon him.

After they finished their after-dinner coffee and brandy, Hillyer leaned over and whispered into Maggie's ear, "I want to make love to you. Now!"

"Do you?" The words were slurred.

"Yes. And you want to make love to me."

"All right." Her voice was low. "But under one condition."

"Name it."

"I want to make love at the Plaza."

"I have an apartment in town. It's more comfortable."

"I want to go to the Plaza." Henry and Selma would be there.

"But we'll have to register at the Plaza. It's a hotel."

"Then we'll register."

There was no room for argument. How was he going to register there? They knew him at the Plaza. They also knew his wife and children. Maggie read his thoughts. "The Plaza, John, or find some other girl to fuck tonight."

Hillyer went to a public telephone. Fortunately he knew the night manager, Robert Connelly. "Bob, this is John Hillyer. I have a problem, and I hope you can help me."

Henry and Selma walked down the wide hall on the eleventh floor to the bridal suite. He opened the door and stood back to let Selma enter first. Hesitatingly, Selma walked over the threshold.

In the months that preceded the wedding, Evelyn had attempted to impress on Selma that a husband had certain conjugal rights. She had forced Selma to read several medical books that explained how humans made love. Selma finally grasped the idea that a man's sexual organ would penetrate her body through the opening between her legs. She grasped it, but she hardly accepted it. Then Evelyn took Selma to a gynecologist, who found everything in order. Even her membrane was intact. The examination threw Selma into shock. Now she could only quake at what might happen to her. But she was a gentle, willing soul ready to serve her mother and God.

In a cab on the way to the Plaza, Maggie drew John's face toward hers. "Kiss me." He bent toward her and was surprised when her arms pulled him forward. As big as he was, he sprawled awkwardly. Their lips came together, and she ground her mouth against his. The inside of his lip seemed to scrape against his teeth. The kiss wasn't passionate. It wasn't even sexual. It was furious. But as an involved party, John was hardly objective. He recovered his balance and slid his hand under her dress to caress her breasts. She helped him by pulling open the front of the bodice so he could feel her more freely.

Henry locked the door of their suite. Selma was standing so close to the door that he bumped into her as he turned. This body contact was the first they had actually had during the entire engagement. Dimly, Selma heard Henry apologizing for bumping into her. She put her hand on his arm. It seemed to burn, but she held it there determined not to let go, not to give in to the terror this night inspired. "It's all right. I know you didn't mean to hurt me."

The cab pulled up in front of the Fifty-ninth Street entrance to the hotel. Maggie adjusted her dress, and she and John got out. He put his arm through hers to steady her.

She pulled away. "I'm fine, John. Not nearly as drunk as you think." She didn't want him touching her as they entered. She wanted Henry, Henry who was with his bride somewhere in the hotel. Well, she would be in bed with someone soon enough. A substitute who happened to have red hair and look vaguely like her love. She was here because she couldn't spend the night alone. So she was going to the wrong man's bed. But she would go there on her own. No help needed, thank you. Tomorrow she would face her own empty bed. But not tonight.

Hillyer picked up a key from the desk without registering. Maggie wondered how he had managed that, and then forgot it.

John locked the door to their room and reached for her. "I need another drink," she said, avoiding his arms. "Order me a double brandy." He was displeased with the delay, so she put her arms around him. "A little patience, and you'll get everything you want and more."

\*   \*   \*

Henry looked compassionately at Selma. He couldn't decide what to do. Should he insist, gently of course, on his rights as a husband? Or should he wait? It would be easier to wait. But was that the wise choice? Sooner or later they were going to have to consummate their marriage. The longer he waited, the worse it could be. For both of them. Anticipation of a dreaded event can be far worse than the event itself. Henry saw a love seat against a wall.

"Let's sit a while and chat." He took Selma's hand and drew her to the love seat. "Don't you think the ceremony and party went well?"

"The bishop had a beautiful voice."

"Who caught the bouquet?"

"I don't know. It's supposed to be good luck, isn't it?"

"Yes. It means that girl will be the next married."

This was going to be just as difficult as he'd expected. It made up his mind. If their marriage had any chance at all of success, it would have to be consummated this very night. So he kept up a steady stream of nothing talk ending fifteen minutes later with, "Aren't you uncomfortable in that traveling dress? It's getting late. Time we went to bed."

Maggie went into the bathroom and took off all her clothes. She hung them very carefully in the closet. Standing naked and looking at herself in the full-length mirror, she cursed both Henry and William for the hundredth time. Hillyer was a mistake, but a mistake she had to make. It seemed forever before she heard a knock on the door to the room, the door opening, a few muffled words and the door shut. Then she heard John's voice telling her that her brandy had arrived.

Selma knew that what married people did together would have to be done tonight, or she would never be able to live through tomorrow knowing that tomorrow night the ordeal was in store for her. "It is late. I guess we should go to bed."

Henry suggested she use the bathroom first. He would wait and change after she was finished. The room faced north and overlooked Central Park with its curving roads, riding paths and reservoir. He could see the four famous twin-towered buildings that dominated the West Side as well as that architectural oddity, the Dakota. On the East Side was Fifth Avenue where the apartment houses were mixed with huge homes that at one time were the residences of the very, very rich. He looked north and could see no farther than the lights of 110th Street.

The door opened, but he didn't move until he heard the sound of the bed springs and the rustle of the covers. When he looked at Selma, it was hard not to laugh. The covers were pulled up to her chin, and she lay motionless. He sat on the edge of the bed and kissed the tip of her nose. She tried her best to smile.

Henry went into the bathroom to change. He thought of Maggie about twenty-five miles north of New York spending the night in her apartment looking at the dark waters of the Hudson. Alone.

Maggie was in a semi-quandary. Hillyer didn't in the least excite her, but she had promised herself as well as him that she would fuck him. She must work then with her own body—arouse herself. It had helped in the past, and it would help now. She would arouse herself and things would take care of themselves. So she forced a gaiety into her voice and called out, "I'll be there in a minute." After a short time she said, "Ready or not, here I come."

Henry carefully pulled the covers back from his side of the bed. He and Selma lay on their backs. Then he turned on his side to face her. "Won't you turn over and look at me? I promise I won't hurt you."

She turned, and ever so slowly, he reached across and gathered her in his arms. It was hard for her not to scream. Henry let her get used to lying in his arms. He did nothing. Fortunately, he didn't have an erection. This wasn't sex. It was a very delicate operation where the surgeon's knife dare not slip.

"Darling." The use of the word sounded strange to him. "Darling, what would you like me to do?"

"I don't know." The answer was almost a wail.

"You know, a body is a little like an automobile engine. Racing it when it's cold can hurt the engine, so you have to warm it up. Let me warm up your body."

Selma was ice-cold with fear, and the idea of being warm appealed to her. "Yes. Warm me."

Henry kissed her mouth. It was the first real kiss Selma had ever received. Bit by bit he moved his hands over her shoulders and back, gently caressing the flesh. He put his hand on her throat and gradually moved it down to her chest, carefully avoiding touching her breasts.

Selma forced herself to lie still. Soon he would touch her breasts. That's what the books said, and he was following what she had read. She did feel a little warmer. Then Henry's right hand rested on her left breast. At least it was on her nightgown where it covered her breast.

Maggie picked up the glass of brandy and took a large sip. The brandy felt warm going down, warming her through and through. The brandy made the idea of fucking Hillyer seem less impossible. He was not as good as someone else she knew, but probably he was better than many, and one had to make do. John Hillyer was waiting for her. She went willingly, even eagerly, into his arms. She had promised him the greatest fuck he'd ever had, and she was going to keep her promise. Her best efforts would go into it.

Henry slipped one hand onto the bare skin of her breast and felt the nipple rise to meet his hand. Selma could feel her body trembling, and this time it wasn't entirely fear. A certain warmth such as she had never felt before was seeping into her loins. They felt wet and soft.

In spite of his best intentions, Henry could feel the beginnings of an erection. Damn it. It was too soon. She wasn't ready. He tried to think of other things, but all he could think of was Maggie. That didn't do any good.

"Don't be afraid," he said. "I'm going to see if the engine is warm enough to start making love."

"What do you mean?"

"I'm going to put my hand on your body and touch you. You'll like the way it feels." He slid his hand down to her belly and to the top of her pubic hair.

Selma lay there thinking, "I must do it. I must."

He rubbed her belly, even tickling it a little. That did feel good, and Selma felt the warmth grow. He let his hand drift further down, entangling in her hair and then past her hair. But Selma's legs were clamped together.

"Open your legs a little. If I don't warm up the engine, the car won't run."

Being compared to a car seemed funny to Selma. She giggled and allowed her legs to be parted. Henry pressed between them and used his forefinger to find her clitoris. To his amazement, she was wet. He rolled her clitoris around with his finger until she moaned with what he hoped was pleasure.

Maggie and John staggered to bed. He certainly wasn't subtle. She wanted to slow him down and asked, "What's your favorite position? What do you like best?" The question seemed to puzzle him. Even so, Maggie took control, the way Henry had controlled her the first night they made love.

Carefully, never stopping the kneading of her clitoris, Henry lifted himself up, lowered his pajama bottoms and got to his knees between her legs. He placed his penis in what he hoped would be the proper position to let the head enter Selma's vagina. She tried not to shrink from the contact. It seemed to be fine until he hit something: Selma's membrane. Henry stopped his movement.
"Darling, listen to me."
Selma had closed her eyes. Now she opened them. "Yes?"
"Do you know that you still have your vaginal membrane?"
"Don't all girls?"
"I have to break it to enter. This may hurt a little."
"It's all right. I won't mind."
He moved back and put a little force behind his thrust. Selma winced, but nothing happened. Three more tries and three more failures. Finally, Henry drove forward with force and broke through. He was inside her when he remembered that virgins bleed. Blood was soaking him. Unable to restrain himself, he kept moving and came very rapidly. The orgasm was full and mingled with Selma's blood.

"Let me be your guide. I'll make love to you," Maggie whispered. She reversed her position and faced John's feet. Straddling him, she lowered herself until she could feel his nose and mouth pressing against her. "Suck me. Suck me hard!" She took his penis in her mouth, shut her eyes and fantasized that it was Henry she was making love to.

The pain was very sharp, and Selma was horrified at the blood. Death was upon her, and she prayed loudly to God that she be accepted into heaven.
Henry hurried into the bathroom to get some towels. He wet them and wiped the blood from her vagina and legs. Then he placed a second towel over the bloody sheet. Amazing how little there actually was. It

had seemed like so much more only a moment ago. He placed Selma on the dry towel and pulled the sheet and blanket over her. After that he lay down beside her, held her inert hand and waited.

"What happened?" she asked, finally opening her eyes.

"We made love. I broke your membrane, and I forgot to warn you that there would be some bleeding. It's quite normal."

Selma listened and thought, How am I going to do it night after night? She knew Henry had tried. But, as her mother had said, sex is a disgusting chore. She might bleed again, and where was the pleasure the books talked about?

Henry, too, lay in bed thinking. He had done his best, and his best wasn't good enough. He knew Selma felt damaged, and he had no idea what to do about it.

She huddled on the far side of the bed in a small clump of misery. After a while her breathing grew slower and more even. She was asleep. So he slipped out of the bed and went into the bathroom to clean up. Only then did he remember that he'd had an orgasm, and he had paid no attention to the possibility of pregnancy. He shook his head in dismay, and after washing, returned to his bridal bed to try to sleep.

Maggie awoke around eleven. Under the circumstances, she felt good enough. John had turned out to be a reasonable lover. With the help of her slightly drunken fantasies, she had made love extravagantly, recklessly, holding nothing back. Her ass hurt a little. Yes, she recalled, they had even done that. But where was he? The bathroom door was open. He wasn't there. There was a neatly folded piece of paper on the pillow next to her. The note said he had left early in the morning. Duties at home and so forth. There was also a check made out for $500. The bastard! Suddenly she felt rotten. She wasn't a whore, but he didn't know the difference. That was what William had meant. To the John Hillyers of the world, all women who fucked the way she did were whores. Ladies, wives would never permit it.

Then fear wiped her mind clear of the insult. Drunk and angry, she had done nothing to prevent getting pregnant.

Disgusted with herself, she went into the bathroom to draw a bath. She was in no hurry to go home, and there was no one to go home to.

# Chapter 11

CRAIG SPEARS lay in his bed wondering if he would ever lift his head again. He knew he had returned to his hotel room in the Algonquin the night before in a somewhat less than sober condition. But it had been a nasty three months— probably the worst three months of his life—and it all began that Monday morning after the weekend at the Carsons. With a $10,000 check signed by William Carson in his pocket, and more due, he had felt that things would work out. That was three months ago.

As expected, he was fired that Monday morning. What he had not counted on was the vindictiveness of Evelyn Wilkenson. She had contacted as many managing partners of major law firms as she knew—and she knew most of them—to tell them how Craig Spears had sold company secrets to the corporations bidding for Wilkenson, Inc. The woman was a barracuda.

Then Evelyn went further. She introduced Barbara to his wife. While it was one thing for Myra to know he was unfaithful, it was quite another matter to be confronted with the living proof, and to face the fact that other people knew about Barbara as well. Myra had asked him to leave and was seeking a divorce on the only grounds available in the State of New York—infidelity.

Thinking about Evelyn Wilkenson, he wondered if the viciousness of her retaliation was a secondary sex characteristic. Wouldn't a man have been content with firing him? He certainly couldn't imagine a man introducing Barbara to his wife. What he overlooked was the fact that Evelyn might have been content with firing him if he'd honored his gambling debt instead of stopping payment on the check he'd given her for her bridge winnings. That was too much for her to stomach. On such petty mistakes are lives ruined.

Beyond career problems, the three months had been financially disastrous. With $10,000 and too much free time, he had gambled constantly, sometimes when drunk. He would have to call his bank Monday to check his bank balance and find out how much he had left of the ten.

It was an effort to get out of bed and stumble to the bathroom. A shower and a shave would help. Also a drink. It was Sunday and the bar was closed, but he was prepared. A pint of gin was stashed in his bureau under his shirts. He dialed room service to bring up a large orange juice and a pot of black coffee.

He finished shaving, managing to nick himself only once. He added a dollop of gin to the orange juice, gulped it quickly and poured himself a cup of coffee. After a second cup he felt almost human.

He started on the front page of the *Times*. The articles were all about the war and the coming election. The headlines and captions gave him all the information he felt either he wanted or needed. When he glanced at the bottom half of the front page, his lethargy disappeared, and he sat bolt upright. There it was, in large type: SOCIETY WEDDING OF THE YEAR. A MARRIAGE OF PEOPLE AND BUSINESSES. He read the article slowly and carefully before turning to the *Herald Tribune*. The same information was in about the same place on page two. The *Times* reporter had chosen to concentrate on the business aspects of the event while the *Tribune* reporter—the society reporter at that—had emphasized the social aspects of the wedding. Spears tossed both papers into the air and capered around the room like a madman.

The deal was done. William would keep his word, and on Monday morning he could expect another $40,000. Fuck Evelyn Wilkenson! Fuck Barbara! Fuck Myra! Everything was going to be A-OK from now on— $40,000! He might open up his own law firm. Fuck'em all! That called for another drink, and he didn't need any orange juice. A good shot of gin to celebrate. Who could he call for the evening? Where was the action? He was back in the game. They couldn't beat him. Not him. Not Craig Spears.

Still thoroughly disgusted with herself, Maggie dressed for work Monday morning, offering up two prayers. One, she should not be pregnant. Two, John Hillyer would keep his mouth shut. She wasn't too confident that God was listening, but one could hope.

Looking in the mirror, she was glad she was a healthy young woman. A good night's sleep had erased the evidence of the weekend. Even without makeup, she looked as fresh as ever—no lines, no shadows, no hollows.

William had had a note delivered to her apartment asking her to stop at his office Monday morning before going on to the labs. A call to Felix from the office would explain where she was. Otherwise, Maggie suspected, he might not know she wasn't there. But the files were in order. The office looked and worked like an office, and they'd even found room for her desk.

She drove past the guard at the outer gate, and he waved a greeting like an old friend. This was the first time in months she'd gone to the main office, and it surprised her that nothing had changed. But why should it change just because she had changed? As she approached the offices on the third floor, her steps grew slower, finally coming to a complete stop about five feet from the unnumbered double doors. She must prepare for Henry's not being there. He and his bride were on a train to Florida, probably somewhere in Georgia right now. She mustn't think about that, or the hurt would show.

Mary O'Toole was opening and sorting the Monday morning mail. Another woman was preparing the coffee. That had been her job for so long she had to force herself to watch and not help. At one point she almost said, "Add some more coffee. They like it stronger."

Mary saw her. "Good morning, Maggie. What brings you here?"

"Mr. Carson asked me to drop by on my way to the labs."

"I'll tell him you're here." She knocked on the door before opening it. "Mr. Carson, Maggie's here."

"Good. Send her in, and bring in the coffee as soon as it's ready."

Mary waved Maggie through. On the way she asked Mary if she would please call Dr. Flam and tell him where she was. Upon entering the room, the first thing she saw was Henry's empty desk. It was absolutely bare. Even the name plate was missing. William noticed her reaction.

He pointed to the couch and chairs. "Let's sit over there. We have some things to talk about."

Maggie seated herself rather primly on the edge of one of the deep chairs. After the familiarities they had exchanged on Saturday, she was uncertain as to what the proper tack was now. And the sight of Henry's empty desk made her realize she was still angry at William for the part he played in marrying Henry to Selma. It was difficult for her to maintain detachment. The coffee was brought in and set on the table. She automatically poured two cups, both black. Then she began to feel nervous. Was it possible Hillyer had talked to William? She asked, "Do you want a report of Dr. Flam's progress?"

"While Henry is away, yes. But first, tell me what you did after I left you at the party."

She gasped. That bastard! He told. All right, she'd deny. She kept her voice even and answered, "I had dinner with John Hillyer at the Beekman Tower."

"Very romantic."

"Not with John." She realized William was simply curious, nothing more. But why that curious?

"I'm glad you took my warning seriously." He paused, then continued. "You noticed Henry's empty desk? That's why I wanted to talk to you. Henry no longer works for the Carson Company." He smiled at her shocked expression. "I exaggerate slightly. He does and he doesn't."

"Would you mind, sir, not playing games with me. I don't understand."

William's face grew flat, even a little grim. "I'll explain. First, I think it might help you to know that in exchange for his agreement to marry the current Mrs. Carson, Henry extracted a price. I suspect your presence in his life made the price a good deal higher than it might have been otherwise."

"Me? How?"

"Henry's in love with you," William added. "He'd be a fool if he wasn't. At any rate, to persuade him to go through with the marriage, I had to surrender a sizeable piece of territory. At precisely four-thirty on Saturday, Henry became president of Wilkenson, Inc. It is a subsidiary of the Carson Company, but he is president and in charge."

There was nothing surprising to Maggie in this information. Or heartening. The reality was that even if Henry did love her, that love had come second to a business gain. He had used her as a trading card to force his father to give him control of the subsidiary. Why not? And more power to him. If you're going to sell out, make sure you get a good price. Hadn't she done the same those years ago when she agreed to William's plan? Her unfortunate accident was falling in love. And perhaps Henry's as well.

"Good for him. The president, with full executive control. Why not? He's up to it." She paused. "But why tell me? I assume you have something more in mind besides keeping me informed."

William wondered what he would have done if faced with Henry's options. One never really knows until one has to choose, but he had an idea he might have chosen differently. The same need in Henry that made it possible for him to absorb the brutal beating Francis gave him made him capable of paying the price of this marriage. William realized that while it was true that he himself had many strengths and few weaknesses, some virtues and vices, his son was of an entirely different cast.

Henry accepted that a decision had a price, and he was willing to pay the price of his decisions, even when the price was exorbitantly high. So high, in fact, that it went beyond William's ability to pay.

His thoughts were interrupted by Maggie. "Have I lost you, sir?"

"No. I lost myself. Anyway, back to business. I have a proposition for you."

"Anything like the last one?" In spite of herself, her voice reflected her hurt and new-found criticism.

"I suppose so. Yes. But in a broader sense, no."

"I'm listening."

"I assume you want to continue your relationship with Henry?"

"Yes, I do."

"And Henry?"

"I believe he wants to continue seeing me." She thought about Hillyer. If Henry knew, he probably would not want to continue to see her.

"But there's a third person to consider."

"I'm all too aware of Selma Wilken—" She had to swallow the lump in her throat before continuing. "Sorry about that. Selma Carson."

"Henry places a high value on not hurting people."

"I'm aware of that."

"Therefore I'm concerned that Selma not be hurt by our continued relation to Henry."

"That makes three people concerned with Selma's not being hurt." Maggie let a tinge of sarcasm creep into her voice.

"Three?"

"You, Henry, and Selma's mother, Evelyn."

"Ah, yes, Evelyn."

"So where are we?"

"I seem to be having trouble making my point." And he was. What had seemed years ago to be a stroke of the highest business acumen now seemed a sordid piece of human folly. At this moment all he could see was grief, grief and more grief waiting for Henry, Maggie and Selma. He shook his head in disgust at the situation he had created. "In any case, as I said, the problem is how you and Henry are going to see each other without Selma becoming aware of the situation."

"As usual, I count on you to have a plan."

"I do. I would like to transfer you to the Wilkenson subsidiary. Your job will be administrative assistant. It will serve two functions."

She considered the possibilities for a moment, and her eyes widened with appreciation. "We'll see each other as often as we like. Working late, working early, taking trips together—everything. And for the other reason, let me think. . . . You'll have a spy in the operation to report to you everything Henry does, so you can keep check on him. Right?"

"That's right."

"It stinks." She caught herself. You do not tell William Carson his idea stinks even if it does. "I'll put it more cogently. You know I love Henry. What makes you think I'll spy on him? Even for you?"

Now William was on firmer ground. "Believe me, there are plenty in that company who will. At least with you reporting, Henry will get the benefit of any doubt."

"Since we agree my reports will favor Henry, why do you want me reporting?"

"Because you'll be close enough to know what's going on. But not after his hide." William saw the doubt in her face and realized some further explanation was necessary. "Remember, he's going head first into a situation with lots of sticky problems, and he's going to stir up a hornet's nest by firing a lot of people. But the incompetent have a way of looking after their own." What he didn't tell her was that hers would be one of three reports he would be getting. The most important, but only one of three.

Maggie wanted to agree. She would be in a position that gave her regular contact with Henry. And as for reporting, William was correct. There were many who would be delighted to make unfavorable comments on their new boss. She would see to it William Carson received essentially accurate, if slightly biased, information. Then there was the job itself. Administrative assistant represented a huge promotion. "When do I start?"

"Now."

"Now? What about Dr. Flam? His work is very important."

"I've already selected another secretary."

"Give me the week to indoctrinate her. Dr. Flam is very special and needs special treatment. If the new girl doesn't understand the kind of man he is, she could cause serious slowdowns in his work."

"All right. I'll see you here a week from today, and we'll drive to New York together to get you started. We're starting on a new building here. It'll take about a year to complete. Until the new offices are ready, you'll commute to New York." Maggie made a wry face. "It has many advantages: theater, opera, concerts, museums, great shopping. Then, of course, there's one other small advantage."

"And that is?"

"The company maintains an apartment in the Pierre for those nights when executives have to work too late to get home."

Maggie had to laugh at the bait. "They must be lined up six deep to use that apartment."

"Not really. The list is limited to two."

"That does make a difference."

"I hoped it might." Even though his troubled vision of her future had sharpened during their talk, his better judgment told him he should end the interview then and there. But his judgment was losing ground to his growing need to blur, if not erase, his image of himself. "I have one more point before we can end this meeting. It has nothing to do with whether or not you accept this new job." Maggie wondered what else he could be thinking. They hadn't discussed pay, vacations, or any of the usual considerations connected with a new job. William had always been more than generous, and she assumed he would continue to be so. "This marriage and Henry's coming of age has made me realize I'm getting older."

"Not so that anyone would notice."

"I notice." All the ugly uncertainties he saw ahead for her, and the guilt he felt at his role in creating them, made him blurt out a startling confidence. "At any rate, I'm having a new will drafted. I want you to know that you're in it."

Maggie stared at him. She could only repeat, "I'm in your will?"

"Correct. But I would request that you not repeat that information to anyone."

"You mean Henry?"

"I mean anyone and Henry especially." William moved to his desk and turned the pages of his appointment book. "I've just noted that we'll meet here next week at this time. Now, unless you have any questions, I have work to do. And Dr. Flam needs you."

"I'll see you next week." She turned at the door to say goodby, but William was already buried in a report.

Mary noticed her leaving. "Are you finished? I have a pile of telephone calls and mail for him."

"I'm finished." Maggie left the office, her head spinning. Administrative assistant! An apartment in the Pierre with Henry! Where was the Pierre? And most amazing of all, she was in William's will. It was too much. Much too much!

By the time she left the building, she was in a mixed mood. How could she have been so stupidly jealous and irresponsible? Bad enough to climb into bed with another man, but not to take contraceptive precautions? What damn stupidity! She had a full week of work and prayer ahead of her.

Mary O'Toole followed Maggie's back as she left the office. Very unusual things were going on in the Carson Company. Mary disliked change. It seemed to her they were rarely for the better. In addition, one of the phone messages she'd taken bothered her. She had to tell the caller that Mr. Carson was in conference and was not taking messages. The man—what was his name? Craig Spears—had become vulgar and abusive. Even a little threatening. She meant to tell Mr. Carson about it. So instead of waiting for his call, she knocked on the door.

"Come in, Mary."

"I've brought you your mail and messages." She hurried on, not wanting to lose his attention. "Sir, one of those messages is from a man named Craig Spears. I seem to remember he's been here several times in the past. But you gave explicit instructions to hold all calls, and when I refused to put him through, he was personally abusive and used language I found offensive." There. She felt much better for saying it.

William's eyes narrowed, and his mouth thinned out in an expression of disgust. "I'm sorry, Mary, and I'll take special care to see that it doesn't happen again. Thank you for telling me."

That was "her" William Carson. If he was going to take "special care," then Mary felt secure she wouldn't be bothered by that man again. She decided to risk a small opinion. "I would like to tell you how excited we all are about the addition of the Wilkenson company. It's so important. Everybody would like to be as much help as possible."

"Thank you. There will be a lot of extra work until the two companies are operating as a team. And you should know that I've made Mr. H president of Wilkenson, Inc. and assigned Maggie to help him. That's why she was here this morning." Then he thought of another change. "We'll now dispense with the title of Mr. H. Please pass the word that Henry Carson is to be called Mr. Carson. I don't think there'll be much difficulty distinguishing between us."

Mary agreed. She could handle the two Mr. Carsons with no trouble. But for Mary O'Toole, there would always be one Mr. Carson— Mr. William Carson.

"Mary, I'm going to call Craig Spears myself. Hold the rest of these for the moment." He waited for her to leave. Then he dialed the local operator and asked to be connected to the Algonquin Hotel in New York. Once connected, he asked for Craig Spears. There was a pause, and he heard a phone ringing. The operator came back on the line.

"I'm sorry, sir. Mr. Spears doesn't seem to be in his room. Shall I try the restaurant or the bar?"

"Would you please? Try the bar first."

"Yes, sir."

Once again he heard the phone ringing. This time it was picked up, and he heard the operator ask if Spears was there. Apparently he was, because the operator asked him to wait. "Mr. Spears is going to a house phone."

"Thank you."

"This is Spears. Who's calling?" The words were slightly slurred. Even this early in the morning Craig was feeling the effects of his drinking.

"This is William Carson. You called me."

"William! I appreciate your returning my call so promptly."

"My secretary tells me you were rough on her. You know she was following my orders."

"I was anxious to reach you. Secretaries have been known to hold some calls and put others through." Now that he had William on the phone, his voice grew expansive. "Please offer her my apologies for anything I said that was amiss."

"I will. Now, what can I do for you?"

"Our understanding, William. You agreed to pay me forty thousand dollars when the Wilkenson deal closed. The Sunday papers report more than a business deal closed." There was silence on the other end of the phone, and suddenly Craig began to sweat. All he had was William's word for the money, and men have been known to break their word for far less than $40,000. "You do remember, William? We made a deal."

Spears' need was obvious, and for a moment William pitied him. "Of course I remember. We have a deal. How do you want the money? Cash? Check? Certified check? And where do you want the funds delivered?"

"A certified check will do nicely. As for delivery, I'll drive up tomorrow and pick it up. Is that all right?"

Until this morning, William had even considered offering Spears a job. But heavy drinking at this time of the morning? Abusive language to Mary? No. A job wasn't feasible. Nevertheless, why not see him? "Tomorrow at ten. I'll have a check drawn and certified."

"Ten o'clock it is." Spears had an awkward moment. "William, I'm embarrassed. I don't have a car. No use for one here in the city. Could you have someone meet me at the station?"

"Of course. What train will you be on?"

"I'm not sure of the schedules. Suppose I leave word with your secretary?" He had another thought. "That way I can apologize for my bad behavior this morning."

"Do that, and I'll see you tomorrow. Goodby."

Craig Spears set the phone on its hook and could barely walk to an easy chair in the lounge. Not, he told himself, that he ever had any doubts. Of course William would keep his word. William was a gentleman. Not some loony-bird of a woman who had no understanding of business and male ethics. Her business now belonged to William Carson. A business grossing over $20 million. And what did he have? A lousy $40,000. Not much for the effort he had put in. Why if it wasn't for him, Carson could never have pulled it off. He had given Carson the information he needed about the patents. And it cost him his job. He had arranged the weekend in which the acquisition had been put together. No weekend, no acquisition. With all that help, Carson would have had to be a total fool not to have made the deal. He wasn't being paid enough. His forehead grew wrinkled, and his eyes pinched as he tried to think of ways to get more out of William. He'd been euchred. Carson had plenty. He'd come up with more money, or he'd pay in other ways. It was only fair. Anyone would agree.

Spears' thoughts began to dissolve. The liquor, the excitement, the general excesses through which he had put his mind and body took their toll. He slumped in his chair and fell asleep, his mouth open, snoring slightly.

The staff of the Algonquin was a sophisticated group. They had to be. It was not unusual for a guest to nap in the lounge rather than going upstairs to his or her room. If a guest wanted to sleep the day away, the guest would be allowed to sleep the day away. So Spears slept on, dreaming the sweet dreams of vengeance he would inflict on all those people who stood in the way of his ride to glory.

He was picked up the next morning at the New York Central station at Hastings-on-Hudson. Spears had managed to miss the early train, and only after frantic telephoning was he able to make the correct connection. William waited for him and wondered about a man who was unable to show up on time even to pick up a sorely needed check. An hour after the time of the appointment, Mary announced with acute distaste in her voice that a certain Mr. Spears was in the reception room. "Do you wish to see him?"

"Don't be too harsh on him, Mary. The man has been through a lot of trouble recently. He may even apologize for his bad manners. Have him shown up. And you meet him at the elevator."

"Yes, sir."

She left, and shortly thereafter, a knock announced Spears. William had to struggle for a moment not to show his shock at the changed appearance of the lawyer. There were deep, dark patches under his eyes, a layer of unhealthy fat blurred his small features, and a belly that didn't seem to come from good living bulged tight against his vest.

"Would you like some coffee, Craig?" It was his standard question before starting a meeting. Usually the answer was either yes or no, thank you. This time he didn't get an answer. Spears went right into what was obviously a not-too-well-prepared speech.

"William, I'd like you to consider renegotiating the terms of our agreement."

Keeping his voice level but thinking it was all so predictable, he asked, "Why?"

Spears leaned forward. "Why! You get a business worth millions, and I get forty thousand dollars. Without me you wouldn't have been able to buy the business. That's why." As William did nothing but keep looking at him, his voice began to weaken. "It isn't fair. I deserve more."

"In the first place, with this payment you will have received fifty thousand dollars, not forty."

"Fifty or forty, what's the difference? It isn't enough."

"It's the amount we agreed upon."

"Show me a piece of paper where I agreed to take fifty thousand dollars."

"That's true. On the other hand, it cuts both ways. Show me a piece of paper where I agreed to pay you fifty thousand dollars." William had lost all his sympathy for the man and found himself growing angry. Had he really thought of hiring him? Could this lack of judgment be another sign of growing older?

The realization that the lack of a written agreement could be a two-edged sword let all the air out of Spears' balloon. He shrunk visibly, and from an aggressive, forward-leaning posture, he fell back against the rear of his seat. Neither his physical nor his mental condition permitted him to maintain any sustained effort in the face of possibly losing the

$40,000. His voice became a querulous whine. "I still think I deserve more money or something." William waited for him to continue. "Maybe a job? That's it! Forty thousand dollars and my job back with the Wilkenson organization. That would be fair."

"It's no longer the Wilkenson operation. It's a subsidiary of the Carson Company, and the president and chief operating officer of the sub is my son, Henry. Do you think Henry will hire you?"

"You can order him to."

William shook his head. "I don't have the authority to order him to do anything. Our arrangement gives him full operating control."

"I don't believe it. You gave up control of a large part of your company? Even to your son? I do not believe it."

"It's true. As I told you, Henry has total control of the operation. Do I make myself clear?"

In spite of himself, Spears was convinced. But why? Why had William Carson given up that much control? Of course. How could he have been so stupid as not to see it? The marriage. It had to be the marriage. He started to laugh. "So you and the old bitch bought him, and the price was the company. I wondered why he agreed to marry Selma Wilkenson." His laughter grew louder and verged on hysteria. "Shit, I wouldn't have taken her even with Wilkenson, Inc. as a dowry."

William grew more quiet. "It was never offered to you." Suddenly he had enough of Spears. He raised his voice for the first time. "I'm going to give you two pieces of advice. The first is, take the money. It's all you're going to get. The second is, cut the booze, the whores, the gambling and whatever else you're taking. The money won't last that long." He reached into his pocket and produced an envelope. "Here's your check. Certified. Take it and get out. The car is waiting to take you to the station."

The lawyer's face changed to something between a snarl and a smirk. He looked at the check, stuffed it in his pocket and left the room. It took a few minutes before Mary reappeared.

"He's on his way, Mr. Carson."

"You saw him to the elevator?"

"I saw him to the car."

"By any chance did he apologize to you?"

"No."

"At least he's consistent."

She left, and William returned to the reports. From everything he read, Henry was going to have one hell of a job. In the few months that had passed, affairs at Wilkenson, Inc. had disintegrated far more than he had imagined possible.

During the ride to the station, Craig Spears was in a fury. Not only had his very reasonable requests for a fair deal been denied, but he had received a lecture on how he chose to live from a hypocrite, a man who sold his son to that hag for a business deal. It was almost funny. Add that to what he already knew, and there was a nice juicy story for the gossip columnists.

He looked at the check. It was made out to him and certified. Forty thousand dollars. As before, the check was drawn on William's personal account. It didn't matter. He would photostat the check before depositing it. Another piece of evidence should he need it. This time he folded the check very carefully and put it in his wallet. Then he pulled a small, leather-covered silver flask from his hip pocket. The prospect of additional money called for a celebration drink. He took a large swig and felt the warmth spreading through his body. He'd show them. He'd show them all. Especially William Carson. And Evelyn Wilkenson.

# Chapter 12

THE HONEYMOON dragged on for an eternity, both Henry and Selma finding it a subtle form of torture. Selma's body was frozen to all pleasure, and though she did her best to perform what she considered her duty as a wife, she hated every second of it. The shock of the bleeding was not repeated, but she lived in constant fear of the return of the searing pain.

There was nothing in the act for Henry except a momentary release, and that was partially inhibited by his realization of Selma's fright. He would have blamed her fear on his carelessness that first night if he hadn't known that Selma had been born to remain a virgin. That she had married was for her a misery.

So it was with lighter hearts that Selma and Henry boarded the train for home. Henry had forgotten the intense jealousy he had felt at seeing his father and Maggie together in the Wilkenson garden and yearned almost painfully to see her again. And Selma longed to see her mother. Then, too, with Henry back at work she would have more time for church. And he would have less time to make demands upon her. She knew she had missed her period, but that wasn't unusual. She'd missed periods before she had married.

The month that went at a snail's pace for Henry and Selma both dragged and raced by for Maggie. Every morning, before leaving for work, she checked her mailbox for a letter from him. If the mail had not yet arrived, she hurried home in the evening to check it again. She stayed home most evenings, sitting in one of the chairs they had shared, and looked out at the Hudson wondering how the deep red sunsets over the Palisades differed in color and texture from the sunrises over the Atlantic that Henry was seeing in Palm Beach. She sat patiently, fatalistically, waiting for the phone to ring, all the while knowing it wouldn't. For, in truth, she expected him neither to write nor telephone. And she gave him the benefit of any and all excuses. The proper time and privacy to write a note couldn't be found. And if it could, what could he say?

151

"Having a good time—wish you were here"? There was also the indelicacy of phoning a girlfriend while on one's honeymoon. One or all of the excuses would do. But the long silence began to make her increasingly uncertain about their relationship.

Maggie, too, had missed her period. This had happened before. Rarely, but it had happened. She was usually not one to avoid reality, but the idea that she was carrying John Hillyer's baby was too much to face. In any case, there was nothing she could do for another month.

Her new job was taking another kind of toll. William had explained she was to observe, make notes and have reports ready for Henry when he returned. The office was located in the Chrysler Building on the forty-eighth floor. It needed refurbishing. It also needed new personnel. The staff customarily reported late, left early and took long lunch breaks. Invoicing was thirty days late and payments worse. The central files had been organized by a woman who had died three years ago. No one else understood the system, so each department did its own filing. A large number of people would have to change their ways or look for new jobs.

One morning William telephoned to tell Maggie that Henry and Selma were on their way home. After that, time seemed to stop. Seconds became minutes; minutes, hours; and hours a full day. A day was forever. But though time stopped for Maggie, it still passed. Maggie went home Friday knowing that if she didn't see Henry over the weekend, she would see him on Monday.

William had spent the month doing little of importance. The company was running smoothly, and as much as he wanted to act on Maggie's reports, he knew he couldn't. It was Henry's responsibility. Any action by him would violate their agreement. So he went to the office, supervised the start of construction of the new building that was to house the Wilkenson subsidiary and played a lot of tennis after work and on weekends at the Westchester Country Club.

He continued seeing Marion on a regular basis, but although he wouldn't admit it, the relationship was beginning to pall. He found himself distracted by thoughts of Maggie and Henry. And the nature of love. In the years since Nathalia's death, he hadn't worried about love. Marion was a wonderful woman, but to think of marrying her would be absurd. Nor would she have appreciated the offer.

In the middle of July, William signed his new will and had it properly witnessed by John Hillyer and the appropriate secretaries. Before the will was finalized, there ensued a short, intense discussion between the two men about the wisdom of Maggie Rhodes' being included in the will. Hillyer started to give his reasons why he felt she should not, including the beginnings of a description of his evening with Maggie after the wedding. William cut him short. He warned Hillyer to keep any gossip about Maggie to himself. In fact, he would hold John strictly accountable for Maggie's good name. The matter of Maggie was dropped. However, the incident told William more than he wanted to know.

Henry called several times during the month. William took the opportunity to give him short summaries of what he had learned about the conditions at Wilkenson, Inc. He did not tell him the source of his information.

The month did not pass slowly for Craig Spears. If anything, it simply disappeared. From the moment he deposited William's check in his bank, the days and nights flew by in a miasma of liquor, women, late-night poker games and finally a long period he spent drugged by cocaine—a new discovery for him. Of all this he remembered little. One morning in the middle of the second week of July, he telephoned the Bank of New York to obtain his bank balance. He was startled to discover that less than $20,000 remained out of the original $40,000.

He insisted upon an immediate accounting and made an appointment for the next morning. After that he returned to his other distractions. It was two weeks before he recovered sufficiently from his entertainments to remember he had a bank and a banker. Another call informed him he had gone through another $5,000. This time he did not ask for an accounting. It was easier to take a drink from the ever-present bottle of brandy and several snorts from the ever-present packets of cocaine. Refinements such as shaving and bathing became a hit-or-miss proposition. Had he thought about it, he would not have been able to remember when he'd had his last full meal.

The two announcements of the Carson-Wilkenson wedding and corporate acquisition were pinned to the wall over his bed. When he was able to focus on anything, he would stare for hours at the clippings and plan what he would do to the bastards.

During this period, he bought a fully loaded .38-caliber pistol. He needed the pistol to protect him and his winnings when he returned late at night to his hotel. That he rarely won was irrelevant. It was only a matter of time before his luck would change. Hatred and hope gradually fused as the life of Craig Spears turned into one long nightmare. All that remained constant was his conviction that William Carson had taken advantage of him and would have to pay for it.

Henry and Selma arrived at Penn Station late on Saturday afternoon. They were met by Jimmy in the family limousine. The luggage was piled on top of the car, and the bridal couple were whisked north to Westchester and Carson House.

William and Evelyn were waiting on the front steps to greet them. After affectionate greetings all around, Henry and Selma were escorted to a suite that was to be their home. Evelyn seemed oblivious as she fluttered around her daughter, but one look at Henry convinced William that whatever he imagined could go wrong had gone wrong.

Speaking softly, he broke a self-imposed rule. "That bad?"

"Worse," Henry muttered.

Evelyn had already gone downstairs to supervise dinner preparations, so when William left, Henry was alone with Selma. She looked around slightly dazed. "Welcome home." He carefully put his arms around her and kissed her on the cheek. "Do you like our new rooms?"

"They're lovely, Henry."

"If there's anything you don't like, we'll have it changed. Oscar has run the estate for years. He'll rearrange anything you want."

"Maybe Mother could live here? She could run the house with Oscar."

The idea of having Evelyn around on any permanent basis was not one Henry would consider for even a fraction of a second. "We'll see. I don't think you'll find the house difficult to live in. Just give it time."

"I'd like to wash up and change."

"Why don't you take a short nap? I'll wake you for dinner."

Selma was only too glad to agree. The best thing about the suite from her point of view was that the bedroom had two large beds.

Henry joined William and Evelyn on the terrace, and the three sat around and chatted. When it was time to eat, Evelyn suggested she go and fetch her daughter. It would give her a chance to have a short chat with Selma. The two men watched her walk across the terrace. Then Henry leaned back and took a large swallow from his gin and tonic.

William took advantage of their moment together to give Henry a brief rundown on the business. He had made Henry's title official. Then he gave him a quick progress report on Dr. Flam's work. Last, but hardly least, he described Maggie's new job and title. Henry approved of everything. He had been puzzled about exactly how he would maintain contact with Maggie without hurting Selma. Now, with his usual foresight, William had solved the problem.

Henry had one concern he could not discuss with William. How would Maggie feel about continuing their affair now that he was married? When he had chosen to marry Selma, his choice had been made with the full knowledge that he might lose Maggie, and though she had expressed a strong desire to go on seeing him, he wasn't really sure she meant it. It was in the nature of the man that his real and deep love for Maggie caused him the most conflict. He knew that the sooner she stopped seeing him, the sooner she would find someone to marry and make a happy, settled life. Maggie was meant to love and be loved, to marry and bear children. She could never have a child with him. But he loved her and needed her even more than he had expected. Maybe they would be granted a little more time together? They would see each other on Monday, and he would have his answer then.

Selma and Evelyn appeared. Henry never did find out what she had told her mother, but whatever it was, Evelyn came out in favor of Henry. As the four of them went into the house for dinner, Selma linked her arm in Henry's.

Craig Spears finished his gin and orange juice and settled down to his usual brandy-laced coffee. For the first time in weeks he didn't feel too terrible. Last night he had won over $4,000, stayed reasonably sober, and held his use of cocaine to a point where he was still alert. As usual, the *Times* and *Tribune* had been delivered with the juice and coffee. There was a large notice in the *Tribune*'s society section about the return of Mr. and Mrs. Henry Carson from their honeymoon in Florida. Spears cut out the notice and added it to the two already on the wall. It gave him an idea. He would see Henry Carson about additional money, and he would take his pistol along. Should he call for an appointment or just appear? He would appear. There were enough employees left who knew him and owed him favors.

Spears grinned as he visualized the scene. He'd threaten to tell the newspapers the truth about Carson's marriage. The society reporters loved that sort of thing, and Carson knew it. He would pay handsomely to keep his name and dear, dear Selma's out of the papers. And once having paid, he would pay again. This could turn out to be a steady income for Spears, a salary he had earned and been denied. He had his gun in any case. This called for another brandy.

The next morning Spears had a rotten hangover. He needed a shave and a bath, but he felt so shaky this morning, he needed a little help first. Actually he needed help most mornings. He took the cellophane bag out of its hiding place, shook a little powder onto the back of his hand, took a sniff in each nostril and waited. It didn't take long. First there was the "pop" as though the world had expanded, and then the good feeling. He could do anything. Why, he didn't even need the gun. He could handle Carson with his brains and guts. He was Craig Spears, and he was smart and hard. He'd take the gun just because.

The feeling of power held while he finished dressing and left the hotel to make a quick stop at the bank. He deposited $3,500 and kept the rest for pocket money.

Maggie awoke Monday morning having spent another restless night thinking and dreaming of Henry. The possibility that he had accomplished a miracle and turned Selma into a willing, even eager partner poisoned her whole being. She was tormented with vivid and detailed pictures of Henry and Selma making passionate love. In these fantasies Selma's rather small, thin body was transformed into a lush sensual figure capable of giving Henry delights such as he had never imagined.

She was surprised that John Hillyer had made no further attempts to see her. It did not occur to her that he was involved in drawing up William's will and her being in the will warned him off. Maggie was both grateful and troubled by the fact that he kept away.

During the weeks of loneliness, Maggie had grown tired and nervous. Sometimes, staring at herself in the mirror, she felt her eyes had shadows beneath them and her cheeks had lost their roundness. She thought she was becoming a different Maggie, no longer the young woman she was familiar with. And she was right.

Maggie's beauty had always been a trifle obvious, an example of fresh air, good food and a made-in-America heritage. But in the past month a change had taken place. She found herself paying attention to the character, the personality, the attitudes of the women she saw on the streets. They were women such as she had never seen, lovely women, exquisitely turned out, pacing the sidewalk with a proud, undulant rhythm of legs and hips as though they owned the earth. Maybe it was the ascetic life she had chosen in Henry's absence? Or maybe her sad foreboding that their time together was ending? Maybe it was simply that she was working harder than ever before? Whatever it was, the Maggie of June 21 was not the Maggie of July 28.

She was ten pounds lighter, but that wasn't it. Rather, it was that her weight was redistributed. Her slightly round face seemed to have lengthened, with the result that her cheeks were indeed flatter, even hollow, her cheekbones far more prominent, her jaw line more defined.

Her eyes, while hardly sunken, had deepened and lost some of their laughter. It was as though she had been brushed by the wings of truth and the vision lingered in her expression.

Her hair had been tamed, and now instead of in wild curls, she wore it rather severely, pulled back in a page boy bob.

Then there were the changes in her body. The loss of weight had not diminished the curve of her hips and breasts; instead, the flatness of her belly and the beauty of her shoulders and neck became clearer. A restored look of breeding that had been dulled by her years in the factory was added to her softness. She became more beautiful than ever before, with the kind of beauty that would last for the rest of her life.

She bathed, applied a small amount of eye makeup and lipstick, and chose a pale gray linen suit with an even lighter gray silk blouse. Her stockings had a slight gray cast, and her simple pumps were gray and white. She smiled a sly, self-mocking smile as she snapped her brassiere in place and adjusted her breasts so they fitted comfortably in the cups. The brassiere reminded her of the day she had first dressed to meet Henry Carson and all the other wonderful days when under-clothes were either absent or held to a minimum.

But this was another Monday, and they were two other people. What was appropriate then was not now. Added to that was her continuing insecurity. She had not heard from Henry over the weekend. That could be significant or meaningless. She was prepared for either event and meant to conduct herself with dignity and grace.

After Sunday services, William had decided to give Henry a first-hand look at the progress on the new building, and he drove him over to the construction site.

"What's your estimate on completion?" Henry asked.

"You'll move in in less than a year. Provided we can close in the building before the first frost."

Henry pursed his lips. That was enough time to decide who would be invited to stay and who let go. For those staying, the transfer would be made as easy as possible. The company would assume all the moving expenses and would find housing equal if not superior to whatever an employee presently had. Both William and Henry wanted to make it as painless as possible.

The next morning Henry arrived at the Chrysler Building at eight-thirty. He got off the elevator on the forty-eighth floor and was appalled to find that the oak doors with Wilkenson, Inc. in heavy brass letters were locked. There was a small white button and a crudely lettered sign taped under it that requested a visitor to "Ring if the Door is Locked." If it weren't so outrageous, it would be funny. He pushed the button and heard the faint sound of a buzzer ringing inside. In a few moments the door opened, and there stood Maggie.

Henry had not planned on their meeting in a public hall. Since William said she would be in the New York office, he'd concocted and discarded all sorts of plots and schemes involving their meeting. He would be formal. Or friendly. He would be warm and affectionate. He could be any number of things, but they all required privacy. Now he was at a loss.

Maggie had arrived at eight. She wanted to be there ahead of him to steel herself for the meeting. It would be a politely extended hand and "Welcome to your new office, Mr. Carson." She planned to wait for a cue from him to make clear their new status. But there he was, and she felt unready.

Henry's immediate impression thoroughly shook him. In a little over a month, a subtle but unmistakable change had taken place in the quality of her beauty. He remembered her face as having a transparency, an openness. Now, its impenetrable surface suggested her nature had arrived at an understanding with itself.

And there was another change. The woman standing before him was an elegant, self-assured being who gave no hint of a childhood spent struggling to survive. Nor did it suggest long years on a factory assembly line, a place Henry had never considered an ideal finishing school for elegant young ladies.

Maggie, studying Henry in turn, thought he looked like a man returned not from a glorious honeymoon, but from a disappointing business trip. This restored some of her self-possession. And, as always, his very nearness had the power to move her deeply. She could not keep her pleasure at his return from showing in both her face and voice. "Welcome home, sir."

Henry laughed with a quick sense of relief, his astonishment at this strange Maggie receding. "I am glad to be home, though home was never like this. Where the hell is everybody?" he asked, following her into the office.

"They get in about nine, plus or minus."

"I thought the hours were eight-thirty to five-thirty."

"Pure hearsay."

Henry grunted. "Give me a quick tour of the offices, ending up at my office."

When they reached Henry's office with its south and west exposures, he went behind the huge, glass-topped desk and sat down. The chair promptly collapsed under his weight. Maggie shook with laughter, and finally Henry smiled a little sourly, remembering William's remarks about his weight. Getting up, he deposited the wreckage outside the office. "How soon can we have a new one delivered?"

"There's an office furniture store on the ground floor. I'll get the biggest and strongest chair they have available for immediate delivery."

"And meanwhile?" He looked around the room. There was a large leather easy chair in one corner as part of a grouping around a small table. He picked it up and placed it behind his desk. When he sat down, the chair sagged but held. "This will do for now. Where do you work?"

Maggie pointed through the open door to an area reserved for secretaries. "That space was empty, so I claimed squatter's rights."

"Does anyone know your job title?"

"No. I was waiting for you to make the announcement."

"Who's the office manager?"

"There is none."

"Christ! How does the office run?"

"Run? It doesn't even walk. Sorry. Bad joke. I've been working on reports covering the operations, department by department. They're ready for you."

"I'll take them now."

All through their conversation she was aware that his glance was averted. As was hers. But when she turned her eyes toward him, he met her glance with an anxious look. She handed him the neatly stacked pile of reports, each carefully clipped. "You can read them now. I'll go and order your chair." She left Henry alone with the reports.

Deep in concentration, making notes on a pad as he went, Henry did not hear footsteps approaching. He was startled when a voice said, "Well, well, if it isn't the new broom come to sweep clean."

Henry looked up, at first not recognizing the man standing before him. It was Craig Spears, but an incredibly changed Craig Spears. His skin hung loosely over small areas of unhealthy puffiness, there were terrible dark patches under his eyes, and he moved in an odd, jerky fashion as though his muscles were at war with their owner and the outcome of the contest had yet to be decided. Without asking, he plopped himself into a chair next to the desk.

"How did you get in here?"

"I walked in. They know me here. I worked here, remember? Before your father got me fired."

Henry looked at his watch. Nine-thirty. Maggie must still be downstairs getting his chair, or she'd have stopped him. "Since they know you, you can get up and walk right out again. No one will stop you." There was going to be one hell of a scene with whoever let this thing get into his office.

Still on his cocaine high, Spears was confident he could handle the situation. His nose was running. It had been running a lot lately. He took out a used handkerchief and blew into it noisily. Then he said, "I'll go after we have a talk."

"No talk. Get out!"

"We'll talk."

Henry became mildly exasperated. He walked around the desk. "You'll leave politely, or you'll leave and there will be nothing polite about it."

It seemed that the "ape" was going to be tough. Spears pulled out his revolver, pointed it at Henry's stomach and said, "We'll talk now, won't we?"

As they faced each other, the gun wavered, and Henry's foot lashed out, kicking the gun across the room. He jumped for the gun while Spears sat in the chair, shocked into immobility. The noise brought people into the outer office. Henry asked, "Who let Spears in?"

No one answered.

Henry emptied the shells from the gun and tossed it toward Spears, who grabbed for it.

"This damn fool came in here with a gun and threatened me." He addressed the onlookers. "I'm going to accompany him personally to the door." Raising his voice so that everyone outside the office could hear him, he added, "I never want to see Mr. Spears in this office again. If I do, I'll fire every single one of you." He realized he had forgotten something. "Yes, my name is Henry Carson."

Henry turned back to Spears, picked him up like a sack of potatoes, slung him over his shoulder and finally deposited him on his feet in front of the elevators. When the elevator door opened, he pushed Spears into it, just as Maggie arrived to see the finish of the incident. Henry saw her and said, "Miss Rhodes, I want to interview the entire staff. We'll take them one at a time, alphabetically. Have them type their names, job titles and duties on a card and give the cards to you. And where's my chair?"

"In your office, Mr. Carson. We brought it up the service elevator and missed the fun."

"That wasn't fun. The man's sick. He threatened me with a gun."

"Shall I call the police?"

They walked together to his office and shut the door. Henry thought about the police. "No. He's probably frightened enough now to stay away. And we don't need the publicity."

"Are you sure?"

"What can the police do now?"

"Arrest him."

"I would have to prefer charges. No." He dismissed the subject and requested she hold all calls and messages, unless from William. He had reading to do.

Maggie had a strong feeling this was a mistake. A man with a gun is dangerous. Henry was treating it too lightly. But there was nothing she could do about it. The entire event would be included in her report to William.

Left alone, Henry began to study the reports again. This time he found himself unable to concentrate. Part of the reason was that Maggie prepared them, and this drew his attention from the reports to her. He had neither written nor telephoned while in Florida, in an attempt to give both of them breathing space. Besides, he wanted to give his marriage every chance of success. It had failed, but he had tried.

Now there was Maggie to consider. He had left a girl and returned to find a woman, one whom he would have to consider in an entirely new way. He saw the long slimness of her body, the fresh curve of her throat, her face paler and thinner than he remembered; and her eyes, her large, blue eyes, rested on him with the quiet poise of a well-bred stranger. She was lovelier than ever before.

He paused in his thinking. Who had been her teacher in his absence? Who had remade her in this image? It was hard for him to understand how the change had come about, and it made him feel like a deposed ruler.

His bitterness surprised him. Shouldn't he be glad that she had bloomed like a great, rich rose? In their time together, she had played planet to his sun. Now she could stand alone, a beautiful, gracious woman whom any man would be proud to have for a wife. Which left the question further up in the air: would such a woman settle for a married Henry as a lover?

The news that each employee would have a meeting with the president produced a stream of people at Maggie's desk asking what he was like and how to behave. She gave each one the same answer. "Mr. Carson is a reasonable man. He expects you to do your job, and that's all. Behave as you would with any employer." Each employee was assigned a number. There were thirty-six, not counting executives. Executives would be interviewed another day.

Though Maggie pointed out to Henry that it would take more than one afternoon to see thirty-six people, he insisted that they try. Those who were not seen during the afternoon would be seen the next morning. Maggie was to sit in on the interviews and take notes, transcribing them the next day.

At one o'clock, Miss Sara Ames from Purchasing appeared. Henry studied the card that gave her title and job description, and asked a few questions. Maggie was introduced as the new Assistant to the President. The staff was to take their orders from her and consider them as coming from the President.

Henry found that Maggie's reports were correct. Morale and efficiency were either very low or non-existent. But the basic problem did not really lie with the office workers, who were, on average, neither better nor worse than most clerical help. The problem lay with senior management, who were more interested in protecting their rights and privileges than in getting the work done. Everything Maggie reported about the lack of systems, lack of clear-cut responsibility, lack of master files and so forth, turned out to be accurate. Straightening things out was going to be like wading through a swamp. Toward the end of the afternoon, William called to find out how things were going.

"Could be worse. The building hasn't caught fire, and no one's jumped out the window."

"Good luck."

"Thanks." Then he remembered. "By the way, I had a visitor this morning. Care to guess who?"

"Male or female?"

"Male."

"Craig Spears."

"How did you know?"

"He visited me. I said no. It's logical you'd be next."

"Did he show you his new toy?"

"His what?"

"A thirty-eight-caliber pistol."

William's voice turned serious. "No. What happened?"

"I took it away from him and threw him out."

"You kept the gun?"

Henry felt abashed. It had been a mistake not to keep the gun. "As a matter of fact, no, I didn't." A further justification was necessary. "If he wanted another gun, he could get one almost anywhere. So what was the point?"

"That's true." There was a pause. "Still, I have a feeling you should have kept it."

"You're probably right, but I didn't."

"How badly did you hurt him?"

"I didn't hurt him. I just tossed him out, with a warning."

William considered the situation. Spears was becoming a nuisance. What could be done? Having no answer, he went on to another subject. "How is Maggie working out?"

"Doing a fine job." Henry's voice had overtones of other things, and William, in rare haste, jumped to a conclusion.

"Is it possible you won't make dinner tonight?"

"I'm not sure." Henry hesitated just long enough for William to realize things weren't yet settled. It gave him a stiff moment when he realized he'd pressed because he wanted the relationship to end. He would have to examine his motives very carefully. Maggie was his son's lover. He had no business having any such wishes. Henry's voice sounded in his ear. "I've piles of paper work. If I have to work late, I'll call Selma and tell her."

"Is there anything else you can tell me about Spears?"

"He looked terrible and was constantly blowing his nose. Maybe hay fever."

"A running nose?" William thought it over and recognized an unpleasant possibility. "Maybe cocaine. Add that to liquor and gambling, and he's going down fast."

"What do we do about him?"

"Be careful. If I'm right, the drugs could trigger any kind of lunatic behavior."

After the morning's experience, Henry was convinced that William was right. "I'll be careful, and you be, too."

"Right. If I don't see you tonight, call me in the morning. Maybe I can help you with your problems."

"All help will be gratefully accepted. Take care." Then he buzzed for Maggie. When she entered, he said, "Let's call a halt for today. We can pick up the interviews tomorrow. I want some time to think about what we already know, and there's something else more important." He told her about his conversation with William. "Try to find out, unobtrusively, who let Spears in. Then ask whether anyone knows if Spears has hay fever or some other allergy."

"Given my position, I can ask some pretty direct questions."

"All right, but be careful. You never know what peculiar loyalties have been built up over the years." She left, and Henry started reviewing the rough notes he had on the employees. A more detailed study would wait for the completion of the interviews and Maggie's transcribing them. After that he would weed out and go on to senior management.

Even for a person with as tenuous a grasp on reality as Craig Spears had, the morning had to be classed as a disaster. After being thrown out of the office, he had stumbled across town to his hotel room. A shot of brandy did nothing for him. First William Carson and then Henry Carson had treated him like dirt. They had forgotten everything he had done for them. The cocaine had worn off, and he felt depressed and exhausted. Without bothering to undress, he collapsed on his bed, finally breaking down in a deluge of bitter tears. He needed another picker-upper, but when he roused himself enough to go to his bureau to get another pinch of powder, there was none left. The morning's doses had used up his supply. And there was no way to locate his source until that night.

He drew the blinds to throw the room into darkness and sank into his chair. His brain whirled with half-thought-out plans, none of which gave him any peace. He looked at the now useless revolver. He would get more shells that night. Settling with the Carsons was more important than gambling, drinking or women. He would have to get back his own and then some. They owed him. The idea of the unpaid obligation grew. When he shut his eyes, he could see William Carson sitting in Westchester spinning his web like some huge, poisonous spider. Henry was not important. Cut off the roots, and the limb would wither. William was the root of his trouble. He would decide what to do tomorrow. Tomorrow, when he had another supply of cocaine. In the meanwhile, he needed brandy and sleep. The brandy was easy, but he couldn't sleep.

Spears spent the day sitting in his chair in the gray, shadowed room sipping brandy until the bottle was empty. By then he was very drunk. The room began to spin, and he felt nauseous. He tried to get to the toilet, but fell sprawling as he entered the bathroom. Semiconscious, he lay for hours in his vomit, urine and excrement. The day had turned into night before he was able to rouse himself. It took a supreme effort of will to get his clothes off and fill the bathtub. The clothes, including his last good suit, were ruined. They couldn't even be sent to the dry cleaner. They were so dirty and smelled so bad that he began to vomit again. This time he made it to the toilet. While the bath was filling, he stuffed everything into a pillowcase and put the pile in the corner of the bathroom. Later, he would drop it into a street corner trash can. Every nerve seemed exposed, raw, on the surface of his skin. He sat in the tub, trembling uncontrollably.

Ever since Maggie had met Henry at the door that morning, she had been "on point" waiting for a signal from him. She had eaten her lunch at her desk, hoping he might take advantage of the lack of people to ask her into his office for a private talk. It hadn't happened.

As the day went on, the tension between them grew. What did he want? His formality seemed far beyond anything business decorum required. She had no idea that she, the new Maggie, had contributed to his caution, failing completely to sense his uncertainties and doubts.

When five-thirty arrived, the office emptied out in the race for the subway. Maggie had to decide if she should wait and face a possible rejection, or leave and face the same question tomorrow. Henry seemed in no hurry to leave. That decided her. She would wait. When she looked at her watch, she couldn't believe only ten minutes had passed. She looked at her watch again. Had it stopped? It hadn't. The little second hand was jumping from point to point as it traveled around the dial.

The next five minutes almost undid her. She knew that unless she did something, her supply of courage would be exhausted, and she would end up going home alone. She forced herself to walk to the closed door and drew her hand back to knock. Just as the forward motion started, the door opened. Maggie stood with her hand suspended in midair, facing Henry.

Henry stepped back and bowed her into his office. They stared at each other in an awkward silence. Henry was the first to break it.

"Sit down. Let's talk. What a bitch of a day. Unless, of course, you have something else to do. A train to catch. Whatever."

The words were spoken hurriedly, and the thoughts were out of sequence.

"My trains run every half hour or so. I have time."

Henry paced up and down the room, looking at his desk, out the window, at the walls, everywhere except at her. Maggie watched him, bewildered. Finally she understood. And the understanding was as startling and inexplicable as anything that had happened to her in the last years. Henry Carson was just as uncertain of her as she was of him, and he wanted her as she wanted him.

It was as though he had read her mind, because they both began to speak at the same moment.

"Maggie . . ."

"Henry . . ."

"Hear me out, please?" He would take the risk. He had to. It was he who had gotten married and caused the separation. If there was going to be a rejected party, it should be him. He sat down next to her and said what he felt had to be said. What he wanted to say. "I love you. I love you as much if not more than I ever did. But if my marriage makes it impossible for you to love me and continue to see me, I'll honor your wishes, but I won't stop loving you."

Maggie couldn't answer. She buried her face in her hands and began to weep. All the tensions, aches, fears poured out in a stream of tears, leaving her cleansed and open. Still crying, she flung herself into his arms. "I love you, my darling. I love you."

They held each other, laughing and crying simultaneously. It was all right. For now, at least, it was all right.

After the emotion of the reunion subsided, Henry gently disengaged himself. "Excuse me for a moment, love. Let's get practical matters out of the way." He went to his desk, called Carson House and explained to Selma that he wouldn't be home tonight.

Selma agreed with relief. She need not be concerned that she might have to be a "good wife." The more often he stayed in New York, the less often he would make demands of her. It would be a blessing if business kept him in New York every night.

Henry and Maggie were now free to enjoy each other. But first, Henry pointed out, there were personal items to buy: a new shirt, underwear, a razor and shaving soap, a toothbrush. That would take several stops on the way to the hotel. Listening to him, Maggie began to laugh slightly hysterically.

"You don't need a thing. I've had more than a month to prepare for tonight."

"I don't understand."

"I bought everything you might need. They're in the hotel room waiting for you. As well as things I need." That was how she had decided to use the $500 "tip" Hillyer had left her. It seemed a fitting way to spend the money.

Henry was silent.

"I hope you're pleased." She had recognized the risk when she had made the purchases. Each item increased her awareness of the fragility of the web that bound them and how easily it could be ripped. That it had held was a blessing, a blessing for which one made sacrifices to the gods. For an instant she wondered what further sacrifices the gods might ask, but the twinge of fright was forgotten in her happiness. She wouldn't count her winnings. Not yet. Not until they had made love with the same intensity and complete union of spirit as before. She kissed him lightly on the nose and murmured, "Let's go! Oh, how I want you!"

Henry looked at Maggie. His body was relaxed yet taut in its relaxation, its stillness being slowly filled with anticipation of the evening ahead. She was at the door, a beautiful, unnerving stranger. For a moment it was difficult for him to contain his emotions, and he pressed his fist to his forehead in regret. He had always refused to allow himself to think of Maggie as a "wife." He couldn't. But what a wife she would have made. What a life they might have had together. If it had only been possible.

He heard her voice soft and quiet. "Henry . . . stop dreaming. We must go." And the shape of her mouth was a shape of pain and tenderness and resignation. She had accepted that he'd been powerless to do other than he had done. That he was powerless to change himself. But her being there was a gesture of acceptance. It solved everything, answered all doubts, as though her meaning was simply to be the woman he loved, who loved him and forgave him. And offered him tonight.

# Chapter 13

DURING the next few months, the self-destructive impulses against which Craig Spears had unconsciously battled all his life gathered strength for their final triumph. Spears' use of brandy and cocaine went totally out of control. His body chemistry required the alcohol, and his endless, deep depressions, alleviated only by cocaine, made the drug indispensable.

In mid-September he received a routine notice from the Bank of New York stating they had returned several of his checks because of insufficient funds. Spears silently cursed them. Along with the printed notice was a handwritten note from his banker asking Spears to stop in and straighten out his affairs. Otherwise, the banker implied, he would have to take more drastic action.

Spears had $455 in his wallet. The overdraft was for several thousand dollars. Worse, one of the bounced checks was for the overdue rent on his hotel room. The Algonquin would redeposit the check just once. Then they would ask him to leave. A quick examination of the envelope in his bureau drawer was somewhat more reassuring. He had a three-day supply of cocaine.

He thought of William Carson. He had managed to buy more shells for his revolver, and next time he would be more careful. Carson had welshed on an obligation. No man of honor could permit another man to welsh on an obligation. He would collect what was his due. He wiped his nose with a dirty handkerchief. Living in this crummy hotel was causing his nose to run. He'd move out as soon as he'd made his win. Tonight's game would see him through. Yes, that would be the start. He'd make a big win tonight. Thousands of dollars. Why not? He'd done it before. He'd do it again. In a mind slipping from reality, the win of $4,000 had become $40,000, and the time when it took place was last week, not months ago.

After he won, he'd see Carson.

William and Henry were sitting in Henry's office going over reports. In the few months he had been in charge, Henry had started the "turning around" process. He had cleaned house of senior management. The beginnings of a central bookkeeping system were in place. Objections at being forced to give up domains of power had been overruled. Anyone who proved too resistant was fired.

The conversation drifted to Maggie. William asked, half joking, "She's working out?"

Henry answered cautiously. "Yes. Very well. Why do you ask?"

Now it was William's turn to be cautious. "Have you told her about Selma?"

"Her being pregnant?"

"Yes."

"No."

"I understand, but sooner is better than later."

"Easier said than done."

William nodded. Since Henry and Selma's honeymoon, William's pessimism about the marriage had deepened. Could they have made the acquisition without the marriage? His business sense told him no. There were too many companies ready to outbid him. Public companies with shareholder money to spend. They would have lost Wilkenson, Inc. But Maggie and Henry would have been together always. Now he knew it was only a matter of time. Sooner or later she would find the backstairs relationship unendurable, and then? . . . Henry would never abandon Selma, especially with a child on the way. Someone as unusual as Maggie deserved a future after Henry with more possibilities than that of an executive secretary. For the moment his hands were tied. The subject so depressed him, he decided to change it. "Have you seen anything of Spears?"

"No, but a friend ran into him at a poker game. Spears was high as a kite and managed to lose his last cent. His check bounced. Don't be surprised if you get a visitor."

"I won't." Here, too, he felt a twinge of guilt. But here, at least, it was uncalled for. The seeds of Spears' destruction were there long before he came in contact with the Carson Company. "What are you doing tonight?"

"Going home, unfortunately. And you?"

"My night with Marion. I've considered suggesting that the four of us make a night of it, but decided against the idea. It's not Marion. She'd enjoy it. But I don't want to suggest to Maggie that the Carsons can't distinguish between a high-priced, accomplished and most excellent whore and a young woman in love with a married man." William had managed to forget the origin of Maggie's relationship with Henry, nor

did he wish to remember the inference Hillyer had made about her actions on the night of Henry's marriage. He had invented Maggie—the
next best thing to having created her—and he wanted to admire his invention.

William and Henry separated on Lexington Avenue between Forty-
second and Forty-third streets. Henry crossed the avenue to catch a train
for Port Chester. Just before entering Grand Central Station, he glanced
back and saw William striding north toward Fifty-seventh Street. Then
he would walk east to River House and Marion.

Maggie had paid a visit to Dr. Charles Benjamin during her lunch
hour to confirm what she had suspected. She was pregnant. If Henry
had been the father, she would have been delighted, and in spite of the
complications, she would have had the baby. But she knew John Hillyer
was the father. So, as much as she disliked the prospect, an abortion
was necessary. The longer she waited, the more dangerous it would be.
She wanted to tell Henry. However, her courage faltered in the face of
what his reaction might be. Not only the loss of the baby, but the loss
of Henry as well. She could stand the first, not the second. She wrote
Henry a note claiming a bad headache and left the office early. She took
the train to North White Plains station, where she had parked her car.
From there it was only a short drive to her apartment. She picked up
food, liquor and wine for the weekend. Maybe Henry would come over?
If so, she would be ready. If not, she would spend the weekend alone.
She wanted very badly to see Henry in her own home. She was frightened,
and there was a kind of safety in being at home. A feeling of security
and permanence lacking at the Pierre with all its comfort and luxury.

Marion was waiting for William, wearing one of her unique cos-
tumes. The color or design of the fabric could never be predicted, but
one could count on its being one piece, easy to remove, with as much
of Marion visible as was strategically possible. She had what William
considered the perfect body and features for her profession. She was
average height and naturally slim with very high breasts, narrow hips
and small buttocks. Weight was not a problem for Marion. Her hair was
straight and dark, worn in a simple fashion, parted on one side and
slicked back, reminiscent of a 1920s flapper. Her skin was olive and rich
in tone. It would never become dry, brittle and lined. Finally, the single
feature one noticed before anything else was a pair of large, oval, deep-
set dark eyes that looked out on the world in a slightly amused way that

combined ageless female wisdom with a touch of the eroticism of the East.

These qualities were combined with an excellent mind to create what amounted to a challenge for most men more accustomed to the typical American standard of good looks. However, during the last few months William had found himself less eager to rise to her challenge. Marion, sensing his waning interest, had used every form of sexual enticement to arouse him, and her repertoire was extensive. She knew she was losing him. The thought saddened her. Not only was he generous and a better lover than any of her other customers, but she cared about him as much as she permitted herself to care about anyone. This night would be special. If, after tonight, she couldn't revive his interest, she would let come what may.

William observed her semi-nude state with a mixture of appreciation and irritation. Appreciation at her effort and irritation at his lack of visceral response. Maybe he was getting old, or . . .

Sitting beside her, naked except for his light dressing gown, it took him two martinis to relax and feel his fondness for her turning sexual. While Marion sipped her sherry, she let her free hand wander over William's chest and nipples. Marion had observed that while a man's nipples were not as sensitive as a woman's, they provided an excellent starting place for seduction. Most men were unaware of their instinctive response to the caress. Her hand wandered down his stomach, ending up stroking his semi-erect penis and cupping his balls.

"Slow down, girl. The night is young." He finished his drink and handed her his glass. "Another, please."

"Three martinis before dinner?"

"Another martini, please. Without comment." He sniffed the air. "I gather from that splendid aroma wafting in from the kitchen that we're eating home tonight?"

"The leg of lamb has about forty-five minutes to go. Along with roasted new potatoes, my special salad and a bottle of Lafite Rothschild." After giving William his third drink, she went into the kitchen to check the meal.

William sipped the martini, idly playing with his penis. In spite of his efforts to control his thoughts, his mind went to Maggie sitting home waiting for Henry's call. He knew she and Henry had not spent as many nights together as either of them had expected. The reorganization of Wilkenson, Inc., along with Henry's concern about Selma now that she was pregnant, limited Henry's free time.

He slipped into a reverie, and somehow Henry's needs became his own. William lost himself in a vision of Maggie. Maggie lying in a hot tub, her hair pinned to the top of her head with soap bubbles reaching her chin. He saw her step from the tub, her body magnificent. Dripping on the bath rug, she walked toward a full-length door mirror, every movement she made bringing out the provocative, full curves of her breasts and buttocks. Her hair was full of lights as she unpinned it and began to brush it.

Marion returned from the kitchen, interrupting his dreams. She saw the bulge in his dressing gown and felt her hopes confirmed. He would stay the night, and by morning be hers again. At least as much as he ever had been.

She slipped off her non-dress and posed naked before him, her whole body an invitation. William responded to her presence and let his dressing gown drop. They met in the middle of the living room and slid to the carpet together. Marion's expert tongue sought his. She turned so she could take his penis in her mouth. William's hand was in her vagina making ever widening circles.

"Lie on your back, darling," she whispered. "Let me invent."

He found a pillow and dragged it under his head. She straddled him, facing his feet. He watched as she lowered herself onto his prick, and continued to watch as she moved up and down. Rising and falling, he could feel her entire vagina.

But he was beginning to lose sensation. In spite of the original excitement, he was getting soft. Marion was in the middle of her orgasm and unaware of what was happening, but she would be aware in a moment. William closed his eyes and fantasized. He seized Marion and took control of her movements. He lifted her up and set her down. His penis became a rock, and his orgasm came rapidly. He felt himself flooding her, and as he came he murmured, "My darling. My love."

Not in all their years together had William used such words. Wise in her business, Marion realized immediately that the words weren't meant for her. Now she understood only too well why William had grown cooler. She wondered who the other woman was. For some reason she couldn't explain, she didn't think they had had sexual relations. Or ever would. It was something in his tone. Isn't that just like a man to fall in love with a woman who is unavailable? But it's not like William, she thought. She had no intention of sharing her discovery. "Not bad, young fellow. Not bad at all. We'll have to think about a double-header."

William lay there. He was shocked by his fantasy, a fantasy of

Maggie. He had to understand what was happening to him, and above all, put an end to this growing desire for his son's woman.

Dragging her dress behind her, Marion went into the bedroom. Now that she knew what was wrong, she had a handle with which to fight. She put on a short, opaque robe.

William was still on the rug. "On your feet, you lout. You need food to revive your lust for life."

William opened his eyes. "Another drink first."

"Another drink?" He must indeed be feeling the pressure. "Yes. Let's get a little drunk tonight."

He smiled. "Exactly my feeling."

"But not too drunk." Marion knew that alcohol and erections did not mix.

William was forced to stop drinking while he carved the leg of lamb. All during dinner he tried to think of an excuse for leaving gracefully. It was important not to hurt Marion's feelings, but he couldn't risk repeating the experience he'd just had. Until he could make love to a woman without Maggie's coming between them, he was not prepared to make love to anyone. He had no doubt he could work through this "aberration," but he needed time.

They finished dinner, and Marion quickly cleared while William waited in the living room. "May I make a phone call?"

"If it's private, use the phone in the study."

"Thank you." Then he called the garage where he kept his car. "Jimmy, bring the car around as soon as possible and wait for me." When he returned to the living room, Marion was waiting.

"I'm getting ready for that double-header."

"Sorry. I just spoke to Henry. There's been some kind of accident at the plant. Henry wants to meet me there now."

Marion wondered why he bothered to lie. He must have called the other woman, and she had agreed to see him. "It won't wait?"

"I'm sorry. It won't."

With a resigned shrug, she said, "I understand. And I'm free tomorrow, if you can break away. Besides, you owe me one." The last was said in a somewhat plaintive tone. She didn't like facing the fact that she'd lost him.

"I'll call you tomorrow." He went into the bedroom to dress. Marion waited for the sound of the shower. She was surprised when he appeared dressed and ready to leave. He wasn't going to another woman, not with the smell of her still on him. Then what on earth was he doing? She saw him reach into his pocket and stopped him.

"Not tonight. Full services weren't rendered to either party. I'll collect after the next performance."

William understood. It was in keeping with the woman. "I'll call you tomorrow."

"I'll be here." She led him to the door and waited, as she had so many times before, until he entered the elevator and the doors closed. She shut her door and returned to the living room. She poured herself a large brandy and wondered who the woman was. Even if William wasn't going to see her, she was the reason the evening ended as it had.

The destruction of Craig Spears' physical and mental stability was complete. His concentration had become monomaniacal. He saw William Carson everywhere he looked: William riding down Fifth Avenue in a large, golden Rolls Royce, William going to the bank with a million in cash, William surrounded by naked women performing every kind of highly erotic act, William sitting in his office dictating a letter that ordered the murder of hundreds of innocent employees. William, William, William!

Spears' assets consisted of one threadbare suit that needed cleaning, one loaded revolver, a small amount of cocaine, a full pint of brandy—with a label that proudly noted the liquor was guaranteed to be six weeks old and flavored with wood chips—and exactly $38.65.

He had found a regular place to sit outside the Chrysler Building, on a reasonably flat top of a twin-hose fire plug from which he could observe the comings and goings of the Wilkenson employees. This day he had seen William Carson arrive, step out of his limousine and enter the building. The car pulled away. William was visiting the company. Spears waited for him to reappear.

It was after six by the time William and Henry appeared together. Spears watched them talk for a moment before separating. Silently, always keeping a block behind, he followed William up Lexington Avenue and across Fifty-seventh Street. By the time he reached Sutton Place and turned the corner, William had disappeared. Spears guessed he had gone into one of the apartment houses or private homes that lined both sides of the street. He would wait, but where? A rough hand on his shoulder jolted him. It was the doorman from the corner building. Spears recognized the building as the one he had visited a few months ago. It had been a large, noisy party. He particularly remembered the curved driveway that one entered from Fifty-seventh Street and exited on Sutton Place. This was one of the few buildings in the city that had such a driveway. People could get out of their cars under the protection of the building and ignore the weather.

"Get a move on. We don't let bums hang around here." The voice had a thick Irish brogue, and the hand that shoved him was calloused from years of holding a night stick when the owner had walked a beat as one of "New York's finest." Spears stumbled around the corner, barely keeping his balance. The buildings were closing in on him. Everywhere he looked he could see smartly uniformed doormen waiting to shove him on his way. But he wasn't a bum. He was Craig Spears, a lawyer and a gentleman. They had no right to treat him like a bum.

His nose was running. It was always running. He pulled out a rag and tried to clear it. Damn that allergy. He needed a doctor to fix him up. After tonight he would have money to go to a doctor. Staggering slightly, he weaved down Sutton Place to Fifty-sixth Street. There it was—an alley between two buildings. The tradesmen entered that way with their deliveries. He slipped sideways into the darkness of the alley. Once again he was in luck. There was a wooden milk box. He could sit on it out of sight of the doorman and still see the street. Spears settled down with his bottle of brandy for a wait.

It took several hours, but his wait was rewarded. A limousine with the license plate CARCO 1 drew up in front of River House. Spears had seen that car often enough in reality and versions of it in his fantasies. It was William's car. He looked for a place closer to the car to hide. There wasn't one. He got up and went out onto the sidewalk, moving as carefully as he was able so as not to attract attention. He was across the street from the car when he saw the door open and a doorman usher William out. He could see William waving away the doorman's offer of assistance. That was good. Moving more rapidly, Spears crossed the empty street and reached the car just as William got in. He opened the door on the street side. William looked up at him, startled.

Spears pulled out his gun and pointed it at William. "Don't make a sound, William." He slid into the car and closed the door. "Just sit there and be a good boy." Apparently the driver had been given instructions, because the car began to move away from the curb. Although Spears didn't realize it, his timing had been perfect. He had opened the door and entered just as William's chauffeur had gone around the front of the car and therefore the chauffeur had no idea that another person had entered the limousine. The glass between the front and rear seats was very dark, giving William maximum privacy when he wanted it. Yes, everything had worked just right, and here he was, alone with William, with a loaded pistol pointed at William's heart.

William sat still and looked at the intruder. Who was it? Suddenly he recognized Craig Spears and relaxed. Even smiled a bit. "Craig, I hardly recognized you." He realized the rumors were true. Spears was already on skid row. "Why don't you put that toy away? We can talk easier without it."

Spears grinned. It wasn't a nice grin. "I think not. We'll talk all right, but we'll talk with the gun right where it is." To emphasize the point, he jabbed the pistol against William's side.

"Then I'm afraid we won't talk at all. You ought to know me better. I never do things under a threat."

Spears was unsure what to do. It was true. As long as he had known William Carson, he had never seen the man waver under any kind of force. But to put away the gun meant giving up his one advantage. William could and probably would order the car stopped and throw him out. The opportunity would be lost. No. He would have to take the chance. The gun would stay. "We'll see. Meanwhile, I'll talk. You can listen." He started on a long speech, going over again what William owed him and must pay him tonight. He knew William kept lots of money at Carson House in his safe. He wanted the money and an agreement that said he was entitled to the money. Not that the agreement made any difference. William would never go to the police. Not with what he could tell them about the Carsons and Wilkensons.

"I'm sorry, Craig. No money." He looked at the figure beside him. The only part of Spears that seemed to be alive was his voice and, of course, the gun. The man's need was desperate. Nothing less could have forced a coward into threatening violence. Were there alternatives? He would like to help, but Spears would misunderstand any offer of help while he held the gun. He had to get Spears to put the weapon away. Then they could talk about help without the threat.

The car had proceeded northward and was now moving up the Grand Concourse. Traffic was light, and they were making good time. His attention returned to the immediate problem when Spears poked him again in the ribs.

"I need money." The words were almost a plea.

William shook his head. "No. Not with a gun pointed at me."

Once again Spears considered. He reached into his pocket and pulled out the bottle of brandy. He took a quick swig. All at once several things happened at the same time.

William's hand came across to knock the gun away. The car swerved sharply to avoid a deep hole in the road and bounced off the curb. In a reflex action, Spears' finger tightened on the trigger. The gun went off, and the .38 slug entered under William's left armpit, splintering his rib cage as it passed through and out the other side. Neither Spears nor William knew that it was a dum dum bullet; it made a much larger hole coming out than it did entering.

Jimmy heard the gunshot, slammed on the brakes and the car skidded to a halt. Spears took one look at William, who had been thrown first against the side of the car by the force of the bullet and then forward when the car stopped so abruptly. Slowly, and obviously in great pain, he was trying to straighten up. Spears was terrified at what he had done. Still holding the pistol, he opened the car door and moved in a lurching run down the center of the Grand Concourse. The sight of a man running down the street was the first inkling Jimmy had that there was another passenger in the car. He slid back the glass divider and looked at William.

"Get me to a hospital. Quickly," William gasped.

It took less than seven minutes to get to Bronx General Hospital. Jimmy ran into the emergency entrance and yelled, "I've a wounded man in the car. Help! Someone help! William Carson is in the car."

The words brought immediate action. An intern on night duty ordered a stretcher. When William was lifted from the car, the intern gasped. He could see the hole in William's right side.

"Get this man into emergency!" The intern had no idea what to do. A gunshot wound of this nature was fatal. He didn't know why the man was still alive.

As William was being carried into the operating room, he regained consciousness. He knew he had been shot and was now in a hospital. He also knew he was going to die. Just like his father, he had been shot by a madman. History does repeat. Maybe not exactly, but close enough. His vision was going. The doctor looked as though he was wrapped in white gauze. It took a supreme effort, but he touched the doctor's arm.

"Take it easy, sir. You'll be all right."

"No. The bullet tore me up." He paused for breath that didn't want to come. Weaker now, he continued, "Tell my son. Tell him it was an accident." He measured his next words very carefully. They were to be his last. "Spears didn't mean to shoot me. It was an accident." With that he died.

# Chapter 14

 "**MR. CARSON**, there's a call from some hospital in the Bronx. It seems important, or I wouldn't bother you."

Henry went to a phone in the sitting room of their suite. Selma remained asleep.

"Hello. This is Henry Carson. Who is this, and what's the problem?"

The voice on the other end of the line was professional. "Mr. Carson, there's been an accident. I'm afraid your father has been shot."

"What! Is he badly hurt?"

"I'm sorry, sir." The voice seemed to gather itself for the effort. "I'm sorry, sir, to have to tell you this. He died ten minutes ago."

Henry was reduced to grasping at straws. "You're certain it's my father? Not some other William Carson?"

"I'm certain. His driver made the identification and gave me this number."

"Jimmy!" The name was yelled into the phone. "Where is he?"

"Right here, sir. I've given him a sedative, but he can talk to you."

"Put him on." Henry waited. "Jimmy? This is Henry Carson."

Jimmy was crying as he spoke. "I'm sorry, sir. I don't know what happened. There was someone in the back with Mr. Carson. There was a shot, and he ran away."

The finality of the words sent Henry into shock. But where another man might have been paralyzed, it produced exactly the opposite effect on Henry. Action. Action that was direct, even logical. But for the rest of his life, Henry could never recall with any degree of clarity exactly what he said or did. He knew only one thing. This was a personal matter. He and no one else would deal with the man who had killed his father.

"Where are you now?"

"Bronx General Hospital."

"Where's that?"

"East Tremont Avenue just off the Concourse."

"Don't move. I'll be there as soon as I can. Now give me the doctor."

"Dr. Greenberger here."

"My father's dead from a gunshot wound. Does anyone have an idea who shot him?"

"I don't know. As he was dying, he said something about it being an accident. That someone named Stears or Spares didn't mean to do it."

"Spears!" Henry said the name in almost a whisper. "Of course." He swallowed. "Doctor, I'm in Westchester, but it'll take me less than an hour to get there. Please keep that name to yourself. You didn't hear a word. Do I make myself clear?"

"I can't do that, sir. The police will have to know."

"I agree. But wait until I get there. My father's been murdered. All I'm asking you to do is wait until I get there. Please!" The agony in Henry's voice would have been hard for a strong man to resist and far beyond the ability of Dr. Noah Greenberger.

"I'll wait for you, sir. But the police will have to be informed of a gunshot death."

"Do that, but hold that name until we talk."

"I guess I can do that."

Henry dressed, took his wallet and other identification. The drive took a little over forty minutes. There was his father's limousine in front of the emergency entrance. Henry burst through the door. "Where's Dr. Greenberger?" he yelled at the admitting nurse.

"Are you Henry Carson?"

"Yes."

"Dr. Greenberger is in that office." She pointed to a door at the end of the room. Henry was through the door before she could add another word. He found himself facing a thin, tired young man with thick, black hair and a shy, almost timid, air. He was dressed in a white surgical gown that was flecked with blood—his father's blood.

"You're Dr. Noah Greenberger?"

"Yes." The doctor's voice sounded as tired as he looked.

"I'd like to see my father."

The doctor shook his head. "I don't think that's a good idea. He's not very pretty."

"I said I'd like to see my father."

"All right. Follow me." He led Henry down a white-tiled hall and through a set of swinging doors. They went down a flight of stairs and through another set of doors. The sign over the doors read "Morgue."

Henry pushed ahead of the doctor. A body covered by a sheet was stretched out on a slab. The sheet had large bloodstains on one side.

"My father?"

Dr. Greenberger nodded.

Henry lifted the sheet from William's head. The white-blond hair was still neatly combed, and his face seemed younger in death. Recent lines of care that Henry had noticed seemed to have vanished. Henry drew the sheet further down to expose the wound—the small, dark hole under the left armpit, and the gaping tear on the right. He turned to the doctor. "How much do you know about gunshot wounds?"

Dr. Greenberger spread his hands in a self-deprecating gesture. "Not that much. What I've seen here. That's about all."

"Ever hear of a hollowed out shell—a dum dum bullet?"

The doctor nodded.

"Think that could cause a wound like that?"

The doctor looked at both sides of William's body. "I'm not a specialist in the field. The coroner will give you a better answer."

Henry covered the body. "I think we ought to have our talk now." Then he noticed the absence of police. "Where are the police? I thought you were going to call them."

"I am, of course. But you were so insistent on seeing me first. An hour more or less won't make much difference now. And we know who did the killing. At least we know a name."

Henry left the room without a last look. William was gone. What remained was to take care of his murderer. They went up the stairs and through the tiled hall. For the first time he noticed the hospital smell.

"Where's Jimmy?"

"Up the street. Having a drink, I guess. He asked me to let him know when you arrived."

"I'll talk to him shortly." There was a pause. Henry's lips grew pale as they pressed against his teeth. "Doctor, what are your plans after you finish your interning?"

"Private practice. No specialty. General practice. Why?"

"How long do you have to wait before you can enter private practice?"

"I have to complete this year as an intern, and then there's my residency requirement."

"How long is that?"

"A year."

"So you have about a year and a half to wait?"

"About."

"Picked a location for your office?"

"Not yet." The doctor laughed. His laugh became a cough as he glimpsed the agony in Henry's face. "It's a little too soon for that kind of a decision. Besides, I don't have the money to pick and choose."

"How much money does it take to open an office in a desirable location?"

"I'd like the suburbs. Either the Five Towns on Long Island, or Westchester, Mount Vernon, or New Rochelle." He thought for a few moments. Unless he totally misunderstood the drift of the conversation, he was about to be offered a bribe. But he wasn't certain for what. Surely Mr. Carson realized that the murder couldn't be covered up. He couldn't agree to that. It had to be the name of the murderer. Carson must know who he is. How much was his silence worth? It might be worth a lot. Enough to open up an office and keep it open for years. "Fifty thousand dollars would do it."

"Fifty thousand dollars? Now I'll tell you what I want for fifty thousand dollars. I want you to forget that you ever heard any names. My father died without speaking. Report the crime at once. You can even tell them you called me, and I was here." He had another thought. "Are you the only one who heard my father speak?"

"Yes. He was very weak."

"If you'll agree to do that, I'll see to it that fifty thousand dollars is deposited in a bank of your choice. Or better, delivered to you in cash. You can do whatever you want to do with it."

The opportunity to open a nice office right after finishing his residency was one Dr. Greenberger couldn't ignore. Had he really heard the dying man say anything he understood? Mumblings. But words? Not really. Nothing distinct. Dr. Greenberger looked at Henry. He was glad he wasn't the person whose name he couldn't catch. The man would be safer in police hands. "I understand what you wish. And as a matter of fact, the mumblings of a dying man are very hard to make out." He paused, then said, "Do you know the Mount Vernon Trust on Gramatan Avenue?"

"Very well. Peter Sayler is the president."

"Can you meet me there at two-thirty on Monday with the money? If you'll pardon the cliché, in small bills. Nothing larger than a fifty."

Henry held out his hand in the traditional gesture of acceptance. Dr. Greenberger shook his hand.

The doctor had one last question. "Won't the police think it strange that you came and left without talking to them?"

"I suppose so. You have my number. They can reach me at home tomorrow. Now where did you say Jimmy, my father's driver, is?"

Henry made a quick trip to the bar up the street, where he met a slightly drunk and grief-stricken Jimmy. The talk produced no further information. The killer had staggered from the car down the middle of the street. Henry was certain Spears headed for Manhattan. He'd heard he was living at the Algonquin. That's where he'd be.

Henry parked in front of the hotel and asked the night clerk if Craig Spears had come in.

The clerk made a disgusted face. "An hour ago. Drunk as usual."

"I want to pay him a quiet visit." Henry slipped a twenty-dollar bill across the counter.

"Try Room 408." He looked at the row of mailboxes. "Like a key? Cheap at half the price."

"I'd like a key." He passed over another twenty. "That buys me something else."

"What?"

"I wasn't here. You never saw me."

"Like that?"

"Like that!"

"As long as the cops don't put on too much heat."

Henry walked up the four flights of stairs and opened the fire door exit to the fourth floor. The lights were dim, and he looked carefully at each room number until he was in front of 408. He entered the room. Outside, a red neon sign was blinking on and off, casting a dim red glow over everything. The shades hadn't been drawn. He looked around. The bed was empty. There was a chair facing the window. It was empty. That left only the bathroom.

He went to the door and placed his hand against the thin, wooden panel. There wasn't a sound. He turned the handle and opened the door. Craig Spears was sitting on the toilet. The lid was down, and he was fully clothed. The smell of urine was very heavy. He was either so drunk or high he had forgotten to raise the lid and drop his pants before relieving himself. Something seemed to rouse him. He looked up and tried to focus on his intruder. When he saw who was there, he nodded.

"I might have expected you." He tried to look past Henry. "No cops?"

"No cops!" Henry crossed the bathroom, hauled Spears up and carried him into the bedroom. "My father's dead."

"Dead?" The word didn't seem to have much meaning to him. "You killed him!"

"It was an accident. I didn't mean to shoot."

"I can understand that, and I don't mean to kill you. It'll be an accident. Except I don't need a gun." Henry's words were hard and sad. Killing Spears would not bring William back, but he had to do it.

Spears heard. He was wet, smelled awful and had neither liquor nor cocaine to shield him from the terror of dying. As for his gun, he had tossed it down an open sewer in the Bronx. He couldn't stop Henry, and he was much too tired to run even if there were some place to run to. The idea of dying had a seductive lure. He only wished he had been able to do it himself in some painless fashion. The fear connected with dying was far worse than actual death could possibly be. He felt his body leave the ground, felt it being shaken back and forth. His head, arms and legs flapped limply. It was too much effort to control their movements. A violent pain exploded in his brain. He tried to scream but discovered he couldn't make a sound. Then the world was gone for him.

It took Henry a moment to realize he was shaking a body that had no movement of its own. He placed Spears on the floor and bent over him. No breath. No pulse. No heartbeat. Spears was dead.

Terror, a deteriorated body, and a combination of drugs and brandy had done their work. Henry's work. Craig Spears died of a cerebral hemorrhage.

Henry picked up the corpse and returned it to the closed toilet seat. He set him on the seat, slumped forward in almost the same position he had found him. When the police found Spears they'd make of it what they would. He felt a small relief at not having actually killed the man. Spears' life had taken its own revenge on him.

He handed the key to the night clerk. "I'd call the police. The man is in the bathroom. Dead. Probably a heart attack or a stroke." What had he accomplished? Nothing! Might it have been better to let the police handle the matter? No! That wasn't the Carson way. They took care of their own. Now he couldn't stand the idea of being alone. Being with Selma was like being alone. He had to see Maggie. He stopped at a phone booth and made a call. Yes. She would wait for him. When he saw her, he'd tell her everything.

Maggie waited anxiously for Henry to arrive. He had sounded almost incoherent. She was frightened for him, for what was bringing him to her. Although he had his own key, he rang the buzzer to let her know he was there. She waited for him at the elevator, and he walked ahead of her into the apartment, sinking into the chair facing the river. She watched silently, waiting for him to tell her what had happened. Then she knelt at his feet and held his legs tight against her body.

After a long time, Henry spoke. His voice was chilling in its lack of emotion. "My father's dead."

"Noooooo!"

"Murdered. Shot by Craig Spears."

"Oh, God! You're sure?"

"I'm sure." He told her of his visit to the hospital and seeing William on a slab in the Morgue. He also told her how Spears had died in his hands. "I don't think I killed him. Not directly, at least."

Maggie thought quickly. "How could you have killed him? You've been here since—whatever time you left the hospital. Since forever."

"Thank you, darling. I don't think I'll need an alibi, but I might. What I'd like to do is lie down and rest before going home." Henry could think of nothing but his loved, lost father lying on that cold marble slab in Bronx General Hospital.

She reached for him. He rose willingly, and they went into the bedroom. William's violent death moved Maggie as nothing ever had before. Not even the death of her own mother and father had affected her so deeply.

"Set the alarm for five, please. I have to get home before the house wakes up." He closed his eyes. She held him close until his breathing became regular. He was asleep.

Then, very carefully, she disengaged herself, got out of bed and went into the kitchen to make a pot of coffee. It was hard for her to imagine a world without William Carson. During the last five years he had been everything to her except a lover. And in so many ways she loved him as one never could a lover. Her feelings for the dead man were so strong that at no time during the hours that Henry slept did she remember that she was in William's will.

She managed to reach one decision. Her abortion. It would wait until after the funeral. She still had a little time.

# Chapter 15

**B**ECAUSE of the nature of William's death, the police insisted his body be held in the city morgue for three days. After that, it was transported to the MacDowell Funeral Parlor in Briarcliff. It stayed there for two days while Henry made arrangements for the burial service. William would be buried in the family plot which he had purchased twenty-two years ago, at the time of his wife's death.

It had been impossible to conceal the fact that William had been murdered, and the murder made headlines in the business sections as well as on the front pages of all the major New York and Westchester newspapers. The obituary page of the *Daily News* carried a small item concerning the death of Craig Spears, a lawyer and well-known man-about-town who had died of a stroke in his room at the Algonquin. No connection was made between the two deaths.

The funeral services were conducted by the Reverend Dr. Arthur Carlson, minister of the Episcopal church William had attended for over twenty years. Since the graveyard adjoined the church, both the service and the actual burial were attended by all the mourners. These included the governors of New York and Connecticut, three United States senators, a number of local political figures, chief executives from a dozen major corporations plus the heads of three large New York banks. Along with the figures of local and national importance were neighbors, friends, employees, household servants, family, and, standing with the family but slightly apart, Maggie Rhodes. Marion Wade attended both the service and the burial. Only Francis Carson was missing.

Henry delivered the eulogy. It was the only eulogy permitted.

The assembled mourners stood under a very blue sky, the kind that occurs in the northeast primarily in late September and October. They watched as the heavy, mahogany coffin with its thick brass handles was lowered into the freshly-dug grave. Henry shoveled the first dirt over the coffin. The rest of the mourners followed in order of their importance. Everyone present was wearing black, dark gray or navy blue. The only color came from the very green grass of the cemetery, the matching green cloth placed over the newly-exposed brown dirt and the brilliant assortment of flowers that blanketed the entire plot.

In the years to come, when Henry thought back on the funeral the most unusual thing he remembered was the lack of anything unusual. The men stood, hard-faced, occasionally reaching into the corner of an eye to clean away a fleck of dirt with a clean white handkerchief, while the women's behavior ranged from the highly emotional response of Maggie, who made no attempt to control her sobbing, to Evelyn, who might have been cast in bronze, given her lack of either facial or body movement.

After the burial, most of the mourners went in a long cavalcade of cars to Carson House, where a large buffet and several bars had been prepared. About five-thirty Maggie looked around. Unless she left promptly, she would find herself alone with only the immediate family. She was entering her fourth month of pregnancy, and although it still didn't show, something had to be done about it immediately. The reading of William's will was scheduled for the following Monday. The time for the abortion was now.

With some hesitancy, she approached Henry, Selma and Evelyn to say goodby. Evelyn had a thin, frozen smile, almost as though she were saying, "Better him than me." Selma seemed to have only a dim awareness of the tragedy that had struck her new family. She understood that William had died and gone to heaven, but the impact of his death and especially the way he had died had made little impression. Henry had been so deeply hurt that he seemed still in a stupor. He would need all the help Maggie could give him once the shock began to fade.

He saw her approaching and left his wife and mother-in-law to meet her. "I'm glad you came."

"Of course I came." What on earth was he talking about? She added in a low voice, "I'll see you Monday at the reading of the will. Unless you can get away sooner."

"At the reading? Are you in the will?"

"Yes. At least he told me I was. And John Hillyer said he'd let me know when and where it would take place. So I guess I'm in it. Didn't he tell you?" Then she remembered. William had instructed her not to tell Henry, so why would William have told him? But now William was dead, and Henry had to know.

"He told me nothing. I knew he had made a new will recently, but I have no idea what's in it. Hillyer's kept it sealed, under William's explicit instructions." He shook his head in confusion.

Something about the exchange told Maggie she would not see Henry before they met in Hillyer's offices. The tone of the conversation had turned abruptly cool. She couldn't say why, but it had.

The gift, if that was what it was, would be minor, but she was concerned about seeing Hillyer again. He was not a subtle man. There was no telling what he might say that could make Henry suspicious of them. She had nothing to do but wait and hope. She never considered not showing up for the reading. If William had placed her in his will, he wanted her there, and she would do as William wished.

Maggie had an appointment to see Dr. Benjamin the day following the funeral. She felt Dr. Benjamin was the most logical person to advise her on the best and safest way to obtain an abortion. Her appointment was for twelve-thirty. She had planned to go during her lunch hour. But since the Carson Company and its subsidiary were closed for the week in memoriam to William Carson, she had plenty of free time for the appointment.

She entered the small, red-brick building on Seventy-third Street between Fifth and Madison at twelve-twenty-five and pushed the bell next to Dr. Benjamin's name. In a few moments the door was opened by Dr. Benjamin's plump, white-haired nurse.

"Good afternoon, Mrs. Rhodes. If you'll find a chair in the waiting room, Dr. Benjamin will be with you in a few minutes." An hour later the doctor was ready for her.

Dr. Benjamin was a short man with small, pleasant features, a thin nose and very bright blue eyes that were magnified by thick, rimless glasses. The most notable thing about him was a mass of wiry brown-and-gray hair which he wore unfashionably long. Although small-boned, he had developed a comfortable bulge around his midsection. His hands were clasped and resting on this bulge.

"Well, Mrs. Rhodes. One look tells me you're just fine."

"I am fine, Doctor."

"Sorry you had to wait. There was a difficult birth this morning. I hope your office won't mind the extra hour."

"No. My office is closed this week."

"Not another depression casualty, I hope."

"Oh, no!" Maggie began to feel the tears forming, and talking became difficult. It happened every time she thought of William, who had been there once to give help and advice and now would never be there again.

Dr. Benjamin was quick to notice. "What is it, my dear?"

This was her first opportunity to talk, and in spite of her resolve not to share her pain at William's death with anyone, she couldn't stop herself from saying something. Her voice choked as she said, "You probably read about it. My employer and friend, William Carson, was murdered last week. The office is closed in memoriam. Though I think"— she managed a short, cheerless laugh— "it's an honor he'd have preferred to have missed."

Dr. Benjamin had read all about the murder. "Do the police have any clues as to who shot him? And why?"

Maggie hesitated just long enough for the doctor to grow curious. Then she said, "Not as of yesterday when I was at the funeral." The doctor's eyebrows shot up, and she added, "My mother was a school friend of the late Mrs. Carson. William Carson was like a father to me." Dr. Benjamin nodded sympathetically. Maggie swallowed hard. "Doctor, I have a favor to ask."

Dr. Benjamin sat up straighter. He was a fine gynecologist and an intelligent man. In thirty years of practice he had heard those familiar words literally hundreds of times. When he was a young doctor, he'd been shocked when a well-bred young lady had asked about an abortion. In time, his attitude toughened. And stayed unchanged. He'd refused help so often, it no longer gave him insomnia. His job was to deliver new life, not end it.

"Mrs. Rhodes, don't ask the question. Years ago I came to a firm decision in this matter. Unless the pregnancy involves *rape* or *incest*"—he watched for a reaction to the two key words but saw none— "I refuse to be of help. In cases of rape or incest, I refer the victims to another doctor with slightly different views. Should you change your mind, of course I'll be delighted to be of service as your doctor. If not, I wish you good luck." He waited for the usual pleading. There was none. She accepted his refusal as though he had declined a dinner invitation. It contrasted sharply with her show of emotion over the murder of William Carson. Was there any connection between the two? Probably not. The grace with which she accepted his refusal persuaded him to go one step further.

"I'm going to give you some advice. But first, would you answer two short questions? Do you know who the father is? And if you do, does he know?"

Maggie bridled at the assumption that there were so many men in her life she wouldn't know who her child's father was. She knew only too well. "I know who the father is. And he doesn't know he's the father."

Dr. Benjamin sensed her outrage at his assumption. He had put it that way deliberately. It confirmed his opinion of her. "Then tell him, and have the baby. If he cannot or will not marry you, put the baby up for adoption. You're a beautiful woman and should have a beautiful baby. There are many childless couples who would love to adopt your child." He broke another rule and added, "Please let me know your decision."

"Thank you, Doctor, for the advice. But, candidly, my mind is made up."

"I understand."

After Maggie left, Dr. Benjamin considered his patient. He was not one given to speculation, but on this occasion, he mused over the possibilities: a murdered millionaire, a widower; a beautiful, pregnant, unmarried young woman who not only worked for the murdered man but was emotionally involved with him and was a friend of the family. Oh, my, my, my!

Later that afternoon, sitting at her kitchen table, which was stacked with notes of names and address books, Maggie considered her options. Years ago, before she started seeing Henry, one of the factory girls had given her the name of a "doctor" in Yonkers on Central Avenue. Just in case. She still had the number. She vaguely remembered a warning, "The guy is an animal," whatever that meant. And she should not pay more than $250. She dialed the number. The phone was picked up on the second ring.

The next morning Maggie drove down Central Avenue in Yonkers. She had made an appointment the moment she'd finished talking to the nurse. The street was very wide, and it was a main north-south artery from New York to Westchester. She drove by the building, made a U-turn and parked across the street. It was ten minutes before her appointment, and she wanted to wait and observe.

The building was an old, two-story wooden house, set well back from the street. It might have been painted white fifteen years ago, but now it needed a new coat of paint badly. The lower story was concealed by a thick, untrimmed privet hedge. There was a gap in the hedge, through which she could see a narrow, unpaved driveway. She guessed that was the way one entered. Her instructions were to park in the rear of the building and ring the back doorbell. As she watched, she saw a dark-green sedan turn into the driveway. A middle-aged woman was driving, and a young woman huddled in the corner of the front seat.

It was now time for her appointment. Maggie thought again about Dr. Benjamin's well-intentioned advice. If only it were possible! But she had made her choice. It was a harsh choice. She had chosen Henry over her baby.

Maggie rang the doorbell. A skinny woman in a nurse's uniform appeared. She had sallow skin and black hair that Maggie recognized as a wig. "You're late. Anyway, don't stand in the door. It might let some fresh air into this pig sty." She led Maggie into a small room with a fly-specked, dirty window. It contained a badly scratched wooden desk and two wooden chairs. "I've a few questions for you." Maggie waited. "First, did you bring the cash?"

"Yes."

"Four hundred dollars?"

"I was told the price was two hundred and fifty."

"Wait a minute." She opened a drawer in the desk and looked at a note. "Yeah. You insisted on a special." She looked again at Maggie and noticed, seemingly for the first time, her simple but attractive skirt and blouse as well as her good looks. "I'll give you a piece of advice. Forget the 'special.' Pay the full price. That way Asshole gets no extras."

"I've only brought two hundred and fifty."

The woman shrugged. "Okay. How many of these jobs have you had?"

"This is my first."

"You in good health?"

"My doctor thinks so."

"Oh, shit! If you have a doctor, what are you doing in this out-house?"

In spite of her decision to go through with the abortion, Maggie began to feel her nerves tighten, and small internal parts of her body began to vibrate. But she refused to permit any hint of her fear to show. "I'm here because I'm pregnant and want an abortion."

"And this is the best you can do?"

"And this is the best I can do."

There were a few more questions. No, she hadn't eaten. Yes, she had taken an enema. How far along was she pregnant? Did she have any idea what the "doctor" was going to do? The woman explained the procedure. He would shave her pubic hair. Then he would insert a device into her vagina so he could see what he was doing. She would be given ether to knock her out. Her cervix would be artificially dilated and her uterus scraped. There would be a little bleeding. She would come to in an hour or so and go home. "Afterward, rest at home for a few days. And no sex for a month. Wait for your next period unless you want to be back here. I'll take the cash now."

Maggie handed her an envelope. The woman—Maggie never did find out either her name or whether she was actually a nurse—counted the money. It was correct.

"Go through that door. Find yourself an empty cubicle and undress. There's a white gown in each cubicle. If yours is dirty, find one that's clean. Put it on and wait. Asshole'll be with you as soon as he finishes the job he's doing now." She snorted. "In one way you're lucky. He's good when he's sober, and he's sober today. But we'll see what you think. I told you there's an extra with the price cut."

"What do you mean?"

"You'll find out. Maybe he won't collect—you can't tell. Anyway, I've wasted enough time with you. There's another stupe due any minute."

Maggie went into the next room. It was lit by two low-wattage bulbs hanging from the ceiling and had four curtained cubicles on each side of a center aisle. The first three had already been used, she assumed, that morning. They were empty, but the gowns were blood-flecked. Disgust and nausea were rising inside her, and she had to go step by step through the process of convincing herself she was doing the right thing, the only thing she could do. But it was getting more and more difficult. There was a semiconscious woman in the fourth cubicle. She skipped the next three and tried the last on the right. It was empty and reasonably clean. At least the surgical gown was clean.

She began to undress. Each successive garment seemed harder to remove. There were wooden pegs extending out of the one solid wall. She hung her few clothes on the pegs. Finally she was undressed. After putting on the gown and tying the three strings that held it closed in the front, she lay down on the cot that was the only piece of furniture in the cubicle. The mattress was lumpy and was covered by a thin cotton sheet. The cot sagged in the middle.

She lay there for about fifteen minutes. It seemed much longer. Then the drapes were parted, and the woman who had taken her money and instructed her poked her head through. "It's your turn. Asshole's waiting for you." Maggie followed her down a short, narrow hall into a brilliantly lit room. She blinked at the contrast. The windows were heavily draped. A table with steel loops for her legs stood in the center of the room. The table seemed a twin of the one in Dr. Benjamin's office and standard equipment for all gynecologists.

The man waiting for her was not standard. He was about five feet tall and weighed less than 100 pounds. Maggie guessed he couldn't be more than forty-five years old, even though the fringe of hair he had left was totally white and his mouth and eyes were deeply lined. His nose was thick and very red with ruptured blue veins showing through. The pores were enlarged and seemed as deep as pockmarks. The only things that gave her an idea he was younger than he looked were a kind of youthful ease with which he moved and his long, tapered hands. The skin was smooth and free of liver spots. They were surgeon's hands, and Maggie wondered what might have happened to the man to reduce those hands to performing abortions. He didn't seem to have anything on under his white gown. She felt a sudden alarm at her own nakedness.

"Get up on the table, and put your legs in the stirrups."

She did as instructed. The robe fell back. She was fully exposed. His fingers probed her vagina. They were both delicate and gentle, as though nature and training meant them to be used for other purposes. He withdrew his fingers and asked, "The old Cunt tell you anything about the special deal?" His voice had the rasping hoarseness that Maggie recognized from years back as coming from constant drinking.

Maggie had heard all the language long ago, but its constant use at this moment stung her raw, open nerves. She made an effort to answer the question. "Your nurse alluded to something, but she wasn't precise."

"My nurse! Get that, Cunt. You're still a nurse." Then he yelled at Maggie, "So she wasn't precise. I'll be precise. You got a hundred and fifty bucks off the price. That'll cost you one fuck. No ass, baby, and you can keep the baby." He opened his gown, and his erect penis was visible.

Maggie shut her eyes to block out the sight. She realized that even if she had paid the full price, he'd have found some other reason. What could she do? She fought against her heaving stomach. Everything began to spin, first slowly, then rapidly. The ceiling was up, then it was down. She fell sideways trying to vomit over the edge of the table. She heard herself screaming as though it were another woman; and without conscious thought, she half fell off the table and ran for the door, down the short hall and into her cubicle. She grabbed her clothes and purse, and without stopping to dress, ran for the outside. Anywhere to get away.

Barefoot, she raced across the dirt yard, threw her clothes into her car, found the key and drove out of the driveway at increasing speed. It was fortunate that there were no cars passing the driveway because she was in no condition either to see them or avoid them.

After some minutes of driving she began to recover her senses and became aware that the white dressing gown was hanging open. She was driving almost completely naked. She forced herself to pull the car over to the curb and tried to find her underwear in the jumble of clothes on the seat. But everything seemed to slip away and evade her clutching fingers, and it was only after a huge effort that she managed to find her brassiere and panties, slip them on and tie the strings that held her gown together. Her shoes, stockings, garter belt, skirt and blouse were left in a scrambled heap on the seat and floor of the car. The effort of putting on her lingerie was enough to cause her to tremble weakly, and laying her head on the steering wheel she began to sob, at first hysterically and then quietly. It was several hours before she was able to start the car again and drive home.

Sitting on the side of her bed, she let the scattered memories of her experience come out, one by one, and join themselves together. The horror would haunt her forever, and nothing had been accomplished. She was still pregnant, and she knew she could not go through another such ordeal.

Something within her had changed. Illegitimate or not, she would have the baby. She longed to cry out her humiliation, her rebellion, her despair. But with William gone, there was no one to talk to, no one to advise her. There were thoughts and more thoughts. A thousand fantastic ideas contended for her attention, but when it came to applying them to herself, they were all impossible. When she finally accepted there was no way out, it was a hard hour to live through. Angry, hurt, ashamed as she was, she would have to tell Henry, and she would have to lie. Slowly she worked out what she would say. It was his child—his baby. Certainly she wished it was, and who knows, maybe it was? Maybe the douche hadn't taken. He might not believe her at first. He might be angry. But she would convince him. She'd have to.

Now she had an urgent need to see Henry, to talk it over as soon as possible. She sat by the telephone waiting for him to call, but the entire week passed without any word.

Henry spent the time at home. He saw no one except Evelyn, who had moved in, and Selma. He was sleeping in one of the guest rooms, so he saw them only at evening meals. The rest of the time he spent behind locked doors in the great library he had shared with William. Now and then he would look over at William's desk expecting to see his father sitting there. Then he would close his eyes and see William's face.

Sometimes he would look and smile at something Henry said. Seeing him in his mind, with so many memories out of order and out of time, he saw, for the first time in all the years of knowing the man, the love his father had felt for him, the son he tried to teach everything he knew.

When Henry opened his eyes they were wet; he wiped them with the back of his hand, thinking it took too long to know things. Much too long. He knew how much he had lost: all the understanding they would never share, all the questions he would never ask and the answers William would never be able to give.

He knew William hadn't wanted to die, and he wished he could believe he hadn't known he was dying. But he couldn't hide from himself his father's last words about Spears. "It was an accident." His father had tried to protect his killer because he knew he was dying. That was the way William was. Henry doubted that he himself would have done the same thing under the same circumstances.

Most of all, he blamed himself for not keeping Spears' pistol. Yes, Spears could have replaced the gun. But somehow he thought if he had kept the gun, William would be alive now. He didn't know why he thought this, but he did.

On one occasion he had picked up the phone to call Maggie, but her presence in his father's will stopped him. There were some questions he would never have asked William even if he were alive. And some answers he didn't want to know.

Then Henry thought about Francis and why they hated each other. He thought back to when he was twelve years old. Puberty had come in a puzzling rush. When he touched his aroused penis, it had felt wonderful. He knew a little about the coupling of men and women. And the idea that if he could find an agreeable girl he could now have sex was very exciting. He was growing up.

He wondered if Francis had ever had an erection. If Francis hadn't, even though Henry was younger he was really more mature. That was very appealing, though he actually felt somewhat sorry for Francis. Francis was much taller than Henry, and at this stage seemed several years older. Although Henry was heavier, some of the weight was baby fat. Later, Henry was to realize Francis had matured ahead of him.

When Henry went to Francis with his great news, Francis suggested a celebration. They stole into the library and broke into William's private stock of liquor. At Francis' insistence, Henry had several glasses of brandy. This was the first hard liquor Henry had ever drunk. He felt warm and happy and didn't notice Francis had stopped drinking after the first drink.

When Henry was drunk but not too drunk, Francis suggested they make use of Henry's new abilities. Henry asked where Francis was going to find girls, and Francis laughed. He said that while girls were useful, they were not a necessity. This puzzled Henry, but he was ready to do whatever Francis suggested. The boys went upstairs to an unused portion of the third floor. When their mother had been alive, she'd come up here to escape from the pressures of running the huge house.

Francis closed the door and told Henry to take off his pants and underwear while he did the same. Henry remembered being shocked at how much larger Francis' penis was than his. Francis then instructed Henry to hold his penis in his right hand and move the hand up and down "like this." As Francis said "like this," he stroked Henry's penis a few times. Henry imitated Francis. He had never felt anything like it, and his penis became large and hard. Soon he felt something stirring inside him. He couldn't control his hand. It tightened, moving faster and faster. As he came, he closed his eyes in surprise at the depth of the feeling. It was over in a matter of seconds.

When he opened his eyes, he saw a small puddle of white liquid on the couch beside him, and his hand and penis felt sticky. He panicked at what he'd done and ran into the adjoining bathroom for a towel to clean up the mess. Francis just laughed. His penis was still hard.

Then he said, "Now I'll teach you a little about the real thing." Henry remembered not wanting to learn anything more from Francis. He knew he was in trouble, but he didn't know just how much trouble. Francis insisted Henry do for him what he had just done for himself. If Henry refused, Francis would march downstairs and tell their father everything. The fear of William's reaction plus the fact that he was still a little drunk made Henry agree. He grabbed Francis' penis and moved his hand up and down. The orgasm came rapidly, but just as it did, Henry gave Francis' penis a twist. Francis screamed and hit Henry as hard as he could on the side of his head.

All at once the boys were rolling on the floor and fighting. They were still half naked. Fortunately for both of them, the first on the scene was William's manservant, Oscar Sorensen. Sorensen recognized at once what had happened. He locked the door, separated the boys and made them get dressed. Then, together, they cleaned up the room as much as possible. William never found out, but from that day on, Henry and Francis were at each other's throats. This was not sibling rivalry; it was pure hatred.

But now, no matter how he felt, he had to call Francis. It took several hours of telephoning, first to Governor Lehman's office in Albany

and then directly to the Canadian Prime Minister, Mackenzie King, in
Ottawa. The prime minister was most sympathetic and promised to have
Commander Carson located as rapidly as possible. If Mr. Carson would
remain by the phone, they would be back to him. It took forty-eight
hours. What with daytime bombing missions and nights in London,
Francis was an elusive quarry.

Henry took the call in the library. The connection was poor, broken
by the sharp crackle of static. Francis' voice sounded thin and harsh.

"I understand you want to talk to me. Why?"

"Because I thought I had to. Not because I want to."

"Again, why?"

"Father is dead. He was murdered."

"How fortunate for you. The Carson Company is now all yours."

"No sorrow, Francis?"

"For whom? Father? You?" Henry waited. Francis had more to
say. "Understand me once and for all, Henry. No sorrow. None. I
disliked him, I despise you. A warning, my dear brother. When this war
is over, whatever I can do to harm you, to destroy you, I will do. My
only regret regarding our father's death is that he won't be around to
witness it." Francis hung up, leaving Henry holding a dead phone.

He'd done what he had to do, and the results were as he'd expected.

The reading of the will was set for Monday at ten o'clock. John
Hillyer arrived in the office early Monday morning. The weekend had
been cold and damp. Monday only added to the clouds that hung, heavy
and black, over the city. A hurricane was moving slowly up the coast.

Conference room A had been made ready the Friday before. In
addition to John, an assistant and a secretary, there were six people
invited to the reading: Henry Carson, Selma Carson, Evelyn Wilkenson,
Oscar Sorensen, Marion Wade and Margaret Rhodes. Though there was
a clause in the will referring to Francis, it was expressly stated he was
not to be at the reading, even supposing he were available. There were
numerous bequests to the servants, and Oscar was there to represent
them. Hillyer wondered what part Maggie would play in the proceedings
and considered again whether, now that William was dead, he should
say something to Henry.

He decided against it. Not only would he implicate himself, but
what was the use? Whatever was in William's will was final. No one
would contest it. And if William, knowing what he knew, didn't care,
it wasn't any of *his* business. After all, Marion Wade was also in the will,

and that certainly wasn't something about which he cared to make a stir. There's no fool like a middle-aged fool in love with a young girl, Hillyer thought. He had no idea he was both right and wrong. Right in that William had come to care far too much for Maggie, and wrong in thinking that his "caring" had anything to do with including her in his will.

Henry, Selma and Evelyn left Carson House together. Henry decided to take a new car. The limousine in which William had been murdered had been scrubbed clean of all blood. It would be disposed of as quickly as possible. Henry was also going to find another position for Jimmy. Anything that might serve as a reminder of what had happened would be eliminated from his sight.

The first thing Maggie realized when she woke that morning was that she had cried in her sleep. But today, she said to herself, there was a reason to be glad. She would see Henry at the reading of the will. And she was relieved to be doing something besides sorrowing over William's death and reliving what had happened at the abortionist. It had been twenty-four hours before she could keep any food in her stomach. But now her thoughts were clearing a way through the horrors she had survived. A train ride to New York and a chance to see Henry would be a vast improvement over sitting alone in her apartment. The idea that William had left her something played almost no part in her thinking.

Marion Wade had canceled all her appointments the moment she read of William's death. Not once in twenty years, except for a few days a month when she had her period, had Marion closed the doors of her establishment. She left River House at nine-thirty. A cab was waiting to drive her downtown.

By nine-fifty the entire group had arrived at the law offices. As they arrived, each was ushered into conference room A where seats had been arranged around a long, narrow table. On one side there were two seats for the lawyers and a third for a secretary who was to take minutes of the meeting. A special chair for Henry had been placed in the middle of the opposite side of the table. On his right were two chairs, one for Selma and the other for Evelyn. There were three chairs on his left: one for Maggie, the second for Marion and a third for Oscar. Each seat had a carefully lettered place card in front of it so there would be no question as to who was to sit where.

Hillyer waited in a small anteroom until the entire group had arrived. Then he welcomed everyone collectively and started on the short preamble he had prepared. "Before I open this sealed envelope containing the last will and testament of William Carson, I would like to express again my condolences to his family and his friends. I feel a sense of personal loss which I recognize cannot approach your own." His speech was cut short by Henry.

"I've heard this before. I don't give a damn how much you miss him. We're here to hear his will. Nothing more."

Everyone in the room was stunned by the hardness and strain in Henry's voice. The sound almost reduced Maggie to tears. It spoke of suffering so deep it demanded privacy. There could be no intrusion. It was not to be shared.

Hillyer lowered his eyes to look at the sealed envelope. "Very well. Miss Evans," he turned to his secretary, "will you please note that the envelope has an unbroken seal."

"Yes."

There was a sharp letter opener on the table. Hillyer heated it with his cigarette lighter and gently worked the blade under the wax, trying to separate it from the paper. About halfway through, the wax snapped and crumbled into small pieces. Looking up, he said, "I'm sorry, but the seal broke."

"We can see that." These were the first words Evelyn Wilkenson had said since entering the room. She'd been puzzling over the presence of Maggie and, to a lesser extent, Marion. What were these two ladies doing at the reading of William's will? Maggie's mother was not an old friend of William's wife, and she knew from the detectives' reports who Marion was. A whore in William's will? She sensed something between Marion and Hillyer, and she could make a good guess what it was. When the seal broke, she permitted herself to express some of the impatience she was feeling. "Will you please get on with the reading?"

"The will is divided into a number of sections. I'll omit those that don't apply, such as the death of an heir before him, and go on to those that do." He started reading a long list of bequests to the servants, beginning with Oscar and running down the list by name and job.

It took over thirty minutes to finish the entire first section. One could see Oscar was pleased. Everyone who had served the family in any fashion for a number of years profited from William's death. Hillyer handed Oscar the prepared list, and Oscar was excused. This was the way William wished it. The sooner the servants knew, the better. After thanking everyone present, including Maggie and Marion, Oscar left.

The next section of the will dealt with charities. The gifts were lavish and covered a wide range of local as well as national organizations.

Then he came to the clauses that dealt with Marion. She was to receive the apartment in River House. Hillyer had been surprised to discover it was owned by William. In addition to the apartment, she had been left a sufficient income to be paid out of the estate to maintain both the apartment and Marion in a very comfortable style. The will stated that if she wished to remain in business, she could, but she no longer had to do so for financial reasons. A certain Mark James was to administer the funds as part of his other functions.

Maggie expected to be next on the list, but to her surprise, she wasn't. Francis was. In addition to the monies that Francis received at the time he lost the company to Henry, he was to receive the income from a $10 million trust. Once again, Mark James was to administer the trust. He would never receive the principal, which would revert to the estate upon Francis' death. There was one additional condition. He was not to contest the will or have anything to do with the Carson Company. If he violated this condition, he would forfeit his inheritance.

Then it was Henry's turn. With one exception to be mentioned later, he was to receive everything else: all stocks, bonds, real estate, cash, Carson House and, most important, all the stock and total control of the Carson Company. Hillyer mentioned that an accounting would have to be made for estate tax purposes, but he suspected the total would be larger than William had realized. It could run well over $100 million.

Finally he turned to Maggie. She had sat through the entire reading with increasing unease. When Oscar and Marion had been treated so generously, she began to wonder if her inheritance was as meaningless as she had expected. Hillyer read carefully and in precise tones. He started by explaining that he, himself, was ignorant of the exact contents of this section of the will. William had written it by hand and had it witnessed in private in the office. This was the real reason for the seal and the care taken that the document's authenticity be beyond question. As he spoke, he looked directly at Evelyn Wilkenson.

"To Margaret Rhodes, my friend and co-conspirator, I leave the sum of five million dollars, net of all taxes, to be paid by the estate. The funds are to be administered by Mark James of the Morgan Bank. At the age of thirty, she is to receive the principal to do with as she sees fit. While I realize this is a substantial sum of money, not only have her services to the Carson family entitled her to consideration, but I have found Miss Rhodes to be a most unusual woman with a capacity for growth equaled only by my son, Henry Carson. It is my fondest hope that this money will enable her to achieve her full potential."

Maggie was stunned. Five million dollars! It was beyond comprehension. Some of the terms— "friend" and "co-conspirator"—were clear. They had been that. The rest of the words were a blur. Five million dollars! Incredible!

John Hillyer understood. Capacity for growth? Who did he think he was kidding? She had been William's mistress, too. He was amazed that a fifty-year-old man could satisfy two highly-sexed women. But that was William.

Henry thought the words unusual. William had assured him there was nothing between Maggie and himself. That was some time ago. Things could have changed. In spite of the depth of his grief, he felt the return of that always-present jagged streak of jealousy.

Evelyn was certain she understood it all. It shook her to think she had shared her confidences with a woman who had sexual relations with both a father and son.

This concluded the reading of the will. Hillyer would take care of further details. He asked Maggie to wait a moment while he returned to the small anteroom to call the Morgan Bank. Once connected to Mark James, he recited the terms of the will. Of course, he would be delighted to administer the various estates, James said. And if Miss Rhodes were available, he could see her right now. Hillyer returned to the conference room and reported his conversation.

Maggie turned to Henry and asked, "Could I, should I see this Mr. James?"

Henry realized she was asking if she should accept the inheritance. "I think you should see Mark. If you're free, go ahead. But I'd like to meet you in the New York office this afternoon. There are some things we must talk about." By agreeing to the meeting at the bank, he was giving his approval to the terms of the will.

Then Maggie remembered. In the excitement, she had forgotten she had made an appointment with Dr. Benjamin, who had been delighted with her decision to have the baby. "I can't see him today, but if I can talk to him, we can arrange another time."

John led her into the second room. "You're a very fortunate woman.

Five million dollars is a lot of money. You don't seem as pleased as one might expect."

"I'd trade the money for his life anytime."

"Would you?" Hillyer seemed to doubt her words.

Maggie grew very angry. "Yes, and don't you make any mistake about it, Mr. John Hillyer!"

Her voice rose almost to a shout, and John backed down. "Sorry—uh—Maggie. I didn't mean to offend you."

Maggie wanted to get rid of him as rapidly as possible. "Then stop offending me and let me speak to the banker."

After a brief introduction, an appointment was made for four weeks later. This would give both of them time to assemble their thoughts on investment strategies. When they returned to the conference room, everyone had left. Maggie was distressed at the distance Henry seemed to be putting between them. What she had to do was going to be very difficult. She hoped she'd be successful. She had to be. The consequences of failure were too dreadful even to consider.

During the time they had been at the reading, the weather had worsened. A cold wind was blowing, and Maggie shivered at the sudden chill. What had William thought she had done or might do that entitled her to such an enormous sum of money? Was it to make up for her falling in love with Henry? Five million dollars for falling in love? That made no sense. Did it? Was it to keep her from disturbing Henry's marriage? No! William knew her better than that. She would never try to break up his marriage.

Her visit to Dr. Benjamin went well. He found her in perfect health, and there were no restrictions on any activities for some months. She would report to him on a monthly basis for the next three months, and she could look forward to giving birth in late winter or early spring.

From Dr. Benjamin's, she went to the office. She asked the receptionist if Mr. Carson had arrived.

"Yes, Miss Rhodes. He asked me to let him know when you arrived."

"Please." She headed toward Henry's office.

She was met by Henry coming to greet her. He was dressed as he had been earlier, but there was something different about him. It took her a moment to realize he'd been drinking. There was just a hint of care in the way he moved and an effort not to slur his words. If she had

not known him so well, she never would have noticed. He took her arm
and led her into his office. With the door shut, he relaxed his effort to
hide his drinking and slumped into the huge chair behind his desk. She
sat on the edge of the small chair beside the desk, a feeling of concern
sweeping over her. It wasn't like Henry to drink too much, and certainly
not during the day. "Are you all right?"

"Splendid. Why shouldn't I be? Wasn't this morning a perfect way
to start a day? Perfect for you, anyway." She cringed at the sarcasm in
the words. "Actually, I had a few drinks at the Harvard Club with Marion
Wade. There seem to be some questions that need answering." Henry
went straight to the point. "Have you ever been to bed with my father?"

"No!" Maggie gave an outraged cry.

"Marion thinks you may have."

"Marion? I never met her until this morning. How would she know
what I did or didn't do?"

"She said she'd known for some time that my father was interested
in another woman. Perhaps in love with her."

"But why me, for God's sake?" William in love with her? The idea
was preposterous. There was a mistake somewhere, a mistake she wasn't
sure how to rectify. A hammer started drumming in her head as she saw
Henry giving the idea serious consideration. And the damning fact was
that incredible five million dollars he'd left her. "What would make this
Marion, whatever her last name is, think such a thing?"

"She was my father's mistress. If anyone would know his feelings,
she would. He was leaving her apartment the night he was murdered.
She thought he left because of another woman."

"Why me?"

"Five million dollars worth of reasons."

Maggie felt a growing certainty that whatever she did, it was going
to be wrong. But she would try. "I'll refuse the money. Would that
help?"

"Of course not. I don't give a damn about the money, especially if
you've earned it. And I have no desire to get in the way of my father's
last wishes. It isn't the money, damn it! It's why the money."

Maggie placed her hands in front of her almost as though in prayer.
Her chin rested against her thumbs. She closed her eyes and shook her
head with pain. "I can't answer that question, because I don't know the
answer."

There was silence, each buried in private anguish. Maggie remembered her pressing reason for needing to talk to Henry. She knew this

was not the time, but her world was turning over, and she wondered if there would ever be another time. She was too weary to carry the burden any longer, too exhausted, too dismayed to think clearly. For the moment she was blind to the repercussions. How Henry might react to what she was going to tell him was lost in a blur of uncertainty, confusion and fear. "Henry, darling, listen to me."

"I'm listening."

"This is very important."

His voice only hardened. "I said I was listening."

There seemed to be no "right" way to say what she had to say. When they were close and their love was strong and without doubts, it might have been possible. Now $5 million stood in the way. She wasn't certain how Henry felt about anything, let alone her. So she would just have to say it and take her chances. The words came out in a rush. "Henry, I'm pregnant. Three months pregnant."

Of all the mistakes she had made in the past or would make in the future, this was the worst. It wasn't until after she had blurted out the words that she realized what a damning interpretation could be placed on what she had said. Her major concern for so long had been with keeping Henry from learning she was pregnant with John Hillyer's child; she hadn't seen beyond that fear.

Henry sat studying his desk. For an instant the words conveyed no meaning to him. Then they surged up and flung him forward with a half-raised arm. But he controlled the gesture and dropped back into his seat looking at Maggie with utter contempt. "And who is the proud father?"

"You are, of course." Her only chance was to try to convince him, to insist it was his child.

"I am?"

His tone and face told her he didn't believe her, but she had to continue to try. "You are! You are! It happened that morning we made love. The morning of your wedding."

"I seem to remember your taking precautions."

"I did douche, but it didn't take."

"That was some day. Two fucks and two pregnancies. I can't say I like the odds."

"Two pregnancies? What do you mean?"

"Selma's also pregnant. That same night, it seems." He lifted his arms and smashed them down on top of his desk. The glass broke and the legs gave way, tilting the desk at an odd angle. He hurled the offending furniture to one side. "Pregnant. Goddamn him! Damn him to hell! That explains the will. I assume you told him all about the joyous event?"

Maggie felt a rising hysteria as she saw the enormous mistake she had made. The five million dollars had changed everything. It made Henry think it was William's child. And nothing could be worse than that. "Your father is not the father of the baby. You are." Her last words were said in a low, stubborn voice.

"Tell me, did you confine your talents to the Carson family? Or did you take on all comers?"

She heard the words through the noise of her world crashing. "There was always only you. Just you."

"Liar! Then explain the five million. My father always took care of his own."

"No. Noooo!" Her voice was a wail of pure pain.

"Yes!" He looked at her with disgust.

"You are the father." Maggie, numb with grief and fear, was reduced simply to restating her position. "You."

"I doubt it. I think you're carrying my half brother, not my son."

"I swear on everything that's holy to me that I never had sexual relations with your father. I don't know why he left me the money. I don't want it! I hate it!" That at least was true.

"My father never did anything without a reason, and there is no other reason except the baby."

Maggie felt all her hope die. They both knew William, and she could see Henry's logic and agree with it. But what would happen if she told him the truth? Sleeping with Hillyer was something she had done under the strain of Henry's marriage. She now realized that if she had told him months ago, there was a chance he might have understood. And maybe even excused it. But now, in his present rage, it would simply confirm her infidelity. And if she had been unfaithful on one occasion, why not on others? William was dead and unable to say he was not the father, or explain why he'd left her the money. She had no choice. Henry was the father. He must accept it.

The irony of the situation was that William had chosen his pawns too well. Henry had fallen in love with her and under conditions that made their marriage impossible. While both Henry and Maggie recognized and accepted the flaw at the heart of their love affair, William, its creator, could not. Unconfessed romantic, unwillingly in love with Maggie himself, his growing guilt over the ruin he felt he had brought to their lives gave him no peace. If Henry even suspected his father's anguish, the reason for the gift would have been obvious. But Henry had molded himself in a false image of his father, as a thoroughgoing pragmatist, and this image permitted no such anguish.

Finally he spoke in a voice thick with anger. "Either the child is mine or it's my father's. In either case, you're carrying a Carson. I'll accept responsibility as the father. After the birth, I'll adopt the child and raise it as my own. Selma will be its stepmother."

Maggie stared at him. "What are you talking about?" It had never occurred to her that she would have to give up the baby. "Exactly what gives you the right to tell me whether or not I can raise my own child?"

"You claim I'm the father. Very well. I claim a father's right."

"But you're not—" She stopped.

"Not what? Not the father, I think you were going to say."

"I was going to say you're not my husband, but you are the father."

Her answer shook Henry and dampened his rage. "No, I'm not your husband. But it's better if I raise the child."

"Why, Henry? Why can't I raise my own child?"

"I told you why. Whether William or I am the father, the baby is a Carson and should be raised as a Carson. Not as the child of an unmarried, if wealthy, single woman. Of course, if the baby is not a Carson—shall I go on?"

Maggie continued to sit, trying to think. One mistake, unadmitted. After that, the necessity to lie and keep lying. With the result that she forfeited the right to the flesh of her flesh, blood of her being, because she had been a frightened fool. She raged against a background that had reduced her to such weakness. The humiliation Henry was inflicting on her merged with the humiliation to which she had subjected herself for allowing the pregnancy to occur. She had never before hated her life as she hated it now.

She heard Henry speaking, his voice sounding dim and far off, and she forced herself to listen attentively. "We've some details to clean up. First, as an heiress, there's no longer a reason for you to work here."

It was as she had expected, but despite her pride, pain and the certainty of the answer, she heard herself pleading, "Won't we be seeing each other again?"

All the hurt, rage and loss he'd been struggling to control suddenly broke loose. He made his answer as direct and crude as he was able. "I'd have trouble fucking my father's woman, though he didn't seem to have the same scruples."

Maggie raged at the attack, though the vulgarity of his words should have told her what a high price he paid for them. The marriage, Hillyer, the pregnancy, the abortionist, the misunderstanding about William's will and now there was no doubt Henry was finished with her. Without realizing exactly what she was doing, she picked up a piece of the broken leg of the desk and, with a wild scream, lunged at Henry, swinging the leg as hard as she could. The leg hit him on the side of his head and knocked him backward off the chair. He tried to catch himself and only succeeded in hitting the floor with his thumb extended, dislocating the thumb. He got up slightly dazed. Maggie stood in front of him, heaving with fury. Henry grasped his thumb and pulled it out so that it snapped back into its socket.

She lifted the piece of wood, ready to swing again, but he caught her arm and easily wrenched it from her hand. Then, holding the bodice of her dress with his left hand, he slapped her face with the back of his right hand, snapping her head sideways. He followed this with a full slap with his open palm. The slap was hard enough to fling her backward, leaving most of the front of her dress still in his hand. She landed on her back on the carpet halfway across the office, her head ringing with the force of the slaps. Even then she was aware he had not used his fist to hit her or he could have killed her.

He went into the bathroom and returned carrying a raincoat. Maggie was still lying on the carpet. He tossed the coat over her.

"Put it on."

She got up and turned her back to him while putting the coat on. It was so large it almost wrapped around her twice. "Thank you."

He knew what she meant and nodded, his eyes filled with shock and suffering. In the space of a few hours he had lost a father for a second and final time, as well as the woman he loved, the woman who had changed the face of life for him. He was about to give up forever a part of his being. His words were very quiet. "I would appreciate it if you would keep in touch. Let me know how the pregnancy goes."

"Yes. I'll have the baby, and you'll raise it."

"I said I would. Would you like it in writing?"

"You keep your promises. People will think whatever people want to think about who the father is. I loved you so much, and you won't believe me, so what difference does it make what anyone else thinks?"

Their eyes met, and he was struck by the lost, even tranquil look on her face. It was as though the external aspect of their situation had vanished for her. She knew they would never be together again, and she seemed to see more deeply than he into the hidden things of love. "Goodby, my love," she said, raising her hand in a gesture of farewell. Then she turned and moved toward the door. After it had closed, Henry Carson put his head in his hands. His eyes were blank and unseeing, his mind unable to sort out or understand what had happened to him or why it had happened. Then he began to tremble. His huge body shook uncontrollably as he sat quietly rocking back and forth, sobbing his grief to the silence around him.

# Chapter 16

MAGGIE sat in Bryant Park in back of the New York Public Library, a heavy rain drenching her. The severe storm that had been predicted all day had arrived. But Maggie felt nothing. Sunk in her own thoughts, she was hardly conscious of the weather. Everything she had struggled against and dreaded for the past months, as well as things she had never imagined possible, had happened. Now she was trying to determine if there was any course open to her. Could she change anything? She had completely missed the obvious, because it had not occurred to her that the man she loved, who loved her, could imagine she could betray him with his own father.

How could he have thought her capable of such an act? And if he could think it possible of her, how could he have thought it of his own father?

From the first, she'd recognized the deep and intense rivalry that existed between Henry and William, a rivalry that existed despite their close father-son relationship. But there were things between them—things such as blood kinship, trust, William's choice of Henry as his real heir, years of living with and knowing each other, the essences of life itself. How could Henry not realize that William was incapable of that kind of treachery?

She again considered telling Henry the truth. What would happen if she did? He might confront John Hillyer, who would deny everything. They had not registered at the hotel. There was no proof. And balanced against the lack of proof on one side was five million dollars' worth of proof on the other side.

It struck her that something terrible must be buried within Henry. Something that neither William nor she had seen. Something that made him view the world, see her, see his father, see anyone and everyone capable of all kinds of betrayals. To trust was to give a weapon to the enemy. The loneliness, the despair, the imprisonment of such a view made her want to reach out in protest, knowing it concealed an inner fear that no outer threat could equal.

Maggie faced the ugly fact of Henry's nature, refusing to let it change her own. Her code was belief in life and in people. She had learned this by surviving so much misery, surviving it to find love in Henry's arms. If he was gone now, it was a senseless accident. But since love was the proper response to the beauty the world had to offer, she would not give it up even now. Even if all she ever had of the world she wanted was her memory of Henry and what might have been.

The rain was growing heavier, and the wind was driving it at a forty-five-degree angle. Leaves were being stripped from the trees a full month before their time. Maggie felt her decision to carry the baby, a decision which had been forced upon her, confirmed again. Any lingering doubts were gone, washed away with the leaves in the storm. The rain-drops mingled with her tears as they slid down her cheeks and dropped into the small but growing puddle at her feet. The wind was rising, and while it hadn't reached hurricane proportions, the trees bent with its force. A weakened branch just to the left of her snapped and flew across the open space only a few feet from her.

She looked around for the first time. The small park was deserted. Water was beginning to soak through Henry's huge raincoat. She could feel her bruised face. It seemed a little tender, but he hadn't hurt her physically. He hadn't intended to.

Another branch snapped. It was time to go.

After Maggie left, it took Henry several hours to recover sufficiently to consider going home. He left the office, hurried across Lexington Avenue, getting soaked in the process, and caught the first train he could for Port Chester.

He arrived home as dinner was being served. While he changed, another plate was set. Evelyn had been eating alone.

"Where's Selma?"

"She wasn't feeling well. I suggested she take dinner in bed. Henry, would you permit me to ask a delicate question?"

He hoped it wouldn't be about Maggie's also being pregnant. Then he realized she had no way of knowing about it. The amazing fertility of the Carsons was still a secret. "I hope it isn't too delicate. It's been a rough day."

Evelyn took a deep breath as though she was about to plunge under water and stay there for a long time. "First, I'm concerned about Selma's being pregnant."

"Why? Pregnancies are quite common these days."

"That may be, but remember, Selma's my daughter. I had a terrible time. I'll spare you the details, but I had to spend the last six months in bed."

"I'm having trouble following you."

"The reason Selma is in bed is because the doctor suggested it. She began to bleed slightly, and Dr. Adams insisted, given the family history, she stay in bed. He'll be here in the morning for a further examination."

"That was very wise. We don't want to lose the baby."

"The point is it is entirely possible, even probable, that the doctor will suggest you refrain from any sexual activity with Selma until the baby is born. That's over four months away."

"So—?"

"Well, I am aware you have been having an affair with Margaret Rhodes." The look on Henry's face should have stopped her, but she hurried on well past the "stop sign." "I see no reason why that affair should not continue. Selma need not know, and—"

Henry lurched to his feet with such violence that his chair fell over backwards. "That's enough!" His rage was so great it made his voice hoarse. "I am aware that you set detectives on us. Now you will mind your own goddamned business!" He leaned over the table, his face very close to Evelyn's. With every word his voice grew louder. "Understand this because I won't repeat it. You are welcome in this house just so long as you mind your own business. I am not the fool John Wilkenson was, and I would think nothing of having the servants toss you out of here, bag and baggage! If Selma must be careful until she has our child, she will be careful. If it means staying in bed or even in a hospital, she will do just that. This subject is closed."

In her entire life, no one had ever spoken to Evelyn Wilkenson the way Henry had spoken, and she was unable to believe it was happening now. "Listen to me, Henry Carson. I am her mother and your mother-in-law. With your father dead, I regard myself as the head of this family. And I intend to see to it that this family conducts itself in a manner that I deem appropriate."

"You're a fool!" Henry went to the butler's pantry and called out, "Please ask Oscar to join me in the dining room at once." Oscar appeared almost immediately. "Mrs. Wilkenson is leaving tonight. Will you see that her clothes are packed and she is driven into the city as soon as possible."

"Tonight, sir? In this storm?"

"Now! The storm is blowing itself out."

"Yes, sir."

Evelyn remained seated. She heard what was said, but she still did not believe it. "I am the head of this household. I'm not leaving. Disregard what Mr. Carson just said."

"Oscar, follow my instructions. Evelyn, you are not the head of this household." To make his point clearer, he added, "Just as you're no longer the head of Wilkenson, Inc. I'm not asking you, I'm ordering you out of Carson House. You're not wanted or needed. Now get the hell out of here!"

He picked up the chair he had knocked over, walked out of the room and slammed the door. Then he went into the library. That night, for the first time in his adult life, Henry Carson drank himself into a stupor.

The next morning, Dr. Adams confirmed Evelyn Wilkenson's prophecy. There was a slight separation of the placenta from the uterine wall. Not serious, but it would have to be watched. All sexual activity must be curtailed.

"I understand. I'm as concerned as you that nothing interfere with the birth. Should we move my wife to a hospital now?"

"There is a family history to be considered. So we'll see. If there's any emergency, check her into New York Hospital. Right now I want her in bed for a week. Then I'll make another examination."

Henry returned to the library to think again about what had happened. He was alone as he had been for most of his life. He thought of his mother whom he never knew and his father whom he had just begun to know. Maggie had been a companion for such a short time. Selma would never be anything except another body in the house. A ghost that would haunt him. Then there was Francis. If there had been any tears left in Henry, he would have wept over Francis. There had been a few years when both young boys had played together and fought together and had been as brothers. He had idolized Francis with the open, unreserved admiration that a younger brother can feel for a handsome, seemingly more gifted older brother. And it had ended as such relationships can end, in disillusionment and betrayal.

He had realized only a few months later what Francis had had in mind that day on the third floor. He was to be Francis' own, private bugger boy. His own brother! Henry closed his eyes in pain at the recollection. Wasn't it a short step from Francis to William's behavior with Maggie, his son's love? It seemed to be in the Carson tradition. Betray those closest to you. Good practice for living in a treacherous world.

He was no longer angry at Maggie. She had cooperated, but in some ways she was as much a victim as he. All the conditions of their lives had conspired to separate them. But at least he had loved her. And no matter what had occurred between his father and her, it did not alter the love they had felt for each other. Though he would never again permit himself the luxury of trusting anyone as he had his father and Maggie, he would otherwise continue to behave as he had in the past. If the world would not be honest and true with him, he would be true to himself. And, as much as possible in an imperfect world, honorable in dealing with it. It was the least he could do as a man.

Toward the middle of October, Maggie received a typed note signed by Mary O'Toole informing her that the New York office was closing at year's end, and Mr. Carson would appreciate it if she would pick up her personal things as soon as was convenient. The note gave her a choice of days and hours to stop by.

Maggie made one call to Mary, hoping to talk to Henry, but she was met by a cool rebuff. "I'm sorry, Miss Rhodes, Mr. Carson is not accepting your calls."

"He won't talk to me?"

"No." Mary's voice faltered slightly.

Maggie accepted this in silence. It was useless to pressure her former co-worker. Mary O'Toole had switched the fierce loyalty she had felt for William Carson to his son. Henry's attitude toward people automatically became Mary's. "I understand. I won't call again. Goodby."

Aside from suffering over her loss of Henry, Maggie spent most of her time at home reading books on investment and making notes of conversations she had had with William or overheard when she worked in the office. As she went over the notes, one fact became clear. William had divided the work between Mary and herself in such a way that Mary handled most of the matters connected with the Carson Company, while, aside from the training that went into making her a suitable secretary for Henry, she handled most of his personal affairs.

She knew more about what he had bought in the way of stocks, bonds and real estate than anyone else, including Henry, knew. It was as though he had started very early preparing her to handle large sums of money. There was no one to ask whether this was deliberate or just happenstance. But since it was William, she believed it deliberate. But if he had not been murdered, she wouldn't have had any money, so why the training? Had he meant to give her money while he was still alive?

If so, why was he planning to do such a thing, and when would the time for doing it have come? It made no sense.

She had been trained to get used to handling money, and it followed from the will that William had been planning something. He was a man in the prime of life and in perfect health. He must have expected to live for twenty or thirty years more. There was no reason to include her in his will except as a precaution. A precaution against what? She had Henry.

Maggie stopped, sat back in her chair, ran a hand through her hair and looked up at the ceiling. The solution had been staring her in the face all along, and she had refused to look at it. Yes, she had Henry, but for how long? He would never marry her. She had seen it that day of his marriage. She had recognized then that she brought nothing to him besides herself, and for Henry, she wasn't enough. Would she have been content to go through life without a husband, without children, without a man to live with in private and be seen with in public? This was what William had doubted. She had been happy, but William saw a day when she would be miserable, when the situation would become unbearable. In preparation for that day, he had put aside those monies, which were not large for him but huge to her, as a sort of passport to another life. Even a dowry for another husband. William had set up the affair as well as the marriage. As Henry said, he "took care of his own." He had certainly taken care of her. Yes, that explained everything. She was certain she was right. And she was half right.

What Maggie would not see, the fact her mind refused to accept, was William's tortured, growing hunger for her. This desire for her was what fueled his feelings of guilt, of remorse. His concern for her was not that of a father but that of a lover.

Though she was satisfied with her understanding of William's motives, it gave no lift to her depressed spirits. She wondered if she would have agreed to his plan if she'd known the outcome. Her answer was a resolute Yes! It wasn't the money. She'd gladly have traded that to have William alive. It was her escape from life on the production line and where it would have taken her. Even more, she had known a great love and been loved in return. She'd had a glowing, if hopeless, vision of all that life had to offer. It gave her a sense of kinship between herself and a loving, striving world. She could go anywhere, do anything, with or without William's money.

Four weeks passed, and Maggie took the train to New York to keep her appointment with Mark James. She was now in her fifth month, and she looked as lithe and lovely as she ever had. Unless one looked very closely, it was impossible to tell she was pregnant. In fact, since she'd felt no impulse to find sexual release, her very remoteness added a quality that augmented her beauty.

Upon arriving at the Morgan Bank, she was met just inside the door by a middle-aged man with neatly combed gray hair and a charcoal gray suit. She told the man her name and whom she expected to meet, and he led her to a glass-enclosed reception room. After a very short time, he returned followed by a younger man, stocky, with sandy hair, wire-rimmed glasses and wearing a better-cut version of the same charcoal gray suit.

"Miss Rhodes?"

"Yes."

"I'm Mark James. It's a pleasure to meet you." He held out his hand.

She shook it. "Delighted."

He looked at her again. "If I may be permitted, I must say you look absolutely lovely. Perhaps being an heiress agrees with you?" Even as he said the words, he would have given a month's salary to recall them.

"Thank you, Mr. James. Perhaps being pregnant agrees with me."

James turned a bright red. It was as though a trap door had opened, and he found himself falling through. In fact, he wished it would open and he were somewhere else. Anywhere except facing this smiling, young woman who had just admitted, cheerfully, to carrying an illegitimate child. In Mark James' world, young, unmarried ladies did not admit to being anything but simon-pure virgins. He was, of course, aware that there were other realities. But it was unheard of to mention them publicly. It was a credit to both his good breeding and lack of a certain type of imagination that he did not immediately connect Maggie's inheritance with her pregnancy. It took about five seconds.

Maggie let him remain nonplussed for a suitable length of time and then suggested that they adjourn to a conference room where he could outline his investment ideas and listen to a few of hers.

They arrived at a small conference room furnished with excellent copies of English club furniture. "Would you like a cup of coffee?"

"Please. Black and no sugar."

After the coffee arrived, they chatted aimlessly. When they had finished, James placed the cups on a tray and moved it to a credenza against the far wall. This left the table clear for his papers. He opened a large folder and arranged the papers in three neat piles.

"Before going into details, I want to explain the basic philosophy behind these three investment portfolios. But I must ask several basic questions. For example, do you understand the differences between stocks and bonds?"

"Yes. I've had several courses in night school that dealt with investments and money management in general. In addition, I was fortunate to be very close to William Carson, who did his own investing." From the look on his face, she realized some additional explanation was necessary. "By close I mean that I worked for him and actually typed the reports upon which he based his decisions. Therefore, I was in a position to watch what he did and monitor the results."

Listening to Maggie, James got the impression he might have to justify his choices. It was in the nature of the man that he actually preferred doing that. His decisions were correct, and he would have no trouble explaining them. In fact, it was always easier when the client had some idea of what went into his thinking. "Excellent. It saves a lot of time if terms don't have to be explained. Of course, should I use a word or phrase with which you're not familiar, please don't hesitate to interrupt."

"I have no hesitation in admitting ignorance."

"In the first place, the bank always attempts to obtain maximum income along with maximum security for the principal. These two conditions aren't always compatible."

"I would say they're never compatible. Isn't every investment some form of compromise? Profit versus security?"

"Precisely. But at the Morgan we also take into account the individual whose capital we're managing. A thirty-five-year-old business man with a substantial earned income has a portfolio entirely different from that of a sixty-five-year-old lady who inherited a sizable sum of money but has no financial knowledge or income beyond what her invested money can earn."

"Exactly where, given those extreme examples, would you place me?"

"Frankly, closer to the lady without financial or business experience."

"I see. Still, you have gone through the exercise of preparing several portfolios based upon different premises?"

"No. It was my understanding you did not have extensive business experience. If I'm wrong, I stand corrected."

"No, you're not wrong. It's simply that I'm having trouble seeing myself as a sixty-five-year-old widow who can't take care of herself. I've taken care of myself most of my life. In any case, please continue."

James pointed to the first of the three piles of papers. "This group represents a portfolio of bonds of the highest safety. Triple A bonds. Mostly utility bonds. You can average two and three-quarters percent on these bonds, or almost one hundred and forty thousand dollars a year income with maximum safety. The next group is a mixture of Single A to Triple A bonds. A number of major industrial corporations are included with the utilities. The portfolio averages"—he consulted his papers—"almost three and a half percent. Your income would be about one hundred and seventy-five thousand dollars. Naturally, the greater the risk, the greater the income." He pointed to the third pile. "These bonds are rated Single A." Struck by a thought, he stopped and asked, "You do understand the difference between Single A and Triple A ratings?"

"We agreed I would interrupt if I had any questions."

"Sorry. But I'd rather be certain than wrong. These are good companies. Single A is a fine rating. Just not the best. Not Triple A. Being slightly riskier, they must pay a slightly higher interest rate. These bonds average over four percent. Your income would come to about two hundred thousand dollars. The incomes are all gross incomes. Bank charges and taxes have not been deducted."

"What are the bank charges?"

"Five percent of your income." He added hurriedly, "For this fee, we manage the funds, income as well as principal. You receive a weekly, monthly, quarterly or even semiannual check, as you wish. The interest is collected by us and placed in a special account where it also draws interest until you receive the funds. If you choose to do your banking with us, the funds are automatically transferred to your account. In addition, we monitor the investments constantly to insure that nothing has changed in the various corporations to reduce the safety of your investments. And—"

Maggie interrupted. "Mr. James, I've listened to your proposals. What I'd like to do now is to make some of my own."

James was taken aback. She seemed to have dismissed all his work. "Are you saying none of my proposals meets your needs?"

"Before I answer that, let me offer a few ideas."

"Please."

"First, I don't need nearly the income even your most conservative Triple A bonds would give me. Also, as I told you, my association with William Carson gave me the opportunity to observe an authentic genius at work. He had some definite ideas that I would like you to consider along with your suggestions."

"I don't follow you."

"Look, let's forget stocks and bonds for the moment. There are other investment opportunities, you know. For instance, you made no mention of real estate. Mr. Carson thought New York City real estate represented a remarkable investment opportunity."

"With buildings half rented and available for the asking? Just pick up the mortgage payments and taxes?"

"Precisely. My living needs can be met very comfortably, even luxuriously, on between thirty-five and fifty thousand dollars a year. At that, I'll be living at three times the scale I am right this minute. Also, I'm twenty-two years old, with no intention of becoming one of the 'idle rich.' After the baby is born, I'll start to think seriously about a new career."

"Then you'll need a house large enough for you, the baby and a housekeeper."

"No. The baby's father will take the child. He's insisted, and for very private reasons, I've agreed."

"But I thought that—" He stopped himself just in time.

"I know what you thought. Apparently, so does everybody else. But William Carson is not the father of my child."

Once again James wished for that trap door. "I really wasn't probing."

"It makes no difference. Henry Carson is the father."

"But why the—" He stopped again. "I am sorry. This seems to be my day for putting my foot in my mouth."

"Why the legacy? It's not relevant. Of course, the information about my baby's father is confidential."

"Of course."

"Let's proceed. Using your third portfolio and assuming a four percent return after your fees, investing about one million dollars will be sufficient to support me in luxury. I trust you to select the best Single A bonds for investment. That leaves four million dollars for other purposes."

Mark James drew back and studied Maggie more carefully. "What do you propose to do with the rest of the money?"

"The United States will be at war within a year. I suggest you take two million dollars and invest it in common stocks of companies which will benefit from the war. No consumer products. Steel, chemicals, textiles and the like. Pick a leader in each industry and only one company per industry. Five industries ought to do it. Then I want one hundred thousand dollars for immediate expenses. That leaves one million nine hundred thousand dollars to invest in real estate. Choose two buildings in top locations—Fifth Avenue or Madison Avenue near Grand Central Station. If you can, make deals that permit a two- or three-year moratorium on interest and amortization payments, just so long as we maintain the buildings and keep the taxes current. We can use the dividends from the stocks to make up any negative cash flow in the buildings. Contact the savings banks that own the buildings and put together a selection for us to review. We'll pick what we think are the best available."

"That's quite a program. Are you certain you want to take the risk? I mean in real estate. The stocks, while not as secure as bonds, can be carefully selected and don't represent that much of an additional capital risk. But real estate? I'm not sure."

"I am. I realize Mr. Carson's will gives you control until I'm thirty, but I hope you'll consider my ideas."

"There's no question but I will. They're not as safe as my plan. And I have a fiduciary responsibility to consider. Still"—he was openly admiring her daring—"it's well within the bounds of a reasonable investment policy, giving weight to your being a businesswoman with the ability to earn outside income."

Maggie smiled inwardly at the shift in her status from little old lady to businesswoman. "Oh, yes. One more thing. Out of that one million nine hundred thousand dollars, I would like you to set up two trust funds based on Single A bonds that will throw off an income of ten thousand dollars each. They are for my two sisters. You'll monitor the funds, making certain their incomes remain commensurate with any rise in the cost of living. I'll supply you with their names and addresses. But on no condition are you to give them any information on how to reach me. I don't want to be thanked."

Mark James considered Maggie. She was indeed an unusual woman. Even more so than he had suspected.

As Maggie left Mark James' office, she felt pleased with how the meeting had gone. And for the first time in a long while, she had a sense of being at one with herself. The months spent with Henry were added to the savings account of her life, where moments of love are stored with "thanks" for having lived them. It was those moments that mattered, that gave life value. She had lost Henry, but she was still alive. And so was her baby. The very act of living would always make demands on her, and she was only too glad to accept them.

# Chapter 17

IN LATE January, Dr. Adams placed Selma in New York Hospital. The bleeding had begun again, and in her advanced stage of pregnancy, it was considered dangerous. Henry drove the short trip from Pleasantville to the hospital in a shiny new black Packard limousine. The car in which William had been murdered had been destroyed, not sold. It was driven to a junkyard, doused with gasoline and set afire. But Jimmy had not been discharged.

While Selma had been home, Henry had played the role of faithful husband. He surprised even himself by discovering that between the companies which were now under his control and running a house, he had neither the time nor the inclination to find a woman. The wound left by Maggie's uprooting had not healed, and this, as much as anything else, contributed to his celibacy.

Maggie lived a quiet life over the winter. Except for twice-a-month trips to New York to see Mark James and once-a-month appointments with Dr. Benjamin, she was content to spend her time alone. Her health was excellent. Dr. Benjamin remarked on several occasions that she was born to be a mother. Maggie agreed. "At least to give birth."

During the winter an idea took shape in Maggie's mind. After the baby was born, she would take the Twentieth Century Limited to Chicago and then the Silver Streak to California. The trip would serve several purposes. It would give her a chance to see a part of the country she had never seen and that interested her; more important, it would sever the tie between herself and Henry. And, finally, it might dull the pain her separation from her baby was going to cause.

Mark James had followed her instructions to the letter. The stock and bond purchases were complete, the trust funds for her sisters set up, and they were in negotiation for the purchase of two well-located office buildings.

Mark approved of her plan to visit California. She'd get away from Carson and the baby. Thinking this, he felt a sense of loss. He'd miss

Maggie. He'd come to enjoy his meetings with her. But it would be good for her, and the bank had many helpful connections in Los Angeles. In addition, there was a branch of the James family in Los Angeles. They were people worth knowing—important and influential. More important, he remarked teasingly, than even Clark Gable or Gary Cooper.

The idea that there were people on the West Coast more important than movie stars was a novel one to Maggie. After thinking it over, the new Maggie realized she was being introduced into another level of society.

Mark James' relations were old California settlers. They had acquired huge land holdings south and east of Los Angeles. Today they symbolized California. And what Mark refrained from mentioning was that in the tight world of Manhattan, Maggie would always be subject to unpleasant speculations as to the source of her money. The groups that would accept her with no questions asked were not the people he thought she should associate with. On the other hand, should she decide to stay in California, with the Morgan Bank and the James family behind her, her position would be socially secure.

Maggie had observed months earlier that Mark James was doing more for her than simply carrying out the terms of William's will. She appreciated his efforts, especially since he asked for no more than the pleasure of her company. They talked about his wife and children, and on several occasions she had spent a pleasant weekend at the James home in Princeton. Sally James liked her, and she liked Sally, regarding her as a sweet, naive woman who took her position so for granted she had no need for social snobbery. She and Mark were very close, and Maggie watched them with affection. Given the proper combination of man and woman, marriage could be a blessing. Perhaps someday even for her!

The winter had been a trying one for Evelyn Wilkenson. Henry had kept his word. She was barred from Carson House. And since it was too dangerous for Selma to travel, Evelyn's only connection with her daughter was by telephone. When Selma had to be moved to New York Hospital, it was almost a relief for Evelyn. Now at least she would see her.

In the privacy of her house, Evelyn had to smile at her new-found maternal instincts. She knew as well as anyone what she had done, and she had little if any regrets about the decision to have Selma marry Henry. That he had turned out to be unmanageable was most unfortunate. She had not counted on that. He could prevent her having any contact with her grandchild. So, she resolved that once the baby was born she would make every effort to restore communication between herself and Carson House. She knew her direct attack on Henry had been a bad mistake. She would not repeat it. She would wait. A different approach, more tact, a surface acceptance of him as the head of his house would bring her the desired results.

As the long, cold winter approached its end, so did the term of pregnancy for Selma and Maggie. Selma lay in bed in her room over-looking the city, unaware of the promise of spring. Whenever Henry had visited the hospital, which was at least three evenings a week and on weekends, he tried to interest her in reading books—about the war, the election, the movies, anything. Selma cared only for her Bible. Months spent in bed had weakened her, and her always limited supply of energy was at its lowest ebb. Her blood pressure showed a tendency to rise for reasons the doctor didn't understand. Dr. Adams was prepared for a difficult birth, but as he assured Henry, difficult births were his meat and drink. He would take care of everything as it arose.

Neither Henry nor Evelyn was satisfied. Dr. Adams seemed too casual and overconfident of his abilities. For once, they cooperated. A specialist, Dr. Charles Benjamin, was called in. Dr. Benjamin listened carefully to the family history, examined Selma and consulted with Dr. Adams. Afterward his words were reassuring, though not as reassuring as Dr. Adams'. "While we have every expectation of a normal birth, we will prepare for any emergency."

"Exactly what does that mean?" Henry asked.

"It means we are doctors, not gods. There are always risks. It's our job to try to reduce the risks."

"Is she in any real danger?" Evelyn asked.

Dr. Benjamin was sympathetic. "Yes, she's in some danger. If she weren't, I wouldn't be here. There's no way of telling how much until she goes into labor." He chose not to mention that her cervix had not expanded the way one would expect at this final stage of the pregnancy. Selma might well require a Caesarean section. Even more troublesome was her recurring high blood pressure. That could pose a truly serious problem. He then left to return to his office and his usual patients, among them Maggie Rhodes.

Maggie continued to have a model pregnancy. It was only a matter of days before she would enter the hospital. Because she had no husband or any suitable companion, Dr. Benjamin insisted she move into a hotel near the hospital. He planned to have her admitted at the first signs of labor. Arriving a little early was preferable to a last-minute rush to the hospital.

When she moved to New York, Maggie wrote a note to Henry making it PERSONAL and PRIVATE. The note let Henry know what she was doing, where she was staying and that she expected to give birth on or about March 21, nine months to the day after she had become pregnant. And she would enter New York Hospital.

The note caused Henry to laugh in spite of himself. The idea of his wife and former love being in the same hospital having babies at the same time was a piece of gallows humor. He would have been even more shaken if he had known that the same Dr. Benjamin who was going to assist Dr. Adams with Selma's birth was Maggie's doctor. If he actually was the father of Maggie's baby, it set a record of sorts. He dismissed the idea as wishful thinking. He was not the father. The baby was his half brother or half sister, not his son or daughter.

On March 22, Maggie, feeling the first pangs of a measured cramp, packed her bags and took a taxi to the hospital. She had called Dr. Benjamin, and they were ready for her. Her room overlooked the city and was one floor above Selma's. She brought several books with her as well as travel brochures about Chicago and the West Coast. Her only visitor was Mark James. Sally James called from Princeton and saw to it that her room was overflowing with flowers. At Maggie's insistence, James called Henry Carson to let him know she had been admitted to the hospital.

On March 22, Selma felt the first contractions that normally led to the birth of a baby. Dr. Adams was dismayed because the baby had neither turned nor dropped to the position where the birth would be simple and natural. He informed Dr. Benjamin, Henry and Evelyn and prepared for whatever might happen.

Henry dropped everything and drove to New York. He wanted to see Selma, but the nurse would not permit him to enter her room. Standing in front of the closed door, he could hear her screaming. As he stood not knowing what to do, he was joined by Evelyn. The sounds of Selma's pain brought back all the memories of her own agony at giving birth. Like mother, like daughter. Only Selma didn't have her stamina. The nurse suggested they were in the way. "Why don't you wait in the lounge at the end of the hall?" Feeling helpless, Henry and Evelyn settled themselves in the lounge.

Then Henry remembered Maggie was also in the hospital. He excused himself to Evelyn, left the lounge, inquired at the admittance desk and found that Maggie was in the room identical to Selma's, one flight up. The continuing series of coincidences began to annoy him.

Things looked exactly the same on the floor above as they did on the floor below. He found his way to Maggie's room, and as before, his way was blocked by a nurse.

"Yes, Mrs. Rhodes is in labor."

Henry listened, but he heard no screams as had come from Selma's room. "Pretty quiet in there, isn't it?"

"She's doing very well. Are you her husband? A relation?"

"I'm related to the baby."

"Then wait down the hall." She pointed in the standard direction. "We have a waiting room for visitors."

"I passed a staircase. Does it go to the floor below? My wife is also in labor one floor below. And Mrs. Rhodes is one of her classmates."

"I see. Use the stairs. It's much faster."

Henry used the stairs and was back with Evelyn in a matter of a minute.

"Where have you been? Dr. Adams has been looking for you. It seemed important."

Henry walked over to the door of Selma's room. He stopped a nurse who was entering the room. "Dr. Adams was looking for me. I'm Henry Carson. How is my wife doing?"

Before she could answer, Dr. Adams appeared hurrying down the corridor with Evelyn running to keep up.

"Mr. Carson, we have a decision to make. You must know the risks."

Henry remembered the doctor's boast months ago that difficult births were his meat and drink. "What is it?"

"Several things have occurred. First, labor has started, and the baby has not dropped or turned. We could wait if it were not for the fact that Mrs. Carson's blood pressure has risen. It's currently 250 over 200. That's stroke territory. We haven't the luxury of waiting."

"What are you planning to do?"

"A Caesarean section. That means—"

"Is there any other choice?"

"We can wait and hope the baby turns and drops."

"What about her blood pressure?"

"Risk it."

"Are you asking for my opinion?"

"No. I'm telling you we want to proceed with the Caesarean unless you refuse permission."

"I give permission."

"All right. Dr. Benjamin has a patient upstairs. Things are progressing normally. The mother is being moved into the delivery room now. He should be able to assist me if necessary."

This last bit of information was too much. Henry brought his hand to his face and looked at the doctor through spread fingers. "I'm almost afraid to ask, but would that lady upstairs be Margaret Rhodes?"

Evelyn Wilkenson's mouth dropped open at the mention of Maggie. "You mean she's having a baby too?"

"We Carsons are a fertile family." He turned to the doctor, who understood nothing of what was happening. "Is it Miss Rhodes?"

"Yes, it's Mrs. Rhodes," answered the doctor, ignoring the "Miss."

Henry looked up at the ceiling and exhaled. "Lord, we thank thee for twice blessing us." At which words, Dr. Adams left Henry and Evelyn, to take charge of his patient.

Evelyn glared at Henry. In the lounge she spit out through clenched teeth, "What do you mean by placing your whore in the same hospital as my daughter?"

"I didn't place her anywhere. Remember, she's wealthy. My father saw to that. Her doctor picked the hospital."

Still glaring at him, Evelyn lit a cigarette. Henry felt almost sorry for her. Even for a non-mother like Evelyn Wilkenson, it must be hard to face the birth pains Selma was having. But when Evelyn spoke, her words were so full of malice, they wiped out any sympathy Henry felt.

"I suggested once that you continue to have sexual relations with Miss Rhodes. I never thought you would behave so crudely as to father her child. Now I understand the five million dollars. I must admit I originally misjudged William. I realize now he left it for his grandchild. But a grandchild by Miss Rhodes? With no heritage? No family? Nothing? That's really too much money."

"How much do you think would have been enough?"

Evelyn exhaled the cigarette smoke. She considered his question as she would any business proposition. "I'd say one million—tops. After all, there are blood ties. But that's tops. And you should have some binding agreement to make certain the child is brought up without any knowledge of you. And that you will never be involved in a paternity suit."

"Very sound advice."

"I'm glad we can agree on a few things. I realize you won't contest the will, but you need an agreement to keep that child out of your life."

Henry had no intention of telling Evelyn that he had insisted on exactly the opposite position. The child would be very much in his life. As a Carson, it could be no other way. He realized he had no idea how Maggie's birth was progressing. Without a word to Evelyn, he went upstairs, pushed open the door to the floor and stopped dead in his tracks as he saw Maggie being wheeled by. She had given birth. When he asked the nurse following the orderly about the baby, he was told it was a boy. Mother and child were in excellent condition. The baby was going to be brought to his mother in a few minutes.

"When will she be able to receive visitors?"

"Almost immediately." She smiled at Henry. "You must be the father. The boy has red hair, just about the same color as yours. You must be very proud."

"Red hair?" Henry grinned a little foolishly. "Does he really?"

"Yes, Mr. Rhodes, he certainly does. And he's going to be a large man, just like you. I can tell from his hands and feet. You can always tell that way."

"Just like a puppy."

"That's right." She gave him a big, happy smile and went on.

Henry was thoroughly confused. Was it possible he actually was the father of the child? The nurse took it for granted he was. Red hair. Size. The elevator opened, and another nurse exited carrying a small bundle wrapped in a soft blanket with a blue ribbon around its wrist.

"May I look at the baby?"

"Are you the father?"

Henry swallowed hard. "I am."

"He looks like you. Same hair. Why don't you hold him for a moment? You can see your wife in a few minutes."

Henry accepted the offered bundle. They were right about some things. Red hair, green eyes and a large baby. He handed the baby back to the nurse with a certain reluctance. "Thank you very much. I'll be right back."

Evelyn was where he had left her. Nothing had changed except for the growing pile of half-smoked cigarettes in the ashtray next to her.

"Any news?"

She shook her head.

Again Henry was undecided about what to do. Should he visit Maggie or wait with Evelyn for some news about Selma? He watched

Evelyn light another cigarette. It seemed more sensible to see Maggie. Up the stairs he went, thinking this was turning into a Marx Brothers comedy with musical beds, except the beds were in the maternity section of the hospital.

He knocked on the door and heard Maggie say, "Come in."

She was sitting up with the baby in her arms. The nurse was with her. "Ah, Mr. Rhodes. I wondered where you were." She turned to Maggie. "Are you up to nursing the baby now? He's hungry."

Maggie grinned at Henry's discomfort. It was funny. Mr. Rhodes! She exposed her breast, and holding the baby in one arm, she lifted the nipple so it could be grasped by the baby's mouth. The nurse instructed her how to slowly work the milk out of the nipple. The baby would get the idea of sucking by itself very rapidly. The nurse excused herself, leaving them alone with the suckling baby.

"What do you think of your child? Isn't he beautiful?"

"Beautiful." Henry was thoroughly flustered.

Maggie's eyes misted for a second. "Don't be concerned. Much as I'd rather keep him, he's yours."

"For that I trust you to keep your word."

Maggie ignored the implication. "How's Selma?"

"They're doing a Caesarean." Watching Maggie nurse the baby was more than he could stand. His loss was too painful. "I must find out what's happening with her." He almost ran out of the room.

Downstairs, Evelyn was still chain smoking. Henry wondered how many packs she carried. "Is there any news?"

Evelyn shook her head. "No, and it's taking too long." A tear ran down her cheek. She hadn't cried in years. "There's something wrong."

They sat and waited. Henry had done what he could, but the sight of Maggie nursing what could be his baby and the fear of what was happening to Selma was muddling his usually orderly mind.

Then they saw the doctors coming toward them. Both were sober-faced. Henry went to meet them. "How are things going?"

Dr. Adams shook his head. "Not well, I'm afraid."

"What's happened?" Evelyn asked. "Is the baby all right?"

"The baby is fine."

"A boy?" she demanded.

"A girl. A perfectly formed girl. Small, but perfect."

Evelyn thought about this. Another girl. Well, nothing could be as much of a disappointment as Selma. And this one might be an improvement. A Margaret Rhodes–type with proper blood lines. "When can I see her?"

"Evelyn, shut up!" Henry exploded. "What about my wife, Doctor?"

Dr. Adams gathered strength for what he had to say. "I'm sorry, Mr. Carson. She died on the operating table."

"She died." Evelyn froze.

Dr. Benjamin answered. "We believe it was a cerebral stroke. She was dead before we could remove the baby. But the baby's fine. Mrs. Carson's blood pressure went out of control."

Evelyn shook off her paralysis and hurled herself at Dr. Adams. She tried to get at his eyes and actually made a long scratch down one cheek. She spat at him as he disentangled himself and backed away. "You fool! You stupid, incompetent fool! You let Selma die! You just let her die! They'd have let me die too, if I'd have let them!"

Henry asked, "Exactly what happened?"

Dr. Benjamin explained as Dr. Adams kept his distance. "We knew her blood pressure was too high. I suspect fear was a major cause. An autopsy will tell."

"There will be no autopsy. If my wife was dead before the birth, how can you be sure the baby is normal?"

"All life signs point toward a normal baby. She's in an incubator as a precaution."

Evelyn had made a rapid adjustment to the facts and shifted her attention back to the living. "I want to see the baby."

"We can arrange for you to see her through the viewing glass."

"I'd like to see her now."

Henry asked one thing more. "Where is Mrs. Carson now?"

"The body is in the morgue pending an autopsy."

"I told you. No autopsy." He realized that despite Evelyn's outburst, the doctors had done their best. Events were not always manageable. He had a daughter, and in the process had lost a wife. "Two more questions, please?"

Dr. Adams had recovered some equanimity. "Anything. I can't tell you how we feel about what has happened."

"I understand. Was there a choice between saving the mother or the child?"

"None. We were proceeding with the Caesarean when the stroke occurred. There was no choice to make. It was made for us."

"When will Mrs. Carson's body be released for burial?"

"As soon as funeral arrangements are made."

"She'll be buried in the Wilkenson plot on Long Island," said Evelyn.

Very patiently, conscious that more than he, Evelyn had suffered the greater loss, Henry said, "I'm sorry, Evelyn. Selma was a Carson, and she'll be buried in the Carson plot next to my father and mother."

By dint of a massive effort, Evelyn held her temper. "As her mother, I won't permit it." She turned to Dr. Adams. "Now I insist on seeing my grandchild. When she's safe, she'll be sent to my house, where she will be raised by me and the appropriate staff."

Even allowing for Evelyn's state of mind, Henry could not allow her words to pass. "Doctors, let me make myself clear. Mrs. Wilkenson may see the baby through the glass window. Period. Under no circumstances are you to allow her access to the baby."

"I'll have you in court. With that bastard upstairs, I think the court might give me possession."

"You do that." He gave further instructions to the doctors. "Please disregard my earlier words. Mrs. Wilkenson is not to be allowed to see the baby. Not through a glass partition or any other way. And when would it be reasonable to take my daughter home?"

"A week at least."

"I see. And while we're discussing babies, Dr. Benjamin, what about Miss Rhodes' child? Will he be able to leave the hospital at the same time?"

"If Mrs. Rhodes has no objections. But I'm confused—"

"I'll put it simply. I seem to be the father of two children today, a boy and a girl. I intend to raise both children. Miss Rhodes has agreed to give up custody of the baby. The papers have been signed."

"I see."

"No, sir, you don't see, but it makes no difference. Evelyn, you'll be welcome at your daughter's funeral. That will be the last time your presence will be tolerated anywhere close to either me or my family. Now, Doctors, I'd like to see my daughter. And my son. Both babies will be called for in seven days."

The two doctors nodded.

Evelyn remained silent. A visit to her lawyer was in order. She would obtain custody of her child, and "her child" was the way she now thought about the baby. Meantime she would see the baby if she had to bribe the entire staff of nurses and interns. She might even ferret the child out of the hospital before Henry came for her. Possession, as any fool knows, is nine-tenths of the law.

Henry and the two doctors left the visitors' lounge. Henry looked through the glass at the two small bundles wrapped in white cloth, one with a pink border and one with a blue. "If I can arrange full-time nurses, wet nurses if possible, to be available, why can't I take both babies home in three days?"

"That's a little fast, but it's possible."

"I believe Mrs. Wilkenson is thinking of kidnapping the baby girl. If she succeeds, it will be harder to get the child back. Possession can be nine-tenths of the law, and I'm certain she is aware of that."

# Part Two
## 1941-1946

# *Chapter 18*

**E**VELYN WILKENSON'S secretary knocked on the door to the library. After a few moments she heard Evelyn say, "Come in." She handed her a message, which Evelyn promptly threw into the wastebasket next to her desk. "I presume that was from Mr. Carson."

"Yes, Mrs. Wilkenson. He insists upon hearing from you today."

"He can insist until hell freezes over."

"Yes, Mrs. Wilkenson."

"Now get out and don't bother me with messages from Mr. Carson."

Joan Aimes left the room hurriedly. Her job as Mrs. Wilkenson's secretary had never been a joy. But since Henry Carson had barred Evelyn from seeing her granddaughter, Evelyn had become a monster.

Evelyn thought about Henry and then, reluctantly, about her daughter. Just thinking about Selma made Evelyn furious. She didn't even have the good sense to live long enough to allow Evelyn to get possession of her granddaughter. With all the advantages that money and the best doctors could provide, Selma had managed to die in childbirth. And to die of something as stupid as a cerebral hemorrhage brought on by terror. It was exactly what one would expect of Selma. Still, no matter how she felt, she must attend the funeral or Henry would suspect something, if he didn't already. She must behave as a properly bereaved mother, even though it meant a forty-eight-hour delay.

The private funeral service for Selma Wilkenson Carson was conducted by the Reverend Arthur Carlson. Evelyn and Henry followed the pallbearers from the church to the small graveyard adjoining it. They stood silently, Henry in a gray suit and his Burberry raincoat and Evelyn in a dark dress, beaver coat and black hat with a thick black veil. Despite a brilliant sun, there was a drabness, a loneliness, a lack of real grief that made Selma's funeral a mockery. It was not the grief-stricken gathering of bereaved that a funeral usually is. It was merely a conventional ritual. Henry delivered the eulogy, as he had months before for William. Only this time it was devoid of emotion. He had so little to say about his wife, and he refused to resort to conventional lies to create a woman who never existed. Selma's life had been brief, unhappy and ended in tragedy. But she had produced a baby who Henry hoped would grow up strong and healthy and who would enjoy a richer, fuller life than her mother had known.

As the coffin was lowered into the ground, Henry glanced to the left. William's stone had weathered the winter well. The plantings, too, had survived. He shut his eyes and pictured his father. Strange, he thought, Selma's image had already blurred, but his father was as intensely real as if he were standing beside him. Every detail of his face, his body, the way he moved, everything about him remained vivid and clear. Henry wondered if the pain would ever lessen. Would he ever be able to forget the last time he saw William alive? He had turned, just before entering Grand Central Station, and seen William striding up Lexington Avenue. Most people seemed to shamble when compared with William. Such as that little man behind him, moving without any purpose, shiftless, furtive. Suddenly a great shock ran through Henry. Like a freeze frame in a motion picture, the scene stopped dead. That little man! Oh, my God! That little man was Craig Spears. Henry realized he had actually seen Spears following his father and had done nothing about it. It simply had not registered. He lowered his face into his hands, his fingertips resting on his forehead and cheekbones and began to sob. Evelyn watched him with detachment, wondering for whom he wept. It certainly wasn't her poor, foolish, dead daughter.

When the coffin was lowered into the ground, Henry picked up the shovel to put dirt into the grave, his face red, tears still streaming down his cheeks. Then the rage at what he had not seen, had not done, overwhelmed him, and he slammed the shovel into the ground so hard the entire blade was buried in the dirt. Evelyn decided there was little she disliked more than an unseemly display of emotion from a man who she knew felt nothing in relation to today's funeral. She turned on her heel and walked out of the cemetery.

Dr. Benjamin was being paged in the maternity section of New York Hospital. He picked up the nearest phone and heard a commanding voice.

"Dr. Benjamin, this is Henry Carson. I'm picking up my daughter and my son in one hour, four o'clock. Have them both dressed and ready."

"I'll meet you at the nursery to sign them out."

Dr. Benjamin hurried down the hospital corridor. He had made no attempt to discover who the father of Maggie's child was; he had assumed it was William Carson. The hospital grapevine had given him other ideas. The nurses whispered about a very concerned, red-headed "Mr. Rhodes" who had put in regular appearances when Mrs. Rhodes was giving birth. The baby looked just like Mr. Rhodes. Dr. Benjamin concluded he'd been mistaken. The red-headed Mr. Rhodes had to be Henry Carson. *Henry*, not William, was the father of the child.

The idea that Maggie's baby was a "love child" pleased Dr. Benjamin. It was so romantic. Despite the distance between their worlds and the obstacles to their marriage, they had fallen in love. Because of that love, Maggie had finally chosen to have Henry's baby, then give up her claim and let Henry raise the child as a Carson. A Carson, legitimate or not, was above reproach.

And now everything had changed. Everything was solved. Henry's wife was dead. There was no longer any obstacle to Henry's marrying Maggie.

Maggie had just finished nursing her son when Dr. Benjamin came into her room.

"I'll be in the nursery in about fifteen minutes with Mr. Carson." Dr. Benjamin nodded to the nurse. "Have the baby dressed and ready to leave. Have the little Carson girl ready too."

"He's taking the baby so soon?" The happiness on Maggie's face faded as the nurse picked up the baby and carried him out.

"Yes," Benjamin said. "But you know this needn't be the end."

"Dr. Benjamin, what wheels within wheels are spinning in your head?"

"May I speak frankly, my dear? As your doctor and a father myself?"

"Please do."

"Mrs. Rhodes, it's clear to me now that Henry Carson is the father of your son." He waited for a reaction. When there was none, he continued. "So I would like to make a suggestion."

"By all means."

His confidence growing, Dr. Benjamin plunged on. "Henry Carson is now a widower. After a proper period of mourning, it would be in the best interest of yourself, Mr. Carson and the baby that he marry you, thus giving himself an admirable wife and the baby a mother."

Maggie closed her eyes. He did not know that when the hospital gossip informed her of Selma's wretched death, she had had a flare of hope. She felt a brief pang of regret for Selma, but along with the regret came a thought: she would tell Henry the truth about Hillyer. She would weep out her shame in his arms. His love for her would come to her rescue. But the more she considered the idea, the less she trusted its success. Selma's death made no difference. Nothing had changed. She answered Dr. Benjamin. "It's a wonderful idea. Dear of you to suggest it. But it's no use. None!"

For a moment Benjamin was baffled. Something was very wrong, but he wasn't sure what. Embarrassed at his mistake, he strained for some fitting way to end the conversation. Suddenly it struck him. "You know, Mrs. Rhodes, you could suggest a name for your son. I could relay it to Mr. Carson."

Maggie gazed at him with a faint gleam of her old humor. "Yes, I am the mother. Why not?" She paused, her mood changing. "Tell Mr. Carson that I'd like the baby named after Mr. Carson's father, William Francis Henry Carson."

Dr. Benjamin lost his composure. "William Francis . . ." His words trailed off. Her suggestion confirmed his earlier suspicions. William was the father. "I'll tell him, of course," he stammered, hurrying from the room.

Promptly at four the Carson Packard limousine entered the circular drive of New York Hospital with Oscar driving, and Henry and the nurses seated inside. Henry and the nurses got out of the car. Henry was racing against time and Evelyn Wilkenson, and he was relieved to see Dr. Benjamin waiting for him in the lobby.

"I told the head nurse to have both babies ready."

"You didn't!" Henry roared.

"I had to," Benjamin answered, not understanding Henry's fear of Evelyn Wilkenson. "How else could the babies be prepared?"

"I brought two registered nurses for that. You should not have said a word to anybody." He stopped. "Even the switchboard could be paid off." He could have kicked himself. William had warned him that if you don't want someone to do or say something, tell them. Don't expect them to read your mind. "Never mind. Let's find the babies."

Dr. Benjamin led the way, followed by Henry and the nurses. Oscar remained with the limousine ready to move as soon as they returned.

The head nurse was waiting at the elevator. "Dr. Benjamin, the baby boy is in the nursery with the blue blanket and the name tag of

Carson. He's ready, and I can give him to you. But the baby girl is in the incubator."

"I ordered her removed yesterday."

"Yes, but her reaction was troublesome, so I returned her an hour ago."

"What was wrong, Higgins?"

Henry interrupted. "Dr. Benjamin, would you please take the nurses and find my son while I have a few words in private with Nurse Higgins."

Dr. Benjamin hesitated, and Henry lost his temper. "Doctor, take Mrs. Rosen and Miss Kelly and find my son! I will find my daughter!" Dr. Benjamin gestured toward the nurses to follow him to the nursery.

Henry glared at the head nurse. "Miss Higgins, Mrs. Wilkenson offered you money to prevent me from finding my daughter. She can't be in an incubator, since Mrs. Wilkenson will be here herself any minute to pick her up. So where is she?" He took out his wallet. "I'll pay you double whatever she offered." Knowing Evelyn only paid on delivery, he added, "And I'll pay you now if you take me to my daughter."

Ethel Higgins was terrified, but seeing the checkbook, she asked, "How do I know I can trust you?"

"How do you know you can trust her?"

"She's already given me five thousand dollars."

Evelyn's getting smarter in her old age, Henry thought. "What's the final price?" he asked.

"Twenty thousand dollars more."

"I'll give you fifty thousand, and an extra five thousand to return to Mrs. Wilkenson for defaulting on your contract."

"She paid me with a certified check."

"So will I." Henry was impressed by Evelyn's knowledge of human nature but not surprised. He opened his wallet, pulled out a check and showed it to the nurse. The check was certified by the County Trust, with an empty space for the amount to be written in. Ethel Higgins was impressed. This must be a very rich man. "Make out the check to Catherine Wilder, my mother, for fifty-five thousand."

Henry wrote the check, and as he wrote he asked, "Where's my daughter?"

"In the nursery with the other babies. I changed her blanket to blue and put my father's name, Reginald Wilder, on her name tag."

"Does Evelyn know that?" Henry handed Higgins the check.

"Yes. She plans to take both babies and return your son."

"Right. Let's go." He followed Nurse Higgins quickly to the elevator bank. They arrived just in time to see doors of one of the two elevators opposite the nursery starting to close. Inside were both his nurses. Mrs. Rosen was holding a baby wrapped in a blanket edged in blue. "Where's Benjamin?" Henry shouted.

"In the incubator room looking for the girl," Kelly answered.

"Miss Kelly, wait for me in the lobby! Mrs. Rosen, get in the car!" Henry yelled as the door closed. He turned to Higgins. "How come Benjamin didn't recognize the baby?"

"Nobody recognizes newborn babies but their mothers." She stared at Henry. "If Dr. Benjamin finds out what I've done, I'll be fired."

"How did Mrs. Wilkenson propose to deal with that?"

"She knows Dr. Benjamin's wife. She meant to pour out her grief over her daughter and say I helped her out of the goodness of my heart."

"Get me the baby, and I'll go one better. The maternity wing will receive a sizable donation from the Carson Company in grateful recognition of Dr. Benjamin's abilities."

Higgins laughed. "Wait here." She entered the nursery. Within minutes she was back holding a baby wrapped in a blanket edged in blue. Henry gasped. He'd been too weary to realize it sooner, but the baby was the spitting image of Evelyn. He hoped she'd outgrow that face. He raced for the second elevator; its open doors were about to close. An eternity later the elevator reached the main floor. Thankfully, when the doors opened, Miss Kelly was waiting to take the baby.

"Another boy?" she asked. "I thought it was a girl."

"Don't ask questions. Move!"

The nurse hurried after Henry. When they arrived at the door, another limousine was parked behind the Carson Packard, and three heavy-set men were running toward the Packard. An older woman in a beaver coat and hat sat in the rear seat of the second limousine, watching.

Oscar had been leaning against the fender of the car, but when he saw the men approaching, he yelled to the nurse inside the car holding the baby, "Lock all the doors." Two of the men jumped him. One pinned his arms while the other began punching him—a left, then a right, then a left. At the same time, the third man tried to smash the side window of the Packard where the nurse sat protecting the baby.

"Stay here," Henry said to the young nurse.

One would not have thought a man of Henry's size could move with such speed. He reached the man trying to break into the car in an instant, grabbing him from behind with one hand and yanking him away as though he were no bigger than a child. Then with his free hand he hit the man squarely in the face. The punch had the full weight of his body behind it. There was the sound of a bone breaking. Henry threw the man into the newly flowering tulips and ran to help Oscar.

The larger of the two men, the one holding Oscar, saw him coming. He released his grip and walked, almost contemptuously, to meet Henry. He was tall and strong. All he saw was a reasonably large, red-haired man in a trench coat. Nothing to worry a professional. When they met, he feinted with his right and hooked with his left, intending to follow the hook with a right cross to end the fight. Henry didn't bother to step inside the hook or actually block it with his arm. He caught the man's fist and held it. Then he caught the automatic follow-up right cross in his left hand and held that. Henry closed his hands, crunching the man's fists. Bones grated together, then snapped. Henry released the man's hands and allowed him to fall to the ground, where he lay frozen with pain. He then turned his attention to Oscar, who, once his arms had been freed, was able to cover his face and most of his body. The third thug, having seen what happened to his accomplices, forgot about Oscar and took off down the street toward York Avenue.

After Nurse Kelly was seated next to Nurse Sobel, Henry helped Oscar into the front seat of the car. "Sit here. I'll drive."

He started to get behind the wheel when he saw Evelyn Wilkenson approaching him. In a minute they were face to face. "Henry Carson"— her face was venomous— "I'll have you up on kidnapping charges."

"Evelyn, you are not a stupid woman. I can't kidnap my own children." He lowered his face so their eyes were on the same level. "Evelyn, leave me alone. If you don't, you'll be very sorry."

Evelyn's response was in character. She spit in his face.

Henry wiped his face, got in his car and drove off.

A week later, when Dr. Benjamin discharged Maggie from the hospital, he was full of news. "I understand you're going to California, Mrs. Rhodes. I've a going-away present for you regarding your son." He wanted to measure the effect of his words, but Maggie's face told him nothing. "Henry Carson had his daughter christened Mary Nathalia Carson and the boy William Henry Carson."

"Thank you, Dr. Benjamin, for relaying my wishes."

"No, Mrs. Rhodes, I can't take credit. I never had a chance to speak to Mr. Carson. It was his own idea entirely. The only difference is that the boy must be known as Will, not William."

The news told her clearly how deeply Henry was committed to the idea that William was the baby's father. "Mr. Carson and I seem to be of one mind. But thank you for your 'best efforts.' Now I must go. The cab is waiting." And she walked swiftly across the lobby.

Later that morning, Dr. Benjamin thought about the strange case of Henry Carson and Maggie Rhodes. His musing was interrupted by the telephone. "Dr. Benjamin here," he said.

"Benjamin, this is Henry Carson. I've tried to reach Mrs. Rhodes. Where is she?"

"She checked out of the hospital. I don't know where she is."

"Damn it! I wanted to ask her something about Will."

"Is there anything I can do?"

"You are not the baby's mother. Will has two webbed toes. The nurses tell me it's neither unusual nor dangerous. It's a hereditary trait. There are no webbed toes in the Carson family, and I don't remember if Maggie—" He stopped and gave a short laugh. "I wanted to know if webbed toes ran in her family."

"I can't answer that. I know she doesn't have them."

"Hmmm . . ." There was a short silence at the other end of the phone. "I'll have to ask her the next time we meet."

"It may be a while. She's off to California."

"Thank you, Dr. Benjamin. Goodby." Henry Carson hung up.

The conversation with Henry confused Dr. Benjamin. His certainty about William's role in the affair was again open to question. In fact, everything was open to question. What had actually happened? What had caused the separation between Maggie and Henry if it wasn't William? He shook his head. There were some things not worth thinking about because one never got answers.

# Chapter 19

**M**AGGIE'S train ride to Chicago was her first experience on a cross-country train. The people, the arrangements—dining car and sleeping quarters—everything in the train fascinated her. By the time she finished dinner, it was too dark to see any landscape, and she fell asleep feeling cheated. But Chicago made up for her loss. It was her first encounter with a city that was American to the bone. It was full of a raw, passionate energy to do and to keep doing. A cab driver told her, "If you can't find work in Chicago, you can't find it anywhere."

The people dressed the same as New Yorkers, and the language was the same, though spoken more slowly, and she heard no exotic accents. Still, they were different. Their faces were different. She saw no Modiglianis. No El Grecos walked the streets. She saw farmlands and silos, tidy houses and trees in their friendly expressions. There was nothing extraordinary about them, and yet somehow she felt almost everything of America was in them. And when she thought of the Golden West, as they called it, she thought how closely the words matched her own vision of a life more fortunate and happy than the one she had known.

Maggie heard the final "All aboard!" with delight. Then the Silver Streak started its soft glide into the West.

Maggie's car was called the "Silver Penthouse." It contained a drawing room, three bedrooms—one of which was hers—and, best of all, the Vista Dome Lounge.

The train had pulled out of Union Station promptly at three-thirty P.M. The trip was scheduled to take fifty hours and thirty-one minutes. Given the two-hour difference between Chicago and Los Angeles, Maggie estimated arrival in Los Angeles at about four P.M. the day after tomorrow. With a new world before her, she slipped into a chair in the Vista Dome Lounge feeling like a visitor to another planet. Outside the window the blue sky trembled over wide fields of newly planted corn.

For most of the trip, Maggie sat hypnotized, missing meals and never noticing. Railway stations, depots, freight cars, station yards, towns—a town named Media—rushed past. Then they were roaring down to the Mississippi.

Maggie slept and opened her eyes in Colorado. She hurried through breakfast to get back to her seat in the Vista Dome. She heard the whistle cry wailed back, far flung, as the train rushed round a bend, and what she saw made her breath stop. She had thought those were white clouds way off in the west, but those white clouds were not clouds. It was snow on the snow-capped Rockies. The roof of America.

Pastures flew by, and hollows and gulches and incredible convolutions of the earth. The train was climbing in the mountains. As the roaring engines moved along the track, Maggie felt a strange wild thrill at being there. The train twisted up grades and snaked round curves. The great splendor of the Rockies was upon her.

As the hours passed, Maggie lost all awareness of train sounds and movement. In the world she was watching, time had no meaning. She felt she was traveling not only in space, but backward in history. This was the land of the Conquistadors and the Padres of old Spain, the land of pathfinders and traders. She felt an intangible kinship with these early seekers and builders of America. They grasped the limitless frontier of the country. America had no limits. It belonged to those who were able to think, feel, and see, and who hungered for it. Maggie hungered for it all.

Plunging down the El Cajon grade, the Silver Streak reached San Bernardino. Then it hurtled on through orange groves and Pasadena. At four P.M. on the dot, the Silver Streak pulled into Union Station, Los Angeles. Within the train was the kind of excitement that the end of a long journey usually awakens. All the expressions from eagerness to apprehension could be seen on the faces of the passengers. The look on Maggie's face alone combined expectancy, fear and hope.

The train glided into the station and slid to a stop exactly three feet from the bumper at the end of the line. Maggie packed, and now she was washed, combed and ready to leave. It seemed a good idea to allow the first rush from the coaches to dissipate before she started looking for Anthony James, Mark's cousin, who was supposed to meet her. Mark had assured her that his California relatives would welcome her. He'd shown her the letter from Angela James, also his cousin and daughter of the late Anthony and Joan James. A snapshot of her brother, Anthony James, Jr., was enclosed. He'd scribbled on the back that she'd recognize him by the rose in his teeth.

The station was almost empty when Maggie left the train. Anthony James was nowhere in sight. Wondering if somehow he'd misunderstood the day of her arrival, Maggie asked two redcaps to help her.

By the time the redcaps had assembled her baggage, the station was empty. Suddenly a perspiring young man appeared at the other end, bounding toward them, waving and shouting, "Miss Rhodes! Miss Rhodes!" He was wearing white flannel slacks, white sneakers and socks, a short-sleeved white tennis shirt and a white cable-knit sweater looped around his neck and tied by the sleeves. Anthony James, Maggie thought. Nice of him to come at all.

Racing up to her, he grinned. "I'm the late Anthony James, otherwise known as Tony or Darling. Take your choice. And you're Miss Rhodes? You *are* Miss Rhodes? And is my face red?"

"It looks pretty tan to me."

"I am late. And I don't ask you to excuse me. It's not a personality flaw. Punctuality is the hobgoblin of little minds."

"I thought the quote involved consistency."

"Educated as well as beautiful. What a pleasant surprise. Why is it one always expects beautiful women to be dumb? The truth is I expected Zazu Pitts."

Maggie felt a mixture of impatience and amusement with this impudent young man. "And for Zazu Pitts you'd be late."

"Later than usual. Plain women bore me." Then, turning to the redcaps, he said, "Boys! Follow me. We'll take the luggage to my car."

"I was going to stay at the Beverly Hills."

"Nonsense. Angela and I rattle around in a thirty-room shack on Wilshire. I'm sure we can find a suite for you." He turned back to the porters. "My car is parked right outside the station. Now let's pick up our feet and move along, boys!"

When the redcaps were out of hearing, Maggie said, "You might call them porters. They are men—not boys."

"I might do a lot of things I don't. I am known to be spoiled, arrogant, a wastrel. Particularly, I waste my talents. But many women put themselves out to be nice to me. Wouldn't you?"

"I try to be nice to everyone." Maggie was slightly angry at his flirtatious teasing. He was so childishly insolent.

Tony James was very tall, slim, and if you were to pass him on the street, you would know without being told that he was a very rich young man. His hair was blond, blonder than it seemed in the snapshot, almost flaxen. His nose was crooked, like Henry's. Maybe he'd bumped into a door or a fist? But the crooked nose made his face more masculine.

Otherwise he'd have been too handsome, his features too perfect. Looking at him as he guided her through the station, Maggie thought that if California hadn't been invented, they'd have had to invent it for Tony James.

They arrived at his car, which was illegally parked in front of the station. A policeman was examining it, undecided what to do. He knew very well what to do, legally, but the car intimidated him. It was a white Rolls Royce convertible. The license plate said JAMES 1. The policeman didn't want to step on the wrong toes. Having seen the policeman, the redcaps stopped some yards away.

Tony said to Maggie, "Wait. I have some official duties to perform."

He walked up to the policeman, had a few words, and from where Maggie stood, she saw money change hands. Then the policeman left, and Tony signaled the redcaps to come to the car. He said to Maggie, "You think I bribed a city official. I didn't. I gave him a gift, a little extra money for a birthday present for his kid."

"How generous."

"I have a generous nature."

"Why did you park illegally in the first place?"

"Convenience. What an observant young woman. Here only a half hour and you've already grasped the intricacies of L.A. parking laws."

"I have a deductive mind."

"That's unfeminine." He opened the door to the front seat for Maggie to slide in next to the driver. She was momentarily confused, then realized why. The car had a right-hand drive. "Did you buy this in England?"

"No. Angel—short for Angela—my sister, bought it in L.A. from Gary Cooper. They're old buddies, and she likes this kind of thing. I thought it would give us the space for your luggage."

The offhand name-dropping amused Maggie. It was so much in Tony's style. But she was relieved that the bags fitted neatly into the rear seat and the huge steamer trunk could be strapped to a special trunk rack.

Tony made a number of detours on the way home, to give Maggie a brief sightseeing tour. She was fascinated to see the Chinese Theatre on Hollywood Boulevard, the entrances to the various studio back lots, the Brown Derby restaurant. But beyond the glamour of Hollywood what really caught her imagination was the Pasadena Freeway. It was a relatively flat road with gentle grades, almost no curves, and off and on ramps that did not interfere with the flow of traffic. Two lanes going in each direction were separated by wide grassy islands. At times the freeway crossed Los Angeles streets—on bridges, so there was never any interruption of the traffic.

Noting Maggie's interest, Tony asked, "Are you a freeway collector?"

"No, I collect omens. I've never seen anything like it in the East."

"I'm glad it was completed in time for you to applaud it. It's part of a network of freeways being planned to cut through L.A. and extend into Orange County. Pretty futuristic thinking, I'd say."

"It is. This state's going to run on wheels. Car wheels. Cars will go everywhere."

"You should be a city planner."

Maggie smiled. "I'd first need a city to plan."

The James house on Wilshire Boulevard looked to Maggie like a house that belonged in another place. But the great red-brick and limestone mass with its multi-mullioned windows and stone balustrades seemed cramped by the surrounding lawn. Maggie wondered what was in the architect's mind to design such a house for such a lot. Though not as huge or as graceful as Carson House, it was still a stately mansion and deserved, if not the 100 acres surrounding Carson House, at least a large area. But like some bad architectural joke, the impressive building was set on an acre and a half plot.

Tony took the car around to stop in front of a great door. He had barely braked when the front door was opened by a man in white duck pants and a white linen jacket.

"Where's Miss James? Our guest has arrived."

"At the pool, sir. With friends."

"No more than five, I hope. Jack, take our guest's luggage to the Blue Room. She'll be up later. I want her to meet Miss James first."

As they walked through the house, Maggie noticed the fine English furniture and eighteenth- and nineteenth-century art objects. There were paintings she recognized by Sir Joshua Reynolds, Thomas Gainsborough and John Singer Sargent. Maggie revised her opinion of Tony James. He could not be simply an arrogant, spoiled young man, to use his own words. Not if he grew up in this kind of home environment.

Behind the main house, Maggie found a typical California scene that sharply contrasted with the mansion's formality. There was a large pool, an elegant pool house, patio tables and chairs and several young people lounging in bathing suits beside the pool. A young woman lay under an umbrella sipping what looked like a martini and writing on a pad. A pitcher of martinis was on the table beside her. Her bathing suit was two pieces of shiny black. The straps were pulled off her shoulders. Her skin, a ruddy brown, was set off by a string of creamy pearls. She had thick, dark gold hair, and her face was cool and lovely. When she saw Tony, she gave one of those laughs that is never reflected in the laugher's eyes. A handsome young man in a visored tennis hat and blue trunks was seated at her feet.

"Angel, this is Maggie Rhodes." Tony moved ahead of Maggie, bent over the blonde woman and kissed her lightly on the lips. "Why, sister dear, your breath is rich with martinis."

"Tony, pet, you know that underneath that scent of martinis is more martinis. How do you do, Maggie Rhodes? Come and meet Dudley. Dudley's family does something in real estate."

Maggie felt uncomfortable. The cool, proud face concealed something. There was an anxiety in her eyes that only someone with Maggie's history would recognize. "How do you do, Angela?"

"Call me Angel, honey. And have a martini. And slip on a bathing suit—you'll feel more at home."

Maggie had been feeling overdressed, but a swimsuit seemed the other extreme. "I didn't bring one. A silly oversight."

"You can wear one of mine. We're about the same size."

"Thank you, but I've had a long train ride. I think I'll skip the pool for now."

Tony teased, "Do you Eastern types know how to swim?"

"I swim like a fish. I also play bridge. And tap dance."

"Can you sit a horse?"

"I'm a marvel on the merry-go-round."

Angel watched Maggie keep Tony in line with approval. "Fine fellow, isn't he? Handsome, a perfect gentleman, and he plays tennis in his sleep."

"Maggie, believe nothing and everything she says about me," Tony said, disappearing into the pool house.

"Do you like Los Angeles, Miss Rhodes?" Dudley asked.

"What I've seen, yes. The openness, the hills around it, the nearness to the Pacific. It's not at all like a city."

"It isn't a city. Los Angeles is six towns in search of a city. But if you like open spaces, the place to see is Orange County. It's the wave of the future."

"Orange County?" Maggie's brow wrinkled as she tried to remember where she'd heard the words before. "What is Orange County?"

"Dear girl, don't take Dudley too seriously." Angel's tone was full of good-natured exasperation. "Dudley's just written a book called *Promised Land*, and he wants me to review it. I review books for the *L. A. Times*. That means I'll have to finish it. And I can't."

"You could. You just don't like it."

"Then it's just as well I don't review it."

"What's it about?" Maggie asked.

"Orange County. It's the Promised Land of California. I live in Newport Beach."

"Dudley's father, Gus Wurdlinger, sells real estate in Orange County. So you can see that he has a natural bias. Dudley, darling, read her that passage."

" 'Time moved with the silent majesty of nature in unfrequented places; innumerable suns rose radiantly above the hills and sank in splendor behind the dark outline of Catalina Island. Summers came with warmth and brilliance, mellowing into autumns of tranquil beauty . . .' "

The words impressed Maggie less than the idea of such a place. "Is it really that lovely? Orange County?"

" 'Gray mists of winter and rains of passing springtime clothed the hills in emerald. Through changing seasons, sand and ocean bay and lifting hills lay in incomparable loveliness! . . .' "

"Dudley, no more. I can't stand it. Give it to Maggie for bedtime reading. If it doesn't put her to sleep, she can give me a précis. All right, Maggie?"

Tony had come out of the pool house in brown trunks. "Maggie, don't be a spoilsport. Go into the pool house and put on one of Angel's thingies."

"Let her alone today, Tony. Swim your laps. I'll take her to her suite. Where did you put her?"

"In the Blue Room," said Tony, diving into the pool. Dudley handed Maggie his book, openly asking for help.

Angel watched her brother swim. "He's so transparent," she said rising from her lounge chair and gesturing at Dudley. "See you at drink time. Come on, Maggie."

Maggie's room was both elegant and comfortable. A George III mahogany armchair and Chippendale four-poster bed complemented the distinctive character of the hand-painted Chinese wallpaper. On the floor was a rare English pile rug, and a Henry Raeburn painting hung over the Carrara marble mantelpiece. Two French doors opened onto a small terrace overlooking the pool.

"What a lovely room."

"Yes, it is. Anthony had excellent taste." Angel stood in the doorway watching Maggie through half-closed eyes. "Mark wrote me you were beautiful and unusually intelligent. You more than justify his claims. I'm very glad you came."

"I'm glad I came too. And I thoroughly appreciate your hospitality."

"Good. I like people to feel indebted to me. It gives me—what do they call it?—a marker. Do you know Tony's room is next to yours? And you share the terrace. It's charming that he gave you the Blue Room. A token of his esteem." She bit one of her pearls and left.

Weeks passed, days of light and shadow, hope and hopelessness, during which Maggie searched for peace and forgetfulness. She did her best not to think of Henry, to live one day at a time, not to look too far ahead and never to look back. The new and strange nature of her life in Los Angeles helped to quiet her sense of loss. She tried new ways of thinking about herself, of behaving, of responding.

She spent a great deal of time with Tony and knew, with a female satisfaction, that he was attracted to her. Actually, she didn't want anything to happen, only for the situation to remain in suspension. She was waiting for someone else, some unique man who would blot out Henry.

Tony took her to the Arabian horse ranch in Pomona, where Maggie tried to ride a horse for the first time. It was by far the most fascinating place she'd been. She loved the horses—the sight of them, the smell, the way they breathed. She understood them, instinctively.

"You're a born horsewoman," Tony said, after she got off her first horse. Then she stumbled, and as he caught her, they lurched together. They looked at each other for a moment.

"I like the way you feel, Maggie Rhodes."

For the first time in a year Maggie felt her body stir. Not as with Henry, but something happened. "Who's Maggie Rhodes?" she asked. "Someone you know?"

"Someone I'd like to know a lot better."

Maggie was at a loss, because she still had no desire to do anything.

That evening Angel gave a party and invited all of Hollywood. There was a profusion of champagne, of caviar, a many-colored, many-toned commotion of lights and sounds and music and people. This was Maggie's first encounter with real movie stars: Robert Taylor, Humphrey Bogart, Joan Crawford, Jennifer Jones, Errol Flynn, and on and on.

"Look around," Angel said. "There's quite a lot to see."

"I am looking around. It's amazing!" Maggie had that unreal feeling that comes from recognizing someone from the screen, off screen.

"See Tony over there." Angel pointed. "Talking to Norma Shearer. He isn't half bad. He's been offered movie contracts."

Maggie looked at Tony. He was an attractive man. Much more attractive in person than many of the male stars she'd admired. They danced together during the evening, and she was surprised at his graceful, easy steps. She danced with other men, too, but Tony had the firmest grip, the strongest lead.

The party went on for hours and wound down with the inevitable swimmers in the pool. Angel asked Maggie to share a last champagne, and Maggie realized that this was somehow a cue. They stood together in the moonlit garden, and Angel asked, "You've been enjoying your stay with the James family?"

"Very much."

"Tony's been enjoying it too. But he'd enjoy it more if you'd give him a chance."

Maggie's color rose. She knew where Angel was headed. "Are you calling in your marker?"

Angel laughed. "In a manner of speaking. And you have to admit that Tony is special. Even in competition with movie stars."

"I admit it. But if you call in your marker, I'll move out tonight and take a suite at the Beverly Hills Hotel." The whole thing reminded Maggie of her bargain with William. And now she no longer needed a bargain.

"Don't be absurd. Do that and you meet no one. You'll be a tourist." Angel continued, reasonably, "You see, I love my brother. And since Anthony's death he's become a bum. Wine, women, song and tennis."

"Did your father die recently?"

"My father and mother. Two years ago. They went on one of Anthony's hunting safaris to Africa."

"What happened?"

"I've no idea. We spent a fortune on search parties. Nothing was found. Not a scrap of shirt. Nothing. Not a trace of bearers and beaters. Or the guide. Or Anthony or Joan. Africa devoured them." She watched Maggie shiver. "Yes, it was terrible. Tony was supposed to go, but just before Anthony left, he broke his ankle playing tennis. It saved Tony's life, and I think he's never forgiven himself." She stopped, and Maggie waited for the rest. "Like everyone who knew Anthony, Tony idolized him. He and Tony spent huge amounts of time together. Anthony even took Tony to his political smokers. Anthony was an *eminence gris* in the sewers of Los Angeles politics."

"Is Tony interested in politics?"

"He was. He was brought up to be." Angel was feeling her way. This was the heart of the matter. "My thought is like this. Since Anthony's death, Tony has become a bum. Women chase him constantly. He always has three on a string: one in bed, one leaving, one coming in. You're the first woman he's taken out continuously, with no one in the wings. But I watch, and you keep yourself at such a distance. He's becoming very unhappy."

"Did he ask you to speak to me?"

"If he knew I did, he'd be furious." She drew a quick breath. "You've been lonely a long time."

"Does it show that badly?"

"To most people, no. To me, yes. Maggie, we're a lot alike. If you let me, I could be a good friend. Can we let our hair down?"

Maggie considered the question. What could she say? She did like Angel. In some ways more than Tony. She laughed. "You want to play 'True Confessions'? Go ahead."

"All right. First, I'm not a virgin and haven't been since I was fifteen. I was seduced by our chauffeur. He was so beautiful. When Anthony found out, he fired him. It didn't make any difference since he went on to other families with other daughters."

"He *can* drive a car?"

"Expertly. Almost as well as he can drive a woman. For the last six years I've averaged about one new lover a month."

Maggie couldn't help remembering. It sounded like her own efforts at sex education.

"Anyway, I am very sexually experienced, and so are you."

"Are you asking me or telling me?"

"I'm telling you. It takes one to know one." Maggie listened. "You've been here over three months, and you have not had a single fuck, let alone a lover. Not Tony, not anyone."

Angel's words sounded harsh. Even crude. But her tone was so concerned, Maggie couldn't take offense. "What makes you so sure?"

"You. You're getting nervous, edgy. You're a woman who needs a man. Like me, you may need a lot of men. But for some reason you're fighting your own nature. Why the chastity belt?" Angel's voice became brisk. "I've let my hair down. Now it's your turn."

Maggie felt a bit overwhelmed. She'd not asked for this special glimpse into Angel's sex life, or for her unwanted confidence and unwanted assumptions. But wanted or not, what Angel had said about her was true. Her body had been sending signals that she'd been trying to ignore. What could she tell Angel? Certainly nothing about Henry, nothing about anything important. A pinch of truth along with a dash of lie would have to do.

"Okay. You're right about one thing. I'm not a virgin, although I didn't start at fifteen with our chauffeur."

"Don't knock it till you've tried it." Angel was surprised to find herself feeling defensive.

Maggie realized her words sounded critical. "Really, I'm not knocking it, and it's a little late for me to try it. Without putting a number on it, I've had my share of men." She thought, so much for the truth. Now for the lies. "The reason for my chastity is I've needed time to heal internally."

"Abortion?"

"No. Right church, wrong pew. Cysts that had to be scraped. My doctor said no sex for a couple of months."

"You've been here longer than a couple of months, so why the continued fast?" Angel sniffed the air. She seemed very serious, thoughtful. "I'll bet you're not aware I have a highly developed sense of smell." She leaned toward Maggie, still sniffing. "My goodness. What is that aroma that permeates the air? Aha! I know! It's Eau de Female."

"Eau de what?"

"Eau de you, sweetie. You smell like a woman in heat. My nose knows. I smell the same way most of the time myself. I'm not suggesting you do anything silly like marry Tony. Just go to bed with him. I have it on the best of references he is very good. It'll do you both some good. You'll get back into action, and maybe he'll get back into politics, where he belongs."

Maggie hedged. "I do like him. He's very nice. But no promises."

"I'll settle for that. At least you didn't say no."


The next night Tony took Maggie to the Hollywood Bowl to hear the Los Angeles Symphony. Afterward they stopped at a bar for a drink. Tony said, only half joking, "You know, Maggie Rhodes, usually I have the courage of a lion. Or a drunk. But you throw me completely."

When they stopped for a red light on the way home, Tony abruptly put his arms around her and kissed her. It gave her a foretaste of what was coming, if she'd accept it. She'd been without a man long enough. She returned his embrace and allowed his tongue to slide between her open lips. A feeling of excitement spread through her body. It was only when they heard the cars behind them blowing their horns that they realized the light had turned green. Tony seemed both surprised and frightened by the intensity of her response. Maggie leaned against the back of the seat, dreaming.

That night she waited for a knock on her door.

But no knock came. She went to bed feeling depressed and lonely. Finally she fell into a restless sleep. Once she threw her arm out to touch someone who was not there. Then she woke up. She had dreamed of having an orgasm. Her vagina was wet. She must have been playing with herself in her sleep because her hand was sticky. Damn that Angel! Maggie *was* "in heat." The room was hot. Airless. Not a typical Los Angeles night. Maggie lay in bed perspiring. Finally she opened her terrace doors and looked at the pool. Someone was swimming. Tony, wearing a pair of white trunks. She watched him complete a lap at the shallow end. When he stood up, she saw that what she'd thought of as white trunks was the one part of Tony's body that wasn't tanned. He was naked.

Maggie couldn't turn away, and as though he felt the pressure of her eyes, he looked up at her room. Standing in the darkness, she was invisible, but her door was open. That was encouragement enough for Tony. His penis became hard. Maggie wanted to escape, to stop watching by closing the door, but found herself caught by her own needs. She stepped out on the terrace, the pull of her body too strong to restrain. Tony watched her. His eyes fixed her to the spot. She didn't love this man, but she wanted him; at least her body did, and her body made the decision.

When he gestured for her to join him, she slipped off her nightgown and stood in the moonlight as naked as he was. She would arouse him as he had aroused her. Then she stopped. It wasn't enough. How could they reach each other?

"Wait," Tony said, and ran to the pool bath house. He returned with an extension ladder and leaned it against the wall, saying, "Shall I climb up or you climb down?"

"I'll climb down," she called in a low voice.

Tony held the ladder and watched her naked body come closer—first her feet, then her calves, then her thighs. He waited. Then her behind. He caressed the cheeks, enjoying the shape of them, and then gripping them firmly with one hand he walked around to the other side of the ladder and buried his face in her vagina, his tongue licking her swollen clitoris. Maggie shuddered and almost slipped backward off the ladder. At last she was on the ground. Tony kissed her as if he were drinking in her whole mouth. His penis pressed between her legs. Maggie's sexual hunger rose to an even higher pitch. He whispered, "Come into the pool. You'll see. It's special."

He took her hand and led her down the broad pool steps into the warm water. Then he set her down on a tile ledge that extended out from the side of the pool just beneath the surface. It was the spot where the circulating water re-entered the pool. Maggie felt the jet pressing between her buttocks. She opened herself to receive it, and quivers of pleasure ran through her body. Tony stood in front of her, kissing her breasts. His hand separated her legs, and his penis pierced her, entered her, filled her. Maggie realized Tony knew exactly what he was doing. He had used the pool for this purpose before. But now he was moving inside her, and all such thoughts vanished. The jet of water made small contractions in her ass, just as Tony's penis caused her vagina to open and close. She felt herself about to come. She was on the brink, but her body couldn't seem to break free. She tried to respond to his rhythm and knew, by the involuntary jerking of his penis and the spurts of semen against her vagina, he had reached his orgasm. He held his still erect penis inside her and moved just enough to keep a pressure against her clitoris. It was necessary to satisfy her. Maggie felt herself almost there, and then the wave receded without breaking. It came again and fell back. She almost screamed at her body in frustration. Suddenly Maggie thought of Henry inside her. Henry, with his ability to make her respond any way he chose. Her body reacted immediately. The last barrier dropped. With a moan of relief she arched forward, and she cried out in half sobs from the joy of release.

Afterward they stepped out of the pool hand in hand.

"You're wonderful," he said. "Wonderful." He kissed her, and they walked, locked together, to the ladder. When she reached the third rung his hands cupped her ass, as though memorizing her exact shape, feeling the firmness, the roundness. She thought they might make love again. Then he let her go, and she knew it was over. She continued to climb up to the terrace. As soon as she was there she looked down and saw Tony carrying the ladder to the poolhouse.

Maggie dried herself and got into bed. She was surprised that Tony made love only once. Still, she'd had an orgasm, her first in a year.

Maybe there were things she could teach Tony. He was so self-centered he hadn't thought about contraception. Tonight was safe. She'd see a gynecologist tomorrow. Angel would have a good one. A diaphragm would be best. Just before she fell asleep she wondered if she'd have had any orgasm at all if she hadn't fantasized about Henry. Probably not, but she wouldn't need him next time.

# Chapter 20

**H**ENRY chose Kate Adams for his return to the sexual world, because they had a history. They'd known each other for years, slept together for years. She had her own money and lived in what she called a "bachelor" apartment on Park Avenue and Seventy-third. But he hadn't seen Kate in over a year. And his feelings for her were somewhat similar to what he might have felt for a male buddy. Except that she was a girl. And very knowledgeable in bed. It could turn out that he'd missed something in Kate, something unique and desirable. Maybe this was what was meant by maturity—lowering your expectations or, to put it more optimistically, accepting the science of the possible. He decided he would reserve judgment about the evening ahead. Reserving judgment was a matter of hope, hoping for the best.

After enjoying a performance of Rodgers and Hart's *Pal Joey*, they ended up in Kate's apartment. Henry had a brandy while Kate went into the bedroom to change. She appeared in a sheer dressing gown with nothing beneath it, and Henry noted that her figure was as good as he remembered, at most slightly fuller. He put down his drink and met her in the middle of the room. She slipped into his arms and lifted her head to be kissed. Henry brought his mouth down on hers, sliding his tongue between her lips to play with hers. His body was responding successfully, but his mind seemed to have separated itself and was observing his behavior with detachment. Even when he slipped his hand under her gown to play with her breasts, it seemed a mechanical exercise. However, in no time they were in bed making love, and Henry was satisfying them both as he always had. He had an orgasm. Kate had several, and her hopes rose. Then Henry reached for his shorts.

"Henry?" Her voice was startled. "Is the bed suddenly too small?"

Henry hadn't caught himself in time. Before the affair with Maggie, he'd always stayed the night with Kate. There was always a fast fuck in the morning. "I'm a father now." He lied to conceal his embarrassment. "I have to call Oscar to tell him where I am."

Kate was soothed. "In the future tell him beforehand."

It was a credit to Henry's discipline that he stayed the night. Kate never sensed the coldness Henry felt. She was satisfied and looked forward to a developing relationship. Henry did not.

Henry had learned something from the evening, something he didn't like. He recognized that he had not fully recovered from his infatuation with Maggie Rhodes; he refused to think of it as love. He would have to try something different. Maybe Kate was too familiar. Maybe he needed a woman with whom he'd had no previous experience. There were a great number of attractive young women who played tennis at the club. He had played occasionally with Madge Reevy, the daughter of Laddy Reevy, the yachtsman. Madge had made it clear that she'd like to know him better. When he'd seen her the previous weekend, she'd mentioned, fluttering her eyelashes—there was no other way to describe it—that she'd be alone with the housekeeper Fourth of July weekend. Her parents were spending the time on Center Island. Henry called her and made a date for the evening of the third. Madge was eager, explaining it was the housekeeper's day off and she'd fix dinner. Henry said, "Fine," and hung up the telephone with a feeling of mild anxiety. There was something about Madge Reevy that struck him as off key.

In the morning he stopped in at the nursery, a room he particularly liked. The windows faced south and west, so the room was light and sunny, and the wallpaper with its Walt Disney cartoon characters gave it a feeling of fun.

When he arrived, Mrs. Sobel was preparing both babies for an outing in the pram. As always, it gave him a moment of confused happiness to see the small boy and girl. He stared at them. It was peculiar. The baby girl bore no resemblance to either himself or Selma, only to Evelyn. Henry thought about Selma. He had felt little for her, and Evelyn had probably felt less. The only trace she'd left on earth was the baby who didn't look like her. Selma might never have existed and Mary floated to shore on a seashell. But Will? He was another question. He was a Carson; everything about him said Carson.

Mrs. Sobel stood aside to allow Henry to observe the babies. "Why don't you pick them up? Children love to be held."

Henry didn't understand why, but he was reluctant to handle the babies. He forced himself to pick up Will first. The baby grabbed onto his neck with a strength that was a boy's strength.

"I think little William is as attractive a baby—"

Henry became furious, putting the child back in his crib before allowing himself to speak. "Mrs. Sobel, the baby's name is Will, not William."

"I don't see the difference."

"I do. I am very serious. If you call him William again, much as I regret it, I shall ask you to leave. The baby's name is Will."

Mrs. Sobel watched him disappear. She liked her job, she liked the babies. Until now she had liked Henry Carson. But to make such a fuss between Will and William was senseless. She sighed. "I'm sorry, William, but from now on you're Will." She shrugged. "Will—not William. What silliness."

Once out of the nursery, Henry stormed into the library. The only thing that had kept him from discharging the nurse was her behavior in the back seat of the Packard while Evelyn's hoodlum beat against the door. He'd permit one mistake. But the next time she called the baby anything but Will she was fired.

He thought about the red-haired, green-eyed baby, especially his toes. He asked himself, as he had so often before, is he my half brother or my son? My half brother or my son? He stared at William's empty chair and bare desk. The only things left were the desk blotter and twin pens set in the black onyx desk set. He tried to visualize his father sitting there. Did you fuck Maggie? he silently asked. Did you? Is the child yours? Is it? Or mine? But no answer came. He must make of the silence what he would. And he wasn't sure. How could he ever be sure?

He went back to reading the company reports. Among all the detail there was one question on which he must shortly make a decision. There were a number of duplications of products between Wilkenson, Inc., and the Carson Company. The most serious was a bandage group. They now had the capacity to produce more than could be sold, plus there was a confusion of brand names. The products were competing against each other and the brand managers had taken to offering "price offs" to hold their market share. Either one product should be killed or the market should be divided. The Carson Company product could be sold to consumers, the Wilkenson product to doctors and hospitals. Then Henry remembered a conversation he'd had with William the year before. Roosevelt had won the election; William believed if Roosevelt won it was only a matter of time before the United States entered the war as a full-fledged ally of Great Britain. Now Henry agreed. That meant wounded men, and wounded men needed bandages. He made his decision. He would divide the markets to avoid brand competition, but he would not cut back on equipment. He would keep all unused production facilities in condition for immediate start up. And he would also order Purchasing to increase their supply of raw material. The rest of the nation could sleep, but the Carson Company would mobilize for a coming war.

By the time he finished reviewing the reports, it was close to six. He must shower, shave and get ready for his date with Madge Reevy.

Madge's house was a typical Westchester house built in the late twenties, an architectural hybrid. Henry drove up the standard half-moon driveway and stopped in front of the house. When he rang the bell no one answered. He rang again. Still no answer. Had she forgotten? He was about to leave in disgust when a second-floor window opened, and Madge stuck her head out. "My God, you're on time! I was showering." She giggled. "Go 'round to the back. The charcoal is set, and there're drinks and ice. I'll be down in a minute."

As Madge had promised, there was a grill and drinks waiting for Henry in the back of the house. He poured himself a stiff gin on the rocks and sat down to wait on one of the white patio chairs. Fifteen minutes passed. Henry finished his drink and poured another. After twenty minutes Henry wondered what Madge would consider a long time. He was halfway through his third gin before she appeared wearing a long white dress with a scooped neckline of a material that clung in all the right places.

"Throw some gin in a glass, thank you. But no ice. It spoils the effect."

"Keeps you sober."

"That's the effect it spoils." The scarlet corners of her lips curved up, but it was less a smile than an invitation to a kiss.

Henry chose the smallest glass on the redwood table and poured two fingers of gin. Madge tossed it off and gave him back the glass.

"That was a sip and a swallow, if you don't mind."

He filled the glass and handed it to her. About half disappeared in her first gulp. "Shall I light the fire?"

Madge rose from her seat and moved closer to Henry. "Light my fire first."

Henry almost laughed but didn't. It was the sort of thing you said to sophomores. Light my fire first. Oh, Christ! He kissed her, but her kiss aroused no hunger in him. It was a charity kiss that promised more than it gave. She pulled away when he pressed harder, probing her mouth with his tongue.

"Another drink, if you please."

"Keep that up, and you won't be able to eat." Let alone do anything else, he added to himself.

"Don't be such a spoilsport."

"Okay. One more and show me where the food is." Again she tossed down half the glass in a gulp. The quart bottle had been almost full when they started, now less than half was left. He could hold his liquor, but could she? "I'll start the food. We could both use some. Later we'll do something about your fire." He cringed at the use of the metaphor.

"All right, if you want to. Now kiss me again." She said it as though she were committing a childish indiscretion, and meant to show off.

This time Henry took her in his arms and drew her close against his body. She smiled as her face came up to his and lowered her lids when his tongue touched hers, lightly tickling the inside of her mouth. He could feel her tremble slightly under his caresses and had to restrain himself from any further foreplay. It seemed too soon. He let her go and turned back to the grill. "Food?"

Madge pointed under the patio table where a paper bag rested. Henry opened the bag. Two small steaks, some wilted greens and two ears of corn. Nothing. Madge was not accustomed to feeding a man. Soon he had the fire rising from the grill, and he poured himself another gin on ice. In a slightly slurred voice, Madge asked for another drink.

"You've had enough for now. After dinner we'll see about a reorder."

"Yes, sir." Madge slumped back on one of the patio lounges. Her dress fell away from her slim, silken legs, and Henry wondered why she wore stockings and a girdle in the heat. Beyond his lack of physical excitement, she was becoming a bore. June, one year ago, had been marked by Maggie's passionate presence. It had been a rare time. Was it the only penny's worth of happiness he would know?

He hurried the meal along, and as they sat down under the umbrella to eat, Madge's left breast pushed up by her wired bra became partially exposed. Henry could see her nipple just over the top of the bra. Dinner was finished in record time. "Now can I have my drink and thank you very much."

Henry handed her a glass with a little gin in it and sat down beside her on the lounge. He kissed her again while his hand caressed her bare breast, and she moaned and writhed so that her right breast also rose from the bra, thus inviting Henry to rub the palm of his hand over both her nipples. Her head fell back, and she began to gasp for breath, a desirous woman. But somehow Henry didn't believe it. He slid his hand under her dress intending to continue his fondling, even if impeded by the girdle. Madge sat bolt upright. She gripped his hand firmly and pulled it away from her body. "No!"

"I beg your pardon?"

"Goodness, you don't have to apologize. It just seems funny to have a man you think of as a gentleman come to see you and try something like that right off the bat."

Henry took stock of the situation. "You mean it's too soon. There's a timetable. Like for a train schedule."

"That's perfectly crazy. What on earth do you mean?"

"I mean that's why you stopped me. Because it's too soon."

"Well, if you're talking about doing anything below the waist, you're right. Not on our first date. I wouldn't think of stopping you from kissing my breasts, or my mouth, or my ears, but below the waist, you can't touch me there."

"I see. How far below the waist?"

"I don't understand what you mean."

"How do you feel about your ankles?"

"Well, of course. My ankles?"

At this point Henry realized the whole thing was one big blunder. He hadn't heard anything like this since he was fifteen. Maybe he'd just been lucky. But his curiosity was aroused. "How about your knees?"

"Yes, sure, you can touch my knees."

"Can I go any higher?"

"No, no higher!" Her voice was very serious. "Not on our first date."

"So then it's not really below your waist. It's below your waist and above your knees that everything stops."

"Yes. Until our second date. Then you can touch me down there." Remarkably, Madge was now stone cold sober.

"Go on."

"On our third date is when I can touch you down there."

"So it is like a train schedule. Each date or station gets us a little closer to the terminal. Does the train ever arrive at the end of the line?"

"If you happen to mean do we ever have real sex, no! I'm a virgin."

Henry started to laugh. "And you're saving yourself for your husband."

"I certainly am. I wouldn't want him to feel, whoever he is, that I was a piece of used merchandise."

"I'm used merchandise."

"Oh, that's marvelous. That's awfully funny. You don't mind if I laugh."

"Not at all. Laugh."

"Well, I mean, everybody knows there's a difference between men and women."

"Not between all men and all women."

"Oh, I know there are lots of girls who don't think anything of doing things like that. But I think it's terrible, and they aren't very nice girls."

"Then I'm not a nice man." Henry rose.

"Now look, I'm sorry if I hurt your feelings. I'm sure I didn't realize anything I said was an insult. Everybody else knows where to stop."

"I'm not hurt," Henry said, "I'm just out of step. I'm wasting your time and mine."

"Well, for goodness' sake, don't feel you have to stay here and be bored. The only thing I'm sorry about is I didn't know sooner. I broke a date with Jeff Harper to go to a movie and everything. It isn't very pleasant to sit here and feel you're boring a person to death."

"It isn't very pleasant to feel like a child molester." Henry felt suddenly depressed. "I'm sure if you call Jeff he'll be delighted to see you. You can even finish the gin bottle. It seems to have no effect. Good night, Madge."

Driving home, Henry considered the evening and adjusted himself almost visibly. He had expected too much. Obviously, he'd been spoiled in the past by the many less narrow, freer women he'd known, like Kate Adams. And most of all by Maggie, whom he had once loved and now could not have. Madge's businesslike approach to sex—it could only be described in those terms—was something he'd never met before. He felt old and weary. He would not go through a replay with other young women at the club. Even granting that, there must be those who had other standards. He was too tired to chance it. Tomorrow he would call Kate Adams, and after that a number of other women he'd known. He could wait as long as necessary for what he wanted. Meanwhile, he'd be seen around town. The world had to be full of possibilities.

In the sun-warmed, sensual world of Los Angeles, the ice around Maggie's heart began to thaw. She could not be certain how much of it was the change in her vision because of the strangeness of California, and how much was response to the attention and nearness of Tony. Although she liked Tony more and more, she knew she wasn't in love.

What she loved was California. She couldn't seem to get enough of it— the look of it, the people. In this new world she found an intoxicating freedom, a freedom it seemed to give to everyone.

This freedom sent her driving around the city, with or without Tony, to stare at everything and everyone with a fevered obsessiveness. Only Hollywood, curiously enough, was exempted. After seeing one movie set and meeting the famous names regularly at the James house, Maggie preferred to keep her distance. Too close a contact with the scandalous and petty private behavior of some of the great stars made it difficult to enjoy their screen performances.

But Los Angeles itself was a magnet. She stared at its buildings—at Pershing Square, at Griffith Observatory, at the Hollywood Bowl—as though they were the baths of Caracalla. She studied the Miracle Mile with the same intensity she would have given to the Appian Way. Something was stirring, some unformed idea forming.

She observed people with the same fanatical intensity, and they often stared back, wondering what was wrong with them or with her. She had a dozen adventures a day. She felt more and more at home in California. It was a world full of strangers who came to invent a new future, even as she was inventing her own. Seated on a bench in Lincoln Park, she met a geography teacher from Boston who now gave speech lessons to actors and actresses. "They drawl, or slur, or twang, or are nasal. No one here comes from here, and no one speaks straight American."

"Yes. The only native I've met is a descendant of the Pomo Indians."

"You're from upstate New York, with a very slight overlay of Manhattan."

Maggie laughed. "You're right, if Westchester is upstate. I lived only a short while in Manhattan. I'm here to stay."

"Well, there's room. This is the second largest state in the Union— 155,652 miles. It almost equals the combined size of New York, Ohio, Maine, New Hampshire, Vermont, Massachusetts, New Jersey, Delaware and Rhode Island." The young woman enjoyed showing off.

"Wow!" said Maggie.

"And only one-fourth of the state has been utilized. Almost forty percent of the people live in the county of Los Angeles. That's a million and a half in this city and another million outside the city limits. Have you ever been to Orange County?"

Orange County . . . Orange County . . . why did the place strike a bell? She remembered her reaction when Dudley said the words. "No.

I've been in and around Los Angeles, and up to San Francisco. That's a beautiful city."

"My brother says when he dies he doesn't want to go to heaven, he wants to go to San Francisco." She laughed. "But if you want to see California's future, see Orange County. Along the shoreline. It's stupefying. I just bought myself a bay front shack in Newport Beach, on Lido Isle, for two thousand dollars. With luck, I'll haul in a sailor."

"Good luck," said Maggie. "Yes, it's time I saw Newport Beach."

The effect on Maggie of her train ride to Newport Beach was one of immense release and an expansion of her vision. If she had felt a sense of freedom before, it was now even stronger. The further south they went, the greater her feeling of escape from all the worlds that were crowded and confined, into one with an almost infinite vista of space, of distance, of promise. She would have stared out the window all the way, but Tony, who had insisted on going with her, required adroit handling. He had been sitting, brooding, through most of the trip. And Maggie felt an obligation to him, the heavier for having so little deep feeling to sustain it. He had been more than kind to her since she arrived. Their sexual life had been reasonably satisfying, and they'd lived together over the past months on terms of easy friendship. But recently she'd become aware of friction between them. Her interest in Orange County irritated him.

"It's so wonderful, so wide open, so much land, so much sky." She tried to convey her enthusiasm.

"I've seen it before. Anthony used to take me with him to Newport Beach when he wanted to sail or check the gambling concessions. Anthony believed in the inalienable right of every man to life, liberty and the pursuit of his favorite vices." He frowned. "This trip is too full of memories."

This was the first time Tony had mentioned his father, and Maggie wasn't sure how to take the remark. "If it makes you uncomfortable, why did you come?"

"I've been uncomfortable since Anthony's death. Being with you is the only time I'm not."

Maggie was thankful that their arrival at Newport Beach made it unnecessary to answer. "We're here!" she said gaily. "Dudley's Promised Land!"

When they left the train, Tony spotted Dudley. He was wearing dirty white ducks and an open shirt. "Doesn't he look like something washed up by the sea?"

"Newport Beach is sea country, so why not? You told him I wanted to speak to his father?"

"Of course." Tony was offended. "Why else would we come to this godforsaken place. You have a yen for Orange County real estate. I think of it as a sickness, like alcoholism."

"Perhaps, once I look around, the sickness will pass." Dudley Wurdlinger approached them on the run. "Glad to see you folks. Glad you came to see the Promised Land for yourself."

Maggie laughed, animated by her eagerness to see everything, the whole scene: sights, sounds and odors; the blazing desert sun so close to the ocean, flashing on people and on the golden shores. Everything about the place seemed to call to her.

"You could fish off the wharf," Dudley was rambling. "We have bass, halibut, mackerel . . ."

Maggie was enchanted. "I don't know how to fish. And I've no fishing rod."

"Oh, there're plenty of bait and tackle stores around. If you still want to later, you can fish off my sloop. Right now you're here to talk land, not fish." He nodded toward the Chevy parked outside the station. "My father's waiting for you in his office."

Gus Wurdlinger's office was on Balboa Island. It was in a wooden building set on pilings. The building extended over the water, and Maggie could see, in several spots where the wooden floor had splintered, the bay below them. On the wall of the office were two large framed pictures. The first was a montage of Balboa Island, Lido Island and the general area just after the storm and earthquake of 1934. The island looked as though it was under water. The second was a huge map of the entire countryside running from Newport Beach to San Clemente. Areas were marked off in different colors—the Irvine Ranch, the O'Neill Ranch. But there was even more land that was unmarked.

Gus Wurdlinger was a very thin, almost skinny man with a full head of white hair cut very short, piercing black eyes and a long, aquiline nose. There was a growth of short black hair that extended out of his nostrils. He wore a gray business suit, white shirt and dark tie. In spite of the fishing village atmosphere of Balboa Island, Maggie recognized this was a no-nonsense businessman.

"Dad, this is Miss Rhodes and Tony James. Now that I caught them for you, I'm going fishing for me. See you at dinner."

"How do you do, Miss Rhodes, Mr. James? My son tells me you're interested in real estate."

"I'm not. She is," said Tony.

"Yes, I'm the buyer." Maggie nodded, smiling. "Tony is along to stop me buying something that happens to be under water at high tide."

"Miss Rhodes, I don't sell land that belongs to the Pacific at high or low tide."

"I'm sorry. I was only joking."

"Maybe so," he muttered, "but there's some that would. Now, what are you looking for? A plot in Newport Beach or on one of the islands?"

"No. No plots. I'm looking for acreage."

"Suppose I call James Irvine? He may have something to dispose of right now."

"I think not." She looked again at the wall map: the Irvine Ranch, the O'Neill Ranch, and then the unmarked land. Here was an earth without fences. This was "it." She knew it, she could feel it; a sharp surge of excitement ran through her. There was something here she had never seen before, something that had vanished long ago from the northeast. It was raw, undeveloped land, land that was the true gold of the earth. It was as though she had landed on Manhattan Island in the seventeenth century and was considering its purchase. "Leaving out the Irvine and O'Neill ranches, what is the average price of an acre of land?"

"Pick a location, and I'll answer your question."

"All right." Maggie walked to the map. She located Laguna Beach and Laguna Canyon Road. "Here. I've heard of Laguna Beach." Then she pointed to other unmarked areas.

"That's a big chunk. We should be able to find something there." He went to an old file cabinet and thumbed through the folders. "Yep. I have three parcels I can recommend. All available and good buys."

"Point them out on the map."

Wurdlinger circled an area south of Laguna Beach with his finger and then two others parallel to the first but farther inland.

"They don't connect?"

"No. The connecting land is owned by a Mr. William Carson who lives back East."

"William owns—I mean owned land here?" Maggie struggled to regain her composure, because even as she said it, she understood why the words Orange County had been so alive to her. And she saw William again in her mind. He was dead, but his truth was with her. It was he who had first mentioned Orange County to her. He had told her this was where he was starting to buy land. But with her head full of Henry she'd only half listened. And now Henry owned the land.

For the first time Tony took an interest. "Do you know William Carson?"

"He was a client of Mark's. He's dead now." She asked Wurdlinger, "Could you put the details of the three parcels together by this afternoon? If the price is right, I'd like to see the land today."

Tony slouched into his chair. "I think I'll take the next train back."

Maggie looked at him. "I am sorry. But since you're bored, you probably should go back." Then she said to Wurdlinger, "I am a serious buyer. I'll give you my credentials after you show me what's available."

Gus Wurdlinger believed that many men were cleverer than he, but he didn't doubt he had more sense of people. He was less concerned about this young woman's credentials than she was. "Fine, Miss Rhodes. Be here at two, and I'll have things ready."

"I'd like a copy of that map on your wall."

"I'll have one marked out for you. I'll include the Carson land."

Maggie and Tony left the real estate broker's office and wandered along the island. They stopped at a small street stand for a snack of clams, which did nothing to lessen Tony's sullenness. "Maggie, you can't be serious about this Orange County thing."

"I'm quite serious, Tony. Let's not discuss it." Actually she knew he didn't want to discuss it. Tony had only one subject—himself. And her interest in anything else exasperated him. They finished their lunch in silence. Tony left for the station, and Maggie continued to wander around Balboa Island.

Wurdlinger was in his office waiting for her. A large map of the area was spread out on a table next to the windows overlooking the bay. Areas were marked off exactly as the map on the wall, but there were four new areas outlined. "Besides the Irvine Ranch and the O'Neill Ranch, I've marked out three properties which I know can be bought now. I've also marked the land owned by William Carson. I checked the county assessor, and the land is still in his name."

She studied the map. The three pieces for sale were on the perimeter of Henry's property. Without making a conscious decision, she was nevertheless coming to a decision. And if she held to it, it would be necessary someday to purchase Henry's land. Another job for Mark. She wanted no contact with Henry.

None of the parcels were contiguous, so she asked Wurdlinger, "What about the land between the three parcels? Is it for sale?"

"Most things are for sale at a price."

"All right. How much land is in each parcel, and what's the asking price?"

"Are you talking cash or terms?"

"That would depend on the price and the terms offered. Are there any mortgages on the properties?"

"We call them 'trusts' here. No, they're free and clear."

"We'd do better if we paid cash?"

"Considerably." The more they spoke, the more she impressed Wurdlinger.

"So what's missing is the size and price of the properties."

Wurdlinger gave her a wide smile. "I wondered when you'd ask that. Parcel A"—he pointed to the piece of land marked A— "is 165 acres. Available for $350 an acre. Parcel B is 700 acres. It's hillier and further from the ocean. That's going for $250 an acre. Parcel C's the largest. It's about 1,200 acres. The owner wants to sell, so the price is $150 an acre."

Maggie studied the map. All the parcels were south and east of Laguna Beach. "When can you show me this acreage?"

"If you don't mind driving over some rough dirt roads, we could make a tour today." Wurdlinger looked at his watch. "It's almost four. If we leave now, the light will hold."

Forty-five minutes later Maggie got out of Gus Wurdlinger's Model A Ford and looked around. She pointed to a small hill near where they had stopped. "If we could walk to the top of that rise, I'd get a better idea of the property."

Wurdlinger agreed. "See that hill over there, the one with the red bush on the side?" Maggie nodded. "The land ends the other side of that hill."

Maggie looked around, she wanted nothing to escape her. Staring in quiet joy at the golden hills that dropped down into the immense Pacific, she felt as if she had come home. The sun was still high in the sky, but the heat had passed. The great body of the earth was collecting into the coolness of late afternoon and evening, resting quietly in the waning light of day. It was, as she suspected, an oceanside desert. And she thought again of William. Work was the religion of his soul, and he had seen her too as a worker, a doer, a creator. He had left her more than money, he had left her with his belief in her courage and talent to find and work for her dream. What had he said in his will? "It is my fondest hope this money will enable her to achieve her full potential as

a human being." This dream would do for her. She'd justify his belief
in her. She would build homes, schools, theaters, factories—a place for
people to achieve their own dreams. It would take years, maybe a decade,
before the land would be ready for development. Meanwhile, it would
take planning.

She heard Wurdlinger speaking, interrupting her musing. "See that
mountain range over there? That's the San Bernardinos, one hundred
miles away and eight thousand feet high."

Maggie followed his finger. "They're stupendous." Then she looked
away, for something more human-sized, and noticed a few trees struggling for survival. "The roots of those trees must go very deep. There's
no water here."

"Yes, but there's no rock in the soil to stop them. The hills are
clay."

"So all one would need is dirt-moving equipment?"

"Depends on what you're planning to move the dirt for."

They moved on to the second site and then the third. The third
site was the closest to the Pacific. From the top of a hill, Maggie could
see the ocean. She remembered a piece of poetry: " . . . And stout Cortez
and all his men gazed at the broad Pacific in wild surmise, silent on a
peak in Darien."

"I bet they were silent. The Pacific sure can get you."

She stood for a few minutes staring at the ocean, picturing tens of
thousands of people living in one of the most beautiful places in the
world. No labor would be too great, no dedication of time and effort too
much if, through it, she achieved something worthwhile. The freeways
were the key. She would draw a line on the map where she remembered
the proposed freeway south would be built. She'd buy all the land she
could between the freeway and the Coast Highway. She wanted everything. It would be her life's work.

The great red sun was sinking into the Pacific when they settled
themselves in the broker's office. Maggie decided a direct approach was
best. First she would give her full banking connections, and when he
realized she had the financing to carry out her plan, he would see it was
in his best interests to work for her. Once all the properties were purchased and construction started, he would be the major broker on what
she now thought of as Mission Nuevo. His commissions would be
enormous.

"Mr. Wurdlinger, let me explain why I've taken up your whole day. If you represent me in my negotiations, it should prove a profitable day for both of us." Wurdlinger made no comment. "To begin, the Bank of America in Los Angeles is one of my credentials." Maggie had recently opened an account. "But Tom Payton, the manager, was referred to me by my New York banker." Wurdlinger remained silent. Nothing this young woman might say would surprise him. "My home was in New York, but I plan to stay in California. I arrived here in June. My friend and chief financial advisor is Mark James, a cousin of Anthony James. Mark James is a senior vice president of the Morgan Bank on Wall Street." Wurdlinger's face was impassive. She was as good as he expected. "I tell you this because I'd like you to handle the purchase of the three properties we looked at today. They will be bought by different corporations. I want no one to guess I mean to assemble a large plot between Laguna Beach and San Clemente."

"Will you be paying cash, or will you want terms?"

"Cash."

"That takes money."

"I have money. If need be, I can arrange additional financing through the Morgan."

"Why do you want undeveloped land fit only for cows and sheep?"

It was a straight question, but she hesitated in answering it. Wurdlinger could tell that Maggie Rhodes was onto something, and she didn't quite trust him. He reached for the telephone. "You've given me your credentials. I'll give you mine." He dialed a number. "I'd like to speak to James Irvine." They waited. "Jim, this is Gus. Would you say a good word for me to a young lady I'll put on? No, sorry, I can't give you her name. But she's interested in land."

He handed the phone to Maggie. "Hello?"

"This is James Irvine." The tone was blunt. "Gus Wurdlinger is a man of his word. I've used him in a number of real estate deals, to buy and sell land. He's always done his best to get me the lowest price when I buy, and he's tried to beat me into the ground when he's represented a buyer and we're selling. I can only say one more thing. He keeps his mouth shut. I don't know who I'm talking to, and I won't know unless you tell him he can tell me. Now let me speak to Gus."

Maggie handed the phone back. She listened. "No. Thanks, Jim." He hung up. "Mr. Irvine wanted to know if you wanted to speak to his son, Myford Irvine. I didn't think it necessary. Now there's one other person you might want to speak to." He made his second phone call. "Is Rowland there? . . . Rowland, Gus here . . . I'm fine. Sorry to interrupt your supper. Look, I've a young lady in my office and . . . oh, shut up, you dirty old man. This is business. . . . Real estate business. . . . Stop clowning. Tell her something good about me. Try hard."

He handed Maggie the phone. "Young lady, I would stay away from that man. As far away as I can. He has a wife, and she can shoot straight."

"Who are you?"

"Rowland Hodgkinson, Chief of Police since 1925, and in sixteen years, except for some trouble every New Year's Eve, I've never heard a word against Gus. He's straight and he's smart."

"Thank you."

"No thanks to me. Thank his folks. Goodby."

Maggie handed the phone back to the broker. "I'll describe my idea. First, I want to buy the three properties. Offer two-thirds of their asking price."

"Half would be better. We might settle for two-thirds."

"All right, half. Then I want to pick up what I can around the perimeter of the Carson property."

"I'll ask again. Why do you want that land?"

"I read your son's book. This is the Promised Land."

"My son's a dreamer."

"Out of dreams come reality. I want to build a planned community in Orange County. In time there will be a freeway from Los Angeles to San Diego and roads connecting the Coast Highway with the freeway."

"When?"

"I don't know. But I intend to work toward its coming. In any case I believe that Orange County will be the ideal place to work and live. The climate is perfect."

"You're willing to wait until the spread of Los Angeles reaches this far south?"

"Yes." She smiled. "And when it does, I'll be ready. Meanwhile we'll use the land to raise cattle and sheep. To cover the taxes."

"If Carson, alive or dead, doesn't sell, you could have a problem."

"I'll handle that."

Wurdlinger did some calculation with a pencil on a scratch pad. "Even if we get the properties at fifty percent of asking price, we're talking about something over $200,000." Maggie nodded. "Where can I reach you?"

"Call Tom Payton at the Bank of America, and he'll get a message to me." She gave him Payton's number. "How soon will you need cash for the contracts?"

"A few weeks. To get the best price, we can't rush things."

"Have the properties surveyed while they're in escrow."

"You were right, young lady, you didn't waste my time." He gave her a card with his office and home numbers printed on it. "In case you want me. Now, can I give you a lift somewhere?"

"I'll check in at Balboa Inn. Go back first thing in the morning."

They said goodby, and Maggie walked up the road to the Balboa Inn. Yes, this was "it." This was the Place. This was the day to be forever printed on her memory as the day that divided her life. One was what she had been. The other was what she would become, when she would prove William's vision of her to be true. Yes, she could do it here. "Here" was simply bursting with the heart, the hope, the life of California to come.

# *Chapter 21*

**M**AGGIE was in her room unpacking her overnight bag when Angel, perspiring, skidded to a stop outside the room and came in. "Maggie Rhodes, you've been out all night, fucking."

"How did you know?"

"You didn't sleep home last night. Was he any good? Worth a pass-along?"

"Angel, you know where I was."

"Tony was mad as a wet hen. He said you had a date. Are the papers signed?"

"We didn't have a date. The papers are signed, sealed and delivered." Maggie pulled out the contracts. "The closing closed."

"Rah! Rah! Rah!" Angel cheered. The friendship between her and Maggie had grown through the months. There was now a bond of unspoken trust. "You are now the proud owner of Orange County."

"Me, the Irvines, and the O'Neills." She silently added the Carsons.

"Still, you are a 'Land Baron.' Now you can afford Tony."

"I can afford him less today than I could yesterday. Land costs money."

"I'm sure you could manage somehow on your co-mingled millions. Maggie, make him an honest man." Angel's teasing, at once spontaneous and practiced, was that of a young woman accustomed to having her own way.

"Given your taste for variety, your fix on my marrying is very strange."

"We in the James family are devoted to marriage. And remarriage."

"Then what about your single blessedness?"

"I'm reviewing my options. Anyway, you're not about to move to Newport Beach?"

"Not unless I've worn out my welcome at the James house."

"Hardly. Tony and I decided not to charge you for breakfast. It's the James plan. An improvement over both the American and European plans."

"You're extending my guest privileges?"

"Permanently. We discussed it last night and voted you an honorary member of the James family. That's worth at least a blue star, isn't it?"

"What happens if I happen to stray from the family hearth?"

"Nothing. And to prove my intentions, have I got a guy for you!"

Maggie laughed. "But what about Tony?"

"Oh, time and tide and things like propinquity and proximity will take care of all that. You haven't a chance."

Tony and Maggie were driving north on the Pacific Coast Highway toward Malibu, where a political luncheon was being given by Helen Gahagan Douglas and Melvin Douglas. Tony had decided to go back into politics and pick up his father's connections in the Democratic Party. He was talking about Anthony for the second time since they'd known each other, and half unwillingly, Maggie let herself be drawn into the new intimacy.

"I've thought about it a lot since his disappearance, and I've decided that Anthony had a God complex. He believed he was a better judge of what made good government than either the voters or their elected officials. In fact he agreed with the thought that democracy was the worst form of government except for all the others. So he worked both sides of the street. Sometimes he was on the side of the angels, hot on reform. Other times he'd close his eyes to the rackets. His thinking was that if it made money, made people happy, leave it alone. If it's not broke, don't fix it."

"He set his own rules."

"Yes. He wasn't in politics for money. Or fame. He was in it for power. And he preferred to be invisible. Working behind the scenes was his specialty. In a way it was lucky he disappeared when he did, or he would have stopped being invisible. The James family could have been caught in a nasty scandal."

"Anthony overreached?"

"Something like that. But when Anthony and Joan had disappeared in Africa, it all came to an end." Tony's voice went flat. "Anthony was grooming me to be his front man. But I don't have his instinct for people. I need direction. I don't know what you really think of me—or if you think of me at all—but you're the most beautiful woman I've met since I don't know when. The sexiest. And the most intelligent. You could help me."

Maggie gave a small sigh. "I'm very fond of you, Tony."

"Fond enough to marry me?"

Maggie looked at him, looked into herself, then back at him. "It's too soon, Tony."

Tony had fully expected her answer, but he'd wanted to go on record. Although he himself wasn't ready, he knew a wife was a political asset, and Maggie could be much more. He trusted her judgment, her foresight, as he'd trusted Anthony's. With her as a wife, he might go far. "I realize that you need time. All I'm suggesting . . ."

The radio had been playing "Stardust" at a low level when abruptly a man's voice broke in. "We interrupt this program to announce that the Japanese Air Force has just attacked the Pacific Fleet at Pearl Harbor. We will bring you further reports as soon as we get them." "Stardust" came back on, and Maggie and Tony stared at each other.

"Oh, my God!" said Maggie. "That means we're in the war."

"It sure sounds like it. Add that to my marriage proposal, and today qualifies for more than a footnote in history."

"Pearl Harbor is headquarters for the Pacific Fleet. I wonder how many people were killed."

Tony's face became somber. "If the fleet's destroyed, the Japs could invade California."

"This country hasn't been invaded since the War of 1812."

"And there are a lot of Japs in California already."

"But they're Americans," Maggie protested.

"Who really knows?"

"Will you be drafted?"

"A James drafted?" Tony sounded more shocked at Maggie's question than he was at the announcement of the attack on Pearl Harbor. "I think not."

At nine-thirty Eastern Standard Time on December 7, Franklin Delano Roosevelt addressed Congress and the nation, calling upon Congress for a declaration of war against Japan. On December 11, 1941, Germany and Italy declared war on the United States. America was in the war.

Tony James, like everyone else, had registered for the draft. But Tony had no intention of being drafted. He used his connections, as well as his experience in sailing a small sloop, to obtain a commission as Lieutenant JG in the United States Navy. The Navy ignored the fact that sailing ships had not been used in seventy-five years and sloops had never been used. Tony did not stop with the commission. Maggie never found out how he managed it, but he was assigned to duty at San Pedro, the port of Los Angeles, one of a handful of officers and enlisted men supervising construction of ships at the shipyard. As General Sherman had said, "War is hell."

Maggie realized her Orange County plan had to be tabled indefinitely. The war changed everything, and she confined herself to rolling bandages, some of which were manufactured by the Carson Company, and, along with Angel, acting as a hostess and dancing partner at the Stage Door Canteen. When Tony had a weekend pass, they saw each other on a steady basis; when he was on duty, she looked to find among the shifting population of soldiers and officers a man sufficiently meaningful to her to free her of all memories of Henry.

Henry Carson was working at home on Sunday, December 7, 1941. Through the fall he had seen signs that convinced him the war was imminent. What most concerned him now was who would run the company while he served in the armed forces. He had not planned on a successor, as William had. At twenty-five a man does not think of a successor. He was at his desk, reviewing a list of executives, when Oscar Sorensen interrupted, telling him to turn on the radio.

Henry went down to the local draft board on the following Tuesday and enlisted. He asked for a stay of induction for thirty days so he could appoint and instruct a successor to run the Carson Company for as long as he was in the service. It took a week for the draft board to process his enlistment papers. One morning, while Henry was still sifting through the histories of the few remaining executive possibilities, Mary O'Toole rushed in without knocking. For her to do this, Henry assumed the building was on fire.

"Mr. Carson, there's a call from the White House. A Mr. Hopkins wants to speak to you."

Henry pushed the papers aside. "Put him on, Mary." He waited.

"Harry Hopkins here. Mr. Carson? Mr. Henry Carson?"

"Yes, Mr. Hopkins."

"I wanted to tell you personally that we've disposed of your enlistment papers. One Carson hero in the armed forces is enough. We need you to be heroic at home."

"What do you mean 'one Carson hero is enough'?"

"Isn't Francis Carson your brother?"

Henry remembered the reports on Francis he'd found stored in William's safe after his death. "Yes," he said grimly.

"Well, the RCAF just released him, and the United States has accepted him into the Air Force as a full chicken colonel. He's a hero."

"What has Francis got to do with me?"

"As I said, you are more valuable at home, running the Carson Company, supplying the Army with products for the war effort. Less colorful, but those are the fortunes of war."

"Is this decision final?"

"It is. You keep on doing what you do best. And Francis Carson will do what he does best."

Henry hung up. He was deeply disappointed and tried to stifle the intense feelings of frustration. He wondered if Will or Mary would believe him in the years to come when he explained why he had not served in the military, any more than he had believed William when William had explained how he was needed to run the factory during the First World War.

The Carson Company was one of the nation's first to win the coveted E for Excellence. It won it not only for its bandages but for producing the various sulphur drugs that saved the lives of tens of thousands of soldiers. And much to Henry's disgust, Francis Carson became a nationally celebrated hero. When President Roosevelt pinned the Congressional Medal of Honor on Francis' beribboned chest in the Rose Garden of the White House and personally changed the chicken wings to stars, making Francis a brigadier general, Henry spent an angry, sleepless night.

On June 16, 1944, ten days after the Allied landing on the coast of France, Henry received an invitation to attend a special ceremony in honor of General Francis Carson. General Carson was to receive his second star for distinguishing himself in the Allied bombing raids that preceded the landing. All chief executives whose companies had won the E for Excellence—the Carson Company had won three—were invited to sit on the dais while General Carson made a speech to 500 people in the Grand Ballroom of the Waldorf-Astoria hotel in New York. Afterwards they would be introduced to General Carson. There was no way Henry could resist the invitation. He wanted to see the "hero" for himself.

Evelyn Wilkenson too had received an invitation to be among the 500 listening to Francis Carson. After thinking it over she decided to accept. Actually she didn't give a damn about General Carson, the hero. What interested Evelyn was Francis Carson, not General Carson. Francis, Henry's brother. Maybe he was the connection she'd searched for all these years.

The reception was a gala affair. Every elected city official from

Mayor LaGuardia on down was present. Senator Robert Wagner and former Governor Herbert Lehman also sat on the dais, along with Francis, Henry and other executives. Since the Senator's son, Robert Wagner, Jr., was an officer in the U.S. Air Corps, the Senator was chosen to make the introduction. He concluded with, "And now I'd like to present to you an American and a New Yorker who symbolizes the finest qualities in the American character. I give you General Francis Carson."

The introduction was met by a long, steady applause, giving Henry a chance to study the brother he hadn't seen in four years. His appearance totally contradicted the impression Henry had of his private life. There was no sign of dissipation anywhere, not a line on his face, no sag to his jaw, no slump to his shoulders. If anything, Francis looked better than Henry remembered. His bright gold hair made his blue eyes seem even more intensely blue. The war experience had done something more, it had added a new, reckless yet confident, authoritative air which commanded respect. Remembering what a similar life had done to Craig Spears, it was astonishing that Francis remained untouched. To all intents and purposes he looked like the American "hero" he was supposed to be.

Then Henry studied the audience for the first time. Here and there he noted a familiar face. And heading up a table near the dais was one all too familiar face—Evelyn Wilkenson. Her eyes were riveted on Francis, and Henry could read her mind as clearly as though she were speaking. "Can this man be used to help me get Mary?" Suddenly Henry would have given a small fortune not to be on the dais. A warning had sounded, and he cursed the curiosity which prompted him to accept the invitation. Preposterous as it sounded, he felt a strong premonition that this evening would lead to disaster.

Francis walked to the podium and began to speak. He praised the courage of American soldiers in both the Atlantic and Pacific theaters of the war and then applauded the civilian population on the home front in supporting the war effort. It was a variation on "They also serve who only stand and wait." That ended the prepared speech, and everyone waited for Francis to step back and thus signal the applause to start. But Francis had a few unprepared remarks to make. He turned and looked directly at Henry. "Of course there are always a few—thank God, in our country only a very few—who have used their positions to avoid sacrifice. Those who have permitted other brave men to risk and to die so that they could stay home and enjoy the luxury of peace and prosperity which they have not earned. I call such men cowards and not fit to associate with decent, brave honorable Americans." Then he started back toward his seat. The audience had followed Francis' eyes to Henry Carson, whose face was now as red with rage as his hair. Then the women in the audience stormed the dais to touch the uniform or shake the hand of General Carson. Henry had to thread his way cautiously through the wall of women. And Francis, seeing Henry's efforts to reach him, nodded to the officers standing beside him and left the stage. As he watched Francis striding toward the exit, Henry gave up trying to get his hands on his brother. Again he had a strong sense of foreboding and wished he had never come. The insult was the least of it. His coming had triggered Fate. Now there was something terrible waiting in the unforeseeable future. Henry knew it, and Henry wasn't a superstitious man.

Gracie Mansion, the home of the Mayor of New York City, was on Eighty-ninth Street overlooking the East River. It was a rambling two-story colonial mansion that originally housed a wealthy eighteenth-century farmer.

Evelyn Wilkenson had no intention that morning of appearing at Mayor LaGuardia's gala reception for General Carson. She had gone to the Waldorf, like Henry, out of curiosity. But she'd heard the attack Francis made on Henry, and she'd noted Henry's response. Evelyn was familiar with hate, and a man who hates is often usable. So she decided to put in an appearance to meet General Carson. Francis Carson.

When Evelyn entered the brilliant public room of the mansion, she found what she'd expected: lights, flowers, waiters flitting back and forth, and a huge crowd whose loud conversation raised the noise level to an overwhelming pitch.

It took Evelyn only a moment to locate Francis. He stood head and shoulders over most of those present. The crowd around him was particularly dense, and Evelyn had to push and shove her way through a tight cluster of people to reach him.

Without waiting to introduce herself, she interrupted the conversation. "I congratulate you on putting your brother in his place. It's something I've not been able to accomplish."

Francis looked at Evelyn. He did not care for what he saw, but that made no difference. "I don't believe we've met."

"We haven't. I'm Evelyn Wilkenson. Your brother is my son-in-law. Married to my late daughter, who died giving birth to my granddaughter."

"Henry is a widowed father?" Francis smiled. "Perhaps I'll send condolences."

"You could do more than that," Evelyn snapped.

"I gather you dislike him."

"More than you do."

Francis made some private calculations. "Madam, we are in a war. If you have something in mind, I suggest you contact me when it ends. If we are both still alive." With these words he moved off into the crowd.

Evelyn watched him. There was bad blood between the Carson brothers. She wondered if it had anything to do with the inheritance of the Carson Company. Francis was the older, but Henry had inherited. She thought about Selma married to Francis and decided he would never have married her. Not Francis Carson. Which was neither here nor there, but it told her something. Even though nothing had been settled, they had met. At least it was a beginning.

# Part Three
# *1948-1953*

# Chapter 22

**T**HE MAROON and black Rolls Royce limousine wound its way through the narrow, hilly roads north of Pleasantville. It was Indian summer, and the entire countryside was aflame with the red and golden leaves of late October. Here and there the chauffeur saw a tree already stripped for winter, the branches bare, etching stark shadows on the narrow road. He had driven this road every day for almost two years. He could have driven it blindfolded.

"Here we are. Drive through the trees and park."

"Yes, ma'am." The car followed the tire tracks its continual coming and going had all but turned into a road. He stopped the car in a small clearing and turned off the motor. He needed no instructions. He would sit and wait until it was time to return to New York City. The next day they would repeat the trip.

Evelyn Wilkenson opened a compartment that contained a powerful pair of binoculars. She picked up a folded, three-legged camper's stool from the floor of the car, slung the brown leather carrying case over her shoulder and walked down a narrow path. Like the trail the car made, the path wound this way and that between the trees, bushes and thickets but always returned to the same general direction. It ended abruptly at a cliff overlooking an abandoned limestone quarry. Just before the cliff was a small open space, and there Evelyn carefully set up the camp chair. Only after she made sure the legs were properly in place did she sit down, take out the binoculars and patiently adjust them to her vision.

The huge house jumped into sharp focus. It seemed as if she could almost reach out her hand and touch it. She began to make a slow sweep of the property. Where were the children? Surely they would be playing somewhere? The stables came into view. Nothing there. The riding ring. Ah! Evelyn breathed a sigh of pleasure. There they were: a red-headed boy and a smaller, slim, dark-haired girl. Though they were the same age to the day, the boy was so much larger he could have been years older. They were both on horses, listening to an instructor who was teaching them to ride. What lunacy was this, teaching a little girl to ride?

In spite of her anger, Evelyn was ecstatic as always at the sight of her grandchild. What were they doing now? Jumping? Oh, no! Will started down the course of low jumps and completed it without a mistake. Then it was Mary's turn. Heavens! She was too young to jump. Evelyn stifled a scream. Mary took the first jump in style, but each succeeding jump grew more ragged. The child was losing control of her horse almost as if she felt Evelyn's terror. The horse's gait became rougher. Then Mary lost a stirrup, hung on for a moment and slid to the ground. Evelyn offered a prayer to a God she didn't believe existed. Please, don't let her be hurt. Please! Her binoculars were fixed on the small body in the dirt. She saw it move. Thank God! She wasn't dead. When the instructor and boy reached her, she was standing up. What were they doing now? Oh, no! Mary was getting back on the horse. The instructor gave her a leg up. Were they all crazy? The child couldn't ride. She couldn't ride. Selma couldn't ride. What made them think Mary could ride? Fools! Evelyn began to tremble, and it was hard keeping the children in focus. Mary was going to take the jumps again. That did it. No matter what happened, this farce had to be stopped before the child hurt herself. She needed a mother who understood how to raise a girl. Mary started down the course again, this time completing it successfully. Evelyn's nerves were so jangled she grew dizzy. It was only when the children left the jumping course to continue practicing a simple walk, trot and canter around the ring did she start to breathe evenly.

By the time the riding lesson ended, the shadows had lengthened and the light was fading. Much as she hated leaving while she might still glimpse Mary, she must return to the car, or it would be too dark to find her way.

Henry Carson had just completed going over the morning mail when Mary O'Toole knocked on the office door. "Come in."

"Mr. Carson, the receptionist says there's a woman waiting to see you. She won't give her name, and I see no appointment scheduled."

"Have the lady informed about our rules regarding appointments." He handed her a stack of letters. "File these. No answers are required."

"Would you like me to speak to the woman myself?"

"Yes. Find out her name, please."

Mary left the office. Almost eight years had passed since the death of William Carson, and each day Henry had seemed to her to grow more like William. It was uncanny. At last the elevator operator opened the door and said, "Good morning, Miss O'Toole." Once downstairs, Carl, the receptionist, told Mary that the lady had left. "When I hung up after talking to you, she was gone."

Mary didn't like that. "Does she know which floor Mr. Carson is on?"

"No. But when I asked for extension three hundred, she might have guessed."

"Then she could have used the stairs. I'd better warn Mr. Carson." Mary turned toward the elevator just as the doors closed. Moving quickly to the stairs, she reached the third floor to hear the angry sound of a woman's loud voice coming from Mr. Carson's office. She ran to the inner door and entered without knocking. The strange woman stood glaring at Henry. They both turned to face Mary O'Toole.

"I'm so sorry, Mr. Carson. Shall I call for a guard?"

"No, Mary. This is Mrs. Evelyn Wilkenson. Evelyn, try to be polite. This is Miss O'Toole, my secretary."

The two women surveyed each other with distaste. They were about the same age and looked surprisingly alike: small, slim, short gray hair tightly pulled back, no makeup. Both looked equally angry.

"Mary, Mrs. Wilkenson's rare feat of breaking and entering entitles her to fifteen minutes of my time and a cup of coffee, if she'd like it."

"I wouldn't like it. I only need enough time to tell you what I saw yesterday and make sure you put a stop to it!"

"Do you want to tell me standing or sitting down?"

"I'll stand." Suddenly Evelyn realized she had trapped herself. If she told Henry what she had seen, he would know she was spying on the Carson House. It would even be like him to find her lookout point, purchase the quarry and fence it in, and then what would she do? She must buy the land first.

"Evelyn"—Henry was relaxing in his chair—"I'd like your opinion. What do you think of limestone as a business? It's a fine fertilizer."

Evelyn's shoulders slumped. It was a bad blow. He'd beaten her, damn him.

"I've known about your spying almost as long as you've been doing it. So I bought the land last year." He sighed. "I said I would not permit you any contact with Mary. Watching her through binoculars from two miles away did not seem to constitute direct contact. I even considered widening the road and providing you with a more comfortable chair. But that would have spoiled some of your pleasure. Now, exactly what is bothering you?"

Evelyn gathered herself together. What she had considered a shrewd move had canceled itself out. She would make one last try, though she expected it to fail. "May I change my mind about the coffee? Black without sugar? And I would like to sit down."

"You always were an excellent general, Evelyn. And now you've learned when to retreat." He buzzed Mary and gave her Evelyn's request. "Bring me a mug. My usual cream and sugar."

They sat on the same leather couch and chairs that had been there as long as Henry could remember. The springs still creaked, and Henry made a mental note to replace them.

"All right." He removed the pocket watch he had inherited from William and placed it on the table where they both could see. "You have fifteen minutes. What brings you here?"

"I've spent so much time on that ridiculous ledge because I feel it's my duty to know how Mary is being raised."

"Is there no end to your obsession?"

"Mary is the last surviving carrier of the Wilkenson blood line. I want her to grow up as a young lady, marry and have children who will have many more children in turn and carry on the Wilkenson name."

"It sounds like a horse breeding farm. What is so special about Wilkenson blood?"

"It is Wilkenson blood. That's enough."

Henry shrugged. "You have twelve minutes. Come to the point. What's troubling you?"

"You do know what your children were doing yesterday?"

Henry took a small diary from his vest pocket. "Yesterday, Will attended his school, Mary hers. They were both home about two-thirty. They had a two-hour riding lesson. Nothing unusual about yesterday."

"Fire that instructor at once!"

"Stop giving me orders. Just tell me what happened."

Evelyn looked back over the years and remembered what had happened the last time she gave Henry orders. So she carefully composed her expression and tone. "Mary fell while jumping yesterday."

"She wasn't hurt."

"The instructor forced her to take the jumps again. The poor child must have been terrified."

"She'd be more frightened if she hadn't done it. Now she knows she can take the jumps."

"Henry Carson, she's the last of the Wilkensons. Nothing must happen to her."

"It's impossible to live without things happening to you. After the disaster you created in raising Selma, would you like me to repeat your mistakes with Mary?"

"She's a Wilkenson. The last of our line." Evelyn was reduced to repeating the most important statement she could make.

"She's also a Carson."

Evelyn had another idea. "She needs a woman's hand in bringing her up. You have not remarried, so I offer you mine. I'll listen to her problems. Advise her."

"You may mean well, but I can't afford your advice. You'll make the same mistakes with her that you made with Selma. We'd have a foolish, frightened, priggish young woman exactly like your daughter."

"Selma was a fool."

"Yes. And you made her into one."

Evelyn forced herself to contain the violence of her feeling. She was absolutely convinced Henry was wrong. Mary should not be exposed to risks like horseback riding. Why was he so stubborn? Her temper changed to sorrow. There was no sacrifice she would not make for Mary, even her own life. She had to spend her last years raising the child. "Will you at least let me see her occasionally at Carson House? Get to know her? In simple justice, Henry, please let me see my daughter."

Henry never knew what he might have agreed to if Evelyn had not used the word "daughter." But her mistake cost her his concession. "Evelyn, Mary is not Selma. She is not your daughter, she is your granddaughter. And my answer is no. No direct contact with the child."

Evelyn slumped in her chair, looking beaten, old, incapable of action. It was strange how the woman could be one moment so formidable and the next so forlorn and wretched.

"If you wish, you can write Mary and send her a picture of yourself. I'll have prints made of the pictures we've taken of Mary since she was born. If she wishes, she can write you. That's it."

Evelyn recognized her mistake, but in truth, she thought of Mary as her daughter. "May I speak to her on the telephone?"

"Perhaps when she's older. I make no promises."

On the way home, Evelyn reviewed the meeting. Very little had been accomplished, and time was running out. Mary was eight. In another year or two it would be too late. Her basic character would be formed. Evelyn had tried all possible avenues to reach Henry—his servants, business associates, even ex-lady-friends—to persuade him to consider the good of the child. Everything failed.

Now she had reached a point where the pathological undertow had grown too strong, overcoming her usual good sense. The need for Mary had become an obsession. She had only one possible ally left: General Francis Carson. She'd thought about him for years, waited for him to return to the United States. Working together, they would not have to persuade Henry; they'd force Henry to give her custody of Mary. She realized Henry might do as he had threatened years ago—he might pull the Wilkenson products from the market—but Evelyn had no choice. If she had to abandon Wilkenson, Inc. to perpetuate the Wilkenson name, she would. The lesser gain would be sacrificed for the greater.

This led to a major decision. She would no longer wait for Francis Carson. She would seek him out. And she knew where to begin. Under the terms of William's will, Mark James handled Francis Carson's inheritance. Mark James would know where to find him.

# Chapter 23

DESPITE the fact that she had known Mark James and his father for years, Mark refused to tell Evelyn how to reach Francis Carson. General Carson had left specific instructions that no one was to know his whereabouts. Mark couldn't violate those instructions. Finally, Mark agreed to send Francis Carson a letter saying she wished to contact him. Assuming Francis approved, then and only then would Mark tell Evelyn where to reach the general. Meanwhile, if she attempted to go behind his back, he would make a second contact with General Carson and suggest he keep his distance since Mrs. Wilkinson was dishonorable.

This gave Evelyn pause. So she waited. And she waited. Finally, late in January, she had a note from Mark James telling her to write Mr. Francis Carson in care of American Express in Rome. After reading her letter, Mr. Carson would decide if he wished to be in touch with her. Evelyn spent days composing a short note to Francis Carson, reminding him of their meeting at Gracie Mansion and their brief conversation about his brother. She suggested that their joint dislike could be used to mutual advantage. Then she waited for an answer. Waiting was hard. An old acquaintance, Charles "Chip" Bohlen, was Ambassador to Italy. He would know where Francis Carson lived. She could then call him directly. But if Francis Carson was anything like Henry Carson, calling could be a mistake. Better to wait as long as possible before resorting to what amounted to a last-ditch effort. Evelyn Wilkenson's restraint was nearly at an end when she finally received a brief note from Francis. He apologized for the difficulty required to reach him, but he'd had so much publicity during the war he had to protect his privacy. He had been wintering in Morocco and hadn't picked up his mail at the American Express office in three months. He would meet her in Rome at the end of March. He included his telephone number. She should call him when she arrived.

On March 25, Evelyn Wilkenson registered at the Excelsior Hotel in Rome. She was met at the station by a young man from the American

Embassy, Ralph Warren, and driven to the hotel in an embassy car. The young man had been instructed to treat her carefully.

As soon as Evelyn entered her room at the hotel, she called the English-speaking hotel operator and gave her the number Francis had given her. Although Evelyn was totally unaware that a miracle was taking place, one did. The number was tried and the proper phone rang in the proper house.

"*Pronto.*"

"Mr. Carson, please."

The female voice switched to English. "Who may I say is calling?"

Though the accent was light and charming, it was easy for Evelyn to tell that the woman on the other end of the line was Italian. She had rarely heard English sound so musical. "Tell him Mrs. Wilkenson has arrived."

"*Certo. Un momento.* One moment, please."

There was a short pause before a man spoke. "Mrs. Evelyn Wilkenson?"

"Yes."

"This is Francis Carson. Where are you?"

"At the Excelsior. When can we meet?"

"Tomorrow at your hotel and go elsewhere for lunch."

"I hoped for something more private."

"We'll have privacy enough. And I am bringing a young lady to Rome. She'll dine with us."

"Our business is private."

"Let's not argue. We'll be at your hotel at twelve-thirty sharp. Wait in your room, I'll ring up."

Evelyn thought how much like Henry he sounded. How much like William. All the Carsons seem to do nothing but give orders and expect them to be followed. "All right. Tomorrow at twelve-thirty. Goodby."

"*Ciao, bellissima!*"

Evelyn hung up. She had waited so long that twenty-four hours, more or less, made no difference. And she could go to the opera. Verdi's *La Forza del Destino* was opening at Caracalla. Evelyn was sure Ralph Warren could arrange a ticket for her. She dialed the operator and asked for the American Embassy.

Later, sitting at the window overlooking the Via Veneto, waiting for the limousine to take her to the opera, she took her first sip of the Italian version of champagne, Asti Spumante. And almost spit it out. If this was their idea of champagne, this was clearly a country with no taste. She braced herself to try another sip. Next week, *servizio* said, they expected a shipment of French champagne. But next week she would be on her way home. Still, she thought, if, with heaven's help, this trip was not a wild goose chase, she'd remember even Asti Spumante with pleasure.

When Francis Carson arrived in Rome shortly after the end of the Second World War, he found the city to be exactly as he expected. Having been declared a *Città Aperta*, an Open City, there was no physical destruction—no bombed-out shells of buildings, no walls of cathedrals without roofs, no unfilled craters in the streets. Even the crumbling ruins of ancient Rome continued to crumble at their own leisurely pace, not hastened along by bombs, artillery shelling or the pockmarks of rifle bullets. Of course there were changes. The *Teatro Reale dell' Opera* was now the *Teatro dell' Opera* and the *Foro Mussolini* was now the *Foro Italico*.

But Francis knew the life of a city depends far less upon the integrity of its buildings than on the integrity of its people, especially the integrity of the ruling classes, the aristocracy of the city; and this most vital part of Rome had been decimated. In all of Europe there was no city more ideally suited to the purposes of Francis Carson.

The capital of Italy was bankrupt. Unlike cities such as Milan, Genoa, Turin, even Venice, Rome had no industry, no factories, no farmland. It had three sources of wealth. First was the wealth of Italy itself, which flowed into a huge bureaucracy. Its second source came via the tourists arriving from around the world to marvel at the glory that was ancient Rome. And, finally, the third source was the Italian nobility, who had built great villas in and around Rome to be close to the House of Savoy, the monarchy, Mussolini and the seat of power. The fortunes of these families came from hereditary land holdings all over Italy, some dating back to the Renaissance.

By the war's end, all three sources of income had failed. The tourist trade had dried up, the government was in chaos, and the nobility no longer had any income. The ruling Christian Democratic Party had little time to run the country. Its energy was spent fighting the threat of an imminent Communist *coup d'état*. Amidst such anarchy, the bureaucracy disintegrated. Of what use were bookkeepers, record keepers, tax collectors, when there were no records or books to keep, no taxes to collect? Even the police were not really interested in maintaining law and order. The elite corps, Mario Scelba's *Celere*, were concerned with breaking up huge open-air Communist rallies. In such a city, Francis Carson could flourish.

The first thing Francis Carson did upon arriving in Rome was to select one of the ruined villas and buy it. He chose the Orsini property. When he bought it, he also bought the daughter of the former owner. The first purchase was as legal and as public as a disorganized government could manage. The purchase of Caterina Orsini was less formal. She went along with the estate.

Francis spent a fortune remodeling the villa so that it now combined the beauty of the Italian Renaissance with the most modern features. But over and beyond the elegance of the villa and anything Caterina might provide, Francis had chosen the Orsini estate for a particular reason. A short distance from the villa was an ancient amphitheater. It was small, sixty feet in diameter, built within a natural bowl-like depression in an otherwise flat meadow. The original Roman owner of the property had made the first improvements on nature. Since it was to be a place for private entertainments, the sides of the bowl were terraced to allow for three circles of couches, tables, chairs. Then there were four wide staircases, descending to a flat, circular wooden stage. The staircases and the circular tiers were made permanent by the skillful fitting into place of huge flat stones, cut from a nearby quarry, over the hard red clay of the land.

Additional stones were used to build a wall twelve feet high, enclosing the amphitheater. Iron rings to hold torches were fitted into the stones. The wall had two huge doors facing east and west, and was faced on both sides with Carrara marble. Six feet outside the wall, a row of heavy columns supported wooden beams, which in turn supported a roof and provided a pleasant place for guests to walk and talk during intermissions.

The west door of the wall opened into a small, stone courtyard which led to a graceful building with many rooms. Water was piped from a nearby aqueduct to this building, which provided the guests with toilet facilities, the performers a place to rest and change, and finally special rooms for those who wished to enjoy more personal and private pleasures.

The amphitheater had the usual four stone pedestals, also faced with Carrara marble, where statues of Roman gods were set: Jupiter, Venus, Neptune and Minerva. Finally, a ring of cypress trees surrounded the structure.

Two thousand years had not been kind to the structure. Weather had rotted the wooden ceiling of the loggia and living quarters. Invading barbarians had broken the noses off statues, then toppled them and carried off all the furniture. During the Renaissance, marble was stripped from the walls and pedestals for use in the Palazzo Farnese in Rome. The wooden stage was burnt in the campfires of one of the marauding bands that ranged Italy during the fourteenth and fifteenth centuries.

When Francis bought the villa, architects and archeologists were employed to give advice and help in the restoration of the amphitheater and guest quarters. What had originally been constructed of stone was reasonably intact, and the cypress trees still stood, but there was much work to be done. Francis spared no effort to restore what had been, rebuilding and repairing all the ruined wood and stone sections of the amphitheater as well as the guest quarters. He went so far as to have furniture makers copy the couches, tables and chairs that the ancient Romans had used.

He made only what he considered necessary changes. In the guest quarters, modern plumbing replaced the ancient facilities. A complete twentieth-century kitchen was added, plus a common room and a large number of cubicles for sleeping. Another change was made in the statues standing on the four stone pedestals; Jupiter, Venus, Neptune and Minerva bored Francis. He chose four deities of a different sort, more to his taste: Caesar, Tiberius, Caligula and Nero. He also had his own ideas for the stage. A series of wooden beams, supported by concrete pillars, allowed a complicated system of ropes, swings, pulleys and even special furniture to be raised or lowered onto the stage. Finally, he provided himself with an alcove at the head of the north staircase. Heavy drapes supported by poles could hide him from view. A single spotlight, fixed to focus on the draped-off space, was the only electrical fixture in the amphitheater. Otherwise, light was provided, as in Roman times, by sunlight during the day and torchlight at night.

The restoration was graceful, elegant and, above all, useful. Now all Francis needed were the proper audience and participants for his "entertainments." And those too Rome, of all cities in Europe, could provide, and Caterina Orsini would know well where to find them.

The nobility of Rome, the great land-holding families, the third source of Roman wealth, had lost the income from their estates, these estates having been confiscated by the new Democratic government and the farms divided among the tenants who lived on the land. No compensation was paid to the former owners. Such great families as the Farnese, Borghese, Orsini, Sforza, Baldesarri, Colona—families whose bloodlines went back to the thirteenth and fourteenth centuries, families who had once ruled the city-states of Parma, Siena, Turin, Genoa, Florence—were summarily stripped of all wealth and power, even the public use of their titles.

The "best of breed" of these families, among whom Caterina had been raised, those most fitted to lead during a time of major social and political upheaval, had died. Died for Mussolini's dream of a new Roman Empire, a *mare nostrum*. Died in Eritrea, Libya, Ethiopia, Italian Somaliland. Died in the brutal cold and deep snows of Russia alongside the German divisions. And, finally, died futilely, uselessly, defending their beloved Italy in the mountains and gorges of the Apennines against the overwhelming power of General Mark Clark's U.S. 5th Army.

What remained in Rome to greet Francis were the broken survivors of the great families: the widows, the aged, and the daughters and sons who had been too young to fight. These younger remnants of the nobility had certain things in common: youth, beauty and completely useless educations. They appreciated Michelangelo, Botticelli, del Sarto, as well as Verdi and Bellini. They could read Dante in the original Italian. But they lived in virtual poverty. Even if there had been work available in Rome, these young men and women would not have considered work a possibility. They had not been raised to work. And if they'd considered the possibility, they would have had no idea how to find a job. Rome had become a world they no longer understood.

All that they possessed were their crumbling palazzos and villas, which they had no way of maintaining, some clothes originally belonging to their parents and, in private, the use of their inherited titles: Principe Farnese, Contessa Orsini, Marchesa Colona. The only thing of value, the only thing that might earn them money for food, was their youth and beauty. So many used this new "coin of the realm" as a form of barter, trading themselves for money to anyone who would pay the price, man or woman. And in so doing, they became thoroughly corrupted; even those with no natural bent for corruption descended the steps to hell.

Francis Carson could have his pick of this group. They flocked to him because, for these penniless, drifting waifs, raised for another age, Francis could provide a day's food, a night's lodging, drugs to wipe out their despair. These young people lived in a kind of wasteland where living had no meaning except surviving from one day to the next. They were the perfect toys for Francis to play with. In another time, he might never have met them, for despite his wealth, his name and charm, he would not have been invited to the homes of the nobility. But now he was their god, and sex was one way they paid their homage to this god. And where Francis Carson was God, he decreed sadism and the orgiastic as the way one should worship him.

Although it had been pouring earlier in Rome and the sky was still heavy with rain clouds, the opening night at Caracalla went on as scheduled. A long battery of spotlights at stage front acted as a curtain, blinding the audience, making it impossible to see the stage. The string of lights was so long, Evelyn had to turn left and then right to see all of them. High above the lights and well behind the stage, a thin arch of stone still stood as a reminder of how solidly the Romans could build. At each end of the lights was a high, stone column that appeared wider at the top than at the base. The clouds were so low and heavy they seemed about to swallow the tops of the columns. Tendrils of moisture floated through the air.

At ten o'clock the row of lights went out. A full moon came out from behind the clouds. The high, thin arch was now clearly visible in the moonlight. And it seemed to Evelyn that the shadows cast by the stone towers converged on her. She shrank down in her seat. Surely the towers were too heavy to stand? They were about to fall on her. The orchestra began. Three great chords. A pause. The same three chords repeated. A pause. The first violins picked up the "fate" theme.

In the sky over a small, highly secluded amphitheater about thirty miles outside Rome along the Appia Antica the same moon appeared. A single trumpet sounded. Three clear notes. A pause. Three more notes. A pause. A strong, clear voice was heard. *"Incominciamo!"* Torches, placed in iron rings around the wall, flamed, one after another, as two naked figures, one male and one female, lit them while racing around the perimeter of the wall. Then they placed the torches they carried into the empty rings waiting for them. The girl wound her arms around the boy's neck and her legs around his waist. They had been lovers since childhood, and it still surprised her to be given food, a bed and enough money to live for a while just for doing what they liked most to do. She trembled with expectation and the effort it took to keep her attention focused solely on the curly hairs of the boy's chest, not to look at the audience. She could hardly wait to be on stage, to feel all their eyes on her. She enjoyed exhibiting herself, enjoyed being stared at. It was almost as good as being made love to. In fact, she felt a heightened sexuality in their presence. She knew her naked body aroused everyone, and the thought of their pleasure, even envy, at the perfection of her mating increased her own passion.

She melted against his chest, feeling his fingers follow the contours of her body. One of his hands slid down to spread over the firm, full cheeks of her bottom while the other sensuously caressed her breasts. A shiver passed through her, touching every nerve, and her eyes glittered feverishly.

There was a tension in the amphitheater, and she felt herself fondled by all the staring men and women. As she arched backward, electricity flowed between her and them. The huge shadow she cast in the semi-lit arena made visible to the audience how willingly she opened, lifting herself up from his waist to receive his thrust. Her long moan of pleasure was blocked by his exploring tongue, and joined together, they stood still as marble statues.

A thrill of satisfaction ran through their bodies when the first voice called out, "*Bravo! Bravissimo!*" Then there was the applause from the twenty-four people in the stone circle. Still holding the girl, the boy walked up the few steps to the center of the stage. He stood in the middle of the stage, waiting.

The man's voice was heard again. "*Adesso!*" A swing dropped to the stage, and the boy sank down on the leather seat and started to swing back and forth. As the swing moved in ever increasing arcs, the girl moved her body in rhythmic rapport with the boy—first away as the swing reached its apex and then back as it reversed direction. The audience edged closer. They wanted to see everything. And the girl felt her response deepen by the wave of desire that swept through the audience. Her body was no longer her own. It belonged to everyone watching her. She could feel the suspense grow, waiting for her release . . . release. Shuddering in ecstasy, she screamed as she came to her climax. "Ah. Aa. Aieeee." Barely glancing at the girl, the boy continued to move in and out of her, and then, still seated on the swing, he lifted her off his sex. As though to emphasize his triumph, he shouted in furious pleasure as several bursts of white exploded between her breasts. Then he smiled as the audience, like some great animal, gave out its own cry of pleasure. He placed the girl back on his lap and slowly, teasingly, licked her breasts clean. When this was done, they slid from the swing, vanishing into the darkness from which they had appeared.

The round of applause was loud. "*Bravo! Molto bene!*" Francis Carson walked to the center of the stage. He was naked except for leather thongs wound around his long legs. His body looked like Michelangelo's "David." His skin was tanned and oiled. He addressed the gathering. "*Amici mei*, you have seen the first act of tonight's entertainment. Servants will pass among you with food, drink, hashish, cocaine, opium. Take what pleases you. There will be a thirty-minute intermission before the finale of tonight's revels, during which you are of course free to do whatever you wish among yourselves." He stepped out of the circle of light.

Francis lay on a couch, his head supported on a bolster, staring out at his guests from between the slightly parted drapes. He inhaled the sweet smoke of hashish through a Moroccan water pipe. Caterina, her dark hair cut short in an Italian boy fashion, was lying next to him on a twin couch. Her nude body was being oiled by a female attendant. "That was one of our more successful efforts. Giuseppe and his sister are very good."

Caterina looked up. Her eyes were large and glazed. "*Sí, caro. Bella.*"

Francis inhaled. "But I am bored with simple sex tonight. I need something else."

A terrified look crossed Caterina's face. "*Caro! Piacere!*"

"No! You have other uses tonight." He snapped his fingers. "Maria."

"*Sí, signore?*" The servant applying the oil answered.

"What have you given La Contessa tonight?"

"An aphrodisiac. And cocaine. As you ordered."

"Excellent. She will perform well. We must not disappoint our guests." Francis sat up and took hold of the hair of a very pretty boy who had been running his lips over his penis. "Paolo, you do not know how to use your mouth. You do not suck hard enough. And you bite. We may have to have all your teeth removed. You must open your throat and use your tongue." He took another full lung of hashish, then glanced down at the boy. "You are a very beautiful boy, but you are lousy with your mouth. Maria?" The maid looked up from her oiling of Caterina. "Take him away." The boy and the servant disappeared into the darkness at the rear of Francis' private alcove. "Caterina, wake up. You will be onstage shortly."

Caterina's eyes opened. "Don't you like me? You prefer the boy?"

"You are the perfect woman, but tonight you are for our friends."

The idea pleased her. She whispered, "Our nice friends?"

"I promise you, you will be pleased."

"Touch me now, *caro*." Suddenly she was begging. "I burn!"

Francis reached between her legs and stroked her. Her body quivered in anticipation. The flesh he did not touch demanded more, and she half rose from the couch, clutching his hand to guide it further inside her. Quite casually, Francis broke her grip and pulled his hand back. "I want you fresh. Do that again, and I'll punish you."

The threat terrified Caterina, and she lay back, panting. No matter how aroused or how deadened by drugs she might be, a threat from Francis always had the same effect. It brought back the horror of the Nazis.

The Nazis had occupied her home six years earlier. She was sixteen. They were a picked group of Hitler's SS, homosexual and sadistic. To them, a young Italian contessa, whose father had died in Eritrea and whose insane mother was confined to the top floor of the villa, was perfect for their games. She became the center of a series of orgies involving sex, drugs and sadism that lasted until the Germans retreated before the invading Americans. By that time the virginal young girl that was Caterina Orsini had accepted her captors and, by accepting her captors, learned to survive and became another woman.

There was no sexual variation, man, woman or animal, she had not experienced and would not experience again if the Nazis demanded it. No drug she had not taken and would not take again if the Nazis insisted. However, there was one thing the Nazis did that could drive her into madness: Caterina could not bear physical pain. In her nightmares, she relived the times when she had been tied to a pole and whipped with electric whips that tortured her body and left not a mark on her skin. Of tongs that pressed exactly to the point where the sinews threatened to tear and the bone to break. The rack that stretched her. The pincers that made her nipples bleed. The pain so great she wanted to die.

Francis Carson rose from the couch and parted the drapes that protected the alcove from curious eyes. It was time to observe his guests at play. It was as he expected. A wind of desire had swept the tiers, and a variety of sexual acts were in progress. There were twelve men and twelve women. Since most of the guests were either bisexual or homosexual, the even division among the sexes was accidental.

Francis' voice rang through the arena. "You have five minutes to finish your current pleasure. The trumpet will sound, and you will separate and return to your places. The finale of tonight's entertainment begins immediately afterward."

In five minutes, the trumpet sounded for the second time. The same three notes, an octave higher than before. Arms, legs, mouths, bodies parted, and each member of the group returned to his or her separate couch. Francis gave the call, *"Incominciate!"*

Again the naked boy and girl appeared and circled the wall, this time snuffing out the torches. They met at the point where they entered, leaving a single torch still lit. With easy grace, the boy lifted the girl to his shoulder, held the position for a moment, and then the girl extinguished the last torch. The arena was now in darkness. The guests waited silently for the final act.

Two flames appeared floating in the air. They flared from torches held aloft by two slender female hands. The audience, their eyes growing accustomed to the darkness, was able to make out a beautiful, naked young woman, her body glistening in the flickering light, being carried on the shoulders of four young men. The young men were almost as beautiful, their bodies lean, muscular, bronze, their heads handsome, with strong molded features. When they reached center stage, a number of slings descended from above. The boy and the girl now reappeared and received the torches from the young woman's hands. They pirouetted away and used them to light a number of candles that had been placed around the stage. Then they vanished again. Now the four men set the girl on the slings so that her legs, arms, body and head were supported, That task completed, they flanked the girl and stood at attention. The tableau held while the onlookers burst into applause.

Caterina opened her eyes for the first time. Reclining languorously on the shoulders of the men, she'd felt her body vibrating with passion, every one of her senses straining in high anticipation. Something familiar had awakened within her, something that triggered an insatiable, restless hunger. The candles cast a flickering unreality around her. Oh how her body burned, enslaved by her need to be used. She wondered how many and what they would do. She writhed and moaned, in the grip of desire so violent it seemed almost devouring.

Then a voice gave an order. "She's ready. You, you, you and you. Take her!"

Out of nowhere shapes appeared, and she was being caressed by many mouths and tongues touching every part of her. Separating her legs, kissing her, biting her, licking her, entering her everywhere at once. She was being taken by a multisexed creature who could satisfy all her desires at once. She seemed to be floating in a dark world of candlelit flesh, feeling soft touches. Each touch brought a new joy. She abandoned herself to all her needs, wanting only to excite everyone to a frenzy of desire. Her eyes, every motion of her body became an invitation to those who watched to satisfy themselves with her or whomever they pleased.

The audience watched in a state of growing arousal. A hand fondled someone's splendidly full buttocks with a seductive, teasing finger. Faces were covered by breasts or buried in pubic hair. Legs were opening for exploring hands gently probing secret places. Ivory and bronze skin, all sexual combinations, were joining together.

Caterina bloomed like some hothouse flower, odorous, moist, with erotic eyes and lips, filling the air with a rich, female perfume, pungent as the smell of the sea. Her mouth opened to close around a thrusting penis. At the same time, sensually persuasive lips were sucking on her nipples. Then someone was kissing her feet and running his hands up the insides of her thighs. He put his hands on her waist and kissed her between her legs. She felt him enter her and closed her eyes to glory in the feeling of his hard flesh sliding in and out of her.

"Stronger! Stronger!" she murmured. She became like a mouth opening and closing around him, currents of excruciating pleasure running through her body until she gave a long cry of joy—only to have her desire renew itself. Her flesh was now like a hot ember, so that everyone was warmed by her nearness. Then someone was pushing against her buttocks. She resisted for a moment, then gave way and felt the thrill of his entrance between the soft walls of her flesh. How well he fitted, and heaving slightly, her body trembled with orgasmic release. And again her desire returned. She reveled in her gluttony, in her eagerness to satisfy everyone and satisfy herself. She no longer existed as a person. Only a mass of senses: touch, smell, taste, sight and hearing in an unceasingly demanding body.

# Chapter 24

FRANCIS CARSON woke the next morning at seven, as refreshed after two hours sleep as if he'd spent the evening reading and had retired at ten. He was due to meet Evelyn Wilkenson at the Excelsior at twelve-thirty, which gave him plenty of time for his morning routine of swimming two miles in the pool. Caterina was asleep next to him and, if permitted, would sleep all day. Usually he permitted it, but today he had a hunch he should bring her with him to meet Mrs. Wilkenson. It was that same kind of hunch that had saved his life many times during the war. He never ignored it. He slipped on a robe and entered the adjoining room. Maria was asleep next to Tomasso, her husband. He tapped her lightly on the shoulder. She was wide awake at once.

"Maria, wake La Contessa at ten o'clock. We are to leave for Rome at eleven-thirty. See she is alert. One benzedrine if necessary. But only if necessary."

"*Si, signore.*"

Francis returned to his room to change to bathing trunks.

Precisely at twelve-twenty-five, Francis, wearing a seersucker suit, white shirt and dark tie, stopped his Alfa Romeo in front of the Excelsior. "Wait in the car, *cara*. I will return with Mrs. Wilkenson."

Caterina wore a simple white dress, white shoes and a white band holding her black hair in place. She looked as fresh and alert as Francis.

"Soon?" she asked.

"Very soon. I suspect Mrs. Wilkenson has been ready for hours."

Evelyn Wilkenson had been ready for hours. She'd had almost no sleep the night before. The meeting with Francis Carson and what she hoped to accomplish kept her awake most of the night. *La Forza del Destino*—the Force of Destiny. Maybe the opera was an omen?

By eight A.M., Evelyn had given up all hope of sleep. After she finished breakast, she spent the rest of the morning waiting, sitting at the open French windows and looking down at the busy crowd on the street. Her waiter was a mine of information. She only wished he could tell her if Francis would agree to her plan. He had to agree. This was the last chance she would have to obtain custody of her child. Only he could help her defeat Henry Carson.

A dark green sports car stopped in front of the hotel. Evelyn held her breath. Yes! The blond-haired man getting out of the driver's seat was Francis Carson. Evelyn left the window to gather the few things she thought she would need for the meeting: a picture of Selma, a picture of Maggie Rhodes taken at the wedding, pictures of the two babies. That was it. The rest would depend upon what action he decided to take. The telephone rang. Mr. Carson was in the lobby waiting for her.

It took a few mintues for them to reintroduce themselves, introduce Evelyn to Caterina, and then to drive to a small trattoria in a poor section of Rome. On the way, Francis showed Evelyn a part of Rome very different from the tawdry, faded elegance of the Excelsior and Via Veneto. They entered the Borghese Gardens. He pointed out a section of a wall and gate called Porta Pinciana. Evelyn was startled to see that people lived in the towers.

"Yes, people in Rome live where they can. In towers, ruins, even in caves in the seven hills."

"That's disgusting!"

"Possibly, but they do live. The alternative is less desirable."

Eventually they drove through a huge monument with a triple arch and into a huge round piazza.

"Piazza del Popolo, Mrs. Wilkenson. A favorite gathering place for Communist rallies."

Then they entered a series of narrow, stone streets with a small trickle of dirty water running down the center of them. Evelyn noted the old ladies dressed in long, black dresses, so different from the Italians on Via Veneto, the hordes of boys, teenagers and younger, who lounged about obviously with nothing to do.

Evelyn was also surprised at the number of horse-drawn carts of all sizes winding their way through the streets, and was revolted by the amount of uncollected horse manure. Here and there men with hand carts and brooms were sweeping it up.

Francis laughed at her reaction. "Yes, the Eternal City will die buried under the horse manure. I can see the piles gradually creeping up the walls of Saint Peter's. Rome survives earthquakes, invaders, conquerors, everything, but not horse manure." He had decided to humor Evelyn. One never knew. Evelyn had no interest in Rome's troubles, but she was interested in Francis. If he wanted to impress her with his knowledge of Rome, she was prepared to be impressed. Until she saw him get out of his car, she had not been certain he would keep the appointment. She had prayed, and this half of her prayer had been answered.

He paused and leaned closer to Evelyn. "Incidentally, I chose this place deliberately. If we ate on Via Veneto, the photographers, the *paparazzi*, might just happen to take a picture of us. I don't believe we want anyone with a record showing we know each other."

When they pulled up in front of the trattoria, Francis called to a boy, "*Giovane, Vieni quí!*" He tore a 100-lire note in half. "*Mezzo per te. Mezzo per me. Guarda la macchina. Quando tornerò, tutto per te. Capisci?*"

The boy showed a mouthful of very white teeth. "*Grazie, excellenza. Ci penso Io.*"

Francis led them into the trattoria. The proprietor took them to a large, relatively secluded table and left them menus and a liter of white wine.

Evelyn studied Francis while she read the menu. There was a family resemblance among all the Carsons. He was older than Henry. Why wasn't he running the Carson Company?

"May I order for you?"

Evelyn put the menu down. "Please do."

Francis signaled for the waiter and gave their orders in rapid, fluid Italian. "Now to business. You've come a long way to see me. Why?"

Evelyn tried to collect her thoughts. To give herself time, she focused on Caterina, who had not said a word since they were introduced. She appeared content to sip her wine and listen. She was an extraordinarily beautiful girl. And a Countess. Quite appropriate for Francis. "The countess, does she speak English?"

Caterina answered. She found Evelyn what she thought of as *non è simpatico*. Unpleasant! Cold, dry, sexless and without any humor she could discern. And to ask the question in that manner was insulting. "Mrs. Wilkenson, though I am an Italian, I am also European. Yes, I speak English. I also speak French, German and some Spanish. What else do you wish to know?"

Her voice was very deep for a woman. It reminded Evelyn of another voice, Maggie Rhodes' voice. She stared at the girl. If her nose were a trifle shorter, she would look like Maggie Rhodes—the same black curly hair, eyes, chin and, as far as she could tell, a similar figure. "My apologies, Countess. I did not mean it the way it sounded. But what I'm about to discuss must be held in strict confidence."

"Mrs. Wilkenson, I would not have brought Caterina if I were not confident of her discretion.

"All right. When last we met, I had the distinct impression you were not fond of your brother."

"Something of an understatement."

"As I mentioned, he has a daughter. My granddaughter." Francis seemed bored. Evelyn knew this part of the story didn't interest him. She hurried on. "But Henry has another child, a boy." Francis' interest picked up, and Evelyn, anxious to hold his attention, poured out the story of Selma, Maggie and William.

When she finished, Francis was smiling, trying not to laugh. "So my brother doesn't know whether the boy is his son or a half brother? And I may have a nephew or a half brother? I certainly don't care which, but knowing Henry, it must be torture. That is a very amusing story."

"Henry has not remarried. I believe he still loves Maggie Rhodes."

"It gets even better. Henry in love with a woman who may have had an affair with our father. Yes, his Puritan soul is in hell. But what has all this to do with me?"

"Don't you see? Henry Carson has acknowledged he is the boy's father. That makes him an unfit parent for my grandchild and unfit to run the Carson Company. Help me, and we can contest William Carson's will. Take both the child and the company from him."

Francis was no longer amused. "I believe you were at the reading of the my late father's will. You are aware what happens to my income if I contest his will."

"Not when we break it. All the clauses will be canceled."

"Mrs. Wilkenson, you want to obtain custody of your granddaughter, and you believe a legal battle will do it. I don't. I think we'd lose. But before I give a final answer, I admit to curiosity. I now understand at least one reason why Henry was chosen over me. However, I would like to be sure. Do you have a picture of your daughter with you?"

Evelyn realized she'd lost everything. Francis Carson would not help her. She would never gain possession of Mary. It took a massive effort for her not to scream at the man. "Of course." She opened the purse and looked for the snapshot of Selma. It was clipped together with snapshots of the children and of Maggie Rhodes at the wedding. "You might as well see the entire 'family,' " she remarked, handing him the photos.

Francis glanced at the picture of Selma. I was right, he thought. Henry would marry her. I never would, and William knew it. He looked at the photos of the children. "She does resemble you, Mrs. Wilkenson. And the boy? Who knows?" Then he looked at the photo of Maggie in the dress and wide-brimmed hat that William had bought for her. "A very beautiful woman. My respect for my brother increases. Respect, not fondness. She looks very like—" Abruptly his eyes narrowed, he studied the picture, then Caterina, then the picture and back to Caterina. "Hmmm. Mrs. Wilkenson, I've no interest in the scheme you suggested, but . . ."

Evelyn seized on the "but." "But what, Mr. Carson?"

"May I call you Evelyn? And you call me Francis."

"Of course."

"Give me your impression of this Maggie Rhodes. Her hair, her figure, her voice. Whatever you think of."

Evelyn smiled for the first time in months. "You see the similarity too. The countess has a Roman nose, and Maggie's a little taller and larger in the bosom. That's the only difference. Even their voices are similar. They could be doubles. What are you thinking?"

"Caterina, look at the picture. Uncanny, isn't it?"

Caterina took the picture. She had no idea what Francis had in mind, but quick to sense his games, she rose from the table. "*Tornerò in dieci minuti.*"

"She'll be back in ten minutes," Francis told Evelyn. "And here's our first course. "*Cameriere, porta la zuppa della contessa in cucina. La contessa tornerà subito.*" Caterina's plate was removed. "Try the soup. It's called *stracciatella*, and it's very good."

Evelyn sipped the yellow broth and tried to guess what Francis had in mind. Caterina returned before they finished their soup. She had been to a nearby shop and now wore a wide-brimmed hat, similar to the one Maggie wore at the wedding.

She walked to the table and curtsied. "*Eccola qua.* What is her name?"

"Maggie Rhodes."

"Maggie Rhodes *è qui.*"

Francis applauded politely. "*Brava! Magnifica!*" Evelyn looked from one to the other. "Evelyn, the plan you proposed was pure nonsense. Furthermore, I've no interest in controlling the Carson Company. But I have an idea which, if it works, may give you custody of your grand-daughter." He glanced at Caterina. "Unless Henry connects Caterina to me."

Evelyn put down her spoon. "Tell me your idea, and I'll give you my opinion of its success." She spoke firmly, but she knew she would agree to anything.

"Of course." Having fallen in love with his plot, Francis was willing to indulge Evelyn's show of independence, up to a point. Unlike Henry, he had a dim recollection of their mother and much clearer memories of how much William had suffered when she died. He knew his father had loved Nathalia, loved her fully, completely until "death did them part." And it was death, Nathalia's death, that parted them. William had never loved again. He was a man capable of loving only one woman throughout his entire life.

Henry was like their father. He also could love only one woman, love her fully, completely, until "death did them part." But in Henry's case, it wasn't "death" that had parted them. It was William. Something their father had done caused Henry to question who had fathered Maggie's child. Francis almost laughed out loud as he realized the full extent of Henry's love for Maggie Rhodes. He loved her so much his love had even affected his judgment about their father. Francis knew under no circumstances whatsoever would William Carson go near a woman his son loved. But William was dead and unable to allay Henry's suspicions. It made no difference. What was important was that Henry loved Maggie and had lost her. Henry's grief would provide Evelyn with her Mary and him with some measure of vengeance. "We'll provide my brother with what he wants—Maggie Rhodes. Maggie Rhodes free from any taint of our father's hot hand or hot anything else. And Caterina is an Italian aristocrat with a family name that goes back six hundred years. She will replace Maggie Rhodes as Henry's love, and if I know anything about my brother, he'll marry her." He turned to Caterina. "Tell me, *cara*, would you like to marry a very rich American? You would, wouldn't you?"

There was a very clear threat in his voice that Caterina heard and understood. "A rich American is an excellent start. Tell me more about him."

"He's not quite as tall as I am, but he's heavier, stronger and has very red hair. I'll tell you more in private."

"Stronger than you?" She found that hard to believe.

Francis nodded. "Si, *cara*. Stronger than I am. And bigger."

Evelyn was puzzled. "But I thought the two of you were, shall we say, in love."

"We are. One makes great sacrifices for love and hate."

"How will Henry's marrying the countess help me get my grand-daughter?"

"That I cannot tell you. Don't look under rocks. But if he does marry Caterina, it will help." Like Caterina, Francis instinctively disliked Evelyn. It was bad enough to spend time with her, but convincing her to accept his plan was too much. He decided to stop humoring her. "Furthermore, you have no choice. Your scheme is worthless, and I'll have no part in it. You can turn down mine. We'll finish our lunch and return to your hotel. Everything will end there."

"No! I agree. I was simply trying to understand what you're planning."

Francis looked again at Caterina and then at the photograph of Maggie. "I need three months. We must change her nose. Leave these pictures and send me any others you have of Maggie Rhodes." He turned to Evelyn and put his hand on her arm. "In the meantime, you must do your part. Do your best not to anger Henry. Try to make yourself as agreeable as possible to him. In three months, Caterina will arrive in New York and stay with you. Shortly afterward, you will give a party in honor of La Contessa. And invite Henry Carson. It is your job to see that he accepts the invitation and meets Caterina. Nothing more. She will do the rest."

"I understand," said Evelyn. And to her dismay she understood more than either Francis gave her credit for understanding or she, herself, wished to understand.

# Chapter 25

EVELYN WILKENSON sat reading a cablegram from Caterina Orsini. "Minor surgery completed. Am fine. Leaving Rome in two days. Sailing U. S. S. United States, first class. Arrive New York, June 12. Meet me. Contessa Caterina Orsini." After eight years of waiting, it had taken a luncheon in a restaurant in Rome to work out a plan that might gain her custody of Mary. It wasn't a nice plan—in fact it was obscene—to induce Henry Carson to marry a woman who was his brother's mistress. She almost felt sorry for Henry. First William, now Francis. But Evelyn believed that the ends justified the means, so she put sympathy aside to review the progress she'd made in preparing Caterina's way.

She had taken the Île de France back to the States, so that she could stop in Paris and buy things for Mary. She bought pretty, feminine dresses, lingerie, hats, bags, special French dolls and a model of the Eiffel Tower. On her return, she had written Mary telling her of the presents and then called Henry to ask permission to send them. Listening to Evelyn on the telephone, Henry realized she had trapped him. If he didn't allow her to send the presents, Mary would be disappointed. He recognized again that the game was not over, and Evelyn had lost none of her skill as a master tactician.

Mary was so pleased with the presents from her grandmother that Henry had to call Evelyn to thank her for Mary. Evelyn suggested Henry and she have dinner at her home, so he could describe in detail how Mary played, and Evelyn would have some idea what the child might need. Give the little girl the benefit of a woman's touch.

Henry had to admit to himself he'd been raising Mary as a "tomboy," and feeling guilty, he agreed to the dinner. A date was set, and that evening Evelyn served roast beef done as Henry liked it with a fine bottle of Lafitte Rothschild. Henry waited all evening for Evelyn's request that she be allowed to visit Mary. It never came. Her only suggestion was that if he were free, she needed an extra man for a small dinner party she planned.

Like all bachelors, Henry had his periods of feast and of famine. At the moment life was famine. Even his fallback, Kate Adams, was away in Europe. Albeit somewhat doubtful, Henry agreed to attend Evelyn's dinner party.

Evelyn Wilkenson knew most of the people in New York worth knowing, both the famous and the infamous, and her dinner parties were well attended. The evening that Henry attended, Evelyn arranged a small but very select, very impressive guest list. She made certain that there were enough attractive, bright, unattached young women who she felt would be as interested in Henry as he would be in them. She wanted him to be accustomed to meeting young, attractive women at her home, so the appearance of Caterina Orsini would not alert him. She knew she took a risk introducing him to women, but she had no alternative. Besides, he'd met so many women over the years and was still a bachelor. The odds were he'd still be one when Caterina arrived.

Henry attended several dinners and parties after the first. And somewhat to her own surprise, Evelyn found Henry interesting. He knew more about more things than she'd realized. If the reality of Mary hadn't been between them, he would have been someone she would have enjoyed knowing better. Much like William. But there was Mary and the Wilkenson name to consider, and that came before everything.

Although Henry enjoyed himself at her parties, he had no illusions. She was the same Evelyn Wilkenson who had sacrificed her daughter for the sake of the family name, the same woman who would use any means—legal or otherwise—to gain custody of Mary, the last of her line. She had the zeal of a religious fanatic.

The day Evelyn received the cablegram from Caterina she sat down with her secretary to prepare a list for the party at which Henry would meet La Contessa. She would have the correct number of people from the Social Register, and people from the arts—musicians, actors, dancers. But no painters. They drank too much and talked too little, and what they said tended to be either obscene or obscure. A few corporate chairmen were included. Limited, narrow-gauged men with even more limited wives, but necessary to offset the quicksilver of the artistic types. A few politicians—they would add to the fireworks.

It took a week for Tiffany to print the invitations. The guest list numbered over 200. The invitation stated that the guests were invited to meet the Contessa Caterina Orsini, who would be spending the summer with Evelyn Wilkenson. Finally, the invitations were mailed. Then Evelyn waited. In spite of her optimism, until she had Henry's acceptance, she couldn't be sure he'd attend. There were many genuine reasons that could keep him away. Twice a day, when the mail was delivered, her blood pressure rose. With each passing day, she grew more nervous. He had seen through her scheme and wouldn't attend? No, that was unlikely. He had planned to be out of town on business? That was possible. With national distribution, the Carson Company had offices all over the country. He could be going anywhere. Three weeks before the party she had not yet heard from Henry. But she meant to wait as long as possible before telephoning. That would place too much importance on his presence and alert him.

Henry had received the invitation at Carson House and spent many hours wondering about it. One thing was clear. This party was different from the others to which he'd been invited, both in size and the meticulous care given it. Who was Caterina Orsini and how did Evelyn know an Italian countess? He wondered if Caterina had something to do with Evelyn's transformation.

He tried finding a connection between the party and Mary, and failed. It crossed his mind that everything Evelyn had done in the past months was in preparation for this party. But why? What was the connection? He could find none. Yet something about the sequence of events nagged at him, and left him undecided whether to accept or send regrets.

Max drove Evelyn to the west side docks to meet Caterina. As she expected, it took over an hour before the first passengers descended the gangplank. She walked to a spot where she could be easily seen. The passengers descended one at a time or in twos, usually a husband and wife linking arms, occasionally an entire family. Suddenly Evelyn gasped. There she was! She couldn't believe what she saw: the same print dress and wide-brimmed hat as Maggie had worn at the wedding. Perfectly copied. And her face—she looked enough like Maggie Rhodes to be her twin sister. Even the same stride, head thrown back. My God! For the first time she really believed it could happen. Francis' idea had seemed only a desperate chance, but it was going to work! She could feel success. And Henry would come to the party. There was no question about it. She waved her arm, and Caterina responded with a wave. When they met the two women embraced.

"You look wonderful. I don't know what to say."

"You think he'll notice me?" Caterina needed reassurance. She was afraid of Francis and she knew she had to succeed.

"He'll notice you. Oh, will he ever!"

Max had no trouble fitting Caterina's luggage into the trunk of the Rolls. Caterina explained, "I brought very little. Francis gave me money to buy American clothes. He said you know the kind of dresses that Maggie Rhodes wears. I have only this." She swirled around, the dress flying out from her legs.

"Tomorrow we'll open a bank account and charge accounts in your name that will be paid by me." Evelyn was euphoric. If she had any questions about the morality of her actions, the questions faded before the shining promise of success. "Now get in the car, and Max will drive us home."

An hour later, Evelyn was in her library. While waiting for Caterina to settle herself in the guest suite, she went over the mail. Suddenly her body relaxed, and she let out a great sigh of relief. A perfect day was now more perfect. Henry had accepted her invitation. To celebrate, she ordered a bottle of Piper Heidseck, 1923. When Caterina finally entered Evelyn said with a flourish, "Henry has accepted. He's coming!"

Caterina looked puzzled. "Didn't you think he would?"

"With Henry you never know. Now let me look at you."

Caterina posed. She was dressed as Evelyn had first seen her: white head band, white blouse, white slippers. But instead of the skirt, she wore a pair of tight, white pants. So tight, Evelyn was amazed the stitches held. Would Maggie Rhodes wear anything that tight? Caterina saw her look and frowned. "Don't I look like Miss Rhodes?"

Evelyn said nothing, still thinking. The line of the pants was so revealing, it was obvious the girl wore nothing under them. Would Maggie Rhodes go without lingerie? Yes, under some circumstances. Never under others. At last Evelyn answered. "You look like her, but I think we'll have to choose clothes a little looser. American girls don't wear things that tight."

"It's the newest fashion in Italy. They'll be wearing it here too."

"I'm certain you're right, but they didn't when Henry knew Maggie. Sit down, and we'll make plans. Would you like a glass of champagne to celebrate?"

"*Si.* I love to celebrate."

Evelyn poured a glass for Caterina and one for herself, remembering how she and Maggie had sipped champagne the day of Selma's wedding. She smiled. Now the mistake would be remedied.

"You are happy?"

"Yes. But we must get to work. There are many things you should know about Henry Carson and Maggie Rhodes. I'll tell you all I know, but then you're on your own." Evelyn handed Caterina a large photo album. "This contains all the pictures I have of Henry and Maggie. Some are quite poor. They were taken at long range by detectives before he married my daughter. Others were taken at the wedding. There are many pictures of Henry, some as recent as a month ago."

Caterina began to study the pictures. *"Molto bello. Un'uomo grande.* Your Henry is a very handsome man. Very big." The pictures of Henry pleased her. The burning feeling she loved was returning. Not the same burning as when she was given drugs to arouse her. Better. It would be a pleasure to make love to this man. If he was as big all over as Francis said, it would be more than a pleasure. She wondered, could she love a man? One man? Be satisfied with only one man? For a sunny moment she felt young again, young and sixteen, before the Germans arrived at the villa. She all but memorized the pictures of Henry. Then there was a good picture of Maggie. Oh! She was very lovely, but she looked so unhappy. "Was this taken at the weddding of your daughter to Henry Carson?"

Evelyn glanced at the snapshot. "Yes."

Caterina closed the album. "You must tell me everything about them. I think I understand Maggie. But if Henry Carson was in love with her, why did he marry your daughter?"

Evelyn spent the rest of the afternoon telling Caterina about William and herself, about Henry and Selma, about Henry and Maggie. Caterina absorbed the information easily. She understood marriages of state and mistresses, royal and otherwise. When Evelyn finished it was time for dinner. Caterina left the library to change, leaving Evelyn to her thoughts.

What a sordid affair she'd gotten herself into. The best she could say was she had more in mind than hurting Henry. If only he would grant her custody of Mary there would be no need to traffic with the likes of Francis. And Caterina Orsini was clearly no better. Francis had told her not to look under rocks. She didn't have to. What was under had oozed out and was in plain sight. Caterina would arrange in some way to disgrace Henry. No, she wouldn't threaten, it would have to be actual disgrace. Nothing less would satisfy Francis. That left one rock she wouldn't turn—how Caterina planned to disgrace Henry. She would leave that to Caterina.

The two weeks before the party went by rapidly. Caterina and Evelyn spent their waking hours together talking about Maggie and Henry and selecting a suitable wardrobe for Caterina, elegant clothes that yet emphasized the roundness of her hips, the softness of her stomach and the perfect shape of her breasts. Her hair was trimmed the way Evelyn remembered Maggie wearing hers. The wild curls were sacrificed to achieve a more sophisticated look. She stopped wearing makeup except for mascara and some eye shadow. The transformation was perfect.

Caterina was amazed by the sights and sounds of New York. The people, the size of the buildings, the electrical energy she felt all around her. Her only difficult times were alone at night. Not when she was asleep, as in Rome—for some reason the terrifying dreams had not managed to cross the ocean with her. It was getting to sleep. There was Henry to think about. She needed more information about Henry. Evelyn would know, but she dared not ask. Besides, she could not rely on anything Evelyn might tell her. A curious woman. Without seeming to, Caterina watched her constantly. Occasionally, Caterina thought Evelyn knew or had guessed everything. Then there were times when she was sure she knew nothing.

Then it was Saturday, the morning of the party. Caterers, florists, extra servants descended upon the house. It was garlanded and festooned as it hadn't been in years. Evelyn's luck held. New York was in the middle of a June heat wave, and Saturday was expected to be the hottest day of the year. The ladies with their light dresses wouldn't need wraps, and the men would be thankful for lightweight, summer dinner jackets. Evelyn decided she could risk a little with Caterina's evening gown. She chose a floor-length white, gossamer chiffon with a thin lining of flesh-colored silk. Two narrow straps over her shoulders held it in place. The dress was meant to be worn with a strapless brassiere, but when Caterina tried it on, the wires distorted the natural shape of her breasts and she refused to wear it. Against her will, Evelyn gave up on the brassiere. As a final touch, Evelyn went to one of the family safe deposit boxes in the Bank of New York and returned with a tiara of diamonds and pearls that had last been worn by her mother. But it was fitting for a contessa to wear a royal headdress. The only other jewelry was a single strand of pearls.

The party was to start at six-thirty. A dance floor had been erected in the garden in back of the house, and Meyer Davis and his band hired for the occasion. A dozen Pinkerton men were on hand to chauffeur the cars to a parking lot rented for the evening. They were to guard the cars as well as keep an eye on the house. To make certain the police cooperated, Evelyn invited Mayor Impellitieri and his wife. "Impy" saw to it that this night New York's finest behaved like New York's finest.

Except for people living on the street, Beekman Place was closed to traffic. At six-thirty-five the first guest arrived.

By nine-thirty the party was in full swing. Evelyn and Caterina spent almost three hours acting as a receiving line of two. Everyone who mattered and many who didn't had arrived, with one noticeable exception: Henry Carson was not there. Evelyn was exasperated and worried. It wasn't like Henry just not to show up. She strongly resisted the impulse to call Carson House. She watched Caterina wandering about, and lovely as she was, she had no shortage of male admirers. Where was Henry? Evelyn knew the party was a big success, for everybody except herself. Unless Henry Carson put in an appearance it would be a disaster.

Caterina wandered from group to group. Everywhere people made much of her. She should have had a marvelous time, but she, like Evelyn, had but one purpose: to meet Henry Carson. And where was he? She was startled by a heavy hand on her shoulder and a male voice whispering in her ear, "What on earth are you doing here, Maggie?" She looked up at a tall, wide-shouldered man with slightly thinning red hair. Was this Henry Carson? Before she could ask, he said, "You're not Maggie Rhodes. You're the Countess Orsini. I arrived late and missed the receiving line. Sorry, but you look very much like her."

"Two questions, please. Who are you, and who is Maggie Rhodes?"

"I'm John Hillyer. Maggie Rhodes is an old friend and a beautiful woman who is not here. Can I get you something to eat or drink?"

Caterina preferred wine to hard liquor. She had not yet had a single glass, wishing to be fresh for Henry. But there was no Henry, and this attractive man wanted to be friendly. Actually more than "friendly"; she knew the signs. She realized she was hungry and thirsty. "I could use something to eat."

Henry hung up the phone and looked at his watch. He'd been talking to Godfrey Moore for two hours. Every detail was now in place. Now the lawyers could start to draw papers on Monday. Evelyn would understand his being late when he told her the news.

It was ten o'clock, and Evelyn refused to give up hope. Still time for Henry to show. She saw her secretary frantically waving at her. What on earth did she want? "All right, Joan. What is it?"

"Mr. Carson called, and he asked me to give you his apologies . . ."

Evelyn's world crashed with such a noise in her head she glanced around the room to see if anyone else had heard it. No, they were eating, drinking, talking, laughing; apparently they heard nothing. She made herself ask, "He's not coming?"

"Oh, no! He apologized for being so late. He's on his way and will be here shortly. He said to tell you when you know why he's so late, you'll understand and join him in celebrating."

Evelyn felt the blood start to flow again through her body. "Thank you, Joan. Now join the party. Enjoy yourself." She hurried away. She found Caterina and John Hillyer standing at the far end of the dance floor. "Excuse me, John. I can't allow you to monopolize our guest of honor. Caterina, there's someone you have to meet."

"Farewell, Maggie Number Two. I will see you later."

"Of course." Caterina let herself be hurried away. Henry Carson must have arrived. "Where is he?"

Evelyn spoke in a whisper. "He called and is on his way. Something detained him, and knowing Henry it was business."

"Then he's coming!"

"Did you doubt it?"

Caterina suppressed a smile. "I doubted it, and so did you."

"Yes, but I shouldn't have. I know Henry." Evelyn and Caterina exchanged a long look. "Now that's settled, mingle. But be ready. And keep away from John Hillyer. He's a fine lawyer—Henry's lawyer, in fact—but he likes women too much. Mrs. Hillyer regularly looks the other way." Although Evelyn told Caterina to mingle, she herself remained close to the entrance. A waitress brought her a glass of champagne, and she walked about in small circles talking to this guest and that, but never straying far from the front door. It seemed like an eternity before at last it was opened and a huge, red-headed body filled the space. Now that Henry had actually arrived she wanted to storm at him for being late. But she bit her tongue.

"Evelyn, I'm sorry to be so late, but when I tell you why, you of all people will appreciate my reason."

"I'm sure I will, but first you must meet our guest of honor. After that you can give me your news." She saw Caterina, her back to them, talking to the small group of Italian opera singers. Perfect, she thought. He'll get the full effect up close. "There she is. Come." Henry followed Evelyn toward a young woman who appeared to be engaged in an animated conversation with a short, plump man. They were talking with their hands as well as with their mouths as he'd seen many Italians do. In fact their hands were flying at such a rapid rate Henry wondered how they avoided slapping each other. Evelyn interrupted, murmuring in the young woman's ear.

*"Scusatemi, Signor Tagliavini. Continuiamo un altra volta."*

*"Certo,* Contessa."

Caterina Orsini turned to face Henry Carson.

Henry's normally high coloring turned white and then red and then whiter than the first time. He looked to Evelyn for help.

"Henry, I would like you to meet Countess Caterina Orsini. Caterina, this is Henry Carson."

Henry fought for his equanimity. He mumbled, *"Tanto piacere."*

"Oh. *Lei parla l'italiano? Meraviglioso!"*

*"Un pò. Un pochissimo. L'ho studiato a scuola."*

"I speak English. We can talk in English."

That was Henry's second shock. She sounded like Maggie. The same low voice, soft yet very clear. Even the slight Italian accent didn't matter. He turned to Evelyn. "Why didn't you warn me?"

"Warn you? I don't understand."

"She looks exactly like—" He stopped. "Never mind."

"I don't understand you, Henry. Anyway, now tell me your great news. Why I wouldn't mind your being so late tonight."

"It doesn't seem so important any more. And even if you don't mind my being late, I mind. I could have met La Contessa hours ago."

"That's charming, Mr. Carson. But the party's barely begun. We have much time. What is your news? I too am curious."

Henry was having difficulty collecting his thoughts. The shock of Caterina Orsini was every bit as strong as Evelyn could have wished for in her most optimistic fantasy. Across the few feet between them, the eyes he knew looked at him, a curl fell across a familiar forehead, the smile lingered, grew stronger, her lips parted: exactly the same. She was Maggie. Maggie without William. Maggie without his need to marry Selma. She was a second chance at everything he'd thought he had lost forever. "The Carson Company and Wilkenson, Inc., of course, is going multinational. We've made agreements with the French and German governments and the unions involved to manufacture and distribute our products there." He neglected mentioning that what had decided him to come to the party was to question Caterina about the feasibility of building a factory in Italy.

Momentarily, Evelyn focused on business, realizing how important Henry's news was. "That's wonderful. You can fill me in later. I love the subtleties of negotiations."

"I mean to. You're my best audience."

Though Caterina had the advantage of knowing in advance what

Henry looked like, she was as startled at the sight of him as he was by her. For there never was a picture that did justice to Henry Carson. The size, strength, vitality, magnetism of the man—none of this could be caught by a camera. A picture showed a big man with flaming red hair. Now she understood what Francis meant when he said Henry was bigger than he was. He filled the room with his presence, dwarfing everyone; made the tall, broad-shouldered John Hillyer seem ordinary. And though his features were not as perfect as Francis'—his nose had been broken and poorly set or not set at all—there was something purely male about his face. This man wouldn't be interested in young boys. She had never before objected to Francis' tastes. Now, suddenly, she did. With a man like Henry, she felt she could be completely satisfied. And she could tell Henry was not a sadist. He might hurt someone, but he wouldn't enjoy it as Francis did. They were brothers and alike. They were brothers and so different. Their father must have been a very wise man to have chosen Henry Carson, rather than Francis Carson, to run the Carson Company.

Evelyn was ecstatic to see that the opening maneuver in their plan had been successful. They met, and Henry was overwhelmed by Caterina. But something unexpected had happened. Alert to nuances, Evelyn could see that Caterina was equally taken with Henry.

Leaving them to their pleasure in each other, Evelyn moved away feeling, all at once, uneasy. How would Caterina's response to Henry influence her future behavior? Evelyn could only wait and see.

By three A.M. the party was over. Meyer Davis played his traditional closing piece, "Good Night, Ladies," and the dancing ended. Henry and Caterina had spent the entire evening together, dancing, talking, drinking, eating. John Hillyer made one attempt to be included in their conversation, saw it was impossible and drifted off. He, as much as Evelyn, understood what Henry saw. The girl was another Maggie, another chance at happiness for Henry. John wished him good luck.

By five A.M. only Henry and Caterina remained, uncaring and unaware of the passage of time. They stood at the railing in the same place that Maggie had once stood with John Hillyer. The party seemed only a few moments long, as they watched the sun rise. Caterina waited for Henry to put his arms around her and kiss her. Once they were in bed, she was certain there was nothing she could do that would in any way shock him, but he had to initiate the lovemaking. Though Henry wanted nothing more intensely than to make love to Caterina, he was afraid to make the first move. Suppose she didn't want him the way he wanted her? Suppose she wanted more time? She was a countess, a Catholic. Suppose she was a virgin? And so it was that their mutual fear of offending each other conspired to keep them apart. Henry cast about desperately for something to say. "Caterina, would you like to visit Carson House? We have horses and a swimming pool."

Caterina smiled. "Yes. That would be nice. I can swim quite well, and ride poorly." She would need to buy a bathing suit, but where?

"I'm sure Evelyn will have no objection to your coming. In fact"— Henry then startled even himself by breaking a cardinal rule—"Evelyn is also welcome. She could meet Mary." He swallowed hard. "I'll go home now and call you around ten. Evelyn was always an early riser. Will you be up by then?"

"Of course." She didn't bother to add that not only would she be up, she would still be up. She was much too excited to sleep.

So it was settled, and the two of them walked through the silent house to the front door. Caterina waited again for Henry to kiss her good night, and though Henry longed to, he couldn't. He settled for taking her hand and kissing it. Then he ran for his car like an embarrassed young boy.

Caterina half understood his actions; this was the respect an honorable man pays an honorable woman.

On her way upstairs, Evelyn appeared. "Tell me what happened."

Caterina stared into space. "He kissed my hand good night."

"Will he see you again?"

"He's invited us to Carson House tomorrow."

Evelyn was astounded. "Us! He invited both of us? Both of us?"

"Yes. He said you can meet Mary."

"Caterina! We've won! We've won!"

"You mean because he's agreed for you to meet the child?"

"You don't know what that means."

Only half listening, Caterina's expression changed. She seemed even younger than she was. "He'll call at ten tomorrow. I need a bathing suit."

"We'll get one tomorrow."

"Tomorrow is Sunday. The stores are closed."

"Ben can open the swim shop at Bergdorf for me. He ate enough of my food last night. What a remarkable evening!" Evelyn ran back up the stairs, leaving Caterina to her own anxious anticipations.

Was it a trick? Henry sat in his bedroom at Carson House thinking. He knew Evelyn Wilkenson was capable of anything. Was it a trick?

The special radiance of her skin? Might that not be some kind of skin makeup Evelyn had discovered? No! There was no such product. She was Maggie and yet not Maggie, for Maggie was gone and she had taken with her the magic of life, its breathtaking poignancy. His perception of its splendor was fading, and he was drying up inside. One day even his buried, eternal mourning for Maggie would dissolve into dust. And that side of his nature—the side that could love, could love and grieve—would have atrophied. Then he would be entirely like William, living only for the Carson Company.

# Chapter 26

CATERINA took a cool bath and sat on her chair, watching the sun rise. She wondered if she dared pray. Were people like her beyond God's mercy? He kissed her hand good night. In Italy, one does not kiss an unmarried woman's hand. Her mouth, yes, but her hand, never. That honor is reserved for a married woman who may not be kissed any other place except by her husband—or her lover. She decided he didn't know their customs. He promised he would call. But would he?

Promptly at ten, Henry called. Evelyn answered the telephone and then allowed herself to be convinced Henry really wanted her to come to Carson House. It was arranged they be there for lunch. After a brief stop at Bergdorf Goodman to pick up two swimsuits, they were driven to Westchester.

The clock on the dashboard of the Rolls read twelve-thirty-two when they turned into the long, gravel driveway leading to Carson House. Two people were waiting at the head of the stone steps: a large man and a small girl. The man wore a blue blazer and white pants, and the little girl was dressed in a blue jacket with a white pleated skirt, white knee-length stockings and white shoes. The sight brought back to Evelyn the memory of her first visit: William in his blazer and gray pants, and Henry almost identically dressed. As the car stopped at the foot of the steps, Henry descended to meet them. In spite of herself, Evelyn wished William was with him. He remained the one man she'd ever met worthy of admiration. They had been equals in so many ways. With him alive, she was certain she would have been spared this dreadful game. She missed him as she would not have thought possible when he lived.

Henry waited for Max to open the door and hold it while Evelyn got out, followed by Caterina. There she was—the face and figure and smile he knew. Maggie's face. With that mouth that never counted costs. His heart went out to her as it had the night before. The similarity in looks, voice and movements was uncanny. He couldn't help wondering how far it went. Did she find him as desirable as he found her?

320

Having no recollection that he was using almost the same words William had used long ago, he said, "Welcome to Carson House, Caterina. And welcome back, Evelyn." He motioned to the little girl on the steps. "Mary, this is your grandmother, Evelyn." Mary held out her hand timidly, then, overcome by emotion, flung herself at Evelyn and hugged her around her waist.

"Thank you! Thank you! For the dresses, the dolls, everything!"

Evelyn picked up the child and kissed her on each cheek, tears in her eyes. Strange, Henry thought. Her daughter meant nothing to her, and her granddaughter means so much. Was it the child or was this another Evelyn?

"We've prepared a light lunch in the enclosed porch."

"Where we ate that first night," Evelyn remarked. She kissed Mary again. "You've become too big a girl for an old lady to hold." She set Mary down and took her hand. As they started up the steps, Henry offered his arm to Caterina. Their eyes met and held. For an instant they seemed to make love to each other. She held his arm close to her body, and again he remembered Maggie.

After lunch the party broke into couples. Evelyn would spend her time with Mary, and Henry and Caterina would be together.

"Where's Will?" Evelyn asked.

"Oh, I should have explained. He's spending the weekend with the Hillyers on Fisher's Island. He's going to Exeter this fall, and John thought he should meet his son who's at Exeter now." Henry turned to Caterina. "Would you like to see the estate? It may not be as grand as anything in Italy, but I think you'll find it interesting."

Henry and Caterina were alone, but caught in their mutual dilemma, Caterina wished she could make Henry understand that right now she could do without seeing the estate. Now all she wanted was to reach for Henry and hold him close, as close as she could, while Henry had to struggle not to take her in his arms, kiss her, caress her. The result was that neither dared express their feelings for fear of offending the other.

Henry had three suggestions. They could take an automobile ride around the estate, or, assuming Caterina could sit a horse, they could ride, or, finally, they could spend the afternoon relaxing by the pool.

Caterina seemed to consider the question. "I think it's too warm to ride. Let's relax by the pool." Henry nodded, happy to please her, and they strolled to the pool house, where one of the maids had taken Caterina's small bag.

So the afternoon waned as they swam and chatted aimlessly, as though the idea of making love was the last thing on their minds. But the sense of time slipping away made Henry desperate. In a few hours she would be miles away in New York. "Look, why don't you and Evelyn spend the night here?" he suggested. "I'll take the day off, and Mary is not in school in the summer. The first draft of the European agreements won't be ready till Wednesday at the earliest. Hillyer and his crew are in New York drafting them. They can be delivered to Carson House just as easily as to the office."

As she listened, Caterina raised her eyebrows, a simple reaction she hoped conveyed both surprise and modest pleasure. "I think that's a wonderful idea," she said too eagerly. Then, catching herself, she added, "We must ask Evelyn." That gave her answer a respectable tone, a restraint she hoped to maintain.

Evelyn agreed without hesitation, so Oscar was instructed to make two guest rooms ready. The ladies were staying the night.

Despite the weather prediction, the heat wave did not break by evening. It remained almost as hot after the sunset as it had been during the day. After everyone went to bed, Henry wandered about the estate, feeling a curious sense of betrayal, a betrayal of Maggie. He explained to her that it was really nothing, that no one would ever mean as much to him as she had, that he was sorry.

Caterina lay on top of her bed staring at the ceiling fan that did nothing to cool the room. She was hot and very uncomfortable. What made matters much worse was that her body wanted him, which increased her discomfort. Finally she decided she couldn't stand it any longer. The pool was secluded, and she would take a swim. Anthing was better than this.

She put on a robe and tiptoed, barefoot, down the stairs and out the door. Then she ran for the pool. There was no moon, and even though she could see the stars very clearly, she could also hear the rumble of thunder in the distance. When she reached the pool, she looked around. No one was there, and slipping off her robe she dove into the deep end of the water. There were several lounges at the end of the pool. She climbed out, grabbed her robe, lay back in a lounge and closed her eyes. The most frightening aspect of her feelings was that, at the moment, she was so obsessed with Henry she was unable to shut out the world, to become deaf and blind and throw herself into some fantasy, which she so often did to replace empty reality.

She lay there in a strange state of lethargy when she heard a noise.

She drew her robe over her body and waited. A huge shadow detached itself from the darkness. It was Henry. He seemed to be talking. Or was he praying? Had he seen her? Caterina was desperate. If he saw her, what would he think? But it was very late, and since Henry expected to find no one, he didn't look for anyone. He dropped his white robe very close to the spot where she had dropped hers. Caterina could not stop looking at him, hypnotized by his body. She stared at his huge penis and her flesh vibrated with desire. And his body—it was even more impressive naked than in clothes. While Francis could have modeled for Michelangelo's David, Henry was far broader, more powerful. He could have been a great sculptor's model for Romulus, the legendary founder of Rome. It seemed to Caterina his body was a throwback to a more ancient time.

He dove into the water and began to swim. After a number of laps he stopped, stood up, walked to the side of the pool and hoisted himself up to sit on the edge, his legs in the water. The night was so still, with no breeze to rustle the leaves, and straining to listen, she heard Henry whisper to himself, "O God! What do I do? Tell me! Tell me! Caterina, help me. Want me! Please want me!" Then he placed his arms behind his head and lay back on the concrete, his eyes closed. Want him, she thought. What have I been doing all day but trying to show you how much I want you? She let her robe fall to the concrete. Then she crept on her knees across the space to the pool. She slid into the pool, leaving only the top of her head, eyes and nose visible. He was about twenty yards away, his eyes closed, still resting on his arms. Caterina took as deep a breath as possible and swam underwater toward him. She would answer his prayer, show him beyond a doubt how she wanted him. The water was clear. She could see his legs before her. Soundlessly, her head broke the surface, and taking another deep, quiet breath, she inched her way toward him. His penis was in front of her face. She opened her mouth and closed it around his sex.

The effect was electrifying. Henry flung himself back and away from her, pulling his penis from her mouth. She grabbed hold of his legs. "*Caro. Caro mio! Caro mio bellissimo. Vieni qui. Vienida me. Amore, amore mio.*" As rapid as his reaction had been, so rapidly did he stop, an expression of absolute disbelief on his face. After that came recognition of what was happening, and for the first time he saw her outside of the illusion in which he had hidden her. Then a joy such as Caterina had never seen illuminated Henry's face. Before she could move, he was in the water holding her, kissing her, caressing her, while her own hands were racing over his body. His hands cupped her breasts, lifting each one to his mouth, sucking her nipples his tongue encircling them. And her hands held his penis, unable to close around it.

The current of sensuality flowing between them made speech difficult. "My love, come inside of me," she gasped. "I want you now."

He carried her out of the pool, placing her on a lounge. Her whole body opened to receive him. Then he took her. Gently he began to move in and out, slowly, then faster, inciting her to come with him, with words, with his hands. She came first. A high, keening sound exploded from her throat, and Henry felt her orgasm, felt the spurt of female juices against his sex. Responding to his own needs, his orgasm followed, filling her as she had never been filled before. Then another orgasm started, longer and deeper. She continued to feel the waves roll through her body, and as each wave subsided another began. Henry remained hard and climaxed again. Like Caterina's this orgasm was longer and even more fulfilling. All he could think of was the miracle that had brought them together, the miracle that had given him such a woman, a second chance at loving and living the way life was meant to be lived.

And for the first time in her life Caterina understood what it meant to make love. Years ago she had been taught all about sex. Now she was being taught loving. It was different. He had penetrated more than her body, he had penetrated her very being. There was nothing she wouldn't do for this man. And she knew he would ask nothing she didn't want to do.

Suddenly Henry realized he'd worn no contraception, and the realization sickened him. His life had been damaged enough by unwanted babies. "You must do something about contraception. I, er . . ." He stopped.

"No, *caro*. I was sick during the war. The Italian doctors are butchers. I cannot have a baby." His face was so troubled she grew anxious. "Does it mean so much to you?"

"Darling, I have two children. That's dynasty enough. I was only concerned for you."

Caterina embraced him. Their concentration on each other was interrupted by a bolt of lightning followed by a peal of thunder. "That was too close. We'll go inside."

She glanced at the pool house. "*Caro*, let's spend the night there."

"You want to?" Henry still had to struggle to believe that this wondrous thing had happened to him.

"Yes. We can make love again and again until you no longer want me."

Henry kissed the top of her nose. "We'll see who tires of the other first."

Another lightning bolt ended their teasing, and holding hands, they ran for the pool house.

It was agreed next morning that Caterina would return with Evelyn to the city and pack a suitcase with enough clothes to spend a week as Henry's guest. Evelyn would return the next weekend. That way she could spend time with Mary when Mary wasn't at day camp. Then, too, she would meet Will, who was due back shortly. As for Evelyn, the only interest she had in meeting Henry's illegitimate son was to see who he most resembled, Henry or William. Naturally she kept this to herself.

On the way back to the city, Evelyn discussed with Caterina her ideas on sex. "He will of course try to seduce you. Men are that way. And you must be aloof. Make him unsure. In the end, you'll find him irresistible."

Caterina was tempted to tell this woman, so wise in some ways, so childish in others, that her advice came too late. But the less Evelyn knew the less she could tell Francis. "Yes, I understand. You're a wise woman." She changed the subject. "How did you find Mary? As you expected?"

"I was surprised and pleased. I don't understand how he's managed, but Mary is much better than I expected. I see now that I still have time. When she does live with me, I'll simply smooth out the rough edges and make her into a lady. A true Wilkenson."

"I see. Though she is 'better than you expected,' you still want Henry to let you raise her?"

Evelyn drew back. All the warmth she had shown when playing with Mary and that had lasted even until the car ride home vanished. Her mouth turned down, becoming harsh and unyielding. So much so that Caterina was reminded of Francis, and her smothered fear of him returned. "The child will be mine and a Wilkenson. That's why you're here, and I'm playing this disgusting game. Remember that!"

Caterina became anxious. Though they had different motives, Evelyn and Francis were united in their desire to damage Henry. She sank back against the cushions of the car. She was the instrument they were using to torture her beloved. Groping in the blackness around her, she searched for an answer. Should she end the farce and tell Henry the truth about herself? Then return to Italy and the life she knew? But that was impossible. When Francis found out, she'd be better off dead. She was as much a prisoner now as she had been during the war.

She broke into a cold sweat, staring straight ahead. There was only one possibility. If she stayed, she might persuade Henry to allow Evelyn to have a say in Mary's education. And if Evelyn could be satisfied, she'd help Caterina defend herself against Francis. It was the only choice she had, to stay and try to work things out.

Henry was waiting for her when she returned to Carson House that evening. All that kept them apart was the presence of the children, two children this time. Will had returned. He shook hands with Caterina like a proper little gentleman and said. "Welcome to Carson House, Countess Orsini. My father and Mary and I are very happy you've come to visit."

"Thank you. I am happy to be here." Caterina smiled at them. "Mary's grandmother sent you both presents." She pulled a large, flat box from the car. The wrapping paper said F.A.O. Schwarz. "It's a model of a doll's house, Mary." Then she reached into the back seat again and pulled out a smaller package from F.A.O. Schwarz and handed it to Will.

"What is it?"

"A model of a fort similar to those the French Foreign Legion used in the Sahara Desert. When I was in Morocco, I saw a fort like this. You could help Mary build her doll's house while you build your fort."

Henry had been watching her become acquainted with the children without his help. Now he interrupted. "Will, Mary, it's time the two of you got ready for dinner. Take your presents with you."

Released by Henry, the children clutched their new presents and ran up the steps toward the house. Watching them, Caterina had a strange feeling about Will. Her family was a very old one, and in the course of hundreds of years of its both brilliant and sordid history, it had its share of children born on the wrong side of the blanket. Illegitimate. And she had an inborn sense of blood ties, legal and otherwise. Knowing Francis as well as she did, now knowing Henry, and having seen pictures of William, she knew the Carson look. The three men were different but at the same time alike. But not Will. The choice wasn't whether he was Henry or William's son. There was more to the story than that. *Mater semper est.* There was no doubt he was the son of Maggie Rhodes, but Caterina was certain neither Henry nor William was the father of the boy. He was not a Carson. She had no intention of saying any of this to anybody, especially not to Henry. Will was being raised as a Carson, thought himself a Carson, and she would live by their fiction.

Her thoughts were interrupted by Henry clasping her hand. "I've missed you all day. Do you want to wash up before having a drink?"

With the touch of his hand, Caterina's fears vanished. "Give me five minutes."

They walked into the house together. She kissed him lightly on the lips, evaded his grasp and ran up the stairs. Henry thought about last night and the way they had made love until morning. Neither had worn the other out. Only time had run out. And now they had the whole week to be together, to make love. He'd told Mary O'Toole if anything came up she could contact him at Carson House. The one piece of business he wanted to be kept updated on was the European contract. Otherwise, the Carson Company could run without him for a week.

The five days passed so rapidly Henry thought time had speeded up. In the evenings, after the children were in bed, Henry and Caterina were free to give full expression to their feelings. They melted together and separated only to come together again with ever increasing tenderness and passion. Once Henry thought about how he and Maggie had made love. She and Caterina were so much alike, each willing to give every pleasure the body could invent. But in making the comparison, Henry let himself be blinded to all the clues Caterina unwittingly gave. Maggie was a beautiful, highly sexual woman who loved Henry and whose natural impulses were to enjoy him and be enjoyed by him. Maggie was a talented amateur. Caterina loved him, too, but the nature of her life had taught her the many ways of pleasing a man as now she was pleasing Henry. There is such a thing as too much facility, too much knowledge, too much ease. Caterina was a true professional. While years ago Henry had worried about how fully Maggie had responded to his needs, now he ignored what then he questioned. Caterina did not make him suspicious. She enchanted him.

Normally cautious, by the end of the week Henry had to restrain himself from asking Caterina to marry him. He was proud of resisting the impulse. It proved he was not "losing his head." He had not "lost his head" over Maggie, even at the beginning. Once again something said to him, "Sleep on it! Be an adult! Don't be a romantic fool! Wait!"

Evelyn arrived Saturday morning with clothes for Caterina and presents for Mary and Will. Henry thought she was overdoing the presents, but she'd been barred from contact with Mary for so long, he'd give her another week before calling a halt. He'd arranged a bridge game for her with some of the better players in the neighborhood, thus leaving himself time to be alone with Caterina. Evelyn was delighted to note that Caterina's room had been changed to one next to Henry's. After dinner on Saturday, she managed a private word with Caterina.

"I had a trans-Atlantic call from Francis."

Caterina felt the words choke in her throat. "How is he?"

"Delighted with the progress. He also asked if you needed any of your medication. I didn't know you took any medication."

"I have—how do you call it?—sinus headaches. Next time Francis calls tell him I need nothing. Now I think it would be wise to stop talking about Francis."

Once again it was decided that Caterina remain for the week. But this week, Henry returned to work. The first draft of the agreements were ready. Caterina spent her days with Will and Mary. The more she saw of Will, the more she was convinced that he was neither Henry nor William's son. Even Mary had a certain Carson look, a way of moving. She was small, dark and thin, while Will was big, heavy-boned and red-haired. But Mary was a Carson and Will wasn't.

On Wednesday Henry went into New York for a meeting with his lawyers. It had become difficult for him to leave Caterina even for a day. There were only ten years between them, but he felt the way an aging man might feel for a young girl. It was a deep, desperate body need, and the need urged him to act against the whole logic of his life, to ask this semi-stranger to marry him. Desperate need can blunt the logic by which one has lived for years. He thought about Caterina and the changes she had brought to his life. It was not only the fact of their passion that had created this change, it was the knowledge that once again someone mattered deeply to him. His anger against the world was quieting down because his own war with himself was reconciled. His heart pounded as he considered his decision. It brought with it a great fear such as he'd never expected and an exultant sense of life such as he'd not known since Maggie. And this time he trusted the future. Holding Caterina's hand he felt he could trust the future because she had given it to him.

When he came home he found Caterina in the pool house. He knelt and kissed her face gently, tenderly. "Caterina, I love you. I think you love me. I ask you to marry me, to be my wife. Will you marry me?"

There was one heartbeat of silence, then she answered, "I love you so much. I married you long ago in my dreams."

Henry held out his arms, and in that brief instant before Caterina sank into them, she did something she had not done since she was sixteen. She begged God for mercy, to forgive her and protect her against Francis and what she knew but refused to accept was coming.

\*    \*    \*

Maggie was seated at her desk in the room that had been redone for her as an office in the James mansion. She had just finished her explanation to Mark James of why she needed additional monies.

"Maggie, is this project necessary? You're on the board of the Los Angeles Symphony and personally sponsoring visiting soloists. That costs money. You're putting together one of the finest collections of Post-impressionist paintings in the country. That costs money. You're backing a small repertory theater. That costs money. Yes, you're a wealthy woman and, between your brains and ours, your stock and bond portfolio is sound. But you keep digging into it for projects, and it's not bottomless. You must stop somewhere. You're not that rich."

"I won't stop at Orange County. What do we do?"

"I think you've underestimated the amount needed for a project such as you've outlined." He was half exasperated, half impressed. "Anyway, you're in good company. General Wood of Sears, Roebuck is also convinced there will be a move away from the big cities, for the same reasons you think—automobiles and improved roads. Can you put together a proposal including a map of the land you own, the land you want to buy, the freeway system and the overall idea of homes, schools, factories, art centers, et cetera? Just broad brush everything."

"What are you thinking?"

"I'm thinking you're onto something very big. Too big for you to go it alone. But if I can put together a syndicate—people the bank advises on investments plus members of the James family—it's possible we can get the project off the ground without your endangering all your own capital."

"How much control do I give up for outside investment money?"

"I don't know. That's why I want the presentation. How long will it take to prepare the proposal?"

"A month at most."

"I'll start lining up a group now." He paused. "I've a bit of gossip you might find amusing."

For no specific reason, Maggie wasn't curious. "Yes, what is it?"

"Henry Carson has remarried. An Italian countess. They say she looks something like you." There was silence. "Maggie, are you there?"

Maggie's voice came from somewhere outside her body. "I'm here, Mark."

Mark realized at once he had made a mistake. If he'd kept his big mouth shut, she might never have heard. Three thousand miles has a way of stopping gossip. Now he tried to dismiss the matter as trivial.

"Well, you should feel flattered. After all, he carried the torch for nine years."

"Nine years? Is it that long?"

From her tone he knew he'd fumbled again. He decided to change the subject. "I think so. Now, about your Orange County proposal . . ."

"You'll have it shortly. And give my love to Sally."

Maggie hung up. She leaned back and looked at the ceiling. Nine years. It had actually been nine years. She was no longer twenty-four, she was thirty-three. It had been one of the consoling deceptions over the years that Maggie had considered herself finished with Henry. Now, in the ninth year of their separation, she was forced to admit her hypocrisy. Every man she went out with, went to bed with over the nine years, she had compared to Henry. He didn't do this the way Henry did. Or that the way Henry did. And in the end, she didn't want him as she'd wanted Henry. And all the while the precious moments of her life were slipping away. It was time to see things as they were.

Her thoughts were interrupted by the sound of someone practicing against the backboard on the tennis court. That brought her to Tony. He'd had other women as she'd had other men, but they always came back together. How many times had he asked her to marry him? Too many to count. Each time she'd put him off, not saying no, not saying yes. She walked to the window. There was Angel practicing her backhand. Maggie shook her head. Angel didn't have affairs, she had marriages. She'd already run through three husbands and was looking for her fourth. That kind of life didn't appeal to Maggie, but it was time for her to give up her dream, her dream that she and Henry would be together again. There was a second Mrs. Henry Carson in the world. That changed everything. "Angel, I want to talk to you."

Angel motioned for her to come down to the court. She was seated on a bench, resting.

Maggie sat down beside her. "I want to have a heart-to-heart talk with you."

"I haven't had a heart-to-heart talk with anyone since my last husband. Heart-to-heart talks have broken up more marriages than screwing in the middle of Sunset Strip. Also more friendships." She sighed. "Okay, what is it, Miss Rhodes?"

"That's it. Miss Rhodes." Angel looked blank. "All right, I'll spell it out. Miss Rhodes is the problem. She's out of date. I want to be Mrs. Somebody. I want Mr. Somebody to say I make the best spoon bread in the world. How do I make it? Well, I take a bowl and break two eggs into it . . . My dear, there's nothing that gives me such a feeling of real satisfaction as cleaning out my downstairs closet . . ."

"Ye gods! Stop it! I got it! You want to get married!"

"Yes, and I would like your permission to ask Tony for his hand in marriage."

"Bravo! You have it."

"I guess I'm slow. It's taken me nine years—"

"Impossible! That would make me thirty-two, and you know I'm twenty-eight. But I've seen you run through more good men. And Tony's had more than his share of stars and starlets. It's about time you two stopped thinking of the opposite sex as a natural resource and started taking life seriously."

"The way you do. We're going to a party tonight. I could propose to him then."

"Oh, no. You've turned him down so often, he might turn you down just because. Men are nutsy."

"What do you suggest? My life is in your hands."

"I'll have a talk with Tony over drinks while you take a long time getting dressed. I'll put the idea in his head. Then in bed tonight give him a double whammy." She giggled. "Once I get my ducks in a row and you do your number, he'll propose. Then you zonk him by saying 'Yes.' I'll be wide awake so you can rush in overjoyed and tell me the good news before he can change his mind."

"Would he change his mind?"

"Let's see." Angel started counting on her fingers and stopped at nine. "We've both been to bed with nine of the same men including my second husband, to whom you introduced me. And they all said you're the greatest piece of you know what around." She grinned. "Excluding me, of course. So you know all about sex, but how many times have you been married?"

Maggie placed her thumb and forefinger together making a circle.

"Exactly. Zero. While I've been married early and often. Maybe I don't know how to stay married, but I do know how to get married. Yes, he could change his mind. But once you tell me, it amounts to an official engagement. The family honor comes into play."

"Very acute. Let's do it your way."

Saturday, August 15. Maggie opened her eyes and looked around. A brilliant sun was streaming in through the curtains, so different from the silver moonlight of her dream. In the excitement of their lovemaking the previous night, they'd forgotten to pull down the shades before dropping off to sleep.

She stretched and turned to look at the naked Anthony sleeping beside her. Unable to resist, she reached over and tickled him. "Wake up, you mutt. It's our wedding day."

Still half asleep, Tony reached over and pulled her to him, but she slipped out of his arms. "Later, later, love. We have to go to our wedding."

He sat bolt upright in bed. "My Lord! Today's the day!" He glanced at the clock on his side of the bed. It was eight-thirty. They were due at St. John's at eleven. His face took on a lascivious leer.

"What's the rush, baby? We have two and a half hours. Let's knock off a quickie, before the stifling bonds of marriage grind our sex life to a pulp." Suddenly he pounced on her.

But she was too quick for him. Yelping, "Help! Rape!" she ran for her robe. "Mr. James, the next time I permit such impertinent intimacies, we are going to be strictly legal."

"Women! All you ever think of is marriage."

"Right. Which is why I have to leave you immediately. It's bad luck for the groom to see the bride on the wedding day before the actual wedding. Lucky nobody ever said anything about the pre-wedding night."

Tony nodded. "I'm not superstitious. Except when I am."

"I will see you in church, my love."

Tony thought how beautiful she was and how much he loved her. Sometimes, though, he worried. He'd never felt this way before. Could it really last?

"I'll miss you," he said as she threw him a kiss and left the room.

At a signal from the sexton, Anthony James came out of the vestry and placed himself with his best man, Clarence "Deke" Duquesne, on the chancel steps of St. John's. That meant that the car bearing the bride was in sight.

"Got the ring?" whispered Deke, who was awed by the responsibility of his role.

Tony felt in the pocket of his light gray suit and assured himself that he had the platinum circle with the engraving "Tony to Maggie, August 15, 1950." The wedding ceremony seemed so formal and frighteningly final. Perhaps it would have been wiser to have a City Hall wedding as Maggie had argued for originally. He handed the ring to Deke.

The Handel march swelled ostentatiously through the stone vaulting, carrying on its wave the echo of many weddings.

As she moved toward the altar, Maggie's eyes lingered a moment on a left-hand pew where she saw a woman in a summer dress and a wide-brimmed hat, weeping. But that was another wedding, long ago and far away. Another time, another place, another bride, another groom.

She shook her head to clear it of memories, to bring back the here and now. The music, the scent of the flowers on the altar, the low murmur of the rector's voice, the faces of people in the pews, all these sights and sounds were mingling in confusion in her brain, so sharply recalling the past as to make her falter in her relation to the present. With an effort she regained her composure.

Tony watched her progress toward him, feeling his own mix of emotions. Maggie looked beautiful, but she was so pale. Tony wondered if she was as frightened as he was. Did he really want to get married? Was all this a disastrous mistake?

Then in an instant she was beside him, and seeing her calm and confident eyes, his feelings of fear dissolved.

"Dearly beloved, we are gathered together here . . ." the rector began. There was nothing to mar the perfection of the occasion.

# Chapter 27

**L**ATER, looking back on the first year of his marriage to Caterina, it seemed to Henry a time of grace. At long last he was a whole man, at peace with himself, in his love and in his work. It was as though Caterina gave a unity to his life that it had never had before. His time spent at work at the Carson Company now passed more evenly, more temperately; he saw his work with more perspective and balance. When he was with Caterina, it was as though all the fire and beauty of life, the magic of nights, the wonder and freshness of mornings were contained in her every gesture. It was not merely that he was in love with her. To him, she was his other self. This was the way he thought marriage should be, the communion of two bodies, two souls. Often he would be filled with astonishment at the strength of his feelings for her, and this time he did not pause to analyze them.

Caterina was equally spellbound, fulfillment and high joy replacing the misery and grief of her years. She was her true self with Henry in a way that she had not been for years. All her guards were lowered for the only man she'd ever loved, and she gave herself without reservation, feeling he was the only man who had truly possessed her.

Yet, underlying all the joy, the tenderness and passion of that year, central to it and touching it at every point was the presence of Evelyn. Evelyn, standing in the shadow of Francis. And inevitably, as time passed, Caterina's relations with the world took on a different tone and color. There were still golden days and starlit nights but now, with increasing frequency, there were also times of terror.

Evelyn would visit them regularly on weekends and regularly remind Caterina that Francis was telephoning from Rome for progress reports. And what reports should she give him? "Having a wonderful time, wish you were here?" Through the long, dark nights when Henry went on business trips, Caterina would lie in bed staring at the ceiling, feeling like a woman who had somehow stumbled out of the sunlit world into a place of ruin and shame. Once, when Evelyn badgered her too insis-

334

tently, she seized her wildly by the arm. "Let me alone! Let me alone! It's too soon! Tell him I need time!"

"Time for what?" Evelyn jerked her arm away.

"Time to think. To think what to do."

What she meant, and what Evelyn sensed, was what to do to save Henry, to save herself. More and more as time passed the images of the past and present swept through her mind in a stream of blinding light. When she remembered Francis and his world, and thought of the obscenities in which he had involved her, she felt agony of regret and loss. And her head, full of nightmare visions, would reel about in terror searching for ways of escape.

Then a miracle occurred, or so it seemed to Caterina. It happened in such a matter-of-fact way she was scarcely aware that a temporary reprieve had been granted. She missed her period. That wasn't unusual, and she saw no specific significance in the fact. Then she missed a second period. That was unusual, and she went to see Dr. Harvey Hurley in White Plains. After he listened to her story about the ineptness of Italian doctors and examined her thoroughly, he had a few harsh words to say about these doctors, who after all, were not members of the A.M.A.

"Yes, one of your Fallopian tubes is completely blocked. I think the second was, too, but some scar tissue has separated. Recently, I suspect. In any case, while it is certainly difficult, it is no longer impossible for you to become pregnant."

"Pregnant?"

"I need a urine sample. If you'll call me in three days, I'll know for sure."

"You really think it's possible?"

"You have missed two periods. You are married. It is a possibility."

On the way home, Caterina's spirits soared. She was certain Henry would be pleased. Yes, he had said something about not wanting to build a dynasty. But a baby, their baby? And she would tell Evelyn who would tell Francis how impossible it was to do anything until after the baby was born. Her wordless prayers had been answered, and she had another year to be the woman Henry loved and perhaps to find a talisman that would protect them from Francis.

Three days later a call to Dr. Hurley confirmed his diagnosis. Caterina could hardly contain herself waiting for Henry to come home.

He arrived carrying a huge attaché case. "We did it, Caterina! Signed, sealed and delivered!"

"What, *caro*? What did you do?"

"We signed the contracts. Not just Germany. Germany, France and Italy, too. Your Italy. Now we have a second excuse to visit Italy. I want to visit the place where you were born and grew up." He was so excited. "You said your family home was sold. We'll buy it back. Do you know the name of the owner? We could write and ask if they'd consider selling."

Caterina had an instant of blackness. This was a complication for which she had not been prepared. "I don't know who owns the villa now. So much has happened since it was sold."

"Claire Booth Luce is our ambassador. We'll call Rome and put them to work."

"Oh, no—not now!" Caterina had to struggle to keep her voice steady. "Now I also have news." She followed him into the library and waited while he set the briefcase on his desk.

"What is it?" He looked at her. "You looked so happy until . . ."

"I am happy." She smiled and, putting her arms around his neck, whispered in his ear, "My husband, my love. You are about to be a father."

"I am a father! Oh! I thought you couldn't have a child."

"It seems I was wrong. I'm two-and-a-half months pregnant."

"Are you sure?"

"There are two dead rabbits to give testimony." She told him of her visit to Dr. Hurley and what he said about the scar tissue. Henry listened, and suddenly Caterina was frightened. He seemed so grave. Suppose he didn't want any more children?

Finally he spoke. "Is it all right for you to have a baby?"

"Of course. Women are made to have babies."

Henry thought of Selma. "Not all women. You know I lost my first wife in childbirth. I don't think I could stand losing you."

"You won't. Don't worry." She had to ask, "Are you pleased?"

"Pleased? I'm overjoyed! This calls for a celebration. Are you allowed to drink?" Selma was allowed to do nothing.

"I'm allowed to do anything I want for now. I suppose when I get too big, we must be careful not to hurt the baby."

Henry sat on the couch with Caterina beside him, and they toasted each other and the miracle that would give them a baby. The idea to find and buy the villa where Caterina had grown up was dropped. For now.

The next morning after Henry and the children had left, Caterina sat at the desk that William had once used. Her thoughts were chaotic.

A child of theirs to follow in Henry's footsteps. In her head she saw a large boy with flaming red hair. He would learn to work with Will. And he would be a Carson. A genuine Carson. But it never occurred to her to challenge Will's heritage.

Now she had only one thing to do. She telephoned Evelyn Wilkenson. "I have news for you."

"Good. Francis called yesterday. I'd like to give him some news."

Caterina smiled. A pregnant woman growing more pregnant every day would not suit Francis' plan. On the other hand Francis was highly practical and, when necessary, patient. "I'm going to have a baby. I'm almost three months pregnant."

The dry voice on the other end of the phone asked, "How does the proud father feel? Assuming he is the father?"

Caterina grew very angry. "He is the father, and he's very pleased. Now you tell Francis there is nothing to do for a year. He must be patient."

"I'll tell Francis next time he calls." She slammed down the phone.

As it turned out, Francis accepted the idea, and to Caterina's bewilderment even sent his congratulations. What she failed to realize was that to Francis the more involved Henry became with her, the more he would be hurt when the time came.

On May 7, 1951, Mrs. Henry Carson gave birth to a seven pound, six ounce baby girl in White Plains General Hospital. It was a fine, healthy baby, coming quickly with a minimum of labor. Henry Carson saw the child through the nursery viewing glass. Her red hair and strong body said Carson. He had another daughter. Just as well. There would be no rivalry between the new baby and Will over who succeeded Henry at the Carson Company.

Caterina was pleased that Henry was pleased; a girl would do quite as well as a boy. After much thinking and rethinking, they settled on the name Elizabeth Catherine Carson.

Francis gave her all the time she needed to have the baby, recover from giving birth and regain her figure, before he made his next move. It was direct, blunt and terrifying. One day Evelyn called and suggested she drive into town and have lunch. They had lunch in the garden in back of Evelyn's house. The conversation was uncomfortable and stilted; they stuck to stories about the children. Will had spent a wonderful year at Exeter, but Mary had caught a severe cold which developed into pneumonia. It was six months before she was well enough to think about returning to school. By then she was so far behind her class, Henry decided to keep her home for the year and engaged a private tutor to help her catch up. Elizabeth was growing rapidly into a beautiful child.

The lunch dragged to a close. Caterina waited for Evelyn to come to the point. When they finished their coffee, Evelyn suggested Caterina join her in the library. She had something to show her.

Once the library doors were closed, Evelyn took an envelope out of a desk drawer. Caterina could see the Italian stamps on the envelope.

"This is from Francis. Open it."

"You have already. Just tell me what's in it."

"There's a second envelope inside—it's addressed to you."

Caterina opened the envelope. There were two black-and-white snapshots inside. Both photographs were of Francis and her, both clear evidence of the obscene sexual practices Francis and she had indulged in. Caterina wanted to scream her disgust at herself to the world, a world that had no interest in listening to her. She put the pictures in her purse, hoping she wouldn't vomit. Of course she would tear them up before she returned to Carson House.

Evelyn continued. "Francis called last night. He wanted to make the point that those pictures are a small part of a large collection, a collection he is certain Henry would find most interesting. Francis thought Henry would adore having shared his mistress with his father and his wife with his brother."

Caterina tried to think of something to say. Anything! She knew Francis. He would do exactly as he threatened. It appeared to her the only person standing between Francis and her was Evelyn. A tide of terror washed over her, and her world began to blur. She found herself unable either to think or to see. Shapes fragmented and colors faded. What had been a small woman in a summer dress became a huge gray mass whirling around her. Somewhere she heard a voice, and she tried to make out the words. But she couldn't understand. It took an enormous effort not to scream and run from the gray thing that was enveloping her. Then, slowly, the tide receded and color began to reappear. The gray mass dissolved. And Evelyn Wilkenson was once again an elderly woman in a blue summer dress.

She flicked the ash of her cigarette into a large ashtray. Her words became understandable. Caterina interrupted.

"If you and Francis continue to pressure me, I will leave Henry. I would rather do that than do what Francis suggests."

"How will you support yourself?"

"I'll get a job in a store."

Evelyn shook her head. She exhaled and the cigarette smoke rose and floated out the door to the garden. "I'll see to it that no shop in New York hires you."

"Then I'll find something in a city where you can't touch me. I am now an American citizen. I can work anywhere."

"I have friends in the State Department. After they see other pictures such as I suspect you're holding and learn about your Fascist father and your life in Italy, you can be deported as an undesirable alien. Once he knows what I know, Henry won't help you."

Caterina paused. So Evelyn Wilkenson had guessed everything. The idea of going back to Italy, with no friends, no money and only Francis, was horrifying. They wouldn't let her leave Henry, and they would make it impossible for her to stay with him as his wife.

She studied Evelyn, who had started this ugly war with Henry for reasons she didn't understand. Was it possible she might bargain with her?

"Evelyn, please explain to me why I must do this thing. Why must I destroy the only happiness I've known? And destroy the man I love?"

Evelyn's answer was blunt. "So that I may obtain custody of Mary."

"But you see her constantly. Almost every weekend. And Mary is growing up to be a fine young woman." Caterina was pleading for some kind of mercy.

There was no mercy in Evelyn. "She's not growing up to be a Wilkenson."

"I don't understand. She's both a Wilkenson and a Carson. She's Henry Carson's daughter."

"That will be changed. Her name will be changed to Mary Wilkenson."

"Her name? What does that matter? When she marries, her name will be changed again. She'll be Mrs. whatever her husband's name is."

"No, it won't."

"I don't understand."

"When I married, my husband changed his name to Wilkenson. So will Mary's husband."

"What kind of a man would do that?"

"The kind of man who wants to marry Mary—marry Mary's position, marry Mary's money. I would not permit it any other way."

Now Caterina understood. The Wilkenson name. She didn't really care about Mary. Had never cared at all about her daughter, or Henry, or even herself. It was the Wilkenson name she cared about. "Then you won't help me with Francis." Her words were quiet, spoken almost to herself.

"Help you! I despise you!" Evelyn was in rage at this woman she had to deal with, a woman she regarded as "garbage." "If Francis, for some unlikely reason, decides to give up this project, I will tell Henry everything I've guessed about you. I brought you here, and you will do exactly as you're told. My stomach turns every time I see you and know you've been with my daughter." Her face came within an inch of Caterina's. "You will help me obtain custody of my daughter, or I will see you returned to the sewer where you belong."

Evelyn's uncharacteristic outburst of emotion had an unexpected effect on Caterina. For once she forgot her fears and remembered who she was, an Orsini, remembered what the Orsini family had been.

"Return me to the sewer! You little dried-up stick of a woman who makes claim to a family name." She slapped Evelyn across the face. Then she brought the same hand back and hit the other side of Evelyn's face. Her large ring with its sharp seal made a cut, and a trickle of blood began to drip down the older woman's cheek. "The Wilkenson name? How old is the Wilkenson name? One hundred years? Two hundred?" Her voice rose. "Your family is one of civilization's bad jokes. In that time what has your family done? They've made bandages, and they've made something to put under your arms so one no longer smells like a human being. And they've made a liquid to keep a man's hair neat and another to change the color of a woman's hair." Her voice became quiet and more intense. "I'll tell you about a family name. My family. The Orsini. We survived the Black Death in the fourteenth century. Six hundred years ago, Evelyn. Six hundred years ago. My ancestors were captains in the White Company, commanded by the great Sir John Hawkwood. We have been Romans, Black Romans, since the fifteenth century. The Orsinis commanded Castel Sant'Angelo and defended it and the Pope against the Lombards in the sixteenth century. They fought with the great Medici to conquer Pisa, fought for the Guelphs against Ghibellines and helped Andrea Doria rule in Genoa. We supported the Este family in Ferrara and opposed Cesare Borgia and destroyed him when he tried to unite Italy under his rule." Her voice changed again and grew harder. "We didn't own a house and a few hundred acres, we owned ten thousand square kilometers of land with thousands of houses and hundreds of thousands of people who lived on the land. We owned them, Evelyn. Owned them."

Evelyn listened. But she was too stunned by the physical attack really to understand.

"And then when it was time for Garibaldi to unite Italy, the Orsini family was among the first noble families to fight alongside his Red Shirts. When Victor Emmanuel I was crowned, my great-grandfather was at his right hand, knelt and swore allegiance to the House of Savoy and a United Italy." She stopped to look at Evelyn. "Your cheek has been branded with the Orsini seal." She held out her hand. "Look, Mrs. Evelyn Wilkenson, who is so proud of a family that has done nothing. Look at the Orsini seal. It has marked you well."

Then Caterina Orsini made a decision, a decision worthy of Francis at his best. They gave her no choice. She doubted Evelyn understood what would happen if she was successful. Francis understood; after their lunch with Evelyn, he had explained precisely the results he expected.

She remembered his beatific smile. "There are laws in the United States, Caterina. Laws which are part of the reason I live in Italy. My country attempts to legislate morality."

She remembered herself saying, "*Non capisco, caro.* I don't understand."

And Francis' smile grew more beautiful. "Forcing your innocent wife to become sexually involved with men and women is a crime, my dear. Giving parties such as we give is a crime. Homosexuality is a crime. Sodomy, not just with a boy but with a girl, is a crime. And for your information, oral sex is considered sodomy and is a crime in my country."

"But certainly Americans do these things?"

"Of course, and the police look the other way." He stopped smiling. "Except when they don't. And it's up to you to see they don't 'look the other way.' "

"You want the police to arrest your brother?"

"Yes. You will accuse my brother of forcing you to commit sexual crimes. And if we are successful, it will be more than a simple divorce. Henry will be accused of debauchery, lechery, sodomy, corrupting the morals of an innocent woman." He laughed. "If you didn't recognize yourself, you're the 'innocent woman.' When he's found guilty, he will go to prison for at least five years."

As she thought about the plan, Caterina changed her mind about Evelyn. Aware of the ways of her country, she was prepared to see Henry go to jail. To destroy Henry. And for what? So Mary could be renamed Mary Wilkenson. Caterina would not permit this abomination. She would go through the motions, acting out Francis' plans to ruin Henry. But she would see to it that the plan failed. Her hatred of Evelyn now outweighed her fear of any consequences. Evelyn, even more than Francis, would destroy her happiness, her life, to change Mary's name to Wilkenson. She made up her mind. At the door she said, "I have one of my headaches coming on. The next time you talk to Francis, tell him to send me my medicine." She would turn Mary Carson into someone Evelyn would not want as a Wilkenson.

Maggie Rhodes James sat at her boudoir table brushing her hair and thinking about the party to come. This made her think about Tony, and she closed her eyes, picturing him. At the same time that Maggie was visualizing him, Tony James was admiring himself in the cheval mirror in his bedroom suite in the opposite wing of the house. He liked the way Adolpho cut his hair. It made him look distinguished and yet still boyish. He liked the way his tuxedo fit. He even liked the few pounds of weight he had gained. They made him look more substantial. A solid citizen. Immensely pleased with his appearance, he walked into the sitting room that served as his home office.

Tony had finished dressing early and found he had time to kill before the evening's dinner party would begin. The party was a house-warming for this splendid house Maggie and he had built to hold their marriage together. Tony intended to use the party to help him make two critical career decisions. There were going to be some very important political figures attending, and as well as he already knew them, circulating among them tonight should tell him what he wanted to know. He thought about Maggie, who had prepared the guest list. It mildly irritated Tony that she knew as many important men as he did, and he wondered how many she had slept with.

It was none of his business, he thought, taking a cigarette from an antique silver cigarette box on his desk. He lit it with the wafer-thin gold cigarette lighter his bed partner of the previous night had conveniently forgotten. Tony looked at the lighter, certain it was a trick to make him call her. Women! Always clutching at a man. He'd have it wrapped and sent back by messenger. Then he sank into a huge leather lounge chair and gave himself up to a feeling of satisfied superiority. Poor Maggie. How could he object to whom she slept with? He had created their "arrangement," an arrangement he was convinced she hated.

Anthony James believed that Maggie was wild about him, that rather than lose him she would have agreed to anything. He hoped that she did not feel a failure as a woman because it had become increasingly difficult for him to consummate the sexual act after only the first weeks of marriage. She simply ceased to excite him. Marriage made sex boring, predictable. It was the chase, not the capture, that aroused him. He knew Maggie ascribed his attitude to some kind of arrested development and felt that living in the James house encouraged him to hang on to teenage attitudes toward sex. So they had bought this property and built this home in an effort to "grow him up." Tony James smiled at Maggie's naivete. He knew the house would make no difference, and his impotence alarmed him. So after a very short time of making a "college try" at fidelity, he gave it up as beyond him. And the first woman he took to bed confirmed his theory. His impotence vanished. He tried to keep his indiscretions discreet, but after a jealous actress wrote Maggie a note, the fat was in the fire. They had to sit down and talk it all out. It was from their talk that the "arrangement" emerged. Of course there were moments when he still desired Maggie. After all, she was a beautiful woman. But his fear of impotence kept him at a distance. Then, too, he was afraid she might misinterpret his gesture, see it as meaning more than he intended. All he was interested in was another one-night stand with a woman who also happened to be his wife.

Tonight he would decide whether to run for public office or to remain behind the scenes the way his father had. He could easily become one of the "boys in the smoke-filled room" who decided who should and who should not be nominated to run for public office. But if he decided that he wanted to become a "public man," he was certain he had enough influence with the "boys" of either the Democratic or Republican party so that he could be nominated to run for some office—probably to the state legislature in Sacramento as a starter. He lit his third cigarette.

It wasn't as it had been in Anthony's time when one could work both sides of the street. Now one was forced to choose: Democrat or Republican. Of course there were still a few people like Bill Knowland, who would be at the party tonight. He had been nominated by both parties for the United States Senate. However, it was wiser to choose. That's why the party was a mix of high-ranking Republicans and Democrats. Senator Richard Nixon had accepted. He had even higher ambitions than the U. S. Senate. Along with Nixon, Governor Earl Warren was coming. The Democrats would be represented by Edmund "Pat" Brown, someone to reckon with in California. Maggie had certainly put together an interesting guest list. He even had to acknowledge she understood him very well. She never exasperated him with questions about which political party's ideas he preferred. The reality they accepted without discussion was that Tony James cared nothing for ideas, only for power. The question to be decided was, Where would power be easiest to acquire? It was time to pay a visit to his wife. He always hated asking her opinions on matters relating to his career, but he never underestimated her advice. Which was another reason why he preferred staying married.

Maggie was selecting jewelry from her mother-of-pearl jewel box when she heard a knock on the door. She decided it was either Tony or Angel. Angel was occupying the main guest suite with her current husband, Andy Farrington. She hoped it was Angel.

"Come in," she said. It was Tony. "My, you look distinguished, Mr. James." She smiled, knowing how he loved flattery.

"I do, don't I? I believe I'd appeal to the women voters."

"Does that mean you've decided to become a 'public man'?"

"No. Not really. I haven't decided anything yet. That decision will come after I decide which party to join." He forced himself to go to the heart of the matter. "I meant to ask you sooner, but every time I thought of it, you weren't around. Offhand, which party do you think I should join?"

Maggie did not say she'd been waiting for weeks for him to ask her. She'd put together the guest list with the answer in mind. The concrete examples of her opinion would be at the party. "Well, look at our guests. Richard Nixon has national ambitions. And a Republican White House is a distinct possibility, providing they can get General Eisenhower to run for the presidency. I believe the Republicans are moving into power. The Democrats are in total disarray. That's why I invited our charming Democratic mayor, Fletcher Bawren. All the money is on him to be re-elected in November. But Bawren has been mayor for fifteen years. I think Norris Paulsen, the Republican, will win."

"That would be an upset." Tony rubbed his chin with his fingers. "Then are you saying I should try to cut a deal with the Republicans?"

"I'm saying just the opposite. The Republicans have nothing but fair-haired boys. The Democrats are in trouble. Their young lions haven't bowed in yet. So there's a power vacuum that a smart man could take advantage of."

"I see," said Tony, irritated that he hadn't thought it through himself. "Well, thank you for the pointers, Mag," he said, and he left.

Maggie watched him slam out and shook her head. What a conceited, self-centered child. He even resented being helped to succeed. Her original instinct had been right. She should never have married him.

# Chapter 28

CATERINA drove home to Carson House slowly, preoccupied with her own despair. Her rage had been replaced by resolution. In being faithful, she had done what came natural for her with Henry. Now she would have to behave differently. Henry was lost to her forever as she was to him. To survive, she must accept this fact.

For his sake then, as well as her own, she must free him of his love for her. She had presented him with selected versions of herself. Now she would let him glimpse another Caterina. He would come to believe that the Caterina he'd known was a magician's trick, a figment of his imagination. Discovering her deceit would cause him anguish, but he would accept it as the truth.

As for herself, to do what she had to do, Henry must become a thing of the past. She must never remember a single one of those moments which once had held the sum of life's meaning. The first step would be the parties. After that Mary. She would spare him the worst of it—prosecution as a criminal and possible prison. But she would not spare Mary. However, Mary was young, Mary would recover, Mary would experience far less than she herself had experienced. Yes, Mary would recover. And so would Henry. But not Evelyn Wilkenson. No, not Evelyn!

Over the next few months subtle changes began to take place at Carson House. The parties increased, attended by the usual friends and neighbors and by strangers to Henry—very attractive young men and women, people Caterina met at openings of art shows when Henry was out of town, at a dance class she took in New York, at a course she attended at the New School for Social Research. There were never enough strangers to disturb the flow of the parties, and Henry enjoyed talking to the people Caterina added to their circle.

At the same time the relationship between Caterina and Mary grew. Caterina bought her clothes, taught her how to improve her swimming, rode with her. They became more intimate. Caterina had no hesitancy in changing from a dress to a bathing suit in front of Mary. And Mary came to imitate Caterina. They talked about the difference between a child and a woman. Caterina explained the menstrual process. She showed off her breasts and pubic hair, which she assured Mary she would develop when she started to menstruate. From menstruation they progressed to childbearing. This naturally included carefully examining Caterina's body to show Mary how babies were born. Caterina then explained to Mary that she was made exactly the same. All women were. Slowly Mary became more physically affectionate. The first time she spontaneously hugged and kissed Caterina she pressed her mouth so hard against Caterina's mouth Caterina felt Mary's teeth and shared the licorice taste of her saliva.

"No, no. That is no way to kiss," said Caterina, giving Mary a feathery, sensuous kiss on the lips. They spent the hour practicing kissing.

As their intimacy progressed, Caterina swore Mary to secrecy. Nothing they did together was ever to be discussed with anyone. It was their secret, a proof of Caterina's love for her. Mary, basking in the attention Caterina gave her, loved the idea of sharing secrets with Caterina. She swore she would cherish their secrets; no one would know. Not Will. Not her father.

Toward summer's end, Caterina asked Henry to add another room to the pool house, a room with special exercise equipment and where they could make love in ways they couldn't in their bedroom. Henry was delighted to do something to please his wife. He even added a few ideas of his own, equipment heavy enough to enable a man of his size to get a good workout. There were padded benches for massages, ramps for sit-ups, ropes for climbing, rings for hanging and twirling, mats for tumbling and finally couches and stools for making love. The lighting ranged from brilliantly full to heavily shadowed. The roof could be open to the sky or closed in time of rain or cold. Caterina had seen a new product in New York, and she added it as a surprise—it was called a Jacuzzi—along with several bathrooms with showers, and male and female dressing rooms.

Then there were the changes in Caterina herself. Caterina now seemed to need new forms of stimulation. It wasn't enough that they made love as they had in the past. She constantly needed greater variety. Henry wondered if somehow, somewhere, he was failing her. Sometimes Caterina seemed to cease to be herself and became a series of apertures used to achieve orgasms. The change was gradual, but as time passed, Henry felt he was making love more and enjoying it less.

Which was exactly what Caterina had intended to happen. Knowing Henry as she did, she deliberately set out to offend him, to change their lovemaking from the magical experience it had been into something less tender, less romantic, more coarse.

And Caterina added new garments to her wardrobe, clothes that revealed more and more of her body. At first Henry was amused at her exhibitionism. While he didn't understand her need for it, since it was reserved for their private pleasure he saw no reason to object. But he felt a change in the atmosphere in which they were living. Beneath the surface calm, he could feel something building up slowly like a wave, something strange and dangerous. It was the newest element among so many novelties in their relationship. Had Caterina really changed into somebody else? It was often hard for Henry to find his beautiful wife, whose every gesture enchanted him, in this sometimes crude young woman.

Then one evening, dressing for a dinner party, Henry looked at Caterina and knew he had been mentally preparing for what he saw. She was wearing a black lace dress that came with a black silk lining. But she had cut away most of the lining, leaving only a small triangular patch in front and a horizontal strip across her breasts. Her buttocks were clearly visible.

"Change that dress, Caterina!"

"*Amore mio*, do not be prudish."

"Change it!"

"No."

Henry reached for her arm, held it in a viselike grip, and with his free hand ripped the dress from her body. "If you want to give them a thrill, go down like that!" These were the first harsh words he had ever spoken to her.

"*Caro*, you are so angry. But as you wish."

Henry winced and looked away. Was this the woman he had married? He felt a sense of degradation.

When it was time for Mary to return to school, Caterina pointed out that if she went to school they would have less time together, so Mary enlisted Evelyn's help, explaining she was too bright for the local private school and would be better off with tutors. Besides, there was her health.

"What's wrong with her health? She looks fine to me," Henry said.

"She's had a serious bout with pneumonia. Do you want her coming down with TB?" was Evelyn's irritated reply.

That almost decided Henry to send Mary back to school, until

Caterina suggested he ask Mary her preference. "I'd rather study with tutors," Mary answered. So Henry surrendered, and Mary stayed home.

The winter passed uneventfully, except that Henry had begun to feel a growing resentment of Caterina. She seemed to be stubbornly determined to outrage him, to make him love her less. He did not understand her behavior, and his natural ardor for her was being sapped by a feeling of betrayal. He began to fear his own desire for her. Sometimes he fought against the impulse to take her in his arms. Some secret purpose was driving her, and though he didn't know what it was, it sickened him.

In the spring Caterina made her next move. She planned a large dinner party, but at this party the guest list consisted solely of those couples she had introduced into the house over the last year. The dinner went smoothly. Caterina's friends, who came from all walks of life—the arts, science, business—were attractive, intelligent, animated conversationalists. Still, Henry had the distinct impression there was something more in the air, an anticipation of other things to come. After dinner, Caterina invited her guests to see the special gym Henry had built for her. Henry had a long-distance phone call to make, so he excused himself from the tour. The call to Europe took longer than expected; it was almost midnight before he could rejoin the party.

Leaving the library, he found the house deserted. Since the cars were still in the parking area, his guests had to be somewhere. Probably the gym. When Henry entered the gym, the room was semi-dark. Caterina, in a leotard, was giving lessons to a couple on how to use the ropes, rings, ramps and mats. The woman had stripped to panties and the man to shorts. Henry watched for a moment trying to decide what to do. Then, hearing a noise, he turned and saw something that made up his mind. Three couples were in the Jacuzzi playing a variety of sexual games. That was enough for Henry. He turned up the lights and gave all his "guests" ten minutes to get dressed and get out.

Alone with Caterina, he felt thoroughly angry. "Who were these people?"

"My friends, and I think you treated them quite rudely." Caterina seemed prepared to fend off his reaction with a casual politeness. "What if they make love in the Jacuzzi? We've done it often enough."

"We're married. And we were alone. If I hadn't walked in, you'd have had a first-class orgy on your hands."

"I would have left."

Henry tried to sound reasonable. "I'm not questioning you. It's your friends I question. Let them play their games in their own homes. Not in mine. Not in Carson House." Henry recognized there was a wide range of sexual mores in the culture, but as far as he was concerned, this was his house, had been his father's house, and here he intended to maintain what he considered to be the standards of civilized behavior. He felt he needed no justification for his anger, and a curious remark slipped out, "When in Rome, perhaps you do as Romans do." He coughed nervously. "What I mean is, this is Carson House . . ." He fumbled for words. "Here they must do as we do. Caterina, listen! You know I've planned to travel all around the country during the next twelve months. I'll be gone two or three weeks out of each month, and I rely on you to make certain nothing like what happened tonight happens again." After he finished, Henry felt drained of feeling. All he wanted to do was get away from Caterina, get away from an idea he refused to face—that she might well have been one of the women in the Jacuzzi.

Caterina said nothing for a moment. She understood more clearly than Henry what was troubling him. He did not know it, but she knew he was having difficulty lying to himself, difficulty disguising his growing doubts about her. This was her purpose: to teach him to despise her, to free him of his love for her. She dared not end her "parties." She needed them as proof for Francis that she had tried to carry out his instructions. So she answered in a subdued tone, "You're quite right. I don't know enough about people in this country. I will be more careful in the future."

"I don't blame you. But next time you give a party, stick to people we both know. No strangers."

Henry walked quickly back to the main house, leaving Caterina alone to change. Why had she married him? That was the question he'd asked himself most often recently. She was not after money. She spent little and was indifferent to the kind of extravagance he could well have afforded. But if she had married for love, what had brought about this change in her? What did she want from him?

He tried to put the whole matter out of his mind. What he had told Caterina was true. He had a very full travel schedule—trips all over the country to set up the Carson Company's own distribution system so they would no longer have to work through regional distributors. The work on the tranquilizers was proceeding with maddening slowness. Felix was extremely cautious. Godfrey Moore wanted him to visit Europe to see first-hand how the competition was doing. He had to make a decision shortly about marketing the tranquilizers. Felix would never be fully satisfied.

\*    \*    \*

Life continued at Carson House. When Henry was home, the routine followed Henry's wishes. But when he was on one of his frequent trips, Caterina turned the pool house into a brothel. At the same time she concentrated her attention on Mary.

Mary Carson had her first period several months after her twelfth birthday. After it was over, Caterina had a long talk with her. Now Mary was a woman, and as a woman she should learn the things women knew.

"A woman! Isn't that wonderful!" Mary sat down on her bed beside Caterina. She loved her stepmother, and if Caterina was going to teach her about womanhood, Mary could scarcely wait to be taught. "Now will I begin to have breasts the way you do, and can I have a baby?"

"Oh, of course. But you are too young to have a baby. However, there are other pleasures which you are old enough now to enjoy."

"There are? What?"

"I'll show you soon enough."

"Please! Soon!"

"Yes, soon."

Caterina knew that this was a precarious game she was playing. If she were to have her full revenge on Evelyn, she must proceed with the utmost delicacy. When Henry went on business trips, Mary slept in their bed with Caterina. Caterina always slept nude, and imitating Caterina as she always did, so did Mary. She grew accustomed to the nearness and feel of Caterina's skin. One morning Mary was awakened by the sound of Caterina moving in bed and making odd noises. She opened her eyes and saw the now familiar naked body of Caterina on top of the covers, her knees bent and her legs apart. She was doing something with her fingers between her legs. Then suddenly she stiffened and groaned. Mary was afraid she was in some kind of pain, and when the spasm repeated she grew more frightened. But the spasm passed, and Caterina lay quiet. She seemed very happy. Seeing Mary's frightened face, she asked, "Were you watching me?"

"Yes. Were you in pain?"

"No." Caterina laughed. "I was in pleasure. I was masturbating. It is what a woman can do for herself when she doesn't have a man or a woman to give her pleasure."

"It didn't hurt?" Mary needed convincing.

"It never hurts." Caterina decided the time was now, but before proceeding she considered for a final time what she was about to do. Mary would be subjected to what Caterina knew was a series of damaging experiences. The question was, how damaging? She knew of so many instances in the long history of the Orsini family when Orsini women had undergone trials far more severe than anything that would happen to Mary. If she, Caterina Orsini, had survived the Nazis and Francis Carson, Mary Carson would also survive. If she didn't, the Wilkenson blood line had grown too thin and deserved to end, and her vendetta against Evelyn Wilkenson would be complete.

She thought again of the pain she knew she was going to cause Henry, and the thought almost made her draw back. But she had given Henry a daughter. A fine, strong daughter with the blood of Dusalina Orsini in her veins. No matter what happened to Mary, it was a more than equal exchange.

She turned to Mary. "Would you like to find out how much pleasure it is?"

Mary was frightened, but she loved Caterina. "I guess so."

"I'll help you."

Mary brightened. "Would you? Could you show me what to do?"

So Caterina carefully instructed Mary in the pleasures of masturbation. When it was over, Mary clung to Caterina with love. She was a woman and had done the same thing Caterina did, felt the same pleasure Caterina had felt. She kissed Caterina on the lips, and Caterina directed Mary's mouth to her breasts and they began again. Caterina was teaching her the satisfactions of lovemaking between women.

About a month later, after reaffirming their vow of secrecy, Mary was introduced to men at a party. But Caterina took no chances. The drugs Francis sent her via Evelyn had been hoarded for just this moment. Mary hardly knew what was happening. Of only one thing was she certain: that she worshiped Caterina and wanted to do everything Caterina did. Imitating Caterina, she moved among the party guests from one man to several men to women to being the "star" of the party. At each level Caterina added a little larger dose of the aphrodisiac, then cocaine and finally heroin. At the end of six months, the corruption of Mary was an accomplished fact. Only a short time remained for Caterina to stay at Carson House. She would move into Evelyn Wilkenson's house and initiate divorce proceedings. While Evelyn still knew nothing about Mary.

One day late in May, Henry received a call from Will. He wanted permission to bring John Hillyer, Jr., home for a week after school ended. John's parents had agreed. "He's fourteen, Dad, a year older than I am. But we're in the same class, and we're great friends. You'll like him."

"I'm sure I will. When do you arrive?"

"June something or other. After finals. I'll call you back after I check with John. We could take the train to New York."

"I'll send Oscar with the big car. He'll take your luggage and anything John Junior needs. He can send the rest home by Railway Express. I'll work out the details with John's father."

Now that the main purpose of his call was settled, Will asked, "How's Mary and Elizabeth and Caterina?"

"Fine, though Mary seems tired the last few months. She may need a checkup." Thinking about Mary made Henry nervous. "Anyway, call me when we can make final plans."

Three weeks later, Oscar drove John Hillyer, Jr., and Will Carson to Carson House. As usual, Henry was working in the library when Oscar brought the boys in. "Tell Mrs. Carson they're here, Oscar, and ask her to join us with Mary and Elizabeth."

In short order Caterina appeared carrying Elizabeth, with Mary walking beside her. There were introductions all around and, watching the boys, Henry was surprised that though Will's hair was red and John's brown, and while John was older and taller than Will, the two boys looked surprisingly alike.

"Will, after you're settled, show John around—the pool, the gym, the stables. And dinner's at seven."

"Great, Dad. Come on, John. Your room's next to mine."

"Attractive boy, Caterina. They seem to like each other."

"I think he's very good looking," Mary remarked.

"Aren't you a little young for John?" He turned to instruct Oscar on dinner and missed the secret smile that passed between Mary and Caterina. Henry tousled his daughter's hair. "Wait a few more years. John will notice you."

Mary flushed at her father's words and ran out of the room. Maybe her silly father thought she was too young, but there were plenty of men who didn't.

Henry asked, "Now what was that about?"

"She's angry. You treated her as a child."

"She is a child. She's thirteen years old."

"She's almost a young woman. You know she had her first menstrual period."

"I didn't know. Did she tell you?"

"Of course. I explained it to her."

He picked up Elizabeth. "Oh, Elizabeth. What have I missed about you?" Henry held the toddler in front of him. "Are you still Daddy's girl? You're not mad at me?"

Elizabeth gurgled happily, hugging him as tightly as she could.

"This is going to be a strong young lady. She's got a fine grip for a two-year-old. I think I'll help the nurse put her to bed."

"Yes, you take Elizabeth, and I'll see to Mary. I'll explain you were only teasing her." Caterina was relieved to see Henry go. She wanted time with Mary, who needed calming and something to raise her spirits. She'd had nothing for three days, and without drugs, Mary became depressed. Any doctor would recognize the symptoms.

Henry nodded and walked upstairs to the nursery, carrying Elizabeth. Something he didn't understand was going on. He thought about Caterina and the last year. When they made love, he would sense in her only a woman's acceptance of carnal pleasure, not the deep closeness they had once shared. More and more his desire for her lacked joy and meaning. It had come to be only the need of a woman's body. Incredibly, the magnificent image of his love had become somehow soiled and tattered. It was as if a great iron door had closed forever in his heart.

And then there was Mary. Did the onset of menstruation explain her moodiness? He had noticed too that her depressions usually improved after Caterina spent time with her. Why? He decided he would skip the sales meetings in Dallas and Chicago. Something was brewing in Carson House, and every instinct warned him to stay in easy reach.

Caterina found Mary lying on her bed. She was so locked into a numbing depression that Caterina hurried to the box in the closet where she kept Mary's drugs. She handed her a small pinch of powder and said, "Inhale. You'll feel better soon." Mary did, and Caterina could see the effect almost instantly. The child had not inherited the Carson constitution. She must be like her mother. "Feel better?"

Mary smiled brightly. "Yes. Caterina, I love you."

"I love you, too, but we have rules. We must be careful when Daddy's home. And now there's Will and his guest."

"I like Will's friend."

Sitting at her bedside, Caterina considered the danger implicit in Mary's statement. She calculated how much time that gave her, realizing she must be out of the house before things came to a head.

Everything was arranged. The guests at her "parties" had signed affidavits. They stated that Henry had been the leader in their parties, that he had introduced Caterina to them against her will, that he had terrified her. It was a heap of rubbish, but with those affidavits in hand, Caterina could see Evelyn calling her lawyers. While Caterina initiated divorce proceedings, Evelyn would instigate action against Henry. Fool that the woman was, Caterina thought, she would not even pause to investigate the testimony. She was so anxious to draw Henry's blood.

But Henry's lawyers would be more judicious. They would investigate. And she was well aware that even a surface probe of her guests would reveal who and what they were. For the first time in months Caterina permitted herself a breath of relief as she thought how all legal action against Henry would collapse. She credited herself with at least saving him from the worst, a public disgrace, saving him because she had loved him and would love him until the day she was beyond loving. But she could not have him. She wiped the thought from her mind. It was enough that she'd wreaked vengeance on Evelyn.

"Why are you smiling?" Mary asked.

"I was thinking of your grandmother," Caterina said. "How do you feel?"

"Wonderful. I think I'll go downstairs now and talk to the boys."

"Yes, do that," said Caterina. "I'm going to my room for a nap."

Will and John spent the next day riding, swimming and working out in the gym. During the day, Henry was at work and Caterina and Mary spent long hours together, apart from the boys. The only time the family got together was at the evening meal. Then Mary made herself the center of attention. She had been a quiet, rather reserved child. Now, it seemed to Will, she was almost too exhilarated, too aware of everybody and everything. Her voice was too loud, her laughter feverish, her gestures exaggerated. She interrupted constantly, and when Henry suggested she let people finish their sentences, she had a hard time fighting back tears.

"Honey," Henry said, "what is it?"

"May I be excused, please?" Mary pushed her chair back.

When Henry nodded, she hurried from the room, and Will watched the concern grow on his father's face. At the end of dinner Henry spoke to John. "Could you amuse yourself alone tomorrow afternoon? I have family matters to talk to Will about."

"Don't worry about me, sir. There's plenty to do around here."

"Good. Will, Oscar will drive you to the office after lunch tomorrow. Your first visit to the Carson Company. We'll spend the afternoon together."

"Oh, great!"

Henry had thought William had made one of his rare mistakes in waiting so long to introduce him into the company, and he didn't want to repeat the error. Beyond that he had another motive. He wanted to question Will about Mary. It would be wise to get the opinion of someone her own age. But he didn't feel free to raise the subject in the house. "Caterina," he said thoughtfully, "I'm setting up an appointment for Mary to see a doctor next week."

"Henry, she's just a growing girl. She's moody."

"A check-up can do no harm," Henry answered, looking at Mary's empty chair.

When Oscar drove Will to the Carson Company, they were waved through by the guard at the gate. Will entered the main reception area and was greeted by the receptionist, who had been warned by Mary O'Toole to expect him. "Mr. Carson is in a meeting. He suggested you look around in the reception room. When he's done, he'll call downstairs and you can go right up."

Will took the badge prepared for him and pinned it to the buttonhole in his suit coat lapel. He looked at the name on the badge: WILL CARSON. Never in his life had he felt so proud to be Will Carson. A part of all this. He looked around the room and was struck by how similar it was to the library at Carson House. There were no books on the walls, but the furniture, the general feeling reminded him of home. Finally he saw the four paintings on the far wall. He almost ran across the room to see more clearly. There was his great-great-grandfather, Francis Carson, 1835–1886. The painting had an odd lifelessness about it. There was no one to tell him it had been painted from a photograph. And his great-grandfather, Henry Francis Carson, 1865–1910. Golly, he looks like Dad, except his hair's blond. Then there was his grandfather, William Francis Henry Carson, 1890–1941. This was the best painting of the three. He would have liked to have known his grandfather. Everyone who remembered him seemed to think he was a swell guy. And the fourth painting, his father, Henry William Carson, 1918–      . Unlike the others, there was a blank for the final date. Will hoped the date would never be filled in. The picture didn't have the detail and quality of his great-grandfather and grandfather. It seemed cruder. But when he stepped back to look at all the paintings at the same time, he could sense the similarity among all four men: the power, the will to work, to risk, to succeed. Will felt intimidated by the pictures and hoped when it was time for his own picture to be added, his mother could know and be proud of him. He wished he knew who, or where, she was, but his father would never talk about her or permit him to ask questions.

His musings were interrupted by a tap on his shoulder. "Mr. Carson just called down. He's ready for you, young man." Will nodded. "Use the elevator. You'll be met by Mr. Carson's secretary."

"Thank you—er, I'm sorry, I don't know your name."

"I'm Carl. I remember the first day your father came to work here. And I hope to be here when you come to work instead of visiting."

"Thank you, Mr. Carl. I also hope you'll be here."

"Just Carl, Master Will. Now you get a move on. Don't want to keep your father waiting."

In fact, Henry was not that busy. He had deliberately delayed a meeting with Felix Flam to give Will a chance to wander around the waiting room. If Will was like him, he'd have spent most of his time studying the paintings of his ancestors. The Carson Company was so much larger and more diversified now. From Felix's report it seemed the tranquilizer was almost ready for marketing now. It would be an important product. And the sooner Will began to think about his future at the company, the better trained he would be to work at the empty desk next to his. Henry still stared at it every day.

He decided he would not ask Will what he did while he waited, but if Will brought up the portraits, it would tell him a good deal. Occasionally it occurred to Henry that Will might not want to succeed him at the company. But he was a Carson. That alone was enough to determine his future.

Mary knocked on the door, opened it, and Will entered the room. Henry watched his expression as he took in the empty desk. If he'd had doubts in the past, Will's expression resolved them. "Sit down, Will." He motioned to the chair in front of his desk.

"Dad, I didn't know you had a Rogues' Gallery downstairs. All those Carsons. What a collection!"

"You found them interesting?"

"Much more than that." Will sounded thoughtful. "It's funny. You grow up knowing you belong to something, but until I saw those paintings, I never really thought how I felt about it."

"And how do you feel about being a Carson?"

"Proud, Dad. Proud."

Henry's eyes blurred. He blew his nose to cover his feelings. "The first time I saw the paintings I felt the same way you do." He smiled. Then his face changed. Before Will's first initiation into the Carson Company, they had to talk about his sister. "Will, have you noticed anything odd about Mary?"

Will was reluctant to answer the direct question. He might get his sister into trouble. But he had been surprised at the changes since last he'd been home, only three months ago.

Henry understood his son's reluctance to speak, so he tried making it easier. "Say it, Will. Nothing will happen to Mary."

"Well . . ." Will decided the best he could do for Mary was tell the truth. "Yes, Dad. She's—maybe 'flighty' is the best word. Sometimes I don't think she's there at all, and sometimes she's too much there. Does that make any sense?"

"Yes. And what about Caterina?"

Now that he'd started talking, Will couldn't stop. "She's changed too. She and Mary act like girlfriends or something. I've seen them look at each other when they thought no one was watching. Funny looks."

That was enough for Henry. Mary was going to a doctor at once, no matter what Caterina said. "Okay. You've told me what I wanted to know. Now, suppose I give you the tour. Would you like to see the factory?"

Henry and Will arrived at Carson House around six. Will had been given a complete tour of the offices, and they had even run through the labs.

"I'm going to wash up before dinner. You find John."

"Oh, John's fine. Probably reading. He's smart, Dad."

"Good. Maybe some of it will rub off?"

Will went straight to John's room, poked his head in, expecting to see him lying on the bed reading a book. What he saw was John lying on the bed with his eyes wide open and fixed on the ceiling. John heard the door squeak and looked up. His wave of recognition was weak.

"What's the matter? You look funny."

"I'm not funny. I'm something else."

"What else?"

"Forget it. It's nothing." Will could see John was embarrassed. "I'd like to call my parents. I bet they want to see me. I could go home tomorrow."

"You want to leave?" Will sat on the bed next to his friend. "Come on, John. We're friends. The Rover Brothers." He used the nickname they were known by in school. "What's the deal?" John's face suddenly reddened, and Will guessed. "It's Mary?" John nodded. "What happened?"

John didn't know how to talk about it. Not without offending his friend. But he didn't know how to get out of talking about it. Not without offending his friend more. "Is Mary all right?"

Will remembered his father's question. "What do you mean 'all right'?"

"I mean does she understand what she's doing? She'll get into a lot of trouble if she's not careful."

"What's that supposed to mean?"

"She's heading for trouble if she keeps doing what she did this afternoon."

"What did she do this afternoon?"

"I was in the gym working out with the weights. Mary came in. She started laughing and dancing around. She had on a bathing suit. Then she took down the top of her suit and . . ."

Will was incredulous. "She what?"

"She took down the top of her bathing suit and began to dance around half undressed. I tried to get out of there, but she grabbed me. Rubbed herself against me and grabbed me . . . er . . . well, you know where."

"I don't believe you."

John didn't want to continue. He couldn't believe what had happened either. "Then she took off her suit and said, 'Kiss me.' Will, she was naked."

"You're a liar!" Will threw himself at John, and they fell to the floor struggling with each other. Will was yelling, "Liar! Liar!"

In spite of pounding John, Will couldn't get him to admit he lied. And eventually John, who was older, bigger and stronger, was able to pin Will to the floor. "Listen, Will. On my honor, on our friendship, on the pact we took to be friends forever, it's the truth. That's why I want to go home. Suppose she tries again? Something's wrong with her."

Will stopped fighting. "All right." He'd known something was wrong with Mary, but this? All the older boys at school talked about girls, and he understood some of what went on between boys and girls. But he couldn't associate that with his sister. The need to know and the fear of what he might find out tore at him. He thought about his father and the paintings on the wall. Those men were able to face the truth. Well, he was a Carson. He too could face the truth. He made himself ask, "What happened next?"

Now it was John's turn to be angry. "What do you think happened? I ran. I've been in my room since."

He got up and helped Will to his feet. "What do I do?" Will asked.

"I don't know. But the next guy isn't going to run away. That's what I meant when I said she's going to get into trouble."

Will thought about the way Mary had been behaving. "I'll talk to her. We're very close. She'll tell me what she was doing. I'll find her and tell you what she says."

John had to ask, "You do believe me? Even if she doesn't admit it, I told you the truth."

Will let out a deep breath. "I believe you. That's why it's so hard."

As he expected, Mary was in her room sitting in a chair, looking out the window toward the pool and the pool house. Her eyes were swollen from crying. Will sat down next to her. "Mary, I just talked to John. Please tell me what happened."

Mary tried to laugh. "Nothing happened. He was too scared, but other men like me."

"What do you mean 'other men'?"

"I can't tell you. It's a secret between Caterina and me."

Will thought about this. He had to persuade her to talk. Suddenly he had an idea and pretended to laugh. "Oh, come on, Mary. That's a kid game. Caterina told Daddy about it. Married people don't have secrets."

Mary looked puzzled. Will was right. For an instant, she was angry at Caterina for treating her like a child. If Caterina could talk to Daddy, she could talk to Will. "Well, men do like me." Will listened, dumbstruck, while Mary told him everything that occurred between her and Caterina, her and other women, her and other men, the parties, the medicine Caterina gave her to make her feel good. Everything. She finished, saying, "You see, I'm a woman like Caterina. I've done everything she's done. I even asked her if you could be invited to our parties. She said you were not a man yet. But I don't think she wanted you. That was an excuse." She sighed. "After you left, she had to go into New York. I thought she'd be back by now, but she isn't."

Will managed to hide his horror while listening to Mary's story. Now he had no idea what to do. "Well, I'm sure she'll be home any minute. See you at dinner."

"I hope she's home soon. I miss her so much."

Will left the room, careful not to run until the door was closed.

\* \* \*

Before John could ask a question, he blurted out, "She admitted everything. And more. Much more. John, she's sick. I don't know what to do."

"What else did she say?"

Will repeated the story. All the way through John kept saying, "Oh, my God!" and "My God!" When he finished, the two boys looked at each other. They were terrified, but both knew there was only one thing they could do. They had to tell Will's father. Everything!

They agreed to do it together. At least they could give each other support.

The boys found Henry alone, having a drink on the porch. He asked, "Have you seen Mary and Mrs. Carson?" Will and John glanced at each other. Henry saw at once something was disturbing them. "Out with it. What kind of mischief have you two gotten into?"

The boys sat facing Henry. Will said, "Dad, I've got to tell you something, and John's here only because he knows it's true and can back me up. Please promise to listen to everything first before doing anything."

"It's about Mary."

"Yes, but there's more."

"Caterina?"

"Yes, but will you let me tell you my way? Please, Dad?"

Henry put his drink on the table. "All right, Will. Tell it your way."

The entire story took a long time to tell. As he went from point to point, he could see his father's face change from amazement to shock to rage to resignation to something he couldn't define but was much worse. When he finished, he expected Henry to turn to John for confirmation. He didn't.

Henry rose slowly. "I want you boys to forget everything you told me. Mention it to no one. No one. Now promise me that."

Both boys answered at the same time. "Yes, sir."

"And I want you to go to Will's room. No matter what you hear, stay there. Your dinners will be brought to you. I'll see you later. Go now." Henry's words were so measured, so controlled, neither boy knew what to think. They weren't even certain he believed what Will had told him.

Just before they left the porch, Will turned. He was about to say, "Dad, it's the truth," but the sight of his father—his head buried in his hands, his body so rigid, the cords of his neck standing out like ropes—

told him he need not say a word. Even as he watched, the hand holding his drink crushed the glass. His father believed everything.

Henry waited to give the boys time to reach Will's room. He rang for Oscar and told him to send their meals upstairs. Then he asked, "Where is Mrs. Carson?"

"I believe she's gone to New York for a few days. She took the Buick and several bags."

"Do you know where she's gone?"

"No, sir."

"Bring Mary something to eat. And tell her to remain in her room. I'll talk to her later." At that moment they heard the sound of the front doorbell. "Oscar, unless it's Mrs. Carson, I don't want to be disturbed."

Oscar left and returned quickly. "It's something from Mrs. Carson and Mrs. Wilkenson. The man says he has to hand it to you personally."

"Very well. Let's get it over with." Henry had a good idea why he had to be served personally, and he was right.

A small man in a dark summer suit was waiting for him. "You're Henry Carson?"

"Yes. Serve the papers and get out."

"I'm sorry. It's my job."

"I know." Henry accepted the two documents, both enclosed in blue folders. He looked at the titles: Mrs. Henry Carson vs. Mr. Henry Carson. A divorce proceeding. Mrs. Evelyn Wilkenson vs. Mr. Henry Carson. A custody proceeding. Henry went into the library to study the papers. He would have to see Mary and hear her story firsthand before the end of the evening. Above all, she had to be protected from further damage.

# Chapter 29

**H**ENRY read the contents of the two Summons and Complaints with growing amazement. Supposedly he organized and participated in a series of orgies and forced his innocent wife to take part in the sexual activities. She could no longer accept his depravity and was suing for divorce. There were a number of affidavits from men and women, some of whose names he vaguely remembered as having been brought into the house by Caterina, that testified to the truth of Caterina's complaint. In each case, the dates and people attending were given.

Henry looked at the dates and turned to his pocket diary. In spite of the wreckage of his life, he was stunned by their stupidity. The Summons and Complaint was sheer lunacy. During each and every date mentioned, he had been out of town—Chicago, Detroit, St. Louis, all over. As always, for tax purposes, he had kept records: airline tickets, restaurant bills, hotel receipts. Now he could use them as proof of his absence. And his lawyers could gather affidavits from people with whom he had spent time in each city. There was no way Caterina could prove he had forced her to take part in revels at Carson House, when he had not been within 500 miles of Carson House. Obviously, she'd lose the suit.

It followed that if Caterina lost her suit for divorce, Evelyn would lose her suit for custody of Mary. If he had not been at those parties, there was no way she could claim he was an unfit parent.

He thought about Evelyn. Would she also claim he had tossed Mary to that scum? Was that possible? No! Obviously, Evelyn had no idea what had happened to Mary. He could not conceive of her endangering Mary's mental and physical health, to say nothing of her morals. What was going on?

Suddenly Henry thought of Elizabeth. She had not been mentioned in either action. Elizabeth! Oh, my God! Was she all right? Was she still upstairs? He dropped everything and took the stairs three at a time to burst into the nursery. Nurse Sobel was sitting next to the crib humming a tune. Seeing him, she looked concerned. "Hello, Mr. Carson. How is Mrs. Carson?"

"What do you mean?" The intensity in Henry's voice frightened the nurse. "I'm sorry." He went on in a much softer voice. "What's wrong with Mrs. Carson?"

"I don't know, but she stopped in after lunch, picked up Elizabeth, held her for a long time and then put her back in her crib. She asked me to take special care of her and left. She was sobbing as though her heart would break."

"Thank you, Dora. I'm sure you'll take excellent care of Elizabeth." He left the nursery and stopped off at Will's room. The boys were seated in the window alcove whispering as though afraid they could be heard through the thick walls. Neither had eaten much of the food Oscar had sent to them. "I wanted to see both of you before I spoke to Mary. Is there anything else I should know? Anything you forgot to tell me?"

Will answered. "One thing. Mary said she suggested Caterina include me in their parties, and Caterina said I was too young. Mary thought that was an excuse. She just didn't want me there. Does that make sense?"

Henry frowned. "Maybe. Now I've some news. Caterina has left. We're getting a divorce."

Neither boy knew what to say. Feeling equally uncomfortable, Henry turned to leave, then remembered something. "And Will, John, don't think I've underestimated how hard it was to tell me that story. I'm proud of you both. Good night."

When he reached Mary's door, he knocked lightly.

Mary answered, "Come in, Caterina." He opened the door. "Oh! Daddy, where's Caterina? No one tells me anything."

Henry sat down next to his daughter with no idea how to begin. He told her a half truth to ease her temporarily. "She's spending a few days with your grandmother."

"She didn't tell me she was going."

"Maybe she couldn't find you when she had to leave."

Mary smiled. "Maybe. I was in the gym with John. He's such a child."

Listening to Mary, Henry realized this was beyond him. It was going to take a very experienced psychiatrist to help her understand what had happened, the right and the wrong of it. The best he could do was give her approval and support. "Will tells me you wanted to include him in your games, but Caterina said he was too young. You thought she didn't want him?"

"She didn't. She loves Will but not the way she loves me." She glanced sideways at her father, smiling, "Why did you say I was too young for John? I can do everything Caterina does."

"I was just teasing."

"Actually he's the one who's too young. He ran away from me today."

Henry nodded, and Mary felt a little better. Maybe her father would help her. "Daddy, I'm feeling funny. Caterina kept a box in my closet with my medicines to make me feel better. I can't open it. Do you think you could?"

"Where's the box, Mary?"

"I'll get it for you." She went to her closet, reached up and took down a heavy padlocked metal box. She handed it to her father.

"It's a strongbox, honey. I'll take it downstairs and see what I can do. Feel any better?"

"Oh, yes. Now I know where Caterina is. But I miss her. We used to sleep together whenever you were on a trip." Everything Mary said made it harder for Henry to maintain his composure.

"You get a good night's sleep. I'll see you in the morning." He hurried out of the room. There might be some clue in the box as to which drugs Caterina had given Mary. The information would be useful to the doctors.

Once in the library, he snapped the lock and opened the box. The packets were clearly labeled: cocaine, opium . . . Henry went to the bar and poured a snifter half full of brandy. He understood Evelyn's involvement thoroughly, but not Caterina's.

Over the last year Caterina had undergone a major change. This could be attributed to her using the same drugs as Mary, but there'd been no signs of any personality disintegration such as in Mary. Primarily, what he'd felt in her was detachment—something mechanical, almost professional, in her responses to him. She'd withdrawn from the intimacy they had once shared. But had she really changed, or had she gone back to something she'd been before they'd married? Henry thought about this for a while and came to an odd conclusion: Caterina had deliberately set out to destroy the love between them. And as he thought about it further, he marveled at how successful she'd been. He tried to examine his own feelings for her. He felt nothing. His real love for her had died months ago. And now, even allowing for numbness and shock, he felt surprisingly little pain at his loss—nothing like the grinding grief he had felt so many years ago when he'd stamped out his love for Maggie. He was primarily concerned about Mary and what could be done, and his anger at Caterina was more like disgust.

Then he turned his attention again to the actual lawsuits. He read Caterina's action first, then he reread it. Something very important was lacking. Nowhere did she claim Elizabeth. He remembered what Nurse Sobel had said. She had left the baby. It had not been easy for her to give up the baby, but she had. She wanted him to have the child. Why? Maggie had given up Will because he had forced her to. But Elizabeth was their child, and they'd been married. Normally, in a divorce proceeding, the mother is awarded custody of the children. He looked at the papers again. There was nothing at all about Elizabeth. He glanced at the affidavits of the party guests. Here was the strangest fact of all. Caterina knew his work schedule almost as well as he did. If dates had to be used, why didn't she use dates when he was at Carson House? Since all the claims were lies, why not lie intelligently and make the accusations harder to disprove? The more he thought about it, the more Henry became convinced she wanted him to disprove the accusations, and do it so thoroughly as to leave no doubt in a judge's mind, should the suit ever come to trial.

He sipped his brandy, continuing to review the situation. Who were the people who lent their names to this charade? Most men and women would be hesitant to admit publicly a connection to anything as sordid as the events they described. Either they never expected the case to come to trial, or it made no difference if it did. Since they had no way of knowing whether he'd fight the action or not, the answer had to be it made no difference to them. That meant in their world sexual profligacy was acceptable. Wouldn't that place their testimony under a cloud?

The more Henry considered it, the more he accepted that Caterina's entire action was a sham. But why? If she wanted a divorce, he would have granted it. With a generous settlement. She knew him well enough to know he wouldn't want to live with a woman who didn't want him. For that matter, he no longer wanted her. What she had done was too self-destructive to be accidental. It made no sense. She would lose her case, and so would Evelyn.

Henry poured another shot of brandy into the snifter. Why Mary? Why had Caterina drawn the child into this farce? To hurt him? He thought of Will. Of Elizabeth. If she wanted to hurt him, why not make a clean sweep? Include Will in the parties. And take Elizabeth with her.

The answer was in Mary. Why had Caterina focused on her? To hurt her? That seemed absurd. And with proper treatment and time Mary might recover. As would he. Suddenly it struck Henry he'd been blind. The answer was Evelyn! Caterina hated Evelyn. She hated her enough to sabotage her entire custody suit, as well as her own divorce. Hated her so much she'd gone further. She seduced Mary and then provided her with drugs to aid in her degradation at orgies. When Evelyn found out, she would be devastated. Caterina wanted to destroy Evelyn.

This logic brought Henry up against a blank wall. Why? Evelyn had brought Caterina to this country. Evelyn had placed her personal imprimatur on Caterina's respectability. He recognized how he'd been gradually ensnared by Evelyn. When Evelyn decided he was ripe, she had introduced him to Caterina. He remembered the first sight of her. Was it Caterina or the fact that she reminded him so much of Maggie that hypnotized him? Evelyn certainly noted the resemblance. Who, then, was Caterina Orsini? And where and how had Evelyn met her? And why did Evelyn Wilkenson want him to marry Caterina Orsini?

Whatever the answer, he now recognized their marriage had fallen in with Evelyn's plan. With his eyes wide open, he'd stepped into the trap. Henry forced himself to go on thinking. Now what did Evelyn gain from his marriage? She could see Mary on a regular basis. But that wasn't good enough. Mary was still being raised as a Carson, not as a Wilkenson. The only way she could be raised as a Wilkenson was if Evelyn obtained custody. Henry knew he was coming close to the truth. It wasn't enough for Caterina to divorce him. She must do it in such a way as to prove him an unfit father. Only then could Evelyn have Mary.

This recognition brought Henry full circle, back to his original questions. Why had Caterina undermined Evelyn's plans? And even gone beyond it to corrupt Mary? The same answer stood. She hated Evelyn. But if she hated her, why had she let Evelyn intimidate her, terrorize her to such an extent that she even made a pretense of going along with the suits? Did Evelyn know something about Caterina's past? Surely Caterina knew he wasn't an innocent? She could have admitted anything to him. She'd lived through the German occupation. Anything was possible under those conditions. Was that it? His gut feeling said no. There was something about Caterina he wouldn't accept, and Evelyn had used whatever it was to force Caterina to do as Evelyn wished. And Caterina obeyed, but in such a way as to subvert the goal. Mary was a pawn in her revenge. Again Henry asked himself what Caterina had done that gave Evelyn such power over her. Caterina wouldn't tell him, and in the final analysis did he really want to know? No! There were some questions better left unanswered.

Henry finished his brandy. Maybe, some day, he would find the final piece to the puzzle. Meanwhile, he would work with those pieces he had. Should he call Evelyn and warn her off, or should he turn the papers over to John Hillyer? The legal way would be easier, but far slower. John would have to gather the evidence. A defense motion filed, pretrial examinations, motions, and so forth. If he made the phone call, grueling as it would be, there was a good chance Evelyn would recognize how hopeless her case was. The one thing he would not tell her was Mary's condition. It would be enough to bar her forever from Mary.

It was a little after eleven. He would call now.

Upstairs in her room, Mary lay in bed unable to sleep. While she had not inherited the Carson constitution, she had inherited both Henry's and Evelyn's brains. Despite her brother's effort to appear casual when she told him about the parties and Caterina, she knew he was shocked. And she'd picked up the same reaction from her father. It made her feel alone and frightened. Every time she'd felt that way, Caterina had given her some medicine that made her feel better. But Caterina was with her grandmother, and her father had the metal box with her medicine. She wondered if he'd been able to open it. If he had, he could give her the medicine. She slipped on a robe and hurried to the head of the stairs. From there she could see the door to the library, with a light shining under the door. She ran down the stairs and was about to enter when she heard Henry talking on the phone. She couldn't hear what he was saying, but she heard her grandmother's name. She opened the door a crack and looked in. Her father was facing away from the door, so she opened it wider and slipped into the room, her bare feet making no sound. She dropped behind the couch and listened.

"Evelyn, before we continue, let me speak to Caterina. . . . Don't argue, put her on." He waited. "Caterina, I don't know why you chose to divorce me the way you did, but we both know your suit is a farce. . . . Now be quiet and listen. It will blow up tonight. There's over twenty-five thousand dollars in our personal bank account. Withdraw it tomorrow. If they call me, I'll okay it. Now put Evelyn back on. . . . Evelyn, pay attention and shut up. I can prove I wasn't even in the state on the days in question. Your suit doesn't stand a snowball's chance in hell of succeeding. . . . I was in Chicago, St. Louis, all around the country on each and every day I was supposed to be here. . . . On June twenty-first I was in Chicago. That's when Edgar Henderson says I— Of course I can prove it—plane tickets, hotels, restaurants and three days of meetings. They're all the same. . . . No, I have no idea if Caterina looked at the dates. She can have her divorce, but not as you planned. . . . Ah, I'm glad you see the light. I'll have my secretary prepare photostats of all the evidence with telephone numbers of people you can contact in each city to confirm I was there. . . .''

He didn't see a small figure slip out of the library and close the door behind her. Mary ran upstairs and threw herself onto her bed. Caterina was going to divorce Daddy. What would become of her? She loved Caterina, and Caterina loved her. Last month she'd been allowed to take the train alone to New York to visit her grandmother. She had almost forty dollars. That would easily pay for the train ticket and a taxi to Beekman Place. She'd see Caterina and Grandmother. They'd help her feel better.

Mary spent the rest of the night halfway between sleeping and waking. One moment she'd be wide awake, and the next moment she could see the sky lightening. Once she sensed Daddy leaning over her bed watching her, and she pretended to be asleep. She'd leave right after he went to the office. After the door was shut, she waited before rolling over and pretending to wake up. Just in case someone was watching her. No one was there. She hurried to her bathroom, washed and put on her best dress. Then she stole down to the garage. Daddy's car was gone, but there were the Olds, the Chevy, other cars, and two trucks used on the estate. A repair man was working on one of the trucks.

"Where's Jimmy?" she asked.

"He drove your father to work, Miss Carson."

She stamped her foot in make-believe anger. "How can I get to the railroad station? I'm visiting my grandmother today."

"Well, I'm going into White Plains for a part for the truck. I'll take you to the station there."

"Can you do it now?"

"Sure. Hop in." He opened the door of the smaller pickup truck. She sat beside him, trying not to wrinkle her white dress.

At the White Plains station Mary bought a ticket and had to wait thirty minutes for the next train. Her body and head ached. She needed Caterina's medicine as badly as she ever had. When the train arrived, she got on. She fidgeted with impatience until it pulled into Penn Station. Mary got off and followed the signs that led to the taxi stand. Since the rush hour was past, she had no trouble getting a cab. She gave the driver the address on Beekman Place and closed her eyes. It was getting harder to control her nerves. Each block seemed to take forever.

Finally the cab drew up in front of the Wilkenson house. Mary paid the fare and jumped out. Climbing the stairs to the door, she rang the doorbell. Then rang again. Finally a maid opened the door. She was new and had never seen Mary.

"What can we do for you, young lady?"

Mary sounded choked. "I want to see Caterina. Caterina."

"Caterina? Oh, the Italian lady. She left last night."

"When will she be back?"

"I don't think she will. Mrs. Wilkenson—er—asked her to leave. She's gone, bag and baggage. I believe she's gone home."

Mary brightened. "Home? To Carson House?"

"No. Home to Italy."

"Italy!" Mary sank down on the steps.

"I have to get back to work, or I'll catch it from the lady."

Mary looked up. "Will you tell her I'm here? Please?"

"I can't. She's left absolute orders not to be disturbed."

"But I'm Mary Carson. I know she'll see me."

"I'm sorry, miss. Orders is orders. She made no exceptions. She'd fire me if I disturbed her against orders."

"But I'm her grand—" The door was shut before she could finish the sentence. Mary remained on the steps. The blue sky had clouded, and rain was threatening. Mary rang the bell again. The same maid appeared.

"Be a good child, go away."

"She'll see me," Mary insisted.

"Miss, I can't let you in. Mrs. Wilkenson would—"

"Please! Please!" Mary started to cry. "Please tell her Mary is here. Me!"

The little girl's sobs overcame the maid's reluctance. "All right. I'll see if she'll see you." Although terrified, the young maid went to the library and tapped on the door. There was no response. She tapped a little harder. Still no response. Then, not daring to open the door, she said in a loud voice, "Mrs. Wilkenson, there's a girl, a child, outside who wants to see you."

A shriek sounded through the closed door. "Jeannette, if you disturb me once more, you're fired. I don't care if the Christ Child wants to see me. I am in to no one! No one!"

Jeannette scurried away. Mary was still sitting outside on the steps.

"I'm sorry, miss. I can't let you in. She said 'no exceptions.' " And the maid shut the door.

Mary walked west on Forty-ninth Street, sobbing. Her beloved Caterina had deserted her. She'd never find her again. And she knew her father and brother thought she'd been bad. Now her grandmother, who had been so nice to her, wouldn't see her. Her head hurt, and she felt nauseous. It was very hard to keep track of where she was walking. Twice cars swerved, just missing her. She reached Lexington Avenue and stumbled uptown. It had begun to shower, and she was soaking wet in a matter of minutes. She saw an entrance to a subway and remembered being on a subway once. You bought a token, put it in the slot and pushed through.

Mary sat on the subway platform bench a long time, and the longer she sat, the worse she felt. She was alone. Caterina, whom she loved, had left her. She felt dizzy. She thought if she walked around she might feel better. A train hurtled into the station coming to a screeching halt. The noise was unbearable. And the shoving people terrified her. She stood frozen in the same spot until another train roared into the station. She moved closer to the edge of the platform. Another train careened by. Each time the sound of the brakes and the people grew louder and more strident. Her vision blurred. Then someone bumped her trying to get to the open door, and she almost fell. Every nerve seemed outside her skin. Noises, touches, smells became intolerable. She moved closer to the edge of the platform. There was a line on the platform that must mean something. She didn't know what. She bent over the platform to look at the rails. There was the sound of another train coming. She knew she should move back, but she was so dizzy and tired she couldn't. It was hard enough to stand still let alone move. The engineer saw a small girl leaning over the edge of the platform. He blew a shrill whistle to warn her. She didn't move; if anything, she leaned over further. Much too late, he slammed on the brakes. The screech of the train mingled with the screams of the passengers as they were thrown forward and the shouts of the people on the platform who saw what happened. Mary never felt the train hit her. She was thrown back against the wall of the station, dead before she hit the platform.

The police were on the scene in less than five minutes. Mary had no identification and was removed to the morgue. At Carson House, Mary was missed at breakfast. A search of her room and the grounds turned up nothing. When Henry was notified, he hurried home to lead a further search. In spite of his efforts, nothing was discovered until a mechanic returned. Yes. He knew where Mary was. He'd driven her to the White Plains station so she could visit her grandmother in New York. Henry called at once and was told Mrs. Wilkenson was not to be disturbed. But Henry was not a frightened little girl, and Evelyn was on the phone in minutes. When she learned Mary had disappeared on a visit to see her, Evelyn turned the house upside down. She discovered almost at once that Mary had been at the door and turned away by a maid following her orders. Then Henry called the police. Half an hour later his call was returned.

"Mr. Carson?"

"Yes."

"This is Sergeant Weinstein, New York Police."

"You've found my daughter, Sergeant?"

"Possibly, Mr. Carson." The sergeant's voice was matter-of-fact. He'd long since lost count of the number of similar calls he had made. "I'm afraid I'll have to ask you to come to New York to make an identification."

Henry knew. He thought how similar the sergeant's voice sounded to the doctor's when his father had been murdered.

"How did she die, Sergeant?"

"We're not sure it's your daughter."

"I understand, Sergeant. How did the young girl die?"

"A subway accident."

"Suicide?"

"We don't know. It could have been an accident. I'd like an identification before investigating further."

"Where is she?"

"The morgue at Bellevue."

"I'll be there." He hung up the phone. There was one more call to make. He couldn't stop himself. "Give me Mrs. Wilkenson."

"Who's calling?"

"Henry Carson." He waited. "Evelyn?"

"Yes."

"I wanted to be the one to tell you, Evelyn. Mary's dead. She was hit by a subway car after being turned away at your door."

The scream couldn't be described.

"Goodby, Evelyn."

# Part Four
# 1953-1960

# Chapter 30

**M**AGGIE led her seven-year-old gelding, Reposo, out of the stables. Once outside, she took a sugar cube from her pocket and held it in the flat of her hand. The touch of his tongue was slight and fleeting. The horse nuzzled her shoulder asking for another cube.

"Later, boy." She rubbed her hand against his velvety nose, and then concentrated on adjusting the stirrups to the proper length for jumping. This done, she mounted Reposo.

When she and Tony picked the land and built their house two years ago, one of the considerations had been that there be enough land for several good riding trails and a large flat area where she could build an exercise ring. She had built a stable large enough to hold four horses and a barn to store feed for the horses. The final building on the property was a small, comfortable house near the stable. The riding master, Robert Tilling, lived there with his wife, Cora. Ever since the stables and barn were completed and the horses moved in, Maggie rode every day at "Bienvenido," the name Tony and she had given their home. Riding had become a source of enormous pleasure for her, almost a compensation for the lack of pleasure she derived from her marriage. There were times when she thought she loved her horses more than she did people. And her affection for the horses and riding overflowed to include Bob and Cora. They were straight, simple people, almost out of place in a city such as Los Angeles. Almost, but not quite. Occasionally Bob would surprise her with his knowledge of matters other than horses.

Bob Tilling was a short man, no more than 5' 3" tall, bald except for a fringe of nondescript gray-brown hair, with a lined, chapped red face, the kind of face one sees on a man who has been exposed to too much sun and wind. He had been an instructor at the Malibu Stables, and Maggie was one of his pupils. When Maggie added the stables to the property, it seemed natural to hire Bob Tilling to work for her full time as both stable and riding master. Cora loved the change. She loved the house Maggie built for them. She appreciated Maggie's allowing her to select her own furniture. She loved the evenings Bob, Maggie and she spent together. And Bob and she loved Maggie Rhodes James. They thought of Maggie as the finest lady in California.

Bob hoisted himself up onto the top rail of the fence and shouted, "Warm up, Maggie. Work him till he breaks into a light sweat before you try the jumps." He watched Maggie take Reposo from a walk to a trot to a canter. If Maggie had ridden as a child, she would have had everything to be a first-class show rider: nerve, strength, natural balance and a love of riding. But she hadn't, so her riding lacked one vital element—the instinctive response to her horse that was only present in one who learned to ride as a child.

Maggie pulled up her horse in front of Bob. "We're both in a sweat now. I think we're ready." Bob watched her take the horse through the series of jumps he'd set up.

When she had completed the course, they looked at the three jumps she'd knocked down. Bob said, "What you need is practice and a better feel for the jumps. You'll improve."

Maggie made a half-humorous, half-disgusted face. "I suppose so. Is Reposo up to trying the course again?"

"Go ahead. The jumps don't matter. And I've enough wrapping on Reposo's legs. You won't hurt him."

The sun had come out, and beads of perspiration rolled down Maggie's face. Her brown shirt was plastered to her back. "Here we go." She thought, "engagement" and "release." Flow with the horse. When she pulled Reposo up in front of Bob Tilling, she asked, "Was that better?"

"Yep. Four jumps were excellent. But you let the reins go slack on two and held them too tight on four. Would B-plus do?"

"It'll have to." Maggie grinned as she dismounted from Reposo. He nuzzled her, wanting his reward. She reached into her pocket and produced another sugar cube. A flick of his tongue and it was gone. "See that he gets a good rubdown. He deserves it. I'm working this morning, but would you like to go trail riding this afternoon?"

"There's lots of work to do in the barn. Call the house when you're ready, and Cora'll tell you if I can."

After changing from her riding boots to brown loafers in the small dressing room next to the stalls, she walked down the well-kept gravel path that led to the main house.

The house was a huge H built on one level, with the main room, kitchen and dining area in the center. In the front half of the H, the right wing was devoted to her bedroom and office suite, while the left wing belonged to Tony. Her suite faced the morning sun; his faced the sunset. The guest rooms, with a special suite at the far end called "Angel's Rest," completed the right wing of the H. Several smaller guest rooms and the servants' quarters made up the other wing.

A six-foot-high, brick-colored concrete wall with tile coping similar to the main house was constructed around the entire compound, enclosing about two acres of land. Inside the wall was a four-car garage, a swimming pool and pool house, gardens, fountains and all the amenities necessary for gracious living. A huge paved parking area for guests was also provided.

The house was the essence of casual elegance, combining architectural grandeur with Maggie's desire for sun and air and comfort. The Southern California sun flashed on the glass and almost seemed to call forth sparks from the redwood and the brick-colored concrete. Only a huge budget could have achieved the deceptively simple look. The interior of the house was in the same mood of informal elegance. The furnishings were all large old Spanish pieces or good modern copies of the original pieces brought by early California settlers. Only Maggie's office was different, being totally modern, almost Spartan, and absolutely utilitarian.

Once in her suite Maggie stripped off her sweaty clothes and considered taking a quick shower rather than a tub bath. The combination of the hot ride and the lack of a current lover made her conscious of her body. She decided there must be some affinity between riding and sex. Maybe that was why so many young girls loved to ride until they discovered boys. Every time she rode she felt sexually stimulated. She glanced at her body in the mirror-panelled bathroom. She was thirty-seven, but there was no hint of the matron about her. Her skin had an allover golden tan, thanks to the use of her patio. The flesh under her chin was firm, as was her entire body. Many years ago she had been concerned about putting on too much weight when she grew older. The opposite had happened. Her body had grown leaner and harder during the last ten years; the horseback riding did it. Turning sideways she could see the result of all the riding. The muscles in her buttocks were larger, while her waistline was smaller. They were a match for her breasts, which showed no sign of sagging. Large, full and round, they could have been the breasts of an eighteen-year-old. Once again she had riding and swimming to thank. The sports had kept her muscles hard and her breasts high. Her legs were powerful and at the same time shapely. Small ankles and knees and strong calves merged with her full thighs.

Looking at herself she felt a fleeting sadness. Hers was a body for bearing babies. Her breasts were meant to give milk. But it wasn't to be. Her life with Tony and their lovers was not a life suitable for children. Now time was running out. How many years did she have before nature's clock stopped? Five? At the most! Something about the thought of children made her pause. She wanted to talk to Mark, and if she stopped to take a shower, she'd miss him.

Slipping on her terry-cloth robe, she went to the desk in her office and dialed the kitchen. "Were there any calls for me, Maria?"

"*Si, signora.* Mr. Wurdlinger from Newport Beach. And Mrs. Chandler wants to talk about her plans for the new music center."

"Thank you, Maria." Maggie hung up. She'd call Mark first. An unfamiliar voice answered her in New York. "Mark James, please. Maggie Rhodes calling."

"One moment, Mrs. Rhodes. I'll see if Mr. James is in."

Maggie smiled. A new secretary? Unless Mark's door was closed, which meant he was in, she knew very well if he was or wasn't in.

The phone was picked up, and the familiar voice said, "Maggie! What's on your mind this glorious, wet spring day in Manhattan?"

"The usual—Orange County. I think it's time we opened negotiations with Henry for that pivotal piece of property he owns."

"Henry?" Mark sounded peculiar.

"Henry! Prices are rising. Someone else could make him an offer."

There was a brief silence, then Mark said, "You're calling me to talk about buying Carson's land in California?"

"Maybe we should start this conversation again. Hello, Mark, this is Maggie of Orange County." She heard Mark clear his throat.

"I gather you haven't heard."

"Heard what? What's wrong that I haven't heard?"

Mark sounded grim. "Remember the last tidbit of gossip I gave you? . . ."

"About Henry's marriage? How could I forget?"

"It was a mistake, so I thought this time I'd shut up."

"This has something to do with Henry?" She had a moment of panic. "Henry's all right? He's not sick?" She was afraid to ask if Henry was dead.

"He's all right, but . . ."

Maggie breathed again. At least she was spared that. "But what?"

The words came in a rush. "He's divorced. His ex-wife's gone back to Italy." He swallowed. "And Mary's dead."

"What?" Maggie couldn't believe it. "She can't be. She's a child."

"Children die too. The rumor is suicide."

"Oh, my God!"

"It gets worse. There are shocking reports from the rumor mill. It seems Mrs. Carson gave some very wild parties." He almost whispered the next words. "Orgies. And she got Mary into them."

"Mary? But she's only thirteen."

Suddenly Maggie felt a sick, shaking fear. "Why did Henry permit it?"

"He knew nothing about it. The Carson Company's grown very big, and Henry travels a lot."

"And while he was away his wife gave sex parties? With Mary?" It was unbelievable.

"That's what I hear."

Now she must face her fear. Her body had known before her mind. She asked the question. "What about Will? Was he involved too?"

"His name's never come up. As far as I know, he wasn't present."

"Are you sure?"

"How sure is sure? He's at school at Exeter. He must be all right."

Maggie felt as if her own life were in peril. She had to be sure. She had to find a way to see Will. "Mark, I'm flying in. I have to see Will."

"Why give yourself the pain? After avoiding him all these years, a strange woman's visit could very well upset him." Mark seemed to be thinking out loud. "John Hillyer's son is also at Exeter. I hear Will and he are friends. I have an idea you might consider. Hillyer's firm is legal counsel for the Rhodes Corporation. We pay them enough in legal fees that I think we can ask John to report to you on Will. He could visit both boys at Exeter."

Maggie considered Mark's suggestion. It was true—seeing Will would cause her great pain. And over the years she'd met Hillyer regularly at board meetings in California. "I'll call you back, Mark." She hung up, wishing she could talk to Henry, still trying to control her fears about Will.

Maggie booked herself on one of the first nonstop flights across the country, on a new American Airlines DC-7. She would leave at nine that night and, allowing for the three hour time difference, arrive in New York at nine Tuesday morning.

Then she called Dorothy Chandler who, fortunately, was out, and left a message that she was taking a quick trip east and would call when she returned. The same message went to Gus Wurdlinger. She called

Mark to tell him she'd be in tomorrow morning, staying at the Park Lane. "What's your schedule tomorrow?"

"Don't worry about it. Do you want me to arrange something with Hillyer?"

"Yes. Tell him I'm flying in and I'm concerned about Will."

"Right. I'll have the limousine waiting for you at Idlewild."

The plane landed on time. She was met by a man in a dark suit and a chauffeur's cap. He wore a card pinned to his coat that read, "Mrs. Margaret Rhodes James." After her luggage was collected, they drove into Manhattan. Maggie found the trip to be both interesting and disturbing. It was the first time in thirteen years she'd been back in New York.

Her mind was obsessed with thoughts of Will and Henry. She prayed that Will hadn't been damaged, all the while mystified how Henry could have married such a woman. And why did she have Mary to her parties? From everything Maggie heard, Mary Carson wasn't an early-blooming beauty, mature beyond her years. She had the Wilkenson looks. This reminded Maggie of Evelyn Wilkenson. She must be devastated by the tragedy. Maggie decided she would have to visit Evelyn. Like it or not, she was being drawn back into her past.

Her night flight and the time lag combined to depress her. But after a shower and a pot of hot coffee, she felt up to calling John Hillyer. The switchboard operator must have been alerted to expect her call, because she was put through to John with no detour to his secretary. Maggie was surprised at how genuinely cordial he sounded. Most of the old arrogance seemed gone. He was sympathetic, and he'd already called Exeter to make arrangements to see the boys. Sounding apologetic, he explained it would have to be tomorrow. "They're already in class, and it's a six hour drive."

"Tomorrow's fine. Could you answer a question?"

"If I can I will."

"Mark told me Will and your son are friends. What is he like?"

"Will? I've never met him. He was supposed to visit us. Then the tragedy happened, and he seemed to prefer going home on vacations."

"Then you don't really know how it affected him?"

"Only what John tells me. He says he's fine. You know things came to a head when John was visiting Will at Carson House. We'll talk more tomorrow. Where are you staying?"

"The Park Lane."

"Fine. I'll call you as soon as I return."

\* \* \*

When Maggie called Mark James, his secretary put her through immediately.

"It's arranged. John is going to see Will tomorrow. He'll report back to me. Now, what about Henry?"

"I've set a tentative appointment for Thursday."

"All right. I'm visiting Evelyn Wilkenson today. She may have some information. I'll ring you after I talk to John."

Maggie hung up and considered whether she should call Evelyn first or arrive unannounced. She decided an unannounced visit was best. She must handle their meeting with the utmost tact. Of all the people affected by Mary's death, Evelyn had to be the most devastated.

Maggie stood on the corner of Beekman Place and Fiftieth Street studying the Wilkenson house. At a cursory glance, it seemed the same as when last she'd seen it. Still black stone, still nestled under the trees between it and the street, still clean white window trim. But on closer inspection, there were several troubling incongruities. The empty garbage cans stood uncovered on the sidewalk. Where were the servants? By ten-thirty someone should have collected the cans and placed them in their wooden bin next to the house. Then she noticed that the leaves that had fallen from the trees over the winter lay undisturbed in the small front garden. Newspapers were piled on the front stoop. Why hadn't they been picked up? And the windows were closed, the curtains drawn. Maggie had an eerie feeling no one lived in the house. She crossed the street, and as she approached, the house appeared more disordered. The sidewalk hadn't been swept in days, maybe weeks. It wasn't like Evelyn to permit this.

Maggie rang the bell three times. No one came to the door. She could hear the bell sounding through the house. Then she saw the fluttering of a curtain in a window overlooking the front door. Still no one came to the door. Now Maggie pressed the button and held it. After several minutes a woman's voice called out, "Go away! Mrs. Wilkenson is seeing no one."

Maggie rang again. The same voice cried, "Go away!"

Maggie called back, "If you don't open, I'll call the police." There was something very wrong here. She thought she heard a gasp at the word "police." "Open the door now!" She pressed the bell again, and the curtain moved. The voice was trying to see her. "Open the door. I insist on seeing Mrs. Wilkenson!"

Then she heard a series of bolts turning, the door opened, and there was a cry of disbelief, "No! You!"

Before the door was slammed shut, Maggie threw the weight of her hip against it and shoved it open. She sent whoever was holding it staggering back across the entrance hall. Maggie followed her and stopped dead in her tracks. What had been a beautiful, graceful entrance hall was a squalid mess. And beyond it, the living room was strewn with yellowing newspapers. There were white dust cloths over all the furniture. The air was rank, as if no one had opened a window in months. The doors to the beautiful library were open, and the chairs Maggie remembered sitting on having champagne with Evelyn were overturned. The table was missing a leg. As for the books, there were more on the floor than on the shelves, books lying every which way as though scattered by a furious hand. Evelyn's desk was a rubbish heap, and there was dust and dirt all over. It was unbelievable.

The woman clutched her arm. "How dare you come back here!"

Maggie surveyed her, an incongruity in this wreck of a house. Her clothes were clean, her face washed, her hair combed. "Who do you think I am? And who are you? Where's Evelyn Wilkenson?"

"You're Cate—" The woman paused, placed her glasses, which had been on the top of her head, on the bridge of her nose. "No, you're not Caterina Carson?" It was as much a question as a statement.

"I'm Maggie Rhodes. Now where is Mrs. Wilkenson? Tell me, or I'll call the police!"

"She's upstairs. She's not well."

"Living in this pigsty would make anyone sick. Who are you?"

"Joan Aimes. Her secretary."

"Where are the servants? Why hasn't this place been cleaned up?"

Joan gave a dry laugh. "The servants quit months ago. She wouldn't pay them. And anyway, who but me would stay here? It's too awful. But she insists I stay."

"Mrs. Wilkenson is upstairs?"

"Yes, but she's sick. She doesn't want to see anyone."

Maggie lost her temper. "Listen to me, Joan Aimes. What I see here disgusts me! And I'll see Evelyn Wilkenson with or without your permission."

"All right. But I warn you, you won't like what you see."

"I'll risk it. Now move!"

Joan Aimes walked up the stairs and toward the rear of the building, Maggie following. She opened a door at the end of the corridor. Whatever Maggie might have expected, it wasn't what she saw. The beautiful room that looked out on the garden and the river—the same room Selma and

Henry had used to change in after their wedding—had been completely redone for a child.

"Mrs. Wilkenson had this room redone for Mary to move into."

"But Henry would never have . . ." Maggie stopped herself. She had no idea what Henry would or wouldn't have permitted. "Where is Mrs. Wilkenson?"

Joan dropped to her knees, calling out in a playful voice, "Come out, come out, wherever you are." In response, a small, bony figure, dressed in a child's dress, high stockings and patent leather shoes and wearing a black wig, crept out from behind a chair. "Ah, there you are, Mary. We have a visitor."

"A visitor?" The voice of the figure was childish, in keeping with her costume. She looked at Maggie and giggled, "My Caterina. You've come back."

Maggie stared at the absurdity that had once been Evelyn Wilkenson. Under the black wig, a wizened old face smiled back at her. "Does she ever realize she's not Mary?"

"Sometimes. Then she goes crazier. You saw the library. She runs around the house breaking everything she can. After a rampage, she collapses, and I put her to bed. When she wakes up, she's Mary again."

"Why haven't you called a doctor?"

"I did once. He wanted to institutionalize her, but I was afraid. You don't know her. If she got well and found I was responsible, she'd see I never worked again. She can be terrible!"

"So you did nothing?"

"I hoped she'd get well. And I fed and clothed her. You see how clean and neat she is." Joan was pleading for understanding from this strange woman who had discovered her secret.

"How did you pay for things? What did you say to telephone callers?"

"I lied. I said she was in mourning and speaking to no one. And to pay for things I . . . well . . . I signed her name. She scrawled her signature. The bank never knew the difference. But I didn't steal. I didn't even take a salary."

Maggie couldn't understand how anyone could be so afraid of Evelyn Wilkenson. She turned to look at the old woman, who had been dancing around the room and now was staring at her. "Evelyn, do you know me?"

The voice changed abruptly. "You're Maggie Rhodes."

"And who are you?"

"Ev . . . Ev . . ." The voice became childish again. "I'm Mary Wilkenson. Caterina, play with me?"

"Miss Aimes, is there a phone that works?"

"Yes, the one in the library."

Maggie smiled at Evelyn. "I'll be right back to play with you."

"What'll we play?"

There was a deck of cards on a table. "We'll play 'Go Fish.' " She hurried out of the room. Once in the library, she called Mark James. "Mark, I'm with Evelyn Wilkenson. This is too much to explain on the phone, but she's sick. She thinks she's Mary."

"She what?"

"She should be in a mental institution. Do you know a good one?"

"Payne Whitney."

"Do you have contacts there?"

"No. But I'll call Tommy. Dr. Thomas Barnes. He's connected to New York Hospital. He'll know who to call."

"Tell him what I just told you. And to send an ambulance and orderlies, in case she becomes wild."

Then Maggie went upstairs and stayed with Evelyn, talking to her and playing "Go Fish." When she heard the doorbell ring, she tried to distract Evelyn's attention. But Evelyn heard the ring and started to crawl under the bed. Maggie managed to hang onto her until Joan Aimes, two orderlies and a white-jacketed doctor entered the room, at which point Evelyn exploded into a whirlwind of rage. She became a wild creature, hurling herself around the room and howling at the orderlies. It took some time for the two strong attendants to get hold of her. She fought them off with her head and her teeth, trying, like a dog, to bite them, herself and the restraints that were being tied to her. She fought until she was exhausted and finally stood quietly in the straitjacket.

Then Evelyn Wilkenson said her last sane words. "Thank you, Maggie Rhodes. Thank you very much. You know, there's nothing anyone can do to me any more that's half the hell my Mary puts me through. Goodby, Maggie Rhodes."

# Chapter 31

MAGGIE spent most of the night wide awake, her mind shuttling back and forth between her memory of Evelyn Wilkenson and the wild-eyed face of the straitjacketed woman she'd last seen. She had read some old, high-melodrama tales of insanity, but she had never felt the terror and pain the actual sight of raging insanity could bring. She doubted that Evelyn would recover; she had escaped too far from the real world into a world of her dreams to ever return. She wondered what had happened that had so unbalanced Evelyn's mind that she chose insanity rather than face it. Was it Mary's death alone—or was there more to the story? There had to be more to the story. Somehow, in some dreadful way, Evelyn must have played a part in the events that led to Mary's death. John Hillyer might have some information. Henry would know more. Maggie had to ask herself if she wanted to know more. The answer to that question came in the form of a very strong premonition. Something waited for her in the future that made it imperative she know all she could possibly know about this terrible tragedy.

Her thoughts about Mary and Evelyn mingled with thoughts about Will, Henry and, surprisingly, William. Older and wiser now, she recognized something in William she would rather not have seen: a willingness to sacrifice his son's happiness, sacrifice anyone, for the Carson Company. That same flaw was in Henry. The company came before all personal feelings. She knew how deeply she felt about the Rhodes Development Corporation and her plans for Orange County, but she doubted she would have asked herself or anyone else to make the kind of sacrifices William had asked to fulfill his dream. How could she know that, before he was murdered, William had had the same doubts about the rightness of his actions?

Maggie spent the next day sightseeing. She reflected briefly on the fact that John had never met his second son. It should be interesting. She felt no reason for concern. Unless one looks for family resemblances, one seldom finds them. There was no reason for John to suspect anything, especially since John, Jr., who lived with Will, suspected nothing. And Henry, who had seen both of them together, suspected nothing.

When she returned from an evening at the theater, there was a message from John waiting for her. He had seen Will and John, Jr. Will was very well. He had been untouched by Caterina. However, it was very urgent for John to see her the first thing tomorrow. He would be at her hotel at eight-thirty.

The tone of the message left Maggie in some doubt. Was it possible, in spite of her feeling of security, that John had noticed something? If he had, what did it mean? She would have to wait until tomorrow to find out. Toward morning she drifted off into a restless sleep, full of dreams in which John and Henry merged and separated and then combined with her in a struggle against some third force. She awoke early. Despite little sleep and troubling dreams, she was waiting in the lobby for John at eight-thirty. John was prompt, and watching him come through the revolving door, Maggie noted he was still tall and broad-shouldered. But he did look older; he was a little thicker in the middle, and his bright red hair was thinning and had streaks of gray. He also looked very agitated. He knew! It was clear that in spite of her confidence he had guessed the truth.

After leading her by the arm to a secluded sofa in a corner of the lobby, his first words confirmed everything. "Why didn't you tell me, Maggie? Why didn't you tell Henry? I don't understand. I'm Will's father, not Henry or William. Me."

"John, that's absurd."

John hit his head with the flat of his hand. "I saw John Junior and Will together. I'm an idiot not to have figured it out. You were in love with Henry. You'd never have gone near William, or he near you. It was not in his nature."

For the first time Maggie's voice showed the bitterness and pain she'd carried all the years. "It's nice of you to think such high-minded things about us now. And how do you propose to convince Henry that you're the father? That is, supposing you are?"

"You still love him, even though you're married to another man?"

"I still love him."

"Then tell him. I'll back you up."

"You will?" This was a new John Hillyer.

"I will!"

Maggie hesitated, then blurted out, "He wouldn't believe you any more than he would me. Remember William's will."

"Forget the will! No one will ever know what was in William's mind. I never understood half the things he did. The point is, I have proof I'm Will's father."

"What proof?"

"The webbed toes, Maggie. Will has them. John Junior has them. I have them. They've run in our family for generations. Has anyone in your family ever had twin toes?"

Maggie shook her head. Although Maggie was astonished, she knew John Hillyer meant every word. "What about your wife? Ellen will be hurt."

John answered as honestly as he could. "Yes, she will. But it was long ago. I was younger and dumber then. I think I can explain it so she'll understand."

"So the truth is to come out at last?"

"It's about time. You should have told Henry years ago."

"Let me think about it. Sometimes the cure is worse than the disease."

"Don't think about it. Do it!" In his eagerness to help, John raised a question that had been puzzling Maggie too. "I think Henry loves you. I think much of the reason he married Caterina was her similarity to you." He paused. "I wonder if Evelyn Wilkenson set a trap for him."

"I think she did. I'd like to know how she met Caterina Orsini." Maggie stopped to think for a moment, then she said, "Look, John, I appreciate what you've offered to do about Will. But think over what you've said. Think about Ellen. A child is not as simple as a fling. And I have to decide what I want to do. But I do thank you for offering."

"We haven't much time. Mark and I are seeing Henry this afternoon to make an offer for that property he owns in Orange County."

"I know. If Henry will see me, I hope to be at the contract closing."

"He'll see you, Maggie. You can arrange to talk to him privately."

"Slowly, John, slowly. One can't push Henry Carson."

"Push Henry? That's like pushing Boulder Dam."

"Isn't it?"

"I've got to run to pick up Mark. We'll call you after the meeting."

"I'll wait for the call in my room. Good luck."

"Good luck to all of us. Especially you."

Maggie watched him leave and returned to her room to sit and think about Will and Henry and her. And what was best for the boy who thought of himself as Will Carson.

The hours crawled slowly over the face of the clock she kept glancing at. One minute seemed like ten, and ten minutes an hour. To help pass the time, she started reading Hemingway's latest book, *The Old Man and the Sea.* She was deep into the book when the telephone rang. It was Mark, sounding dazed.

"I think it went well. We haven't cut a deal yet, but Henry seemed willing to sell."

"You sound peculiar. What's the problem? The price?"

"I don't think so." He was puzzled. "Henry has kept track of everything you've done in Orange County . . ." Maggie wasn't surprised. She expected as much. William would have done the same thing. "But he wants to meet with you alone and suggested tomorrow morning." A note of "banker's caution" crept into Mark's voice. "Any idea why he'd want to meet with you alone?"

"No. I'm equally anxious to meet with him, though. Did you set an appointment?"

"I wanted to check with you first. We're in a private office at the Carson Company."

"May I speak to John, please?" There was a pause while Mark handed the telephone to John. "John, what do you think's in his mind?"

"I haven't a clue. But it gives you a chance to do what we discussed. I'm still behind you."

"Thank you. First, though, I have to hear why he wants to see me." Maggie had an idea. She remembered Henry used to get in by eight. "Ask if I can join him for coffee. He'll tell you when."

John was back in a minute. "He said he'll expect you at eight-thirty tomorrow."

When Maggie hung up, she felt wrung out. She hadn't realized until this moment how worried she'd been that Henry wouldn't see her. But not only was he willing, he had suggested it.

That night every nerve in her body seemed to start with separate wakefulness. It was as though a great blaze of electric light had been turned on in her head, and her whole past was reenacting itself at a hundred different points of consciousness. Memories crossed her mind— memories of working for William, of meeting Henry, of nursing Will. She had a tragic but sweet vision of lost possibilities. But she had not yet reached the stage where a woman can live on memories. It was happpiness she still yearned for, and the idea of seeing Henry made everything else seem unimportant. If she told him the truth about Will, would he believe her? Would he believe John Hillyer's proof?

* * *

She arrived at the Carson Company headquarters ten minutes early, wanting to park outside the gates and study the changes. There was a major one. Instead of one old, three-story red brick building with white trim, there were now two buildings with a small parking area in between the buildings and much larger lots on either side of the two buildings. She remembered William had planned the second building at the time he had purchased Wilkenson, Inc., a duplicate in style and construction of the first. However, the gate with the guard house and the guard inside hadn't changed.

Maggie had dressed very carefully for the meeting. She had chosen a very simple navy blue linen dress with a straight skirt and navy blue and white spectator pumps. Even though her legs were tanned from her life in California, she decided to wear hose. Earlier that morning, when she fitted her breasts into a brassiere and slipped on her panties, she thought of the days when she never wore a brassiere, when panties were a thing to be discarded before Henry arrived. She shook her head. Her knowledge of Henry's ex-wife, and an intuition as to the kind of clothes she must have chosen, made it important for Maggie to place distance between her own image and Caterina's. If nothing else, she would be a Lady with a capital L.

Now it was eight-thirty. Time for the meeting. She drove up to the guard house and the guard stepped out.

"I'm Mrs. Anthony James. I have an appointment with Henry Carson."

The guard checked a list. Then checked it again. "I'm sorry, Mrs. James. Your name isn't on my list. Are you certain your appointment is with Mr. Carson?"

Maggie hesitated. Henry couldn't have forgotten. "Try Maggie Rhodes."

"Is that your name?"

"My maiden name. The gentleman who made the appointment may have used that."

"One moment, please." Maggie could see from his face that although he'd found the name, he wasn't taking any chances. He picked up the phone and made a call. Then he returned to the car. "My apologies, Miss Rhodes. Mr. Carson is expecting you." He pointed to the parking area between the two buildings. "See that Chrysler limousine at the end? There's a space reserved for you left of it. And the entrance is on the left."

"Thank you." Maggie drove to the proper parking space. The limousine had to be Henry's. There was another space to the right of it. It had a concrete curb in front of it making it impossible for anyone to use it. She looked at it and her vision blurred. The name William Carson was painted on the curb. She swallowed hard, saying to herself, Please God, don't let me cry. After several deep breaths, she regained her composure and entered the building.

An old man was seated at the reception desk. Maggie recognized him instantly. Would he remember her?

"Maggie Rhodes!" He stood up, his smile so broad it seemed about to split his face. "They told me to expect you, but no one said you'd become such a great lady."

Maggie had no idea what to say. "It's nice to see you, Carl. And you don't look a day older than the first day I came to work."

"Ah, get on with you. I promised Master Will I'd greet him the first day he came to work, but I don't think I'll make it."

"Yes, you will. Who would ever take your place?"

"We'll see." He handed her a badge. "Maggie Rhodes" was neatly hand-lettered. "Miss O'Toole asked if you wouldn't mind waiting. You remember her. She wants to come down and say hello before you see Mr. Carson."

"Of course." Maggie remembered Mary's coldness after she and Henry separated. But she couldn't blame her. Mary did what she was told; her loyalties belonged to her employer.

Maggie walked to the portraits at the far end of the room. Four generations of Carsons. And Will would be the fifth—if she didn't tell Henry about his true parentage. If she did, there was no telling what Henry would do. She remembered his long-ago words. "Of course, if the baby's not a Carson . . . Shall I go on?" There was no doubt that he'd disinherit Will.

The date of William's death, 1941, was engraved beneath his portrait. Maggie studied the painting. He would have been sixty-four today. She couldn't bear looking at him any longer and turned to Henry's portrait. He ought to sit for a better one. If Andrew Wyeth could be persuaded to leave his beloved Chadds Ford, he'd be the ideal painter.

There was a light touch on her shoulder. It was Mary O'Toole, and to Maggie's eyes she seemed to have grown smaller. Or had Maggie grown taller? She didn't remember towering over Mary in the past. She probably did, even if it hadn't seemed that way. Mary's hair was almost white now. Otherwise she looked about the same.

Mary's concern about their last conversation was evident in her hesitant, "Good morning, Maggie. It's been a long time. How are you?"

Maggie tried to put Mary at ease. "Well, Mary. And how are you?"

"Growing older like everyone. I can't complain." She paused, then decided to say what she'd come downstairs to say. "I want to apologize for my rude behavior the last time we spoke. Mr. Carson was distraught over his father's death, and he upset everyone. It's no excuse . . ."

"I understand. And it was so long ago."

Her few words served their purpose. Mary resumed her efficient secretary role. "Fine. Then let's hurry. Mr. Carson's waiting, and we don't want to keep him waiting, do we?"

Maggie smiled at Mary's assumption, which was exactly the opposite of Carl's. To Carl she was a great lady. To Mary they both were still Henry and William Carson's secretaries. "No, we don't want to keep him waiting."

Henry Carson paced the floor of his office nervously, unsettled at the idea of seeing Maggie. With the years, he had accepted that he would never know whether William and Maggie had had an affair. For all their sakes he hoped they hadn't. Putting that aside, he now accepted Will as his son and heir and looked forward to the day Will would sit at William's desk learning from him as he'd learned from his father.

A knock on the door announced Maggie's arrival. He stopped pacing and went to greet her. He opened the door and stood still. Oh, God! He'd forgotten so much. Forgotten her beauty, her grace, her natural elegance. Even how tall she was. Somehow, he remembered her as smaller, less vital. And there were other real changes in her personal manner—a different way of standing, of walking, all probably formed by her life in California. She seemed almost another woman. And despite all this, there was an instant surge of recognition between them that no amount of time or distance could alter. He reminded himself he had to say something—anything.

"Good morning, Maggie. How kind of you to drive all the way here." Oh, Lord! How dumb! Was she supposed to walk? He thought she might laugh at him.

Maggie was not about to laugh. She too had forgotten so much. Oh, yes, she remembered he was big, had red hair and a slightly crooked nose. He, like she, had become more ordinary in her mind, similar to other large, attractive men she knew. Now she recognized what a truly imposing man Henry was. The young man she'd once known, who was still in the process of formation, had, as a mature man, fulfilled all the promise of youth. Seeing him, loving him, and faced with the full extent of her loss, Maggie had to fight back her tears. She forced herself to make a polite reply. "It was no trouble. I was delighted to drive here to meet you. The office seemed so fitting." Oh, Christ! How clumsy. Couldn't she have found something more appropriate to say?

"Would you come in, please? The coffee's waiting." He found he could move, step aside and let her pass.

Maggie's eyes scanned the room. William's desk was still there. No one had used it in fourteen years, but it was polished and ready for Henry's successor. There were the wooden file cabinets she'd organized for Henry. He hadn't replaced them with new, metal cabinets. She wondered if he still used her filing system.

"Sit down, Maggie. I'll do the honors."

"No." She hurried to the coffee table. "Cream and sugar?"

"Yes." As he sat down, the couch creaked, and Henry made his usual mental note to do something about the springs. He knew he wouldn't. He'd wait until the couch collapsed under him the way that old chair had caved in the first day at Wilkenson, Inc. He smiled at the memory.

"A penny for your thoughts, Mr. Carson."

"I was thinking of the time I broke the chair in the office in the Chrysler building."

"And I bought you a new one at the furniture store."

Struck by the same memory, they both stopped laughing. That day Craig Spears had made his first attempt to get money from Henry, and Henry had not thought to take his gun away—the gun Spears had used to kill William.

To hide their thoughts, they both spoke spontaneously. "You look so . . ."

Henry said, "Sorry. Ladies first."

"I was thinking how well you look."

"Thank you. So do you. I recommend hard work, lots of exercise and much more trouble than one thinks one can stand. Best way to stay young."

The awkwardness of the conversation was apparent, and Maggie tried to make things easier by pouring coffee. It would give them time to gather their thoughts. As she sipped her coffee, she wondered how much of what had happened she was supposed to know. She decided if she didn't try to hide anything, she would not have to remember what she did or didn't say. "Henry, about Evelyn Wilkenson."

"What about her?"

"I visited her when I first arrived in New York."

"I know you did. Why?"

"I was concerned about the influence your ex-wife might have had on Will. I wanted to find out if Evelyn knew anything."

"Caterina had no effect on Will. Only Mary."

Knowing Henry, loving him, Maggie was one of the few people in the world who realized how badly Henry had been hurt, not only by Mary's death but by what had been done to her before she died. She understood and accepted the effort he was making not to let her or anyone see his real grief. His grief was a private matter, and he would bear it as best he was able.

"I know you were responsible for her being institutionalized," he said, interrupting her thinking. "Payne Whitney called last week. So did her lawyers. It seems she never changed her will after Selma's death. A bad joke on her. Now I'm the executor of her estate. I have to see the hospital officials to make the necessary arrangements for her to get the best of care." He studied Maggie. The question was a hard one to ask. "Was she rational when you saw her?"

"Only briefly."

"Did she explain anything about what happened?"

"If you mean why she introduced you to your ex-wife, no."

"Did she tell you how much Caterina looked like you? Did anyone?"

"Everyone!" Maggie grimaced. "And I don't like it. I have enough trouble answering for my own actions. Feeling responsible for someone else is too much."

Without any effort on Henry's part, the conversation had arrived at one of the reasons he'd asked to meet with Maggie. He wanted to find out how he would respond to the real Maggie Rhodes. He hoped his response would tell him some things about himself. Specifically, it might tell him how much of the instant attraction he felt for Caterina—an attraction that was so strong it overpowered his usual hard-headed appraisal of people and situations—had actually derived from his love for Maggie. Were any of his feelings for Caterina real? Did any of them belong to Caterina alone?

"You are not responsible for another's actions simply because you happen to look alike," he said, clenching his fists, "or for other people being misled by the mistaken identity."

As he said the words, time seemed to stop in the room. Henry had never been at peace with his love for Maggie. He'd been a young man then with limited experience and far too proud of his limited experience. It had made him suspicious of the ardor and passion of Maggie's response to him. He had failed to recognize it as the simple, happy coincidence of two similar natures. The truth, he now realized, was that no matter what experience Maggie had had prior to meeting him, their relationship was based on love—the love they felt for each other.

The nights he had spent with Caterina seemed to have so much in common with the nights he had spent with Maggie that he had been misled, in part at least, because he had wanted to be misled. He had thrown himself into his illusion with every ounce of his creative passion, adding to it all the time, decking it out with every bright memory and similarity to Maggie that drifted into his head. No amount of hard facts or incongruities could challenge what he had stored up in his heart.

But while Caterina and Maggie had seemed so similar and had both loved him, he was now aware of a crucial difference between the two women. Couldn't Caterina's love have been an escape from horrible memories and despair beyond his ability to understand? Even, possibly, a terrified attempt to stave off death? Whether it had been things that had happened to her during the Nazi occupation of her family's villa that had caused this or something else entirely made no difference. To save herself, Caterina would accommodate to anything, to anyone.

If he extended that thought beyond sex, where would that take him? Evelyn had trained Caterina to be Maggie Rhodes. And she had learned her lessons well, so well it was possible she had believed herself to be the role she played. But she could play other roles—witness her sickening corruption of his daughter as an act of vengeance against Evelyn Wilkenson. What she had done to Mary made Henry wonder if he had ever met the real Caterina Orsini. He suspected that what was true and belonged only to La Contessa Orsini had been lost years ago, long before he'd met her. And if there were no "real" Caterina, what he had loved was the role she'd played, the role of Maggie Rhodes.

As the sun evaporated the ground mists, gradually Henry's troubled vision cleared. He had loved the same woman twice. While the copy was gone forever, the original, the real Maggie Rhodes, sat here in his office with business to transact. What a pleasant mundane matter. She wanted to buy his land in Orange County. "This may seem like an effort to change the subject, and it is. Somehow your being here has helped answer some questions that have troubled me. I thank you. Now let's get on with the day's work. You want to talk about my land."

Maggie wished she knew what questions she'd helped Henry answer. However, she said nothing. "Um—yes. I understand you'll consider selling. But you haven't set the price."

"I've known for some years you've been purchasing land on the perimeter of my property. I've even seen the land. It's a lovely spot. I admit, while I have no idea why William originally bought it, now I can see why you want to buy it. When will the freeway reach that far south?"

"I don't know, but it will. I've seen the master plan." She couldn't restrain her curiosity. "Would you mind telling me how you discovered my corporation was buying land? And I was involved?"

Henry smiled. "I was first approached by a group wanting to purchase my land some years ago. They offered what seemed a good price. Naturally, I wouldn't sell without checking. So I called a top New York real estate agent and had him find the best broker in Orange County— Gus Wurdlinger."

Maggie held her breath. She would be very hurt if Gus had talked.

Henry caught her expression. "No, Maggie. Gus claimed to know nothing. So I contacted the largest landowners there, O'Neill and Irvine. They put me onto an escrow company. After that I simply hired a company to do a title search over the last ten years. The Rhodes Development Company kept showing up. So I turned down that first offer and waited for your group to approach me. Mark did a first-class job trying to get me to set a price."

"But you didn't."

"I had another idea. I wanted to see you again. For personal and business reasons. Tell me in your own words what you see in Orange County."

Delighted with the opportunity, Maggie spent the next twenty minutes explaining her theories about the movement of people away from the cities and the kind of community she planned to build. Her ideas were grander and more imaginative than Henry had expected.

When she finished, Henry put down his cup of cold coffee and clasped Maggie's hands. "I think that is as bold a venture as any I've ever heard." He dropped her hands self-consciously. "I understand land is now selling for between $500 and $750 an acre. I own about fifty thousand acres. At $600 an acre, that comes to thirty million dollars. Does that sound reasonable?"

Maggie's hands still tingled from his touch. "It sounds high. Your price per acre is right, but that's for smaller parcels. Given the acreage, I think the price should be lower."

"What do you suggest?"

"Depending upon the actual survey, between $350 and $400 per acre, tops." Maggie knew she would pay his price, but not without trying for a lower one. Henry shook his head. "I've another idea. How many acres does the Rhodes Development Corporation own now?"

"Why should I tell you that?"

"It'll save time. I could find out without your telling me."

"We own about 100,000 acres."

"And how much has been invested so far in buying the land?"

"We started when the land was much less expensive. So far we've invested about thirty million dollars."

"Hmmm. Now I have a question I'd appreciate your answering, and I have no way of checking the truth of your answer."

"Ask your question. If I answer, it will be the truth."

"How much of the corporation do you own personally?"

"What!"

"I asked what percentage you own."

"I heard you. What use is that information to you?"

Henry leaned forward. "Maggie, trust me. I have an idea, and I need the information to judge if the idea is feasible."

When Henry Carson said "Trust me," Maggie accepted that he would not use the information against her. "I own fifty-five percent of the corporation."

"Fifty-five percent? And how much cash have you invested yourself?"

"A little over three million."

"So for ten percent of the investment, you own fifty-five percent of the corporation. Mark did a fine job for you. I want to do some numbers work. What's the capitalization of the corporation?"

"One million shares."

"Issued and outstanding?"

"Two hundred thousand."

"There's eight hundred thousand shares in the treasury?"

"That's right."

"I don't need the cash. All I'd end up doing is paying a long-term capital gain to the government. Maggie, I've fallen in love with your idea. I'll take stock, sixty thousand shares, for my property. That would bring the capitalization to two hundred and sixty thousand shares and the acreage to one hundred and fifty thousand acres."

Henry was practically giving her the land. How could she object? She had one concern. "With two hundred and sixty thousand shares issued and my owning only one hundred and ten thousand shares, I could lose control of the corporation."

"Not if I assign to you the voting rights to my stock in perpetuity."

Maggie's business sense made her look this gift horse in the mouth. "Why, Henry? That amounts to a freebie."

"I think you deserve a chance to make your dream come true. And when it does, my stock will be worth a lot more than thirty million dollars. And maybe this is my way of saying thanks for many things I don't want to discuss. Including Will." Maggie managed to keep her self-possession. "Yes, Will. He's a Carson through and through. In no time he'll be sitting at that desk." He pointed to William's empty desk. "He loves the company as much as I do, and he wants to run it just the way I do. Do you realize, Maggie, he'll be the fifth Carson to head up the Carson Company? Almost a dynasty."

Throughout the meeting Maggie had kept in the back of her mind the possibility of telling Henry who Will's father really was. Now, looking at Henry's face as he spoke of Will, seeing the pride and confidence he had in Will, she knew that telling him was impossible. Will had been raised as a Carson, thought himself a Carson, and he loved the Carson Company as much as any bloodline Carson had ever loved it. She had no right to rob him of his heritage, his dream. She had her own dream, which Henry had just made more real. Henry had his, and Will had his. She would tell John Hillyer her decision. That was that.

Now it was time for her to leave. "Will you make a note of what we've agreed to? I'll have John draw up the papers."

Henry went to his desk. He wrote the terms of the deal on a piece of note paper, then signed his name. "John will think I've been to the 'funny farm.' He'll hate the lack of legalese. Tell him he's representing both sides in this transaction, and I expect him to protect both our interests."

As he handed her the paper, their hands touched again. Both Maggie and Henry held the contact a fraction longer than necessary. When Henry withdrew his hand he gave a small, embarrassed laugh. "At least now we have an excuse for talking and seeing each other again."

"Yes. If you don't mind, you'll be hearing from me regularly."

"And when I get to the Coast, I can have dinner with you and your husband."

"Thank you, Henry." When Maggie reached the parking lot, she looked again at the space reserved for William. Then she pictured the name Will Carson in the space where her car was parked. She'd done the only thing she could do. "God," she said softly, "please make it the right thing. Make someone happy."

# Chapter 32

OWNING Henry's property made Maggie impatient. The maps of Los Angeles and Orange County were crisscrossed with a series of lines, some solid, some with dashes and some with dots. The lines moving south were dashes and dots. The network of solid lines in the city of Los Angeles was only starting to creep south. Maggie knew that at some future time the freeways would reach her property. It had not yet happened. And folding her hands in her lap, she closed her eyes and offered a silent question to the heavens: When, O Lord? When?

Her request for inside information from God was answered by a telephone call on her private line. It was Angel.

"This is the only time I've ever had a flock of martinis without a sense of guilt. I'm not even smashed. You know why?"

"Why?"

"Because I'm toasting him. Drinking for his sake. Wait till you meet God's gift. I want you and Tony to come to dinner Washington's Birthday."

Maggie glanced at her appointment diary. She had a meeting with Dorothy Chandler on the twenty-first to discuss plans for the music center. One didn't break appointments with the Chandlers. Not if you wanted to have anything to do with the performing arts in Los Angeles. Washington's Birthday was free. "Yes, I can be there. I haven't seen Tony in a week, so I can't answer for him. Who's his latest?"

"Maggie, dear, do I detect a note of irritation? One would think you cared."

"I do, in my own way. He's drinking more and paying less attention to his job. There are only twenty-six Democratic assemblymen in the legislature, and they need every vote they can get. He's never around. And now that our version of a political boss is in jail, who's going to protect Tony?"

"You're referring to Artie Samish?"

"I am. That quaint stunt Artie pulled for the magazines, posing with a ventriloquist's dummy dressed as a bum and referring to the dummy as his 'legislature.' That certainly endeared him to everyone."

"Artie is an original. Once he told me he could tell at a glance what a man would sell his vote for—a baked potato, a girl, money."

Maggie had no doubt what bought Tony's vote. "He understands the legislature better than the I.R.S. That's why he's in jail. Anyway, the word is out. Pat Brown's tired of Tony's 'fuck you' attitude, and with no Artie Samish around, the Democratic Party could find itself minus one Tony James."

"Pat Brown should have more faith."

"The nominations are coming up. Suppose Tony doesn't get re-nominated?"

"Right now I'm more interested in men than in politics. Let's find my brother. You can't meet God's gift unless you arrive as a happily married wife."

"What is God's gift's Christian or Hebraic name?"

"I'll give you one clue: Mark James sent him."

"J. Pierpont Morgan. But he's dead."

"You'll never guess. I'll put on my rubber hip boots and wade through the sewers of the city. Tony will be wallowing in one of them."

"If you don't find him, I'll come alone."

"Nope. You'll come as a happily married couple or not at all."

"Why? We never played that nasty 'what's yours is mine' game."

"I guess I'm jittery because this one isn't mine yet. He's been here ten days, and he avoids my advances as if I were infectious. So don't tease me. I'm off to find your spouse and remind him of his wedding vows. 'Bye."

Maggie hung up, wondering about Angel's sudden attack of puppy love. It wasn't her style. Then she forgot about it and went back to thinking about Mission Nuevo. Was she ready to start site planning? She made a phone call to Richard Phillpotts of Phillpotts Association.

"Mr. Phillpotts?"

"Yes."

"This is Margaret Rhodes of the Rhodes Development Corporation. Mr. Phillpotts, your firm was recommended as experts on site planning. It's time for a site planner and model maker to look at what we own and what we want to do."

"How many acres do you own, Miss Rhodes?"

"Approximately one hundred and fifty thousand." She heard Phillpotts gulp. "Of course, I don't need architectural details in the models. Just squares, rectangles, circles, and so forth."

"Miss Rhodes, your place or mine?"

"My office for starters. I have maps, surveys, topographical layouts here. Would tomorrow at ten be convenient?"

"You are joking. For a project such as you propose, anyone in my business would cancel a trip to paradise."

"If you have a paper and pencil handy, I'll give you directions."

Maggie dabbed perfume behind each ear and then pressed the intercom button for Tony's suite. The phone rang several times before he picked it up. "Tony, I'm ready. Are you?"

"Almost. Angel likes her guests to be late."

Tony's voice was slurred. "You're starting a bit early, Tony."

"It's going to be a long, boring evening. But for Angel, anything. In five minutes we'll be in our golden pumpkin off to meet Prince Charming."

"You have your fairy tales mixed up. Meet you at the front door in five."

Maggie insisted on driving. Tony was not so smashed that he couldn't walk or talk, but too smashed to maneuver the hazardous roads running down through the canyons.

By the time they turned into the circular driveway of the James house, Tony was in better shape. Getting out of the car, Tony looked at the house wistfully. "You know, Mags, I kind of wish we'd never left. This is home to me."

"I know. Why not have Angel set up your old rooms? When it gets too late, you could stay here. Angel won't object."

Tony took out his key ring and put a key in the lock.

"Don't you think we ought to ring to say we're here?" Maggie rang the bell.

"This is half my house. If they're doing anything, it won't be in the entrance hall or living room. Angel doesn't mind voyeurs from her own class—just not servants."

By the time a Mexican-American girl in a maid's uniform appeared, they were standing in the great hall. "Mr. and Mrs. James, Miss James say you fix yourself a drink on the terrace. She will come pronto."

"Thank you," said Tony, straightening his jacket. They walked through the house to the terrace. The bar was set up.

"Martini?"

"Vodka please." Maggie watched Tony make drinks and was relieved that he settled for a light scotch and soda. They sat on high stools next to the bar, sipping their drinks and waiting. Before long they heard voices coming from inside the house.

The door opened and Tony chortled, "Darling, Angel Cake!"

"Dearest, Tony. Glad to see you're still a member of the family."

Maggie put her drink down, swiveled around on her stool and felt her head spin. Before she could find words, the tall, strikingly handsome man stiffened and exclaimed, "Caterina! *Come qui?*" The words were barely out before he caught himself. "Oh! I am sorry. I mistook you for someone else. Let me introduce myself. I'm Francis Carson. You must be Tony and Maggie James."

"I'm Tony James," he said, stretching out his hand to Francis.

"A pleasure to meet you." He gave Tony an understanding smile. Deeper than understanding, it had a quality of eternal reassurance in it. It concentrated on Tony with an irresistible prejudice in his favor. It understood him just as far as he wanted to be understood, believed in him as he would have liked to believe in himself.

While the two men spoke, Maggie had a chance to regain her composure and study Francis Carson. He was still tall and erect as she remembered from those days long ago when she'd seen him in the small church in Pleasantville. Now his blond hair was cut very short, almost a crewcut. And she could only marvel at the deep tan he'd acquired in the brief time he'd been in California. What was most unnerving was he'd called her Caterina. That meant he knew Henry's ex-wife. She'd have to let Henry know as soon as possible.

After shaking hands with Tony, Francis turned his full attention to Maggie.

"You appeared surprised to see me, Mrs. James. Do we know each other?"

"No. You said I reminded you of someone?"

"Yes, someone I knew quite well in Italy, where I've been living since the war. A great lady. One of the few true aristocrats left in the world." Francis gave Maggie a winning smile, another in his repertoire of smiles. The smile said in effect that he had committed a childish error. She must forgive him because it was not a matter of any moment. "I will never forget her," he continued. "She made a lasting impression on my life."

His smile had changed. There was an element of sadness in it. She was supposed to understand he'd suffered some deep sorrow connected to this Italian woman. And one does not question a stranger about his deep sorrows. It was a perfect performance and deserved loud applause. Maggie doubted Francis would appreciate her applause. Now she understood his remarkable suntan. It wasn't a California tan; it was the Mediterranean sun that had turned him that color. She sat quietly, afraid if she spoke she might give something away. Then, realizing her silence was becoming awkward, she said, "Everyone looks like everyone else."

Angel had seen the byplay, and her eyes narrowed. There was something going on she didn't understand. Tony was oblivious. The sight of Francis filled him with excitement. There was something about him that reminded Tony of his father. They even looked somewhat alike, both big men with blond hair. Francis Carson was even taller than Anthony and carried himself with an air of authority such as even Anthony could not match. "Somehow your face is familiar. Are you well known?" he asked.

"Tony! Doesn't the name Francis Carson mean anything to you? Or you, Maggie?"

Before either could answer, Francis intervened. "Angel, it's been years. Why should anyone remember?"

Once again Maggie admired his performance. The modest war hero. Let Angel be his straight man.

"Maggie, Tony, how could you forget General Francis Carson? One of our country's great war heroes?"

"I remember!" Tony exclaimed. "Next to Audie Murphy, the most decorated man in the entire military service. General"—he shook Francis' hand again—"this is indeed an honor."

"I just happened to be at the right place at the right time. And, thank God, in none of the wrong places."

Maggie marveled. How did he do it? The man was actually blushing. You could see the red under his tan. She made an effort at enthusiasm. "You were one of the wartime legends."

Francis held up his hands. "Please! No more! I spent years living abroad so people would forget. Let's not rehash tiresome ten-year-old public relations articles."

Angel was subdued. "Sorry, Francis. I mentioned it only because I'm so proud to know you."

"What brings you to sunny, smoggy California in February? Business, pleasure or chance?" Maggie asked.

Francis ranged over the possible answers. He certainly was not about to tell her his personal truth—that he considered his first attempt to injure Henry a failure. Mary's death meant nothing to him, and via Caterina he'd provided Henry with another daughter. All in all, it was a disgustingly even exchange. While the loss of Caterina might have caused Henry some private torment, Henry would soon recover. Even letting him know that Caterina was his whore would have been meaningless, a petty victory at best. What he hungered for was a public disgrace of Henry Carson. There was only one blow from which Henry would never recover—a blow to the Carson Company. And as long as he remained in Italy, there was nothing he could do to bring that about.

So he'd decided to return to the United States, to put his huge income and his great reputation as a war hero to use in the most effective way he could think of to destroy Henry Carson. Now he was concerned about his original blunder and what the consequences might be. How was he to know that Mrs. Anthony James was Maggie Rhodes? And, more important, was she still talking to Henry all these years later? If she was, would she consider his mistake important enough to report to Henry? If she did, how much would Henry tell her? Henry was a proud man. Would he subject himself to the pity and even scorn of his ex-mistress? Francis doubted it. Besides, what was done was done. He could not undo his mistake. Even if the worst he imagined came to pass, there was nothing either Henry or Maggie could do to stop him. So he decided to tell her a part of the truth. The public part. "I believe I'm going to settle here. I like the climate, and"—his voice became self-deprecatory—"you see, my father left an income. I am wretchedly wealthy." Maggie tried to recall exactly what William's will had given Francis. As she remembered, it was a sizable income for life with no control over the principal.

She was fairly confident he had no idea that she too was a beneficiary of William's will, or he would somehow have made her know it. Maggie brought herself back to the conversation. Francis was saying, "Once one has enough money, I think it's a waste of time to try to earn more."

"But you have to do something."

"I agree, and since business doesn't interest me, I'm considering other possibilities."

"For instance?" Tony was as curious as Maggie.

"Politics." Francis looked at Maggie. "You asked why I came to California. It's simple. Back East, take Massachusetts for example, there's an old saying that goes something like this: 'The Lowells speak only to the Cabots, and the Cabots speak only to God.' There, ancestry counts. Here, no one cares. So few people were actually born here, there's little if any ancestor worship."

Of those listening, Angel had the most difficulty adjusting to the idea of her heroic Francis in politics. He was so clean, so honest. Drawing from her experience of her father and brother and their associates, politics appeared to be no place for an honest man. "Are you sure, Francis? Our father was in politics. It's a dirty business."

"Angel, dear, I'm in politics."

"Tony, dear, you are a living, strutting example."

"Let's leave family out of this," said Tony. "What about Earl Warren, Bill Knowland, Goodie Knight and a raft of others?"

"And what about Artie Samish, Bill Bonelli, and I can give you a longer list?"

"It sounds like the military," said Francis. "A few men—they could be generals, majors or mess sergeants—were on the take. The majority weren't. I well remember checking out the fuel tanks of my squadron with a dip stick to make sure they had really been filled, and ten percent didn't end up in the black market. Sometimes I had to order a tank to be refilled, but usually I didn't. There are good men and bad men in every field."

"Angel Cake, didn't you tell General Carson that your brother is in the California legislature?"

Angel half apologized. "I had other things to talk about."

"I'm a first-term member of the assembly. And if you're interested in politics, I might be useful." Tony was more wide awake than was natural for him. It crossed his mind that General Francis Carson—wealthy, handsome, with great personal charm and that air of sincerity mixed with authority—was a natural. He might do Francis and himself some good by introducing him to a few men. "Have you registered with any party?"

"Not yet. I've only been here three weeks."

Maggie watched Francis, feeling a great purposefulness in the man. The kindly mixture of human tolerance and a certain half-naïve conception of the world was not in keeping with what she suspected of Francis Carson. Only the dip stick in the fuel tanks rang true. Francis was in the James house, interested in politics, and Tony was an elected official. Wasn't that stretching coincidence thin?

Tony hurried on. "Which party do you think you'll join?"

"First I want to know where each party stands."

Tony had heard the same rumors Maggie had heard about Pat Brown becoming annoyed with him. If he brought General Francis Carson into the party, it might make up for some of his lapses. "I could help you meet a few of the men in the Democratic Party here."

Maggie waited. There it was. The shy, appreciative smile.

"That's very generous, but as your guest, enjoying your hospitality"— the last was directed at Angel— "I feel I'm taking undue advantage. It's too much like using people."

"Everyone uses everyone for one thing or another." Angel grinned. "And it gives me a marker on you."

"Just being yourself is enough of a 'marker.' " Francis smiled, and this time the smile was a delicate compliment promising all kinds of possibilities.

Maggie understood Francis was playing a highly calculated game, a game with a purpose she didn't grasp.

"At any rate," he was saying, "should any of you ever go to Italy, to Rome, I extend the hospitality of the villa I own there. And that might, in some way, compensate for your kindness to me here. The villa is a gracious place that I entirely restored."

"You bought your house from an Italian family?"

Maggie sensed Francis' hesitation before he answered. Again, trapped by his original mistake, he told the truth. "Yes. I bought one of the villas of the Orsini family." He smiled at Maggie. "The name of the great lady I confused you with is Caterina Orsini. Buying her villa was how I came to know her."

A hand bell rang in the house, and Angel said, "Dinner is served."

As the two couples entered the long, graceful dining room, Angel looked up at Francis adoringly. "Would you mind doing the honors, opening the wine and carving the roast? It's lamb, nicely pink inside, as you said you like it."

"Not at all," said Francis, thinking to himself, Isn't Lady Luck a fickle creature? After that rotten luck with Maggie Rhodes, Tony James was the perfect political contact. He glanced at Tony—Tony with his good-looking American face that would stay adolescent until it became puffy and middle-aged. Yes, he would do. He was the perfect dupe.

The next day Maggie was on tenterhooks, knowing she must call Henry. And of course this was the day Tony elected to stay home and laboriously explain to Maggie his thoughts and plans for Francis. She listened patiently, knowing full well his reasons, wishing she could think of a way to stop him without raising his suspicions. The idea of Francis Carson in a position of political power gave Maggie a chill.

Shortly before dinner, when Maggie had about given up on calling Henry, Tony returned to his own suite to shower. Within fifteen minutes, he called Maggie on the intercom to tell her he was leaving. "I'll check you tomorrow or the day after." And he was gone. Some minutes later Maggie heard his Cadillac convertible roaring away from the house. The last sound she heard was the tires squealing in protest as he took the first of a string of sharp curves that led to Latigo Canyon Road and finally the Pacific Coast Highway.

Maggie looked at her watch. Six-fifteen. It was too late to call the Carson Company, so she would call Henry at home. When she realized she didn't have the phone number of Carson House, she had a pained feeling. She'd had the number years ago and had thrown it out with all the numbers left over from that life. If the number wasn't listed, she'd have to wait until morning and call him at the Carson Company. It was listed. The phone rang several times before it was picked up.

"Carson House."

"Good evening." The man's voice sounded like the estate manager. If only she could remember his name. But so much of her life ended with the loss of Henry that, in self-defense, she had blocked out as many people and details as possible. "This is Mrs. Anthony James. I'd like to speak to Henry Carson."

"One moment please, Mrs. James. I'll see if Mr. Carson can come to the telephone."

She waited only minutes, but in her state of extreme anxiety, it could have been an hour. Her eyes wandered all over her office, focusing on the model of Mission Nuevo that Richard Phillpotts and his model maker were creating.

"Maggie!" Henry's voice was full of happiness. She was so startled she almost dropped the telephone. "Where are you?"

With a leap, her heart went out of her as it had when she saw him in his office. "I'm in Malibu. I think I have something important to tell you."

"Oh?" The happiness faded from his voice. Her tone conveyed her anxiety. "What is it?"

Now that she had to tell Henry her news, she wasn't sure how to do it. There were so many deep, personal matters involved.

Henry sensed her reluctance three thousand miles away. "Out with it, Maggie. You have something to tell me and are afraid to. Say it!"

The use of her name was like an embrace and gave her courage. "I ran into your brother last night. He let something slip that might be important."

There was a long silence. "So Francis is in Los Angeles." His voice was calm and his words measured, but Maggie knew what it cost him. "How long is he staying?"

"He's going to live here. Henry, listen!" She was deep in it with him, no matter where it led. "There's something more important."

"With Francis there always is."

"When he first met me, he was startled. He . . . he made a mistake. He called me . . ." She was afraid to say it.

For a moment the silence hung heavy between them. Then Henry finished her sentence. "Let me guess. He called you Caterina."

The words were spoken with such resignation, such a deep loathing for Francis and even himself that Maggie felt way out of her depth. "I'm sorry. I simply meant to tell you he must know your ex-wife, that he might have had something to do with what happened."

"It would appear he did. And what a fool I was not to have guessed. Evelyn could never have come up with Caterina. That takes a Francis." The words said everything—everything about family hate and blood feuds.

"What's Francis really like? What kind of a man would do such a thing?"

Henry told her everything he had learned about Francis from reading the reports sent to William during the war. He finished with, "I can only assume he continued to live the same way in Italy. And with Caterina."

"He bought the Orsini villa outside Rome."

Henry was weighing and judging. "It does follow. What does he plan to do in Los Angeles?"

"Enter politics. And my husband"—she spit the word out like an epithet— "is so charmed with him he's going to introduce Francis to his political friends."

"Your husband is in politics?"

"You didn't know?"

"Maggie, I've kept track of some of your business activities because I thought it appropriate. It didn't seem appropriate to pry into your private life."

"Tony is a member of the California State Assembly."

"Francis should do well in politics."

"I don't understand. With his life-style? They'll massacre him the minute they find out."

"You spent the evening with Francis. How did he look?"

"Too good to be true."

"Not dissipated? Dissolute?"

"Anything but."

"Do you understand now?"

Maggie's first feeling was fear. She had been trying to see what kind of man Francis was, and now she did. "He can control his natural inclinations."

"Indefinitely. To achieve his ends. On the other hand, it would be wise for us to make sure he can."

Maggie heard his use of the word "us," and in spite of the trouble she saw coming, the fact that they were acting together was more important to her than anything else. "What are you thinking?"

"Would you do me a favor?"

"What do you want me to do?"

"Hire the best detective agency in L.A. I want Francis tailed twenty-four hours a day. I want to know where he goes, whom he sees, what drugs he takes, if any. If he does slip, we'll be the first to know. Would you do that for me?"

The necessity for the question almost made Maggie sob. She hadn't realized how much of her still lived in a time when such questions would have been unnecessary.

"I know exactly how to find the right detective."

"Good. Get monthly reports and special reports should Francis do anything unexpected. Send them to me along with the bill."

"I'll keep you well posted." There was nothing more to say, yet she didn't want to end the conversation. After a brief pause, she said awkwardly, "I'll let you know whom I've hired when I hire them."

"Thank you, Maggie. Good night."

Henry put the phone down and leaned back in his chair trying to arrange his attitude. He'd never be rid of Francis. And Francis in a position of power as an elected official? That spelled trouble. The best he could say was he was forewarned. Forewarned is forearmed. Maybe. Only time would tell if that was enough to keep Francis at bay.

# Chapter 33

THE NEXT MORNING, after Maggie finished her workout with Reposo, she had a short talk with Bob Tilling about detective agencies.

"Call Michael F. X. Dunne on Sunset Boulevard. Tell him I sent you."

"How come you know Mr. Dunne?"

Bob shuffled around and made an X in the dirt with the edge of his work shoes. "Well, you know the racing racket. It draws all kinds of people. You can't imagine the stunts that have been pulled by so-called 'improvers of the breed.' When the stunt is so raw they want the guy but not the publicity, the Racing Commission goes to Dunne."

"He'll do. Thanks." She changed subjects. "I think I'm feeling the reins."

"You are. I thought we might raise the jumps to six feet. Give us a year more, and you might make a good showing in some local events."

Maggie grinned. "Thanks a bunch. Reposo might. Me, I'm not so sure."

Reposo had grown tired waiting for his sugar and was trying to squeeze his nose into Maggie's pocket. In the process he slobbered over her pants. "Stop it. Here!" She held the sugar cube in her hand. "You need as much attention as a lover," she whispered in his ear. Out loud she said, "Take care of him, Bob. I'll call Mr. Dunne."

In light of his political ambitions, 1954 was a fortunate time for Francis Carson to arrive in Los Angeles, California. For over fifty years the Republican Party had controlled the state legislature. Considering the political picture, it struck Francis that the Republican Party hierarchy of California was as entrenched as its counterpart in the Northeast. It survived by perpetuating itself. What use would it have for a newcomer?

So it was not Tony's cajoling that persuaded him to throw in his lot with the Democrats, but his grasp of things to come. The qualities of mind and personality that would propel him upward were emerging.

With his effortless style and confidence, he could be thoroughly charming, a fine diplomat without seeming to be diplomatic. He was a hard worker, a good soldier, and his energy and industriousness were qualities not apt to be overlooked by the decision makers in the Democratic Party. Especially since, at the moment, his obsession with Henry went far deeper than his need for power and helped him maintain a balanced view of his ambitions.

So Francis Carson allowed himself to be sponsored by Tony James. In the hope of regaining some of his lost prestige, Tony took Francis to Democratic Party headquarters in the old Lincoln Building in downtown Los Angeles to introduce him to his "friends." He hoped the celebrity of Francis Carson would rub off on him, and if Francis turned out as he expected, he'd be a welcome addition to the party. This would also work to Tony's advantage.

Tony's strategy succeeded. Neil Haggerty, executive secretary of the California Federation of Labor, and Jesse Unruh, a rising young Democrat, were clearly interested in meeting General Francis Carson. They liked his modest but knowledgeable manner.

A petite lady with blonde hair, as much a tribute to her Scandinavian heritage as to the California sun, walked across the room. It was Elizabeth Snyder. Tony grabbed Francis' arm. "Hold it, fellas. I want Francis to meet Elizabeth." He dragged Francis across the room, whispering, "Francis, smile. She's chairman of the Southern Ladies Committee. If she wins the July election, she'll be head of the Democratic Party of California." He stopped in front of the woman. "Elizabeth! I want you to meet Francis Carson."

The vivacious little lady paused and glanced at Francis. He gave her his best smile. Elizabeth Snyder was a professional politician. She had seen many a politician's smile, and she wasn't as impressed as Francis would have liked. Quick to sense her cynicism, the smile disappeared. "I'm new in the state, but I hoped I might be of some help in the coming election."

"In what way, Mr. Carson?"

"I've had extensive experience speaking before crowds. There must be some candidates who could use someone to speak before Rotarians, Elks, various district groups, while the candidates appear at large rallies."

Tony thought he'd bungled the introduction. "Elizabeth, if you knew Francis' background, you'd know what a prize I've captured. He's Major General Francis Carson, winner of the Congressional Medal of Honor, the Distinguished Flying Cross, the Purple Heart. You remember him?"

Elizabeth Snyder took another look at Francis. This time he did not make the mistake of smiling. She liked that. He was perceptive. "Yes, you visited our city in 1945."

"Briefly. There's no reason why anyone should remember."

"There is, and if they don't, we'll remind them." She thought for a moment. "Yes, we can use you. Providing you don't object to working for a woman?"

"Of course not."

"Fine. I'm running to be the first lady chairman of the Southern wing of the Democratic Party. The Party in California has two wings. Control of the party alternates every two years. It's the Southern group's turn."

"Sounds quite civilized. It avoids things like Gettysburg."

"Exactly. We can't fight among ourselves and also win against the Republicans. At any rate, the Party can always use good men and hard workers. You can fill in for Tony as his legislative assistant at those small groups when he's too busy to show."

Tony knew he wasn't going to be dumped. He would be renominated, and all was forgiven.

"What are your hours? When do you work?"

"My hours are my own. I've an independent income. And politics will be my work."

"Is your income earned or inherited?"

"Inherited."

"Better if you earned it, but one can't have everything. I'll see you here tomorrow at ten, and we'll review Tony's campaign schedule. Good meeting you, General." And she was gone.

Francis spent the next months working with Tony and Elizabeth Snyder. She was unlike any woman he had previously known. You could rely on her word. She was on time to meetings, and presented her positions clearly and decisively. District leaders listened attentively and responded enthusiastically.

Tony was another matter. It was impossible to know whether or not he'd show up for a meeting. He could be drunk, with a woman or sleeping off a drunk. Francis realized that Maggie knew all about his women, and she and Tony had reached an "arrangement." He briefly considered approaching her as another way to attack Henry. When he spotted detectives tailing him, he assumed Angel had hired them, and he let the idea drop.

In July, Elizabeth Snyder was elected the first lady chairman of the

Southern Democratic Party. And, as such, she became the de facto chairman of the California Democratic Party. Since Francis had contributed in some small part to her victory, he had a new and powerful friend in the Democratic Party. At the same time, thanks to the tireless efforts of Francis Carson, in November Tony was re-elected by a landslide.

When the legislature went into session, its first act was to pass Elizabeth Snyder's bill requiring every candidate to list his or her party affiliation. The bill's success was due, in part at least, to an impassioned and convincing speech delivered by Assemblyman Anthony James. The entire legislature was impressed by what seemed to be a "new Tony." Only Elizabeth Snyder, Tony James and Francis knew the speech was written by Francis Carson. And only Maggie James knew they knew. She was also aware how chancy it was that Tony had made it to the assembly to make that memorable speech. The report from Dunne gave her some of the facts. It refrained from mentioning that Francis found Tony, less than sober, with a seventeen-year-old senior from Sacramento High School. A thousand dollars got rid of the girl, who was well aware she was a minor. Then a gallon of coffee and two quarts of fresh orange juice made it possible for Tony to function. Watching from the balcony, his hands gripping the brass railing, Francis held his breath. Finally the speech ended. The applause brought home to Francis how much influence an intelligent elected official really had. Tony had no idea how to use the respect he'd won. Francis would.

After the speech, Elizabeth Snyder introduced Francis to Roger Kent, concluding with a smile, "Besides all the help he's been in other ways, this is the man who wrote the speech for Tony James."

Roger Kent, chairman of the Northern District of the Democratic Party, had a keen eye for political talent. "I look forward to working with you in two years."

Each month a report from Michael F. X. Dunne and Associates arrived in its plain brown envelope for Maggie. Each month, unless Francis was involved in a rescue operation involving Tony, the report was the same: *"Re: Francis Carson.* Nothing to report." After a year, they had taken to heading the report: *"Re: Saint Francis."*

Nineteen fifty-six was the year of the presidential election. Early in the campaign Francis decided Eisenhower couldn't lose. He was the father figure of the country, a great military man who understood civilians.

Francis decided to support Adlai Stevenson although, like others, he thought Stevenson too quick to talk, too slow to act and indecisive. Tony needled him about it with the latest Stevenson joke. "He had to make a speech in East Cow Pasture, but first he wanted to know if there was time to go to the bathroom. When his aide said yes, Stevenson's next question was a lulu. 'Do I want to go to the bathroom?' " Tony doubled over laughing. "And that's your man?"

"That's my man," answered Francis, not bothering to add that he believed Stevenson's elegance, wit and literacy brought a new vitality to the Democratic Party. A whole generation of educated Americans was behind him, the very people Francis wanted behind him someday.

Maggie wished with all her heart she could stop Francis. What was worse, she understood exactly how astute he was. He would make political capital out of backing Stevenson. It might be the wrong race, but it certainly was the right horse.

And so it proved. Francis campaigned tirelessly up and down the state for Stevenson—speaking to farmers in overalls in northern farm communities and flying south to speak to sparsely attended meetings of businessmen and their wives in San Diego. During the course of the campaign he came to know Attorney General "Pat" Brown. Brown, a politician's politician, was undecided about running for the U.S. Senate against the incumbent Republican. When Francis and he talked, Francis was firm. "Don't run. Eisenhower's coattails are too long and wide. There'll be a Republican sweep on the national level."

"I notice that hasn't stopped you from working for Stevenson."

"He never discussed with me whether or not to accept the nomination."

"You would have said, 'Don't run'?"

"I would have said, 'Run.' He's good for the party image."

"I agree."

Brown gave him a curious look. "And my running isn't good for the party?"

"Your running would be a waste of your valuable political status here in California."

Brown took it in. The idea didn't trouble him. It was simply a fact. "Thank you for reminding me of what I already know."

When, as Francis predicted, there was a Republican sweep on the national level, Brown made a mental note that Francis Carson was well worth watching.

Maggie stared at the *Los Angeles Times* headlines. Sutter and Collier, two Republican senators, had broken from the party and voted for a Democrat, Hugh Burns, to be president pro tempore of the California state senate, the first Democrat to hold that post since 1891. It wasn't simply unusual, it was unheard of. What was she missing? She reread the article. The state senate was now evenly divided: twenty Democrats, twenty Republicans. Everyone assumed the Lieutenant Governor would break the deadlock by selecting a Republican to be the senate president. And then, out of nowhere, this upset. Maggie was deeply troubled.

She reread the report from the Dunne agency. Francis had arrived in Sacramento shortly before the vote. He spent more time with Republican senators than with men from his own party. He lunched with them, had drinks with them, dinners. He was seen with both Sutter and Collier. But that didn't mean a thing. Did it? It made no sense. How could Francis Carson, a legislative assistant to Tony James, persuade men of the stature of Sutter and Collier to vote for a Democrat? Could he? Was it possible? She hoped to heaven he had nothing to do with it. If he had been instrumental in that vote, the catalyst, it would give him a huge leg up in the Democratic Party. It might make his rise unstoppable. No! She refused to believe it possible.

Francis sat at his desk in Tony's office in Sacramento reading the same article as Maggie had, when Roger Kent entered.

"I don't know how you did it, but I'd like to know when the gentlemen will present their bill and what it will be."

"I didn't do anything, and as far as I know there will be no bill. The senators voted their consciences."

"And if you're wrong and either senator presents something special? A park? A highway? A school?"

"I told you there was no deal. Our party can vote on the merits of any proposal suggested."

"I'll relay your opinion to Senator Burns. And, Francis, from both Hugh and me, well done! The party will look for some way to reward you. You've a future with us."

Shortly after this conversation, Francis left for Los Angeles. The idea that he might be closer to his goal than he'd realized made him consider another problem. There was something about a single, attractive bachelor that set gossips chirping: homosexual, homosexual, homosexual. He'd heard the scuttlebutt on Stevenson, and if it could happen to a man of his stature, there was no reason to assume that he, an unknown, would be spared. Until now his energies had been so taken up with political activities that his self-imposed celibacy had not been burdensome. Realizing he'd established himself as pure in heart and spirit, he decided it was time the "pure in spirit" married. The obvious woman was his long-time hostess and sister of his closest friend, Angela James Monroe Farrington, et cetera. Francis began to pay unusual attention to Angel. He took her to the theater, to the opera, to dinners in small, out of the way restaurants, art shows and festivals. He encouraged her to try to reclaim her old position as a book reviewer for the *Los Angeles Times*. He did what had to be done. Saint Francis accepted the role assigned to most saints—martyrdom.

One night, after an evening of dinner and the Philharmonic, Francis took Angel home. They had a brandy on the terrace, and though they'd done this many times before, Angel sensed tonight would be different. It was. Francis undressed her, caressed her and carried her to bed. There was a minimum of foreplay, with almost none of the attempts at arousal that usually accompany lovemaking. He parted her legs, entered her and both came almost at once—Angel because she'd been on the verge of an orgasm for the last hour, and Francis because he'd been celibate so long.

It seemed to Angel afterward that he'd made love like a teenager, and she thought it was the monastic life he'd led. She decided he needed a course in sex education, and she was the one to give it.

Dunne's reports told Maggie what was happening. She was curious as to Francis' motives in finally succumbing to Angel's charms. One afternoon, while visiting Maggie, Angel coyly mentioned what Maggie already knew—that at long last she and Francis were "a thing." She went on to explain how naive Francis was and how she was teaching him everything she knew. Maggie choked on her martini.

"What's so funny? Don't you think I know how to screw?"

"Of course, but . . ." Maggie stopped. How could she tell Angel that Francis could teach her games she'd never imagined? "Well . . . er . . . I guess his innocence surprises me. It's hard to imagine women not trying to give him lessons."

Angel's insecurities exploded. "Like you, for instance?"

"Not like me. Remember, we don't poach."

"That was before Francis Carson. I can't help wondering if you know him as well as you do his brother, Henry Carson!"

Maggie put her drink down. So Angel knew. Probably Francis had told her. But what else did she know? She had better find out. "Francis and Henry are brothers. So what?"

"So what! Maggie, I may act like a damn fool at times, but I'm not.

I remember the land you bought from Henry Carson. The price was so cheap, he almost gave it away. That told me you know Henry Carson very well."

"And as a shareholder, you should be delighted."

"I am. Whoopee! What about Henry Carson?"

"Nothing about Henry Carson. Angel, lay off. It's none of your business."

"I don't give a damn about Henry Carson. It's Francis Carson I'm thinking about. Is he to you what Henry Carson may or may not be?"

"No! He's nothing to me. Never was. Never will be. The only things we have in common are you, Tony and politics."

"If you haven't slept with him, how would you know what he does or doesn't know?"

"I don't. I have no idea what he doesn't know."

Angel knew she'd stumbled onto something regarding Henry Carson that Maggie wouldn't discuss and that caused her pain. Angel was much too fond of Maggie to want to add to that pain, so she looked for an easy way to change the subject. "I accept. But let's have no more startled looks at my teaching Francis about sex, because I am."

Maggie realized that Angel was trying, in part, to spare her any further discussion of Henry, and she appreciated her friend's understanding. She raised her hand. "If you say so, it's so. Friends?"

Angel raised her hand, and the two women touched palms, similar to an Indian greeting. "Friends."

"I'll let you know when the wedding is set." She grinned. "I told you once I know how to get married. Maybe this time I'll know how to stay married?"

Francis proposed within a month, and the date was set for June. Before he proposed, Angel and he came to an agreement. If they were to marry, they had to move out of the James house in Beverly Hills. Francis explained to the unhappy Angel that as a liberal Democrat who expected to be nominated for office, either state or national, the huge house on Wilshire Boulevard in Beverly Hills was not appropriate. When Angel objected, pointing out that Tony was a politician and kept his suite in the James house, Francis dismissed her argument. Tony never wanted the kind of career he wanted. And in fact Tony's career was ending. His drinking, his whoring, his legislative irresponsibility had destroyed it. Both Elizabeth Snyder and Roger Kent were fed up with Tony James. Angel had no answer for Francis, and when he added that he'd like her to look at a house on La Mesa Drive in Santa Monica, she agreed. At least it was Santa Monica and the very best section. Even if the house was smaller, it wouldn't be that small.

In August 1957, something Francis had been waiting for finally happened. The Republican Party, having been in power for so many years in California, lost all perspective. They thought they could afford to fight among themselves, with the result that the highly conservative senior senator, William Knowland, decided not to seek re-election to the United States Senate. Instead, he would campaign for the Republican nomination for governor. In so doing he would oppose a member of his own party, the moderate incumbent governor, Goodwin Knight. The Carson family was having dinner at the James house on the evening of the announcement, and Francis was jubilant. "It couldn't be better. They're handing us the governor's mansion on a silver platter."

"What do you mean?" Angel asked.

"He means . . ." Maggie started to explain and caught Angel's hostile look. "Well, it's a house divided," she finished lamely.

"Whose house?"

"The Republican house, Angel baby." Though he was well into his fourth martini, Tony was still sober. And sober, he was a shrewd political animal. "It's going to be a head-on clash between the liberal and conservative wings of the Republican Party."

"Keep your fingers crossed, my dear, that the conservatives win the primary." Francis couldn't contain his glee. The sheer foolishness of the Republicans amused him.

"Why?"

"Because, like any loving wife, you want your husband to get ahead."

As events turned out, the conservatives did win. William Knowland, the known enemy of organized labor, was nominated by the Republicans to run for governor, and Goodwin Knight finally agreed to accept the nomination for the United States Senate. The Democratic Party almost danced in the streets. They knew that Knowland intended to run on a platform supporting a "right to work" law, which every union man considered "union busting." It gave a worker the right to work at a union shop without joining the union.

Francis Carson was the first to put into words what everyone was thinking, that now was the time for Pat Brown to run for governor.

"He's the right man in the right place at the right time. If ever a state was asking for a Democratic governor, California is."

"Agreed!" said Neil Haggerty. "And every union member will walk the precincts spreading the word on Knowland. And getting the vote out for Pat."

Francis was at his desk at the new Democratic headquarters at 311 South Vermont Avenue when he received a call from Jess Unruh. If he was available, Howard Ahmenson, banker, art collector and a major political money raiser and contributor, wanted to meet him. Of course he was available. "When and where?"

"Today at headquarters. Sit still. We'll be there in an hour."

The two men met, and after a short conversation, Ahmenson thanked Francis for his time and left with Unruh. When Jess returned, he shook Francis' hand.

"You're in. Ahmenson thinks you'll make a great candidate, and he's prepared to support you."

"Assembly or senate?"

"Neither. We've an opening on the national level. Congressman from the Twenty-third District."

Francis went to the large map on the wall which showed the various congressional districts. He allowed a small smile to cross his face. The district included Santa Monica and Venice. His prophetic intuition still held. He could win in that district. Neil Haggerty's union organizers would be of great help.

The next day he caught Tony early, before he was drunk.

"Tony, I've a suggestion you might take seriously."

"I'm listening."

"Instead of running this year, how about being my campaign manager?"

"You're running for office?"

"So I've been told."

"For what?"

"U.S. Congress, Twenty-third District."

Tony hated Sacramento. Hated campaigning. Hated everything about holding public office. When he'd made the decision to become an elected official, he hadn't realized just how much he'd be in the public eye, how much the party would monitor his actions. Sometimes he thought they followed him into the men's room. And if Francis won, he'd be in Washington. A bigger city, less visibility. He had no idea why Francis wanted him, and he didn't care. He held out his hand. "I'm with you all the way."

"Just go easy on the booze till after the election."

"I'll watch myself."

Francis knew why he wanted Tony as his assistant. It was only a matter of time before Tony got into serious trouble. Tony was his brother-in-law, and Francis preferred it to happen as far away from his district as possible.

The election was a landslide for the Democrats. Pat Brown was elected governor; Clair Engel defeated Goodwin Knight for the United States Senate; Alan Cranston was elected state controller; and Francis Carson was sent to Washington as a freshman congressman from the Twenty-third District of California. Francis' victory was obvious from the moment the vote count began. He had made the defeat of the "right to work" law the major issue in his campaign, and he emerged from the campaign as Neil Haggerty's man.

When Maggie called Henry to tell him the results, she sensed the concern in Henry. "Washington is a lot closer to the Carson Company and to me than the California legislature."

"I know. And he's taking Tony with him."

"All I can do is keep my left up."

"What can I do to help?"

"Just keep me informed if you find out anything."

"I will." Maggie hung up and called Angel. With Tony in Washington, Angel was her closest contact to Francis. And Angel would be alone, in need of cheering up. Since her marriage to Francis, Angel's drinking had increased. This would make it worse. As far as Tony and she were concerned, they'd lived apart for so long, it made no difference.

# Chapter 34

**H**ENRY CARSON replaced the telephone receiver, breaking the connection to Switzerland. He leaned back in his chair and considered what Godfrey Moore had told him. Hoffman La Roche was ready to introduce their newest drug, a tranquilizer. They even had a name for it—Librium. Unless he wanted to play catch-up, the Carson Company would have to begin to market their own product. Several years ago Felix had asked for "one more year," and that one more year had become three. Felix still wasn't ready. Henry buzzed Mary O'Toole.

"Mary, set up an appointment with Dr. Flam at the labs this afternoon. If he's tied up today, make it for tomorrow morning."

They had bought Wilkenson, Inc. in June 1941. Now it was April 1958, almost seventeen years later, and they still hadn't marketed the product. It was hard to believe. He wondered what William would have done to hurry things along. What could William have done that he, Felix and the Carson Company research staff hadn't done? This drug was not another cough drop or hair tonic. They must be certain there would be no unpleasant or dangerous side effects. Twice during the last ten years he had thought they were ready, then something turned up. The first time there was a marked decrease in the birth rate of rabbits. The second time they discovered that taking an overdose of the drug could cause temporary paralysis in the hands and feet of a few people. Finally, after three years of testing on animals and then humans, these problems had been overcome. The rabbits bred like rabbits, and for the hypersensitive there seemed to be nothing more than an occasional "tingling" in the fingers and toes if they took too many pills. What else could turn up?

"I've set an appointment with Dr. Flam for tomorrow at nine-thirty."

"Tomorrow morning will do, Mary. Thank you."

In matters pertaining to the Carson Company, Henry Carson answered to no one but himself. His decision, first to market their products nationally through their own distribution system, and then to manufac-

420

ture and market their products internationally, was prompted by what he thought best for the Carson Company. Whether the company netted $15 million or $25 million after taxes in any single year was meaningless. What mattered was the gradual, sound growth of the company and the expansion of its product lines. He had already achieved both goals. He had inherited from William a company grossing about $75 million, even after the acquisition of Wilkenson, Inc. In fiscal 1957, the Carson Company grossed over $300 million and netted close to $20 million. The net would have been greater had Henry not spent as much as he did on research and development in the search for new products.

While no executives were ever given stock options, they all were part of a very generous profit sharing plan as well as a privately funded pension system that far exceeded anything a publicly-held corporation could afford. After all, both the profit sharing plan and the pensions were paid by the company. And since Henry Carson was the company and the company was Henry Carson, in essence they were paid by Henry Carson.

Now he had to make a decision on the latest product, the tranquilizer. No one else could make the decision, and no one else would have to answer for its success or failure. All Felix could do was give his opinion on the status of the product. Felix couldn't decide what the Carson Company would do.

The next morning Felix and Henry met in Felix's lab office. "You want another year, of course?"

Felix had struggled with this question all night and had been unable to come to a solid decision. He was still uneasy. "Yes, Henry, I want another year."

"You've already had three extra years." While Henry's words sounded impatient, his voice was concerned. He was trying to understand the reluctance of his Vice President for Research and Development, for whom he had considerable respect as well as great personal fondness. "Why, Felix? What haven't we tested for over and over?"

"If we knew that, I'd have tested for it years ago. And so would the F.D.A. It's hard to solve a problem when you don't know what the problem is."

"Or if there is a problem?"

"Or if there is a problem."

Henry came to a decision. "I've never marketed a product before that you haven't 'signed off' on. And I don't want to now, but we have no choice. I don't know what you're worried about, and you don't know what you're worried about. I still want your approval. So, I'll wait three more months, ninety days. Meantime, we'll gear up for production of Placidium. That's the name I've given the product. If, at the end of ninety days, you can't give me a sound reason why we should not go ahead, Placidium will be marketed."

Even though Felix didn't like it, ninety days was more than he'd expected. Henry had shown great patience. He had not one single, solitary, concrete reason for not giving his okay on the product. And if he couldn't find out in another ninety days what was gnawing at him, he would have to "sign off." He owed it to Henry to stop dragging his feet. Maybe he'd been on the product so long it scared him?

Henry left for another meeting, on a product that would hold a man's hair in place without using oil. Felix started a systematic investigation of all their research reports. He prayed that it would either lay to rest his doubts or give him a reason more concrete than a "bad feeling" for objecting to marketing Placidium.

The ninety days zoomed by in a blink, and at the end Felix had no more answers than when he'd started. Another meeting was held, this time in Henry's office. The manager of the Ethical Division of the Carson Company was there along with the head of marketing and people from their advertising agency, who had layouts for the packaging, the advertising and the actual design of the pill. Henry Carson made it clear to everyone that nothing was to be done without his personal approval. His initials were to be on every design, every piece of promotional material, every claim made for the product, every piece of advertising, everything. Felix sat quietly throughout the entire meeting. When the meeting broke up, he waited for everyone to leave. Then he handed Henry a piece of paper.

Henry looked at it and held out his hand. "Thank you, Felix." He put his arm around his friend and walked with him to the door. They shook hands. Felix left for the labs. Henry returned to his desk and reread the paper Felix had handed him. "I approve of the marketing of Placidium and sign off on the product. Felix Flam, Vice President, Research and Development."

The first six months of marketing Placidium went like a textbook case used at the Harvard Business School. The product did exactly what it was supposed to do. It calmed nervous, high-strung people who had problems that seemed to them, for the moment, to be insurmountable. Tense salesmen attending sales meetings made presentations that were well received. Nervous performers took a pill and stopped throwing up before going on stage. Mothers with frayed nerves were able to react to the noise and commotion of their children reasonably, without resorting to screams, slaps and abusive behavior. Even high-strung children, borderline hyperactive children, took a pill and were able to concentrate in school, to conduct themselves in ways that led their teachers to marvel at the change. Run-of-the-mill, everyday neurotics took the pill and could function without the ever-present fears that oppressed them. Anxious expectant mothers took Placidium and lost their fears about giving birth. And as proven in lab tests, there were no withdrawal symptoms when one stopped taking the drug. Indeed, some of the tranquility induced by the pill seemed to remain as a residual effect. Reading report after report, Henry wondered if, had Placidium been available at the time, Selma would have had a stroke brought on by her fear of giving birth.

In 1959, just before Memorial Day weekend, the first disturbing report arrived on Henry Carson's desk. It was a letter from a small hospital in Tulsa, Oklahoma. Henry read the letter twice. Three mothers had recently given birth to seriously deformed babies. One baby had no hands; his arms ended in stumps. Another baby had only one fully developed leg; the other ended at the knee. And a third baby, a girl, had no legs at all; she had a torso, a head and arms, but no legs. There was no history in any of the three families of deformed children. The only thing the doctors found in common among all three mothers was that they were nervous, and three different obstetricians had prescribed Placidium. The hospital wanted information as to whether the Carson Company had any information on this possible side effect. Henry called Felix Flam immediately and asked him the same question. The silence at the other end of the phone was an answer in itself.

Finally, Felix was able to say, "Of course not."

"What information do you have on tests with pregnant women and their control groups?"

"We gave the tranquilizer to pregnant women throughout all stages of their pregnancy."

"And there were no instances of deformed babies?"

"None, but . . ."

"But what?"

"Henry!" Felix was almost weeping. "I missed it. *Gott in Himmel!* I missed it. Now I know what it was!"

"Now you know what?"

"We gave the drug to women in all stages of pregnancy, but not to women throughout the entire nine months of pregnancy."

"I don't see the difference."

"If a woman who was part of the test group became pregnant, we continued giving her the drug for the usual three month period. Each group was tested for three months. If a woman was in the fourth month, she was given the drug from the fourth month through the sixth month. Or the sixth through the ninth month. But we never gave a pregnant woman the drug for nine months in a row. We never thought to. Give me the name and telephone number of the hospital. I'll check and call you back."

Henry paced the floor. When the phone rang, he hurtled across the room. "Yes, Felix, what is it?"

Felix's voice seemed to come from far away. "It's not good. In all three instances women were placed on Placidium by their personal physician prior to pregnancy. The gynecologist maintained the prescription throughout the nine months of pregnancy. Three cases are too many to be a coincidence."

"I'll order the drug pulled off the market immediately and production stopped. Also, we'll have to send letters . . ." He stopped. "Be in my office tomorrow morning at eight-thirty. Also marketing, manufacturing, distribution and our ad agency. We've got our work cut out for us."

"Yes, Henry. Tomorrow at eight-thirty." Henry knew where the blame belonged. Felix may have missed this crucial area, but the ultimate responsibility for marketing the drug was his. He should have paid attention to Felix's reluctance. Given more time, he might have discovered the danger in taking Placidium for the full nine months of pregnancy. God only knew how many tragedies had or would occur for which he was responsible.

During the morning meeting, Henry considered what could be done that he or his staff had overlooked. In addition to recalling the product and notifying doctors and druggists via mail, telephone and telegram, he decided to do something never done before. The Carson Company would place full-page notices in every major newspaper in every city in the United States warning the public about Placidium. Thank God he had not yet gone international with the product. Time would also be bought on television and radio to warn the public. The cost was immaterial. So much more than money was at stake.

Once the public announcements hit the media, the flood gates opened.

Hundreds of babies had been born to mothers who had been taking Placidium for the entire term of pregnancy. Not all babies were born deformed, but enough were to prove the danger of the drug. The entire Carson Company as well as the Carson and Flam families were stunned. Henry Carson and Felix Flam both felt personally responsible for each and every deformed child. Henry's family, Will and Elizabeth, tried to understand what happened. Henry attempted to explain, and finally both children, though Elizabeth was only seven, grasped what a great tragedy had occurred. Henry's children and John Hillyer, Jr., a semi-permanent house guest, stood fast in their love and concern for Henry. Felix Flam's family too gave loving support to their father. But the world didn't understand the mistake. The world offered no sympathy. The world would not forgive. And neither would Francis Carson.

The right of Congress to investigate events, both public and private, primarily for the purpose of passing laws that would improve the ability of the government to protect the people of the United States against the selfishness and greed of other citizens, is an old right dating back almost to the formation of the country. The first congressional investigation took place in 1792. In 1927, the United States Supreme Court had decided unanimously that an individual who had not committed a crime could be subject to a subpoena as long as the intent of the committee was to investigate and the investigation had legislative functions—to propose new laws or reforms on existing laws.

Freshman congressman Francis Carson did his homework well. This was the opportunity for which he'd waited. It was his reason for returning to the United States, his reason for entering politics. It was for the joy he would feel in destroying his brother that he'd willingly undertaken the life of a Spartan, in opposition to his natural inclination. Henry Carson had made a terrible mistake, and Francis Carson would use that mistake to ruin him, and in doing it ruin the Carson Company.

Francis approached "Mr. Sam" Rayburn, the long-time Speaker of the House, and petitioned to have a special subcommittee formed to investigate the actions of the Carson Company and to propose new laws to strengthen the powers of the Food and Drug Administration. The disaster of Placidium should not occur again.

Who was better suited to chair such a committee than he, Francis Carson? He, Francis Carson, was the brother of the man responsible for the outrage. Who knew better the inner workings of the Carson Company than he, Francis Carson, deliberately concealing the fact that he had had no association with the company in his entire life. And now his name was tainted. His own reputation as a man of honor was at stake.

The Placidium scandal was front-page news, and Mr. Sam knew a hot issue when he saw one. He also saw the possibility of a great political gain for Francis Carson and, since Francis Carson was a Democrat, a political gain for the Democratic Party.

There was an old tradition in the House of Representatives that permitted a one-man subcommittee to investigate in a very narrow area of legislation. This case fitted that definition perfectly, so, ignoring the fact that Francis was a five-month-old freshman congressman, Sam Rayburn authorized the formation of a subcommittee with Francis Carson as the chairman and sole member for the purpose set forth in Francis' petition. Mr. Sam's authorization was equivalent to passage by the entire House of Representatives.

In two months Francis put together his staff: a group of young, ambitious lawyers looking for an issue to bring their names before the public and investigators with no illusions about where the investigation would go.

Subpoenas were issued to Henry Carson, Felix Flam and the Carson Company. Investigators were to be allowed access to the company records for the purpose of determining what procedures had been followed to test Placidium for side effects. One month was allowed for the investigation. Then, on July 16, 1959, Henry Carson and Felix Flam were to appear before the subcommittee together, with counsel, prepared to answer any questions relevant to the congressional inquiry.

While Henry had been expecting something like this, the fact that Francis was the sole member of the subcommittee gave him pause. He consulted with John Hillyer, who consulted with his Washington office.

"I'm sorry, Henry, but one-man subcommittees are legal. It is only unusual that Sam Rayburn would allow your brother Francis to chair the committee. That could work to your advantage."

"How?"

"If you control your temper, Francis may overreach his authority. Rayburn isn't a fool, and he's not about to permit Francis to turn the investigation into a vendetta."

"How can he stop him?"

"If necessary, he'll remove Francis from his post as chairman."

Henry shook his head. While John was right in theory, he knew Francis Carson better than anyone else. He had only one opportunity. Since he was allowed an opening statement, he would use that statement to present both his and Carson Company's role in the Placidium disaster. He would tell the truth. Let Francis try to prove otherwise.

During the months after the scandal became public, Maggie was in constant touch with Henry and a source of great strength. Every time Henry saw a picture of a deformed baby, a small part of him died. And every time Maggie called, that part of him that was dead was reborn. Will, too, was a great support. He had been proud to be a Carson and was still proud to be a Carson, and would always be proud to be a Carson. Elizabeth insisted upon remaining in school in spite of the daily cruelty she was exposed to at the hands of other children. Henry considered suggesting she remain home until the worst of the scandal died down, and decided it was a poor idea. It would diminish the strenuous effort on his young daughter's part to accept what it meant to be a Carson, at a time when the Carson name was not an advantage but a burden. Will and Elizabeth drew together to shield their father and themselves against the world.

Felix Flam, Henry and John Hillyer all registered at the Mayflower Hotel in Washington on Wednesday, July 15. They were to appear the next day. John Hillyer explained he would be there as both Henry's and Felix's personal attorney. Wilson Warfield, the head of their Washington office, who was familiar with similar proceedings, would represent Henry, Felix and the Carson Company.

At nine-fifteen on the morning of July 16, 1959, Henry Carson led a group of men to Capitol Hill. They had been told the investigation would be held in the Longworth Building, an imposing structure built of white granite seven stories high with the main entrance on Independence Avenue between New Jersey and South Capital Streets. As an offshoot of the Interstate and Foreign Commerce Committee, the subcommittee was assigned a committee room on the fifth floor. Henry's knowledge of what he would find was limited to what he had seen on television during the Senator Kefauver hearings to investigate organized crime in interstate commerce. He found it ominous that a subcommittee from the House version of the same parent group, Interstate Commerce, had been assigned to investigate the Carson Company. When the small party entered Room 1505, the first words were muttered by Wilson Warfield.

"Son of a bitch! There's a television setup. That's been illegal since 1954 without our express consent. I'll insist the cameras be removed."

Henry stopped him. "No. The press and public will believe we have something to hide."

"Listen, everything you say, every twitch of your mouth, every time you clench your hands will be seen on TV. It's hot in here. No air conditioning. When you sweat and dry your face, you'll look guilty. Do you remember Frank Costello's hands? Just the way the camera showed him wringing his hands told the world he was guilty."

"It would be a bigger mistake to order them removed. If Francis can take the publicity, we have to."

The room was small. Four rows of benches, able to seat fewer than fifty people, were in the rear of the room. Then there was a low wooden railing which separated the benches from the two long tables with wooden chairs set up for the attorneys who would represent the committee and the lawyers who would represent Henry and the Carson Company. Facing the tables and looking down on them from a platform was a podium with nine chairs behind it that ran most of the width of the room. There was a door off to one side from which the congressmen, in this case one congressman, would enter. Just to the right of the middle of the podium and below it, but still on the platform, was a seat for a stenographer and a machine for the stenographer to make a transcript of the hearing. The walls were all paneled in dark oak. Only the ceiling was white. The original hanging lamps had been replaced by modern fluorescent fixtures which gave a discordant note to the old-fashioned room. The four small windows were open, and fans turned slowly in between the lighting fixtures. While one could hear the traffic along Independence Avenue, neither the open windows nor the fans provided much of a breeze. If one added the heat from the television lights to the heat of a sultry day in Washington, everyone present would drip perspiration.

After everyone was seated at the table, Warfield went over the ground rules again with Henry and Felix. In some ways it was like a trial; in others it was not. They would be under oath to tell the truth, but instead of a district attorney asking the questions and a defense attorney following up with cross-examination, all the questions would come from the chairman of the subcommittee. All the attorneys could do was advise their clients if the questions passed over the line established by the purpose of the investigation or if the questions violated their constitutional rights. There would be no cross-examination of a witness except on points of fact. Opinion was permitted to be entered provided it was clear it was the "opinion" of the witness and not established as a fact. Finally, as Henry knew, he was going to have the opportunity to make an opening statement before any questioning.

About nine-forty-five several men entered the room and sat at the table reserved for the committee's attorneys. Witnesses, who would re-port on what they had learned from their investigation of the Carson Company, sat behind the railing. As the time approached for Francis Carson to start the proceedings, the television cameramen and reporters entered and took their places behind several special sections of benches that had been roped off for them. When Henry looked at Felix, he saw a terrified man. This seemed to Felix like the Spanish Inquisition. All Warfield's words to the effect that this was not a trial but an investigation meant nothing to him. Even worse than the "trial" was the knowledge that he, not Henry, was responsible for what had happened. He felt personally responsible for causing the births of close to one thousand deformed babies. In the months since the facts came to light, this plump, round-faced man with a placid if slightly disorganized air about him had become a thin, haunted creature. His hair had turned white. His suits hung on him as though they were three sizes too large, which now they were. His hands trembled, and he had developed a twitch—half shutting his right eye and raising his upper lip before answering any question.

Finally Francis and the congressional stenographer appeared. Francis wore a dark suit, a white shirt, a black tie—a combination ap-propriate for a funeral. His brilliant blond hair and deep tan provided a sharp contrast to his otherwise somber appearance. And as the television lights came on, Henry saw the glint of a gold pin in the left lapel near the buttonhole of his suit jacket.

During the morning, Francis called the congressional investigators one at a time. He established how long the Carson Company had been working on the product. Then he stated for the record that another similar product, Miltown, was already being marketed. So far there was nothing for Henry's lawyers to object to. Under oath each expert said the same thing. They had examined the lab notebooks of the Carson Company and Dr. Felix Flam and had confirmed the company had been testing Placidium for many years. No, they had no idea why, after so many years of testing, the Carson Company finally decided to market the product. No, there was no evidence that the company had ever tested Placidium on pregnant women for a full nine months.

"Is it possible that there were other lab records and books you did not see?"

"That is always a possibility."

"Were there any missing years or gaps in time between the entries?"

"Many. Sometimes there were months between entries."

"Is that consistent with usual laboratory procedure?"

"No. It's unusual."

Felix muttered to Wilson Warfield, "If I had nothing new, why should I write something?"

Warfield shook his head. "He's giving the facts and stating opinions. There's nothing I can do."

"It's possible there are missing notebooks covering those time frames?"

"Yes, sir."

Felix stood up. "You lie," he screamed. "There are no missing notebooks." Then he collapsed in his seat, his face buried in his hands. One could hear his sobs over the sound of the traffic and the whirr of the ineffectual fans. The cameras, with their red lights shining, zoomed in on Felix.

Francis was stern. "If the gentleman can't control himself, he must leave the room until he can." Henry put his arm around Felix as though to shield him from Francis. The sobbing ceased, and Francis returned to the questioning. "What would you say are the odds that there are missing notebooks?"

Warfield shot to his feet. "With all respect, Congressman, the question of 'odds' is out of order under the rules of this investigation. Your witness stated there is a possibility that there may be missing notebooks. We must accept possibilities, but you're trying to show there is a probability of there being missing notebooks. That goes too far."

Francis smiled. "Good point, Mr. Warfield. We'll move on."

And all over the United States millions of radio listeners and television watchers were convinced Francis Carson was correct, and there were missing notebooks.

After several more questions, the experts who had examined the Carson Company were excused. They were replaced by a dapper little man with thin brown hair which he wore slicked back, a brown mustache and brown suit. He was sworn in.

"Give us your name for the record, sir."

"Gunter Harte."

"And your nationality?"

"I am a Swiss citizen." His English was perfect.

Henry sat up. He had a premonition of what was coming.

"And for whom do you work?"

"I'm a consultant in the ethical drug field."

"Tell us in your own words what you know that might give us additional information on this matter."

"Certainly. While everyone knows of Miltown, a product similar to

Placidium being marketed in the United States, very few people know of Librium, also similar to Placidium, about to be marketed in Europe by Hoffman La Roche. It's only a matter of time before Hoffman La Roche will receive F.D.A. approval to market Librium in this country."

"Why is that important?"

"Carter-Wallace, the manufacturer of Miltown, is a fine small company. They would not present too much of an obstacle to the Carson Company's successful marketing of Placidium. But Hoffman La Roche is a giant. Larger than the Carson Company. Once they capture a market, it would be very difficult and expensive for the Carson Company to penetrate the same tranquilizer market."

"Then it was important that the Carson Company market their product as soon as possible?"

"Of course."

"And, in your opinion, was Mr. Henry Carson or the Carson Company aware of the plans of Hoffman La Roche?"

"It is not my opinion, sir, it is a fact. I myself gave the information to their representative in Switzerland, a Mr. Godfrey Moore."

"And how were you able to obtain such confidential information?"

"I apologize, sir. That is confidential. Obtaining that type of information is the way I make my living."

"You were paid by the Carson Company to spy for them?"

"I was."

John's hand tightened on Henry's shoulder. He whispered, "Is that true, Henry?"

"Of course. We all keep track of each other. But what has that got to do with our knowing about the side effects?"

"Nothing, actually. Your brother is building a case to show why you might have marketed the product even knowing about the side effects."

"Then you can state for the benefit of this committee that the Carson Company knew of an important rival product soon to be marketed in the United States?"

"Their agent in Switzerland is a competent man. I would assume he informed his employer."

"Thank you, Mr. Harte." The television camera followed the dapper little man as he left the room. All over the United States, Americans now understood that the Carson Company had a strong motive for marketing Placidium immediately despite possible knowledge of the side effects. And there was the matter of spying. Did Americans really use "spies" to find out what their competitors were doing? It seemed too close to Russian spying on the United States. The word made the audience of millions watching or listening uncomfortable.

"That was a nasty blow he got in there," Warfield whispered.

"Dr. Flam, are you able to answer questions now?"

Felix looked at Francis Carson, then he glanced at the television cameras. His right eye half closed and the side of his mouth twitched. If one didn't know Felix, it looked as though he was winking at the cameras and trying not to smile. "I'll do my best, sir." The oath was administered.

"Good! Dr. Flam, where did you earn your degree?"

"At the University of Vienna."

"And why did you leave Vienna?"

"The Nazis were about to enter Austria. We're Jews."

"I understand. You couldn't stay. And you came to the United States—when?"

"Nineteen thirty-six."

"With your excellent credentials, you must have had many job offers."

"No, sir. There was a depression here. It was very hard."

"How long did it take you to find a job?"

"After learning to speak English, it took over a year."

"All that time. You must have run out of money."

"We were careful, but it was difficult."

"And where did you find employment?"

"Mr. William Carson hired me."

"Mr. William Carson, the president of the Carson Company?"

"Yes."

"The father of Henry Carson?"

"Yes."

"And of course you were grateful?"

"Yes."

Warfield whispered into Henry's ear. "Your brother would have made a good lawyer. He's not after Flam, he's after you."

"I know."

"So there's little you wouldn't do for Henry Carson?"

"I'd do anything for Mr. Carson. I owe him so much."

"Does anything include hiding laboratory notebooks that showed you and Henry Carson knew the side effects of Placidium?"

Felix screamed. "There were no notebooks. We had nothing."

"Dr. Flam, I've gathered you learned nothing new during the last three years of research and testing. You had your approvals from the F.D.A. Why didn't you market the product three years ago?"

"I asked for more time. I felt we'd missed something, but—"

Francis interrupted. "You felt you missed something. And Henry Carson, a man running a successful business, allowed you three years to fool around on your hunch you missed something?"

"Yes, sir."

"I think any businessman would find that hard to believe." And all over America, businessmen who had refrained from making a decision regarding Henry Carson and the Carson Company, shook their heads. On a man's hunch? Three years? No, sir! There had to be more than a "hunch." Carson knew something was wrong with the product. "Why did you suddenly decide to proceed? Were you satisfied at last?"

Felix held out a piece of paper. "This is a copy of a note I gave Mr. Carson. I signed off on the product."

Francis signaled one of his men. "Would you bring me that paper?" He read the note aloud. " 'I approve of the marketing of Placidium and sign off on the product. Felix Flam, Vice President, Research and Development.' Interesting. This seems a copy. Do you have the original?"

"No, sir. Mr. Carson has the original."

"But there's no entry in your lab notebooks about your signing off on the product."

"It was between Mr. Carson and me. It didn't belong in a lab notebook."

Warfield whispered to Henry, "Do you have the original?"

"Yes. But I won't let Felix hang alone for this. He gave me the paper as a gesture. Felix didn't want to market the product. He was still worried."

Wilson Warfield stood up. "With all due respect, Mr. Carson, I don't see how Dr. Flam's signing off on the product relates to your legislative mandate."

"What it relates to is whether Henry Carson and the Carson Company, with full knowledge, sold a product to the public as dangerous as this one."

"That is a matter for a grand jury not a congressional investigation."

"Probably, counselor. We'll move on. Dr. Flam, were you aware of the plans of Hoffman La Roche?"

"Yes."

"Is it your opinion that that was the reason why the Carson Company went ahead with marketing when it did?" Felix looked at Henry. "Please answer the question without coaching from Mr. Carson."

"Yes. It was one of the reasons."

"And the others?"

"Mr. Carson waited three years for my approval. Finally he ran out of patience."

"In sum, he waited for you to solve the side effects of Placidium, then got tired of your failure to do so and proceeded without a solution."

"No. That's—"

Francis interrupted. "That will be all, Dr. Flam."

"No. You've made a mistake. Henry knew nothing about any—"

"That will be all, Dr. Flam. Strike that last remark from the record." Francis looked at the large clock over the door. "Well, it's twelve-fifteen. Before we break for lunch, does anyone have anything to say?"

Wilson Warfield rose. "For the record, I'd like to say it seems to me, Mr. Carson, you are more interested in your brother, Mr. Henry Carson, and the Carson Company than in proposing legislation that might help prevent a disaster similar to the one we're dealing with."

Francis smiled at Wilson Warfield. "Obviously, you are entitled to your opinion, and if Henry Carson were my client, I might make the same accusation. This inquest is adjourned for lunch. We'll reconvene at two o'clock this afternoon."

Henry Carson, Felix Flam and their lawyers had a glum lunch. Both lawyers were of the opinion that Francis was building a very strong case not only against Henry and the Carson Company but, if he went that route, in favor of much more stringent controls over any new drug marketed in the United States. They had no idea what to do.

At two o'clock everyone was in place. Francis beamed at the cameras and at the group below him. "And now I think it's time for Mr. Henry Carson to be sworn in." The oath was administered. "Do you have a statement, Mr. Carson? One for the record?"

"I do."

"Proceed."

"Thank you, Mr. Carson." Henry stood up and walked to the spot he had chosen during the morning hearings. It was on the platform in front of the podium. Since he was standing and Francis was sitting, the television cameras were able to get both their faces in the same frame. "To begin, on my oath as a man, neither I nor anyone in the Carson

Company had any idea of the disastrous side effects caused by Placidium. And let there be no mistake, we acknowledge that Placidium is the cause of the deformed babies. Now I ask each and every one a simple question. Why would anyone in his or her right mind market a product, knowingly, with such a flaw? A flaw that would not appear twenty or thirty years from now—as for example in certain suspected carcinogenic agents—but a flaw that would appear within one year of marketing. The Carson Company grosses over three hundred million dollars a year. Our net profit last year was over twenty million. And I own every single share of stock in the company. I have no concern with a board of directors, with the price of our stock, or even with profits as such. Without the Carson Company, my personal net worth is close to two hundred and fifty million dollars. By most standards I am a very rich man. I am not desperate to make money on a dubious product. So, unless you think I am a madman, why would I knowingly market a product which can only damage my name and my company when I have absolutely nothing to gain from its sale? And a great deal to lose. Second, the Carson Company is contacting every parent of every child born with a birth defect due to Placidium. I have planned to go beyond the insurance settlement, even if it involves my entire personal fortune, to make certain that the victims of this dreadful mistake will be taken care of for the rest of their lives. And, at that, I see no way of ever making amends for our mistake. And a mistake is what it was, despite all your innuendos. No one at the Carson Company had any knowledge of the side effect of the product when taken continuously over nine months of pregnancy. As to Hoffman La Roche, of course we knew their plans. And of course that knowledge influenced my decision to go forward. Undoubtedly, Hoffman La Roche were aware of our plans and have been aware of our plans and were pushing their people to beat us to the market. It is true I waited for three years for Dr. Flam to 'sign off' on the drug. And three years is a long time. But my relationship with Dr. Flam is an old and trusted relationship. I wanted to be sure, so I waited. I can only say I wish I had waited longer. Waited forever. But Dr. Flam, as he has said, had no concrete reason why we should not proceed, so, in the face of the coming competition, we marketed our product. I was wrong, and Dr. Flam was right. That brings me to the question of missing lab notebooks. There are no missing notebooks. There never were any missing lab notebooks. Once again, do you people take me for a madman or a fool? We are dealing with a congressional investigation for the purpose of proposing new legislation to prevent a disaster of this sort from ever occurring again. The Carson

Company is hiding nothing! No notebooks! That would be committing a crime. Why in God's name would I commit a crime now? For money? To avoid bad publicity? Could anything be worse than the publicity my family and I have already received? To avoid criminal charges? There are no criminal charges. But if I attempt to deceive the Congress of the United States, to lie to the American public, to hide evidence, I risk discovery and certainly criminal charges." Henry paused for a moment to control himself. "My next statement goes beyond the scope of this investigation, but in a way it does not. When our father"—and as Henry said "our father" he gestured toward Francis—"chose me over my brother to run the Carson Company, he made his decision based upon his knowledge of both of us. Congressman Francis Carson has never set foot in the Carson Company in his life. He has no idea of our research procedures, how we make our marketing decisions. And yet he has the arrogance to insinuate that there are missing notebooks. How would he know that? Has he seen the notebooks on our aspirin product? No. Or on hair tonic? No. Are there missing notebooks there as well? He would not know. And yet there he sits on the podium, by virtue of his being a member of Congress, and makes insinuations about procedures of which he knows nothing, and which have nothing to do with his mandate from Congress and are based solely on his personal hatred of me. A hatred born of events that happened in our childhood and are not part of this hearing. So help me God!"

Francis was livid as he leapt to his feet. "And I say, Henry Carson, you are a liar. You did what you did knowingly and with total disregard for the public welfare. The same disregard that enabled you to avoid serving during the war." In his rage at Henry, a rage inflamed by what he now saw as a possibility of Henry's escaping him, Francis lost perspective and his usually sound judgment deserted him.

"I thought you would get to that point," Henry replied. "Actually, I tried to enlist several times. Harry Hopkins finally wrote me stating I would not be allowed to enlist. My duty was to stay home and run the Carson Company." Henry handed the letter to the stenographer. "He also thought that one 'hero'—you, Francis—was enough for the Carson family. Which brings up another point. I address myself to the Congress of the United States. Who was so rash, so foolish, as to permit this circus to go on? To set one brother against another, against a brother whom he hates, and allow that brother to turn a congressional investigation of a highly serious matter into a personal vendetta? And if this question puts me in contempt of Congress, then, gentlemen, I'm in contempt of Congress."

Henry stepped off the platform and left the room.

The television networks had a field day. This was the best daytime show since the Kefauver hearings.

Wilson Warfield stood up. "Mr. Carson, I would like to suggest adjourning this hearing until Monday. It will give everyone time to cool off."

"I agree, Mr. Warfield. Monday at two o'clock." Francis thought the delay would give him time to prepare a contempt citation, which he felt Sam Rayburn would have to sign. He was mildly concerned about the attack Henry had made on him, but it would probably be overlooked by the foolhardiness of his attack against "Mr. Sam" and Congress. Henry Carson versus the Congress of the United States was even more than he had hoped for.

# Chapter 35

**M**AGGIE and Angel were glued to their television sets most of the day watching Francis Carson investigate the Placidium case. Though both women saw the same program, their reactions were so dissimilar they might have been viewing two different programs. To Angel, it was a simple matter. Her husband, Congressman Francis Carson, had proven beyond question that the Carson Company knew, prior to marketing the tranquilizer, what would happen to the babies of pregnant women who used the drug. She wasn't as quick to condemn Henry Carson. After all, he wasn't a scientist. There was a remote possibility he had been fooled by the lies of that man Flam. As for Henry's charge that Francis was conducting a personal vendetta against him, she dismissed this idea with a shrug. Hadn't she and Tony fought all their lives? That didn't mean they would try to destroy each other.

Maggie's interpretation of the program was entirely different. The Carson Company and Henry Carson had made a serious mistake in marketing Placidium, but it was not a willful, deliberate attempt to profit from the misery of innocent people. And the fact that Francis Carson sat alone as the chairman of the subcommittee seemed to her as thoroughly prejudiced an act on the part of Congress as she had ever thought possible. Her only question was, How did it look to the public? After listening to Angel, she spent several hours telephoning everyone she knew, asking if they'd seen the hearing, and if they had, what was their opinion? The results were discouraging. The majority were impressed by Francis Carson and thought he had done a magnificent job in bringing out the truth. The animosity he supposedly felt for his brother was dismissed as a "smoke screen" thrown up by Henry Carson to hide the truth.

When Maggie finished her telephone canvass she analyzed the results. The better educated, more intelligent among her friends and acquaintances tended to accept Henry's story, but nobody believed the shifty-eyed Felix Flam. Was he crazy? He even had the gall to "wink" at the camera, which amounted to saying he was lying. By the time she finished her analysis Maggie was desperate. If this was a reasonable sampling of public opinion, Henry was in serious trouble. Accepting this fact, Maggie acted. She would fly to Washington and see Francis Carson herself. As someone in no way connected to the creation and marketing of Placidium, she could attack Francis Carson in ways that Henry could not and would not.

She called United Airlines, booking a seat on the "Red Eye" to Washington. The flight, which left at midnight, would land in Washington International Airport at nine A.M. If everything went on schedule, she'd be in Francis' office by ten o'clock. Then they'd see who had the better nerves.

United Airlines Flight 9 landed at Washington International Airport at ten minutes to nine. And, as planned, she was at Francis' office almost exactly at ten o'clock. From that point on nothing went as she'd expected.

To begin with, there was no one in the office but a secretary sitting at her desk filing her nails. Maggie looked at the young woman, with her overblown figure, bleached blonde hair and nail file. Obviously Tony had hired her, and she wondered why Francis permitted it.

"Excuse me," Maggie said. "Where is Congressman Carson?"

"I don't know. He'll be here when he gets here."

"And his legislative assistant, Mr. James?"

"What's it to you, honey? He'll be around."

Maggie got angry. "Now listen to me, Miss Peach Blossom of 1949, I am Mrs. Anthony James. Francis Carson is my brother-in-law. I said I want to know where he and my husband are. If you don't know, call Mr. James at home and ask him where Mr. Carson is."

Her anger had absolutely no effect on the secretary. "If you're Mrs. James, you should know where he lives. You call him."

That stopped Maggie in her tracks. She wasn't going to tell the secretary that she avoided all knowledge about Tony, including where he lived, what he did, whom he saw. She looked around the office. This was the outer room of a two-room office suite. She spotted an old picture of Tony standing on Dudley Wurdlinger's sloop on the desk nearest the entrance to the inner office. The sight of the young Tony James in the snapshot made her heart ache. Why had Tony gone so wrong? How much was her fault? She had married him without loving him, but if she had actually loved him, would he have turned out to be more of a man? She didn't think so. Everything Tony had become was in Tony before she'd met him. It would have been the same no matter whom he'd married. In fact, it might have been better if Tony had never married; then the disintegrating influence of the life he chose would have hurt no one but himself.

There was a large Rolodex on the desk next to the picture. Probably Tony had his address on one of the cards. She sat down at Tony's desk and turned the knob of the card file. The blonde girl jumped to her feet.

"Get your cotton pickin' hands off that!" She tried to yank the file away. "That's office property."

Maggie didn't argue. She stood up and slapped the girl as hard as she could. Then she slapped her again and shoved her backward onto the couch. The girl's dress slid up, revealing a garter belt, stockings and the briefest of bikini panties. She asked herself again why Francis permitted Tony such license.

The girl was making frantic attempts to pull her dress down without rising from the couch. She was afraid Maggie would slap her again. This was not her first encounter with a jealous wife, and now she believed Maggie was Mrs. James. Maggie had just found Tony's telephone number and address when he walked in the door. One glance told Maggie he'd been up all night drinking.

He noticed the girl on the couch first. "Get off that fucking couch and sit at your desk!" Then he saw Maggie. "What the hell are you doing here, you bitch?" The hatred in his voice shook Maggie. They may not have been lovers in the last years, but they had been friends. "Of course," he sneered. "That circus yesterday got to you!" He laughed. "Wait till Monday. We ought to charge admission."

Maggie hadn't seen Tony since before the election nine months ago. The physical deterioration she had noticed then was an early warning of what she saw now. Tony had put on twenty-five pounds. His skin, always so tan and healthy, was red and blotchy. His eyes were circled with dark, puffy rings, and his nose was swollen, the pores noticeably larger. His hair was shaggy and unkempt, and he needed a shave. She guessed he hadn't been near a razor in three days. And his clothes! Tony's clothes had always been casual but elegant. Now he looked as though he'd been living in that one dark blue suit for a week. The pants were baggy, the coat wrinkled; his tie showed sweat marks around the knot, and his shirt collar was torn. He wasn't the Tony James she had known for eighteen years.

"Where's Francis, Tony?"

"Are you upset, dear wife, because your lover is on the griddle?"

"What are you talking about?"

Tony's voice rose. "Francis told me everything. Henry Carson was your lover before you came to California. You married me because he married some whore Francis found for him. What a joke! When I think of the time I wasted worrying about your good opinion of me, I could vomit. And all those years you were itching for Henry Carson."

"There's no limit to you, is there?"

"Screw it, baby, none!" Tony was yelling. "You've made a fool of me long enough."

"You've managed it all by yourself. With things like that." She glanced at the secretary who was now at her desk enjoying the fight. "Where is Francis?" Maggie asked again.

"None of your fucking business."

"Tony, I promise you, Francis won't thank you if you don't tell me where he is. Or find him for me."

"Go fuck yourself!" Maggie realized Tony was giving vent to a rage she'd never seen in him before. In some way Francis had intensified the worst in Tony's nature, subtly encouraging his insecurities and weaknesses. Why would Francis do that? she wondered. Why make an already wretched man more miserable? The answer came as though she had always known it. This was the real Francis. Not Saint Francis but Francis the corrupter, the sadist. It gave him pleasure to inflict pain.

"Get your fucking ass out of my chair!"

"Washington seems to have limited your vocabulary." Maggie was fighting to stay cool. "Tony, I know every cheap whore you've been sleeping with for the last four years. I know every time you were drunk and almost missed a roll call vote until Francis got to you. I even know the abortionist Francis found for you when you made those two sixteen-year-olds pregnant. And I also know how many times you've had a dose of clap, who gave it to you and the doctor Francis took you to. The *Los Angeles Times* has been after the James family for years. And you're their key. Now, where is Francis?"

When she finished, Tony's whole body was shaking. "He—he's over at the House with Sam Rayburn. They're going to issue a contempt of Congress citation against your beloved Henry Carson." Tony seemed to recover some strength. "After that's done, you can visit him in jail."

"If that happens, there will be two Carsons in jail. The other one will be Francis."

"Now that's a very interesting threat. Would you care to step into my office and give me some details?"

Tony and Maggie turned to face the voice. Francis Carson was leaning against the door. Neither Maggie nor Tony had any idea how much he had overheard, but Maggie assumed he'd heard enough.

"It would be my pleasure."

"Thank you. And Tony, you look like something that spent the night in a compost heap." Francis' voice was even, but it had the cutting edge of a razor. "Go home, bathe, change your clothes, get a haircut and shave. I never want to see you in my office again looking and smelling the way you do. If Mr. Sam ever saw you in the House looking like this, he'd kick your ass so hard you'd land in the gallery."

"Sorry, Francis. I had a hard night."

"I'll expect you in Monday morning like the legislative assistant of a congressman. Not a bum."

"Yes, Francis. See you on Monday." Tony almost ran to the door.

"And now, Maggie, would you like a cup of coffee before we talk seriously?"

Maggie couldn't help marveling at Francis' methods. On the one hand he encouraged Tony's deterioration. Then, without missing a beat, he whiplashed him, telling him to straighten up. And Tony took it, even enjoyed it. "Yes. Black with no sugar."

"Mary Ellen—or is it Ellen Mary?—bring us a pot of black coffee with two cups and saucers." Francis showed Maggie the way into his office. She couldn't help being impressed. If one liked modern furniture, Francis' office reflected superb taste and a generous wallet. From the Matisse, Picasso and Roualt prints to the geometrically patterned rug designed by Edward Fields, to the Barcelona chairs by Mies van der Rohe, to the huge slab of marble that served as his desk, the office was a showpiece. Another side of Francis that Maggie had never seen, since he'd let Angel furnish their Santa Monica home in a totally hit or miss fashion.

While they waited for the coffee, Francis thought about the conversation he'd overheard, realizing the mistake he'd made years ago. The detectives he had spotted had not been hired by Angel but by Maggie, and undoubtedly at Henry's request. Tony had behaved like a class A fool. And their close connection left him vulnerable. Tony had become excess baggage; he must do something about him. Then he considered Maggie, and he was surprised at how much he admired her. She was ready to fight for Henry in a way he'd never before seen a woman fight for her man. He recalled their brief conversations about politics over the last years. She had a quick and intuitive understanding of its complexities, grasping more than many who were directly involved in the process. What a woman she would have been to stand behind him in his rise! Of course it was impossible, but what a pity! He could well understand Henry's loving her. For the first time in his life Francis had a fleeting moment of regret that his way of life made it impossible for a woman like Maggie to accept him. He smiled.

Maggie saw the smile and misunderstood it. He was so confident he could smile without knowing what she was going to say. She didn't think he'd be smiling when she finished.

Mary Ellen or Ellen Mary brought in a molded wooden tray with Dansk cups and saucers on it. She set the tray on a stainless steel and glass table and turned to leave. Francis stopped her. "Two things, Mary Ellen or Ellen Mary."

"It's Mary Ellen O'Connor."

"Miss O'Connor, I've noticed you come to work looking like a whore. I've been too busy to tell you. Change, or I'll fire you. Also, Mr. Anthony James is off limits to you, both in and out of the office. Do you understand?" The girl nodded, speechless. "Good. Get out and close the door." He waited for the girl to leave, and then his entire personality underwent a change. His harshness evaporated, his charm returned. "Permit me to pour you a cup of coffee."

Maggie said, "Yes," watching the graceful way he poured the coffee. She then came straight to the point of her visit.

"What are your plans Monday regarding the investigation?"

"I'll question Henry. He'll continue to insist he's innocent."

"He is."

"That's irrelevant. When I've finished questioning him, I'll serve him with this paper." He pulled a document out of his breast pocket. It had a blue covering. "It's a contempt citation. Sam Rayburn has agreed to place the motion before the House Monday morning."

"At your request?"

"At my request."

"And if you withdrew your request, what would happen?"

"Mr. Sam is reasonable. If I had a good reason not to proceed, he might listen."

"You have a good reason not to proceed."

"I do? Tell me the reason."

"Caterina Orsini and Italy."

"Henry told you about her?"

"Many people told me. And we both know any serious investigation of your life in Rome after the war, before you arrived in California, would produce very newsworthy headlines."

"I see. You would launch this investigation?" Francis smiled a gentle smile. "Then you must realize I have some cards too. Henry believes you had an affair with our father. He's unsure if Will is his son or his half brother."

Maggie had expected this counterattack. It was inevitable that Evelyn Wilkenson would have told Francis the story. "Will is Henry's son. You have no proof he isn't."

"Proof, Maggie, can be manufactured. I can produce excellent forgeries, hotel check-ins and the like, that would prove you and William spent nights together." He shrugged. "Of course, I know you and I knew my father, and we both know the idea is nonsense. But Henry is a jealous ass—otherwise he'd have recognized the truth in the first place. Now he'll believe the worst."

Maggie, at her most tense, still sounded matter-of-fact. "I'll risk your forgeries. They can do no more harm to Henry and me than has already been done."

"I realize that, but what about Will?"

"Yes, what about Will?" Maggie had expected this too. Carefully—for she had a double purpose—she must keep Francis believing she'd jettison everything, even her son. "I'm prepared for the necessity that Will will have to survive any scandal."

"It will be a scandal, since I am fully prepared to see it gets all the publicity it deserves. If the Placidium investigation has troubled him, wait until he starts asking who his father is."

Maggie understood Francis better than she could have had she cared for him. He was bargaining with her. Now was the time to make her proposal. "Since we are discussing a matter of mutual blackmail, let's say we are temporarily deadlocked."

"But we might reach a point where we'd see eye to eye?"

"The hearings have been televised to a wide audience. The reaction has been very favorable to you."

"I know. Why would you be here otherwise?"

"You have enough evidence to propose a law broadening the powers of the Food and Drug Administration, which, after all, was the purpose of the investigation. There's a California senate race next year. With the reputation you'll have achieved and my help, you could get the Democratic nomination for the United States Senate. Remember, Eisenhower can't run again. Jack Kennedy will probably get the Democratic nomination for president. You could run one hell of a campaign in California."

"You'd support me?"

"If you drop the contempt citation against Henry."

Francis thought about Maggie's connections in the state. She knew everyone of note and worth on the political scene, on a first-name basis. Her parties were actually political meetings. "Also, you'd forget Italy?"

"And you'd forget William."

"That's an even exchange. Maggie, you are quite a lady. Wait outside a moment while I make a call."

"Make your case to Sam Rayburn as strong as possible." Her voice was businesslike. "Or we all go down in flames together. I won't spare you."

A chastened Mary Ellen was busy typing a release that covered the previous day's hearings. Maggie couldn't help feeling sorry for her. She thought she was an adult playing in an adult world, but the truth was she was an innocent compared to the real adults who ran the world. Maggie considered briefly apologizing to her for hitting her, but decided it wouldn't do Mary Ellen any good. Mary Ellen would have to work out her own survival like everyone else.

In a few minutes Francis opened the door. "Come in, Maggie. The coffee's cooled off." He waited for her to settle herself, then said, "Mr. Sam wanted Henry's head. This is the best deal I can cut. I'll put Henry on Monday afternoon. He'll of course deny everything. This time I'll accept his denials as true."

"They are the truth."

"Of course they're the truth. Do you think I believe Henry Carson, that pillar of righteousness, would palm off a drug like Placidium on the public if he knew the truth? Flam blew the research. And so did the F.D.A. My legislation will see to it that in the future the agency has the money, the facilities, the staff to reproduce all the research tests presented to them by drug companies on new products. Only when they're fully satisfied will they license a drug for distribution. But two things must happen first."

"Go ahead."

"First, Henry will offer an apology to the Congress of the United States for the suggestion that he holds them in contempt. And then"— Francis couldn't help laughing—"he has to apologize to me personally for the insinuations he made as to my motives."

Maggie considered what she had accomplished. It was as good as she could do, and the hardest part was yet to come—getting Henry to agree. To apologize to Congress was one thing, to Francis was another.

"Sam Rayburn wants Henry to apologize to you personally? As well as Congress?"

Francis inclined his head to the side. "He does indeed."

Maggie didn't believe him, but there was nothing more to say. "When do you need an answer?"

"Monday at ten. If he won't apologize, Mr. Sam needs time to put a roll call vote together."

"I'll call you at ten." Maggie stood up. "Francis, pray to whatever dark gods you pray to that I can persuade Henry to apologize to you. Remember what you said the evening we met. Well, this time you'll be in the wrong place at the wrong time. *Ciao, caro.*"

Watching her go, Francis thought—a warrior woman. No quarter given. He had a vicious appetite for hating people who got in his way, but, perversely, he admired Maggie. Thinking this, he took the contempt citation with the blue cover out of his pocket and tore it up. The form had been blank. Yes, luck was a fickle lady. How could Maggie have known that though the rest of the country thought he was a bloody hero, the great and cynical Mr. Sam had been in a quiet fury. Unlike anyone else, Mr. Sam had seen through Francis' scheme, which was why Mr. Sam was Mr. Sam. He'd recognized that Francis had maneuvered him into believing it was all simple, political ambition, that he was on the side of the angels. What Francis hadn't realized was that, coming from Texas and knowing the West, a family blood feud was not that uncommon a matter. Mr. Sam had listened with his third ear to what Henry Carson said about Francis Carson, about the obsessiveness of his desire for revenge. To Mr. Sam it made absolute sense, especially when he followed Henry Carson's logic. The man was not a lunatic, and he had not a straw to gain by marketing a product so immediately dangerous. In addition, as Mr. Sam had pointed out to Francis Carson in slow, unsparing words, Francis had deliberately lied to him. He said he knew the workings of the Carson Company when the fact of the case was he knew nothing. In sum, the whole investigation, though it might be useful for other reasons, was actually the result of Francis Carson's efforts at vengeance for some old family hate. Mr. Sam did not believe a congressional investigation was the place to settle a family feud. When he told Francis never to try to manipulate him again, Mr. Sam almost lost his temper. And now Francis was to end the hearing. All he wanted was Henry Carson to apologize to Congress. No more, no less. And don't tell him when to call for a contempt citation.

Maggie knew none of this, for which Francis gave thanks. He would introduce a major piece of legislation which would carry his name. He would be elected to the Senate. And if Henry Carson took it into his head Monday afternoon to apologize to him as well as to Congress, Mr. Sam could hardly object to such a display of brotherly affection.

That afternoon Maggie met with John Hillyer and Wilson Warfield. She outlined everything Francis had agreed to, omitting the bargaining that led to their understanding. Warfield was more skeptical than Hillyer. "I can see Sam Rayburn accepting a public apology to Congress. But he comes from Texas. He's not a man who would use Congress to settle a blood feud between brothers. It's not in his character to ask Henry to apologize to Francis."

Maggie agreed. "I believe Francis Carson added his own footnote. Can you call Sam Rayburn's office and find out the truth?"

"Not until the investigation is over."

"Then we take a chance on breaking the deal. Except that apologizing to Francis will be the hardest bone for Henry to swallow. What do you think, John?"

"What we're dealing with is Henry's pride. If Henry apologizes to Congress and then adds an apology to Francis, Rayburn certainly won't kill the deal."

Warfield thought it over. "No. He might be surprised but that's all."

"There's your answer, Maggie. I think Henry should apologize to Francis too, even if we find out later it was unnecessary. There's an old legal joke called 'Pay the Two Dollars.' In this case, the 'two dollars' is Henry's apology to Francis."

Maggie gave in. Then they decided between them that since Maggie had made the arrangement, it was up to her to persuade Henry.

"Where is he?" she asked.

"At the airport with Felix. Sending him home. Felix blames himself for everything. Henry is trying to soothe him. He'll be back any minute."

"Is there somewhere I can wash up? Where's the ladies' room?"

"Down the corridor. I'll have my secretary show you the way."

It took about twenty minutes for Maggie to wash her face, freshen her makeup, comb her hair and feel human again. And better ready to face Henry. Although they had spoken many times on the telephone, Maggie hadn't seen him in the five years since she'd bought his property in Orange County. As then, the prospect of seeing him was both exciting and frightening. At least this time she knew what to expect. The television cameras had provided very sharp close-ups. He had seemed about the same, though now he was forty-three.

When she returned to John's office, she found Henry, John and Warfield waiting for her. Henry had not anticipated the appearance of Maggie at this time, and in later life he was to remember the events of that afternoon in vivid detail. Her presence, her attitude, seemed to say their reunion was natural, to be taken for granted. It was as though she had reappeared simply to calm his troubled spirit. With one warm smile she removed, for the moment, all thoughts of Francis and Placidium from his mind. Everything about her seemed to say she was not afraid.

"You took Felix to the airport?"

"Yes. He's not needed for Monday's hearing. Being with his family who loves and believes in him will do him more good than anything else." He hesitated, then a faint smile touched his lips, the kind of smile with which one regards—with bitterness and pride—a possession purchased at an excruciating cost. "And what brings you to Washington, Maggie?"

Maggie became suddenly aware of the others in the room. "John, Mr. Warfield, would you mind leaving us? I want to explain to Henry what's happened."

Henry stood quietly, holding the recaptured sensation of what he felt for her every time thay met.

"She's pulled off a miracle for you, Henry. I hope you take advantage of it," John said, closing the door after himself and Warfield.

Henry looked at Maggie, neither hiding what he felt nor implying any further demand. "What is this miracle I should accept?"

Maggie had tried not to allow herself to know with what tension and longing she'd wanted to see him. During the five-year gap she'd been East often enough, and Henry had been on the West Coast equally often. They both realized, without having to say it, that they'd been avoiding each other. To see each other again, with only the right to behave as polite business associates, was asking too much. She sat down and closed her eyes for a moment, and when she opened them, Henry was standing over her. She saw his face with loving clarity, and she did not want to think of the outer world, of the ugliness that had brought them together. Simultaneously, she knew she had no right to be here unless she could help him. She felt frightened as she heard herself saying, "I've persuaded Francis to persuade Sam Rayburn to end the hearings."

For a moment it seemed Henry was living through an unlivable moment. "You saw my brother? You persuaded him?" He backed away from her.

She felt as if a shudder had run through his body and then run into hers. "It was strictly blackmail. I did what you couldn't do. I threatened him with exposure of his life in Rome." She added, with a desperate effort, "I also used Caterina."

There was a pause, and then he asked, "And what did he threaten you with in return?"

"With opening up the question of Will's parentage. You or William."

"And you said—?"

"I said Will would survive it."

She did not know how long Henry stood looking at her, because the first moment she fully grasped was when she felt his hands on her arms. He pulled her to her feet, burying his face in her shoulder. Then her hand moved gently over his hair, thinking she had no right to do it but unable to stop herself.

When he finally let her go, he said, "Maggie! Maggie! Maggie!" his voice sounding as if a confession resisted for years was breaking out. "You remarkable woman! You outplayed that bastard!" He took her hand and held it to his lips, not as a kiss but as a gesture of respect.

"No. It was a draw." Maggie pressed her lips together not to moan. "There's more, Henry. Francis has a price."

Henry continued to hold her hand. "Of course. Francis always has a price. And it's never low."

"One is that you apologize to Congress for your words of contempt."

"That's not high enough. What else?"

"Forgive me, Henry." Maggie felt weighted with exhaustion. "That you apologize to Francis, personally, for your insinuations." She rushed on. "The hearing Monday afternoon will proceed on schedule. Francis will question you, and you will deny that either you or the Carson Company had any knowledge of the side effects of the drug. This time Francis will take your word, and you will apologize to Congress and Francis. The contempt citation will then be dropped."

Henry slumped in a chair, and seeing his despair, Maggie felt a need to fight his battle, to fight for him, for that integrity in his face and the courage that fed it. But there was nothing more she could do. "All right," he said at last. "Every man builds his world in his own image. I built mine, the Carson Company. And if it was almost destroyed, Francis is only an accessory. I'm responsible. When does he need an answer?"

"Monday morning by ten."

"That gives us the weekend." He had not meant to say that. He had always been able to keep Maggie at a distance, but now he had no power to let her go. "Would you consider staying in Washington until this mess is over? Monday evening. I'm sure you could get a hotel room. And if I wear a mustache, we could have dinner and go sightseeing together without too many people asking for my autograph."

Maggie recognized the need in his eyes. It was the same need she fought within herself. For the first time, it struck her she was holding him to her as surely as by a physical touch, and the seconds that passed, brief and tense to endure, were the most satisfying form of contact. It gave her an almost frivolous sense of triumph.

Henry added awkwardly, "Of course, if you'd rather go back to California, I'll take you to the airport."

"I'd rather keep you company over the weekend."

"Separate bedrooms, of course. Probably I shouldn't have bothered saying . . ." He let the sentence hang.

"Naturally. I'm a married woman. We need no additional scandal." She tried to steady herself, dropping all thought of triumph or of who had the power over whom.

For years neither had known, until they spent the weekend together, the sense of lightness, of emancipation, the glow of freedom that they felt in each other's presence. Through the two days that followed, Maggie was childishly humble, almost apologetic for her joy. It seemed to her that the weekend was a long summer day out of a carefree youth she had never lived. And Henry in turn felt that no problems existed; nothing could ever make him leave her again. Then Monday morning came, and they said goodby over coffee in the breakfast shop of the hotel. Watching him leave, Maggie thought that all he was seeking was already his. It only took his capacity to see the truth: the truth of her love for him, the truth of William. Yet she had no way to reach him, no power to give him sight, no power to pierce the barrier he'd set up. There was no power except his own desire to see the truth.

At ten A.M. Wilson Warfield reported Henry's agreement to Francis Carson. The scheduled meeting of the special subcommittee would take place in the same room as on Thursday. There were a few vacant seats in the rear, and as unobtrusively as possible, Maggie slid into one.

Henry was reading from a speech prepared by Warfield. "I—um—I—" He faltered as if his lips were stiff. "I would like to offer my apologies for anything I might have said last Thursday in this room which intimated that I lack respect for the Congress of the United States. I have nothing but the highest respect for that great body of men and women, and I so state publicly under oath." He paused. Maggie saw the deep cut of bitterness at the corners of his mouth. The seconds clicked by as he fought to continue. His fingers gripped his thighs in a claw-like grip Maggie understood. If Henry released his hands, they would control him, and he would end by seizing Francis' throat and crushing it. Finally he mastered himself; the pain had burned itself out. The events no longer had any meaning to him. He continued. "I would also like to single out my brother, Francis Carson, and apologize to him as a congressman and as a man for any implication that I lack respect for him or feel any contempt for him as a congressman and a gentleman."

Francis smiled at Henry, a faintly superior smile. The television cameras zoomed in on the handsome face of Congressman Francis Carson. All over America, citizens of the United States were thinking that Francis Carson was a man to watch, a rising political star. And in California, Edmund G. "Pat" Brown agreed. Very interesting, he thought. Francis is now a national figure. He could be the man we're looking for to run for the U.S. Senate.

# Part Five
# *1960 – 1970*

# Chapter 36

THE PLACIDIUM investigation proved to be a triumph for Francis Carson. While it did not ruin Henry Carson or the Carson Company, it did much to further Francis' political career. Immediately after the investigation, Francis drafted a bill that became known as the Carson Amendment. The bill provided the ways and means for the F.D.A. to prevent future drug disasters and broadened the powers of the F.D.A. to test and retest all data submitted by the pharmaceutical companies.

When Congress was not in session, Francis ranged up and down California making speeches to all manner of groups from the Napa Valley farmers to the arch-conservatives of Riverside. With television emerging as a primary means of communication, Francis' striking good looks and his capacity to handle the new medium made him a center of media attention. At no time did he announce he was campaigning for the Democratic nomination for the United States Senate. No! He was visiting the folks to become acquainted with their problems, so that he could act on behalf of every Californian when in Washington. The performance was worth watching. General Francis Carson, the war hero, and Congressman Francis Carson were merged into one by a very simple device. As Henry noticed during the committee hearing, Francis had taken to wearing a gold pin in his lapel. No one found out what the pin was until Francis allowed the wind to turn the lapel of his suit so the underside appeared. A small ribbon could be seen under the lapel. It was sky blue and covered with white stars. An alert photographer, helpfully placed by Francis in a convenient spot, snapped a picture of the ribbon. Thus, without his reminding anyone, it became known that Congressman Carson always wore his Congressional Medal of Honor. It was his way, he explained, of saying how proud he was to have served his country.

In answer to a direct question, he replied, "Yes, I still hold a commission in the U.S. Air Force Reserve." Francis gave the questioner his favorite smile—mainly modest and yet aggressive. "At my age, the commission is primarily a courtesy. There are so many younger men with faster reflexes who would do a better job. Of course, if there ever was a need, they know where to find me."

The reporters searched their morgues, and soon pictures of General Francis Carson along with Congressman Francis Carson were appearing on the front page of the *Los Angeles Times*, the *San Diego Chronicle*, the *San Francisco Examiner*, the *Oakland Tribune* and many smaller papers. When Francis Carson was nominated as the Democratic candidate for the United States Senate in 1960, it came as no surprise to political insiders, including Maggie Rhodes James who had worked diligently for this man whom she personally despised.

He wasn't the first one- or two-term congressman who had run for the Senate. Richard Nixon had done almost the same thing. He was first elected to Congress in 1946 and then to the Senate in 1950. In 1952, as Eisenhower's running mate, he became Vice President of the United States. And now Nixon was running for President of the United States. Francis asked himself if history would repeat.

The 1960 election split California. When the absentee ballots were counted a week after the election, Richard Nixon had the solace of having carried his home state by a little over 35,000 votes. Almost too close to call. Francis Carson had no such problem. He won with a margin of 600,000 votes and became the junior senator from California. It was happening according to the plan he had made six years ago in his villa outside Rome.

On October 21, 1961, a columnist in the *Washington Post* made a reference to Tony James. Though it was a veiled and guarded reference, it was one which immediately identified Tony to those whose business it was to make such identifications. The column referred to a rising star on Capitol Hill whose legislative assistant was seen regularly squiring the wife of a traveling foreign diplomat to parties where unusual events were known to take place. Francis had extricated Tony in the past from similar situations. This time it had hit the papers, and that made up Francis' mind. Tony would have to go, no matter how long and loud Angel screamed. Francis Carson would let nothing stand in the way of his Washington career.

Originally his ambition had been simple and single-minded—ruin Henry Carson. The investigation he had chaired had been a step in that direction, but it was only a step. Henry and he were not quits. Not as long as either of them lived.

But something had happened to Francis in his search for revenge.

Something he had not counted on. Washington had happened to Francis. He had discovered power, the greatest aphrodisiac of them all. To be a principal player in the power game was very strong stuff indeed. And he was never in awe of the Kennedy people. For all their flash and reputation, he considered himself more astute and more worldly. In many ways he was right. Francis was a strong figure where too many men were corporate men or gifted clerks. This put him in a position to drive them toward programs and policies they themselves would never have conceived or dared. Slowly Francis was evolving into a true man of power.

As time passed, his trips to the villa became fewer. On his most recent visit Maria provided him as usual with a beautiful boy. There was a sensual excitement, but a part of him was bored. The thrill was nothing when compared with the exultation of rising on the Senate floor to deliver an important speech in support of or against a particular bill. To hear the Senate applaud, the press applaud, his aides proud and delighted— what greater triumph was there?

He remembered Caterina the last time he'd seen her. Her face was gaunt, her body thin, almost to the point of starvation. Francis had no objection to helping Caterina destroy herself. It was the least he owed her for falling in love with Henry and bungling his first direct attack. He remembered again his patron saint, Lady Luck. If his original plan had succeeded, he might not have returned to the United States and entered politics, thus never discovering his life's work. For that reason alone, he allowed Caterina the right to destroy herself in the comfort of his villa, instead of in the gutters of Rome.

Francis thought about the years of sensuality spent in his Roman villa, and all the years before that. Something within him had changed. He would do nothing now that might in any way compromise his rise to power. If need be, he would lead a celibate life. Angel was drunk so often these days, she was almost useless as a sexual partner. She had never seen and would never see his villa. He'd settled that matter by telling her he'd sold it. Thinking about Angel and her drinking convinced him he must do something about Tony. The only question was what.

The hotel on the edge of the northwest section of Washington had seen better days. Since the war, it had been replaced in the pecking order of hotels by a half-dozen new, high-rise buildings in better locations with larger rooms, more elaborate dining facilities and the one thing a successful hotel in Washington required—many small conference rooms. The Castleton had no conference rooms. Its main attraction was that it required no luggage upon registering. If a couple wasn't planning to stay more than an hour or two, and paid in advance, the night clerk dismissed the need to register entirely.

Nicole was exhausted. It was now eleven o'clock. She and Tony James had arrived two hours ago, and nothing she did seemed to arouse Tony. Maybe he was too drunk? Or no longer interested in her? She thought of all she had done, but her extensive repertory was useless; Tony remained impotent. It was an affront to her simple theory of sex. A man had only to accomplish three things: the first was to get an erection, the second was to caress her briefly (Nicole was easily aroused), the third was to enter her and stay hard for at least a short period of time. Once entered, Nicole could achieve a satisfactory orgasm in minutes. She tried to give pleasure and expected pleasure in exchange.

Tony lay in the middle of the sagging mattress. He'd had too much to drink at dinner, and he was tired of Nicole. He needed a new woman. Sooner or later, usually sooner, he lost interest and needed a replacement. Actually Nicole had lasted longer than most—almost a month. Maybe what was said about French women was true. They knew more about sex. Right now he didn't know or care.

Nicole whispered, "I am sorry, *chéri*." She had resigned herself to a wasted night. She would not see Tony James again. If there weren't such a man shortage in Washington, she would never have dated him anyway. Once he might have been handsome, but no more. "*Chéri*, you will drop me off in the usual place?"

"Like hell! Get yourself home!" He staggered to his feet.

Nicole reached for his hand. "This is not a safe neighborhood for a woman to be alone."

"Don't worry. You're a mess. No one will bother you."

Abruptly Nicole grew angry. "Tony, look at yourself. You are the mess."

Her biting words released a rage in Tony he had suppressed for years. If a woman couldn't arouse him, he always hated her. He wanted to hit the woman, punish her for her failure. Who could this one complain to? Not her husband. Without warning Tony slapped Nicole's face. "Ugly, fucking bitch!"

Nicole's head rocked sideways, stunned by the slap. She slapped Tony back and tried to knee him in the groin. In a drunken daze he staggered just far enough to one side so her knee hit his hip. He knew exactly what she had tried—the bitch, female stunt. To hurt a man, hit his balls.

His rage against all women exploded. He hit Nicole in the stomach, then in the breasts. He hit her in the mouth, and bleeding began. Then he hit her nose. There was a crunch as the cartilage broke. Nicole fell back on the bed, her hands over her face, trying to protect herself. Tony crouched over her, punching and swearing. "Try to kick me, you bitch! Kick me!" Finally, he had strength left for one last punch, and leaning back, he hit straight down. His blow landed on Nicole's pelvic bone, one of the strongest bones in a woman's body. After all the other blows the punch gave her little additional pain. However, sharp pain in Tony's knuckles cut through his fury. He thought he'd broken his hand. He glared at the woman who had been trying to arouse him only moments ago. Blood was running from her nose and mouth. Red welts covered her body. She moaned softly, almost to herself. "Stop, Tony! Please! You hurt me."

"Kick a man in the balls!" he screamed, staggering into the bathroom. Cold water seemed to help his hand. Then he stared at himself in the full-length mirror opposite the toilet. His belly was fat and bloated and bulged over his waist. His chest muscles sagged like an old whore's tits. He stumbled back into the bedroom. Without glancing at Nicole, he looked for his clothes. Now he wanted to get out of the room, out of the hotel.

Nicole was making the low, soft sounds that the badly hurt make, partially to assure themselves they are still alive and able to make sounds. Tony looked for his underwear, then thought, To hell with it. There were his loafers. He slipped his feet into them and tried getting into his pants with his shoes on. Tony fought his trousers. He won the battle but at a cost. In order to get his pants over his shoes he had to rip the bottom of each pant leg. But at least he was half dressed. Next came his shirt. He tucked his shirt into his pants without buttoning it. Next his jacket. He got his arms into the sleeves without a struggle. He was ready to leave. He glanced at the body on the bed.

Nicole had turned on her side and lay in a fetal position, her legs drawn up tight against her bruised body. Tony left the room without shutting the door. Any guy passing was welcome to have at her.

He staggered down a strange street. Then another street. He had no idea where he was. He passed a few women, and those he approached ran from him. He wondered why they ran. Did they think he was some kind of pervert? Or a rapist? The streets were darker than those he was used to. The houses had lawns that weren't kept up. The hedges were overgrown, and from what little he could see, the century-old red-brick three-story buildings needed painting. Even the sidewalks were broken. Occasionally a car passed him, moving rapidly. Suddenly frightened, it occurred to Tony it was too late to be in this kind of neighborhood. He stood under the street light to check his wristwatch. Where the hell was it? Goddamn it! He must have left it in the room with that stupid cunt. The watch was gold. He'd never get it back. And it had belonged to Anthony. It was all that damn bitch's fault. At least he still had his wallet.

Tony weaved around a corner. It seemed to him he saw a glow in the distance. That meant lights. And lights meant people and taxis. He started shuffling toward the lights. It was hard concentrating on his footing. The sidewalks were uneven, and he was very tired. Breathing was an effort. He didn't see a shadow detach itself from the wall of a house. The shadow followed him for a block, gradually closing the distance between them. The shadow was in no hurry. His sneakers didn't make a sound. Many blocks lay between them and the bright lights. Closer. Still closer. Now the shadow was only a few feet behind Tony. One leap and an arm snaked around Tony's neck, cutting off his breath. The knife against Tony's back wasn't needed. The shadow became aware he was the only thing holding his prey erect. He loosened his grip, and Tony slumped to the ground. A quick hand in Tony's jacket, and a wallet changed ownership. His watch. The dudes always wore watches. No watch! Shit! Tony lay still. Why take chances? There was that nice, white throat exposed in the dim light, with not even a necktie. Slash. The heavy knife cut through the fat and muscle. Blood squirted from the severed artery. The man had been alive. He wasn't now. The shadow melted into the blackness that dominated the neighborhood.

Francis Carson arrived at his office early, before the secretaries or anyone connected with his staff, eager to start reading the most recent reports on his desk. Because of his remarkable war record he had been able to maneuver himself onto two of the most important Senate committees: the Foreign Relations and the Armed Services committees. When Francis had received his assignments he knew almost nothing about Vietnam. Now he was as good an authority as anyone. For Francis had one of his strong sixth-sense hunches that where he stood on the Vietnam issue would one day influence his career. And he always trusted these hunches. But he found himself in a quandary. He was at odds with the Administration. If the Chinese had failed to conquer Vietnam after trying for 2,000 years, we the Boy Scouts of the Western world didn't have a chance of a snowball in hell. And yet Kennedy was sending in more and more "advisers" to South Vietnam. Why? Was Kennedy crazy or was he?

One by one Francis' staff drifted in. All except Tony James.

At nine-thirty-six Francis was interrupted. "Yes?"

"Mr. Carson"—his secretary sounded frightened—"there's a policeman on the line who wants to talk to you."

"What about?"

"Mr. James."

It irritated Francis to realize he should have attended to Tony sooner. "Put him on." There was a pause. "This is Senator Carson. To whom am I speaking?"

"Sergeant Thompson, Sixth Precinct."

"What can I do for you, Sergeant?"

"Has your assistant Anthony James arrived this morning?"

"Not yet. Why?"

"Senator, we found a man with his throat slashed and his wallet missing last night. We think it's Anthony James."

Francis was properly concerned. The sergeant gave him the address of the morgue. Francis said he would drop everything and hurry over to make identification. They could be wrong. He hoped not.

The autopsy showed that although Tony's heart was in terrible condition, and he had enough liquor in his stomach and blood to be considered drunk, the immediate cause of death was a severed artery. The motive was robbery. Both his wallet and watch were missing. There was some confusion over the lack of underwear, socks and a tie, but the police had no reason to connect those things with his murder. Everyone assumed he'd been with a woman, left her somewhere the worse for wear, and stumbled into a part of town where he shouldn't have been in his condition. He was murdered and robbed. The next day Francis noted a small article, two paragraphs, that said the wife of the French military attaché had been attacked near the embassy and seriously, but not fatally, injured. She couldn't identify who had attacked her or why. While Francis suspected the two events fitted together, he thought it well worth forgetting.

Once released by the police, Tony's body was flown to Los Angeles as quickly as possible. The fact that Francis was a senator helped speed the release of the body. He was buried in the family plot at St. Michael's Cemetery. There were three mourners: Maggie Rhodes James, Angela

James Carson and Francis Carson. Maggie felt a resigned sadness, remembering everything lighthearted and outrageous about Tony the first time they met at Union Station and on so many other occasions when they were young. Angel was in deep mourning, having completely erased all knowledge of what Tony had done to destroy himself, holding fast in her memory only the picture of the golden-haired older brother whom she worshiped. Francis Carson delivered the eulogy at the funeral and again thanked Lady Luck. He, better than anyone, knew how fortunate he was that Tony, with no help from him, had managed to remove himself from the path of Francis' career. And done it with greater finality than Francis might have dared.

After the funeral they separated, Maggie returning to Malibu, and Francis and Angel to Santa Monica. Once home, Angel began to drink, steadily and hard. As the liquor took effect, all the resentments Angel had built up over the time Francis spent in Washington and away from her erupted.

"You prick! You are a bastard! For the last two years you've been away eleven out of twelve months, playing 'doctor' to every cunt in Washington."

Francis tried to be reasonable. "That's foolish. Some days I put in eighteen hours working. Even if I wanted a woman, I wouldn't have time."

"You smug son of a bitch! You only married me to get the James' backing for a political leg up. Tony told me all about it!"

"If so, it was a mistake in judgment. Neither you nor Tony has turned out to be an asset."

"Poor Tony." Angel was heaving with drunken sobs. "You murdered him." She started to shiver and tried to pour herself another drink. But the bottle was empty. "I need a drink. Whenever I think of what you did to my poor brother—his throat—" Angel struggled to rise from the couch.

Francis went quickly to the bar and took a full quart bottle of Tanqueray gin from the shelf. Pulling a handkerchief from his jacket pocket, he opened the cap, using the handkerchief to handle it. Then, wiping the bottle with the handkerchief, he handed it to Angel, who was still trying to rise. "Here. Have all the gin you want."

"You bastard!" Angel grabbed the bottle. "You probably poisoned it." She took a sizable swallow. "You know and I know that you had Tony killed. No matter what the police think or what the press says about the great Senator Carson." She kept swallowing between outbursts. "I'm going to open a full investigation, and you and your steely blue eyes and your solid gold career will go up in a puff. Pouf!"

"Do that, Angel. By all means."

"Bastard!" Angel took another swallow. "You think they won't find anything. I know better."

"Angel, sometimes my arm gets tired whipping you. Don't you understand that no one will listen to you? Your reputation precedes you. You're a drunk. You've been a drunk for years. Like brother, like sister."

"I'll kill you. I'll kill you!" Angel took a stiff swallow from the bottle and tried again to get up from the couch.

"Yes, kill me," said Francis, experiencing a vast satisfaction.

"Don't you threaten me, you bastard."

"It's my impression you're threatening me. Have another drink."

"Don't tell me what to do, you prick! Noooooo." She stopped swallowing suddenly. "I . . . don't . . . feel . . . good. . . ."

"Then have another drink, Angel."

"Leave me alone. . . . I . . . will . . . do . . . as I please. . . ."

"I'm going out to a restaurant and get some dinner." Francis stared at Angel. The total value of this effort was to make him realize again how little he cared.

"Don't you dare go away! I . . . feel . . . so sick. . . . Help me . . ."

When Francis turned at the door, he saw Angel slumped unconscious on the floor. The gin bottle was almost empty. Good riddance, he thought, to the Princess of Beverly Hills.

When he returned to the house three hours later, an ambulance was parked in the driveway. Damn it! Someone called the hospital. There was always a chance they'd been too late.

This time Lady Luck deserted Francis Carson. Not only did Angel recover completely, she told Maggie, her first visitor, that she was leaving Francis. He had tried to kill her by forcing her to drink a full quart of gin. He was also responsible for Tony's deterioration and death. Although Maggie convinced Angel there was no way to prove her wild charges, Maggie's feelings about the destructive nature of Francis Carson were reinforced. She called Michael Dunne and put him on the case.

Dunne's report came in. There was no evidence to implicate Francis Carson. His statement was simple. He had left before Angel passed out. Naturally, if he'd been there, he'd have taken her to the hospital. Alcohol poisoning could be fatal. There was no way to confirm this statement.

And no way to disprove it. There was one, small puzzling item. While Angel's fingerprints were all over the bottle of gin, there were no prints on the bottle top. Not one. The police noted this too and dropped it. Francis Carson was a United States senator, and Angel Carson was a borderline alcoholic. Dunne doubted that a case of attempted murder could be based on a bottle top without fingerprints.

# Chapter 37

WILL CARSON and John Hillyer, Jr., graduated from Harvard in June 1961. After graduation, they spent the summer touring Europe together. They found girls in every port. When they weren't girl scouting, Will would stop in to introduce himself to the heads of the Carson Company divisions in the various countries. They returned to the United States, weary but exhilarated, in need of another short vacation. But they'd run out of time. They were now men and must begin men's work, following their separate ways on their different life paths. Though, for both of them, economics and sociology had formed the core of their undergraduate work, Will's interest was in the practical application of his knowledge in the market place, while John, Jr., had a more theoretical cast of mind. In keeping with their different leanings, Will would sit next to Henry at William's old desk at the Carson Company, while John went off to begin his graduate work at M.I.T. in the fields he thought most influenced human events. So, for the first time in eight years, the two young men said a real goodby.

On June 25, 1964, the four o'clock Boston shuttle landed at La Guardia Airport. Will and Elizabeth Carson waited impatiently inside the terminal for John, Jr., to arrive. Will had seen John only occasionally over the last three years. John had taken two Masters degrees, one in sociology and the other in economics. Elizabeth hadn't seen him at all since he'd started working for his degrees. Now she had her nose pressed against the window trying to catch a first glimpse of him.

She had gone to a hairdresser for the first time in her life in honor of John. The shop had been warm with brilliantly vulgar wallpaper. The woman behind the reception desk was round, fat, her head like a black powder puff set on a frilly, pink dress. The more Elizabeth sniffed the warm, scented air, the more certain she became that they wouldn't understand her. That is, the real her. They might do her hair all wrong. But the powder puff head nodded, acknowledged her appointment, led her through the shop, settling her behind a curtain in a small cubicle. Waiting there alone, Elizabeth wished she hadn't come. It was all a mistake. She'd end up looking frightful. It was only the tugging, hopeful feeling in her heart that made her stay. John was coming. John, Will's best friend and her very best dream man. She wanted John to realize how grown-up she was. She wanted to be beautiful for him. Will was always teasing her about being a tomboy. If John thought she was beautiful, that would show him. But suppose the hairdresser did everything wrong? She started to squirm, and just at that moment, steps sounded. A slender, young, dark-haired man entered. His name was Rudy, and when he smiled at Elizabeth with real appreciation, she knew everything was going to be all right. And it was. She could tell by the look in Will's eyes when she arrived home.

Will watched her now, his face a study. When John saw her last, she had been a tall, gawky ten-year-old with a mass of curly red hair surrounding her face. Now she was almost fourteen and had matured beyond anything anyone had expected. She was 5′ 8″ tall, and while slender, her figure, in tight jeans and one of Will's old shirts, had a definite femaleness about it. Her breasts had filled out, her hips widened, her waist narrowed. Her features were clearly defined: a strong jaw, wide mouth, generous lips. Her brilliant green eyes drew the world into them, and by the time she reached her late teens, she'd have those elegant, high cheekbones he remembered her mother having. Liz was going to be a true beauty. If he hadn't known her age, he would have guessed it to be sixteen, seventeen or maybe even eighteen. The red curls were now shaped to her head, and she really was a knockout. Will felt displeased with himself. Brothers weren't supposed to look at sisters as if they were girls. They should hardly notice them or feel anything but affection or exasperation.

Suddenly they both saw the tall, broad-shouldered figure of John, Jr. They waved, and John, spotting them, ran to greet them. Will and John shook hands and hugged each other in the fashion of Europeans. Then John saw Elizabeth.

"Liz? . . ." He gave her a faintly astonished, admiring look that pleased her enormously. "You are Liz, aren't you?"

"Yes, I'm Liz." She tried to smile. She wanted to hug him the way she had when she was a child. But she wasn't a child now. She felt herself blush because she wanted to kiss him, to put her arms around him and press against him and feel his cheek hot against her kiss, the way she felt Will's cheek when she kissed him. Oh, she wouldn't kiss John on the mouth—not on the mouth! She wouldn't dare. Would she? Why not? She threw her arms around John and kissed him squarely on the mouth. "Oh, John, I've missed you so much!"

Will watched Elizabeth clinging to John. While his smile remained fixed, he wished she'd let John go. Liz wasn't a child any longer. She should behave herself. He fidgeted, trying to hide his irritation. Finally he slapped her smartly on the behind. "Okay! Hands off, kid!"

"Ouch!" Elizabeth was indignant.

"Come on. We still have a drive ahead of us."

John extricated himself from Elizabeth's grasp, feeling uncomfortably warm. "Girls sure do grow up quickly, don't they?" He grinned at Will and then looked at Elizabeth. "How old are you now, Liz?"

"She's thirteen," Will answered.

"I'm twenty-five."

"Thirteen? Good God!" Then John thought about it. "Of course, but I'd never have guessed."

"I'm thirteen going on twenty-five. I had a birthday every month this year. That's how I caught up with Will."

"You are something." John still tasted the sweet shock of her kiss. "If somewhat precocious."

"I proposed to you when I was ten. Are we still engaged to be married?"

"Sure. If, when you're older and wiser, you want to marry a poor, struggling economist."

The words sounded strange to Will, and although he couldn't analyze his feelings, he thoroughly disliked the idea of Liz marrying John. Just talking about it made him wince. Will was an intelligent young man. Had the girl been anyone but his kid sister, he wouldn't have felt so embarrassed. Now he felt ashamed as he realized he was jealous of his sister's interest in his best friend. His only defense against what he didn't understand was sarcasm. "He'll be able to afford to marry you when he wins the Nobel Prize."

John started to laugh. "That means we shall never marry. There is no Nobel for economists."

Elizabeth's cheeks burned. And the stupid thing was she didn't exactly understand why she was so angry at Will. He was only teasing, but he was always teasing. She tried to swallow her irritation. "My brother would prefer for me to be a spinster."

"Aren't you a little young to worry about such things?" John picked up a peculiar tension between Will and Elizabeth. It caused him to concentrate entirely on Will. "How does it feel to be an important executive in the corporate world?"

"How does it feel to be a rising young economist?"

Both of them knew they'd escaped from some unexpected awkwardness, and both of them meant to avoid letting it happen again. They walked toward the car, filling each other in on their work, hopes and accomplishments to date.

"Between working for Dad and going to Columbia night school to get my M.B.A., I live between marketing reports and textbooks."

"And I live between Margaret Mead, Nimroff and Paul Samuelson. Sociology plus a little anthropology added to economics. It's like jumping on a horse and riding off in all directions at the same time."

Beneath their words their voices showed their fondness and mutual concern. There was a current of intimacy that flowed between them; each was almost as interested in the success of the other as in his own. What about me? Elizabeth wanted to interrupt. What about me? Don't ignore me! I'm here too! But she said nothing, walking silently between them to the car.

"By the way," Will said, "I've set us up for tomorrow night with two Sarah Lawrence girls."

"Which one has the apartment?"


As Will turned his Mercedes 300 Cabriolet into the long driveway leading to Carson House, John looked at the estate with admiration. It was as perfect as ever, from the elm trees and white stones bordering the driveway to the huge, gracious three-story house that seemed, as it aged, to have grown out of the land. The ivy, originally planted by Will's grandfather, now covered most of the house, making the walls as one with the hedges and the sweep of the beautifully kept lawns.

When Will stopped the car at the front steps, Henry and Oscar were waiting. "Hello, John. You've been away too long."

"Thank you, sir. I'm glad to be back."

"Oscar will see to your luggage. We've set up your old room next to Will's. If you'll excuse me, I'm expecting a call from Europe. I'll see you at dinner."

John watched Henry leave. "Will, your father must be fifty, but he looks and moves like a man of thirty-five."

"I know. I'm afraid he's about to start a new career."

"Like what?"

"Like I don't know, but he's very interested in politics. He thinks Washington could use the advice of more businessmen."

In spite of his promise, Henry did not join them for dinner. Will, Elizabeth and John sat later in the enclosed porch waiting for him. He was still in the library talking to Godfrey Moore in Switzerland. Will and John were discussing the upcoming election involving Goldwater and Johnson, as well as the Vietnam issue. Exasperated at being ignored, Elizabeth burst out, "Come on, John, we know Johnson thinks he's Roosevelt. With Roosevelt it was the 'New Deal'. And saving the world from Hitler. With Johnson, it's the 'Grand Society'. And saving the world from communism."

"It's the 'Great Society'. Not the 'Grand Society'," Will said, impatiently.

John smiled and asked, "Miss Carson, would you be interested in giving a lecture at M.I.T. titled 'The Psychology of L.B.J.'?"

Elizabeth swallowed a giggle and answered, "Thank you, but no lectures until I graduate. But to continue, and don't interrupt me, Will Carson, I am certain we all realize that between Johnson and Goldwater, Johnson is the greater menace. You gentlemen will agree that Johnson has Congressional support?"

"And Goldwater doesn't. Very astute, young lady."

"Miss Rabbit Ears doesn't miss a word at the dinner table. She can quote Dad by heart."

"Yes I can. If you want to be a genius, find one and follow him around. Dad's a genius. He says we can't afford a war. Anyway, not with the 'Grand Soc . . .' I mean 'Great Society' programs."

Why doesn't John stop her, Will wondered? He surely couldn't be interested in the second hand opinions of a thirteen year old, even a bright thirteen year old?

"And you don't think he can raise taxes?" John had the grace not to laugh at Elizabeth's gaffe.

"Raise taxes in an election year? Goodness, I couldn't pay higher taxes. I mean, if I paid taxes." Elizabeth was flattered by the attention John gave her. It went to her head, and she went on and on, throwing in every bit of information she'd heard—opinions on budget deficiencies, inflation and even the rising cost of raw materials for the Carson Company.

Will listened, his mind filled with growing resentment at the play she was making for John. Once she looked at him, uneasily, and he looked away. He was really irritated. What a spectacle she was making of herself. Like a puppy dog wagging her tail and leaping around John. Will hated the whole thing, and why didn't she stop? Why didn't John stop her? Maybe he was collecting disciples?

As though he'd heard Will's thoughts, John turned to him. "I suppose you know all this by heart?"

"By heart! It's usually served up with dinner at Carson House. Dad doesn't trust Johnson. Talk about the election, the budget deficit, the possibility of inflation, it all comes with the main course." Will knew it was ridiculous, but he was torn by a double jealousy: Elizabeth's interest in John and John's noticing her. He was angry with himself, and mystified. He repeated, "Our Miss Rabbit Ears doesn't miss a trick."

John still appeared impressed. "She has some of it garbled, but I think she has a good grasp of the fundamentals."

"See!" said Liz. "I'm not such a dumdum, Will Carson." But even as she said it, the hurt look in Will's eyes made her lose confidence. She felt uneasy with herself because she knew that flirting with John had somehow put her in conflict with Will. The whole thing made her tired and unhappy, and she wanted to get away. She went to the door. "I'm going to get Daddy. He's been on the phone for hours. They're talking about some new drug."

"We introduce most of our new drugs in Europe," Will said, watching her leave. "The F.D.A. here makes it too difficult to get marketing approval in this country."

"I know. That's why we've lost our lead in new medical products to Germany and Japan."

"And the result is the United States public doesn't get the best medical care available." Will grew quiet, seeming to struggle within himself. John felt a sense of intrusion which he couldn't explain, and he waited for Will to speak first. Somewhere the evening had gone wrong, but he couldn't put his finger on where or why.

Then Elizabeth returned. "Dad said he'd be with us in a minute to help me settle the problems of the world." She smiled affectionately at Will. "Of course I do give you some credit for my superior education."

Her eyes met Will's, and he knew it was a kind of apology for monopolizing John, for flirting the way she had. He smiled back, and his face grew open and relaxed. "I'm glad to hear you admit it."

John watched the brother and sister with relief. They were making up for some quarrel he didn't understand. But he was pleased that they now seemed content with each other and themselves. This was like old times.

It was hard for Maggie to realize it had taken twenty-five years for the San Diego Freeway and the Santa Ana Freeway to link up and reach her property. She had been twenty-three when she started. Now it was 1966, and she was forty-eight years old. Other than retouching the few gray hairs that crept in among the black curls, her appearance was still that of a woman in her mid-thirties. No face lift. No body lift. Nothing.

She and Richard Phillpotts studied the scale model of Mission Nuevo: houses, schools and shopping malls; a country club with golf, tennis facilities and a swimming pool; motion picture theaters; a building that served both as a legitimate theater and concert hall; a small art museum; several two-story office buildings and others for light manufacturing; and finally open stretches of untouched land, land that would remain exactly as Maggie had seen and loved it twenty-five years ago.

Shortly, she would leave for New York and a shareholders' meeting to obtain final approval for work to start on Mission Nuevo. Bank financing, both construction and "take out" loans, were already arranged. This time Maggie had wanted the meeting held in New York. She hoped Henry would attend, and if not, they might at least have a dinner together.

Henry did attend the shareholders' meeting of the Rhodes Development Corporation. Not only did he attend, he defended all of Maggie's positions. One shareholder group objected to her putting aside so much "wilderness" land. Another felt she included too much "affordable housing" instead of more expensive homes which could be sold for higher prices and greater profit. Henry's defense from the floor put an end to opposition. Maggie received a vote of approval to proceed with construction on the first phase of Mission Nuevo.

She and Henry went to dinner that night at the Café Pierre in the Pierre hotel, with its memories of a lifetime ago. Other than Mission Nuevo, the subject they most shared in common, and with an even deeper interest, was Will.

"He's fine. Brilliant. I put him in charge of a whole new product group—disposable and diagnostic equipment for hospitals. Within ten years it should be the greatest division in the company. And Will's built it himself. He sits at William's desk"—he caught himself—"it's Will's desk now, and he makes decisions as though he were born to the job."

Maggie smiled. "And wasn't he, Henry? Wasn't he born to the job?"

"Yes. He's a year older and better trained than I was when I began."

"Do you think he can really do it? It's so large."

"I know he can."

Maggie had to restrain herself from reaching across the table to take Henry's hand. It was an intimate gesture such as they never permitted themselves. Even the simple, human act of shaking hands was calculatedly cool.

"We both have reason to be proud." Her words were so natural, so assumptive that they were Will's parents, Henry accepted them as true as never before. "Does he have a serious girlfriend yet?"

"No. And I wish he did. Oh, he has girls, girls, girls. He calls them all 'doll.' And changes them the way he changes socks."

"He's a Don Juan?" Maggie was astonished.

"I do not pretend to understand Will. When he isn't scolding her, the only girl he treats with real affection is Liz. I've seen him break dates with very pretty girls just to take her to the movies."

"If she were his mother, I'd say he was becoming a mama's boy. But a sister's boy?" Maggie laughed uncomfortably. "I've never heard of that."

"I said I don't understand it."

"I don't either." It gave Maggie a good deal to think about on her flight back to California.

Several weeks later, Henry was sitting alone in the library at Carson House, his elbows on his desk and his face in his hands. During his dinner with Maggie he hadn't told her all his news. Now he knew why. For several months he'd been receiving feelers from the Johnson Administration regarding his availability for the post of Secretary of Commerce, and he'd given Washington reason to hope. It was only after the nomination had actually been offered that he was able to force himself to look at the realities governing the nomination. It would require Senate confirmation, and Francis Carson would fight his confirmation using the Placidium disaster as his weapon. His children would have to relive that horror; the Carson Company would be damaged; and in the end, Francis would win. He would not be confirmed. So he'd done what he had to do. Turned down the appointment.

Now a kaleidoscope of events passed before his eyes, stretching back almost thirty years. There was a thing called "original sin." It was true. Every single horror that had happened in his life could be traced back to the original sin of marrying Selma Wilkenson to acquire the Wilkenson patents, when he loved and should have married Maggie Rhodes. First Selma died giving birth. Then William, whom he loved even more than simply as a father, was murdered by Craig Spears, whose life had been ruined by the merger. Then he may or may not have killed Craig Spears. He would never really know. After that, he lost the woman he loved because of something he didn't understand. And in losing her, he lost his father for a second time. In large part because of his love for Maggie, he'd married Caterina, and while that marriage gave him another daughter, it cost Mary her life. That in turn drove Evelyn insane. So much tragedy brought about by an effort to obtain control of patents that in the end proved defective—patents that led to the births of a thousand deformed babies and the distress of several thousand parents. Finally, when he had a chance to serve his country as a cabinet minister, the same sin arose again to destroy the possibility. And as a final irony, his success in business would have been achieved without the Wilkenson patents. He hadn't needed them.

He considered the life he now lived that so much resembled the life William had led. Both lives were barren. He and his father were alike. He had a vision then which had never come to him before. For the first time he understood the central truth of William's existence. His father had been so much in love with his wife, he could never love again. He was the same way. He loved Maggie as he would never love another woman. William and he. So much alike.

Henry leaned back. A thought that could only be described as heresy struck him. Was his commitment to the Carson Company, and all the business success that went with it, worth the inner deprivation? Silence and emptiness seemed to symbolize his past. And as for the future, he felt as though the house, the world, were empty, and he was alone in a lifeless universe. There was only one thing he could do. He would not permit what happened to his father and himself to happen to Will. Will's commitment to the Carson Company must never interfere with his personal happiness, with his finding and loving a woman of his choice. Once it had seemed to Henry that the world offered a great deal over and beyond marriage. Now he could conceive of a love so strong, so fulfilling, that it would only broaden until it became the center of his life.

Will would have such a life full of tenderness and passion. The cycle of single-minded devotion to the Carson Company must be broken. That was all he knew, all he could do to make amends for the past.

# Chapter 38

THE USUAL White House leaks had informed Francis Carson of Henry's being considered for a cabinet post, and he'd prepared himself to fight the nomination exactly as Henry had expected him to. When the same sources let him know that at the last minute Henry had refused the nomination, Francis had been disappointed at the lost opportunity. However, there were several actions he could take regarding Henry Carson.

Francis rang for his legislative assistant. "Clark, set up a file on Henry Carson and the Carson Company. Inform the Library of Congress and the Senate clipping service I want a copy of everything in print and on radio or television that mentions either Henry Carson or the Carson Company."

"Do you want copies of their TV and newspaper adverstising?"

"No. There are government agencies monitoring the media. Ask Linda to get Dr. Maguire at the Food and Drug Administration, and when I'm finished, Mr. Ornstein at the Federal Trade Commission."

Francis waited for the call to be placed. "Hello, Dr. Maguire. This is Francis Carson . . . I'm well, and you? . . . Excellent. Dr. Maguire, my sources tell me the Carson Company is at it again. . . . No, not another Placidium. That would be too raw even for them. I'd suggest you take a second look at any of their new products you're currently testing. . . . Yes, I realize that could delay licensing for months, possibly years. . . . We don't want another Placidium, do we? . . . Right! . . . No thanks necessary. We all have a job to do. . . . Delighted to help. . . . Goodby."

The second call followed immediately. "Hello, Mr. Ornstein. This is Francis Carson. . . . I'm very well, thank you. And you? . . . Excellent. Mr. Ornstein, I caught a commercial last night on television. A cough drop. The Carson Company manufactures it. They're making some very strong product claims. . . . Yes, they made Placidium. Of course it's nothing like that. I'm merely suggesting you put a special watch on Carson Company newspaper and television advertising. . . .

Yes, the public must not be deceived. . . . No thanks necessary. We all have a job to do. Delighted to be of help. Goodby, sir."

Francis hung up the phone. Too bad Henry never took the company public. A call to the S.E.C. would have been next. For the moment he'd done what he could. From now on, two key federal agencies would be breathing down Henry's neck.

It was the spring of '67 and time to consider his future. Every step from now on must be judiciously planned. Stupidly, he had supported the open-ended Gulf of Tonkin Resolution. Having made that mistake, at least he'd had the sense to disassociate himself from Johnson's Vietnam position while still supporting the Great Society programs. However, the question was, What was really going on in Vietnam? The answer was bound to influence his immediate career decisions. None of the claims of success put out by the United States Military Command could be proved, and the war cost money. The Administration admitted to $800 million per month. As a member of the Armed Services Committee, Francis estimated the cost as over $2 billion per month. That meant huge government deficits, deficits which left very little money to implement the Great Society programs—and the people helped most by these programs made up the core of Francis' constituency.

He studied the private reports sent him from California's Democratic headquarters. After losing the race for governor of California Richard Nixon had retired from politics. Now he'd come out of retirement with a vengeance. He was campaigning around the country, stating that Johnson was probably "impaled" on the Vietnam war, and if so, extremely vulnerable in the 1968 election. Francis realized it all depended on what was happening in Vietnam. And there was only one way to find out the truth. Since he was a senator, a member of the Foreign Affairs Committee and still held the rank of major general in the Air Force Reserve, he could visit Vietnam and decide for himself.

Francis arrived in Vietnam to be heartily greeted by Ellsworth Bunker, the American ambassador. The briefing was detailed and highly optimistic. Bunker was optimistic. General Westmoreland was optimistic. But off-the-record talks with junior officers and reporters were far less optimistic. The undertrained, undermotivated, overequipped South Vietnamese and United States forces never lost a battle. They never won one either. When confronted, the Vietcong and North Vietnamese melted into the jungles, only to return after the South Vietnamese and U.S. forces left the area.

Francis spent the next three days on a helicopter gunship as part of the elite First Air Cavalry, taking part in the operations and sharing the daily personal risks. Although for his benefit the copter flew closer to the ground than regulations allowed, he saw neither a single member of the Vietcong nor a North Vietnamese soldier. The gunship bombed and strafed huge land areas, but no one knew if they hit anything or anyone. The bad joke was that "kill totals" were estimated by assuming so many deaths per bomb and so many deaths per minute of machine-gun fire.

When Francis was leaving Saigon, Ambassador Bunker was still optimistic. "Senator, I guess you can tell your constituency we have the lid on the kettle."

"Mr. Ambassador, we're getting our asses kicked in." Ellsworth Bunker looked shocked. Francis continued, "I have only one suggestion to make."

The ambassador was wary. "Hmmm. Yes, Senator?"

"We've lost the war. When the North Vietnamese are ready to attack, you'll find out how badly we've lost. Still, there is a way out."

Bunker smiled his gentle, New England patrician smile. "Yes?"

Francis smiled back at the ambassador—his elegant, aristocratic smile. "Gather all the U.S. troops around Saigon. Launch a huge sweep, say a radius of one hundred to one hundred and fifty miles. The V.C. and N.V.A. will vanish as usual, so casualties should be light."

"I don't understand, Senator."

"Try to, Mr. Ambassador. Once your sweep is complete, make a public announcement that you've cleared the area of V.C. and N.V.A. and won the war. That's crucial, sir. The announcement that we've won the war. Then put your men on every plane and ship available and get the hell out. Leave your equipment. We'll arrange a ticker-tape parade up Broadway in New York. When the Vietcong and North Vietnamese take over—and they will—it will be the South Vietnamese who turned the glorious victory we handed them into a crushing defeat. Good day, Mr. Ambassador."

Francis returned home convinced Johnson was "impaled" on Vietnam, and so, totally vulnerable. Francis stepped up his attacks. He spoke before many different groups comprising every segment of the United States: Martin Luther King's Southern Christian Leadership Conference, the League of Women Voters, the annual Governors' Convention, the C.I.O. Each group was given a speech that attacked the war, and that was tailored to show how the war harmed that particular group. Francis was all things to all people while he waited for the North Vietnamese to strike.

On January 31, 1968, they did. For the first time the Vietcong and North Vietnamese did not melt into the jungle. They attacked the South Vietnamese and U.S. troops in the cities and deltas. They fought and won and held territory. It became known as the Tet Offensive. Two days later, on February 2, Lyndon Johnson held a press conference pronouncing the Tet Offensive a failure. Television provided pictures that proved it was a huge success, and President Johnson appeared foolish and uninformed. Now the President faced the election even more weakened than Richard Nixon had foreseen.

Senator Francis Carson looked for a "stalking horse," someone to run against the President in the New Hampshire Democratic primary and prove he was vulnerable. Francis was on the verge of announcing his own candidacy when Eugene McCarthy, senator from Minnesota, challenged the President. Francis preferred this. He was not ready to campaign seriously for the presidency and disliked taking a position from which he knew he must later retreat. McCarthy took forty-two percent of the New Hampshire vote, and Francis watched his own man, waiting in the wings, grow restless.

Then events speeded up. In a dramatic television broadcast, President Lyndon Johnson announced that he was pulling back on bombing North Vietnam, and that he would not be a candidate for the presidency.

Within days Bobby Kennedy announced his candidacy. This was the man Francis had been waiting for, and he did everything possible to make himself available to Kennedy. When they stood together on campaign platforms, they complemented each other perfectly. Kennedy: average height, slim, longish dark hair that kept falling over his right eye, intense, brilliant. Francis: tall, powerful, shortish blond hair, handsome, deliberately less intense, equally brilliant. The Democratic Party leaders evaluated the two, Kennedy from New York and Carson from California. The two states with the most electoral votes. A promising combination.

The possibility of such a Democratic ticket prompted a call from Maggie Rhodes to Henry Carson. After their standard greetings, Maggie came to the point. "What do you think of Francis Carson as Vice President of the United States?"

"Is it possible?"

"According to my sources, if Bobby Kennedy is nominated Francis will be his running mate." There was a prolonged silence. "You did hear me? Francis may be our next vice president. Unless he's stopped."

"Can you come East? This is too important to discuss on the phone."

"I've booked an eight A.M. flight on United. I'll be at Kennedy Airport at four forty-five your time."

"My chauffeur, Robert, will meet you. You can stay at Carson House while we discuss Francis." Maggie hesitated just long enough for Henry to add, "It's a big house. You'll have your own suite. And you won't bump into Will. He and Liz are visiting John Junior in Cambridge."

A wave of emotion swept over Maggie at the prospect of spending the night under the same roof as Henry. She had many good reasons for wishing not to stay. Still, she would, for it would be accepting the pain of being close to him, and the pain would be proof to herself of the unselfishness of her motive in contacting Henry. "All right," she said. "Tell your chauffeur to wear a name plate."

By the time she arrived at Carson House, Maggie had the start of a plan. After dinner they closeted themselves in the library—Henry at his desk and Maggie at Will's. Before presenting her idea she reviewed Francis' prospects.

"You know how involved I am in California politics, so I speak with some authority when I say he has a real shot at the nomination."

"Why?"

Maggie understood the seriousness of Henry's question. It expressed the essence of what made Henry Henry. Francis had done him irreparable damage. Francis had conducted an obsessional vendetta against him. But Henry was not Francis. He did not believe in an eye for an eye. He truly believed vengeance was God's. To make any move to stop Francis from becoming vice president, he needed reasons independent of himself, reasons that concerned the nation's welfare.

"I'll simplify," she said. "His qualifications are almost too numerous. He was one of the first senators to oppose the Vietnam War. When George Meany placed the labor movement behind the war, Francis still spoke out against it, at the risk of losing organized labor, a large part of his political backing. Going further, Francis, in an election year, has called for higher taxes and a tighter control on the money supply to fight the inflation he sees coming." She spoke rapidly and rationally. "He also supported every effort to extend voting rights to blacks and other minorities through the Civil Rights Act and the Voting Rights Bill. He's fought job discrimination on the basis of sex, race, color, religion."

"He looks better and better." Henry's voice was dry.

"He fought to pass the Great Society programs: medical care for the aged under Social Security, special job training for minorities, federal aid to primary and secondary schools, creation of the Department of Housing and Urban Development to fight inner city slums."

"A truly remarkable senator."

"To the voter, it looks like he has great personal courage, stamina, intelligence—a true leader. And as a Democrat, I know he's a born winner."

"You've convinced me," Henry said. "Why then are you here to prevent his nomination?"

"I'm here because neither you nor I nor anyone, including Francis Carson, I think, knows what Francis really believes and where he really stands on any of the issues I've mentioned. We only know what he says and does. And that's not necessarily the same thing. Francis is incredibly astute. He may simply sense the public mood, put his fine mind to work, and then take a stand he believes will win him votes. There are only two facts about his nature that we do know—he is sadistic and destructive. These traits are well hidden, but when he chooses to exercise them, he can quite effectively destroy a human being." Her eyes held him. "Take Tony. During all the years I knew him, and eight years of married life, he was a debonaire, lazy playboy who drank too much. When he went to work for Francis in Washington, he became something else. In less than three years he deteriorated into a fat, vicious slob. In less than three years he was dead."

Then Maggie recounted Angel's experience. "Angel drinks too much. Has for years. But Angel wouldn't drink a full quart of gin at one sitting. That's suicidal, and she's not suicidal. Putting aside her accusation that Francis egged her on to suicide, the Dunne agency reported a lack of fingerprints on the bottle cap. Yet Angel's prints were all over the bottle. I think Francis opened the bottle for her and somehow goaded her into drinking herself to death."

"That's a serious accusation."

"This is a serious matter. I believe we're dealing with a highly deceptive, dangerous man. Add Tony and Angel to everything else we know about him and we must ask, Who is Francis Carson? Remember the sadism and destructiveness of his life in Rome. And the virulent attacks he has made on you. And what do we see? A terrifying personality buried within a great man. A man who is a chameleon. Who, when he chooses, can be humanistic, fearless and upright—a brilliant statesman. But what is this man when he is truly himself? An amoral sadist who has developed a taste for power and who, I believe, hates losing. So much so that I think if he were in Johnson's place now he would, without a blink, order the atomic bombing of Vietnam. He's neither afraid to die nor afraid to kill. Even millions."

Henry thought of their lifelong feud and how it started. It was true. Even as a child Francis could not accept defeat. He would go to any length to destroy opposition. "An acute analysis of Francis."

"I've watched him. Francis Carson would rather die than accept defeat. That quality made him a hero. That same quality can also make him a 'man on horseback,' a terror to the country. Given power, he'd think nothing of blowing up the world, if *not* blowing it up meant he would lose his power. The death of billions of people, his own death, none of it would mean a thing to him." She'd almost run out of breath. "Do we dare allow the survival of the entire earth to depend on the decisions of such a man?"

"How do we stop him?"

Maggie recognized that this situation gave her no right to be squeamish. She had come with a definite purpose, more than the simple longing to see Henry. But the secret hope she always carried with her suddenly showed itself, and a sense of her lifelong loneliness returned with redoubled force. She felt herself forever shut out from Henry's innermost self. To state her idea with all its complications was to intrude on his privacy. And she would be the intruder.

Henry understood her embarrassment, and his guarded look became one of understanding. "Suppose I make it easy for you. We have the same idea. Francis' life in Italy is his Achilles' heel." His voice showed no emotion. "I've a man standing by in Switzerland, Godfrey Moore. You met him here once."

Maggie had a glimpse of her past, of that other evening when she'd sat next to Henry at William's great formal party to introduce Selma Wilkenson. She could always relive that night in its minutest detail. "I know who you mean."

"Godfrey knows everyone. It's the life he leads. If anyone can get data on Francis, he can. He's waiting for my call to know if to proceed."

Henry picked up the phone. The conversation was promising. Moore had friends in Rome. In a few weeks he'd be back to Henry with a progress report.

Maggie left the next day for Los Angeles to await results.

# Chapter 39

THE WARMTH of seeing Henry remained with Maggie even after reaching home. One morning she woke up with the thought, I'm only fifty-one, and then shook her head. It was too late for such summer dreams, but surely not for a quiet harvest of friendship, of comradeship.

As for Henry, the time Maggie spent in Carson House had not been easy. He'd had to deal with all the regrets and stifled memories of an inarticulate lifetime. But at least he felt an iron band removed from his heart. He felt they were joined in a higher purpose about which he need not feel guilty. And then there was the blessed fact of her nearness.

Maggie waited, and the longer she waited the more tense she grew. It became apparent that unless Francis Carson was stopped in his tracks, he would be the Democratic candidate for vice president. The Democratic primaries were six weeks away. Then her private line rang. It was Henry.

"I've news . . ." Henry sounded like a man who'd caught a glimpse of hell. "Godfrey just left. I have what we need."

"Moore made a personal delivery? . . ." She stopped. Of course. The material was so loaded he could not trust the mails. "Francis is campaigning in California for Bobby. Come to the Coast. We must see Francis now."

"In a week. I have family business to attend to."

"We're almost out of time."

"I can't leave yet." His tone was weary and adamant.

"All right. Let me know your flight. I'll meet you at the airport. You can stay here at Bienvenido. There's a spacious guest suite." She desperately wanted him to stay at her house. "Henry . . ." She started to ask about the material and stopped. "Nothing."

"You want to know what Godfrey brought? You'll see."

Henry arrived in six days. Maggie met him as planned, and they drove to Malibu in silence. After they made the last turn on the twisting driveway, Henry saw the house, and his first words were, "It's as beautiful as the pictures."

"You've seen the magazines?"

"Of course. It's been featured in *Architectural Forum*, *House Beautiful*, *Architectural Digest*. It's even better in reality."

Maggie braked to a stop in front of the main entrance. A servant was waiting. "Juan, this is Mr. Carson. Show him to the guest suite." She said to Henry, "I'll wait for you in my office. Juan will show you the way."

Within a few minutes there was a knock on Maggie's door. "Come in." Henry was carrying his attaché case. "Sit down." She gestured to a chair next to her desk and waited.

Henry opened his attaché case and removed two large brown envelopes. He handed one to Maggie. "Do you read Italian?"

"It's close enough to Spanish so I'll get the drift." There was a series of affidavits, signed and notarized by someone at the American embassy in Rome. As near as she could make out, all the affidavits stated that between 1946 and 1952, with a few dates between 1958 and 1962, Francis took part in orgies at his private amphitheater—orgies during which he had sexual intercourse with boys and girls and distributed to guests, as well as used himself, drugs including opium, cocaine and hashish. Each affidavit had a second paper attached to it on which were listed numbered exhibits. She handed them back to Henry and waited. There had to be more. These were accusations by Italians living in Rome. Francis would deny everything. Henry handed her the second envelope. As he extended his hand, the bones on the back of his knuckles stood out as though they would break through his skin. His fingers seemed paralyzed, unable to open, unable to release the envelope. Finally, by some great internal effort of will, he dropped the envelope on Maggie's desk.

Maggie opened it carefully. Inside were a number of pictures, each pasted to an 8 1/2 x 11" piece of white paper. The sheets were marked Exhibit 1, Exhibit 2, and so forth. Having picked up Henry's struggle, it took Maggie a few moments to focus on the pictures. Then she turned white, red and white again. Maggie was hardly an innocent. She'd seen enough hardcore pornography in her life for the pictures alone not to shock her. But these pictures were insane. They featured Francis and her. She had to take hold of herself to accept it wasn't her. It was Caterina. Caterina and Francis. Caterina and Francis and another woman. Caterina and Francis and another boy. Two boys. Two girls. Many variations. The pictures showed Francis in every conceivable sexual act with boys, girls and Caterina. Always Caterina. Then there were pictures of Francis whipping Caterina, who was either tied to a post or spread-eagle on a table. Maggie so completely identified she could almost feel the terror Caterina was feeling.

Halfway through the pictures, Maggie stopped looking. This was a woman Henry had loved and married. The mother of his daughter. She tried not to imagine what Henry felt.

Henry broke their silence. "Godfrey found her at Francis' villa, almost dead, her body wrecked by drugs. She weighed eighty pounds. Caterina told him who to see to get the affidavits. She gave him the pictures. The only ones Francis hadn't burnt. He never knew she had her own collection. She prayed someday they would have a use." Maggie tried not to flinch. "For the past sixteen years Francis kept her supplied with drugs, but he permitted no treatment. She died two days after giving Godfrey the pictures." His control wavered. "I'm late because I had to arrange for her body to be flown here and buried in the Carson plot."

"Does Elizabeth know?"

"No. I'll tell her her mother died in Italy, and I had her buried here. I'll think what else to say later."

As Maggie listened to him, her pity quickened. She could feel his shame, sorrow, anger and frustration. She longed to reach out to him, but she knew that such expressions were forbidden. There was a sudden returning memory of their last night in her apartment, and she felt as close to him as she had felt then. She knew exactly what he felt, as thought they were one person, emotionally. She wanted to hold him in her arms, against her breasts, and by her love to draw the pain from him through her body. But she could do nothing. Action of any sort, the right as well as the wrong—if the difference existed—was not possible. Any false move might break him. Her wisdom reduced itself to being quiet, to creating minimum vibration.

And it proved to be enough for Henry, giving him back his purpose— they were working together for what they must do. Finally he was able to ask, "Where is Francis?"

Maggie hesitated before answering. The cold breath of her fear, a sharp ugly view of what Henry might do to Francis on meeting him, stopped her. Yet the identity of spirit they shared was now so complete, he understood her unspoken concern. "Don't worry. I won't touch him. Trust me."

"He's in his house in Santa Monica."

"Dunne?" Maggie nodded. "It's seven o'clock. Call him, Maggie. Tell him you want to see him tomorrow morning. Don't mention me."

Maggie made the call. "Francis, Maggie here. . . . Well, thank you.

And you? . . . Francis, something's come up. I'm going to L.A. to-morrow. Could we meet on my way in at your place? In the morning? . . . Ten-thirty it is. See you. Bye."

"I could use a strong drink. Do you have any Scotch around?" Henry asked.

"Gallons. I'll join you."

Francis sat in his study sipping white wine and soda, reading a letter from Rome. Caterina was dead. But instead of being buried in the Orsini vault, the American embassy had claimed her body and shipped it some-where. Clearly America. Francis dropped the letter on his desk. He had never liked or trusted coincidence. Caterina's death, her body being claimed by an American and now Maggie's call reeked of coincidence. His mind made a quick connection. Where was Henry? The answer to that question would tie things together.

It was ten-thirty on the East Coast. Information gave him the num-ber of Carson House, and he dialed directly.

"Carson House."

It was an old man's voice. Oscar Sorenson? "Henry Carson, please."

"I'm sorry, Mr. Carson is on a short business trip. Who's calling?"

On impulse he said, "Francis Carson," and was rewarded by an audible gasp. "No message, Oscar. Thank you." He hung up. Henry would be with Maggie tomorrow. What were they planning? He'd know soon enough.

The drive from Malibu to Santa Monica was short and, for once, free of traffic snarls. When Maggie drove into the combination driveway and parking area in front of Francis' house, they were ten minutes early.

"Come," Henry said. "We're early. But Francis is waiting."

As they approached the front door, it was opened. Francis was indeed waiting. "Maggie, how pleasant. And Henry. Should I be surprised?"

Standing there in a pair of slacks and a tennis shirt, Francis appeared thoroughly at ease, but Henry, knowing better, replied, "No. But I'm sure Oscar was."

"Did he call you or did you guess?"

"I guessed. You did what I would have done."

"Come in. Would you like to tell me why you're here?"

Watching the two men together, Maggie felt the futility of it all. What she and Henry had come to do was indeed harsh. It came down to the essence of tragedy—a tragedy for Francis and perhaps for the nation. But the risk was too great. There was something sinister, something evil in Francis Carson that might appear at any time. It was something only they knew, and that knowing made them completely responsible.

"There's not much to tell," Henry said. "More to show you."

"Why don't we go into my study? Follow me, please." Francis motioned to two chairs and settled himself behind his desk.

Henry unlocked his attaché case and handed Francis the first of the envelopes, the one with the affidavits. Francis skimmed them rapidly. Maggie studied his face for a change of expression. A small smile appeared—possibly at memories, possibly at the current situation.

"Of course I'll deny everything. Your affidavits are not from the most creditable sources. No major newspaper, magazine or telecaster will touch them. A scandal sheet might." Henry ignored this and handed him the second envelope.

Maggie observed both men patiently, intensely. This was the first time in decades she'd seen them together, stripped of their corporate and political roles. Now she noticed that, next to Henry, Francis seemed slimmer, elegant, more as she remembered William. What a waste! What a dreadful waste! Francis studied the pictures without any reaction. How could he look at those pictures and not react?

Francis scanned each one briefly and then placed it face down on his desk, keeping them in the same order as he'd been given them. Henry's legs were crossed, his hands quiet on his lap. The small smile on Francis' face remained fixed. Then Francis combined the pictures with the appropriate affidavits and reviewed the entire package. There was silence in the room. It seemed to Maggie the only sound she heard was her own breathing. When Francis finished he handed the package back to Henry.

"Would you mind telling me how you obtained those pictures?"

"Caterina gave them to a friend of mine. They were what was left of a larger collection. The photographers always gave her prints of anything involving her. She said you never knew."

"Quite so. Would I have let her keep them if I'd known? There's a moral in all this. Had I followed my usual practice, after Caterina betrayed me with you, I'd have thrown her out to die in the gutters of Rome." Momentarily he frowned in self-disgust. "I'd have found and burned the pictures, and we three would not be sitting here this beautiful spring morning." He moistened his lips. "There are copies of these?"

"With two lawyers, my banker and a fourth person. They have no idea of the contents of their envelopes. But if I do not contact them at regular intervals, they have instructions to open the envelopes and distribute the contents to interested parties."

"Newspapers, radio and television."

"And the political leaders of both parties. Plus the Senate majority and minority leaders."

"Let me think. Have you missed anyone? No." He folded his arms across his chest. "All right, you're here to make a deal. What is it?"

"First, under no circumstances can you accept the nomination for Vice President of the United States. Second, your term as a senator has four years to run. You can serve out your term, but you cannot run for re-election in 1972."

"I'm being retired from politics." Francis stood up and walked to the French doors. He opened them and stood very still, looking up at the sky. Then he turned and stared at Henry. "Why? Why have you stopped with my career, Henry?"

"It's enough for me. It protects our country from you."

"It would not be enough for me. If our positions had been reversed, I would have ruined you entirely. You would not have been able to show your face without people staring and children throwing stones at you."

"I think you'll have enough trouble living with yourself."

"I would have made absolutely sure that you had no life to live."

"We're different."

"We are. Is there anything for me to sign?"

"No. Would you like to keep the package?"

For an instant Maggie thought Francis' composure might crack. "No. I need no reminders of my stupidity. Allow me to show you out." He led them to the door. "Goodby, Maggie. Henry, I don't know why I keep underestimating you. It's been that way since we were children."

The drive back to Malibu was not a victory celebration. In retrospect, Maggie realized it was more like a funeral. They had buried a rare man who, but for a twist in his nature, a twist he himself didn't understand, could have been one of the nation's greatest leaders.

When Robert Kennedy was assassinated on June 5, Francis watched the event on television, feeling he had already died. He used the uproar that followed to make a quiet announcement. He was retiring immediately from the Senate. Reasons of health were given. He saw no sense in postponing the end of his political career. That part of his life was over forever. He would return to Europe and North Africa to resume the life he had given up in 1954, fourteen years earlier.

# Chapter 40

**H**ENRY paused before opening the door to his office. With the exception of vacations and occasional days sick, this was the first day in his twenty-nine years at the Carson Company that Mary O'Toole wouldn't be waiting for him. She had retired. It wasn't age; it was arthritis. At seventy Mary was as spry and alert as ever. The disease had finally made typing and taking dictation too painful. Henry offered her a number of positions which didn't require typing or dictation, but after thinking about them, Mary refused. She was an excutive secretary, and if she no longer could function as one, she'd rather resign.

Mary stayed until a satisfactory successor was found. Friday, August 29, 1969, was not a happy day for her. She had been with the company fifty-two years, the last forty as excutive secretary, first to William Carson and then Henry Carson, and her departure was painful—for Mary and other long-time employees. It made Henry aware that although he was fifty-four, his time too at the Carson Company was limited. Will was almost twenty-nine. In ten years at most, no matter how he felt, Henry must step aside and allow Will his rightful place. To stay any longer could blunt Will's ambition and nerve.

Finally Henry shrugged off the feeling of awkwardness and opened the door to meet Mary's successor, a younger version of Mary—the same light voice, brown hair smoothed down, conservative dress and neatly-manicured hands with short nails.

"Would you like me to bring you your coffee, Mr. Carson?"

"Please. My usual cream and sugar. Has Will arrived?"

"Not yet, sir. He called saying the traffic was heavy."

Henry began going through his mail. The bulk was routine, and he made his usual separations: discard, file, hold for reply. There was one exception. A letter marked Personal and Confidential was mixed into the pile.

He opened the envelope and read the short note with puzzlement. John Hillyer, Jr., was apologizing for canceling the week he was to spend

487

with them at the end of the month. Furthermore, he would not be able to spend any time with them for a year or so. He must finish his book as rapidly as possible. His publisher was pressing him for its completion. Henry neither understood nor believed what John had written. Why the formal note? John was like a member of the family. Why not a phone call? Curious, Henry examined Will's mail. There was another envelope marked Personal and Confidential and postmarked Cambridge, Massachusetts. When Will arrived, they would decide what they should do, if anything.

By the time Will burst in, Henry was on his second cup of coffee. "Sorry I'm late. The Triboro traffic was a mess. Robert Moses is right— a bridge from Oyster Bay to Connecticut would cut traffic in and out of New York."

"And get you to East Hampton faster." Henry grinned. "Where's Liz?"

"Heading home. She dropped me off on the way. Say, you okay?"

"I'm fine. Look at the letter on the top of your pile."

Will scanned the letter, his face repeating the puzzlement Henry had shown. "I take it you didn't expect it either. What does he mean his publishers are pressing him? This isn't hot journalism. It's a scholarly work on economics and sociology. Five years would make no difference."

"The answer is it makes a difference to John," was Henry's reply. "The last time we saw him was over Memorial Day weekend, and he said nothing about the book."

Will was groping in a maze of questions. "Suppose I call him now and ask him to visit us next weekend. Saturday afternoon to Sunday evening won't take that much from his work."

Will made the call, and John's response showed he'd been expecting it and was prepared to say no to whatever Will suggested. "But it'll only be for a day. . . . Everyone needs a break now and then. . . . Why on earth didn't you call me? . . . You didn't want to argue . . . that's no excuse. Liz wants to know when you're coming down. She starts at Barnard in three weeks. . . . I'll tell her no such thing! You tell her yourself. . . . John, if you won't come here, I'll fly up Saturday and we'll— What?" Will's voice dropped. "All right. I'll climb off your back. Sorry. . . . Okay. If you change your mind, call. Bye." Will hung up the phone, a helpless, baffled look on his face.

"I gather he won't visit us or let you visit him."

"Right. He insists he needs an uninterrupted year. You, me, Liz— we're *persona non grata*." Will paused a moment, thinking. "And we can't call his family for news. He'd be pissed!" Henry's expression agreed, and Will made a face. "Damn it! I don't understand."

Neither did Henry, but he was starting to be afraid to understand. He couldn't admit it, because that would mean admitting a great deal more. "Let's forget it for now. Go over your mail. Then I want to review the marketing reports for the disposable sterile syringes and the whole group of new disposables you're introducing this fall."

Summer drifted into fall. In spite of a private probe Henry sent out through his scientists to M.I.T., no information was forthcoming. The winds blew, the leaves fell, Thanksgiving came and went, and no word from John. Then came Christmas and New Year's, the ice and snow, and still no word from John. It became increasingly difficult for Henry to prevent Will and Elizabeth from barging in on John. It wasn't that Henry wasn't concerned. He was very concerned. The mystery of John's self-imposed isolation was perfectly understandable, but only on the basis of the sharpest of reasons. So it was not simply a matter of respecting the wishes of another person no matter how strongly you disliked it. It was also knowing what you feared and why. They must wait until John was ready to get in touch with them. Will accepted his father's dictum with a fair, actually an excessive imitation of patience, remarking only that having and keeping a close friend could be a ball buster.

Just after Easter, John broke his silence with a phone call to the Carson family at home. All three Carsons got on different extensions. They all noticed the same thing at once. John sounded strange—weak, exhausted and at the same time elated.

"I've done it. I finished the book. The publisher is very enthusiastic." For a moment his enthusiasm banished all strangeness and carried his listeners with him.

Will's reaction was instantaneous. "Wonderful! When will you be here?"

Henry listened as John became evasive. "I still have things to clear up. In about a month you'll have me camping on your doorstep."

"Why don't we visit you?" Elizabeth wasn't happy waiting a month.

"No. I've still things to clean up. When I'm done, you'll see me."

"About time." Will tried not to show his anxiety over the exhaustion he heard in John's voice. "Give us a date, man."

Henry interrupted. He'd heard the same fatigue Will heard and didn't want John badgered. "Then we'll see you in a month? More or less."

"More or less."

"Fine, John. Thank you for calling. We've been concerned."

"Right, sir. Take care, Will, Liz. See you soon." He hung up.

The Carson family gathered in the library. Now it was out in the open for Will and Liz to talk about, and Henry to listen. Nothing had been changed by John's call. And nothing could be done about it. Like it or not, they still had to respect his wish for privacy.

The time passed. April became May and then June. Still not another word from John. Without telling her father or brother, Elizabeth tried to reach him. The operator said the line had been disconnected. A letter to his address was returned marked "Address Changed. Unable to Forward."

When she told Henry and Will, Elizabeth was even more alarmed by the fact that her father didn't reprimand her for breaking their agreed-upon discretion. Henry only listened, and though he said nothing, the moment had come for him to find out the truth. The first thing he did was call John Hillyer, Sr.

"John, Henry Carson here."

"Hello, Henry." John sounded so bleak, Henry hated to go on.

"I don't want to pry into family business, John, but what's going on with your son?"

"You've talked to him?"

"Twice in a year. Now his phone's disconnected and mail's returned. Do you know what's happening?"

"Yes, Henry. We know."

"Can you tell me?"

"I promised John I would tell no one. Especially the Carsons."

"How sick is he, John?" Henry had waited a year to ask that question.

"Very. Don't press me. And please don't tell Will or Liz."

"I promise. When can you give me further information?"

"By midsummer. Did John tell you the M.I.T. press is rushing his book through? It should be out in August."

"Four months. That is fast. Remember, John, we love him too."

"I know. I'll keep you informed."

Having given his word, Henry could do nothing to ease Will and Elizabeth's anxiety. He gave them a glib report of his conversation with Hillyer, Sr. They pretended to believe him, but it added to their concern. Something was very wrong. Their father didn't lie easily.

John, Jr.'s book was published in August. It received a front-page review in the *New York Times Book Review* and a major review in the

*New York Review of Books.* The *Atlantic Monthly* devoted an entire issue to the theme, with comments by prominent economists and sociologists. Even the mass market magazines, *Time* and *Newsweek*, featured the book. What John had done was a massive socio-economic study of the origins of two systems of government, capitalism and socialism. He showed how capitalism was linked to an "economy of scarcity" and the "patriarchy," while socialism could thrive only in an "economy of plenty" and then the "matriarchy" would prevail. The thesis was highly controversial, and the book regarded as a seminal work from a new and original thinker.

On Tuesday, September 8, 1970, almost one year after John told them about his book, Will was alone in his office when Jane buzzed him.

"Mr. Carson, there's a man downstairs who insists upon seeing you. Walter says he has no appointment." Jane looked at her pad. "He says his name is John Hillyer."

"John!" Will tried to temper his excitement. "Junior or senior?"

"I don't know."

"Okay. I don't care. Send him up. Find out while he's on his way."

Jane buzzed him shortly. "It's John Hillyer, Junior."

"Hold all my calls. No! First call Mr. Carson—he's at the labs—and tell him John, Junior's here. Then leave us alone."

"Yes, sir." Jane left. She had never seen Mr. Carson so agitated. Who was this John Hillyer, Jr., to cause such commotion? She decided to meet him at the elevator. She hurried out of the office and saw a tall, thin man walking slowly toward her. "Mr. Hillyer?"

"Yes."

"I'm Mr. Carson's secretary. I thought I'd show you the way."

She opened the door for him and hurried ahead to open the heavy inner door. He looked frail, he might not be able to push it.

"Thank you."

As Jane closed the door, she heard the stranger say, "Hello, Will," and the response, "John, what the hell . . ." Then the door closed and Jane went to her desk to let Mr. Carson know John Hillyer, Jr., had arrived.

Will stared at John. Though he tried not to show shock, it was apparent. John had lost pounds of weight. His skin was white, and much of his hair had fallen out. What was left was lifeless and hung limply in patches around his head. His large bone structure stood out like a skeleton. Only his lips and eyes retained color, and they stood out against his pallor in startling contrast.

"May I sit down, Will? Standing gets harder every day."

"My God! Let me help you."

"It's not that bad yet. That's why I wanted to see you now."

Will sat facing his friend. "What's wrong, John?" He didn't want to be told.

"Leukemia." He struggled for an instant, then went on with a small wave of energy. "But I cheated them. They gave me three months, and I've lived a year. And I wrote my book. I actually finished it, and it's good."

"I've been reading it. It's damn good. But how, John? When?"

"How? Who knows how? Maybe someday someone working for the Carson Company will understand and be able to prevent it. I felt tired about a year ago and went for a checkup at Mass. General. They said leukemia and gave me three months. That's why I couldn't see you. Or Elizabeth. The only breaks I took were for treatment at the hospital."

"How are they going? What do they say?"

John shrugged. "They've done what they could. I'm not counting the time in days yet, but it's not months either. A few weeks, I think."

"John!"

There was a shadow of John's old grin. "Ain't it a bitch?" Then his smile faded. "Don't laugh. I don't want to see Liz looking like this. So don't tell her. Not yet."

"I've already called my father."

"It's all right. He knows. He guessed months ago I was sick."

Will had known his father knew more than he'd said and now admitted to himself that in the last months he'd steadily avoided pressing him. "How long has he known?"

"Since June. Don't mind, Will. He doesn't know how sick I am, and my father made him promise not to tell you."

"I knew he knew something. I should have made him tell me."

"I'm glad you didn't. What could you have done? And I wanted to spare you as long as possible."

"I don't want to be spared." Will's words were a cry of protest against what life had done to his friend and against his own fear that had prevented him from sharing John's anguish. If he couldn't share the physical torment of the disease, he should at least have shared the mental agony.

Gentle as always, John reminded him of a fact. "Will, the choice was mine. And I chose not to tell you."

As if for the first time in his life, Will saw John whole, saw how the conditions of his nature had their own necessities and were different from his own. He saw the ways of life as a tangle designed of joy and grief; it was not given to any man to command or control them. The best he could do now was accept John's reality as John saw it. "All right. Now what can I do to help?"

"Nothing. I go home from here. In two weeks I'll enter Sloan-Kettering. Then, depending on my strength, we'll see how long I stick around. I'll call you after I sign in, and then you can tell Liz. You can visit me too, if you want to." He braced himself and stood up.

"Oh, John." Will hugged his friend.

"Easy, Will. I'm fragile. Therapy and radiation do rotten things." Will dropped his arms. "Look. Don't weep too hard for me. Very few people ever accomplish what they want to in life. I've done better than most." He saw Will make a motion to walk with him. "No. Stay here. I know the way out."

Will stood in the middle of the room and watched his friend cross the carpet to the door, brace himself again, open the door and disappear. September 7, 1970, marked a dividing line in Will's existence. That morning Will Carson grew up. Later on he would think of his youth as the time when he thought a grown man didn't cry. Once the door was shut, Will sank to the floor, his head against his knees, and sobbed.

Maggie was in her office comparing the August reports of work done by the various contractors with the monthly progress payments from the Bank of America and the Morgan Bank. The work was on schedule. A large tract of houses and a shopping mall were completed, and construction of the factories and office buildings was nearly finished. Each house in the tract was sold, and most of the factory space and all the office space rented. Mission Nuevo was going to be a success, as big a success as she'd hoped for. She was interrupted by a phone call.

"May I speak to Miss Rhodes, please?" The voice was vaguely familiar.

"This is Maggie Rhodes. Who's calling?"

"John Hillyer."

"John!" This was not John's usual booming telephone voice, so loud she often held the receiver away from her ear. "John? How are you?"

"Not so well. It's our son, John, Junior."

"His book is brilliant. You must be so proud."

"We are. Maggie, can you come East tomorrow?"

"What's wrong?"

"He died this morning."

"Oh, my God! What happened?"

"Leukemia. Ellen and I have known for a year."

"What can I say?"

"Nothing. The funeral is the day after tomorrow. I must talk to you." Maggie knew what was coming. "We've lost John. Will's my other son. I want him."

"Does Ellen know?"

"I'll tell her. She'll understand."

"John, please wait. After the funeral we'll talk."

"Henry and Will and Liz will be here. You can come with them. The funeral will be on Fisher's Island. The Hillyers have been buried there for one hundred and fifty years. You'll come, Maggie, won't you?"

"I'll be there."

Maggie hung up. John, Jr., was dead. She'd only seen pictures of him. Still, she could identify with John's grief. Suppose it had been Will? Will! Now John wanted to replace the lost John with Will. That mustn't happen. Will Carson must remain a Carson. Anything else would make a mockery of all their lives: Will's, Henry's, hers. She studied her appointment book. Six months ago Angel had committed herself to a sanitarium for alcoholics. She was due out in two days and expected to spend months at Bienvenido. Now Maggie wouldn't be here to greet her. With Will's future at stake, she must fly East. She called Angel.

"Honey, I've a problem. John Hillyer's son—you've seen Hillyer's name on company reports—is dead. I must fly East for the funeral tomorrow."

Angel grew frightened. "When will you be back? I need you."

"The funeral's the twenty-sixth. I'll try for the twenty-seventh. The twenty-eighth the latest. Your suite is set up. I'll be gone only a day or two."

"I'll be fine." She heard Angel making an effort to accept the situation. "I'll see you on the twenty-eighth."

Maggie's next call was to Henry. She tried to explain John Hillyer's motives in wanting her at the funeral as due to their long legal association on Mission Nuevo. Maggie knew Henry wasn't convinced, but she had to leave it at that. Unless she was successful with John, Henry would know John's reason soon enough. Meanwhile, she would spend the night at Carson House and helicopter to Fisher's Island with Will and Elizabeth.

\*   \*   \*

The funeral was even more grim than her worst fears. A young man, with much to offer the world, the only child of the Hillyers, the best friend of Will and Elizabeth had died a senseless death. Even nature acknowledged the loss. The fringes of a September hurricane brushed Fisher's Island threatening to make a miserable day worse.

Before John shoveled the first bit of sand on the grave, Elizabeth tossed a small toy dog at the foot of the coffin. John was a voyager into unknown parts, a Viking, deserving a Viking's funeral. Maggie waited, standing off a bit from the family, and after John placed the shovel in the sand, he approached her.

"I'm sorry to have dragged you here, Maggie. I've wasted your time." She studied the tall man with thin, gray hair, almost all the red gone. Though in his early sixties he looked fifteen years older. "I couldn't tell Ellen. She doesn't want another son. She wants John, and I can't give her another John."

"Nobody can. It's wiser not to try."

"I suppose so. In any case, Will remains a Carson."

Henry, Will, Elizabeth and Maggie hurried from the funeral to the helicopter. The weather was worsening, and they didn't want to get stuck on the island. Also, the Hillyers needed to be together alone, to accept, if not be reconciled to, John's death. When the helicopter landed in Stamford, the wind was beginning to let up. Henry had a suggestion.

"The rain should stop in an hour. Instead of driving through it to Carson House, let's stop at a good restaurant I know of on Route Seven and have dinner. It's late, Maggie. You can take a plane tomorrow morning."

Maggie's reservation was for the next day. She had been prepared to stay over and fight it out with John. But now something else had caught her attention, and it gave her just as strong an incentive for staying. When Will and Elizabeth weren't quietly depressed, they were at each other's throats. Maggie didn't like what she was seeing.

Even at the restaurant they never let up their quarrel. They were constantly and bitterly sniping at one another. Elizabeth had been gracious with her, but every time Will showed the same courtesy, his sister bristled with irritation. It was as though he must not pay attention to any woman but her. At the same time, it was impossible for them to have an easy, civilized conversation. They quibbled and criticized and argued continually over nothing. Liz sounded like a teacher reproving a schoolboy. Will's tie was the wrong color for his shirt. And why did he take so long with the menu when he always ordered steak? And why no scampi? Then, seeing Will's face, Liz was sorry for what she'd said. But Will was hurt and retaliated in kind. Why did Elizabeth choose to wear stockings with a run? And why did she keep losing gloves, pens and umbrellas? Liz became extremely ladylike. Will was punctual only at the Carson Company. She or anyone else could wait and wait. Will then observed that though mathematically gifted, she couldn't balance her checkbook. Which provoked Liz to remark that he didn't mind that someone named Felice couldn't balance a checkbook, that he allowed Felice to order him around, bully him and take advantage of him as if he were a child. Which caused Will to state that the clown, Gregory, she wasted her time with could only read by moving his lips. Maybe she enjoyed feeling superior? At which point Liz started to cry, and, immediately contrite, Will begged forgiveness. The quarrel ended by their making up and agreeing to spend all the evenings for the next week together—no Felice, no Gregory. They'd talk about John. Then they excused themselves and hurried to the pay phones to break all current dates.

Watching them go, Maggie realized that their continual bickering was a way of defending themselves against their own deep feelings for each other. Now alone with Henry, she asked, "Is this their usual routine? Or is it John's death?"

"Both. John stood between them like a lightning rod, even when he wasn't around. They've always been close. As children, I was glad. Some brothers and sisters hate each other, need I say, but Will was always protective of Liz. And she took his words as gospel. Now that they're older, I'm not sure I handled them properly. They're too close. The fighting and teasing is continual, and always ends the same way. They make up, close ranks and shut out the world. Except John. Now there's no John."

As he spoke, Henry felt acute concern. Not one to evade facts, he recognized that his two children, half brother and sister, were far too committed to each other. It wasn't healthy, and if it wasn't checked, there was no telling where it might lead. Knowing them, he didn't believe their emotional ties would ever be translated into a destructive sexual relationship. What was more likely was their choosing to live lives devoid of intimacy with anyone but each other. A series of meaningless affairs, sexuality without tenderness, a parallel of both his and William's arid existences. What could he do? Was it his place to bring it out in the open? With John dead, he knew he would be grappling more and more with this question.

Maggie had retreated into a corner of the booth, struggling with her own emotions. This was the first time she'd seen Will since the nurse had taken him from her at the hospital. All her long-suppressed desires for a child, for children, were crying for recognition. She'd known this was going to happen, and up until now she'd been able to master any unseemly show of love for her son. She had even been prepared to leave for the Coast as planned, knowing that, with the passage of time, what was now so agonizingly alive would retreat into its accustomed place in her heart where it would remain dormant, next to her love for Henry.

However, it was not that simple. This was something she hadn't counted on—Will and Elizabeth falling in love. It was a fact that she must now include in her thinking. The situation had changed. It made a hash of all her plans for Will's future, a mockery of all her years of sacrifice. If Henry knew Will was not a Carson, would he forget twenty-nine years of living together, of watching a baby grow into a boy, into a young man and finally a man? He'd boasted of Will Carson's brilliance. Would he feel the same about Will, fathered by John Hillyer? She didn't know. And would Will thank her for the truth? If he gained Elizabeth but lost the Carson Company? Henry had traded his personal happiness for the company. Was Will like his father? That Henry wasn't his natural father begged the question. He was his father in terms of Will's life experiences and Will's commitment to the Carson Company. She was completely unprepared for any of these questions and moved back from them like an open chasm. If she did nothing, she wouldn't be judged, save by herself, which was her own wretched business.

Will and Elizabeth returned to the table, holding hands. It was apparent at once that they were now at peace with each other, all rivals having been disposed of. With John's death as an excuse, they were able to plan a week together without any guilt.

Seeing them together, Maggie realized they were strongly drawn to one another; she should no longer sit back and take no action. She grew angry at her cowardice. She must accept the unthinkable, that Henry would disinherit Will. It was a genuine possibility. She could not allow Will and Elizabeth to live the lives she and Henry had lived. The cycle of devotion to the Carson Company at the sacrifice of personal happiness had to be broken. Also, Will was her son, and heir to Mission Nuevo. It was an inheritance worth having.

During the drive back to Carson House, Maggie took her measure of Henry and decided the sooner he knew the truth the better. She even knew where she would tell him the truth.

Once they arrived at Carson House, the emotionally exhausted Will and Elizabeth went straight to their rooms, leaving Maggie and Henry alone in the library.

"Remember the restaurant in Tarrytown where we first lunched?"

"Of course. I eat there regularly."

"I was sure it still existed. Could you meet me there for lunch tomorrow? I'll take a later plane."

Henry had been aware of something troubling Maggie on the entire drive home. This was no casual request. "Of course. Shall I call for you here?"

"No. Lend me a car. I'll meet you there."

"I'll arrange for the Chevy. What time?"

"Early as possible. What I want to talk about may take a while."

"Noon. I'll clear my schedule so we can take as long as necessary." He had the impression that she was afraid of further conversation. When she saw he would not ask questions, her relief was apparent. "I look forward to our lunch," was all he said.

Although Maggie woke early, she lingered in her room to give Will and Henry time to leave for the office and Elizabeth for Barnard. In the lonely hours of the night her mind had swarmed with images of what good or harm would result from her determination to talk to Henry. Yet she could see no way out. The thing had to be done. The reasons which had forced her still existed.

By the time she'd bathed and dressed and breakfasted, it was almost nine-thirty. Since she still had plenty of time to get to Tarrytown, she stopped at the small cemetery next to the church in Pleasantville. Now there were four graves. In addition to Nathalia, William and Mary, Caterina Orsini Carson was buried there. This time Maggie had prepared and brought with her four dozen roses. One dozen for each grave.

After arranging the flowers as best as she could, Maggie sat again on the stone beach alone with her heart, yielding to her doubts and fears. At moments she held her breath, praying for guidance. It was then she glanced at the new grave: Caterina Orsini Carson, 1927–1968. It spoke of a life impossibly hard and bleak. And wasn't Henry's marriage to her living proof of the results of ignoring the demands of the heart? She remembered the pictures she'd seen of Caterina and Francis, and her hesitation crumbled. Love, marriage, children were the very essence of life, and Will should have the freedom to choose. It was more important than the Carson Company, than Mission Nuevo.

Maggie made two wrong turns on her way to the Tarrytown restaurant and was five minutes late. Henry was sitting, sipping a martini and looking out the window at the Hudson. It was the same table they'd sat at a lifetime ago. She composed herself to enter the room. "Henry?"

"What!" He'd been so lost in thought, she startled him. "Maggie. I've ordered you a martini. Is that all right?"

"Fine. I've learned to drink since we were last here."

She sat down, following Henry's eyes out to the river. "I've also learned more about Henry Hudson. You were right. It wasn't a happy ending."

"The luck of the draw." He finished his drink.

She drained her glass. "Sometimes we make our own luck."

Henry only glanced at her and asked, "Want another?" When she agreed, he ordered a second. The drinks arrived, and they sipped them in silence, Maggie reaching for time, mulling over the best way to begin.

"Could we order lunch, Henry? I've an old story to tell. So old, if it waits a little longer it will make no difference."

"As you wish. Enrico." He motioned for the waiter to bring the menus. They ordered and waited for the courses to arrive. He was giving her all the time she wanted, but, wordlessly, she felt him press her for the reason they were lunching. When the food arrived, they tried not to look at each other, making small talk while they ate. The minutes passed rapidly, but they lasted long enough to renew Maggie's sense of what she'd undertaken.

Henry had the impression of watching her standing on a solid shore, preparing to plunge into possibly treacherous depths. They looked at each other now, and Henry's face showed an intensity of interest, of questions. He only wished he could help her.

A strange moment passed; and first vaguely, then with an increasing clarity, an idea occurred to Maggie as to how to go about it. She would start with the ageless words of all storytellers but tell the story as it actually happened. "Henry," she began, "long ago and far away there was a duchess by the name of Eleanor, Eleanor of Aquitaine. And this young duchess inherited one of the finest landholdings in the feudal world. It spread from the river Loire to the foothills of the Pyrenees, from the central heights of Auvergne to the western ocean. It was wider and fairer than the lands of her overlord, the King of France. It was even richer and more congenial than the Island of Britain. With such a dowry, the Duchess of Aquitaine was indeed a rich marriage prize. Perfect for Henry Fitz Empress, Duke of Normandy, who would one day be Henry II, King of England."

"I know the story very well, Maggie. Why . . . ?"

"Why am I telling you this? You'll see. I read about them in a history book. Years ago. And I learned a lot about royal marriages from my reading. Or marriages of state. When choosing a wife, the property of a great heiress far outweighs any romantic emotions a feudal lord might have for an ordinary woman."

"I know. Why are you interested in royal marriages?"

"Because that's how I came into your life."

Henry's face suddenly went bleak. "You mean these days they don't have to involve landholdings—there can be other reasons for a marriage of state?"

"Yes." Maggie smiled. "And since I knew I could never marry you, I decided to be what Rosamund was to Henry II. Your mistress, to use that old-fashioned word. Or your lover—perhaps that's more accurate? The book gave me the idea."

"And we happened because you read a book?"

"It wasn't that accidental. William gave me the book to read." She saw Henry frown and hurried on. "Dear, he was thinking of you. Since you were about to make a marriage of state, he assumed you would need a friend for 'off-castle' nights."

"And he put the idea into your head with a book?"

"Yes. But he didn't force me. You know your father. At the time, I didn't like the idea. And after William thought about it, he didn't like it either. So he offered me a number of alternatives."

"You didn't take them?"

"No. I chose you. I'd seen you. I was attracted. And I certainly didn't like the prospects my life held out to me. No one on the village green ever interested me." She half laughed. "So I decided to allow history to repeat itself."

"You would be my Rosamund?"

"Yes. Isn't it odd that you and the king are both named Henry?" She faltered for an instant. "Then something unforeseen happened. We fell in love." Maggie said this with neither pride nor joy. "And I believe this gave William additional second thoughts. He'd spent his life serving the Carson Company. And he foresaw you would do the same. This made him realize there'd come a day when between work and home and family, you'd have no time for me. Then what? Where would I go? What would I do? He didn't want this Rosamund to end up in a nunnery. Or any place where she wouldn't have a chance at a fuller life than the one from which he'd rescued her. And suppose, William thought, he was no longer around to help in finding that other life? Even kings die. So William set aside a small property holding for this Rosamund. Something negotiable in the market of misery. Just in case something happened to him before you and I came to the parting of the ways."

"Our King William could see a long way ahead."

"He could see everything. He was splendid!" Maggie was now saying things as they came to her, unable to hold them back. "So Henry and Eleanor, or to be precise, Selma, were married. And Rosamund, or Maggie, wept at the wedding. She hid her tears with a special formula called gin. During the reception she met a baron who looked a little like Henry. King William warned Rosamund/Maggie to keep away from the baron. But the special formula which covered her tears dulled her other senses as well. And she didn't. She and the Baron spent the night together. Henry's wedding night. It was a stupid mistake. And as with so many stupid mistakes, it had its consequences." Watching Henry, Maggie knew he wanted her to continue. He wanted everything to come out so that he should know the truth at last. "Anyway, Rosamund, I mean me—I was so ashamed at my stupid mistake that I didn't say a word to my Henry. Or a word about the consequence. Then the storm broke." She took a deep breath and exhaled. "William was murdered. And Henry, you, went into a state of shock and grief. When William's will was read, giving me a small holding, enough to make me an heiress, you thought William was responsible for my mistake. And its consequence. A baby boy. Since the boy was either yours or your father's, you decided to raise him as, let's say, royalty. And you named the boy after the royal house, Carson, never knowing he wasn't of your dynastic line. That the boy's father's name was Hillyer."

"John Hillyer?"

"The same."

"Will isn't a Carson?"

"Not by blood, but certainly by training."

"Why didn't you tell me sooner?"

"Because I wanted Will to have a future. I had the same Carson Company mania you have. I thought it best he be raised as your heir."

"You don't think so now?"

"I think you've done a wonderful job with him, but he and Elizabeth are in love. And they'll never be able to marry if they think they're both Carsons." Henry was at one with her to a degree and on a scale, with an intensity and an intimacy, that it took an effort for her not to reach out to touch him. "I don't think the Carson Company should come between them the way it came between us after Selma died." Now she had said it all. She'd followed her instinct, and he could feel anything he might feel. If Henry could accept what she had told him, would it lay a new basis on which they could all meet? When his eyes met hers, she saw his confusion. She felt sorry for him, sorry for herself, but it did not prevent her from taking this chance for absolute clarity. "If you choose to disinherit him because he isn't a Carson, of course you can. I think it would be a mistake. But if you do, he and Elizabeth will have Mission Nuevo anyway."

Henry looked at anything and everything except Maggie. He looked out the window, thinking he'd been a fool not to see the truth sooner. John Hillyer—red hair, Will and John, Jr.'s twin toes. And then there was Maggie and William themselves. He'd known for years, without accepting the knowledge, that it was impossible for William to have touched his son's woman. Henry had been too proud, too jealous, and under the lash of a madness, a madness that lingered long after William's death.

At last he faced Maggie. "Would you do me a favor, please? Would you go back to Carson House? I'll join you there shortly, and we'll talk more."

Maggie nodded. She hadn't been sure beforehand and still wasn't sure where it would all end. Yet she felt strangely happy.

Henry drove to the cemetery and sat on the same stone bench Maggie had earlier in the day. After some minutes, he knelt next to William's grave and begged his father for forgiveness and help. And it seemed to Henry that William answered him.

At last he understood his father, seeing his love affair with Maggie through William's eyes. Selma, if she'd lived, was his wife and the mother of his child. No matter how great the sacrifice, he'd have chosen his marriage. And Maggie deserved more than a part of his life, a part that would grow smaller as the demands of the Carson Company, a wife and children grew larger. So William, with his clear, logical mind, had planned ahead. His will was nothing more than an example of his unique foresight. Seeing their coming breakup, and seeing too, in Maggie, the potential for becoming a great lady, the great person she now was, he'd made certain she'd have the opportunity. Had he lived, he'd have done the same thing, possibly using other means. When his sudden death occurred, he couldn't explain what should not have needed explanation. Henry was left only to wonder at his own perverseness, his blind jealousy that had kept him so long from seeing the truth.

Maggie waited for Henry in the library of Carson House, facing what she had done. She had her moments of fear and of doubt that come to all who wait to see the results of their actions. When he entered the room at last, he went straight to the chair where she sat. He paused, looking down into her face, and even before he spoke, she knew Will was safe.

"What a fool I've been."

"So have I."

"But I'm less so now." He didn't hesitate. "I'm better, I think, than I've been in thirty years. You gave me back my father. How can I ever thank you?" His words helped her to smile. "I've missed him for a long time." Then Henry knelt in front of her chair and looked up at her face. "William saw to it that history didn't repeat itself."

"Yes. This Rosamund certainly has had a better life then the original."

"I'm not sure this Henry has. And that's why I think it's time to put an end to the idea of marriages of state. If Rosamund's son is in love with Henry's daughter, and she with him, why shouldn't they marry for love instead of property? Though I don't think either of our properties will interfere with their love."

"Henry!"

"If Will is not Carson by blood, he'll be a Carson by marriage. And in every other way." He stopped for a moment as though speech had failed him. Taking Maggie's hands in his, he brought them slowly to his lips. The touch of her skin gave him courage to continue. "Also, there's the unfinished story of Henry and Rosamund. So many years have been wasted, but there's still time left for Henry and Rosamund to be happy together. Would Maggie, no longer Rosamund, consider Henry, no longer Henry II, Carson's hand in marriage?"

Maggie let his question ring in her ears. "Rosamund/Maggie would be proud to marry Henry II/Henry Carson."

"Would Maggie . . . ?" Henry gave a sheepish grin, "consider a fling with an old lover prior to her royal marriage?"

"What do you have in mind?"

"I bought a small building. It has a special apartment with a living room facing the Hudson."

"Oh, Henry! My building?" Her voice broke. "And you still have the apartment? My old apartment?" She knelt facing him. Slowly, uncertainly, frightened at what they were about to do, their arms crept around each other, gradually tightening. Then their mouths touched.

The tips of their tongues touched, and a joy such as Maggie had not felt in a lifetime fired her blood. Her senses, so alive and ardent, her body in such a great fever that she wanted him now, wanted him as she always had, always would. It was Henry who was able to make a first move toward reality. Very gently he drew away from her embrace.

"Wait. This evening we'll meet and spend the night at the apartment."

"Oh, yes!" Waiting would be the kind of agony she remembered and longed for. Her whole body was crying out for him. It was worse than hunger or thirst, this yearning for his flesh. "It's four now. Let's make it six at the apartment?"

Henry waited at the apartment. Everything was ready. He'd removed the dust cloths, straightened up what the monthly maid missed, and put sheets on the bed. The steaks were in the refrigerator, the wine open, breathing. He'd also bought bottles of gin, vermouth and brandy. In spite of their response to each other, Henry was frightened. It had been so long. Suppose he couldn't measure up. She was not the semi-innocent for whom he'd orchestrated a seduction all those years ago. She was a beautiful woman who was as experienced as he was. Maybe more? He was as excited, as aroused as he had ever been in his life. Even the decision as to what to wear had been a crisis. His usual Brooks Brothers suit was out of the question. Finally he'd settled on slacks, a sport jacket, and loafers which he could easily kick off. Damn it! Where was she? The buzzer rang.

"Hello?"

"Mr. Carson, there's a lady . . ."

"Bring her up." He went to the door and waited. He heard the elevator machinery start. Christ! He was edgy! He glanced around the living room. Drinks ready? Yes. Gin, vermouth, two glasses and an ice bucket. What was taking the elevator so long? His impatience mounted. Then the doors opened and a tall, lithe figure appeared around the corner of the hall. Maggie Rhodes had arrived. She was always more vivid in life than in memory. He stood aside to let her enter the apartment, and she did with enormous confidence.

"I picked up the fixings for dinner. Martinis await you in the living room." She tossed her jacket on the couch and sat in the chair that was always hers. Henry fixed her a martini and stood looking at her. Damn it, he thought. I don't need a drink. I need her.

Maggie rose and went to the window. She sipped her drink and studied the Hudson. Then Henry could no longer contain his need. He moved toward her, pressed himself against her and held his hands over her breasts. She wore no brassiere and her breasts were as full and firm as he'd remembered. She put her drink down, turned in his arms, reached up and brought his mouth down to hers. He felt a great joy, only hoping he could satisfy her as completely as in the past. His mouth opened and her tongue entered. It probed and tickled and excited him. She reached down to caress his penis, while his hands unbuttoned her blouse. He fondled first one nipple, then the other, feeling them spring into life. He could feel his own erection. She'd have to be careful, or she'd have an orgasm in her hand.

Suddenly she withdrew her hand. "Remember what you said that first night? 'We can make love or we can do more.' I didn't know then what you meant. I didn't know there was a whole world of sensuality that was more than fucking. You taught me so much."

He drew her into his arms, his mouth delicately kissing her ear and murmuring, "You let me. You said 'I want to do what you want to do.'" Then he kissed her neck where the veins were palpitating. As he kissed her, he undressed her, removing her blouse and loosening her wraparound skirt. One hand stole softly downward and found her naked body waiting for him.

Her eyes blurred with the violence of her desire, and she opened his pants so that they dropped to the floor. He kicked off his loafers. His underwear followed. She rubbed her whole naked body against his, and together they moved toward the couch.

Maggie slipped backward on the couch. Henry knelt before her, his tongue played with her, entering her. She closed her eyes and felt a dozen hands touching her everywhere, a thousand tongues licking her. She panted, her hips arching up to his far-reaching tongue, her legs drawn back so he could caress more deeply. Suddenly her whole body shuddered, and she came with a moan of unbearable pleasure.

"Now what about you?" she said then. Henry stood up, his full erection standing out like a spear, waiting for Maggie. "Lie down on your back, darling." She crouched over him, gradually lowering herself until the tip of his penis just touched her clitoris. She gyrated back and forth against it, then bent to kiss it, tasting a bit of herself, of her juices, along with a small, salty bead oozing out of the tip. Henry knew he could prolong his pleasure no longer, and he wanted to climax within her. He felt her open and close around him. She raised and lowered herself, raised and lowered herself in an erotic dance over his penis. A beautiful high, thin feeling, like a taut violin string, began to vibrate in Henry. It grew and grew, each vibration becoming longer, higher, harder to control. Just as his insides felt as though they would erupt into Maggie, she settled herself on him, and he felt the flow of female juices pouring against his penis. Thrusting forward with a gasp of joy, as if he had reached the central point of her being, Henry exploded, flooding her with his thick, male semen. Their mingled cries of ecstasy filled the air. It was as though their veins and arteries had joined and their nerve endings entwined themselves to become part of a whole. He could feel her blood running through his veins, propelled by the throb of her heart, and when she'd reached her orgasm, he'd felt her nerves quiver and vibrate with desire and release. Her orgasm was his orgasm. They were one and the same. The joining was so complete he was surprised, even shocked, when, after a long time, his penis softened a little and he separated from her. It seemed unnatural, as though one person had divided into two, because they weren't two. Her blood still ran in his veins and his in hers. Her nerves still sent their special signals to his brain as his did to hers. Finally he lifted her off him and held her flat against his body, her breasts crushed against his chest, her belly pushing against him and his penis, still extending up between her thighs.

"Oh, my darling! My love," he heard her say, and the words were the words from a long-lost youth. "What a long time we've waited."

He had a moment of alarm, thinking about the lack of precautions, and he laughed at his own absurdity. That too belonged to another time.

Maggie read his mind through the sudden tension of his body. "No, my love. It's too late to be concerned. But we've a lifetime ahead of us for pleasure. And the whole night before us now to make love."

Henry's body was still so alive with desire for her, he thought there weren't enough hours in this night to satisfy him.

Maggie's plane was to leave the next morning at ten A.M. from JFK. She would return in two weeks and they would marry. After calling Carson House so Will and Elizabeth would not worry, Henry drove Maggie to the airport. On the way they decided that when she returned they would tell her son and his daughter of their true parentage. They kissed goodby in the car, and Henry watched her disappear through the TWA terminal. It was a miracle. After so many years alone, of living without his love, he would have the rest of his life to make up to her for his blindness. It would be hard restraining himself, not telling Will and Elizabeth the truth. Until Maggie returned.

*    *    *

Maggie's plane landed at LAX at one P.M. She had been too lost in her own thoughts to notice the sudden appearance of dark clouds that wiped out the ground view and grew darker and thicker as they came in for landing. When she left the plane and caught a glimpse of a *Los Angeles Times* headline, she realized what was happening. There was a ranging fire in Los Angeles County, especially the northern part of the county. Malibu was in the middle of the worst of it. She rushed to a telephone booth. When the telephone was answered, she felt an instant relief that didn't last. "Maggie! Where are you?" It was Bob Tilling.

"At LAX. What's happening?"

"We're closed in by the fire. I'm in the compound trying to keep everything watered down. The horses are with us, but the stables are gone."

"Is Angel all right?"

"She took a car and tried to race the fire down to the highway. I hope she made it."

"I'm coming to get you."

"Don't. No one can get through."

"A helicopter can. I'll—" The phone went dead.

Where could she get a helicopter? Western Helicopter Service. She'd used them to do aerial mapping of her property. It took money, persuasion and a strong promise to turn back if the fire made landing impossible, but she convinced them to rent her an Alouette and a pilot. Normally a five-seater, it could carry eight in a pinch. Enough room for Bob, Emma and any servants remaining.

While the news of the great fire didn't make the same headlines in the *New York Times* as it had in the *Los Angeles Times*, it was thoroughly covered. The first thing Henry did after reading about it was to call Maggie's private line. No answer. Then he placed a call to the manager of the Carson Company distribution in Southern California. It was serious. Donahue said huge areas of the Los Angeles basin had gone up in flames, and the brush fires were still not under control. The manager explained that September had been very dry, and the fires were fanned by the Santa Ana winds that approached 90 to 100 miles per hour. Henry had an impulse to fly to California, but when he called the airlines, he found that LAX was closed. He decided to wait at Carson House for Maggie to call. Didn't she understand he would worry? After an hour of waiting and still no word, he started making calls to the *Los Angeles*

*Times*, the mayor's office, the various fire departments, the James house. Angel wasn't there. His hope for a future life waited at the end of each call, and he was not above straining to find it. He carried off the phoning with courage, his calm voice concealing his desperation, but the more calls he made, the more hopeless he felt. Each courteous, merciless reply came back, "We don't know who has survived . . . We can't even get into Malibu yet . . . We're setting fire breaks now . . ." and so on. He felt like begging and couldn't find anyone to beg to.

As the afternoon wore on and there was still no word, another mood slowly took hold. There was nothing he could do. Wherever Maggie was, she was. Whatever happened had already happened. If Maggie didn't call, it was because she couldn't call. He would have to wait. But the walls of the library were closing in around him. He saw himself walking down a long, dark tunnel that was growing smaller and smaller.

Henry waited for the six o'clock news. Although they usually dealt with local events, this time the lead item was the great fire burning in Los Angeles. The WNBC station cut away to their Los Angeles outlet, KNBC. A very sober-faced man gave the news to the nation—the vast acreage lost, the number of people trapped, the number dead. No one yet knew how many were missing. He finished his brief report with the announcement of one death. "Los Angeles will mourn the loss of one of its great citizens, Mrs. Margaret Rhodes James, who died trying to reach her property in Malibu to rescue friends and workers trapped in her house. A number of firefighters watched helplessly as they saw the helicopter explode in midair and crash . . ."

Henry pushed the remote control button and shut off the television set. He sat quietly as the full effect of what he'd lost swept over him. Without Maggie nothing could be. No life. No future. Nothing but an endless succession of meaningless days. A leftover life to live. He stretched his arms out and slumped forward across the top of his desk. Slowly, beat by beat, the great heart of Henry Carson broke.

# Coda
# *1983*

# *1983*

**H**ENRY WILLIAM CARSON was dying. No doctor told him so, but he knew it and so did everyone else. It wasn't that Henry was carrying well over 350 pounds on a 6′ 2″ frame. He had weighed that much for the last ten years. Or that his ankles, feet, wrists and hands had become swollen. That had happened before, and Henry had gone on eating and drinking as usual.

This time something else had occurred. Henry could no longer sleep. Until recently, whenever Henry put his head on a pillow or the back of a chair and closed his eyes, he fell asleep for as long as his body needed to recover from whatever excess Henry had subjected it to. Now when he lay down he fell asleep but woke up in minutes, coughing. The doctors told him it was the fluid in his lungs that woke him. What they did not say, but Henry knew, was that his heart was becoming too weak to pump the blood necessary to clear out the fluid.

As a result, Henry had taken to trying to sleep in his extra large, black leather club chair. It carried both his weight and girth. Now he could not sleep even in his special chair. It was just a matter of time before his heart gave up.

He had stopped going to the office. The Carson Company would have to survive without him soon enough, so they might as well begin now. Besides, there were Will and Elizabeth to carry on. He had other things to do, all the things that a man worth about $500 million and the sole owner of a business that annually grossed over $2 billion had to do before dying. The death of a very rich man is a complicated business.

For the last month Henry had devoted the mornings to working at Carson House in Pleasantville and the afternoons sitting on a special stone chair on the flagstone terrace that faced south and overlooked the hundred-odd acres of the Carson estate. Did Henry regret not taking his doctor's advice about losing 100 pounds five years ago when there was still time? Henry did not. That would have meant depriving himself of something he might want to eat or drink, and it had been years since Henry deprived himself of anything he wanted. And what would the deprivation have accomplished? Given him five or ten more years of life? It wasn't worth it.

Henry had done about everything there was to do in life. He had received his share of triumphs and tragedies, whether deserved or not, and until this final dying process, except for occasional swollen ankles and feet, he had never known a day's sickness. While sixty-seven isn't three score and ten, Henry felt it would do.

The family was waiting for his death. Now he watched a large Rolls Royce pull up to the broad stone steps leading to the front door. He watched the rear door open and stared at the man who stepped out. His brother, Francis William Carson, had arrived. Henry examined his brother from a distance. Although two years older than Henry, Francis was still tall, straight and lean. His hair was thick and blond, with no sign of white. Maybe the light was playing tricks? In any case, Francis looked fit. There was no doubt as to who was going to outlive whom. They'd fought bitterly all their lives. He had won some of the battles, and Francis had won others. Francis was going to win this one. So be it. His thoughts about Francis were interrupted by the approach of a servant.

"Your brother, Mr. Francis, has arrived. Would you like to see him?"

Henry felt the small itch of irritation. Francis was the only man who could still anger him. "No. Tell Mr. Francis I'm not up to seeing him. Maybe tomorrow." The servant departed, leaving Henry alone with his thoughts. He closed his eyes and tried to rest.

The next morning Henry sat in his chair basking in the warm sunlight pouring through the window. He had not slept at all the night before. He had Francis to think about. At dawn he had showered and dressed and was now waiting for time to pass to go down and have breakfast with his brother.

Finally it was nine-thirty, and he lumbered over to his bureau mirror. Henry William Carson studied his reflection with grim amusement. He had certainly become a hulk, an over-350-pound hulk resulting from overeating, overdrinking, and no exercise. His face and neck were now round with layers of fat. His red hair had turned white. He supposed he looked older than his years, but it didn't concern him. Since Maggie's death, he cared for one thing only, and it certainly was not his appearance. It was training Will and Elizabeth Carson to run the Carson Company and Mission Nuevo, without his standing by to check their multi-million-dollar decisions.

Will's training had begun when he was fourteen, but he had never expected the twistings of fate to make necessary the training of Elizabeth. Yet once Will came into his inheritance from Maggie, it was apparent that two Carsons, not one, were needed to carry the huge responsibilities of the Carson Company and Mission Nuevo. Nor, in Henry's mind, could authority be delegated to an employed president. All policy decisions must originate within the Carson family as they always had.

So after Will and Elizabeth were married, Henry had taken over Elizabeth's business education. She would handle the Carson Company when Will was occupied with Mission Nuevo. It particularly pleased him that she took to the complexities of business as though she'd been born to it. And she had. She was a Carson to the core, and observing her decisions he was satisfied that, by now, she missed almost nothing. He sometimes thought he pushed her too hard, but dismissed the idea as unworthy. Though a woman and young, she was as much up to the demands as Will. She could read cash flow projections, marketing reports, product analyses and so forth with the same speed and acumen as he did.

He turned from the mirror in which he'd hardly seen himself. It was time to meet Francis for breakfast. Why had Francis left his palace in Morocco to be on hand for his death? Probably celebrating at a distance wasn't gratifying enough for him. Even after fifteen years his hate was still virulent. That was a long time. A long time too since Maggie's death. It would be thirteen years Tuesday of next week. He didn't think he cared to see the anniversary.

The elevator he had installed five years ago for his own personal use was waiting for him. Slowly, it descended to the main floor. The doors opened automatically, and Henry firmly, with a certain majesty, walked toward the porch and his waiting breakfast. By the time he reached it, the servants were waiting for him. Robert, his chauffeur and now all-around helper, stood behind a huge wooden chair. Henry went to his accustomed place at the table, and Robert pushed the chair until it touched the back of Henry's legs. Then Henry settled himself into it, mildly surprised not to find Francis waiting.

"He's strolling around the grounds," Robert explained. "He suggested meeting in the library after your breakfast."

Henry nodded and set about eating. He took his time as he always did. An hour later he had finished his third cup of coffee with cream and sugar. It was time to see Francis.

Robert hurried to help him move the heavy chair. When Henry

stood up, moving it himself, Robert was startled. Henry hadn't moved that chair or any chair in over a year. It seemed to Robert that Henry walked toward the library with a lighter, more rapid stride than he had in some time. Robert wondered if the doctors were wrong, and there was more life left in that huge body than they realized. It was a matter of "will to live" as much as anything.

In the library, Henry found Francis sitting on the leather couch, waiting. He stood up to greet him. Francis was as tall, straight and handsome as ever. Apart from some white hair mixed in with the sun-bleached yellow, Francis had hardly changed in fifteen years. A little thinner, maybe. Now, even more than when they were younger, he reminded Henry of their father. Henry greeted him and sat down behind his desk.

"You look well, Francis. The years have been kind."

"You look outrageous. As big as a house. Why, Henry?"

"Why not? I like indulging myself." He was struck by his desperate tone. Francis would outlive him by decades. Why was he so desperate?

"You haven't the right to die."

"I haven't the right?"

"Not while I'm alive. If you die, what's left?"

"You. You're left."

"Yes, and you are part of me." There was something awful in his eyes. "If you die, I have no reason to live. How will I spend the hours of my days?"

The conversation had become bizarre. "Francis, you sound insane. What are you talking about?"

"I'm speaking about the one thing that gives me reason to live. You. And the plans I make. You didn't think I'd give up, did you?"

Henry reared back, amazed and pitying, then shook his head. "But you've done nothing for years."

"I have not yet found the right plan. Foolproof and faultproof. When I do, I will strike."

Henry was confounded. It was true, and it was sheer lunacy. But it was true. As long as he was alive, Francis' life had purpose. Even if that purpose was only to scheme and dream and concoct fantastic plots for destroying him. A thousand dreams, a thousand plots that, once made, were discarded in favor of new dreams, new plots. The idea of Henry ruined and disgraced gave purpose to Francis' life. But no plan was good enough. Each plot was flawed. Still, next month, next year, he would find a way.

"You've wasted your time." Henry regarded him with disgust. "There's nothing you could do that's worse than life has done."

"What has life done? The Placidium investigation left you unscathed. And your career, your life, didn't end when you lost the Commerce post. But when I retired from the Senate, mine did."

"I see." He paused. "You know Maggie died in the L.A. fire of 1970."

"She was very special. And you loved her."

"I'll always love her."

"Fortunately, I was well rid of Angel. That damn fool wife of mine tried to drive a car through a wall of fire." Francis' voice grew thoughtful. "So Maggie died, and you mourn her by killing yourself. Pound after pound. Fool! I suppose she told you before dying that Will wasn't your son. Or William's. Even Caterina guessed that much." A smile flickered on his lips. "Who was Will's father?"

"John Hillyer."

"That fits. And explains Will and Elizabeth's marriage. And those red-headed children. I didn't think you would condone incest."

"If you like, you have my permission to visit the Carson Company to see the portrait wall in the reception room. Five generations of Carsons, and the latest is the most unusual. Elizabeth and Will run the company together. The portrait is of both of them."

"I'm not interested. You know you're a disgusting sentimentalist."

"I am. I learned the value of sentiment from loneliness. Should you visit the cemetery, you'll find Maggie's grave there too. I had her remains flown back and buried in the family plot. She almost was a Carson." Henry found himself irritated at the pathetic waste of Francis' life. "At any rate, I think this conversation is ended. I will die when I choose to die."

Francis stood up. "Will I see you at dinner?"

"I never miss a meal. Every pound counts."

Francis left. After the door shut, Henry leaned back in his chair. It was almost over.

That night after everyone was asleep, Henry got up and dressed himself. He left a note for Will and Elizabeth on his bureau saying that if he missed breakfast they should come for him at the address scrawled below, and he left a set of keys with the note. Then, for the first time in five years avoiding the elevator, Henry walked down the main staircase and to the garage. Years ago he'd had his old La Salle completely restored for just these trips, and the mechanic, who kept all the many Carson cars running, maintained the La Salle in perfect condition. The running board and high seats made it possible for him to get in and out of the car without help. Now he squeezed his body behind the old-fashioned wooden wheel, started the engine and backed out of the garage.

The drive to the apartment took less than thirty minutes, seeming to go more quickly than usual. He used his key to open the building door and soon was in the apartment, seated in his chair overlooking the Hudson. Tonight he was more tired than usual. For the first time in a week he floated in the kind of drowsy reverie, a time of magic when anything is possible, that comes before sleep. He turned his head to look at the vacant chair close to him and slowly his expression grew animated as it had not been for years. Whatever he saw, it communicated pleasure to an exquisite extreme; an expression of rapture crossed his face. As though the words were wrung from the depths of his being, he whispered, "Maggie . . ." and then "Darling . . ." and then "Thank God you've come."

To anyone watching it would have seemed he was speaking to an invisible presence, listening to words only he could hear. But hear them he did, and when he spoke, his voice was that of a younger Henry. "I knew you would come tonight. Everything is finished. I did what I had to do. I can go with you now."

For Henry, Maggie was there. He got up from his chair and reached for her hand. "It's been a long time, Maggie. Too long." For an instant he turned and looked back at a very large man with thick white hair seated in a chair. Before darkness came he heard Maggie say, "Don't look back, Henry. That's over and done with. Come with me. We're together at last."

At Carson House, Henry was missed at breakfast. When Robert entered his room, found it empty, and saw the note, he called Will and Elizabeth at the Carson Company. They rushed home.

"Where is this?" Will asked, reading Henry's note.

"It's that old building Dad bought years ago."

"Yes, I remember. We'd better hurry."

Elizabeth's eyes were wet. "It won't help. Dad knew what he was doing."

They met Francis in the hall. "What's going on? Where's Henry?"

Will showed Francis the note. "He's there or he's not."

Francis faltered. "Would you do me a favor?" he was pleading. "When you find Henry, please call and give me the news."

"Of course."

"Thank you." Francis watched them leave.

Will and Elizabeth parked their car behind Henry's La Salle in front of the small apartment house. They used the keys to let themselves into the building and then into the apartment. Henry was seated in a chair facing the Hudson River, and they walked around the chair to stand reverently before the body of the man who had been Henry Carson. His eyes were closed, but his face was so radiant, he seemed to have died experiencing some revelation of joy.

"Liz, he died so happy. Something wonderful must have happened."

"Yes." Tears were spilling down her face. Not maudlin, wasteful tears, but tears of sorrow and real acceptance. "If there's a God, he's with her now."

"I'll miss him so much, but it's all right."

"It's all right. Look at his face."

Will called Carson House. When he reached Francis he said, "We've found him. He died last night in his sleep."

A hospital in White Plains sent an ambulance, doctors and orderlies. Will and Elizabeth followed the ambulance to the hospital. From there the body would be transported to the same funeral parlor Henry had picked for William forty-two years ago, the MacDowell Funeral Parlor in Briarcliff.

When they returned to Carson House, Robert took them aside. "I haven't wanted to worry anyone unnecessarily, but Mr. Francis hasn't been seen since you called. And the door to a room on the third floor is locked from the inside."

"We may have to smash it in. Come on, Robert." The three of them hurried up to the third floor room. The door gave under the weight of both men. They found Francis in the bathroom, dead. His service revolver was in his hand. A note was taped to the door:

*My apologies for my suicide at Carson House and in this, our mother's, room. But everything started here, so it seemed appropriate for everything to end here. I'll use the bathtub. You should have no trouble cleaning up the mess.*

*Francis William Carson*

Francis had pinned his Congressional Medal of Honor, the actual medal, not the ribbon, to his shirt.

* * *

Two days later there was a double funeral. Though many distinguished men and women would have attended the funeral of Henry William Carson, a man of property and honor, and General/Senator Francis William Carson, a man of courage, the Carson family decided the funeral would be a family affair. After the service two short eulogies were delivered, one by Elizabeth, the other by Will. Then the coffins were lowered into twin graves.

The brothers reposed side by side next to William Carson. Nearby rested Caterina Orsini Carson and, with Will's eternal gratitude, Maggie Rhodes Carson. Here Henry and Francis lay composed and serene, seeming to have found at last, beyond the wrath of their spirits and the ruin of their lives, that place of peace and order to which their vast journeyings among the high places of our country had never brought them. The bold-hearted Carsons were at rest. The autumn sunlight fell softly where they slept.